Gunny Malone

by Janie Downey Maxwell

Thanks for being my best friend for so many years! Love you Janie

Portland, Maine USA

Thanks to my many wonderful editors:

Bill Maxwell, Doris Barrell, John Linscott, Sallie Hunter, Debbi Pierce,

Sarah Fletcher, Babs Lightfoot, Meg Springli, and Andrea Peabbles.

Table of Contents

	Prologue	1
1	The Early Years, Dunquin, Ireland	4
2	A Tin Whistle, Holy Days, and Seals	18
3	The Booley	51
4	The Smithy & The Priest	76
5	Working Life	97
6	James, Matt, and Thomas	111
7	Love	147
8	Shrovetide	167
9	The Wedding and the Accident	178
10	Bedridden	194
11	Life in the Hills	221
12	The Graveyard	259
13	Catherine	272
14	The Blaskets	284
15	Patrick, a Poet, and a Pig	312
16	A Calling	336
17	Lord Ventry Builds a School	358
18	Maggie & Larry	375
19	Life in the Village	393
20	The Famine	411
21	Tom Milliken Pays a Visit	430
22	The Loss of a Murphy	456
23	The Fire	462
24	On Board	481
25	Home	490
	Epilogue	497
	About the Author	499
	Books used to research this novel	500

~ **Prologue** ~

The old woman sat in an ancient rocker close to the turf fire, willing the heat of the fire to warm her aching bones. A small front window was propped open to allow the cool ocean breeze into the room. A lone seagull brayed over the low, stone house as surf pounded against the heavy black shore rocks. The air smelled of the sea, and peat, and tea. The chair creaked as the woman rocked on a worn, circular hearth of flat, black stones. Her face was deeply wrinkled, her large, dark eyes covered with a light film of blue. White curls escaped from a loose bun secured with a few pins at the back of her neck. Veins stood out on the backs of her hands, but her long fingers were still straight as they fingered the frayed pocket of her apron. She wiped her eyes with the back of one hand then laid both hands on her chest to help warm herself.

"Miss Malone, if you're cold I could close the window."

She pushed up straighter in the rocker. She was surprisingly tall with wide shoulders. "No. I like the air to be cool in front of a fire." She stretched and wiggled her stockinged toes, then turned her gaze to her gentleman caller. She studied his pale face, his kind brown eyes, the round glasses perched on his nose—so familiar except for the short, salt and pepper hair. "Where was I?"

"If you're tired, we could start again tomorrow."

She chuckled. "No. You asked me to tell my story. I just don't know where to begin."

He drummed his pencil against a thick pad of paper as he waited. She eyed him with pursed lips. He stopped drumming, cleared his throat, and smiled. "When I was growing up, my father said no one could tell a story like you. He told me all about you."

She laughed and the volume startled him. "Your father told you all about me? I hardly know all about me myself. And when it comes to storytellers, the one you should hear is my father. He's the story teller."

"I'd love to talk to him. Does he live here on the Blaskets?"

The old woman glanced at him, confused. "No," she shook her head. "He never lived here." She hesitated. "He's gone now."

"Did he die during the famine?" he asked gently, pencil poised and ready.

The old woman stared at him. "No." She turned back to the fire and was silent.

The writer started to drum his pencil, but caught himself mid-beat. He listened to the pounding surf outside. He had barely made it across the choppy channel on the boat ride from Dunquin. The sailors had warned him he most likely would not get back to the mainland for at least a week. He looked at the old woman. Her eyes were closed. He could see it was going to be a very long, unproductive week stranded on a desolate island on the stormy west coast of Ireland.

1

He was startled when the old woman started to speak, her voice low and husky. "When I was a girl, there was nothing to do at night but sit around the fire listening to the old folks tell the stories. Everyone's too busy these days to listen to the old stories."

The writer scooted his chair in a little closer. "That's why I'm here. You may be part of the last generation to live on this island. I'm hoping to keep your stories alive by writing them down."

"You're writing about the Blaskets but I didn't grow up here. I'm from the mainland. From Dunquin."

"Then let's start there." He poised his pencil. "Tell me about Dunquin."

She shook her head. "There's not much to tell. It was a long time ago."

The writer blinked and eyed his blank sheet of paper. Hadn't his father also mentioned that Miss Malone could be quite stubborn?

The old woman rocked back in her chair and puffed out her cheeks. "It's funny what you remember—a piece of a conversation, a place you visited, part of a certain day. You remember the surprises, and sometimes the most mundane things. And of course you remember the people—so many people."

"I'm interested in anything you want to tell me. Others can fill in the details you leave out. I have plans to speak with several people here on the Great Blasket island, and next week I'll spend time with the old folks in Dunquin, Ventry, and Dingle."

"Old folks." Gunny interrupted. "We weren't always old, you know?"

The writer chuckled. "Point taken."

The old woman sighed. "Would you like a cup of tea?"

"I'd love one."

"Good. There's a bucket of water there by the door. The tea cups are on the cupboard behind you. The tea is in the top drawer. I like my tea weak, and hot, and sweet."

"Weak and hot and sweet," he said, pushing up from his chair. "I think I can take care of that." He grabbed a blackened tea kettle from an elaborate iron crane by the fire and walked to the cupboard that divided the house into two rooms. Behind the cupboard he spied two small beds and a large sea chest. He yanked open the heavy top drawer of the cupboard with a squeak. Inside he found a wooden box and several old, bent spoons. He flipped open the lid of the box and carefully placed three large spoonfuls of dry dark leaves into the kettle as his father had taught him. Then he filled the kettle with water from the bucket, set it on the top arm of the crane and swung it over the fire. He returned to the cupboard and picked out two chipped, stained cups. "Where do you keep your sugar?"

The old woman thought for a minute. "I don't remember," she said softly. She sighed and rocked. Some days she couldn't remember what she'd eaten for her morning meal, but she could remember the past. The past was always with her. She'd have no problem telling this man her story.

2

"Never mind," he said behind her. "I'm sure I can find it." He spied a small glass dish at the far end of the cupboard. He pried open the crusty lid with a spoon and put a heaping spoonful of sugar in each cup. When the steam whistled from the kettle, he moved the crane away from the fire and poured out two cups of tea. He handed one to the old woman, then took the second cup and sat down in his chair. The old woman stared into the steam rising from her cup. He cradled his hot cup and listened again to the pounding surf. He closed his eyes, the pad of paper and pencil neglected at his feet.

"I suppose it's best to start at the beginning," she said.

The writer set his cup down on the hearth and picked up his pad and pencil. The old woman paused. When she did not continue, he reached again for his tea.

She started to rock. The heavy old chair squeaked in response. "Did I mention that I grew up in the village of Dunquin? My father was Robert Malone, the horseman. My mother was Eileen Malone from Ventry. My mother never did like living in Dunquin."

The writer gripped his pencil, tea forgotten. "Tell me about your mother? Did she look like you?"

The woman grinned. "We couldn't have been more different. She was tall like me, but with the straightest black hair you've ever seen. And a stern, stern face. I can count the times I heard her laugh. She would tell you we were nothing alike. She often said I was more like a fairy than a girl. One of my earliest memories was of her standing by our front window. It looked a lot like that window there…"

~ **Chapter 1: The Early Years, Dunquin** ~

Eileen Malone leaned against the wall by the front window and watched the rain fall in the muddy grey yard beyond. She sipped weak tea from a small tin cup. She was tall and had always been considered handsome despite her small brown eyes and heavy brows. She rested her cup on the windowsill and ran a hand over her straight black hair to make sure the bun at the base of her neck was secure. It had rained every day for the past two weeks and the air inside the house was heavy and cold, the dirt floor and rough stone walls damp despite the best efforts of a smoldering turf fire. She winced at the sound of her bickering children behind her. Their sharp voices pounded in her head.

"I want to sit next to Da. You always get to sit next to Da," Gunny whined. The girl was tall for two-and-a-half, her voice loud and strong. She leaned against her father's strong, lean body as he sat on his stool carefully packing tobacco into his pipe. Gunny's head of soft dark curls tickled his nose and he gently brushed her hair away from her face.

"I'm older and I'm the boy, so I can sit anywhere I want," Michael retorted, holding on to the stool with both hands and kicking at his sister. Though only five, Michael had the look of a small man, with a large head and heavy arms and legs.

Gunny squealed and dug her long fingers into her brother's armpits. "I'm not moving," he grunted, "no matter what you do." Gunny dug her fingers in harder and Michael tried not to laugh. "Go away, you stupid girl," he said, pulling down tighter on the stool. Gunny yanked her hands away and jumped onto his back.

Eileen heard a leg of the stool snap and watched both children pitch onto the hard dirt floor.

"Can't a woman have peace in her own house?" she muttered, glaring at her husband who sat, slowly sucking smoke from his pipe, untroubled by the chaos around him. She pushed past him and pulled Michael up by the arms. He kicked at her, then pulled away and sprinted toward the back room, just missing hitting his head on the heavy wooden table in the center of the room. He collapsed onto the thin goose-down mattress in the back room and sobbed. "You always take her side. I had the stool first."

"What's got into you, woman?" Robert said, pulling Gunny up from the floor and into his arms. She buried her face in her father's worn shirt and breathed in his warm, smoky scent.

"What's got into me?" Eileen stammered. She paced past him like a caged animal. "I hate this house. The windows let in no light. The roof leaks. The walls are filthy from having the animals in here all winter. Half the yard is filled by a filthy dung hill. We've had nothing but rain for weeks, and have nothing to eat but potatoes. Only an idiot would be happy living here."

4

Robert cradled Gunny in one arm and wiped at her mud-streaked face with the tail of his shirt. "Our house is no different than the house you grew up in. And do you suppose it rains less in Ventry than it does here in Dunquin, my Lady?"

Eileen turned to the windowsill, her head high; her shoulders stiff. She gripped the tin cup but the tea had grown cold, and the cold cup was no comfort. She swirled the black leaves. "Ventry was beautiful," she muttered, resting one hand against her high forehead.

Robert chortled behind her. "Ventry was beautiful. Until Lord Ventry evicted your parents so he could expand his gardens around Ballygoleen. Have you forgotten that bit of ugliness?"

"Yes, but if he hadn't…"

"But he did. And when you had nothing left and nowhere to go, you married me."

"There were others."

"Oh, yes. Whatever happened to your good friend Moss?"

Eileen turned and glared at her husband with his strong chin and thick black hair, so different from Moss' large round head and thinning hair. "You promised you wouldn't mention him," she hissed. She slammed down the tea cup and grabbed a turf from a pile near the hearth. She placed the heavy brown brick of dried turf roughly on the fire and knelt to poke the embers with a long iron rod. The turf slowly caught fire and she held her hands over the warming flame. "Moss only had the money for one passage to America," she said in a quiet voice. "He promised when he got there and was settled in that he'd send money for my passage."

Robert leaned forward over the little girl and touched Eileen's back as she knelt in front of the fire. Her back stiffened at his touch. "Something must have happened or he would've written."

Eileen glanced over her shoulder. Was Robert mocking her? With the back of one sooty hand, she wiped away her tears leaving a wet smear of ash across her right cheek, then turned and looked hard into her husband's deep blue eyes. "Don't act like you care. You never liked him."

Michael crept in from the back room and slid past his father. He propped up the broken leg on the stool and sat down, grinning. The broken leg gave out, spilling him onto the hearth. Gunny howled with laughter and slid down from her father's lap to wrestle with her brother.

Eileen stared vacantly at her son. "And what about Michael looking so much like his father?"

"Now that's something you promised you would never mention," Robert said in a quiet voice.

"I can't help it," Eileen whined. "I look at his little round face and I see Moss Barney. I look into his brown eyes and I see Moss' eyes. Then I hear Moss laughing at me," she spat toward the fire.

5

Robert chucked. "Moss had a horrible laugh."

"His laugh was not horrible," Eileen said in a quiet, strained voice.

Robert stood and pulled a fresh plug of tobacco from his nook to the right of the fireplace. "All right, it wasn't horrible," he smiled. "But it was odd. His whole manner was odd. And it wasn't just me who thought that. Everyone said so." He cut off a piece of tobacco with his pocket knife and stuffed it into his pipe, then took up the fire tongs and plucked a coal from the fire. He took a long drag from the pipe, making small popping sounds with his mouth as the tobacco lit, then sat back down on his stool and stared into the fire.

"I didn't think Moss was odd," Eileen muttered defensively.

"Clearly, you didn't," Robert scoffed and shook his head. "When Moss worked with us in the stables he didn't know one end of a horse from the other and never got a lick of work done with all his talking. He'd go on and on about how someday he was going to America, about how he was going to be somebody."

"Moss wasn't good with his hands like you are. He was more of a thinker. Moss liked to read."

"Something I never learned," Robert grunted, pulling at his pipe.

"You don't have to read, you have other skills. Moss worked hard to better himself."

Robert snorted. "I suppose you pictured yourself living with him in a Great House, hiring servants like me to tend to your horses."

Eileen stared into the fire. "With a fine garden out back and a coach to travel in," she said wistfully.

Gunny screamed as she fell facedown on the rocky corner of the hearth. Eileen pushed Michael away and scooped up the girl to assess the damage in the dim light. Gunny stared at her mother, too shocked to cry. Eileen fingered a growing lump on the girl's forehead. "Don't even think of crying," she said sternly as Gunny sniffed trying to catch her breath. "You have to be careful playing with boys."

Gunny pushed away from her mother's cool hand and slid down to the floor. Michael ran laughing to the back room with Gunny tight at his heels.

Eileen awoke with a start. Her head was heavy and her nipples ached; she knew she was with child again. She pulled the thin wool blanket to her chin and stifled a sob. Robert woke, bleary eyed, and reached for her. She pushed his hand away and whispered the news. He rolled onto his back and grinned. "About time. No house is happier than one crowded with children," he crowed.

She shushed him. "This house is already too crowded. Gunny is finally eating with the rest of us and sleeping all night. A new baby means starting all over with the crying and sleepless nights, and wet pants, and wet breasts..."

"Children are God's blessing," Robert said, reaching over and gently squeezing her shoulder. "You should praise the Lord that we have children who will care for us when we're old."

"Look at them," Eileen whispered, pointing at Gunny and Michael twisted together in the other bed, their crusty eyes closed and small mouths open. "Michael hardly remembers to come in at noon to eat a meal. Gunny never listens and she's so loud and dirty. You think those two will take care of us?"

"Stop with your nonsense. Perhaps this next child will be caring and kind."

Eileen curled on her side, covered her face with her hands, and wept.

Within a month, God heard Eileen's fervent prayers and after several days of cramping, she felt her body give up the child in her womb. She was exhausted and drained from the pain and loss of blood and stayed in bed for a week. Robert did the best he could to get the cow milked, the eggs collected, and the potatoes boiled for each meal, but there was little he could do to keep the children quiet and away from their mother's bedside. As Eileen prayed for peace, Robert prayed for the day she would once again be a help to him.

Six months later, Eileen went through the same cycle of dread, then relief. The second loss left her feeling even weaker than the first. In the mornings, she felt tired and achy and found she often needed to rest before she prepared the evening meal. Her occasional headaches became more frequent and gained in intensity. When her head ached, she stuffed the front window with a blanket, and insisted the front door be kept closed. The only light in the house came from the weak glow of turf embers while she lay in bed with a wet flour sack draped over her eyes. When she was having a spell, Robert kept the children outside as much as he could, but they had to eat. Over meals, it tore at his heart to see his wife stumble about with her ashen face and deep-circled eyes wincing at the sounds of life around her.

At night, when the fire was smoored and everyone was tucked into bed, Robert tried to comfort his wife, to wrap his body around her to warm her, but she shied from his touch, insisting that they not lie together again until she was feeling better. But their time apart turned from weeks into months, and then into years.

"We live together as if you were my sister," Robert whispered one warm summer evening as they lay barely touching on their small, straw-stuffed mattress.

"I'm sorry. We could touch but that that might lead to more. Do you want me to die and leave these children with no one to look after them?"

"They're five and eight and pretty much take care of themselves now," Robert grunted.

Eileen turned her back to Robert, pulled the blanket up around her face, and went to sleep.

"Your mother's having a spell," Robert informed the children one spring morning over a meal of boiled potatoes, "And the Old Lord's prize mare is ready to foal—so we're going to Ventry," he said, raising his eyebrows to make the work sound interesting and important.

Gunny's dark brown eyes opened wide. "How will we get there?"

"We'll walk. It's only about two hours. If we're lucky, the Lord will lend us a horse if we need to be there again tomorrow."

The little girl gasped. "And we're going with you? Mam said horses are dangerous."

"They are dangerous," Robert said with a chuckle. "But I'll be with you," he said, patting Gunny's head of thick, black curls.

Michael pouted. "Matt and Mac McCrohan asked me to go fishing. I want to go fishing, Da."

Robert shrugged. "Fine. Go fishing. You can come with us tomorrow if we go back. Just be sure to stay out of the house and out of your mother's way today," he said, listening to his wife's snores from the back room. He pulled six hot potatoes from the embers with a long poker and dusted them lightly with one hand. He tossed two potatoes to each child which they slipped into their pockets. He pocketed his own potatoes for the day and they left the house without a word of good-bye.

Eileen sighed deeply when Robert told her that his work in Ventry was done and that he and the children would be home again during the day. "It's been such a nice, quiet week," she said softly.

"You can at least pretend you're glad we're back," Robert said.

Eileen washed the spoons and bowls from their morning meal with sand and well water and stacked the tinware on the cupboard. "It was peaceful without you here, that's all I'm saying. I'd hear you slip out in the morning and then sleep till it got too warm. I made eggs for my morning meal and had the fire to myself. No one asked me to get them anything. There were no slamming doors, no arguments, no noses to wipe. Isn't there more you could do in Ventry? Or take the children down to the strand? Or something?"

"What's troubling you this fine morning, sweet Eileen? Is it your head?"

Eileen pouted and blew out a small puff of air. "We have no eggs."

Robert laughed. "We have three laying hens. Maybe you need to look harder for the eggs."

Eileen glared at her husband. "I know where the hens lay, Robert. And I'm telling you we have no eggs."

"So our chickens aren't laying?" Robert asked.

"Oh, they're laying all right," Eileen snapped.

"I don't understand."

Eileen leaned in and gripped Robert's arm. "The chickens are laying over at Fiona Burke's house. They are up in that rotten thatch roof of hers."

Robert laid a large, warm hand over his wife's tight grip. "And how do you know that?"

Eileen pulled her hand away. "Would you like to run this house? You seem to know more about eggs than I do."

"I never said...," Robert started, but stopped at Eileen's glare.

"There's only one thing to do. I'm going over there and get my eggs off her roof." She pulled on her apron and slammed the door on her way out.

Eileen and Fiona Burke had done nothing but quarrel since the day the Malones moved into the last house on the road out of Dunquin. Robert had grown up in a rambling stone house down near O'Leary's pub, but when they were wed Eileen insisted they move into their own house, away from his parents and the pub, and this was the only house they could afford. The Burkes lived just slightly down the hill on the opposite side of the road.

Fiona Burke had grown up in her little house at the base of Mount Eagle, and lived there now with her aging mother and five boys. Fiona's husband, Gabe, had drowned the previous fall while fishing in a storm only a few weeks before Fiona gave birth to her fifth boy. The rest of the boat's crew had managed to get to shore on the Blasket Islands, but Gabe's body was never found. Eileen was convinced he had run off to get away from Fiona and the pack of wolves she was raising. Fiona's oldest, the twins, were around the same age as Michael, and her third boy was about Gunny's age, but Eileen insisted that her children not play with the Burkes.

"They are not our type of people," she explained to the children.

Eileen sneaked up over the hill side of Fiona's house and crawled out onto her rotting thatch on the roof searching for eggs. Fiona was inside cooking porridge for her boys who never seemed to have enough to eat. As she stirred the pot, lost in thought about a piece of weaving she was working on, bits of ceiling started to fall into the pot of boiling cereal. Fiona slammed the spoon into the pot and raced outside, sure that one of her boys was up to no good. To her shock, she saw instead the bottoms of two worn boots and Eileen Malone sprawled across her sagging roof.

"Woman! What are you doing on my roof?" she screamed.

"I am getting my eggs back is what I am doing," Eileen yelled as she dug her hands into thick layers of rotting thatch.

"Are you crazy? Get down. You're knocking thatch into my porridge. The whole roof may cave in with your weight on it."

"Your thatch is rotten. It's no wonder my chickens are roosting here." She held up a handful of moldy thatch and threw it at Fiona's feet. Fiona kicked at the blackened straw. A few white worms wiggled free of the dark mass and she squished one with the toe of her boot.

"Ah ha!" Eileen gloated from the roof, holding up a small brown, speckled egg. "I knew my best hen was laying here."

"You've lost your mind. What makes you think that's your egg?" Fiona demanded.

Eileen propped herself on an elbow and held out the egg as evidence. "This has the look of my best hen's eggs. Do any of your hens lay eggs like this?"

Fiona could not recall having seen any speckled eggs before, but who knew? Her boys did most of the egg gathering.

Eileen slowly pushed her way back off the roof and onto the adjoining hill. More thatch crumbled and fell into Fiona's kitchen. When Eileen got her footing, she stood and brushed rotten straw from her soiled apron. "I've seen my hen over here with your chickens. Oh, this is my egg all right." She marched home, chuckling, as Fiona's curses dimmed behind her.

Gunny was surprised when her mother bustled into the house and prepared a thick oat cake for their morning meal. "Our best hen was laying elsewhere," Eileen explained. "Sometimes you have to look hard to find a treasure in this village."

It was late April. The sun was warm, and a cool breeze blew salt air in off the ocean. Across the rolling hills, tucked between the ocean and the shadow of Mount Eagle, the farmers of Dunquin were hard at work in their fields. It had been a dry winter with little rain or snow, and the soil was cracked and harder to work than usual as the farmers hauled cart after cart of sand, and seaweed, and a year's worth of dung from their yards to work into the depleted soil.

Like the rest of the men in Dunquin, Robert Malone had three fields to plant—each one around a half-acre. His fields were mixed in with those of his neighbors. Each man had one field of good land for growing oats, and two fields of less desirable land for planting potatoes. The acre of potato fields would supply the family with enough potatoes to live on for almost ten months, but the seed had to be planted by May Day or neighbors would talk. The oats that were planted in the last field would be thrashed in the fall, and the ground kernels saved to help them through the lean days of summer. Robert had been out every day for weeks getting his fields ready and today was finally the day to plant.

"Take the children with you so I can clean the house," Eileen said in a soft voice from her stool in front of the fire as Robert headed out the door, cap in hand.

"We're putting in the seed today, Eileen," Robert said sternly. "This is no work for children."

"I'm in no mood for their foolish games. Take them with you."

Robert sighed and pulled his cap down tight onto his head. "How's a man supposed to get his work done?"

Eileen stood, hands on hips, and stared at her husband.

Robert looked down at the hard-packed dirt floor. "Michael, Gunny," he yelled up into the loft. "Come down. You're going with me."

Eileen tapped her foot as the children scrambled down the ladder. She gave them as a half-smile as she pushed the trio out into the yard and bolted the door behind them. She added a brick of turf to the fire and put on the kettle for tea.

Gunny hummed an uneven tune as she skipped along beside her father's small hand wagon carrying three sacks of oat seed. At the age of five, she was taller than most six year olds and easily kept pace with her father and brother. "When we get to the fields, I'm going to help plant," she announced as she hopped along backwards, letting the stiff wind push her curls up around her face.

Robert eyed his spirited daughter. "We'll see."

When they reached the oat field, Michael spied the McCrohan boys making a stone fort along the edge of the field and raced off to build with them. The McCrohans lived along the main road to Ventry, just down the hill and across a fallow field from the Malones. Their house was larger than most, with a wide yard to accommodate the forge which was built along the creek. John McCrohan was the village smithy. He was tall, with a thick neck and strong arms, and was one of the best story tellers in the village. When Gunny sat at his feet at the nearly nightly gatherings at the McCrohan house, she reveled in his rich, deep voice and in his smell of smoke and sweat.

John McCrohan and Robert Malone had been friends since they were boys, and now Michael was fast friends with the McCrohan boys. Matt was eleven, the same age as Michael, and was the oldest in the family. Mac was eight, the same age as Gunny. Neither boy wanted anything to do with "little" Gunny Malone.

Gunny looked away from their fort making and smiled up at her father. "What do we do first?"

Robert sighed. "I don't have time for you to be playing with the seeds, Gunny," he explained. "Why don't you sit and watch."

Gunny's eyes filled with tears and she felt her throat tighten. "I don't want to sit and watch," she said in a quiet voice. "I want to work."

Robert hesitated. He hated it when the girl cried. "All right. You can help —if you promise to listen and keep out of trouble."

Gunny squealed and hopped up into his arms. He tried to toss her into the air as he done when she was younger, but she was too long and heavy for that now. He set her down awkwardly on the rough dirt road and patted her head, then reached behind her and took a rumpled, empty sack from the wagon. He slashed it open with his pocket knife, folded it in half, and wrapped it twice around her small waist. He tied the cloth in the back leaving a large open pocket in the front, then took a dip of oat seeds in a tin cup and filled the pocket. She tucked her hands under the full pocket and grinned.

Robert knelt in front of her, resting his hands on her shoulders, and looked her in the eye. "Listen to me and think about what you're doing. We don't have one seed to waste."

Gunny licked her lips and shook her head, black curls bouncing. Robert reached into the seed pocket and held out an open fistful of seeds. "Your job is to place the seeds in the little rows I'm going to make. I want one little seed to drop at a time into the center of the row. I'll follow behind you and cover the seeds with dirt. Do you think you can you do that?"

"You know I can, Da," Gunny said with an impish grin.

Robert straightened. "Good. Now wait here while I make the first furrow."

Gunny watched as her father took his furrowing tool and walked across the field turning a long, strait row in the freshly fertilized dirt. She ran both hands through the seeds in her pocket while she waited. The seeds felt cool and tickled as they flowed around her fingers.

He returned to her side. "Now it's your turn. Work as slowly as you need to. Don't leave any gaps or you'll bring bad luck to the field."

Gunny cocked her head to one side and eyed her father. "Mam says there is no such thing as bad luck, that we each make our own luck."

Robert chuckled. "So today make your own luck by getting these seeds planted in straight rows."

Gunny slowly dropped seeds from her small right fist into the narrow row. At first the seeds stuck to her fingers, and two or three would drop at once. When that happened, she carefully picked up the extra seeds and placed them in the next open space in the furrow. She was finally able to get one seed to drop at a time through her fingers and her pace quickened. Robert worked slowly behind her covering the seeds. A few times he wanted to tell her to hurry up, or to say that having one or two seeds out of place was all right, but he admired her determination to stick to his rule. At the end of the first row, they had planted a long, straight row of oats with not one seed out of place. Robert admitted to himself that her seed row was much tighter than any he had ever planted. And his back didn't ache from stooping over to place the seeds.

Michael ran out to the field to see what his father and Gunny were doing. "What do you mean Gunny gets to help?" Michael complained. "Why don't I get to help?"

"Because you didn't ask," Robert said firmly as he started with his furrow tool down a second row. Gunny followed behind, planting a neat, tidy line of oat seeds, humming to herself, and smiling all the while. Robert glanced back at her and grinned. She was his girl.

The next day, Robert announced that they were ready to take on the potato beds. Gunny was tired from planting the oat seeds but looked forward to another day in the fields with her Da. Michael decided that fishing was more interesting than planting, and disappeared along the trail to find the McCrohans as Gunny and her father hiked to the higher fields.

The potato fields looked nothing like the oat field. Robert had dug long trenches to loosen the soil, then added manure to create hills for the potato seeds. As the plants grew, he would add more soil to the hills to give the roots room to make more potatoes. Robert took Gunny's seed apron from the wagon and filled it with cut seed potatoes. The pocket apron was much heavier than the previous day, filled with the lumpy eyes of potatoes, each of which would produce a new plant. He grabbed a sack of cut seed potatoes for himself, and headed across the first field. Gunny loved the smell of the freshly turned soil and dragged her toes through the dirt as they walked. When they got to the far end of the field, Robert handed her a small shovel.

"Dig a small hole in the hill about a hand's width down. Put in one seed and cover the hole. Then move to the next hill."

"Your hand or my hand?" Gunny asked.

Robert laughed. "My hand."

Gunny did as she was told. At the end of the first row, her legs and back ached from stooping and shoveling. She stood to stretch and watched as her father moved quickly onto his third row, lugging the large sack of seed potatoes. She took a deep breath and started into her second row.

Gunny insisted she spend each day now with her Da, either weeding in the fields or making the long walk to the stables in Ventry. Staying home with her mother meant cooking and mending and housework—all of which was boring. The air inside the house was smoky and stagnant, and her mother snapped at her and insisted that she work quietly. Her father gave Gunny a job and let her do her best work. He didn't care if she hummed or sang. She could breathe when she worked outside with her father.

Lord Ventry sent Sean Fitzpatrick to find the horseman, Robert Malone. Sean galloped into the small Malone yard on a large, spotted grey steed. He was fifteen and small for his age, and the horse looked huge underneath him. He slid down from the horse and tied the reins to a post by the door. He knocked three times in rapid succession. Robert opened the door and was surprised to see the boy in his yard. Sean's mother worked as a maid in the big house and Sean had pretty much raised himself with the Lord's horses. Robert couldn't recall ever having seen Sean outside of the Lord's stables. His small face was as red as his hair and was covered with beads of sweat from a thundering ride through the hills around Mount Eagle.

Sean took a deep breath and his words caught in his throat. "The Lord's prize mare refuses to eat and we can't find nothing wrong with her. You're to take this steed and go to the stables at once. She's the Lord's favorite. Someone will pay if she dies."

Robert pulled on his jacket and hat. By the time he was at the door, Gunny also had on her shawl and hat. Sean glanced at the girl. He had seen her before at the stables and didn't like her. She walked right up to the horses to talked with them as if she was raised in the stables.

"The Lord didn't say anything about bringing a girl with you."

Robert swung up into the saddle, then reached down and roughly pulled Gunny up into his lap. "She hardly weighs a thing," Robert insisted. "She won't slow me down."

Gunny's breath caught in her throat. She had never been on a horse this size and her legs barely straddled the horse's wide back. She gripped the horse's black mane and fell back against her father as he spurred the large beast down the hill through the fallow field, then south toward Ventry.

Lord Ventry's large black mare was lying down in her stall. Robert knelt, muttering, and ran his hands over every inch of the horse's large frame. She gave him a weak whinny and he clicked in response. No bones appeared to be broken. He felt around her head and across her belly applying soft pressure along her stomach and at each of her joints. She didn't have a temperature and nothing appeared to be swollen or painful. She whinnied again and Robert nickered in return. Was this perhaps a kinked intestine? If that's the case, she's done for, he thought. He stood and rubbed the back of his sweaty neck with his right hand, bumping his cap onto his forehead. He stared down at the horse, head tilted slightly to one side.

Gunny squeezed past him and squatted near the mare's head.

"Be careful, Gunny. If she's in pain, she may bite you."

Gunny looked the large mare in the eye and placed a small hand on each side of the horse's long black head. The horse stared back, her large brown eyes dewy and soft. Gunny pet the horse's velvet black nose as she muttered little clicks and snorts. Then she ran her hands up along the horses head toward her ears. When she got near the horse's right ear, the mare shook her head and pulled away.

"Da, did you look here?" Gunny asked, cupping her hand around the warm, black ear.

"The horse is not eating and won't stand, Gunny. It's likely something's wrong with her insides, not her ears."

"When I have an earache I feel dizzy and my whole head hurts. And I don't feel like eating," Gunny said.

Gunny held the horse's head steady while Robert held a candle up to the horse's right ear. Inside, he could see a dark mass deep down in the ear shaft.

The surrounding skin was red and swollen. How could he have missed this? Could the problem be as simple as ear mites?

"You may be right, child. Her ear looks bad." He pulled a bottle of mineral oil from a high shelf and heated some in a tin cup over a candle. When the oil was warm, he poured it into the horse's ear, and then took a long swab of fabric wrapped around a small stick and carefully cleaned out the thick, black mess. The horse waited patiently while he worked, then sat up, shook her large head, and struggled to her feet.

Robert laughed. "It looks like she's already feeling better. What made you think to look in her ear?"

Gunny squinted at her father. "I asked her."

The horse whinnied and tossed her head.

Robert looked at Gunny. "You have a gift," he said.

The little girl grinned.

Sean Fitzpatrick ran into the stables, sweaty and pale from his run back from Dunquin. "What do you think..." he started, then stared amazed to see the horse on her feet and pawing at the feed bags. "Well, I'll be. You are the horseman." He wrapped his arms around the horse's thick neck, then ran to the back of the large stables. He returned with a plump sheep dog pup and held it out to Robert. "Old Blue had a litter a few months back. The other pups have been claimed, but no one wanted the runt of the litter. How'd you like him?"

The pup had long, silky black hair and one white paw. His right ear fell slightly forward over light blue eyes. Gunny reached out and stroked the soft fur on the puppy's head. He grabbed her fingers in his mouth and gave her a playful chew. Gunny laughed and pulled the pup from Sean's arms into her own. "Da, can we have him?"

"Give it back, Gunny," Robert said sternly. "A dog eats more than we can spare these days." Robert's old sheep dog had died the year before and truth be told, he wasn't sure how he would get his sheep in for sheering without a dog. He looked at Gunny's intent face as she muttered into the pup's soft ear.

"How much?" he asked the boy.

"Half a pound."

"I haven't got a half pound. Put the dog down, Gunny. We have to get home."

Gunny held the pup's soft head against her cheek and closed her eyes. "Da, we need a dog. You know we do," she said in a voice too mature for a five-year old.

"He's small," Sean said. "I'll give him to you for five shillings."

"I only have four."

"Then I'll give him to you for four."

Gunny whooped and held the pup up over her head while her father dug in his pockets for the coins. Gunny put the pup down and he raced to the back of the stables with Gunny in hot pursuit.

"Gunny, remember he's a working dog," Robert bawled after her.

"What'll we name him?" Gunny yelled back.

"Shep, of course," Robert said without pause.

Gunny walked up to her father and clung onto his leg. "Wasn't Shep the name of our last dog?" she asked, then knelt and clicked her tongue to call the pup.

"I call all of my dogs Shep."

Shep wiggled up to Gunny and licked her hand. She ran her hand over his smooth, black head and he rolled onto his back so she could pet his belly.

"Shep," she said. The dog twisted upright and looked at her. She grinned. "See how smart he is? He already knows his name."

John McCrohan and Robert Malone sat on short three-legged stools on the uneven dirt floor in front of a low peat fire, smoking their pipes and sipping at small jars of whiskey. The McCrohan house was crowded with six McCrohan children plus several other children from the village including Michael and Gunny Malone. Kate McCrohan kept one eye on the fire and the other on the children as she sat on a third stool briskly patching worn clothes. She kept her stool close by John's and occasionally reached out to gently touch his arm or leg. When the fire waned, she knelt to stir the embers and added a new brick of turf. The only other light in the room came from a dim oil lamp that hung along the front wall.

Robert enjoyed a few quiet moments with John each evening before there was a knock at the door and the house filled with the voices and heat of friendly neighbors. John was one of the few men in the village who could read, and his selection of a newspaper story each evening brought friends from the village in for a nightly discussion. Eileen Malone rarely attended with Robert. The local women would occasionally ask Robert about Eileen, but she wasn't from the village and wasn't generally missed. Each guest arrived at the McCrohans' with a stool to sit on. The men brought pipes and tobacco; the women brought a basket of mending and bit of food to share. John started most evenings with a reading from the paper. New stories led to old stories— of Brian Boru, the High King of Tara; of Grania O'Malley, the Irish pirate queen; of St. Brendan, the Navigator; of St. Bridgit, the saint of healing and inspiration; and of the brave Fianna warriors. Everyone contributed to the conversation, but Robert Malone and John McCrohan were recognized as being the two best story tellers.

Some of Gunny's earliest memories were of sitting at her father's feet listening to the old stories. Gunny loved how her father used his whole body when he told a story, leaning forward to create suspense, and clapping his hands to describe a thunderstorm, to cap a phrase, or to break a spell. Robert's face animated the characters he described—his eyebrows raised in surprise, or fell in misery. John favored the mysteries and spoke with a lowered voice and his hand at his mouth to punctuate the secrecy of a moment. He ruffled his hair when he told tales of change brought about by the north wind, and smoothed his hair when he told tales of true lovers reunited.

Gunny loved falling asleep in front of the fire listening to the stories, and especially liked when her father picked her up to carry her home, placing her in bed next to Michael, and gently tucking a blanket in tight around both of them.

~ Chapter 2: A Tin Whistle, Holy Days, and Seals ~

Gunny sat in the loft by the chimney surrounded by chickens, chicken feathers, and dirt, and listened to the drum of rain on the thatch roof. It was mid-April but the weather felt like it had been borrowed from March. Michael was off as usual with the McCrohan boys and her father said it was too wet to work in the fields. She rolled onto her back and thrust her hips into the air, dangling her dirty bare feet over her head. She held her breath until she saw stars, then flopped back down onto the rough, wooden floor. A chicken nesting nearby squawked and pecked at her hand. She ignored the bird, and turned onto her stomach to crawl to the edge of the loft on her elbows. She raised her head just high enough to spy on her mother stitching by the dim light of the fire.

"Stop staring at me," Eileen muttered without looking up. "You're nine years old today. Go find something to do."

"There's nothing to do. I wish you'd had more children so I'd have someone to play with."

"If you can't find something to do, I'll find something for you."

Gunny scooted to the back of the loft and leaned against a pile of old wooden boxes. Weak, grey light dotted the floor from the small rain-speckled loft window. She rocked back and felt the boxes shift behind her, then jumped, hitting her head on the damp roof, as the top box tipped off the stack and spilled its contents with a crash. Chickens squawked and flew out of the loft in every direction.

"What was that?" Eileen yelled, shooing the crazed, exiting birds away from her stitching.

"Nothing," Gunny said loudly as she crouched and flipped the wooden box upright, then felt about in the dim light for the contents. She thrust an old rusted iron pan and two wooden plates back into the box. She spied a glint of metal on the floor, and reached over to grasp a long, thin tube. She sat cross legged and ran her hand over the cool, dimpled surface, then crawled to the edge of the loft, pushed one remaining chicken aside, and held the treasure out toward her mother.

"What's this?"

Eileen squinted up at Gunny then returned to her sewing. "That's my Mam's old whistle. Put it back where you found it and clean up the mess you made."

"I already cleaned it up. Can I keep the whistle?"

Eileen hesitated. "It belonged to my Mam."

"Why did Grandmam have a whistle? Did she play it?"

"Maybe when she was little. I don't remember." Eileen set her mending in her lap and pushed a loose strand of hair away from her eyes. "Put that away and come down. Your da'll be home soon from the pub and will want to eat. We need fresh water from the well."

Gunny remained in the loft, rolling the cool, tin whistle between her dirty palms. "But your Mam has passed and this old whistle is just wasting away up here. Do you know how to play it?"

"No," Eileen laughed. "I'd never play a whistle."

Gunny put the whistle to her mouth and blew. A high-pitched shriek filled the room. She pulled the whistle from her mouth and smiled. "That was loud!"

"That was dreadful!" Eileen said. "You'll bring on a headache sure enough. Take that whistle outside if you must blow on it. And don't forget to get the water."

Gunny scrambled onto the ladder and jumped down the last few rungs. She grabbed the wooden water bucket by the door and hurried outside with Shep tight at her heels. The rain had dissolved into a heavy mist. She set the bucket down in the yard and sat on the rough bench that ran along the front wall of the house. She looked at the small instrument. She remembered seeing Gabe Burke play a tin whistle once at a gathering at the McCrohans'. She covered up all of the holes as best she could with her small hands and blew. The sound was muddled and low. She uncovered one hole and the pitch went up slightly. She uncovered another hole and another until she reached the same high pitch she had made inside.

"I can still hear you!" Eileen shouted through the door. "Take that whistle with you to the well."

Gunny leap off the bench, clicked for Shep to follow, and raced up the muddy path toward Mount Eagle, whistle in hand, the water bucket sitting forgotten by the sodden bench.

Gunny played the whistle everywhere she went that summer, in the fields, along mountain paths, and at the shore. She started off teaching herself the old tunes she'd heard at the gatherings, then made up new tunes that were sometimes jarring, sometimes sweet. Her mother didn't cringe now when she played inside and she had even been asked to play a few times at the McCrohans'.

Through the long, cold winter she played in front of a low peat fire until her cheeks hurt, and her long, thin fingers ached. Eileen pretended indifference to the music, but her father sat near her as she played and often teared up at her high and low trills, shaking his large head as the tunes pulsed through him to the beat of the wind.

Gunny woke from a tangled dream on her mattress in front of the fire. She had moved out of the back room two months before, just after Christmas. Michael was large and sweaty and took up too much space in their shared bed. She tossed her thin blanket aside, unsettling two chickens who were roosting at her feet. A dull light filtered through the front window. When the chickens re-settled in the loft, the front room was quiet and still. She took a deep breath of smoky air and smiled.

"St. Brigit's Day!" she whispered to the walls. Today was the first day of spring. The winds would be warmer now, and the seas calmer. Starting today, she would spend every minute outside with her father preparing the fields for planting. She pushed up from her mattress and looked out the front window. A light rain was falling in the yard. Oh, well. Rain on St. Brigit's Day was lucky. She stood and stretched, then felt a cold, wet nose on her leg. She gave Shep a quick pat on the head and squatted in front of the fire to stir in a few bog sprigs. When the sprigs caught, she added a brick of turf and warmed her hands. She would need straw to make St. Bridgit crosses. She'd take Shep with her up into the high fields. She heard a rustle of covers from the back room.

"Don't get any ideas about being outside all day," Eileen whispered loudly, coming up behind her. "I want this house neat and tidy for St. Bridgit."

"Do you love St. Bridgit? Or do you just like that I have to help you clean the house today?"

Eileen ignored her daughter and glanced out the window. She shook her head. "Rain. How miserable is that?" she said, rubbing her hands in front of the fire to warm them.

Gunny tied on her apron and grabbed her shawl and the bucket by the door. "I'll get the water." She pulled her shawl up over her head and paused. "Are you going to make a fruit cake?"

"I doubt we have enough flour or butter."

Gunny clucked her tongue and pointed. Shep obeyed, racing past her out the door. "St. Brigit gave fruit cakes to the poor. We should make a fruit cake to remember her."

"We are the poor. And who remembers us?"

It was a week before Easter and Eileen was once again turning the house upside down, cleaning for a high holy day. Gunny dragged the kitchen table and stools outside and rubbed them down with sand and water. While they dried, she took the frying pan, potato pot, cooking tongs and flippers to the yard and scrubbed them with sand. The black metal pots still felt greasy even after she scrubbed each one several times. She eyed the pots. They were black and thick with fire-hardened ash. She frowned and looked around the yard. She wasn't sure how else to clean them. How was it that Michael was always absent when there was hard work to be done?

Robert slipped out of the house to join Gunny. Eileen had given him strict instructions about cleaning the yard. He leaned on the low stone fence, one hand on his hip and the other rubbing the back of his neck as he eyed the crowded space. They'd be moving the dung hill soon enough to fertilize the fields. He looked at the broken stool tucked under the front bench. Two legs were still perfectly good and they might need those to mend another stool. The bent wheel from the wagon leaned against the front wall draped in his old fishing net which needed mending. Those should stay right where they were. He glanced at the cracked butter churn. He could probably fix it. He glanced up at Gunny and shrugged. Really. What was there to clean?

Gunny took a deep breath and looked up from her work. "Da, if you go to Dingle this week, could you get me a new ribbon to wear on Easter Sunday?"

Robert dug his hands into his pockets and looked out across the fields. "You know we have no money for ribbons."

Gunny set the blackened potato pot aside and sat on the front bench. "All of the other girls'll have a new ribbon or new shoes or a new hat for Easter. I never have anything that's new."

Robert sat down next to his daughter and took her red, chapped hand in his. At ten, she was nearly as tall as her mother. "There's no girl in this village with a face as fine as yours. You don't need a ribbon to outshine them all." Gunny blinked back tears and said nothing. Robert glanced at her beautiful face. "You still want a ribbon, don't you?" Gunny gave a slight nod. Robert lowered his eyes and squeezed her hand. "I'll see what I can do," he said rising from the bench.

Gunny stood and gave her father a quick hug, then wiped her face with the back of her hand. "Thank you."

The front door opened in a cloud of dust. "Are you two going to talk all day or are you going to work?" Eileen leaned the broom against the front wall. "Nothing comes back inside until we whitewash the walls. Robert, this yard is still a mess. Make yourself useful and help me pull the mattresses outside. Gunny, bring out the blankets and sheets and give them all a good shake."

Robert grinned at Gunny and stepped briskly around her into the house. "Now, Eileen. What is it you need help with? Gunny and I have fields to ready. We can't be about your women's work all day."

Gunny awoke to a cold house. It was bad luck to light a fire on Good Friday. She shivered and pulled her thin blanket tight around her not wanting to give up the tiny bit of warmth she had under the covers. She watched her mother pull the last string of salted herrings from above the hearth. "These're hard as rocks," Eileen said squeezing each dried fish. "We've no kitchen to add to our potatoes. Go down to the strand and find some winkles and limpets for our Good Friday meal. The full moon last night should have pulled them to shore."

Gunny stuck out her tongue. "No one likes winkles and limpets but you."

Eileen stared at her daughter. Gunny tried to look away, then reluctantly tossed her blanket aside and sat up on her small bed. She yawned and stretched while Eileen stared, then got up with a grunt, pulled on her apron, wrapped her shawl around her shoulders and headed out the door, clicking for Shep.

"Your dog's gone with your father. Don't come back until you have a full apron," Eileen reminded her.

"I'm hungry now," Gunny muttered.

"We fast today until our evening meal."

Gunny sighed and pulled the door closed behind her. She grabbed a rake from along the front wall and walked out to the road dragging the rake behind her. Her feet were tender after a winter in tight boots, but she enjoyed the rough feeling of dirt under her feet. On Good Friday, girls were allowed to wear her hair down and her tangled black curls fell down her back and around her face. The sun was warm, the air cool, and the sky clear as she headed down the hill into the village. She stood up straight as she walked past the large white church, skipped past the pub, and raced out onto the low black rocks that lined the strand. The beach was deserted except for Matt and Mac McCrohan who were carrying a small boat and a couple of long oars down to the water. A cool breeze whipped foam off the incoming surf.

"What're you doing?" she yelled.

"What does it look like we're doing?" Matt yelled back. "We're going fishing."

Matt and Mac McCrohan looked like their father. They both had thick, curly brown hair, and long, thin faces. Gunny picked her way across the slick, wet rocks and jumped onto the hard-packed sand. "You're not supposed to work on Good Friday."

"We aren't working. We're fishing," Matt retorted.

"That's not a very big boat."

"That's not a very big boat," Matt mimicked, glancing over his shoulder at the girl. "I suppose you have a bigger one?"

Gunny paused. She didn't usually talk to Matt McCrohan, even on the evenings they were the only two still awake listening to the stories at the gatherings. "I only meant that it doesn't look big enough to be out on the ocean."

Matt turned, still grasping his end of the boat, and eyed the girl. She was tall and her skirt hung awkwardly short around her calves. The wind blew her long black curls around her slim, pale face. Gunny clutched her rake in one hand and held her hair back with the other, trying to meet Matt's stare and wishing she had pinned her hair in a bun after all.

"You're a girl," Matt snorted. "What do you know about boats? Come on, Mac," Matt said, pulling the boat and Mac toward the water.

"Maybe she's right, Matt," Mac said hesitantly, holding tight to the back end of the boat. "Maybe this boat isn't big enough to go out on the ocean."

Matt looked at Mac and cocked his head slightly to one side. "We worked all winter on this boat. We made it small so the two of us could paddle without help from anyone. Remember?"

"I was just saying…"

"Don't. We came to fish. Let's get this boat in the water."

Mac still didn't move. "Maybe we should try it in a tidal pool first. To make sure it floats and all."

Matt shook his head and dropped his end of the boat. "You're not afraid to go out with me, are you Mac? Tell me you aren't afraid."

"I'm not afraid," Mac paused. "I was only wondering…."

Matt turned sharply on Gunny. "See what you started? Why don't you get back to your women's work collecting shore food and leave us alone?"

Gunny gasped. Women's work? She was sure she could out-dig and out-plant Matt McCrohan any day. "Fine. But don't expect me to fetch help when that little dingy of yours goes under the first wave."

She turned and ran onto the slick rocks and raked furiously at the first bed of limpets she found. She glanced over her shoulder as the two boys pulled the small boat out into the surf. Matt yelled for Mac to get in and Gunny watched as Mac's legs flailed out behind him as he scrambled into the rocking boat. She leaned on her rake and held her breath as Matt hauled himself into the boat, and they awkwardly secured the oars on the dowels. After nearly tipping once more, they rowed the small craft unsteadily out to sea. As they rounded the western spit of land that defined the strand Matt's yelling faded, and the sound of pounding surf and gulls filled the air once more.

Gunny set the rake aside and squatted beside a large tidal pool, tucking her skirt in around her bare feet. She sang to herself as she plucked a large periwinkle from the bottom of the pool. The small creature pulled inside his curled, black shell. Gunny held the snail near her mouth and hummed a steady note. The animal emerged from his shell at the vibration. "Just me," she said smiling at the doomed creature, and tucked it deep in her apron pocket. She plucked a dozen more winkles from the icy cold water then stood to warm her reddened hands and looked out to sea. She spotted Mac and Matt in their small boat far out on the horizon. They were rowing evenly together now. "Boys," she muttered as she watched. "Why do you have to act so smart about everything?"

Her stomach rumbled as she moved from one tidal pool to the next, plucking out dozens more winkles and stashing them in her deep, wet apron pocket. Then she retrieved her rake and scraped a few dozen more white limpets off the black rocks. She added the limpets to the winkles in her pocket, rinsed her hands in a tidal pool, and picked her way to the shore across the slippery black rocks. The boys were rowing back toward the beach and she hurried to leave. The last thing she wanted was to talk to Matt McCrohan again.

Gunny tossed the rake aside and pulled the large black pot from under the front bench in the yard. She shook the crustaceans loose from her apron pocket and covered the mouth of the pot with a wide plank of bog wood, then opened the door and leaned inside to announce that the evening meal had arrived. Eileen, Robert, and Michael were kneeling in front of the cold fireplace in the darkened room. Eileen turned to nod at Gunny then continued with a softly muttered prayer. Christ had suffered on the cross between noon and three on Good Friday and midday was a time of prayer. Gunny grabbed a small corked bottle from a box near the hearth, slipped it into her wet apron pocket and tip-toed back toward the door.

"Where do you think you are going?" Eileen asked over her shoulder in a quiet voice.

"I'm going to the holy well to get water," Gunny whispered. She closed the door before her mother could object, sprinted around the house and raced down the hill. The holy well was across the road from the tall white church at the center of the village. She entered the quiet yard by the well and paused to catch her breath, then dropped to her knees and searched through the grasses till she found a small stone. She placed the stone in the deep rut left by years of pilgrim tracings that ran between the stones of the well. She circled the well three times tracing the ancient pattern. At the end of the third pass, she tossed the stone into the well for good luck, then leaned in and dipped the small bottle into the cool, dark water. When the bottle was full, she corked it and stared at her wavering, reflection. She felt a hand on her back and nearly dropped the bottle. She turned with a gasp.

Father Begley laughed. "I didn't mean to startle you, Gunny. See any fish in there today?"

Father Begley was a short, heavy priest with thinning grey hair and a wide smile. The sleeves and hem of his black cassock were ragged and worn, the front stained from years of over-eating and wear. He broke a sweat with the least exertion and had a sweet, musty smell about him.

"No, Father," Gunny said, leaning against the well. "No good luck for me. But I have Good Friday water for whatever ails my mother." She held up the small bottle for the priest to see.

"Think it will work?" Father Begley asked with a wink.

Gunny smiled. "It's always worth a try."

Fiona Burke walked into the well yard and gave Gunny a half smile. Gunny glanced away. She wasn't supposed to talk to Fiona Burke. She backed out of the yard, dashed across the dirt road, pushed open the heavy, creaking iron gates in front of the church, and slipped inside. She crossed behind the church and waded through the long grasses to two graves that lay side by side in the south end of the old graveyard. She squatted in front of the stones. Robbie and Margaret Malone. 1811.

"Hello, Gramps. Hello Nana," she said. "It's Good Friday." A bee flew past her and she waved it away. "I hope you're well. I'm hungry but we're fasting." She stared at the silent stones. "I'll tell Da I stopped by to see you. And we'll pray for you tonight." She dropped a little holy well water on the graves, then hurried back through the church gates. When she pushed the gates closed behind her, the rusted hinges groaned and she felt the hairs rise on the back of her neck. Most of the girls she knew would not go into the graveyard, even on Good Friday. Gunny reminded herself that everyone in the graveyard was a neighbor or kin. There was nothing to be afraid of.

She hurried home, hoping it was late enough in the day that they could finally light a fire and eat a meal. As she approached her house, she saw smoke rising merrily from her chimney and broke into a sprint.

Gunny rose early on Easter morning to watch the sunrise with her father. When Robert left for the high fields to slaughter a lamb, she returned to the house to attend early Mass with her mother and Michael, tying her hair back with a tattered, old black ribbon.

"Today is the most important holy day, because today is the day Christ rose from the dead," Father Begley announced from the pulpit to an audience of mostly women and children. Gunny yawned and wiggled uncomfortably on the hard bench. Her stomach rumbled loudly.

"Easter is the most important holy day because it's the end of Lent," she muttered to Michael who nodded in agreement. Eileen pinched her arm to shush her but Gunny didn't care.

When they got home, she and Michael spent the rest of the day decorating and eating eggs. That night, the family shared a rare meal of lamb and roasted potatoes. Even Christ would be thankful for a meal like this, Gunny thought, after a month without eggs or meat.

They finished the evening at the McCrohans'. When they arrived, the house was already crowded with neighbors. Eileen joined in for a short while but waited uncomfortably near the door until Robert walked her home. Gunny and Michael stayed late into the evening as their friends and neighbors drank, and laughed, and told stories, and the young people of the village danced set after set to the tunes of two fiddlers, a drummer, and a fine new singer from Ventry. Gunny fingered her whistle in her pocket but no one asked her to play. Perhaps another night.

Kate McCrohan was one of the best bakers in the village and every Easter made a yellow cake decorated with fresh, spring flowers. The cake this year glistened from its perch on top of an over-turned butter churn near the fire. At the end of the evening, Kate awarded the cake to the two best dancers. The winning teens ate a few bites, then passed delicate slivers out to everyone else. When the cake was gone, with only a few crumbs left on the floor for the chickens to peck at, the crowd dispersed and Gunny and Michael happily stumbled up the hill to their quiet, dark house.

It was May Day morning and Gunny was out collecting flowers to make a posy. She paused to look across the steep field of tall grasses and bright yellow flowers. Long beams of sunlight broke from the mountain behind her and cut through the mists in the valley below, highlighting the cluster of houses nestled in the heart of the village of Dunquin. There was no smoke coming from any of the grey stone chimneys and the air smelled strangely clean. As the sun rose higher behind her, the mist slowly dissolved to reveal light dirt roads and dark, freshly plowed fields. With no trees to block the view, she could see all the way from the field by her house to the light dancing on the distant grey-green ocean. She set aside a handful of cowslips, buttercups, and furze and pulled out her whistle. She played a mournful tune to greet the morning, then called Shep and headed home with the scraggly collection of limp, yellow flowers.

Inside the damp, dark house, she groped to fill a tin cup with cold well water and placed the flowers on the table. She took a broom of heather twigs and started to sweep out the barren hearth.

"No fire!" Eileen called hoarsely from her bed in the back room. "People will steal anything that leaves our house this morning and that includes smoke. If someone takes the smoke, we won't have any butter all summer."

Gunny raised her hands to show that the only thing she had was a broom. Eileen pushed herself out of bed, tied on her apron, swiftly pulled her hair back into a small bun at the nape of her neck, then sat at the table and rubbed her face.

Robert gave a loud yawn behind her, rose and stretched, his long arms reaching the low ceiling. "Morning," he said, leaning hard on the table. He touched the cup of yellow flowers on the table and smiled at Gunny. "Happy May Day." He walked to the cold fireplace and reached for his pipe in the cubby hole to the right of the fire place.

"No smoke!" Eileen shrieked.

Robert gestured toward the window with an elbow as he cut off a bit of tobacco from a black, wrinkled plug with his pocket knife. "Calm yourself. There's smoke coming from the McCrohans' chimney. Kate McCrohan's already cooking."

Eileen pulled open the door and peered down the hill to make certain that Kate had indeed gotten her fire going. "What a silly woman to light her fire so early on May first. She'll be lucky to have any butter at all this summer." She turned to Gunny. "So get a fire going. Michael," she yelled into the back room. "Get up and make yourself useful."

Gunny scrambled in her father's cubby for the tinder box. Her mother usually smoored the fire at night to keep it alive until the next morning, but on

May Eve, they let the fire die out. Eileen had only recently showed Gunny how to start a new fire. Gunny took a handful of bog deal from the box and placed it near a brick of turf in the fireplace, then took the flint rock and struck it hard against the steel file. She kept striking, watching for a tiny spark to light the dry shavings of ancient pine her father had pulled from the bog and dried.

Michael sat down heavily on a stool next to her. "I don't know how you do that. I can never get a fire going."

Eileen leaned across Michael, hung a pot of water on the crane, and swung the arm of the crane out over the fire. "Go see what we have for potatoes. I think we're nearly out."

Michael ambled to the back room and stretched out under the bed. He felt around in the dark and rolled the last of the potatoes out into the open space between the beds. The potatoes were small and wrinkled. "You're right. There's not much here."

He yawned and crossed back to his stool to watch Gunny work. When a tiny spark finally lit on the deal, she tossed the rock and file aside and cupped the small nest of deal in her hands, gently blowing on the spark until it ignited. She placed the glowing deal back in the fireplace next to the turf and added loose tinder until the familiar smell of peat returned the house. She stood up and dusted off her hands.

"Now that the planting's done, will you go fishing with me?" Michael asked Robert.

Gunny walked to the back room, pulled the loose potatoes into her apron and dumped them out on the table. Eileen shook her head and pulled the flour box open. She stirred her hand through the rough oat flour. "How do we ever get through the summer months?" She turned to Robert and Michael. "No fishing today. It's May first. Lord Ventry will be hiring for the season."

Robert shook his head. "I saw our fine Lord last night at O'Leary's pub. He arrived on foot with a brace of hares in one hand and a bottle of a whiskey in the other, his hunting dogs all barking and slobbering around him. He said he's in town first to collect rent. Then he'll talk about hiring."

"I hoped he'd let the rents go another year. You're best to be away from the village then," Eileen said. "There's turf to be cut."

"Indeed there is. And the bog is one place you'd never find the Old Lord. I'll go see John McCrohan about getting the bog spade sharpened."

"Make sure you're home again before dark," Eileen snapped.

Robert stood and gave his wife a kiss on the forehead. "My dear. I'm only getting a spade sharpened. How long can that take?"

Robert returned around noon with a sharpened spade, a belly full of poteen, and a smile on his face. Gunny whistled for Shep and they headed off pushing the small barrow up the steep mountain path.

The bog covered several acres of land about a mile up the mountain. Four other men from the village were there footing turf on the open, black hillside covered with heather. Robert joined them to share what news they had of the Lord's whereabouts. Michael and Shep wandered off in search of bird eggs while Gunny stretched out on her stomach on a flat grey rock and watched as her father got to work at an opening along the wall of peat, making a straight cut down the back side of each brick of peat, then making a side cut using the second blade of the spade. Gunny's eyes grew heavy as she watched the rhythmic moves of her father as he formed brick after brick, making sure to keep a straight line with each cut.

The bog was a mix of ancient trees and leaves, at places up to ten feet thick, the soil acidic and black. Occasionally as they dug, a man would strike a solid branch that had been preserved through the ages and everyone would stop to dig out the bog deal, so useful for starting fires. Once Ned Murphy had found a golden box in the peat. Gunny tried to stay awake from her perch on the rock, keeping an eye out for any buried treasure the men might have missed.

When Michael and Shep returned eggless, Robert insisted the boy take a turn cutting before they moved the first load of turf bricks out of the bog. Gunny watched as Michael awkwardly slung the spade. His movements were not rhythmic and smooth like her father's. At thirteen, his legs and arms were heavier than her father's and he looked as if he were attacking the soil. The cuts he left behind were jagged and uneven.

Gunny plucked the small violet flowers off a heather plant that was growing next to her rock and made a pile of the tight blooms. She breathed in the spicy smell left behind on her fingers, then snapped off a heather sprig and tossed it at Shep who was napping in the shadow of the rock. The dog's eyes opened and he rolled onto his back. Gunny reached down to scratch his belly.

"Gunny," Robert yelled. Michael's cutting lesson was over. Gunny brushed the pile of heather off the rock and ran to help with the hauling. She worked in tandem with her father and brother as they passed the soggy bricks to her to stack in the barrow. No other girls from the village helped stack turf at the bog and she liked that.

"We'll cut a few more rows of the black bottom peat today," Robert grunted. "Then we'll need a few passes of sphagnum peat for our summer fires. Shouldn't take us more than a week"

Gunny followed Michael as he grumpily pushed the heavy barrow up the narrow path to a higher field. They dumped out the first load of soggy bricks and laid them out in rows to dry, then returned with the barrow, dirty and wet, to wait for Robert to finish the second cut and the third. By the end of the week, they were all tired and sore, but knew they would have fuel for the winter—if the weather cooperated and the turf dried properly over the long summer months.

Michael and Gunny returned to the high field in July to place the bricks of turf upright against one another in sets of three to help the turf dry farther. In late August, Robert joined them in the high field and declared that the turf was dry. They loaded the first round of solid, heavy bricks into wooden creels on their backs and carried the turf home to the yard.

"We moved nine creels and few barrows of turf today," Robert informed Eileen when they got home. "The whole rick is now safe and we will enjoy a warm winter."

"God be praised," Eileen said lightly, envisioning a long, stuffy winter in a house filled with peat smoke, animals, and family.

Robert joined the other men at the pier at dawn to load up the nets for a day at sea. He rarely fished with the other men in the village, but the herring were running and everyone had to pitch in to help bring in the heavy loads of fish from the choppy waters. The villagers owned six large curraghs which required eight men in each boat, with two at each oar. The curraghs were made of a sturdy frame fitted with slats of wood covered with tarred paper. They were tough enough to sail on the ocean, but light enough for four men to carry.

Robert's father had practically lived on the water, but Robert found he preferred the feel of the earth beneath his feet. He knew he needed the fish to help keep his family fed through the winter, but still hated the panic he felt each time a boat shifted beneath him.

With all of the men in the village fishing, Matt and Mac McCrohan had been left behind. Matt was bored. He sprawled out along the bench in the forge and watched his younger brother pump bellows made from two long boards stitched in a leather casing, and attached to the stove by a long, black pipe.

"How about we hike up the hill and catch us some trout?"

Mac stopped pumping the bellows, pulled a glowing iron from the fire with his tongs, and moved unsteadily to the anvil. He took up his father's heavy hammer with both hands and beat on the red-hot bar. When the bar had cooled to black, he plucked up the horseshoe with the tongs and held it toward the weak light that eked in through the ash-covered front window. The horseshoe was uneven and misshapen. He sighed and tossed the cooling "U" into the fire to try again.

"The stream belongs to Lord Ventry," he grunted.

At ten, Mac was much smaller than his older brother, but his arms and legs were thick with muscle. He stood, one hand on a hip, and brushed away the sweat on his brow. He gave the bellows a few quick pumps to get the fire hotter. Matt leaned against the wall of the forge and chewed gently on a bit of straw.

"First off, the old Lord lives in Ventry. That's miles away. And second, how could he possibly know if one or two of his precious fish are missing? The men are all out fishing. Why shouldn't we be fishing? No one will see us."

"I have work to do."

Matt laughed. "Work? I don't think anyone is going to be buying those misshapen horseshoes of yours."

"Poaching is a crime."

"It's only a crime if you get caught."

"Da was mad when we brought the fish home from the stream last time."

"So this time, we'll stay on the mountain and cook the fish before we come back. We'll bury the skin and bones. No one will be the wiser."

Mac shook his head. "I don't want to get in trouble." He glanced at his older brother. Matt stared back at him, eyebrows raised. Mac sighed and tossed the large hammer aside. "All right, I'll go with you. But if we catch any fish, I won't eat them."

Matt grinned. "That's a good lad. Grab some fish hooks from Da's box, will you? I'll get some line from the house."

Gunny climbed the steep mountain path with a crock of butter for Michael. She had spent the morning with her mother learning how to make it.

"If you are going to eat so much butter, you'd better learn how to make it," Eileen had chided her.

Gunny watched as her mother took the cooled milk from the night before and skimmed off the fat into the butter churn. Eileen showed her how to put the wooden churn paddle in and how to secure the lid. After a few minutes working the plunger, Gunny was bored. "How long does this take?"

Eileen lifted the lid to show Gunny that the fat was starting to clump on the insides of the churn—but that most of the milk was still milk.

Gunny churned for a half hour before Eileen opened the lid again to see the results. This time, large lumps of butter were mixed in with the milk.

"No fairies about today!" Gunny said, looking at the gleaming clumps of butter as Eileen crossed herself.

Eileen helped Gunny carefully pour the mix of butter and milk onto a cloth she had fastened over a large bowl. The buttermilk passed through the cloth leaving yellow lumps of butter behind. Eileen scraped the plunger and insides of the churn with a small wooden paddle and added the last butter scrapings to the larger clumps on the cloth, then wrapped the cloth tight around the butter and squeezed the remaining milk out into the bowl. Then she opened the cloth and scraped the butter off with the paddle and kneaded the butter lumps together on the table until they were smooth and milk free. She scraped the finished butter into a butter firkin and smoothed out the top with the back of the paddle.

Gunny eyed the small butter crock she was carrying to Michael. She wondered if her brother would appreciate all the work that had gone into making the butter. Michael was living in the booley fields for the summer tending to the Malones' small herd of sheep and their single cow. All of the livestock from the village was moved each spring to the booley fields high in the hills. Local teens watched over the animals through the summer until the lower fields were harvested. Then the animals returned to the village for the winter to graze on the stubble left in the fields, and to warm the houses at night.

Michael's small clochain was tucked in just below the peak of a long ridge; other round stone huts thatched with heather dotted the mountain ridge, but the fields were quiet. Gunny crouched down through the doorway and peeked inside Michael's hut. It was like an animal den with a low ceiling of smoky thatch and soiled straw strewn about on the dirt floor. The fire pit at the center was overflowing with ash. She placed the butter crock on a high shelf near the door, and then slipped back outside to the fresh air. She whistled for Shep. She didn't miss her brother, but she did want to see the dog.

Two boys who were up in the higher fields tending their sheep heard her whistle and gave a wave. She knew they'd tell Michael she was there. She waved back and hiked down the mountain. It was late afternoon and the warm summer sun lit the fields around her. She felt the heat wash through her and paused to let the rays settle on her face. She pulled out her whistle and breathed out a tune to bring her father's boat home. She watched the village men rowing out along the horizon, and matched the pace of her tune to the rowing as the tiny curraghs headed back toward the pier. She heard voices behind her and ducked behind a large rock. Matt and Mac McCrohan walked by, laughing and tossing rocks ahead of them on the path.

"Have you ever had a finer meal?" Matt asked. Mac laughed and confessed that he had not.

When the boys passed, Gunny headed home. It was well past dark when Robert finally trudged into the house, pale and smelly, but happily rolling a barrel of gutted, cleaned, and salted herring in front of him.

"We packed twenty barrels today—enough for each man who fished, with a few left over to sell in Dingle."

Eileen pried the lid off the barrel and smiled at the silvery treasure inside. Gunny made a string of fish to take up to Michael at the booley the next day. They each had an extra helping of fish that night and praised the Lord for their bounty.

In late September, Robert announced he was ready to lift the last of the potatoes. Once the potatoes were harvested, Michael and the other teens could return with the grazing animals from the booley.

Gunny walked with her father to the fields. She had learned to love harvesting potatoes. Each scraggly, dry plant held a host of surprises below—there were large spuds, and tiny spuds, and sometimes no spuds. The first spade full of dirt was the best—seeing the solid, brown spuds emerge through the dirt along the lines of spidery potato roots. The smallest spuds would be saved to use as seed potatoes. The largest would be shredded to make stampy. They moved load after load of heavy potatoes by barrow to the house and stored them under the beds, in the loft, and in large wooden boxes that lined the low, stone walls. By the time they moved the last load, every bit of Gunny was covered in dirt but her smile. She grinned as she held up the largest potato from the harvest to show her Mam. "Time to make stampy," she announced.

Eileen swept at the dirt around her. "There's no sense grating a perfectly good potato when you can boil it and be done."

"But stampy is so delicious and Michael will be home tonight. I'll do the grating," Gunny said.

"Not until you wash. Out to the well with you. Both of you."

Gunny grabbed the bucket and raced her father to the well. He limped up behind her, stiff from a hard week of work. Gunny splashed cold water across her face and hands. Robert shook his head as the girl sprinted back to the house. By the time he got there she had already changed into a clean apron and had a large pile of grated potato in front of her. She squeezed out the water onto an old rag, and tossed in a little flour and some salt. He watched from his stool by the fire as she slapped a large spoonful of butter into the fry pan and placed it on the coals of the fire to heat. She added the potato mixture by spoonful to the hot pan. Bits of butter and potato sputtered and snapped in the pan and the small house filled with the delicious smell of crisping potato.

Michael trudged through the door the Shep. His clothes were filthy and he smelled like an animal. Eileen sent him to the well to wash while Gunny proudly set the stampy pan on the table. When Michael returned, they sat at the low, wooden table and bowed their heads.

"Lord, we are thankful for another year of harvest," Robert intoned. "We have a fine crop of potatoes, and the oats came in pretty well too so we won't have to eat many of the turnips from the kitchen garden, God be praised. We have cabbage and onions and a fine barrel of herring. And the cow and sheep were well tended to by Michael and everyone is home again for the winter."

"And we have stampy that is getting cold!" Gunny whispered from behind closed eyes.

Robert continued, "And we have stampy that is getting cold. God be praised. Let's eat."

"The horse races start this week in Ventry. It's quite the gathering," Robert mused from his stool in front of the fire as he slowly drew in on his pipe.

"You're not going," Eileen said flatly from her stool never lifting her head from her mending.

Robert frowned. "I thought maybe you'd like to go with me," Robert said, resting a warm, calloused hand on her back. "The harvest is in. It's time to celebrate."

"No," Eileen repeated in the same flat tone.

"Then maybe Gunny will go with me," Robert said, pulling his hand away. "Her tales on the road shorten the way."

Gunny glanced down at her parents from the loft where she was searching for chicken eggs. She hated being talked about as if she were not in the room.

"You're not going, and Gunny's not going either."

"Gunny would love the horses. The races don't run long."

Eileen set her mending in her lap. "It's not the races that're the problem. The days are all innocence. It's the nights that bring the trouble with the drinking and the dancing and the fighting. You know that as well as I."

"We have a bit of money from the harvest. Gunny," he yelled up into the loft. "Are you off to the races with me?"

Eileen pushed a short bit of thread through her needle and snapped up a new stocking to mend. "Do what you please," she muttered.

Robert chuckled and went to the back room to find his hat.

"You shouldn't go to the races with your father," Eileen hissed at Gunny as she climbed down from the loft. "He'll start drinking and forget he even brought you along."

"Da doesn't drink much," Gunny said with a slight frown.

"You haven't seen him at the races. He turns into the biggest ninny hammer in the county."

"Don't listen to her," Robert said, grabbing Gunny by the arm and heading her out the door. "We'll have a grand time."

Gunny and Robert joined several other villagers on their way to Ventry. Everyone was lively and the chatter was loud. Gunny laughed as her father sang along with the other men.

"But why complain when the future is dim,
For our love is the jug that's full to the brim."

As they neared the strand in Ventry, Robert corralled the thirsty Dunquin villagers into the first pub they passed and ordered a gallon of porter to share. Gunny slipped out the door and wandered down toward the water. She watched as several men finished constructing platforms along the road to the strand which were soon populated with vendors selling sweet cakes and whiskey to the visiting crowd. By noon, a large group had assembled along the rocks by the shore and the first race started. Gunny was amazed at the size and speed of the large horses as they thundered past her down the long flat stretch of sand to thunderous applause.

At the end of the first race, she searched through the crowd for her father but couldn't find him. She watched a few more races, then slipped back through the crowd and returned to the pub. Robert was there at the same table with the same crowd. She squatted by the door and listened as he finished telling one of his longer stories about Grania, the Pirate Queen. When he was done, he toasted his friends and ordered another gallon of porter. Gunny sighed. When the sun finally set, she grabbed her father by the arm and leaned against his shoulder.

"I'm hungry, Da. Let's go home."

Robert looked at her surprised. "No races, then?"

"It's dark, Da. The races are done."

Robert laughed. "The races may be done, but we can't go home yet. We need a bottle of whiskey for the road and a few sweet cakes for your mother." He bounded out the door, and caught the last vendor who was closing up for the day to make his purchases.

A high full moon helped light their way along the uneven dirt road back to Dunquin. By the time they crossed the small bridge that marked the entrance to Dunquin, Gunny was nearly asleep on her feet. They crossed behind the McCrohan forge and stumbled up the steep field to home. Stubs of harvested oat stalks cast deep, silvery shadows. Gunny clutched at her father's hand, and when they were in sight of the house, gathered her last bit of strength and sprinted inside. She had already fallen into bed when her father burst through the door.

"Eileen. Get up! Stir the fire," Robert yelled. "I have sweet cakes and whiskey!"

Eileen moaned. "Do you know what time it is?"

"Yes, I do," Robert said in the same loud voice. "It is time to eat sweet cakes and tip a glass of whiskey with your lovin' husband."

Eileen rolled out of bed and pulled on her shawl. "How were the races?" she asked, stifling a yawn as she knelt and stirred the fire back to life. Gunny pulled herself out of bed and sat down heavily at the table. Michael stirred briefly, then fell soundly back to sleep.

Robert poured his wife a few fingers of whiskey in a glass jar, and then poured a second one for himself. "The races were lovely. As always. A toast!" he announced, handing Eileen her jar.

"What're we toasting?" Eileen asked, taking a seat on her stool and stifling a yawn.

"We're toasting fine horses, fine whiskey, and fine women."

Gunny watched surprised as Eileen tipped her glass back and downed the whiskey in a single swallow.

"Ahhh," she breathed. "That is fine whiskey. And let's see what you have for sweet cakes."

Robert sang the road song again as Eileen cut the sugary cake in slices, and passed a small piece to Gunny. Gunny hadn't had a bite to eat all day. The cake melted in her mouth. It was the best thing she had ever tasted. She closed her eyes to enjoy the sensation and could barely get her eyes open again. She grabbed a second slice of cake from the table, and stumbled to bed as her father poured another few fingers of whiskey for Eileen and proposed another toast.

"It's Puca Night," Robert said from his stool by the fire. "On Hallow E'en, the fairies and the dead are out. You children must be careful to not be stolen away."

Michael scoffed and kicked the toe of one boot in the dirt floor. "I don't believe in that rot. I'm headed out with the boys. We'll make our own mischief," he said as he grabbed his cap and headed out the door.

"After you bring the animals into the yard," Robert yelled after the boy. Gunny watched her brother leave. She didn't know if he was brave or stupid. She would never go out alone on Hallow E'en.

"I hope the fairies don't take him," she said to her father, blinking her large brown eyes and holding her hands to her chest.

Robert sighed and pulled on his cap. "I'll go check on him. Don't eat without us."

"The fairies would never take your brother. You're the one that's likely to disappear," Eileen said, dropping potatoes into a steaming pot of water that hung from the crane over the fire. "We'll make Champ tonight. That'll bring the boy back even if the fairies have him." She poked at the potatoes with a knife. When they were soft, she pulled the pot from the crane and handed it to Gunny. "Go pour off the water."

Gunny took the pot from her mother. It was awkward and heavy and the hot water started to slosh as she walked. Her mother took the pot back from her. "Give me that."

Eileen took the pot outside and poured the potatoes and water into a loosely woven basket on the front bench. The water flowed out through the gaps in the basket. She shook the basket, placed it in the pot, and brought both inside. She placed the heavy basket in front of Gunny at the table. "Now we peel."

Gunny eyed the full basket. Everyone usually peeled their own potatoes when they ate boiled potatoes for dinner. "Peel all ten? They're steaming hot."

"All ten, and yes, they're hot. Don't burn yourself."

Gunny grabbed a large potato and tossed it from hand to hand, blowing on it and willing it to cool before she gave up and put it back in the basket. She watched as Eileen expertly skinned the jacket off her potato using a small knife, and placed it in the pot. Gunny took off her apron, folded it a few times, and used it to pick up a hot potato. She peeled it slowly and carefully then tossed the clean white spud in the pot. She worked beside her mother until the last potato was peeled and back in the pot.

Gunny ran to get the smooth, wooden nell from the cubby to the left of the hearth. "This is the part you let me do when I was little."

"You're still little," Eileen said, though Gunny was not little anymore. At eleven, she still had a baby face but was nearly as tall as Eileen. Eileen watched Gunny club the offending pot of soft potatoes. She inspected Gunny's work and pounded out a few missed lumps. "Not bad."

Gunny beamed while Eileen cut up raw cabbage and onion and mixed it in with the hot potatoes. She added a few cups of scalded milk, butter and salt, then scraped the mixture into the center of the pot and added a large pat of butter at the center of the mound. "Done!" she declared.

"Robert Michael!" Eileen yelled the names out the door as if they were one. Robert walked the cow into the house and tied her up to a peg near the fire. Michael was not with him. Robert leaned back out the door. "Champ!" he yelled. Michael sprinted into the house, tossed his cap aside, and joined his family at the table. Robert said a quick grace, and everyone grabbed a spoon and dug into the delicious Hallow E'en treat.

After they ate, Michael headed out to find the McCrohan boys. Robert and Gunny followed while Eileen, feeling a headache coming on, stayed home to clean up from the evening meal.

The McCrohan house was full of villagers, talking and cracking roasted nuts, drinking whiskey and telling stories. Gunny looked around the cozy room She didn't know many of the children from the village. Eileen told her they were not "her society." Nick O'Leary's daughter Maeve sat by her father near the fire. Gunny had seen Maeve before at O'Leary's pub. Gunny eyed the girl with her straight brown hair and fresh apron. She had a little round face and short, pig-like nose covered in freckles. Gunny watched as Maeve nibbled intently at a large piece of yellow cake. Gunny wondered where she got the cake. Maeve stared back and stuck out a cake-covered tongue. Gunny shook her head and slipped outside. Maybe her mother was right about the village children.

Most of the teens from the village were out in the yard. Gunny watched as the boys dipped for apples in a big tub of water, stripped down to their waists with their hands held tight behind their backs. Watching them chase after the apples with their tongues and mouths made her howl with laughter while the older girls giggled in a small group.

One of Maeve's older sisters passed out dried beans to several young couples in the yard. Gunny watched as each couple stood side by side and tossed their beans into a bucket of water. If both beans sank, the couple would have a long, happy marriage. If both beans floated, the wedding would occur

36

but the pair would always bicker. If one bean floated and the second sank, the wedding was off. The game had some couples kissing and others arguing. Gunny wondered if she'd ever play the bean game. She slipped back inside in time for the stories. By midnight, her head was too heavy to hold up and she leaned heavily on her father's knee. Her father jostled her awake.

"Time to head home," he said. "Your brother left an hour ago."

Gunny nodded sleepily and pulled on her shawl. She clung to her father's hand as they hiked up across the dark field to their house.

"Da, do the fairies really come out on Hallow E'en?"

"They do, girl. This is the night the fairies move to their winter quarters. Never be out on this night alone, Gunny. Even with a black-handled knife or a nail in your pocket you could be carried away. And what would we do without our Gunny?"

Gunny squeezed her father's large hand. She loved how his hands were both warm and rough. "If the fairies took me, I suppose Mam would say, 'Well, at least this place is a little quieter now. But who will help me make my stampy!'"

Robert laughed at Gunny's fine imitation of Eileen, and gave her hand a squeeze.

On Christmas Eve day, Robert and Michael packed the small hand wagon with two plucked hens, a few dozen eggs, and several cabbages and turnips from the kitchen garden to sell at the Christmas Market in Dingle.

"We are off to bring home the Christmas," Robert announced as they headed out of the yard.

While they were away, Eileen and Gunny hauled the furniture, pots, cooking utensils, bowls and spoons outside. Eileen whitewashed the walls inside while Gunny worked in the windy, cold yard, scrubbing the furniture and kitchenware with sand. They worked together to shake out the bed linens then hung them over the low, stone wall to air. When the whitewash inside was dry, they reassembled the house, built up the fire to warm their hands, and waited for the men to return.

The sun was just starting to set when they returned. Michael set a large, fat plucked goose on the table with a grunt, and stumbled to his stool to unlace his tight, leather boots. Robert tossed his cap onto a peg by the door and pulled a flask of whiskey and twist of tobacco from his jacket pocket. He proudly showed them to Eileen and Gunny, then carefully stashed them in his right cubby. Eileen looked disappointed until he tossed her a small bag of dried fruit for her Christmas fruit cake. While she sorted through the bag, he pulled a new fry pan from behind his back and slid it onto the table. Eileen gasped. She clutched the new pan to her chest and ran her hands over the clean, hard surface, then held out a hand to Robert. He slipped her a small bag of sweets to give the children on Christmas Day and sat to have a smoke.

While Eileen mixed flour and fruit for their Christmas cake, Gunny wove strands of green ivy into garlands and looped them carefully over the fireplace. Then she dug out the insides of a large turnip, carefully fluted the edges with a knife and placed the decorative vegetable on the sill of the front window. She added a small white candle and bit of holly and stood back to admire her work.

Robert and Michael hauled in a bog log from the yard. The wood fire would burn throughout the evening and into Christmas day. They ate a light meal of salted fish with a little milk and flour for sauce and a few small potatoes. After their meal, Robert said a short prayer and lit Gunny's candle in the front window. They held hands and prayed, then returned to their stools by the fire to wait for the fruitcake to finish cooking in the large pot set on the uneven coals of the fire. Gunny slipped out into the crisp, night air to see the candles burning in front windows all the way down the hill to the village. "If Mary and Joseph came through Dunquin tonight, they would know they were welcome," she thought.

"It's cold," Eileen said from inside. "Come in and close the door. We'll have some tea and fruit cake then head to Mass."

"Snow!" Gunny yelled through the open door as a few large flakes drifted down past her and melted in the dirt of the yard. Eileen, Robert, and Michael joined Gunny outside.

"This is a good sign," Eileen said. "A green Christmas makes a fat churchyard." She twisted an arm through Robert's to keep warm and watched as Gunny and Michael laughed and raced about the yard trying to catch snowflakes on their tongues.

The family walked to Mass together, tiny snowflakes whirling about them. Everyone in the village was at the church. Even those who had moved away and had new families returned home for Christmas Mass. There were candles in every window and the pews were full to the doors. Gunny looked around at the familiar faces bathed in candlelight as the priest told the story of the Christ child. The villagers prayed and sang the familiar hymns, then bustled home in the chill winter night.

Gunny knelt next to her bed by the fire to say her Christmas prayers. She peeked at her father, pipe to his mouth in front of the wood fire.

"Da, is it true that anything you wish for on Christmas Eve will come true?" she whispered.

"No, but it is true that no prayer will go unanswered."

"Isn't that the same thing?"

"No, Gunny," he said, tucking her wool blanket tightly in around her as she crawled into bed. "There is no guarantee that wishing for something will make it happen. What is guaranteed on Christmas Eve is that your prayer will be answered. The trick is recognizing the answer to your prayer. Sometimes God is less direct than we'd like Him to be."

Gunny tried to stay awake to hear the cows in the byre speak, but like all other years, she fell asleep before Christ gave the animals the ability to talk. "I wonder what that old cow would say to me…" she muttered as she fell asleep by the fire. Robert patted her on the head, then crawled into his own bed by Eileen, held his wife's hand, and slept.

The family dressed warmly the next morning and headed out the door for Christmas Mass. The snow had stopped in the night, but an inch or two of powdery white crystals had collected on the brown grasses along the long, dirt road into the village. Gunny skimmed snow from the grass tops as she walked, and tossed a small snowball at her brother. He ignored her and walked on with her parents. She sighed and joined them on the trudge down the hill.

Christmas Mass was short and they were soon back home. Gunny and Eileen made a pot of tea, then put the goose on to roast while Robert and Michael left to hunt for hare tracks in the snow. The men returned late in the day with two thin rabbits. Robert hung them on the door outside, promising to take Gunny with him on the next hunt. They ate the delicious fat goose with roasted potatoes and shared their Christmas sweets, then listened to Robert tell Christmas stories as the last of the Yule log burned away.

The sun was out and the air warmer the next morning. Michael headed out at dawn into the high fields with Shep to catch and club wrens to celebrate St. Stephen's Day. Gunny tagged along and collected straw to finish her St. Stephen's masks. By noon, Michael had killed four small birds and raced them down to the McCrohans' forge while Gunny returned home. Matt McCrohan had been captain of the Wren Boys since he was ten, and the parade would start again this year at the forge. Cornelius Foley, and Maurice and Edmond, the Burke twins, were already at the forge with their birds when Michael arrived. Mac McCrohan ceremoniously tied Michael's dead birds to a large furze bush and the six boys headed out to hunt again.

By late afternoon, the bush was full and Matt ordered Mac to get the old straw masks from the forge. As captain, Matt got first choice of masks. He picked an oval one that was shredded along the right side, the tie barely holding it onto his head. He grabbed the carved wooden sword that could only be carried by the Captain of the Wren Boys. The other boys pulled on the remaining worn, straw masks and the parade was ready to start.

Gunny walked into the yard of the forge with a tall stack of new straw masks. Michael groaned behind his mask.

"What have you got there, girl?"

"Your masks are all worn out. Everyone will know who you are."

Matt pushed his mask up off his face and the whole right side collapsed. "Everyone already knows who we are."

The other boys jeered and told her to go home. Her face reddened, but as she turned to leave, Matt grabbed the stack of masks from her. He looked at the top mask and smirked. It was a cat mask with sharp, pointed ears, wide eyes, and whiskers made from striped straw. The look was fresh and the weaving tight. He tossed the cat mask to the ground and grabbed the next one in the stack. This was the face of a wolf with long, thick ears, a narrow snout, and fire-blackened nose. He dropped the rest of the stack and held the wolf mask out in front of him.

"This is good. What else have you got here?"

Gunny squatted to collect the stack of masks Matt had tossed aside, but the other boys surrounded her, grabbing at the masks of seals, birds, and dogs. They each tied on a new mask and turned to Matt. He eyed the results, then slowly tied on the wolf mask, grabbed the bush of dead birds, and whistled to the boys to fall in behind him.

Gunny grinned as the boys headed off down the street howling, and stopping at every house to beg for a few pennies to "bury the wrens." The only houses the Wren Boys skipped over were those where there had been a recent death. A few villagers complained every year when the boys came begging for money, but it was an insult if someone was not visited. The parade ended at O'Leary's Pub where the small collection of coins was used to buy porter.

Gunny amused herself through the winter collecting a variety of straw from the high fields which she wove into masks and mats and small rugs. Eileen scoffed at her work and used the straw pieces as fire starters. After the spring planting was done, Gunny decided to teach herself to twist rope. Even her mother wouldn't burn a good piece of rope.

She had twisted short bits of rope from straw to tie the masks, but for farming rope, needed longer strands of grass. She hunted for grass for several days in the fields far from where the animals grazed, and hauled bundle after bundle into the yard. She stuffed the water bucket full of grass and leaned against the stone wall to wait for the fibers to soften.

After an hour, the blades felt flexible. She sat on the bench in the yard, bucket at her side, and used a fingernail to split the first strand of grass into tiny strips. She twisted the long, thin strips against one another until she had about an inch of rope. She eyed her work. The piece was lumpy and uneven, much like what she had made to tie the masks. She tossed the short rope aside and tried again, working slower and making the weave much tighter and finally produced a length of strong, even rope about three inches long. She gave a whoop and set the piece down to rest her hands. The rope unraveled in her lap. She kicked the bucket sending water and soggy grasses across the yard, then grabbed the empty bucket and went to fetch water for the evening meal.

The next morning, she filled the bucket again and started over. She worked in the yard all morning until she had a strong, even piece of rope about a foot long. She proudly tied off the ends to prevent any unraveling and eyed her work. The rope was strong, but thin. What if she were to weave using reeds from the strand? The reeds there were tall and strong and much thicker than grass. She emptied the bucket, and whistled for Shep, then remembered he was up in the fields with Michael. She looped the bucket handle over her arm, and set off playing her tin whistle as she marched down the steep, dirt road into the village.

It was a warm spring day with a cool wind coming in off the water. Matt McCrohan, Cornelius Foley, and Maurice and Edmond Burke were sitting along the rocks by the strand. Gunny walked past them and crossed to the far shore eyeing a large bed of reeds. The reeds were taller than her, and dried hard, with deep wet roots that held them fast to rock and sand. She tried snapping them off, then pulled up a few by the roots. Her hands were red and sore from the effort. The next time she came she would bring a knife.

She filled her bucket with cold sea water and jammed her small collection of reeds into the bucket to soak. She found a rock to sit on, turned her face to the sun, and closed her eyes. The sound of the surf mixed with shouts and laugher from the boys as they whacked each other with long stalks of seaweed as they played in the low ocean surf. She opened her eyes and took a stalk of reed from the bucket and split the softened fiber into strips with her fingernail. The reed fibers were much thicker than the grasses and her first piece of twisted rope had a fine speckled brown look. She looked up from the work in her lap. The shore was quiet; the boys were no longer in the water. A single gull dipped past her, cawing. A stiff breeze blew in from the ocean and lifted the hair from her face. She glanced around. Matt McCrohan was standing on a rock just behind her. She looked down and concentrated on her work.

"What are you doing?"

"What business is it of yours?"

"You're not spying on us, are you?"

Gunny tossed the short, twisted rope into the bucket and stood to face Matt. "A girl has a right to be on the strand. You don't own this beach, Matt McCrohan."

Matt took a step toward Gunny. "Actually, we are the Fianna and we do own this beach. You must be the French Queen come to spy on us."

Gunny eyed Matt warily. "I'm not playing, Matt," she said taking a step backwards and nearly losing her footing on a loose stone. Matt took another step toward her. Gunny held up her hands. "Don't get near me. You're all wet."

"Lads!" Matt yelled over his shoulder to the other boys who were crouching in the rocks behind him, snickering. "The French Queen says we are all wet." He turned and faced Gunny, hands on his hips. "What should we do with the French Queen?"

The boys came up from behind him and circled around Gunny. She swallowed hard. Cornelius Foley pulled her hair out of the loose bun she wore at the nape of her neck and shouted, "Let's throw her in the water!"

"Yes," the Burke twins shouted in unison. They each grabbed one of Gunny's arms. Matt grabbed her kicking legs, and they ran with her down across the slippery rocks, and tossed her into the low surf. The boys laughed when Gunny came up sputtering, her hair hanging in long, damp curls along her chest. She staggered to the shore and squatted at the edge of the water, her head on her knees, her hands covering her face.

The boys stopped laughing.

"Gunny, we didn't mean to hurt you," Matt said as he approached her. When he was in close range, Gunny stood and flung a ball of hard, wet sand directly at him. The knot of sand hit him squarely in the chest. He was shocked a girl could throw so hard. He hesitated for a moment, then scooped up a large handful of wet sand and ran after her, rubbing the sand into her hair and stuffing some down her shirt. Gunny laughed and pushed him away. He lost his balance and stumbled into the surf with Gunny on top of him. She splashed water in his face until he raised his hands in defeat, then retreated to the nearby rocks to catch her breath.

Matt held out a hand. "French Queen. You put up a good fight. We will now retreat to the Valley of the Mad for a supper of grass and spring water," he said flopping back on a flat rock.

"I have a better idea," Gunny said, pushing at Matt's leg.

"Yes, French Queen?" Matt asked from his prone position.

"Let's go to your house and ask your mother to make us some cake."

Matt sat up and looked at the pack of sandy, wet boys. "Who votes that we ask my mother to make us some cake?"

"Aye," they yelled and ran up toward the road, looking back to make sure Gunny was coming with them. She snatched her bucket, dumped out the reeds, and raced after them.

Mac McCrohan was coming down to the strand to look for Matt and ran into the ragged group just outside O'Leary's pub. He caught Matt by the arm. "What are you doing walking with a girl?"

"Mac," Matt said with a look of shock on his face. "Please show some respect for the French Queen. We tried to capture her but she put up too good a fight." He bowed low to Gunny and gave her a wink.

Mac was speechless. Matt slung a wet, sandy arm around his younger brother's shoulder. "Gunny's not a girl, Mac. She's the French Queen."

Gunny gave Mac a look to say, "Try to argue with that" and ran ahead to be the first one back to the McCrohan forge.

Gunny was hanging a pot of tea on the crane by the fire when her father emerged from the back room. He stretched up to the ceiling, then grabbed his hat from the peg by the door.

"Where is your mother gone off to so early this morning?" he asked, cutting a couple of thick slices off a loaf of oat bread and putting them in his pocket.

Gunny took her mending out of the nook to the left of the fire and sat on her stool. "Mam said she was going to the market at Ventry. She'll be home by early evening. Where're you headed, Da?"

"To hunt for seals with the McCrohans. Michael," he called to the boy who was still in bed. "Get up. You're coming with me."

Michael rolled out of bed with a groan. "Why so early?"

"We have to get to the islands and back before dark."

Gunny chewed on her bottom lip. "You hate to fish, Da. Isn't hunting for seals just as bad?"

"It's worse, but John McCrohan needs the help and we need the meat." Robert leaned down to kiss her cheek. "Don't tell your mother where we've gone. We'll be back soon, God willing."

"Who else is going?" Gunny asked innocently from her stool.

"The McCrohan boys."

"Then you only have five," she said. "You could use a sixth person to cross the channel."

"And who might you have in mind for that?"

"I could do it."

Robert hesitated. "We could use someone to steer. The channel can be tricky."

Gunny tossed her mending in the basket and stood. "Please, Da! You can't take Michael and not take me."

Robert looked her pleading face, her hands folded under her chin. She had just turned twelve and was tall and muscular. He rubbed the back of his neck.

"I'll ask John—but don't get your heart set on it. And not a word of this to your mother. Bringing in seals is no easy thing and it's not pretty either. None of us would go seal hunting if we weren't desperate."

Gunny moved next to him and threaded her arm through his. "Are we really going to the Blaskets?"

The Blasket Islands lay just off the coast of Dunquin and were the westerly most land in all of Ireland. Gunny had seen them looming just off shore all her life but had never been there. The channel that separated the islands from the main land wasn't wide, but it was deep and fast. Gunny had heard her mother rant many times about her brother who was killed on the Great Island—that it was a cursed place.

"Your brother fell from a cliff," Robert would always reply. "There's no curse. Your brother was clumsy. It was an accident."

"There are no accidents," Eileen always muttered.

Robert, Michael and Gunny hiked down to the pier. The sun was just starting to break through a heavy mist that rose from the water and the grey ocean seemed to blend with the air. John and the McCrohan boys were already at the pier readying John's large curragh. Waves lapped gently against the dock and bounced against the thin sides of the tarred boat. Matt and Mac eyed Gunny suspiciously while John and Robert talked quietly to one side.

"What's she doing here?" Matt asked Michael, giving him a nudge in the ribs. Michael shrugged and nodded his head toward his father.

Robert returned to the pier and nodded to Gunny. "You can come but you're to do as you're told. The seas are calm today. John says we shouldn't have any trouble."

The boys moaned and grabbed the long oars from the boat rack. Gunny stood awkwardly on the dock waiting for instructions. She was clearly no longer the French Queen.

Robert squinted out across the water and glanced down at Gunny. "God be with us and make this a good day for rowing. Amen," he said quietly wiping the sweat from his hands on his worn jacket, then caught Gunny's chin in his hand. "Remember. Not a word to your mother about any of this. I told her last night we'd be hunting at the caves under Slea Head."

Gunny felt a small thrill in her stomach, and smiled. She liked keeping secrets from her mother. Today was going to be a good day.

John McCrohan squatted near the end of the boat and gave Gunny a quick lesson on steering. "Push to the left to turn right. Push to the right to turn left. Do you think you can do that?"

Gunny shook her head of curls. The men climbed into the boat first, then the boys. Robert reached up to help Gunny into the boat. She ignored his hand and clambered into the rear seat by the rudder and turned to face her father and brother on the bench just opposite of her. Matt and Mac sat on the center bench, each securing a long oar to the side of the boat. John McCrohan sat in the furthest bench and took up two oars by himself. Robert pulled the aft rope from the dock, and they rowed out into the still channel toward the Great Blasket island.

"The best seal caves are out toward the west end," John said as he set a strong pace for rowing. The others fell into a steady rhythm and the boat was quiet except for the sound of the oars slicing through the quiet water and an occasional grunt from one of the rowers.

Gunny sat quietly in the stern hardly daring to breath. The feeling of being out on the water was scary and exciting. She clutched the rudder and watched the oars move in unison as the island in front of them slowly emerged as the sun broke apart the morning mist.

"Steer us around to the left of the island, Gunny. Make sure we don't come in close or we'll get caught in the surf," John said brusquely.

Gunny pushed the rudder hard to the right and the boat shifted direction turning past a beautiful strand of sand. She took a deep breath and held the boat on a steady course as the sun burned off the last of the mist.

"At the gob head, bear right and we'll cross down the south side of the island," John directed.

Gunny did as she was told. Her arms were starting to ache with the effort, but she held fast to the rudder. The cliffs on the south side of the island were high and black. The surf crashed against the dark, glistening rocks. After they had rowed for another thirty minutes, John told everyone to slow as he looked for the opening to the seal cave. He explained that the seals lived in a small cove they'd see just before they got to the next adjacent island, Inis Na Bro. A low moan from the shore echoed above the sound of the surf. The moaning grew louder as the men stopped paddling and the boat floated in toward the shore.

"Someone is in trouble out there," Mac whispered.

"No," John said. "That sound means we're close. Those are seals you hear."

The unearthly moan picked up in intensity. It was hard to believe any animal could make that sound.

"All right gentlemen, row her in easy," John said. "We're in the right spot. There's a strand just behind that small inlet, protected by a big rock. We won't get smashed on the shore if we slip in just right."

Gunny looked where John was pointing and steered the boat as best she could in that direction.

"Power now," John yelled as the boat got closer to the opening.

Everyone pulled hard and the boat rounded a large rock and moved with speed toward a short, sandy beach. The sound of sand and rocks on the bottom of the boat announced that they had arrived. John thrust his oars along the inside wall of the boat, leapt out, and pulled the curragh up along the strand. The others followed his lead, stashing their oars and stepping out into the cold water. Gunny was the last one to scramble out, holding her skirts high to keep them out of the shallow surf. The water was bitterly cold on her bare feet.

John grabbed a length of rope and two large clubs from the boat and headed east toward the caves. The others followed.

"Stay with the boat, Gunny," he yelled back. "We won't be long."

Gunny waved as the small group of hunters rounded the bend. When they were out of sight, she brushed the sand off her damp skirt and looked out into the cove. It was small, but nicely protected, with gentle waves and a smooth, rocky beach. She heard a noise, and turned. A large seagull sat on a rock wall behind her, preening. Behind the gull were a number of crumbling stone houses and behind the houses there was a tall field of grass. The grasses had not been grazed on in years and would be wonderful for making rope. She wished she had thought to bring a bucket. She stepped into the yard of the nearest crumbling stone house. The deserted village was so quiet she could hear herself breathing. She walked pass the shell of the house and onto a narrow dirt path that took her past other roofless houses and a building that looked like it had once been a church. Beyond that lay the old oat fields, now covered in grass and heather.

She explored for an hour before she heard shouting from the strand and came running back to the boat. John and Robert were rounding the path back to the strand, each dragging a large seal carcass behind them. Their faces were grim, their arms and faces spotted with blood.

"Where are the boys?" Gunny asked, out of breath.

"Mac was bitten by a seal. Michael and Matt were walking with him," John said, pulling his seal toward the beached curragh. "Robert, help me get these seals into the boat. Then we'll help the boys."

Gunny gasped and ran around the bend. Matt and Michael were walking unsteadily on the slick black rocks with Mac supported between them. Mac's face was pale, his jaw line set in pain. Matt was bare-chested; his shirt was wrapped tightly around Mac's left arm. The shirt was soaked through with blood. Gunny hopped across the black rocks to meet them.

"What happened?"

"Get back, Gunny," Matt said. "We have to get Mac to the boat."

Gunny stepped aside to let the boys pass, then ran beside them onto the strand.

"Lay him down in the bottom of the boat with the seals so he doesn't fall overboard," John directed. Matt and Michael helped Mac into the boat. He squatted between the two dead seals. The smell was nauseating and his face grew greener.

"Lay down. Rest your arm on that seal," John told his youngest son. "Make sure to keep the bite up above your heart. That'll slow the bleeding."

Mac moaned and leaned back, resting his bloody arm gingerly on the dead, brown, speckled seal. He looked up at the sky, blinking back tears.

"We'll get you home as quickly as we can."

Mac nodded weakly.

"Don't you have a brother here on the island?" Robert asked. "Should we fetch him instead?"

"Donal's here on the Great Island but there is no doctor on the Blaskets. We're better off getting Mac back to Dunquin where we can send for the doctor in Dingle." John turned to Gunny. "Once we're clear of this inlet, you'll have to row. We need to get home as quickly as possible and you'll have to man Mac's oar."

"I am sure I can row as well as I can haul turf." Gunny felt excitement rise deep inside her chest.

John shook his head. "We have no other choice."

John pulled the boat out into the surf and everyone scrambled in and mounted their oars. Matt took up both his and Mac's oar. With the weight of the seals, the lip of the curragh sat much lower in the water. Gunny could hardly keep her grip on the rudder as the men rowed hard to break through the incoming surf and back out of the protected cove. Once they were in open water, John told Gunny how to tie the rudder in place. She thought about how helpful that might have been on the way over. When the rudder was set, she slid past her father and brother and onto the bench next to Matt. Matt started to protest, but John shushed him. Gunny took Mac's oar from Matt and did her best to match his rhythm rowing. As they rounded the gob head of the Great Blasket, a stiff easterly wind greeted them as they turned toward home.

"So much for our still day," Robert said. "Damn the wind."

"We'll put up the sail," John said. "This may actually be a blessing." He pulled out the sail rigging, nearly tipping the boat in the choppy grey water. Gunny clutched the rail of the boat and held her breath. She stared down at her feet resting in a puddle of seal blood and sea water. Mac moaned behind her. Perhaps next time the men went hunting for seals, she would not be so insistent about joining them. John hauled up the sail and the boat took off at a fast clip. John scrambled past them across the benches and untied the rudder. "We'll be home in no time, son," he muttered to Mac.

When then neared the pier at Dunquin, John pulled down the sail and they rowed in to the dock. John leapt from the boat when they were still a foot away and pulled the boat in close behind him. He pulled Mac carefully up off of the seals and placed him gently on the dock. Matt and Robert tied up the boat and Gunny collected the oars in silence.

John touched Mac's pale face. "You'll be fine. Don't forget to breathe."

Mac attempted a weak smile. "I'm all right, Da. It just hurts a bit, that's all."

John patted him on the head. "Matt, get your brother up to O'Leary's and tell someone to ride to Dingle for a doctor. Michael, go up to the forge and bring the wagon down so we can get these seals home."

Michael loped off up the road while Gunny stood awkwardly by. John glanced at her. "You did a good job in the boat, Gunny. Good as any boy." Gunny blushed and kicked a dirty toe in the dirt.

Matt looped Mac's good arm over his shoulder and helped him stand. Mac nearly crumpled as pain pounded through his arm and up into his chest. His knees felt weak. Matt gripped him hard. "Stand up, Mac. I can't carry you. You'll have to do some of the work."

Gunny stood to the side, not sure how to help as Mac swallowed hard and tried to concentrate on the road under his feet. He took a tentative step, and then another. Gunny followed behind as the two McCrohan boys limped up the steep dirt road to O'Leary's pub, then hurried inside ahead of them to let Nick know they were coming. Nick sent his daughter, Maeve, off to ask the priest to fetch the doctor. Maeve scurried past Matt as he pushed his way in through the door and laid Mac on the floor near the bar.

"Gunny, go down to the pier and ask Da to cut a hunk of seal blubber from one of the seals," Matt directed. Gunny started to question the order, then turned and raced out the door on her new mission. Nick O'Leary brought Matt hot water and a clean flour sack and knife. Matt turned Mac's face away, and gingerly unwound the bloody shirt from his brother's arm. The seal had taken a deep bite from Mac's forearm and the wound was ragged and bleeding heavily. Matt felt faint but tried to stay focused as he carefully ran hot water over the large gash. When Gunny returned with the bloody lump of seal blubber, Matt pushed it down into the wound and wrapped a tight bandage of flour strips around Mac's arm.

"Are you sure you want to do that?" Gunny whispered. "Shouldn't you wait until the doc arrives?"

Matt grunted and continued wrapping the packed wound with the clean cotton strips. "My grandfather used to hunt seals all the time. He said that seal blubber is the only cure when a chuck of flesh is missing like that."

"I'm glad you listened to his stories," Gunny said, her nose wrinkling at the stink of the seal blubber.

Matt tied off the wrap and wiped sweat and blood from his hands onto his pants. "His arm will be sore but it should heal."

Mac lay on the floor staring up at the ceiling. Gunny watched his lips move and wondered if he was praying.

The doctor brought Mac home from O'Leary's to a frantic Kate McCrohan. He had inspected Matt's wrapping, and left it in place. He told Mac not to move his arm for at least a week and told Kate to watch for signs of infection. She paid him for what little work he had done and watched as he trotted off on his small, brown horse back to Dingle. She tucked Mac into bed and sent Matt out to the yard to clean up.

Gunny crept home exhausted. She slid into the house, not sure if her mother was home yet. The house was empty except for Michael who sat on a stool smoking his pipe in front of a cooling fire. Gunny's clothes and hair were sticky with salt water and seal blood and she smelled dreadful. She washed in the yard and pulled on her extra shift, then knelt and stirred the fire. She sat on the stool next to Michael and closed her eyes. She felt like weeping. "What happened out there?" she whispered.

"I don't know exactly," Michael said, taking in a long, slow mouthful of smoke. "John told us to wait on a bridge of rock that's out in front of the seal cave. John and Da tied ropes around their waists and told us they'd pull on the ropes when they wanted help getting out. Then they swam into the cave with their clubs. Everything was quiet, then there was a terrible barking and yelling. Next thing we knew, seals were flying out of the cave in all directions and the ropes went taut. We didn't know if we were supposed to pull or not. Mac started screaming for his Da to come out. Next thing we knew, Mac dove or fell into the water and landed on top of a seal. She must have thought he was attacking her and bit his arm to get away. Then Da and John were safe on the rock and Mac was out there floundering in the water. Matt dived in and hauled him onto the rock bridge. Blood was pouring out of his arm." Michael paused taking a pull off his pipe. "It was something."

"Poor Mac," Gunny said.

"Poor Mac, nothing," Michael scoffed. "He's the type who always gets hurt."

"Don't be mean."

Michael shook his head. "If it weren't for Matt, Mac might not be here. It was just like that time when we were little and Mac fell into the river after that big rain."

Gunny grinned. "Mac got stuck on a rock in the middle of the river and was too scared to move. I remember Matt yelling and yelling at him to swim to shore and Mac out there, his arms wrapped so tight around that rock. Matt finally had to swim out to get him and came back with Mac clinging to his back. I thought they were both going to drown."

Michael snickered. "Matt was so angry by the time they got to shore I thought he was going to drown Mac anyway. When Mac tried to thank him, Matt stormed off."

"Maybe Mac should stay on shore from now on."

Eileen pushed the door open. "Help me unload the cart. Is your father back from hunting seals?"

Michael scooted outside to unload the cart leaving Gunny to spin the tale for their mother.

"Da's down in the field with John cutting up the seals. I'm surprised you didn't see him on your way in."

"They got a seal?"

"Oh, yes. Two"

"I'm surprised I didn't see them on the road back from Ventry." She glanced around the house. "Did you get any work done here today?"

Gunny pursed her lips. "A little. I spend most of the day collecting grasses for rope."

"God be praised your father has returned home once again from the sea with no incident," Eileen muttered. "Help me get a meal ready."

John and Robert worked into the evening gutting and cleaning the two large seals. When they finished, each man had a barrel of salted seal meat plus a quart or so of seal liver oil to burn in their lamps. They returned to the shore to scrub down their clothes with sand and seawater, though they both continued to smell of seal blubber for weeks. They returned home in their soggy clothes, shook hands, and each rolled off a barrel of pork toward home.

~ Chapter 3: The Booley ~

It hardly rained the summer of 1820. The villagers at Dunquin spent every minute they could in the fields and along the shore soaking in the unusually hot summer sun. But at harvest, the potatoes were small and few and the oat crop was about half of what it should have been. October brought the first rains to the region in months. Gunny sat twisting rope by the fire listening to the rain on the thick, thatch roof as her parents talked quietly in front of the turf fire.

"I have one ridge of potatoes yet ungathered," Robert said to Eileen. "I'll lift those today but even then we won't have enough to get us through the winter. And we don't have enough oats to sell at the Dingle Market to buy more taters."

"How'll we pay our rent?" Eileen asked shaking her head, then touching the bun at the back of her neck to make sure the pins were all in place.

"The Old Lord'll be by soon with his hunting dogs sniffing around for money. I'll ask him for more time."

Eileen's face darkened. "I was counting on straw from the oats to replace the leaky thatch on the roof."

"The roof will have to wait." Robert leaned over and squeezed his wife's hand. "There is nothing to be done. We'll get by as we have before."

Eileen pulled her hand away. "We get by on nothing! How are we magically going to have enough food this winter?"

Michael stomped into the room and pulled off his cap shaking droplets of rain onto the damp, dirt floor. "Mam, I need new boots. There is no sole in my right boot and only half a sole in my left."

"We have no money for new boots. You'll have to wear an old pair of your Da's this winter."

Michael slumped down on his stool. "I can't wear Da's boots! The other boys will know they're not mine."

Eileen knelt by an old wooden box near to the fire. She pulled out a mud-caked boot and knocked the thick dirt off onto the hearth. "Soon as I find this one's mate you'll have yourself a new pair," she said digging deeper into the box. She pulled out a second boot that was in worse shape than the first and set them side by side on the hearth. "Clean 'em up no one will know the better." She picked up her broom and briskly swept the dry mud into the fire and sat back down on her stool. Her glare dared Michael to object to her offer.

Michael grabbed the boots from the hearth and stormed outside slamming the door behind him. He ran down the hill toward the McCrohans' house. When he got to the river by the forge, he flung the boots in. "I'd rather go barefoot than have the other boys tease me," he yelled up the hill toward his house, and headed off in the rain to see if Nick O'Leary would credit him with a pint.

Robert could not sleep. He twisted to one side on the small, lumpy mattress and sensed that Eileen was also awake. "We have no choice," he muttered near her ear. "We'll have to send Michael into service in Dingle."

"I won't have it," Eileen said quietly. "It's an embarrassment to our good name."

"Things're worse than they've been in past years. Would you rather be embarrassed or starve to death?"

Eileen was quiet. "You and John could hunt for seals again. That meat got us through the summer."

"John said it was the last time he'd hunt for seals and I can't do it alone."

"But everyone's harvest was poor. Surely Lord Ventry will understand."

Robert grunted. "There's no telling with him."

"Couldn't Michael work on one of the larger farms in Ventry? Dingle is such a big town and Michael's only fifteen."

"There won't be any farm work until next spring and we need money now. Michael's a big strong lad. I asked Daniel Murphy about him. He said they could use him at the shop."

"You talked to Daniel Murphy before you talked to me?"

"Last time I was in town I mentioned to Daniel that we might need to send Michael out for work. Now that the potatoes are in, it's clear—the boy must work."

Eileen tossed back the rough, wool blanket and got out of bed. Early-morning light lit the dusty front window. "I'll kill and roast a chicken. It will be our last meal with Michael until Christmas."

"Are you sure we can afford to lose a chicken?" Robert asked.

Eileen glared at her husband. "We're losing a child," she whispered. "What difference does it make if we lose a chicken?"

Michael stuffed his spare pair of trousers, a worn woolen shirt, and three pairs of mended stockings into an old flour sack and grabbed his jacket. He pulled his cap down tight on his head, kissed his mother on the cheek, and walked out into the yard at an uneven gait. Eileen had put strips of worn flour sacks layered with newspaper in his old boots but there wasn't much she could do about the heels that were worn nearly flat.

"The fairies took that old pair of boots I gave you?" she called after him. "You're sure?"

Michael stopped in the yard and hung his head. "I told you. I set them by the back door and they disappeared."

"Your first pay, you're to buy yourself a new pair of boots," Eileen said, pulling on her shawl and walking out into the yard. A burst of cold wind whipped a tuft of loose thatch from the roof and bits of straw blew around them. She tucked a stray brown curl behind his ear. "We can wait till your second pay to get money toward the rent."

Michael pulled away from his mother and scratched at the side of his head where she had tucked the curl. "Yes, Mam." He stood awkwardly, not wanting to take the first steps toward Dingle.

"You're ready, then?" Robert asked, walking briskly into the yard with Shep at his heels. "I'll walk with you a ways."

Michael turned to look at this mother. She hesitated, then reached to adjust his hat, her eyes full of tears. She pulled hot potatoes from her apron pocket and handed two to Michael and two to Robert. "These'll keep your hands warm for awhile—at least until you get hungry." She brushed at a smudge of dirt on Michael's worn jacket. "Behave yourself. Mind your manners. And don't embarrass us."

"Yes, Mam."

Michael ducked away from his mother's fussing and walked with his father down the hill through the barren, muddy fields.

Gunny did not want to say good-bye to Michael. She sat by the fire twisting a long strand of rope enjoying the quiet house. She glowed at the thought of her brother leaving home. There would be no more bickering over chores and no more sharing of meager food at the table. She was amazed at how much food Michael ate these days. But then she thought the times when she and Michael had shared secrets and played games and hiked together to the booley. It was already strange having only two children in the family when most families had five, six or more. How was it going to be with only her in the house?

Gunny grabbed the bucket and raced out into the yard. Her mother stood staring down the hill, her shawl clutched tight around her chest.

"I'm going for water," Gunny said, chucking the last bit of grass and water out into the yard. She raced down the hill and reached Robert and Michael as they turned onto the road toward Dingle. She gave Michael a push on the back. "Don't forget about us, eh?" she said, out of breath.

Michael turned and looked at his tall sister with her red cheeks and tangled black curls. "Forget that ugly face?"

Gunny stuck out her tongue, then smiled. Michael gave her a gentle punch on the arm and she watched as they headed off toward Dingle, talking head-to-head with Shep at their heels.

John McCrohan finished shoeing Lord Ventry's new hunting horse. "Matt, can you walk this filly to Ventry? I have two pots to repair for Bitsy Kavanaugh."

Matt ran a hand along the broad neck of the large cream mare. "I'd rather ride her than lead her."

"You're used to riding a work horse, Matt. Lord Ventry's hunting horses are bred for speed. There's a big difference."

"I can feel the difference, Da," Matt said running his hand farther down the horse's broad back. "Of all the work you do, the only part I like is occasionally being around these horses."

"Then perhaps you should spend more time with Robert Malone. He's the horseman, not me."

"Do you think he could get me work at the Ventry stables?"

John turned to Matt. "No. We're Blackies. You need to learn to work iron."

Matt grunted. "You know I've tried it and I hate it. I don't want to spend my life waiting around for some old lady to stop by and tell me her pot needs a patch."

John cleared his throat and looked down at his boots.

"I didn't mean to offend you, Da," Matt said in a serious voice. "You like this work. But a life of fire and smoke is not for me ..."

"You never got over that burn you got as a boy."

Matt grimaced and rubbed at this thigh. "I still have a scar where that poker landed."

"I know you do. I'm sorry."

"Da, Mac is the one who wants to follow in your footsteps."

John looked up at Matt, noting his son's clean hands and smooth face, and frowned. "This job is good enough for me and was good enough for your grandfather and for his father before him."

"I know, I know," Matt said searching his father's face. "Maybe if I spent more time with you..."

John brightened. "I'll save one of Bitsy's pots to work on with you when you get back."

Matt swung up easily onto the tall horse's back and patted her broad neck. "Sure, Da. As soon as I get back."

"Matt, I told you to walk that horse to Ventry."

"It'll be quicker riding, Da," Matt said pulling the right rein to turn the horse out of the small yard. "And as soon as I get back, I'll work with you in the forge. I promise."

Matt kicked at the spurs. The large horse tossed her head and sprinted out of the road. Matt appeared to be barely hanging on as they crossed the bridge toward Ventry and out across John's oat field.

"Matt! Remember the hollow!" John yelled as Matt nearly toppled the large horse in a sharp dip in the field. John grimaced as Matt righted himself, then thundered on through the field and up over the hills toward Ventry.

Matt arrived home past dusk bragging about his fast ride on the Lord's new filly. By then, John's furnace was cool and Bitsy's second pot sat unmended.

"Matt, you must be more careful with the Lord's horses. A poor man can't reach into his pocket to make things better," John said as Matt finished off a second helping of boiled potatoes.

Matt watched a silent look pass between his parents and John said nothing farther.

After his sprint to Dingle, Matt was no longer happy riding their workhorse, Nella, at a slow pace. With each delivery around the peninsula, he pushed her to ride a bit faster. At first, she could only sprint for short distances, but eventually kept up a good pace. When Matt called her from the field, she would whinny loudly and run to meet him with her long ears tipped forward and her large dark eyes alert. Often when Matt mounted her, she'd look around at him and paw till he gave her a click of the tongue that told her the race was on. After a long run, Matt brought her bits of apple to eat, and spent time brushing her rough tawny coat and cream-colored mane as if she were a champion racer.

Their favorite place to ride was along the strand. When the deliveries were done for the day, Matt would ride as hard as he could along the straight part of the road between his house and the church. When the children in town heard him coming they would cry, "Clear the road! Matt McCrohan is coming!" He would give them a wave as he raced past before thundering out along the beach and into the surf.

"Matt," John admonished his son on more than one occasion. "You ride that horse too hard. I can hear the two of you coming a half a field away. You are going to wear her out."

"We're fine, Da. She loves it. You worry too much."

Gunny was first up, as usual. She washed her face in the basin on the table and wiped her face on the back of her sleeve, a new habit she was trying to develop. She stirred the fire and added a turf, ate a few spoonfuls of cold potatoes from the pot on the hearth, then cut off a thick slice of bread and placed it into the pocket of her apron. She patted her leg for Shep to follow and slipped out the front door. Her father hadn't finished manuring the fields; her time was still her own until the planting started. The early spring air felt cool on her damp face, but the sun rising in a cloudless sky promised a warm day.

She was anxious to get back to her work building a fairy village in the foot hills of Mount Eagle. When she got to the ancient ogham stone along the path from the booley huts, she veered to the right with Shep tight at her heels. She counted her paces as she crossed through brush, high grass, and smooth grey rocks, always keeping the sun to her left. At the count of one hundred she stopped and knelt. Where were the small cairns of stone she had used to mark the gates of the village? Where were the tiny houses decorated with bits of rock and shell she had brought up from the strand? She had even built a small bridge over a tiny creek. Here was the bend in the creek but no bridge. Gunny stood hands on hips and looked around. Shep bounded up to her.

"What happened to everything we worked on yesterday, Shep? Did the fairies not like it and took it apart overnight?"

Shep looked quizzically at the girl, waiting to hear a word he understood.

"Or, maybe one of the boys from the village was spying on us and knocked everything over after we left. Fairies and boys! I don't know which is worse."

Gunny took a deep breath, then set about collecting rocks and mosses to start again. Shep lapped up water from the creek and wandered off to investigate an interesting smell.

"Don't go running off. With Michael working in Dingle, I need you to take the cow and sheep up to the booley," Robert announced to Gunny as she hurried through her morning meal of boiled potatoes, thinking through her latest plans for houses in her tiny village.

Gunny gasped. "But we have to start planting."

"I'll plant without you this year. We need to get the animals up to the high fields before the first seeds go in. You should leave first thing in the morning."

Gunny was stunned. It hadn't occurred to her that she would inherit Michael's summer chore of watching the animals in the booley. Once she helped get the crops in, summer was her best time for playing with Shep in the fields, hiking the ridges of Mount Eagle, or finding grasses and bird eggs along the creek.

Eileen sat at the table blowing the steam off a cup of hot tea. "I talked to Cate Mitchell after Mass last Sunday. Her girl, Ashling, and Ellen Kavanaugh are headed to the booley this summer. It's their first time as well. I told Cate the girls could share Michael's clochain with you."

Gunny slammed her spoon on the table. "Michael's clochain is tiny. There's not even a chimney. When the fire is lit smoke comes right up through the roof. It looks like a dung hill after a summer storm."

Robert chuckled at Gunny's apt description.

"I can't live there," Gunny continued. "Not all summer! And I don't know those girls. You told me to never play with the village children."

"Michael never complained about living in the booley," Eileen snapped.

"Michael wasn't smart enough to know he was living in squalor," Gunny retorted.

Eileen set down her mug of tea and grabbed Gunny's hand. "How dare you say that about your brother? His father..." she started, then cleared her throat and changed direction. "Your father told you to take the animals to the booley."

"Fine. I'll live in the booley all summer with two girls I hardly know. You'll be glad to be rid of me." Gunny pushed away from the table, whistled for Shep, and pulled the door closed behind her with a slam.

Eileen leaned in toward her husband. "She has too much opinion for a girl, Robert. She's strong and willful. I can't control her."

"Neither can I," Robert said pushing away from the table. "That's how she was born and that's how she is. The booley may be the very place for her."

The next morning, Gunny washed her face and ate, then sat glumly at the table, kicking a bare foot hard against one leg of the table until her mother got up. While Eileen made tea, Gunny grabbed a clean apron, a blanket and her spoon and jammed them into the water bucket. There was an old, patched pot and rusting fry pan at the clochain so she could cook potatoes. She reached into her apron pocket to make sure her whistle was there, then looked around the tiny house. There was nothing else to pack.

Eileen swept around Gunny. "Praise the Lord you'll take the animals out of here today. What a mess," Eileen muttered. Gunny wasn't sure if her mother was talking about the sheep and cow or about her. "I don't have any butter for you to take," Eileen continued. "Now that the cow has calved, she'll soon have milk to share and we'll have butter again. In the meantime, you'll have to get by on potatoes. I'll have your father bring up a sack. We don't have many left so don't eat them all at once."

"Why don't I live on grass and water like the cow."

"Don't be smart with me, Gunny."

"Better smart than dumb," she muttered turning toward the fire.

"What did you say?"

Gunny turned to face Eileen and said clearly, "I didn't say anything." She grabbed the bucket with her goods, whistled for Shep and left the house. Once outside, she took off at a run toward the booley.

"Wait!" Eileen yelled behind her. Gunny stopped and looked back. "You forgot the cow and the sheep."

Gunny gasped. "Can't I get settled in first?"

"No. Take the animals with you. Your father and the other men from the village are already planting. The last thing they need is to have a hungry cow and a herd of sheep trampling down the new seed."

Gunny marched back to the house, pulled a long length of her homemade rope from a peg near the front door and tossed it over the cow's head. The cow blinked her large brown eyes at Gunny. "Don't look at me like that," Gunny snapped. She whistled for Shep. The dog sprinted in from the road and stared at her. She pointed at the sheep. Shep lowered his head and started to circle behind the timid animals. They clustered together, then skittered onto the road to get away from the staring dog. Shep stayed close behind as they trotted up the steep path.

Gunny trudged behind the sheep with the cow, her small calf following close at its mother's heels. Gunny had spent time with Michael in the booley fields each summer. It was the idea of having to stay in the booley all summer that she resented. She watched as Shep ran the sheep up into the high field, then left the path and walked toward the booley house, pulling the cow along behind her through furze and heather. The tiny thorns of the furze plants pinched and tingled on her bare feet, but boots had to be saved for cold, winter days. When they reached the high field, she pulled the rope from around the cow's neck.

"Stay here," she ordered. The cow lowered her head to graze and the small calf hovered timidly behind her.

Gunny looped the rope around her waist a few times and marched down the back side of the hill to the clochain. The nearby clochains would soon be occupied by other teens from the village sent to watch over their family's livestock for the summer. Gunny opened the small wooden door of her new home and peeked inside. The room smelled sour and was dusty with ashes. Gunny set down her bucket of supplies and went back to the high field. She pulled a few heather plants up by the roots and tied the plants together with the cow rope to make a small broom. She returned to the clochain and gave the hut a thorough dusting and sweeping and set her supplies on the high shelf near the door. With the house in order, she headed out with the bucket to fetch water for her evening meal.

When she returned from the nearby spring, Ellen Kavanaugh and Ashling Mitchell were standing outside the doorway of the clochain peeking in. Ellen was a small girl with thin dark hair that frizzed in clusters about her small, oval face. Her hands and feet were tiny. Gunny looked down at her own large feet and blushed. Ashling was taller than Ellen but was still much shorter than Gunny. Ellen had a massive head of bright red curls and a spray of freckles across her nose and chin.

"Excuse me," Gunny muttered as she stepped around the girls and into the clochain sloshing water on their bare feet.

"I can't believe we have to live here all summer. Look at this place. It's a mess," Ellen exclaimed in a small, reedy voice.

Gunny whipped around. "A mess? I spent the last hour cleaning."

"It's not a mess, Ellen. It's a clochain, that's all," Ashling said, her red curls bobbing. Her mother had warned her that Gunny might not be a suitable housemate. Ellen and Ashling locked arms as they entered the small hut and looked around.

"There is barely enough room for us to sleep. Where will we keep our things?" Ellen whined.

Gunny looked at the two empty-handed girls. "What things?"

"We have to go and get our clothes and food," Ashling explained, raising her eyebrows and speaking slowly so Gunny would understand. "We wanted to come and see the place first."

Gunny stared at the girls. "You left your cows and sheep in the village? What if they're off right now stamping down the new seed your fathers have been working so hard to plant?"

Ellen and Ashling stared at Gunny, mouths open.

"I suppose someone else is watching them," Ellen said with a wavering voice.

"Well, don't suppose, girl! Go and get those animals. We can't have them ruining everyone's crops, can we?"

"Mam!" she yelled as she entered the house. "The first milk is in." She set the bucket down and clapped her hands. "We'll be dipping our potatoes in butter tonight."

Eileen rose slowly from her stool. "Must you always be so loud? You'll put a curse on the butter before I even start." She took a long wooden spoon and stirred up a few small lumps of butter. "You were in such a hurry to get here the milk is already starting to clump. But there's not enough here to skim off the cream. I'll have to use it all. The first batch will be a little watery." Eileen looked up at her daughter's eager face. "The milk has to cool overnight to clabber. There'll be no butter until morning. Take the other bucket and go back to the booley. And make sure you look after that cow and calf. The cow will keep us fed this summer and the calf will bring in a fair price soon at the Dingle Market."

Gunny returned to the booley and filled her pot with water to boil potatoes. The village girls watched her work.

"Do you mind if we add our potatoes to your pot?" Ashling asked.

Gunny shrugged. "Do what you want. But first we have to build up the fire. We don't have much peat up here. We need bracken from the fields."

"We can help with that," Ellen offered.

Gunny frowned. "Good. I wasn't planning on doing all of the work around here."

The three girls headed to the high fields. Gunny checked on Shep who was keeping an eye on the collected flock. She fed him a handful of cold potato then set about collecting furze. When Ashling and Ellen returned to the hut, Gunny was shocked to see a thorn branch mixed in the furze.

"What's this?" Gunny asked holding up the small, prickly bit.

"You said to collect bracken," Ellen said.

"A fairy thorn is not bracken," Gunny said shaking the branch at them.

"It looks the same as the ones you gathered," Ashling retorted. "How do you know that one's a fairy thorn?"

Gunny sighed and said in her most Eileen-like voice, "A fairy thorn is any thorn that was not planted by man. So pretty much all of the thorns in the booley are fairy thorns. Don't touch them. And never burn them in a fire." Gunny sighed. "You two have a lot to learn."

"Well, I think that's nonsense," Ashling said, her pale face reddening. "If a branch is dead then why not burn it?"

Gunny examined the thorn branch, ignoring Ashling. "Where did you find this?"

"In the high field past where the cows like to graze."

Gunny set the thorn branch just outside the low, wooden door. "We'll return it tomorrow. Don't anybody touch it tonight."

When the water was boiling, Gunny dropped in their small collection of potatoes. Ellen kept watch and let the other two know when the potatoes were soft. They each fished out two potatoes and sat on the floor with the potatoes on their laps resting on small tin plates. Each girl carefully peeled the jackets off of the hot potatoes using a long thumb nail.

At first they ate in silence, then Ellen and Ashling started to talk about other friends in the village. When they ran out of gossip, Ashling turned to Gunny.

"Tell us about growing up on the mountain, Gunny."

Gunny hesitated. No one had ever asked her to talk about herself. She looked at the two expectant faces and set her plate aside. At first she hesitated but then cleared her throat and started in. She soon had the girls laughing and sharing their own stories, and by the end of the evening, knew her father would be proud of her storytelling, especially the stories she told about her mother. The girls continued to talk long after the fire died down that first night, surprised to find they weren't so different from one another after all.

The next morning, Gunny took the thorny branch to the high field and used a small twist of rope to attach the branch to a dead thorn bush. Ellen and Ashling watched in amusement.

"From the stories you told us last night, it doesn't sound like you care a fig for what the priest or your parents have to say, but you don't dare cross a fairy, do you?" Ashling said with a smile.

After a week in the hills, the girls were best friends. During the day they sat together in the high fields and watched over the sheep and cows. Each sheep had a distinguishing mark cut into her ear so they could easily be sorted for sheering in the fall. Each family had three sheep: one for wool, one to eat at the end of the summer, and one to sell at the market.

While the animals grazed, Gunny played her whistle, and the girls told stories and made up silly rhymes. The girls loved Shep, though he would only come when Gunny whistled for him. They milked the cows each morning and evening and returned home for a brief time each day to deliver a bucket of warm milk to their hungry households.

On nights when they were short of food, Gunny made a small cut in the neck of one of the cows and drained a quart or so of blood into the frying pan. She talked to the chosen cow as she bled it; the cows never seemed to mind the pinch in the neck. When she was done, she carefully pinned the vein shut and twisted a piece of hair from the cow's tail around the pin to keep it in place. The girls added whatever they could find to the blood—wild mushrooms, green sorrel leaves, or bird eggs mixed with milk, then fried the mixture until the edges were hot and crisp.

One late afternoon while Ellen and Ashling were off to the village delivering milk, Gunny sat on a large, flat rock finishing a slice of oat bread thickly spread with fresh butter and watched the small collection of black-tailed sheep. She liked the way the sheep's coloring contrasted with the sharp green of the summer grasses. There were several new lambs covered in black spots. Gunny watched as they wandered a few feet from their mothers, then raced back to nudge their mothers before venturing out again.

She pulled out her tin whistle and played a grazing tune she had been working on. The low sounds moved with the wind, and the high sounds blended with baaing of the sheep. She looked up from her rock perch. Matt McCrohan was standing on the path just past the rock, watching her. She stuffed the whistle into her apron pocket and looked away.

"Don't stop. I liked that," he said.

Gunny rolled her eyes. "You probably thought it was too loud. Most people do."

Matt shook his head. "Was it your own tune? It was good."

Gunny blushed and whistled for Shep. The dog raced down from a nearby hillock and she ran her hands through his silky black hair, then squinted over at Matt. "I don't know if you mean that or if you're teasing me."

"I mean it," Matt said. "Play some more."

Gunny hesitated, then pulled the whistle from her pocket and put it to her lips. She looked over at Matt. "I can't play with you looking at me."

Matt held up his hands. "Fine." He turned his back and sat down on a nearby rock.

Gunny took a deep breath and started again, breathing and playing with the wind and the fields and forgetting that anyone else in the world was listening.

"I wish we had known you when you were little, Gunny," Ashling said one cool night in late July as the girls huddled together around a cozy fire in the clochain.

"My mother made Michael and me keep to ourselves. Sometimes Michael and I would sneak into the village and spy on you from behind your stone walls."

"I remember seeing you with the McCrohan boys, and my da telling me he saw you footing turf with your brother," Ashling said as she stirred the fire and added a little fairy-free bracken for more heat. "I thought you were enchanted. You seemed more like a fairy than a girl to me."

"I used to watch you working in the fields with your father," Ellen added. "You were always as dirty as the men."

Gunny held out her dirt-crusted hands and laughed. "I still am!"

"I saw you fall in the creek by the forge one time," Ellen said. "You acted like you didn't care and you stayed in the water splashing around."

"I remember that. Matt pushed me in when I wouldn't do as he told me. "

"Matt McCrohan," Ellen said dreamily. "Who do you think he'll marry?"

It had never occurred to Gunny to consider who Matt McCrohan might marry. Ashling leaned back and grabbed a small green apple from a box by the door. "Let's see if it's one of us!" She took out her knife and started to peel the apple.

"What're you doing?" Gunny asked.

"Haven't you played this game before?" Ellen asked.

"Maybe not," Gunny said, not wanting the girls to know she had no idea what they were talking about.

"I'm going to try to peel this apple without breaking the skin. When the skin falls to the floor, it will form the shape of a letter. And that letter will tell us which girl Matt McCrohan is going to marry," Ashling said.

Gunny looked puzzled. "How can that be?"

"It's a game, Gunny," Ellen said in her small, adult voice. "Let's see what the apple peel says."

Gunny and Ellen watched as Ashling peeled the apple, then held the last bit of peel with her knife and let it drop dramatically to the floor. The peel fell in a random squiggle on the hard-packed dirt floor.

"I don't see a letter," Ellen said, disappointed.

"I don't know a lot of letters," Gunny said," but I know that's not a G. I'm safe."

"What do you mean you're safe?" Ashling asked, astounded. "You wouldn't want to marry Matt McCrohan?"

Gunny scoffed. "Matt has a quick temper. It's not a bad one, but it's hasty. I don't like that. And I'm not getting married anyway."

"You have to marry someone," Ellen said soothingly. "Don't you want a house and children?"

Gunny looked as if she had bitten into a sour apple. "A house and children? Me?"

Ashling looked over at the door. "We should be quiet. I saw Matt and Mac McCrohan up in the fields today. They're over in the next clochain tonight."

"Da asked me to watch their sheep this summer. There's no need for them to be here." Gunny said in loud voice.

"Gunny, if you don't have a house and children of your own, then you'll be a spinster," Ellen whispered. "You'll live with your parents all your life and when they get old you'll have to feed them by hand. You should find a man and get married so you can move out."

"And instead live in his house and feed him by hand when he gets old? And take care of his old dottering parents? No, thank you."

"Everyone gets married," Ellen said.

Gunny shook her head, lay down on her straw mat, and tucked her blanket in around her. She closed her eyes and was asleep in minutes.

On Midsummer's Eve, all of the village teens gathered in the booley for a bonfire. They worked off and on through the day collecting bracken, then pulled rocks up around the fire and sat watching the tinder snap, sending bursts of live cinders up into the air.

"Someone should tell a story," Matt said.

Ellen, Ashling and Gunny exchanged glances, but said nothing The Wren Boys muttered about not being good story tellers and the crowd grew silent.

"Well then, I can tell the story of Brian Boru, High King of Ireland," Matt said loudly. He told the tale with great flourish and everyone agreed that his rendition, though shorter, was nearly as good as his father's.

Gunny felt her stomach flutter at the end of Matt's tale. She cleared her throat and took a deep breath. "And now for the tale of Grania, Ireland's pirate queen," she said. She launched into the tale picturing her father's broad gestures and trying to remember all the fine details of the story. When she finished, the small group was silent. Gunny blinked and stared into the fire. Had she done so poorly?

Ellen grabbed her hand. "That was a powerful, good story, Gunny. Please tell another."

Gunny took a deep breath and shook her head. "I think that was the only story in me tonight. But how about a whistle tune to say good night to the fire?"

The teens tightened their circle, leg against leg, arm against arm, as Gunny played a tune so fine it tamed the fire and welcomed the stars.

By September, the days were shorter, and the high fields covered in yellow flowering ragwort. Robert hiked to the booley to let the teens know the harvest was in; it was time for them to return home. He continued on to the bog to bury half-dozen firkins of butter to keep through the winter, then hiked on to Dingle with the calf in tow to sell at the harvest market.

Gunny reluctantly closed up the small clochain, and whistled for Shep to bring in the sheep one last time. The booley teens walked together behind the small herd of sheep and cows down the steep mountain path. Gunny's house was the first on the path back home. She clutched Ellen and Ashling and they all promised to stay friends. They waved back at her and continued on together to the village. Shep corralled the three Malone sheep into the small yard where they would winter with the cow, grazing on the stubble left in the nearby fields, and adding a new layer of fertilizer to the kitchen garden for the next planting season.

Gunny washed her hands and face and tried to braid her hair for the Hallow E'en gathering at the McCrohans'. Her hair was too thick and curly for the braid, and she yanked out the ribbon and tied her hair in a simple tie at the back of her neck. She grabbed her shawl, and headed off down the hill.

Ellen and Ashling were already at the McCrohans' and the girls squealed when they saw one another. At twelve, and after a summer on her own in the booley, Gunny was feeling very grown up—until Ellen and Ashling started flirting with Matt McCrohan, Cornelius Foley, and the Burke twins. Then she felt out of place. She was expecting the warm feeling of the summer booley, but that magic was gone. She found a stool in front of the fire and sat amongst the adults and the younger McCrohan girls and poked at the fire. She noticed Mac McCrohan leaning against the far back wall, looking as awkward as she felt.

Ashling pulled her up off her stool. "Come outside. We're going to play the bean game." Gunny started to object but was glad when Ashling pulled her out the door and thrust a bean in her hand. "Come on, Gunny. Give it a try."

Gunny glanced around at the boys who were all older than she was and were starting to look like men. She laughed and the sound came out with a snort. "Don't I need someone to toss the bean with? Where's that dog of mine? Shep?" she called, giving a shrill whistle for Shep to join her. She doubled over at her own joke, then glanced down at a pair of leather boots in front of her. Matt McCrohan grabbed a bean from the bowl.

"You're not my dog," she said glancing up at his face and giving a second, weak whistle for Shep.

Matt caught her by the arm and smiled. "You came out here to drop beans, Gunny. So drop your bean." He held her hand over the bucket of water. Even though he was three years older than she was, they were nearly the same height. She tried to chuck her bean away, but it stuck to the sweaty palm of her hand. She shook her hand violently and the bean dropped with a soft plunk in the water. Matt tossed his bean in at the same time. One bean rose and the other sunk.

"See?" Gunny said pulling her hand away from Matt and turning to the girls with a nervous giggle. "I told you I would never marry."

Matt pulled two dry beans from the bowl and handed one to Gunny. "Try again," he said. He held her hand out again over the water and they dropped the dry beans into the bucket. Once again, one bean floated and the other sank.

"That's your bean that's floating," Matt said. "My bean is down there on the bottom having a lovely marriage."

Gunny shook her head and grabbed an apple from the tub near the door. She took a big bite and let the juice run down her chin. "I don't think so, Matt."

"Who taught you such lovely manners?" he said with a grin.

Gunny wiped the apple juice from her mouth with the back of her sleeve, then leaned forward until her face was only inches from his. "You think you know everything."

"I may not know everything—but I do know some things," he whispered, holding her close by the arms. Gunny felt the blood rush to her face. She pulled away and let out another high-pitched laugh, then stepped inside and pushed the door closed behind her. She grabbed her shawl and said a quick good-bye to Kate McCrohan and the McCrohan girls, then slipped back outside. The teens were huddled in a close circle, laughing and tossing beans into the pot. Matt was standing by Ashling, their arms lightly touching at the elbow. Gunny walked quickly to the edge of the yard and sprinted home.

Michael returned to Dunquin for a few days at Christmas and proudly presented his father with a bottle of whiskey. "Mr. Murphy said even the poorest families shouldn't be without whiskey on Christmas Eve."

Robert grinned. "I couldn't agree more. And God bless Mr. Murphy."

Michael tossed Gunny a long red ribbon and handed Eileen a packet of bacon. Eileen wept as she unwrapped the heavy brown paper package. They had not had meat in months.

On Christmas morning, Eileen sliced thick strips of bacon and placed them in a pan to fry while Gunny cut four slices of oat bread and propped them in front of the fire on small wooden toasters. Eileen liked both sides of the bread to be evenly toasted with butter spread from edge to edge on each warm slice. Gunny squatted by the fire near the toasting bread threading the silky red ribbon through her long fingers while the first side of the bread browned, thinking back on the summer in the booley and about the night with Matt and the beans. The smell of burning bread brought her back to the moment but the first batch of toast was lost.

Eileen watched her carefully as Gunny sliced four more slices of bread. Gunny remained vigilant this time as Eileen added eggs to the pan of crisp bacon. When the food was ready and on the table, the family sat down and held hands.

"Lord bless this fine meal," Robert said.

"Amen," the family responded, and they ate.

When there wasn't one lick of food left, Gunny collected the bowls and spoons while Eileen sat down with a cup of hot tea in front of the fire. Robert took his pipe out of the right cubby and blew through it. He took the new plug of tobacco from the cubby and cut off a half-thumb to fill his pipe. Michael sat next to him and held out his own pipe. Robert smiled and cut off a half-thumb of tobacco for Michael then held a coal from the fire in the tongs over Michael's pipe. Michael sucked on his pipe, making loud popping noises till the tobacco lit. When Robert's pipe was lit, the two men sat side by side smoking, wordless. At the end of the week, the new plug of tobacco and whiskey were gone and Michael returned to work in Dingle.

A brutally cold winter turned into a surprisingly warm spring. When Robert was ready to plant, it was time for Gunny to return to the booley. She rose, washed her face in the basin of cold water and dried her face with the back of her sleeve. She whistled for Shep, and headed for the door, her bucket of supplies swinging jauntily from her hand.

"I'm surprised to see you so happy to go this year," Eileen said stifling a yawn. "What's your hurry?"

Gunny had grown even taller over the winter and was nearly Robert's height. She had started her women's cycles over the winter. Her new curves looked like nothing but trouble to Eileen.

"The booley wasn't as bad as I thought," Gunny said stuffing a corner of bread in her mouth. "I'll be back soon with milk for butter!"

But that summer the booley was different. Ellen's family had been evicted when they couldn't pay their rent and had moved to Ballyferriter to live with Ellen's aunt. Ashling was still in the village but her parents sent her little brother to the booley; he was living in a different hut. Gunny lived alone in Michael's hut, played her tin whistle to keep herself amused, and watched over a small flock of sheep with only Shep for company.

Matt McCrohan arrived in the booley on a warm day in early July. John McCrohan had purchased a few new sheep and insisted that the boys get them settled in the booley; he thought the McCrohan girls were too young to live so far from home. Matt had convinced Mac to go up in the spring so he could fish. But now Mac wanted time in the forge, and Maggie watched as Matt trudged reluctantly to the high fields. He checked briefly on their sheep and cow, then spotted Gunny sitting on a high flat rock twisting a long piece of coarse rope, her skirt tucked up around her long legs, her black curls pinned loosely away from her face.

"I haven't seen you around much," Matt said trying to sound casual.

"I've been in the booley—working," Gunny said, pulling a fresh blade of wet grass from a small bucket at her feet. "Where've you been?"

"Fishing. Mostly. What're you doing?" Matt asked, walking over to Gunny's rock perch.

Gunny looked up from her work. "What does it look like I'm doing?"

Matt smiled and sat next to Gunny. "It looks like you're making rope." He watched her hands as she worked. "Do you make a lot of rope?"

"Yes, Da uses it at the stables in Ventry," Gunny said without looking up. "Mam uses it for clothesline. And as you can see," Gunny hooked a thumb under a thin piece of rope around her middle, "a nice piece of rope makes a fine belt."

Matt reached over and fingered the wet piece of rope Gunny was twisting in her hands. "Nice."

Gunny gently pulled her work away from Matt's hand and pushed a stray curl from her face with the back of her hand. "There's not much else to do up here," she said, concentrating on her rope twist.

"You used to make fairy villages."

Gunny blushed and pinched the rope tightly between two fingers. "How do you know about that?"

"I used to stumble on them every once in awhile when I was out hunting rabbits."

Gunny winced thinking that Matt had seen her tiny towns. "So I suppose you were the ogre who stomped out my fairy villages?"

Matt laughed. "I never stomped out your villages. And there's lots to do up here. Listen to the wind. Sit. Read."

"You can read?"

"Sure, Da taught all of us to read. Every night he has us read to him from the Dingle newspaper."

"So what have you read lately?"

Matt stood up and brushed off the seat of his pants. He trotted down to his clochain and returned with a yellowed newspaper from Dingle. He showed the front page to Gunny.

"The Dingle paper mostly has local news—who sold what, what is for sale at which shops. The interesting stuff is about what is happening in the rest of Ireland."

"You mean outside of Dingle?"

"Yes," Matt said. "There's a big world outside of Dingle."

Gunny was irritated at his tone. "I know it's a big world, Matt." She scooted away from the boy and concentrated again on her work.

"Would you like to see what this says?" Matt held out the paper under Gunny's nose.

Gunny glanced at the sheet then elbowed it away. "I know some letters. I know how to write my name. Mam says that's enough for a girl."

"Is it enough for you? Da has taught all of my sisters to read, even little Susan."

Gunny pinched the piece of rope between her fingers to keep it from unraveling and looked at Matt. He was tall even when he was sitting down. He had a strong chin and wide cheekbones. His face and arms were bronzed from his time out fishing. His hair was long, brown and wavy. His green eyes were light at the center and dark around the edges. She caught herself looking too long into his bright eyes and turned back to twisting rope. "I don't suppose you could teach me how to read," she muttered.

Matt grinned. "I can try. The question is—can you learn?"

Gunny grunted and shook her head.

Matt leaned forward to catch her eye. "Of course I'd need a favor in return."

Gunny remembered the time Matt pushed her into the creek, their sand fight at the strand, and his days prancing through town leading the Wren Boys. She tilted her head and waited for the latest challenge.

"Teach me how to make rope," Matt said.

Gunny laughed. "Making rope is easy."

Matt was startled by the volume of her laugh. "God, girl. That's a big laugh." He couldn't help but smile, then offered Gunny his right hand to shake. "Reading for rope? That seems like a fair trade."

Gunny shook Matt's hand with her free hand. When she went to pull her hand back, Matt held it. She looked into his green eyes and was surprised to see warmth there. Matt let go of her hand and picked up the paper.

"Hmmm. Now where should we start…"

"It's simple, Matt. But you have to concentrate."

"I've seen you make rope plenty of times and you never seem to be concentrating at all." Matt worked for a few more minutes, biting his tongue between his teeth as he tried to mimic Gunny's smooth twists. He looked at his lumpy string of rope and threw it aside. "I'm terrible at this. Let's read."

"You can't give up. I told you I'd teach you how to make rope and I'm going to teach you to make rope," Gunny said handing him new strands of wet grass to start over.

Matt took the long blades of grass and held them up over his top lip.

"How do I look with a moustache?" he asked.

Gunny twisted her piece of evenly twisted rope into a tiny heart and tossed it to Matt. "You're impossible to teach."

Matt glanced at the tiny knot. "Show off," he said, pushing the knotted heart into his pocket. "I may be impossible to teach, but I'm a very good teacher. Let's go back to reading."

Reading was only slightly easier for Gunny than rope making was for Matt. Learning her letters was a little like walking through brambles. Matt used a black slate and piece of chalk to show her each letter which he made her copy over and over under, mimicking his neat handwriting. She would move forward then get snared in deep tangle after deep tangle. But as the summer progressed, clusters of letters started to make sense to her as words, and the words finally flowed into sentences. What she read in the Dingle paper wasn't particularly interesting but the idea that she could learn something without a person telling her about it took her breath away.

"Imagine if someone wrote down stories instead of news. Think of all the stories we've been told. What if someone wrote them all down so others could read them?"

Matt grinned. "There are stories in books. I've been teaching you from a newspaper because that's all I have. In Dublin, I hear they have vaults filled with story books."

The idea was incomprehensible to Gunny.

When they needed a break from learning, Matt took Gunny up to the high open fields past the grazing sheep to snare rabbits. Robert and Michael had never taken her rabbit hunting. Matt squatted on the edge of the field and pulled Gunny down next to him.

"Patience is the most important tool for hunting rabbits," he whispered.

"You're telling me about patience?" Gunny asked loudly. "This from the boy can't sit still for five minutes to twist a piece of rope?"

Matt snickered. "I don't need to learn how to twist rope. That's what I have you for." Matt ruffled her hair. "Now be quiet. If you want to catch a rabbit, you have to figure out where the rabbits enter and exit from a field. We're looking for a narrow spot in between the barrow and where the rabbits eat and drink."

Matt found rabbit scat along a narrow grassy path and he and Gunny retreated to a large rock to lie and wait. As they watched, a single rabbit appeared from a mostly hidden hole, then another pair hopped across the field using the same path.

"For the next part I need a bit of your rope," Matt whispered near Gunny's ear. "Since you make your rope with grasses from these fields, this is going to blend in beautifully."

Gunny sat up and untied her rope belt and handed it to Matt. He showed her how to make a small noose, then cut a short branch off of a nearby shrub and tied the noose to the stake. They returned to the rabbit path and using a flat rock, drove the stake into the ground.

"Make sure the stake is tight in the ground," he said. "That's what holds the rabbit after he's caught." Matt set the noose at the narrowest part of the trail, a few fingers off the ground, and loosely draped over neighboring twigs. He left an opening about as wide as his fist. "Make this about the size of a rabbit head and ears." He set twigs on each side of the noose to prop it open. "When the rabbit goes through the noose it will tighten on his neck and you'll have yourself a fine meal. Just be sure you don't set traps you can't get back to."

By noon, they had caught a fine fat rabbit which Matt showed her how to skin. They skewered chunks of rabbit meat on furze branches and slowly roasted them over an open fire on the mountain. Any time Matt asked, Gunny was happy to go hunting with him. Matt enjoyed hunting with Gunny. She was more daring than Mac and didn't seem to mind it when she got wet or dirty.

"I don't suppose you'd fish with me," he asked one hot day in late July.

"Sure. I'll fish."

"I mean up here in one of the Lord's streams. You know it's illegal."

Gunny shrugged. "I've never seen the Lord get up as far as the booley. How would he know we were fishing here?"

Gunny twisted fine fishing line for the occasion and finished off the piece with the tiniest line twisted from pale horse tail hairs she got from her father. Matt brought new sharp hooks that Mac had made, and they added fresh water fish to their growing list of summer fare.

Ashling hiked up to the booley one day to see Gunny.

"What do you mean Matt's teaching you to read? Why do you want to read? No wait. You're spending time with Matt McCrohan. I'd learn whatever he wanted to teach me. So, do you like him?"

Gunny shrugged at Ashling's spill of words. "Matt's all right. He's terrible at making rope, but he's a terrific hunter. Slow and patient. We haven't had to bleed a cow once this summer!"

On Midsummer's Eve, all of the teens came up from the village to join the booley workers. Ellen surprised Gunny with a visit, and she and Ashling were careful to not collect any fairy thorns when they collected bracken to add to the bonfire. The bonfire burned hot and strong through the evening while the large group of teens told stories and sang. Gunny closed the night with a merry tune on her tin whistle, then volunteered to stay by the fire until it went out.

Matt was one of the last to leave the fire circle, then turned and sat down next to Gunny as she stirred the burning embers making small sparks jump into the night air. "You're not afraid to be out here at night alone with the fairies?" he asked.

"No. I thought maybe I'd sleep under the stars," Gunny said with a smile.

Matt took up a stick and poked at the fire. "You've changed, Gunny. Just last year you hesitated to tell the tale of Grania and weren't sure about playing your whistle in front of everyone. Now it's like you are the village storyteller and musician all in one."

"A storyteller and musician... Mam says I need to act more like a girl."

Matt chuckled. "When have you ever listened to anything your Mam told you?"

Gunny grinned. "I have to grow up some time. Mam says I have to get married and keep a house and raise a dozen children…"

Matt looked at Gunny in the firelight. Her black curls spilled around her strong face and long torso. She glanced up at Matt and he looked away.

"You could be a gypsy and go about the countryside telling fortunes."

"Unlikely."

"Maybe the Fianna will come and capture you and take you away to France."

"Doesn't the French queen die at the end of the story?"

"I could teach you to sail and you could become a pirate queen, like Grania."

"I don't think a pirate's life is one for me."

Matt shivered. "It's chilly out here. Sit closer to me."

Gunny scooted closer to Matt. He draped an arm around her and hugged her tight against him. She was aware of every part of her body that was touching his and after a moment stiffened and edged away slightly.

"No, snuggle in," he insisted. "That was warmer."

Gunny looked Matt in the eye then moved next to him. She felt an odd rush, a flutter in her stomach as he once again draped an arm around her. She smiled. She was happy. Happy to be outside with a warm fire in front of her and cool air around her. Happy to look up and see a sky full of stars. Happy to be with Matt.

When Gunny brought the milk home the next morning her father was waiting for her.

"I heard you had a bonfire up at the booley last night."

"We had a small fire for midsummer. The smoke blew all over the cow this morning as I walked her out to the fields so she'll be full of milk. I singed a few hairs on her tail to be certain."

"Did you see any of the good people last night?"

Gunny smiled. "I did see some good people. There were fairies everywhere."

She told her father about the little sparks of light that rose out of the fire and up into the hills. She did not mention her time alone with Matt. Robert took a long drag off of his pipe and smiled.

"I remember fine times up in the booley."

Gunny wondered if her father had ever spent time there snug by a fire discussing life's uncertainties with a friend.

The first Sunday after August 15th was Gleaning Day, the day to harvest the oats. Everyone was out in the fields: young and old, men, women, and children. The strongest villagers cut the oats while others gathered the freshly cut stalks. Michael was home from Dingle for the day and Gunny watched as he and her father worked side by side slicing through their field of oats. At sixteen, Michael was as tall as her father and had a strong swing with the scythe. When they reached the last patch of uncut oats, Robert called the family together.

"A moment of silence, please, to witness the cutting of these last sheaves of oat."

Gunny handed Robert a small bottle of water. He uncorked the bottle and sprinkled holy water over the uncut stalks.

"Now we'll cut these stalks, and put out the hare!"

Robert took out his scythe and with one swift cut, felled the last sheaves. He glanced down the hill and yelled to John McCrohan who still had a good bit of field left to cut.

"John McCrohan! We have sent you the hare this year! How is it you're not finished cutting?"

John was slowly making his way through his field, cutting oats with his wife and four daughters collecting the sheaves behind him. He yelled back to Robert, "Perhaps if you had planted more oats, you'd have more to cut."

Robert laughed and scooped up the last few sheaves of oats and handed them to Gunny. "Use these grains for our evening meal. And please weave something elegant from the holy stalks."

John walked up the hill to talk to Robert and admire his cut field. "You had great speed with your harvest. Michael is tall and strong! Dingle has been good for him."

"You have two sons, John. Where are they?"

John shook his head. "Matt was here earlier but left to fish."

"He should be around to help on Gleaning Day."

"He says his time is better spent fishing. I can hardly get him to put his boat away come October he's so stubborn. He hardly listens to me anymore. And Mac, well, he headed home at midday to get water and never returned. He's probably at the forge. That's work I can't seem to keep him away from."

"So you were left to work with your wife and four girls. It's no wonder you're not done. Michael is headed back to Dingle, but I'll lend you a hand."

Kate McCrohan and the girls picked up the last bits of loose straw while John and Robert worked together to haul the oats to the forge.

"Much obliged, neighbor," John said. "We'd have been at it past dusk without your help." He sharpened his and Robert's scythe and wrapped them carefully in straw rope for next year's harvest.

"Now would be a good time to celebrate at O'Leary's," John stated.

"Any time is a good time to celebrate at O'Leary's," Robert replied.

That Hallow E'en, Gunny was amazed that instead of sitting awkwardly by the fire, she was now at the center of the circle of teens, laughing with Ashling, Matt and Mac, Cornelius Foley, the Burke twins, Maurice and Edmond, and the two oldest McCrohan girls.

After a second serving of Kate's apple pie, Robert Malone announced that he was ready to leave. "Come along girl," he said to Gunny. "These old bones are tired."

Gunny frowned. "I'd like to stay longer. We haven't been out yet begging for cake and apples. And I made a new straw mask to wear this year." She held an intricate cat mask up to her face and meowed.

Robert looked at the willowy cat in front of him. When had his daughter grown so tall? "Make sure someone walks you home."

"I'll walk her home, Sir," Matt said.

"See that you do," Robert said, pulling his hat off a peg near the door. He turned and looked at Matt and Gunny. "And don't come by our house begging for the Muck Olla telling me my farm won't prosper if I don't give you food. I'll not contribute!"

Gunny moaned and pushed her father out the door.

An hour later, the Hallow E'en marauders returned with their booty. Apples. Nuts. Someone had even contributed a few eggs and another neighbor gave them a small bag of unspun wool. They had walked Ashling home in their turn through the village. John McCrohan and the McCrohan girls had gone to bed. Kate McCrohan was sweeping off the hearth as the house filled once again with boys—and Gunny.

"What do you want to do now? Want to hike out to the circle fort? Remember last year we heard what sounded like a party of ghosts there," Cornelius suggested.

"Let's go to the graveyard," Gunny said. "I've never been there on Hallow E'en to see the dead."

"You're silly to believe such nonsense," Matt said, staring into the low turf fire.

"I don't think ghosts are nonsense. I rather like the idea of my grandparents coming home to visit each Hallow E'en."

"You're like a fairy, Gunny" Maurice said awkwardly. "All high revel and evil spirits," he said, touching her lightly on the arm.

"Evil spirits?" Gunny said with a frown, moving her arm away. "You're bad company, Maurice. You boys are boring." She yawned. "Matt, will you walk me home?"

Matt glanced at her from his stool by the fire. "I thought you were all for seeing a headless ghost or being taken off by the fairies?"

"That you say don't exist."

"I'm going to stay with the Wren Boys, Gunny. You can walk yourself home. Here, take my black-handled knife for protection in case the fairies try to get you," he said giving Cornelius a wink and holding out his knife toward Gunny.

Gunny batted the knife away, and the boys all laughed. Kate McCrohan stopped sweeping and eyed the gang of boys. "Matt. Walk Gunny home."

Gunny crossed to the door and looked back at Matt. "You told my father you would."

Matt yawned and shoved the knife into his pocket. "I'm tired, Mam. Gunny only lives one field away. What could possibly happen to her on the way from our house to hers?"

Mac stood up from his stool in front of the fire and brushed his hands off on his pants. "I'll walk you home, Gunny."

"No, thanks" Gunny said glancing at Matt. "Matt said he would walk me home." She raised her eyebrows at Mac daring him to take another step toward her. "Besides, you'd have to walk back here by yourself and you are more the type than me to be taken off by the fairies."

The boys guffawed at her ribbing, and she joined in the laughter. Matt stood up nearly knocking his stool over. "I'll walk with you. You're nothing but trouble under all that black curly hair. Just let me pull on my old Grannie's shawl so anyone who sees us will think you're with a ghost—not me."

Even Kate giggled as Matt draped a tattered old shawl around his head and hobbled about the room, crooning. "Come along, Sweetie. This old woman will get you home."

Kate McCrohan swept at Matt. "Stop that silliness," she said with a grin. "You'll bring on a curse from the dead."

Matt slipped out the door with a loud cackle and pulled Gunny out behind him.

Gunny stormed off ahead of him into the field.

"Wait up. I thought you wanted me to walk with you."

Gunny stopped and turned on him. "Why is it you're so pleasant when it's just the two of us, but any time we're around anyone else you're rude to me?"

Matt shrugged and kicked at the dirt. "I guess I don't want anyone to think I like you."

Gunny blushed. "God forbid."

With Matt and Gunny gone, the fun was over and the boys headed home. Mac watched as his mother built up the fire on the hearth instead of smooring it for the night. She set a bowl of water on the table and lit a candle for any dead visitors who might stop by.

"Mac, remind Matt to leave the door unlatched when he comes in," Kate said. "We don't want any disappointed ghosts stopping by for a visit and not being able to get inside."

Mac shivered. "Mam, do you really believe that ghosts come by on All Soul's Eve?"

"I'm not certain, Mac, but there is no harm in being hospitable, is there? If the dead can protect and help us in any way, I'm not going to say no."

She tousled Mac's rough head of black curls and went to bed. Mac eyed the burning candle and unlatched door. He pulled his sweater close around him and sat on a stool waiting for his brother to return.

~ Chapter 4: The Smithy & The Priest ~

It was a warm day in late November. Robert had been gone all week in Ventry breaking in a new horse for Lord Ventry. Gunny looked up from the front bench at the sound of approaching horse hooves. She tossed her rope work aside as her father wheeled into the yard astride a tall, black horse.

"He's beautiful," she gasped. "Can I ride him?"

"I can barely ride him myself," Robert said. "Be careful standing near him. He likes to kick. Reminds me a bit of the Old Lord."

"Oh, no," Gunny protested. "The Old Lord isn't half as pretty as this horse."

"I thought I finally had him in control, but now he's just gone and thrown a shoe. I hope John McCrohan can get a new one on him."

Robert dismounted and walked the pawing, snorting beast down through the fields to the forge. Gunny ran along beside her father. As Robert tied the horse up in the yard, they heard raised voices inside the forge. Robert paused, then knocked gently on the door and pushed it open. "Should we come another time, John?"

John was standing, hands on hips in front of the forge fire. He face was red and sweaty. "No," he said. "Now's as good a time as any."

Mac stood behind his father quietly working the bellows. Matt brushed past Robert and Gunny and stormed out into the yard.

"I've got a fighting steed outside who needs a shoe," Robert said softly.

John sighed. "And I've got a fighting steed inside who needs a smack in the rear," he said, shaking his head. He walked outside wiping the sweat from his brow and paused to catch his breath.

"Are you all right?" Robert asked.

John sat on the bench in the yard and rubbed his forehead. "I had trouble pulling a wheel off of the Kavanaugh's old cart. Now my arm is aching something fierce," he said rubbing his left arm. He stood and shook out his broad shoulders. "It'll pass. It always does. Let's have a look at the fine horse you've brought me."

Gunny sat on the bench and watched John work. The horse shied when John first touched his neck, then relaxed as John ran his hands down the horse's sides, muttering. When the horse was breathing evenly, John grasped the horse's right front hoof and studied it for size. He disappeared inside the forge and emerged with a new shoe. He lifted the horse's hoof again and took a hoof-pick from his leather apron to gently clean the mud from the animal's foot. Using a sharp knife, he smoothed the bottom of the hoof, leaving just enough to nail to. He carefully placed the new shoe on the foot, smooth side down. It was a perfect fit. He nailed it on one hole at a time, then clipped the nail ends where they protruded out the top of the nail and filed down the sharp points with a rasp.

"He won't be able to throw that one for awhile," he said, patting the horse's muscular neck. "He's actually very well-behaved."

"He is for you," Robert laughed. "I've never seen him stand still for so long."

The horse whinnied and shook his newly shod foot.

"I owe you, John. You do good work."

John rubbed again at his arm. "I wish everything in life was so easy to fix."

"Take care of yourself, eh?"

"Yes, I have a batch of nails to make then I'll call it a day."

Robert patted the horse's strong neck and he nuzzled his snout into Robert's hand.

"I wish we had a horse like this one, Da," Gunny said dreamily.

Robert swung up into the saddle. "This is not a working horse. He's good for nothing but the hunt." Robert spurred the horse around. "I am headed back to Ventry. The Old Lord will be frantic that we've been gone so long. Tell your mother I'll be home in a day or two."

Matt came running up the hill to the Malone house early the next morning. He knocked and entered shouting for Robert. Gunny was stirring the fire and turned with a start.

"Can't you wait until a body opens a door before you come bursting in?"

"Where is your Da?" Matt asked, out of breath.

"He's in Ventry. Why?"

Matt spun on his heels and headed out the door. "I'll find someone else."

Gunny walked into the yard and watched as Matt sprinted toward Fiona Burke's house. "You won't find any help there," she shouted after him. "I saw Maurice and Edmond head off earlier today with their fishing gear." She grabbed her apron and chased after Matt. He was nowhere to be seen, then came running around the corner from Fiona's house, his face white.

"Who're you looking for?" Gunny asked tying her apron behind her. "What's the matter?"

"Something is wrong with Da. He can't breathe. I need someone to ride to Dingle to get the doctor."

Gunny felt helpless. They needed someone with a horse. She pictured the fabulous black steed that had been in her yard only the day before. "Why don't you or Mac ride Nella?"

"I want to stay with my father. And Mac can't ride worth anything."

"What about Ashling's father? He has a horse."

"Of course," Matt said taking a shallow breath. "Will you go fetch him? I want to get back to Da. Mam is frantic with worry."

Gunny was already racing down the road, her loose hair flying behind her as she ran.

By the time Patrick Mitchell returned with the doctor, there was no helping John McCrohan. He had taken his last breath in his wife's arms an hour before, surrounded by his astonished children.

His wake lasted two days. Everyone in the village of Dunquin and in all of the nearby villages knew and loved the blacksmith and storyteller. The McCrohan house was full of men, women and children, laughing and telling stories. Kate did her best to feed everyone. Matt shook hands with men he had never met, many of whom told him what a good man his father was and what large shoes Matt had to fill.

"Drink up, gentlemen," Father Begley said at the start of the second day, "to make up for the loss of liquid from our eyes."

Villagers filled the streets for John's funeral parade from the house to the church. Father Begley prayed over John at the church, and again out in the graveyard. Kate McCrohan was stoic through the day, but the night after the funeral when the children were finally asleep, she looked at her empty marriage bed, and wept.

At the age of seventeen, Matt was the man of the family and the new village blacksmith. Gunny hardly saw him through the winter. On the first nice spring day, she sprinted down the hill with a new bit of fishing line in one hand and a rabbit noose in the other. She stood in the doorway of the forge and held up the gifts.

Matt paused mid-swing and wiped sweat from his forehead with the back of his hand. "We're not children in the booley anymore, Gunny," he snapped and returned to pounding a helpless bit of iron on the anvil. "I have a business to run, a family to support. You wouldn't understand. Mac, pump up the fire. This forge isn't hot enough to work a bit of ribbon."

Mac raised his eyebrows to Gunny then pumped furiously at the bellows.

Gunny sat on the bench and tossed the line and noose to the floor. "I just thought…"

"It's hot in here," Matt interrupted. "And dark. Why is the air so dry?" He coughed and rubbed at his smoke-stung eyes. "Mac, the fire has to be hotter. Why won't this metal bend?"

Mr. Kearny poked his head into the forge. "Good morning, Matt. My horse has thrown a shoe."

Matt threw his hammer to the floor. "Mac, find a shoe for Mr. Kearny. I need some air." He pushed past the elderly man and out into the light of the yard.

"I'll take a look at your horse," Mac said. "Her name's Esther, right?"

"Yes, Esther," Mr. Kearny said, eyeing the young teen. At fourteen, Mac had filled out, but his face still looked boyish. "She's been here many times. John was so good with her," Mr. Kearny said uncertainly.

Mac stood up to his full height, and led the man out into the yard. "Don't worry, Sir. I'll have your horseshoed in no time," he said in his lowest voice.

Robert was sitting with Father Begley at O'Leary's Pub talking how much they missed John McCrohan, gone these three months, when the elderly priest pushed back on his bar stool and the stool tipped out from under him. The old priest struck his head hard against the bar. He was a heavy man and Robert struggled to help him to his feet. His bristly grey hair and sheen of sweat on his brow gave him the look of a newly awakened spirit of the night. He had a large red welt along one temple.

Robert grimaced. "The devil may be in you tonight, Father,"

"Oh, yes the devil is in me," the priest agreed in a hoarse voice, rubbing gently at the spot on his head.

"Would you like me to walk you back to the rectory?"

Father Begley waved a hand in front of his red nose. "No, no. It's only a few doors down. Perhaps the walk will exorcise the devil right out of me." He hiccupped loudly and smiled at Robert. "I'll see you on Sunday. God bless you and keep you till then."

"God bless you and keep you till then," Robert muttered after him, holding his breath as the stout priest staggered first to the right, then to the left, then finally gained his forward momentum and headed out into the dark of the devil's own night singing, "When we went a typsying a long time ago…"

When Maeve O'Leary went to fetch water the next morning she found Father Begley slumped along the side wall of the pub with his teeth clenched shut and his eyes wide open. She touched his stiff, cold hand and backed into the pub to get her father. "Father Begley's outside," she gasped. "He doesn't look so good."

Nick wiped his hands on his apron and walked outside. He studied the inert body propped up against the rough stone exterior of the pub. "I've seen worse," he said. He hoisted the heavy little priest onto one shoulder, brought him inside, and hefted him onto the floor near the base of the bar.

"Take off his shoes and run hot water over his feet," Nick instructed Maeve.

Maeve did as she was told, unlacing the Father's worn leather boots, and gently pulling them off his stiff ankles. She poured a bucket of hot water over his white, swollen feet, but it did no good; the priest did not stir.

"Hmmm. Let's pour hot butter down his throat," he said. "That's the only other cure I know."

Maeve heated butter, but they could not pry the old man's mouth open and Nick declared the old priest dead.

Father Begley's wake went on for three days, and the church was full to the last pew for the funeral which was performed by a visiting priest who could only pretend to know Father Begley as well as the villagers had known him.

It was three months before a new priest arrived. The ladies of the village eyed him during the first church service, hardly wanting to close their eyes for prayer. Edward Jessey was tall and muscular and had fair, wavy hair and bright blue eyes. He had a fresh look about him with no hair on his face.

"The church cares nothing for Dunquin," Bitsy Kavanaugh complained to Eileen. "Look at how young he is. The church has once again sent us the scraps."

Eileen nodded in agreement with a sly smile on her face. He might be young but he wasn't bad to look at. Each Sunday, more women attended mass to hear the virtuous Father Jessey preach. He had new ideas—that the men in the village should attend Mass more often. That they shouldn't spend so much time in the pub. That old Father Begley had died because he was unprincipled. That their tiny shanties and meager fields of oats and potatoes were punishment for their sins. The women listened, staring at the new priest's hands, his hair, and his deep blue eyes.

When he requested help cleaning out the rectory of Father Begley's things, a dozen women showed up, including Eileen Malone and Bitsy Kavanaugh. The rectory was cluttered with a mish-mash of chairs and tables, oil lamps and floor mats, most worn out and all filthy. The women hauled everything out into the yard while the new priest sat on the front wall, deep in prayer. Eileen tapped him gently on the arm. The Father opened his eyes, peered at the mess in the yard, and said, "There is nothing here that is fit to be in the house of the Lord. Don't bother cleaning this. It is contaminated by the Devil. We'll burn everything."

The women looked at the old furniture and wiped the devilish filth from their hands. They had done the best they could. How could they know Father Begley's goods were contaminated by the Devil?

"But what will you do for furniture?" Eileen asked.

"I'd rather sleep on a simple mat than sleep on filth," Father Jessey replied.

The women pushed the furniture into a pile and brought out coals from the priest's fire. The furniture slowly caught fire, furniture finer than any the women would ever have in their own homes.

There had been no gatherings at the McCrohan house since John McCrohan's passing, and the teens of the village now gathered at O'Leary's pub. Gunny sat at a back table sharing a pint of porter with Cornelius Foley. He bored her but at eighteen had money from fishing to buy her porter. She tried to listen to him as he droned on about the day's catch, but her mind wandered to Matt. She hadn't talked to him in months. Plenty of boys seemed to want her attention these days. At fourteen, she was as tall as any of the men in the village and had a full figure and bonny laugh. But she missed Matt and dreamed of their summer nights in the booley sitting around a fire, telling stories, talking, and laughing. She stood and straightened out her skirts.

"I must be off."

"But I was in the middle of a story," Cornelius protested.

Gunny leaned down and gripped his freckled face in both of her hands and kissed him lightly on the cheek. "You'll have to finish another time," she said. "I just remembered I have to be somewhere." She raced out of the pub, up the winding dirt road, and into her house. She grabbed the potato pot and ran out the door.

"Where're you going with that pot?" her mother called after her.

"I'm off to the forge to get it fixed," Gunny yelled.

Eileen scrambled to the door but Gunny was already halfway down the hill. "Have you lost your mind?" she yelled.

"No," Gunny yelled, "But somehow I've lost a friend and maybe this pot will bring him back."

"There is nothing wrong with that pot," Eileen muttered after her retreating daughter.

Matt and Mac were working in the forge. Mac looked somber as he pumped the bellows in his long-sleeved shirt and heavy leather apron. Matt stood by the anvil, hammer raised over a glowing iron rod. He was a head taller than Mac, his shirtless upper body toned from six months of daily work in the forge. Sweat gleamed on his face and brown curls of hair pressed against his wet forehead. They both looked up as Gunny pushed the door open, clumsily holding a large potato pot with a handle that looked like it had been severed with a blow from a sharp rock.

"What do you want?" Matt snapped.

Gunny stood in the doorway with the pot staring at Matt.

"If you need something, tell me. Otherwise go away. I have work to do."

Gunny walked in and set the heavy pot at Matt's feet then fluffed out her mass of black curls. "My mother was wondering if you could fix the handle on this pot," she said coyly.

Matt slammed his hammer down on the cooling iron rod. "This metal is too cold to work, Mac." He heaved an unfinished bit of railing at Mac and turned to Gunny. "Leave the pot," he said, indicating a stack of pots that sat waiting to be fixed. "I'll get to it."

Gunny did not move.

"What do you want? I told you I'd get to your pot."

Gunny looked at the large pile of broken pots. "It looks like this'll take awhile. Do you have another pot we could use while you fix this one?"

Matt tossed his hammer to the floor and stalked to a large pile of pots, horseshoes, wheels, and posts that were jumbled together along the back wall of the forge. The forge had never looked like this when John was alive. Matt dug through the pile until he found an old patched potato pot. He thrust it at Gunny. He was close enough to her that she could smell his sweat and feel the heat radiating off his body.

She licked her lips. "I haven't seen you around," she said softly.

Matt stared at the tall girl, his green eyes hot with anger. He pushed sweaty hair up off his face. "I don't have time for your nonsense, Gunny."

She touched him lightly on the chest and he pushed her hand away. She gasped and picked up the patched pot to leave. She held it out in front of her. Her mother would never accept this pot. Mac hesitated, then pulled Gunny's pot from the pile and examined the handle.

"This doesn't look bad, Matt. I think I can fix it."

Matt snatched the pot away from Mac and threw it back into the pile. "I told Gunny I'd fix it later."

Mac's right hand stung from where he had been holding the pot when Matt tore it from his hand. "I just thought..." he started, picking up the pot again, but Matt interrupted.

"You just thought what? You thought you could run this shop better than me?"

Mac looked at the pot in his hands and at the cluttered shop around him. "Maybe."

"Maybe?" Matt repeated. "Why are you always so indecisive? If you think you can do a better job than me why don't you just say so?"

"I never said I could do a better job than you," Mac said standing up a little straighter in front of his taller brother. "I was only offering to help fix this handle."

"Who did father leave in charge of this forge, Mac? You, or me?"

"You," Mac said in a soft voice rubbing at his sore hand.

"That's right. I'm the one who's responsible for the welfare of this family. If you think you can do a better job then go ahead—fix that pot. Fix all these God-damned pots for all I care." Gunny and Mac watched in silence as he pulled on his shirt, pushed the door open and left.

Mac fingered the handle on Gunny's broken pot and set it down near the anvil. "Thank you," he said quietly with a broad grin on his face. He pulled a hot bar of iron from the forge and picked up Matt's heavy hammer. "I'll have a new handle for you in no time."

"I think Matt's lost his mind," Gunny muttered.

"No, he hasn't," Mac said, the hammer pealing against the anvil. "But he will if he keeps trying to work with iron. Maybe now he'll let me do this work and he'll go fishing. I really can't thank you enough," Mac said with a wide grin.

Gunny waited while Mac hammered out a delicately curved handle. After carefully fitting the handle on the old pot he added a twist to each end of the rod, then dipped the finished work in cold water. A hiss of steam filled the room. He presented the pot to Gunny with a flourish.

"Nice," Gunny said examining the fine new handle. "You're good at this."

"I've been practicing. When what I make isn't perfect, I try again, unlike someone I know…"

Gunny grinned at Mac and left the forge with a flip of her skirts.

At the first harvest after John's death, Kate McCrohan insisted they have a gathering.

"Your father liked nothing better than having a house filled with people and stories. I want you to invite everyone in the village," she told her children. "I want things to be like they used to be."

Matt scooped a bite of potato into his mouth. "Things will never be like they used to be." He felt his eyes burn with tears and cleared his throat.

Kate leaned over and squeezed his hand. "I know this has been difficult for you."

Matt pulled his hand away and stood. "I'll be in the forge."

"You're not coming to the gathering?" Kate asked.

Matt shook his head. "I'm in no mood."

Kate grinned. "I'd say you're in a mood."

"Mac can fill in for me. Can't you, Mac?"

Mac lingered over his bowl of potatoes and said nothing.

Father Jessey was livid. Since moving to Dunquin, he had done his best to warn his flock against sin, but now things had gone too far. He stood before his congregants at Sunday Mass, looking at the faces of mostly women from the village. His lips were tight, his face red.

"I have warned you about drinking. I have warned you about dancing. But last Sunday night at the McCrohans', what did I see? I saw young people drinking and dancing. Together. In a hot, crowded house."

Bitsy turned to Eileen. "Kate McCrohan is only now getting over John's death. Father Jessey shouldn't criticize her…"

Father Jessey stared at the Bitsy and Eileen as they whispered in the right front pew.

"Your daughter was there, Mrs. Malone. I saw her."

Eileen's hand flew to her mouth and she blushed deeply. The priest continued.

"I have tried to accept that O'Leary's is always busy. But in all my days as a priest, I have never heard so much ruckus coming from one house as I did last Sunday night."

"All his days as a priest?" Bitsy muttered to herself. "How many days could that have been?"

Eileen waved her hand to shush Bitsy. She did not want to draw the priest's ire again. It was surprising to hear angry words coming from the mouth of one who looked so angelic. Father Begley had never lectured anyone about spending time at O'Leary's or about the evils of drinking, or dancing. The two women sat quietly with the other women in the congregation and listened as Father Jessey insisted that the frivolity stop or there would be hell to pay.

Over the winter, Father Jessey's focus began to narrow in on Gunny Malone. No matter where he was in the village, day or night, weekday or Sunday, if there was trouble, he usually found Gunny at the center of it. He hiked up the steep road to the Malone house and found Robert sitting on his front bench in the sun.

"Good day, Mr. Malone," the young priest said, slightly out of breath from the long climb. "I hope I'm not disturbing you."

Robert stood and extended a hand. "You're not disturbing me at all. There's not much to do until we start readying the fields for planting."

Father Jessey shook the man's large hand. His grip was strong and warm. The priest glanced around the messy yard and cleared his throat. "I thought I might see you in church but since that has not happened since Christmas Mass, I had no choice but to walk up here. We must talk about your daughter."

"Gunny," Robert said. "My daughter's name is Gunny."

Father Jessey sat down on the long front bench. "Yes, Gunny." He patted the seat next to him and Robert obediently sat. "Your daughter is headed down a bad path. One minute I see her skipping about, tossing that head of black curls. The next she's at O'Leary's drinking and singing with the boys. And that whistle. No decent girl plays a whistle. I insist that you put a stop to her frivolity before she meets an untoward end."

Robert laughed. "Gunny has high spirits. No harm will come of it."

The priest stood and paced in the yard. "High spirits can be tolerated in little girls. But Gunny is practically a woman."

"She'll be fifteen next month."

"Fifteen," the priest muttered. "Then this is easy to solve. She must be married before a bastard child is created. I'll have none of that in my parish."

"Just because a girl dances with boys doesn't mean she is going to have a bastard child."

"Trust me, Mr. Malone. I have seen this before. You must take action now."

Robert stood. "You may've seen this with other girls, but you don't know my Gunny. She'd never cause me shame."

"She is already causing you shame," Father Jessey thundered. "I found a houseful of young adults again last Sunday night at the McCrohans. They were packed in there, singing, and dancing, and telling stories."

"We've always gone to the McCrohans' in the evenings. The gatherings have just started up again. I was there myself last week."

"Mr. Malone. We are talking about the souls of our children."

Robert stood chest to chest with the priest. "I hear you and I disagree. Thank you for stopping by." The priest took a step back, then turned with a huff and headed back down the hill to the village.

Father Jessey signaled to Eileen to wait for him after the congregants left after Sunday services.

"Gunny was not in church today," he stated, tight-lipped, arms crossed, eyebrows raised.

Eileen shook her head. "If you continue to chide the teens from the pulpit, I doubt you'll ever see any of them in this building."

"We're not talking about the other teens. We are talking about your daughter. Mrs. Malone, the oats are on the swing from green to gold."

"The oats? Are you talking about Gunny?"

"Well, I am certainly not talking about farming," the slim priest said with the slightest of smirks.

Father Jessey showed up again at the Malone house. Gunny was surprised to see the priest in his dusty, deep black robes when she opened the front door. "Father Jessey," she said, stuffing a half a slice of bread into her mouth and swallowing. "What brings you here?"

"You, Gunny," Father Jessey said sternly. "Please step outside."

Gunny wiped her hands on her apron and joined the priest in the yard. Father Jessey paced. He stopped when he reached the edge of the dung hill. He gagged at the smell and spun toward Gunny. "You must come to church. You must change your ways."

"You care about what I do?" Gunny crossed to him and lightly rested her hand on his arm. "This is the first time you've talked to me directly."

He felt the heat of the girl's hand through his heavy black robe. He wanted to take a step away but instead took a deep breath and looked into her dark brown eyes. "God told me to look after his children."

"After me?" Gunny said, squeezing his arm then resting her hand on her hip. She liked that the tall man was nervous around her.

"Well, not you specifically," Father Jessey said looking away from her. "He charged me with all of his sheep."

Gunny laughed a hearty whoop. "I am not a sheep, Father. None of us in Dunquin are sheep. And we got along just fine before you showed up with your silly edicts and condemnations." She shook her head and turned to go inside.

Father Jessey took a step toward her. "The church will teach you to understand the one true God."

Gunny whipped around and stared. "I actually know God quite well," she said evenly. She stepped closer and the priest took a step back. "I know God when I'm walking in the hills and when I see a storm sweep in off the ocean and when I see a baby lamb born in the fields. And that God," said Gunny, stepping as close as she could to the priest, "is very much a believer in stories, and song, and joy. Unlike you!"

"That's a pagan god you are talking about," Father Jessey said, grabbing the girl's arm. "That is not our Father."

Gunny jerked Father Jessey's hand from her arm. "Your Father is not my Father," she said with a steady voice. "My Father is joyful."

"Is your Father going to save your soul, Gunny? Only the church can save you from this dirty existence."

Gunny snorted. "Save me? With incense and holy water? If you want to save me, get rid of the English landlords. While you're off in that haven you call a church, honest people are doing honest work fishing in God's oceans and raising potatoes in this depleted soil—only to have everything taken by them." Gunny kicked hard at the dirt. "While you waltz around in your fancy robes, real people are hungry so we have to get our hands a little dirty. Do you ever get your hands dirty doing the work of the church?"

Father Jessey wiped sweat from his soft, uncalloused hands against his robe. "You are too young to understand the ways of the church, Gunny."

"You're wrong, Father. I understand the ways of the church." Gunny tapped her finger gently against his chest. "You try to make us feel guilty for being human beings. You ask us for money and tell us it'll make us feel better. Well, I don't feel guilty and I don't feel bad, Father. I'm going to enjoy life and you're going to have to accept that." She brushed past him and slammed the door closed behind her. Inside, she leaned against the door and smiled. She hadn't known those words were inside her.

Father Jessey stood in the yard. He felt a shiver pass down his spine and swallowed hard. God was testing him. God, and the church. How dare they send him to this dirty little village on the edge of nowhere? And how dare this girl defy him?

Eileen chucked the potato peels from the evening meal out onto the dung heap. She dipped a cloth in the water bucket and wiped potato residue from the large wooden potato bowl and stashed it on a shelf by the door. Robert sat on his stool and stared into the fire. He took a wisp of straw from the turf pile, held it over the fire embers until it caught, and held it over his packed pipe, sucking until the tobacco lit. He let out a long breath of smoke.

Eileen picked up the broom and swept around him. When she was between him and the fire, she leaned her broom against the mantel. "It's time Michael was married," she announced.

Robert pulled his pipe from his mouth and stared. "What brought this on?"

Eileen pulled her stool next to Robert's and sat. "I was talking with Bridget Guhan today. You remember her son, Paul, who got married last Shrove?"

"Not really," Robert said without interest. "Everyone gets married at Shrove."

"Never mind. The point is that Bridget told me Paul's new wife has been a God-send helping out around the place. And that made me think that perhaps Michael should be married."

Robert stared at his wife. "You have Gunny," he started but knew better than to finish the thought. Gunny was rarely in the house these days and she never cleaned or cooked. "And who would marry our young son? You must have someone in mind."

"I was thinking… about Maeve O'Leary."

Robert pictured the short round girl who worked behind the bar at O'Leary's, with her large face and beady eyes. "Maeve's got to be around the same age as Gunny," Robert objected.

"She's fifteen. I asked Nick. That's plenty old enough to be married. And O'Leary's is a successful pub. The way I see it, if Michael marries Maeve, we might get back some of the money in her bride's dowry that you've spent over these many years."

"Maeve O'Leary?" Robert shook his head and sucked gently on his pipe. "She's a funny little thing. What makes you think Michael will like her?"

"I'm the one who has to like her and I like that she can cook and clean and will bring us a good dowry. I've thought this through, Robert. I want you to ask Nick for her hand before she gets any older. Go talk to him tonight."

"I'll talk to Michael first. He should have a say in who he marries."

"Father Jessey says that marriage is a parental decision. There is no need to bring the boy in on the discussion. Unlike his sister, Michael will do as we ask."

"Three years ago we asked him to work in Dingle."

"And he did. He went willingly," Eileen reminded her husband.

"That's true," Robert said thoughtfully. "Michael never complained about his work or about handing over his pay to us. Still, marriage is more permanent than working in Dingle."

"You're stalling."

Robert stared into the fire. "You're right, I am. I'll go to Dingle tomorrow and talk to Michael. As long as he is not opposed, I'll ask Nick about the match."

Eileen stood and clapped her hands. "How nice it will be to have someone around here to help." She knelt in front of Robert and rested her arms across his lap. "Go down to O'Leary's tonight and try to strike a bargain."

Robert could not resist Eileen on the rare occasions when she smiled at him. He kissed her on the forehead, grabbed his jacket and hat, and headed down the hill to talk to Nick.

Robert walked to Dingle the next morning to deliver the news to Michael. It was mid-February. The air was cool, the sun warm, and the two-hour walk passed quickly.

The bells above the door at the Murphy's jingled. Michael was surprised to see his father in the doorway, but not as surprised as Robert was to see Michael. The boy had surely grown another inch since Christmas. At eighteen, his chest and arms were broad, and his chin harbored a thick shadow of hair.

"Son, I wouldn't recognize you if I didn't know you worked here."

Michael laughed a deep laugh. Robert hardly recognized that either. Where had his little boy gone?

"What do you need, Da? I'll help you load it." Michael smiled at his father.

"It's not what I need… It's about your mother."

Michael's eyes opened wide and his chin went slack. "What's wrong with Mam?"

Robert raised his hands and shook his head. "Nothing's wrong. I worded that poorly. I'm here about what your mother wants."

"Oh. Knowing my Mam, she wants a bit of sweet cake. Or she has a complaint about the flour I brought home at Christmas."

"Too simple. This is your mother."

Michael looked puzzled.

Robert cleared his throat. "Perhaps we could step outside for a moment?"

Michael looked around for Daniel Murphy. He spotted the broad-backed man unloading boxes near the front window of the store.

"Murph," he yelled over to his employer. "I have to step out for a moment with my Da." Daniel Murphy waved and Michael and Robert stepped out onto the street.

"You'll have to be quick, Da. I have work to do."

Robert took a deep breath. "Your mother would like you to come home and get married."

Michael's mouth fell open. "Mam wants me to marry?"

"Surely you must have thought about marriage, Son."

"No, I haven't thought about marriage. I'm a hired hand here in Dingle. I didn't think I had any prospects for marriage."

"Things have been better for us lately thanks in part to the money you send home. It's time you returned to the farm."

"And what will we do for money?"

"It's Gunny's turn to work. I talked to Mr. Murphy about her last month even before this whole marriage idea came up. She'll work here and you'll come home."

Michael grinned "Have you told her yet?"

"No," Robert said looking down at his boots.

Michael howled with laughter. "I can't picture my sister working inside—and living in a town."

"She has no choice," Robert said sharply. "Your mother is at her wits end about what to do with your sister. The priest has been practically haunting our house."

Michael's smile faded. "The priest? Is Gunny in trouble?"

"No, she's not in trouble. She annoys the priest with her singing and dancing—and with that damned tin whistle of hers. And Gunny should work. It's time."

"All right," Michael said touching his father's arm. "Now give me the bad news. Who does Mam have in mind for my match?"

"We'll talk on the way home."

"Da, I can't leave now. I have work to do."

"I'll explain everything to Daniel."

"So the wedding will be…?"

"Three days from now on Shrove Tuesday. I'm sure there'll be other young couples marrying this week."

Michael whistled and shook his head. "I'll get my things. I can't believe I'm headed home. And I can't wait until you tell me who the lucky girl is."

Gunny pushed open the door at O'Leary's and was greeted with the familiar smell of porter and tobacco. Matt was at a back table with Cornelius, the Burke twins, and Ashling. Ashling was sitting next to Matt. From the number of glasses on the table, it looked like they had been there for awhile.

"Hey," Gunny said as she walked up to the table eyeing Matt. "I thought you never left the forge these days."

"A man has to rest from time to time," he said with a wide smile, raising his glass of porter.

"I'm looking for Maeve. Has anyone seen her?"

"She's out back," Ashling said in a smooth voice, leaning across Matt and pointing toward the wide kitchen door.

"Thanks," Gunny said. She pushed the swinging door open and walked into the kitchen. Bowls and spoons and sacks of flour and sugar were everywhere. Maeve herself was covered in flour. Somewhere amongst the mess, something smelled delicious.

"So this is where you work," Gunny said looking at the cluttered space. "I've never been in Nick's kitchen before."

Maeve smiled at her new sister-to-be and wiped sweat from her brow with the back of her sleeve leaving a wet smear of caked flour across one eyebrow. "You spend most of your time out front. With the boys. I've seen you."

Gunny raised her eyebrows. "Well," she said looking awkwardly around the room. "So you work here in the kitchen," she repeated.

"Not for much longer! Tomorrow I'll be married to your brother and living a life of luxury."

Gunny muffled a laugh. "Have you seen our house?"

Maeve waved a hand in front of her face. "I know where you live. Somewhere up near Mount Eagle."

"Yes, in a tiny little house at the end of a steep climb on the way to a craggy old mountain. And you've met my mother?"

"I've spoken with her a few times. She's lovely."

"She may have been lovely during your matchmaking. Living with her may bring a few surprises," Gunny said with a chuckle.

Maeve nodded her head. She had no idea what Gunny was talking about but didn't want to think about it any farther. All she knew was that she no longer had to stand behind a bar and serve stout to drunken villagers. She couldn't exactly remember who Michael Malone was but he could be no worse than any of the other men in the village.

Gunny handed Maeve a small lace collar. "Mam said you should wear this tomorrow at the wedding. It belonged to her mother."

Maeve wiped her hands on her apron and took the bit of lace from Gunny. "Oh, it's pretty!" She put the collar around her large neck and tugged on the ends to try and attach the closure. Gunny cringed at her efforts. Maeve finally gave up and tossed the collar onto a table amongst assorted rags, pots, and empty food sacks. "Oh, well," she said taking up a long wooden spoon and stirring the contents of a pot hanging over the fire. She took a long sniff. "Ummm. I'm making a nice porridge with currants. Do you want a bite?" She held the stirring spoon out toward Gunny. A large bit of porridge dropped to the floor. Maeve kicked it away with a smile.

"Maybe another time." Gunny gingerly picked the hand-made lace collar up from the table and shook off the flour. "Perhaps Mam has another gift she can give you."

"Tell your mother that I'm making a cake for the wedding tomorrow." Maeve pointed to a large pot that was sitting on the hearth covered in coals from the fire. "I love cake!" she added.

Gunny looked at the plump girl with her wide smile. One tooth on the upper right was missing. "I remember that about you," she said with a half grin then backed out the kitchen door into the pub.

"Gunny," Matt called as Gunny headed toward the door. "Why don't you join us?"

Gunny looked at the crowded table. Ashling gave Gunny a look that said, "Don't you dare."

"Ashling doesn't look like she wants me to join you," Gunny said flatly.

Ashling's face turned nearly as red as her hair. She smiled warmly. "Of course I want you to join us, Gunny," she purred. "We're old booley friends, aren't we?" She reached behind Matt's chair and draped an arm lightly across his broad shoulders. Gunny noticed a long red hair resting near Matt's vest pocket.

"See, Gunny?" Matt said a little too loudly. "Ashling doesn't mind." He scooted her chair away from him with a squeak, nearly tipping the girl onto the dirty pub floor to make room for Gunny. Gunny pulled a chair from a nearby table and squeezed it into the space between Ashling and Matt and sat down.

"Why are you here a midmorning?" Gunny asked, looking at the pasty faces at the table.

"We're having a porter to pass the time," Cornelius said, taking a long swig from his nearly empty glass and giving Gunny a long wink.

Gunny felt uncomfortable sitting between Matt and Ashling. She pushed her chair away from the table and stood. "I should go. I have to help my mother clean the house for Michael's wedding."

"Why're you cleaning? The wedding party'll be here at the bride's house— at O'Leary's. We came early to get the best seats," Matt joked.

"My mother cleans whenever she has an excuse." Gunny flashed back to the cluttered kitchen that lay beyond the wall behind the bar. "And won't she be surprised when Maeve joins us in our clean little house tomorrow."

"Maeve's a great girl. She can down a porter in no time flat," Maurice said in clear admiration of the girl's talent. Edmond shook his head in agreement.

"That's... quite a skill," Gunny said. "All right. I'm headed home." She looked around at the sleepy faces. "Don't you all miss the sunshine? Wouldn't you rather be out fishing or hunting... or something?"

The teens replied in unison, "No," and roared at their collective humor.

"Gunny," Ashling called after her when she was near the door. "I hope you don't mind that I'm here with Matt. It's so nice to have him out with us again."

Gunny turned. "Why would I mind?" she said with a smile, and sprinted home clutching the delicate wedding collar tight in her fist.

Gunny sat quietly on the hard pew of the church staring up at the tall ceiling timbers. It was Shrove Tuesday and three couples stood at the altar joining hands. Watching Maeve and Michael stand before Father Jessey and exchange vows was nauseating. Maeve O'Leary would soon live with them in their tiny house. How was that going to work?

The ceremony concluded with loud shouts and chatter among the happy couples and attending families. Gunny trudged behind her parents and the newlyweds as everyone headed to O'Leary's for a combined wedding celebration. Robert dropped back to walk with Gunny and to break the news about Dingle. Gunny stopped in the dusty road, mouth open and eyes burning as the others continued on toward O'Leary's.

"I'm to move to Dingle? In two days time?" Gunny said trying to take in her father's words.

Robert nodded and looked down the dusty road after Eileen. "Your mother needs help around the house and we both know you are not suited for that. Maeve is."

"So you had Michael marry Maeve to replace me?"

"Maeve isn't replacing you, Gunny," Robert tried to assure his daughter. "We have to be practical. Your mother and I are not getting any younger. Michael will help me on the farm and Maeve will help your mother in the house. Someone has to bring in money, and that someone is you."

"But you'll have the bride's dowry. And I've always worked on the farm with you. Michael doesn't know a thing about planting or when to harvest..."

"You spend more time these days drinking and gallivanting around than you do helping me on the farm. And Michael is strong. He'll be of help. He'll learn."

Gunny gasped. "You never complained before about how I spend my time." She paused and her eyes narrowed. "You're sending me away because of Father Jessey, aren't you?"

Robert looked down the road toward O'Leary's. Gunny grabbed her father by the shoulders and made him look her in the eye. Robert tried to meet her gaze but his focus fell to his dusty shoes.

"I knew it!" Gunny said taking a step away. "That scheming priest got to you."

Gunny spun around and sprinted back toward the church, hair and apron strings flying behind her. She ran past the high stone wall, pushed open the rusting, iron gates and bounded through the open doors. The nave was deserted. Her footsteps echoed as she ran up the center aisle of the church then took a right to the side door that lead to the priest's rectory next door.

She had never been in the priest's private quarters. She pushed open the door and peeked inside. The room was large but had no furniture, no rugs. A small turf fire burned low in the fireplace. Beyond the front room was a second room with a mat on the floor. A crisp white shirt lay on a stool near a small tin washstand. Father Jessey crossed near the mat with his robe pulled up over his head. She was surprised at the priest's lean, muscular frame. She gave a low whistle.

Father Jessey frantically pulled his robe up over his head to see who had entered his home without knocking. When he saw it was Gunny, he covered himself with his robe as best he could. "How dare you come in unannounced," he admonished. "Turn around while I dress.

Gunny turned her back to the priest. "Sorry, Father. I couldn't wait to tell you the good news."

Father Jessey snorted behind her back as he struggled to pull on his shirt. "I pray that it's news of a marriage and not of a baby."

Gunny whipped around. The priest was still buttoning his shirt but Gunny didn't care if she embarrassed him. "It's nothing of the sort, Father. Da is sending me off to work in Dingle."

Father Jessey rolled up his shirt sleeves and pushed back his tousled, blond hair. He turned Gunny away from his room and toward the fire. "I told your father you should marry. I never said anything about sending you away."

"What gives you the right to tell my father anything?"

"So I should keep quiet and allow you to turn the head of every boy in this parish? I see the boys fighting over you. It will lead to no good," he said, kneeling to stir the fire.

Gunny wanted to rake her dirty fingernails across the back of his clean white shirt. "There are no boys fighting over me, Father Jessey. Why would you say that?"

He turned to face her. "I speak the Divine truth of the Lord. And I was correct to counsel your father that you should be married."

"But instead he's sending me into service in Dingle."

The priest's face darkened. "I disagree with his decision. Young women shouldn't be allowed out by themselves. I'll warn Father O'Sullivan in Dingle that you are headed his way."

Gunny saw red and raced back through the door of the rectory, out through the empty church and onto the road. She glanced down toward O'Leary's. She would hear singing and raucous laughter. She sprinted instead up the winding dirt road to spend one last night in the only place she had ever called home.

Gunny angrily packed her clothes the next morning, loudly moving in and around Michael and Maeve who were trying to sleep in after a late evening of wedding festivities.

Eileen sat with her basket of mending in front of the fire. "Leave them alone," she whispered. "Let them sleep."

"I'm looking for my whistle," Gunny muttered.

"Leave it. You'll have no time for that at the Murphy's."

Gunny found her whistle deep in the pocket of a soiled apron she had stashed in a corner of the room. She yanked open the front door and chucked the whistle outside. It hit the front stone wall with a dull ping and bounced into the dirt. "Are you happy now?"

Eileen said nothing as she continued to mend one of Robert's stockings with neat, tight stitches.

Maeve stumbled out of the back room and sat down at the table, yawning. "Is there any tea" she asked blearily.

"Of course there is, dear. I'll get you a cup," Eileen said, setting her mending aside and rising. "Pay no attention to Gunny. She's not happy about her move to Dingle but she'll be gone soon and won't trouble us anymore."

Gunny growled at Maeve and stormed outside, slamming the door behind her. She plucked the whistle from the dust by the front wall and spent the day in the deserted booley fields. She played her most mournful tunes on the whistle until they made her cry. When the sun dipped low in the sky, she started home, then headed instead through the fields to the McCrohans'.

Kate and Mac were sitting quietly by the fire with the four McCrohan girls, the dishes from their evening meal still on the table. Gunny delivered the news of her departure. They were all shocked and the two youngest girls piled into Gunny's lap and cried.

"No, Gunny," they said patting her long curls. "You can't leave Dunquin. Who will tell us stories and play the whistle for us?"

Gunny pulled the slightly dented whistle from her pocket and ran a hand over the cool metal. "I might as well toss this old whistle in the creek. It's caused me nothing but trouble. And no one will want to hear my playing when I'm trapped out in some old shed behind Murphy's General Store."

The girls sobbed and hugged Gunny good-bye.

"I'd better go," she said, standing and looking around the familiar room. "Da wants to leave for Dingle first thing in the morning." She turned to Kate McCrohan. "Is Matt around? I'd like to tell him this news myself."

"He's out in the forge," Kate said, giving Gunny a short hug.

Mac gave her a small wave and shrugged his shoulders. "I'll see you sometime in Dingle, I guess," he said and walked quietly into the back room.

Gunny knocked on the worn wooden door of the forge. When no one answered she pushed the door open and walked in. Matt was sitting by the fire, head in his hands.

"Are you all right?" Gunny asked.

Matt glanced at Gunny then turned to the fire and rubbed his eyes. "Too much porter last night. I have a headache. What do you want?"

Gunny hesitated. "I came to tell you good-bye."

Matt looked up. "Good-bye? Where're you going?"

Gunny took a shallow breath. "My father is putting me out for service. I leave tomorrow to take Michael's place at the Murphy's in Dingle."

"A girl can't replace a man," Matt scoffed.

"Well then I'm either not a girl or Michael's not a man because I am replacing him at the Murphy's."

Matt grunted and rested his hands again against his face.

Gunny pulled up a stool and sat down next to him. "You look as bad as I feel."

Matt shook his head. "Don't compare yourself to me."

"I wasn't comparing myself to you…"

Matt stared at Gunny's slim face. "At least you're getting out of here," he started, then his voice trailed off. "Why did you come out here?" he grunted. "You probably want me to walk you home, don't you? Good old, Matt. The one everyone depends on. Well you can't always get what you want, Gunny."

"You don't have to walk me home," Gunny said quietly and stood. "I can get across the field. What did you used to say? What could possibly happen between your house and mine?"

Matt stood, pulled off his heavy leather apron, and threw it on the floor by the fire. "From what Father Jessey's been preaching, most anything can happen when it comes to you. I'll walk you home," he said, taking hold of her arm. She pulled her arm away and walked out the door ahead of him.

A dark orange moon was rising over Mount Eagle, shining strange, dull light across the stubble in the field. They trudged in silence through the rough, muddy field. Halfway to her house, Matt pulled Gunny to a stop and turned her around to face him. "I'm sorry I yelled at you," he said in a quiet voice.

"That's all right."

"No, it's not. You've been a good friend and I've been nothing but dreadful to you lately."

Gunny paused. "That's true," she said with a smile.

Matt cupped Gunny's face in both of his hands and stared into her deep, brown eyes. "Shut up and listen to me. I'm being serious."

Gunny wrapped her hands around Matt's hands. "I'm being serious too. Sometimes we're friends and sometimes we're not. I'm used to your ways. It doesn't matter anymore. You'll never see me again." She was surprised at the burst of warm tears that flowed down her face to her chin. She pulled away from Matt's grip and wiped her face and nose with the back of her sleeve. "I don't know why I'm being such a baby," she laughed. "You'll probably leave soon too. You always said you were going to sail away, or move to Dublin to do something big. Times change. People leave."

Matt reached out and took Gunny by the shoulders. He pulled her in tight to his chest. "I don't know what Dunquin will be like without you," he whispered into her mass of black curls. He turned her face softly toward his and kissed her on the mouth.

Gunny pushed away from him, breathless, but left her hands resting on his chest. "You'll be fine. You have your work and your… friends." She shook her head. "Forget you knew me, Matt, and I'll forget I knew you." She lifted her skirts and ran the rest of the way home across the moonlit field.

~ Chapter 5: Working Life ~

Gunny woke early and stuffed a clean apron, a few pair of stockings, her good skirt and a second shirt in an old flour sack. She dug a spoon out of the box on the cupboard and grabbed her fraying red hair ribbon from a peg by the door. She stuffed them down in the sack and looked around the small house.

Robert sat at the table. "I know you don't agree with my decision, Gunny, but sometimes one has to make sacrifices for the good of the family," he said in a quiet voice so as not to wake the rest of the family.

Gunny grabbed her muddy boots from the hearth and tossed them out into the barrow in the yard along with the stuffed sack. "I'm ready when you are," she said coldly through the open door.

Robert stood and stretched. "We're in no hurry. I told Murph I'd have you in Dingle sometime after Shrove. How about some toasted bread before we go?"

"Don't let me hurry you, Da."

Gunny remained in the open doorway staring at her father as he cut two thick slices of oat bread and set them on small toasters in front of the fire. He sat on his stool to watch the bread brown. He could feel Gunny's stare along the back of his neck and knew how the sheep must feel when Shep stared to move them to a new location. When the bread was just starting to brown on one side, he gave up and slipped the barely warm slices into his jacket pocket. "We can eat these later."

Gunny pulled her shawl off the table and walked outside. She whistled for Shep who bounded into the yard, gave her a quick sniff, and then sprinted off toward the booley. She gave another sharp whistle and Shep came bounding back. "This way," she said in a stern voice pointing down the hill. "We're going to Dingle today."

Robert hesitated in the doorway. "Don't you want to wake your mother, brother, and Maeve to say goodbye?"

Gunny turned and pushed the barrow out of the yard. Robert had to trot to catch up with his tall, determined daughter. They walked in stony silence down through the bumpy field to the McCrohans'. Gunny eyed the yard by the house and by the forge, hoping to see Matt one last time, but the yard was empty. She steered her barrow left onto the road and crossed the bridge by the forge out of Dunquin.

"That wind is something today," Robert said as they left the confines of the village.

Gunny didn't respond. Her father's words blended with the echoes that were rattling around in her head.

"Your mam and I are not getting any younger."

"I have no choice but to put you out to service."

"I never told your father to send you away."

"You'll have no time for that whistle at the Murphy's."

"I don't know what it will be like in Dunquin without you."

She continued at a fast pace, walking slightly ahead of her father. She usually loved the walk to Ventry but today hardly noticed the new spring growth by the side of the road, nor smelled the fresh sea air blowing in from the ocean. They continued on through Ventry and east into Dingle.

As they neared the large town, she thought back on the stories John McCrohan and her father used to tell about the town, how Queen Elizabeth used Dingle as a trading port to ship butter, wool, hides, fish, and meat to England. About the times the Celts rebelled against her rule, and she had them tortured and killed. Gunny imagined herself as a captured Celt being led to slaughter as she walked with her father along Upper Main Street and into the village. When they passed the holy stone near the corner of Chapel Lane, Gunny ran her hand along the long, smooth bullan in the road, and down into the cup-shaped pits on the rock. It had rained recently and holy water nestled in nearly every cup to wet her fingers.

As they passed Green Street onto Main, Gunny saw the sign for the Murphy's Store. She had been to the shop several times with her father to buy household items, sweets, and whiskey. She never imagined that one day she would live there.

The small bell over the door jangled as Robert pushed the door open and entered the shop. Gunny set the barrow to rest by the side of the road and followed her father inside. Daniel Murphy lumbered over to meet them. He was a tall man with large arms, beefy hands, and red cheeks. As the two men shook hands, Gunny felt the shop darken and close in around her.

"Hello, Murph," Robert said in a low voice. "Gunny has come to join you, as promised."

Gunny grunted and felt the noose tighten around her neck. Murph held out a large hand to her. "Welcome."

Gunny pulled her right hand from deep in her apron pocket. She looked down at the floor and weakly put her hand in Daniel Murphy's firm grip. His hand was warm and calloused, the hand of a working man.

"I'm happy to meet you," Daniel said. "Let me introduce you to my wife, Joanna. You'll be spending most of your time with her."

Joanna was stocking shelves behind a large counter along a side wall of the shop. She was tall, slender, and pale. She flicked a short wave at Gunny and continued moving packages onto the shelves. A small boy clung to her skirts as she moved.

Daniel nodded toward the boy. "We'd like you to spend time with Jamie to give his mother more time to work. Do you like children, Gunny?"

Gunny had never thought about whether she liked children. "I suppose I do. I like the McCrohan girls." Gunny paused. "I was teaching them how to play the tin whistle when I left." Gunny pulled the long cool whistle from her apron pocket.

Robert reached over and folded his hand over hers to take the whistle from her. Gunny's grip tightened around the small instrument. "You won't be playing that here, Gunny," Robert said stiffly, looking Gunny intently in the eye.

"Oh, a tin whistle, is it?" Daniel said. "I used to play one. May I see it?"

Gunny yanked her hand away from her father and eyed Daniel's open palm. She hesitantly handed him the whistle expecting it was the last she would see of it. Daniel ran a finger along the holes in the top of the instrument. "I used to have a whistle like this when I was growing up." He chuckled and shook his head. "The sound of the whistle in the house made my Mam crazy mad," he said giving Gunny a wink and handing the whistle back to her.

Gunny laughed nervously. "My Mam is the same way so I usually play in the hills."

"Did you ever play late into the night around a bonfire. Ah, it's a mysterious sound the tin whistle. The pitch can come right from your soul and move about with the wind."

Gunny nodded in agreement and slipped the whistle back in her pocket.

Daniel eyed her. "Perhaps you could teach Jamie to play. You'll find him to be... a serious child."

Gunny glanced at the boy who was peeking out around the end of the front counter eying the two strangers. Gunny caught his eye. He looked down, blushed, and ducked behind the counter.

"It's a wonder your wife ever gets anything done with him clinging on to her like that. Don't you have any other children for him to play with?" Gunny asked.

Robert moaned. How could she ask such a question? Hadn't he raised her to have better manners?

Daniel shook his head. "No. My poor wife nearly passed over when James was born. It took them both a long time to recover. It's been five years and we've had no more children. It's a shame. Bad luck, really. But at least we have a boy."

"Speaking of boys," Robert said, anxious to change the subject. "How will you get along without my Michael here to do your heavy lifting?"

Daniel shook his head to clear his thoughts and focused on Robert. "Michael was a fine worker but there are other strapping lads about. I'll find help if I need it. And right now, having a girl around might be a bigger help." He smiled at Gunny then turned to watch his wife and son at work. His smile faded and he turned back to Gunny and Robert. "Well, Gunny. Let's get you settled in and ready to work."

* * *

Gunny collected her bundle and worn boots from the barrow outside. Robert took Gunny's shoulders in both hands. "Be helpful, Girl, as if you were working for me. We'll see you no later than Christmas."

It was not yet March. Christmas was a long way off. Gunny felt like crying but she bit her lower lip instead and attempted a smile. "Sure," she said. "I'll see you at Christmas." She knelt and gave Shep a scratch behind the ears then watched as her father pushed the empty barrow west on Main Street with Shep leading the way.

Gunny walked into the shop and pushed the door closed hard behind her. The bells jangled loudly. She turned around. Joanna and James were staring at her. She stared back. She would slam any door she felt like slamming.

Daniel walked her up two flights of steep stairs and showed her to a room tucked into the eaves of the house. "I'll leave you to get settled," he said clumping back down the stairs.

Gunny had never been so far off the earth and hated the feeling of not having dirt beneath her feet. The room was small and cold with an angled ceiling and no fireplace. There was an iron bed and a little table with a wash basin, a pitcher for water, and a neatly folded cloth. She sat on the bed. It squeaked under her weight. She wiggled around and the bed squeaked louder. She tossed her bundle and boots into a corner of the room and walked across the smooth wooden floor to look out a tiny window in the gable. She could see the roofs of neighboring houses and down the hill, Dingle Harbor. She felt hot tears burn at the corners of her eyes. She hated this room. She hated Dingle. And she hated her father and her mother and that damned Father Jessey for doing this to her. She angrily pulled her hair into a tight bun at the nape of her neck, squeezed into her tight boots, laced them up part-way, and headed downstairs to start her service.

Joanna showed her around the small shop. The girl mumbled from time to time while Joanna explained what went where. Joanna could tell she was not listening. "Why don't we have a cup of tea instead in the kitchen," she said. "You must be tired from your walk."

"No," Gunny said, looking away from her employer.

"Would you like something to eat?"

"No."

Joanna looked around the shop. "Things are a little slow and it's about closing time. Why don't you go to your room and rest. I'll call you when I need help preparing our evening meal."

Gunny rolled her eyes. "Yes, ma'am." She turned and trudged up the two flights of stairs.

Joanna returned to the shop and raised her eyebrows to Daniel who shrugged. James scrambled out from under a low shelf and hugged his mother

99

tightly around the legs. A customer entered the store and the couple returned to their work.

Gunny sat on the squeaky bed and pulled off her boots. Her chest felt tight and her feet and head ached. She thought about running away, but where would she go? She couldn't go home. Maybe she could find Ellen in Ballyferriter. Or maybe she could live up in the hills. How long could she survive in the hills? It was spring. She should wait until the weather got warmer, then flee. She lay down on the stiff bed and closed her eyes. The room slowly darkened. She listened to the unfamiliar sounds below her, and then the house grew quiet. She woke several times in the night when she turned over in the unfamiliar space, her head filled with nightmares of trying to run but not being able to move, of opening her mouth and not being able to speak.

The next morning, she limped down to the kitchen in her boots, her stomach rumbling. Beams of sun lit the clean kitchen floor. She squinted. The light made her eyes hurt. Joanna was standing at the kitchen table emptying a pot of drained, boiled potatoes into a large bowl. James was seated at the table.

"Good morning, Gunny. I looked in on you last night for the evening meal. You were sleeping. You must have been exhausted. Would you like something to eat?" Joanna asked.

"No," Gunny said as she stood slumped in the doorway by the stair.

There was an awkward silence.

"Well," Joanna finally said. "Well." She sat at the table next to James. Gunny watched as she took a potato out of the bowl with a large fork and quickly pealed the spud with a small knife. She set the potato skin on a second plate and carefully mashed the boiled potato on her plate. She added a little salt and butter. It looked delicious. Joanna handed her son a spoon, then took one herself and they both dug into the steamy mix on the shared plate.

Joanna looked up and caught Gunny's eye. "Are you sure you don't want a potato?" She indicated the bowl on the table. "We have plenty."

Gunny shook her head and remained slumped in the doorway by the stair.

"Well then," Joanna said, standing and straightening her apron, "Let's get to work. Jamie can finish those last few bites."

Joanna took the peel plate to the back door and tossed it onto the dung pile. By the time she returned to the table, James had finished his morning meal. Joanna took the potato plate and the peel plate and carefully placed them in a large basin on a small table under the kitchen window. "You can wash those later."

Gunny shifted uncomfortably from one leg to another.

"Are you all right?" Joanna asked. Gunny did not look well. Her hair was tangled and her face was puffy.

"You don't have a byre in this house."

"No, the animals sleep outside in the shed in the yard."

"Where do you...?" Gunny couldn't finish.

"Where do we...?" Joanna tried to help.

"Where does one relieve herself?"

"Oh, my goodness. There is an outhouse behind the cow shed. In the yard. Do you want me to show you?"

"No," Gunny said, brushing past the thin woman and out the door. "I'm sure I can find it."

Joanna and Gunny worked in the store through the morning. James was never far from Joanna's side as his mother explained what went where, what cost what, and what questions Gunny might expect from customers. They moved from paper to newspapers, from salt to spices, from graters to butter churns.

"You told me most of this yesterday," Gunny said sharply.

"I wasn't sure you were listening."

Gunny was bored. She had never liked indoor work. "Just tell me what you want me to do," she grunted.

Joanna studied the girl. "Daniel's making deliveries. I was hoping you might help me with..." She hesitated. Did she really want this surly young woman working with customers? She took a quick breath and continued, "Why don't you dust? We pick up a lot of dirt from the street." She pulled a rough cloth off of a stack behind the counter. "Run this over the tops of..."

Gunny grabbed the cloth from Joanna. "I know how to dust," she interrupted and stormed off toward the back of the store.

Joanna heard a loud sneeze and watched as the girl wiped her nose along her sleeve then slapped the cloth along the top items on the shelf. The bells above the door jangled and Joanna turned to greet a customer.

By the time the store closed, Gunny was ravished with hunger and felt a little faint. She straightened the last shelf to ready the store for business the next day as Joanna had instructed and followed the family into the back room. The smell of turf, boiling potatoes, and salted herring filled the small kitchen. Joanna set out plates for each of them. Gunny pushed her plate away and sat slumped at the table, head in her hands.

Daniel looked at her. Her hair was a snarled mess. The cap Joanna had given her to wear was on crooked. Her hands and fingernails were dirty. He didn't remember having so much trouble when Michael started working. "Gunny?" he asked in a soft voice.

Gunny nodded without taking her hands away from her face.

"You need to eat something."

"I'm not hungry," Gunny muttered from behind her hands.

"I can see that you're not happy. Would you like to go home?" Daniel asked.

Gunny felt her chest heave. She choked down a sob and leaned back in her chair, one hand over her eyes and the other wrapped tightly around her chest. She took a deep breath and tried to compose herself. When she opened her mouth, she was surprised at how weak her voice sounded. "I don't have a home to go to, sir. I'm not wanted in Dunquin."

Daniel and Joanna looked at one another. They had not heard anything about this from Robert Malone.

"Did you do something wrong in Dunquin?" Joanna asked.

Gunny pulled her hand away from her face and crossed her arms. Tears brimmed in her eyes. She took a deep breath and wiped her face on the back of one sleeve. "I don't know what I did. One minute, I was living my life like I'd always done, and the next, I was unwelcome and unwanted, and replaced by some fat pig of a girl who can cook!"

Joanna didn't understand, but her heart ached for the girl.

"Dunquin is a stupid place," Gunny continued. "We have a stupid priest who wants to change everything. The people there are stupid. Oh, why am I telling you this? It's not like you care." She pushed her chair away from the table and fled upstairs.

Daniel and Joanna turned back to their meal.

"Do you want to go and talk to her?" Daniel asked.

"Not really," Joanna said, eyebrows raised. "Do you?"

"No," Daniel said with a soft laugh.

Joanna looked at her son as he methodically spooned bites of buttery potato into his mouth. Joanna reached over and touched her son's hand to get his attention. He moved his hand away from her touch and continued eating. "Don't be getting any ideas from her, Jamie," Joanna warned.

James did not look at his mother as he continued eating.

"Let's give her another night and see how she is in the morning," Daniel said. "If she's no better tomorrow, I'll pay her for the week and send her home."

"She says she can't go home," Joanna said.

"Joanna, she's not our problem. If she's no help to us then she has to go back."

James set down his spoon and grinned.

When Gunny descended the stairs the next morning, she looked even worse than the night before. She had not bothered to pull her hair back and heavy black curls twisted around her ashen face. She stood by the stairway yawning and rubbing at her red eyes as Joanna, Daniel, and James sat eating their morning spuds.

Joanna took a deep breath. "Gunny, you can't be seen like that in the store. Go upstairs and wash your face and fix your hair."

Gunny glared at Joanna. How dare she tell her what to do?

Daniel chuckled. "Truthfully, girl, you'll scare our customers away. Go upstairs and make yourself more presentable."

Gunny stomped up the two flights of stairs to her tiny room. She swung the door closed and was surprised when there was no slam behind her. She spun around. James stood in the doorway, looking terrified, having caught the fast-moving door as it closed.

"Go away," Gunny snarled. "This is my room."

James continued to stand in the half-closed doorway.

"Go away! Are you deaf as well as addled?"

She pushed the little boy through the doorway and slammed the door in his startled face. She threw herself on the bed and tried to weep, but no tears came. She pulled the mattress and blanket off the creaky bed, dropped onto the heap and held her aching head in her hands. She heard a small knock on her door and ignored it. There was another knock.

"Go away," she snorted from her heap on the floor

The door swung opened and James stepped into the room. He took a deep breath holding onto the door for support. "They say if you don't behave better, they'll send you home," he said in a soft but clear voice.

Gunny looked up from her pile on the floor. "You can talk," she smirked at the little boy.

"Of course I can talk," James said quietly.

"Well, I don't want to talk to you. I don't want to talk to anyone. I want to be left alone."

"All right," James said and left quietly closing the door behind him.

Gunny stayed in her room all day, sleeping on the heaped pile and mattress and blankets on the floor until the sky finally darkened. She woke at dawn the next morning. Her legs and back ached. She was exhausted, thirsty, and starving. She lay on the heap and watched as the morning sun lightened the room. There was a small knock at the door.

"Go away, James," she uttered in a hoarse voice. "I am not talking to you."

The door opened. Joanna stepped into the room and looked at the mess on the floor. "I see you've re-arranged things."

Gunny flipped over and buried her head in the thin blankets. "Sorry for the mess," she muttered from the pile.

Joanna sat on the edge of the bare metal netting of the bed. "You've had a day to yourself. I hope you're feeling better. Do you want me to help you get the mattress back onto the frame?"

Gunny looked up at Joanna's kind, concerned face. She rolled off the pile onto the floor and nodded. The two women lifted the mattress back onto the frame. Joanna straightened the bedding while Gunny washed her face in the basin of water then wiped her face dry with her sleeve.

"You have a cloth for that," Joanna said pointing at the white cloth that lay untouched next to the water basin. "That will save your sleeve from getting so wet."

Gunny looked blearily at the white cloth. "I thought that was for dusting," she muttered. She took the cloth and wiped her face. The rough clean cotton felt good against her burning cheeks.

Joanna looked at the beaten girl. "Gunny, I know it wasn't your choice to come here."

Gunny grunted and leaned on the windowsill looking out the window at the roof tops beyond.

"Look at me, Gunny," Joanna said gently. Gunny glanced at Joanna, then back out the window. "Daniel and I are ready to have you return to your parents." Gunny stifled a sob as Joanna continued. "But Jamie, for some reason, wants you to stay. Why do you suppose that is?"

Gunny shrugged her shoulders. It wasn't like she'd been nice to him.

"Jamie is a smart little boy," Joanna said. "Sometimes he sees things that no one else sees—and he sees something in you, Gunny."

Gunny walked to the small table by the window and caught herself with both hands. She saw stars around her eyes and leaned forward, weak and out of breath.

"We are going to give you another chance," Joanna said, "but you have to work with us. Daniel was thinking you might feel more at home if some of your duties took you outside. Would you like to help getting the cows up to the pasture? And maybe help with deliveries?"

Gunny took a deep breath. "I'd love to take the cows up to the pasture," Gunny said quietly. "I'm good with cows. And I can help with deliveries. I'm quick. I used to run everywhere in Dunquin."

"We aren't monsters," Joanna said looking at the haggard girl.

Gunny smiled weakly. "I know that. I just want to be able to live my own life."

Joanna sighed. "It's difficult as a woman, Gunny. But that's enough talk for now," she said, standing and wiping her hands on her clean apron. "You haven't eaten in days. You must be starving. Jamie is waiting for us in the kitchen. He refused to eat this morning until you came down."

Gunny reached out and touched Joanna on the arm. "I know I've been dreadful," she said.

"Yes, you have," Joanna agreed, giving Gunny's fingers a quick squeeze. "How about some eggs? Eggs always taste good when you haven't eaten in awhile. And toasted bread. Do you like butter?"

Gunny looked down at her feet, then grinned at Joanna. "Yes, I like butter."

* * *

Gunny moved about the shop that day in a fog. She listened to Joanna and Daniel's instructions and got almost everything wrong. In the late afternoon, she felt more like herself helping Daniel with two meat deliveries. She was surprised at how big Dingle was when she and Daniel hiked down to the Mall that ran along the river, then out along Dingle Harbor.

That afternoon, after eating a huge portion of potatoes and boiled fish, Gunny washed the dishes, then reminded Daniel about the cows. Daniel smiled and opened the door. She pulled on her shawl, and followed him up the hill off of Upper Main Street to the community pasture. He pointed out which two cows were his and left Gunny to her work. Gunny had no problem getting the beasts to follow her back to the shed.

After the cows were settled, she sat on the dirt floor of the shed, leaned against a stall, and pulled off her tight, leather boots. She slipped her tin whistle out of her apron pocket and blew a few notes. The two cows eyed her and continued chewing their cud. Gunny tried a fast jig, but it didn't match her mood so she tried a slower ballad. The haunting tune sent her mind to a time on the hillside in the booley. She pictured the spring flowers blooming on the rocky hillside and watching the sun set and the dew rise. She opened her eyes. Someone was watching her from the doorway.

"Hello, James," she said.

"Hello, Gunny."

"So you know my name?"

"Sure, I know your name," James said taking a tentative step into the shed.

"I noticed your parents call you Jamie. Do you prefer that to James?"

"My name is James."

"I've heard you call your parents Daniel and Joanna. Why do you do that?"

James paused. "That's what everyone else calls them."

Gunny grinned and looked down at her whistle. She ran a finger over the cool metal surface. "Did you like the whistle playing?"

"Sure, I did."

"Want to learn how to play?"

"Sure, I do." James walked stiffly toward Gunny and sat on the floor next to her mimicking her cross-legged posture.

"You're not trying to be friends with me, are you?" Gunny asked. "You know I may not be here long."

James studied her face. "What's wrong?" he asked.

"Nothing," Gunny said, shaking her head.

The boy waited. Gunny leaned back against the stall and took a deep breath. "Everything is wrong. I can't go back to Dunquin. I don't have any friends here, and I miss my dog Shep. I have to wear these damned boots every day, and the spring flowers are starting to come up in the booley. I miss singing and playing my whistle, and hearing stories around the fire at night at the McCrohans', and going to O'Leary's Pub…"

James sighed. "Dunquin sounds perfect."

"It does?" Gunny turned and faced the boy. "Well, it's not. There were a lot of times when we didn't have enough food to eat. And you should meet my mother. And Father Jessey. Now there's a story."

"I like a story."

"Do you?"

"When you're sad, a story takes your mind off your troubles."

"What do you know about troubles? How old are you? Five?"

"I'm nearly six and I have troubles, Gunny."

Gunny looked at the boy's sincere face. "I suppose you do," she said in a quieter voice.

"All those things you miss, you could do them here," James said.

"I'm in service, James. I have to work to earn my keep."

"I hear we have a fine harbor. You could take me there and play your whistle along the way and tell me stories."

"You've never been to the harbor?"

"Daniel and Joanna are too busy in the shop to be walking about town with me. And besides, they say I'm too little to go outside." James imitated his father's low voice, 'Keep Jamie in the house. He's too little to be out on the streets.' Then he continued in his mother's quiet voice. 'Jamie is shy. I'll stay with him here at the shop.' But I'd rather be outside. I'm more like you, Gunny, really I am."

Gunny chuckled at the boy's animated story telling. "So why don't you tell your parents you want to go outside?"

"If you take me then we won't have to bother them," James said expectantly.

Gunny looked into the little boys eyes. They were brown like hers, but softer. "We'll see, James. I have a lot of work to do."

James looked at the floor. His bottom lip began to quiver.

Gunny heard her words echo in her head—she sounded like her mother. "Now don't fuss. I'll ask them." She reached over to touch his arm and he pulled away. She had seen him do that with his mother. "You know, I think you are a very smart young man."

James chewed on his bottom lip and smiled.

The next morning, Gunny's eyes blinked open. She looked around at the white walls and tidy space of her room and defied the iron bed to squeak as she pulled the warm covers up tightly under her chin. Her stomach growled. She moaned and tossed the covers aside. She washed her face in the small basin on the table by the bed. She started to wipe her face on her sleeve, then stopped and used the cloth to rub her face dry. She folded and placed the cloth by the basin and proudly fluffed out her dry sleeve. She pulled on a clean pair of stockings and her boots, and descended the stairs for a new day of service.

Robert rambled about the house and the fields. He kept thinking he saw Gunny out of the corner of his eye, then remembered that she was in Dingle. He chatted with Michael as they worked the fields, but the boy was mostly quiet and was no substitute for Gunny with her stories and whistling and singing.

At the house, Eileen tried to be kind to Maeve but after a week her patience ran out. She eyed the girl sleeping in the back room. The sun had been up for hours. "Maeve. Get yourself out of that bed. There's work to be done."

Maeve stretched and yawned and blinked blearily at Eileen. "The work will still be there when I get up. We never used to get up so early. Father kept the pub open late after Mother died so we'd eat late, go to bed late, and get up late!"

"You're not running a pub anymore, Maeve. This is a farm and some chores are best done in the morning."

"Like what?" Maeve questioned, hauling herself out of bed and shuffling out to the fire to pour herself a cup of hot tea.

Eileen took a deep breath to calm herself. "I need you to take on Gunny chores—getting the fire going, putting water on for tea and potatoes, feeding the chickens, taking the sheep and cow out to the yard, sweeping out the house."

Maeve slumped at the table. "I've been meaning to ask you," she said. "Don't you think it's odd having a cow, sheep, and hens sleep in the house at night?"

Eileen was shocked. "It's not odd. Everyone brings their animals inside until they go up to the booley in the spring."

Maeve shook her head. "Well, we would never do it at the pub."

"This house is not a pub!" Eileen said, exasperated.

Maeve sipped loudly at her tea then picked a bit of tea leaf from a front tooth. "The kettle is nearly empty," she said. "Will you make more tea?"

Eileen simmered. "If anyone is going to make more tea, it'll be you." Eileen grabbed the tea kettle and pointed to the door. "The spring is a short hike up the hill. You'll see the path. Take the bucket with you as well. Gunny brought a bucket of fresh water into the house each morning. That's another morning chore."

Maeve glanced at the empty water bucket by the door. "I only need tea water now. I'll fill the bucket later."

Eileen asked Kate McCrohan to have her girls look after the Malone cow and sheep in the booley that spring in exchange for a share of the Malone butter.

Each afternoon the girls brought her a bucket of fresh warm milk. Eileen showed Maeve the churn, but Maeve said she didn't really like making butter. She also didn't appear to care much about housework. When Eileen complained, Maeve explained that when she was on her feet for too long, her ankles swelled. Maeve's saving grace was that she loved to eat and insisted on making fresh bread every day. Eileen assured herself that she'd be able to change the girl over time.

As bored as Maeve seemed to be during the day, she was animated and lively when Michael returned home in the afternoon. She practically ran circles around him, talking, telling him about her day, and asking him for small favors. Michael seemed a bit overwhelmed by the attention. He tried to smile and talk to his new wife, but preferred sitting in front of the fire smoking his pipe and talking to his Da about the day's events until the family sat down to eat— where his new wife would continue with her chatter.

"Maeve," Robert said one night, trying to be kind. "When a man returns home in the evening, he needs a bit of time to himself. If he doesn't have much to say, you must leave him be."

"Leave him be? I'm stuck here in the house all day with her, and when my husband comes home I expect him to listen to me," she said with teary eyes.

"Michael," Robert said, glancing at Michael. "It's best to ignore a rough-spoken woman."

Maeve slammed down her spoon. "Ignore me? He's my husband and I insist that he listen to me."

Robert turned to Maeve. "You'd be better off biting your tongue than making so many demands on a new husband."

Maeve burst into tears and ran to the back bedroom, sobbing loudly and thrashing about on the bed.

Michael whispered to his father without looking up from his plate, "What do I do, Da?"

Robert shook his head. "I have no idea. Arguing with her seems as useless as striking cold iron with a hair ribbon."

Eileen sat quietly, listening to the three of them, wondering what she could possibly have done to deserve such punishment from God—and wondering how Gunny was faring in Dingle.

At the end of a long, warm summer, Nick O'Leary sent word through the village that everyone should join him at the pub for an announcement. The Malones had just walked in when Nick climbed up onto the bar to tell everyone that he was immigrating to America. The pub fell silent. What would Dunquin be without O'Leary's Pub?

"Have no concerns about this place," Nick went on, hauling his brother up onto the bar with him. "My brother, Micky, has agreed to move from Ballyferriter to run things. Maeve was my last concern here in Dunquin," he said smiling down at his daughter, her mouth open and her cheeks flush. "As you know, my three older girls moved to Virginia years ago. I didn't think I'd ever be able leave after paying Maeve's dowry, but my older girls have sent me passage money and I'm off."

A few villagers smiled and wished Nick well. Others had little to say. Everyone knew someone who had moved to America—and they were never heard from again. Emigration was the same as death to those who stayed behind.

Nick helped Micky down from the bar. "I believe this calls for a celebration. Robert, help me roll out a barrel of porter and a gallon or two of whiskey. Let's do some dancing." With the promise of free porter and whiskey, the atmosphere of the room livened.

Maeve sat glumly next to Michael at a table near the door. "Da was waiting for me to marry so he could leave. My sisters never liked me and now they're taking him away," she whined.

"Now, now," Michael said, trying to comfort his wife by patting her on the arm. "You have me."

Maeve pulled her arm away from Michael's touch and ran to her father. She hugged him tightly around the neck, then dipped a glass of porter from the bucket and headed off to the kitchen to find something to eat.

The next morning, Robert, Eileen, Michael and Maeve walked with Nick O'Leary to the crest of the hill past the bridge by the forge. He had a small sack of goods on his back and did his best to ignore his daughter's moans and sobs as they walked.

"I was feeling old but now I feel young again. I'm off to see new lands and hear new stories. I'll miss you all." He gave his youngest daughter a peck on the cheek and headed off at a jaunty pace toward Dingle. "I'll write!" he yelled back to Maeve as he disappeared over the crest of the hill.

~ Chapter 6: James, Matt, and Thomas ~

Joanna flew about the kitchen getting ready for the day while Gunny sat and ate a plate of boiled potatoes. Joanna eyed the girl. "Would you mind helping with some mending today?"

Gunny looked at the full basket of clothes near the table and blinked. "Mam did most of the stitching at our house but I can give it a try," she said with a half smile.

Joanna pulled a little wooden box from the shelf and opened it. The box held several neat rows of thread, a packet of pins, three sharp needles, and a small pair of scissors. "You'll find everything you need in here. Jamie's good pants need to be lengthened and both knees need to be patched."

Gunny leaned over and picked up the small pair of pants. She fingered the worn fabric at the knees. "I have no idea how to lengthen but I'm sure I can patch," she said.

"Patching will be a help. I have a large order to fill this morning for Mrs. McCallister. You know how fussy she is. Come get me if you need me." Joanna wiped her hands on her apron, straightened her cap, and exited through the house door into the shop.

Gunny tossed the sewing box into the basket and dragged the basket closer to the fire. She dug around in the bottom of the pile and found a few scraps of loose material. She cut a small square, pulled thread from a spool, and quickly sewed a patch onto one knee. She selected another color fabric for the second patch, threaded the needle with a new color of thread, and patched the second knee. She tossed the pants onto the top of the basket and went out to the shop to help Joanna.

"You're finished already?" Joanna asked as she packed up the last box for Mrs. McCallister.

"It was only two patches," Gunny said with a smile.

While Gunny was cleaning up that night from the evening meal, Joanna inspected the loose patches on Jamie's pants. She looked around for the scissors, and found the sewing kit tipped out into the mending basket. Only a few spools of thread were still in the kit. She dug around in the basket to locate the missing spools and carefully reassembled the box. She found the scissors on the mantel, then sat down in her chair by the fire and pulled out all of the stitching on the pants. She tossed the mismatched patches aside, pulled matching fabric from the basket, cut two neat squares and started the work again.

Gunny watched as she stitched. Joanna was so intent on her sewing that Gunny was sure the house could collapse around them and Joanna would take no notice. Gunny asked to see the pants when Joanna was done with the first knee. She looked at the stitches around each matching patch. It was as if a tiny mouse had done the work.

"Could you teach me how to stitch like this? My Mam tried a few times but told me I was too hard to teach. I'll try to be better with you."

Joanna was threading her needle to start in on the second knee patch. She smiled a little half smile. "I suppose I could teach you."

Gunny pulled her stool closer. Joanna set her work aside, selected a needle from the box and handed it to Gunny. "What do you have that needs to be mended?"

Gunny pulled up her apron. "My front pocket has pulled loose. Will this do?"

Joanna fingered the thin fabric. "Perfect. Take off your apron so you have plenty of room to work. And find white thread to match. Thread is expensive. Make sure you don't waste any."

Gunny took off her apron and sat on a stool next to Joanna. She closed one eye, threaded a short piece of white thread, and handed the fabric to Joanna. Joanna took the apron and ran the first stitch up from inside the pocket. "You want to hide the knot, like this. See? Now take the tiniest fold of cloth and hide your needle inside until it comes out at the crease in the fabric. Then go back down through the fabric right next to where the needle came out. No one should be able to see your stitches on the front of the apron."

Gunny took the apron from Joanna and tried to mimic her work. "How did you learn to sew?"

"From my grandmother."

"Did your mother stitch?"

"Oh, no, my mother hated sewing. She was more of a… robust woman. She liked to be outside. Or out in the shop drinking with the men."

"I can't picture you drinking with men. You must be very different than her. Did she like spending time in the garden like you?"

"No, my mother hated keeping up a kitchen garden. It was too much work, she'd say, without a predictable outcome. But my grandmother kept a fine, full garden, and loved to stitch."

"It's funny how things skip around like that. I'm not much like my mother either. I used to pray that I was a fairy changeling, dropped into an unfamiliar house. I wish I had known my mother's Mam like you knew yours."

Joanna reached out for Gunny's apron. She held a clear corked bottle of water over the work to magnify the stitches. "Oh, my."

"What's wrong?" Gunny asked.

"Nothing," Joanna said. "These stitches are beautiful. They're small and nicely spaced. You have a real feel for stitching, Gunny. You just needed a little direction."

Gunny glowed while Joanna returned to her own mending. Her mother had never told her she'd done anything beautifully. "Does it bother you to talk while you work?" Gunny asked.

"No, I like it. I can stitch and listen at the same time," Joanna said in a soft voice.

"Would you like to hear a story then?"

Joanna chuckled. "A story while we stitch. What a treat. I'll call James. He won't want to miss this."

"What do you like to cook, Gunny?" Joanna asked over their morning meal.

Gunny paused with her spoon partway to her mouth. "I can make my own meals if that's what you're asking."

Joanna shook her head. "I don't mind cooking. I was only wondering what you like to eat."

"I don't know," Gunny said thoughtfully. "We ate potatoes most days. Sometimes we added a little boiled fish or other kitchen from the shore. We ate porridge and eggs through most of the winter to help make the potatoes last into the spring. In the spring and summer, Mam made oat bread that we ate with milk and butter. And we ate things from the kitchen garden."

"That's pretty much what we eat," Joanna said. "I wasn't sure what to cook when you weren't eating."

"I'm feeling better now," Gunny said. "I can help you cook. And as soon as the cows calve, I can help you make butter. Mam showed me how. Where's your churn?"

"I've never had any luck with butter," Joanna blushed. "I take our milk to the market on the Mall and sell it. I buy butter on occasion. If you can make butter, we'll sell it in the store."

"I'll do it," Gunny said with a smile. "All I need is a good churn and the blessing of the fairies."

"I have plenty of churns out in the shop," Joanna said with a smile. "You're on your own making a deal with the fairies. You know, if you make butter, I'll make a big bowl of Champ with a huge dollop of butter right in the center."

Gunny laughed. "My Mam used to make Champ," she said picturing her kitchen table in Dunquin with a heaping bowl of hot mashed potatoes and a large well of butter pooling at the center. Champ made her think of Hallow E'en which made her think of the McCrohans which made her think of Matt. Her mouth went limp and her eyes became distant.

"Did I say something to upset you?"

Gunny shook her head and cleared her throat. "No, ma'am. I just had a moment of missing home."

"Would you like to go home for a visit?" Joanna asked gently.

"No," Gunny said with too much energy. "My parents want me in Dingle. I think everyone in Dunquin would prefer I stay in Dingle."

Joanna studied Gunny's long face and large brown eyes. The girl's eyelashes were thick and dark, and her cheeks rosy now that she was eating again. "Are you happy, Gunny? Is there anything we can do for you?"

Gunny smiled. "I thought I would hate living here, but I don't. I like working in the shop. And I like you and Daniel—and James," Gunny added. "You're good people."

Joanna stood and wiped her hands on her apron, her face flushed. "Well, fine. You'll let me know if you need anything," Joanna stated, then turned and left to open the shop.

Gunny walked with Joanna to the Dingle pier to buy fish. A line of men passed by them in single file.

"Why are they doing that?" Gunny whispered to Joanna.

"Doing what?" Joanna asked.

Gunny waited until the men passed. "Why do they walk that way?"

Joanna looked after the men. "They're from the Blaskets. I hear on the island that the cliffs are steep and the paths narrow. The men learn to walk in single file—and they can't seem to break the habit when they come here to trade. We see them here in Dingle whenever there's a helping east wind along Dingle Bay."

Two men at the back of the line carried a large bulky bundle between them. Gunny watched as they took out dozens of rabbit skins and sat down to barter with a pier shopkeeper.

"Look at all those rabbit skins. There mustn't be a single rabbit left on the island."

Joanna shook her head. "I take it you've never been to the Blaskets."

"I went there once to hunt for seals," Gunny said.

"You went seal hunting?" Joanna asked, surprised.

Gunny pushed her curls away from her face and expertly twisted her hair into a loose bun. "My da and John McCrohan hauled in two seals the day I went. We ate sea pork all winter."

"Well maybe it was the wrong season for rabbits. Daniel used to go over to hunt before we had the shop. He said you could hardly walk out there without stepping on a rabbit."

Gunny shivered. She loved rabbit stew but the idea of an area teeming with rabbits was unsettling. She watched as the Blasket traders shook hands with the shopkeeper and handed him two empty sacks.

"They've made a trade for salt," Joanna explained. "The shopkeeper will fill their bags with salt and have them ready on the quay for the trip home to the Blaskets. The men are now free to shop and drink."

The cows had calved and were finally producing milk, and Gunny was busy at the churn. When she had three firkins of fine, sweet butter, she headed to the butter market to make her first sale. On her way home, she heard peals of metal striking metal and stopped at a large forge behind The Mall along the Dingle River. She peeked inside. The shop was much larger than the McCrohans'. The oven was blazing with two assistants working the bellows. Several men were talking near the fire. A large, blackened smithy glanced up at Gunny then returned to his work.

She stepped inside and ran her hand over pot cranes and pots, tools, wheels, and fence railings. She took a deep sniff of hot fire and smoky metal, then slipped out the front door into the cooler air and headed home. As she passed Bridge Street, a raspy voice called out to her.

"You there. Young girl. Whiskey?"

Gunny looked around. The voice came from a small blue house tucked in between two larger houses near the forge. There were several men standing in the yard of the house sipping at small glasses. An elderly woman stuck her head out the front window and called again to her. "Would you want to come in for a whiskey?"

"Me?" Gunny pointed at herself. "I don't drink whiskey."

"Everyone drinks whiskey," the old woman cackled.

A man in the yard raised his glass to her. "Mrs. McGilly's not a shopkeeper so she's not allowed to sell whiskey inside. But she can sell it if we stand outside."

"So we do," the other man said raising his glass.

"I see," Gunny said as she hurried off up the street.

She burst through the Murphy's' door and laid several coins on the counter in front of Joanna Murphy. "I sold our first butter," she said. "There are so many people in this town and everyone has something to sell when you have a little change in your pocket."

Joanna counted the coins and smiled at Gunny. "Good you resisted temptation. You have enough money here to buy yourself a new pair of boots. And we have enough butter left to make all the Champ we want."

"At Hallow E'en," Gunny said.

"Why wait?"

They collected fresh onions and peas to add to the potato mix and ate Champ until they were sure they would never eat Champ again. That night Gunny lay awake on the iron bed, her stomach full, and her thoughts wandering to the milk market, the Smithy, and old women selling whiskey in her yard. She felt her stomach flutter at the excitement of discovering a whole new world in Dingle.

While Joanna and Gunny enjoyed working together, each day brought a few challenges.

"Gunny, I am missing two bowls and two spoons," Joanna said one night as the girl scrubbed out the pot from an evening meal. "Do you have any idea where those might be?"

"No," Gunny said truthfully.

"Well," Joanna said, one hand on her hip. "I think I saw some dishes in your room. Do you have a tea mug up there as well?"

"I'll look when I go upstairs tonight."

Joanna sighed. "Everything has a place here in the kitchen. I like to keep things in order so I can find them when I need them." She looked at Gunny's soaked, ragged apron. "And I hate to mention this after you took such care with the stitching, but your apron looks terrible. The next time you wash it, you may want to fold it squarely to help keep the fabric straight."

Gunny groaned. "An apron works just as well if it's wrinkled or flat."

Joanna took a deep breath. "It matters how you look, Gunny. If you want people to respect you, you have to look respectable."

On Gunny's fourth Sunday in Dingle, Joanna asked she if she would accompany her to Mass. Gunny hesitated. She was not looking forward to meeting the new priest. "I'd love your company," Joanna added.

Gunny stood up straight. She was good company. "Of course I'll go. I'll just pull on a clean, unwrinkled apron."

They walked the few short blocks to St. James Church on Main Street. The building was tall and fort-like. Gunny sat peacefully through the service gazing up at the sweeping white plaster ceiling and studying the details of the tall filigreed glass windows. After Mass, Joanna insisted that Gunny meet Father Owen. Gunny waited nervously while the priest spoke with other parishioners. Gunny picked out the words on a large plague along a side wall as she waited.

"Dedicated to John Fitzgerald, Knight of Kerry, 1741."

Gunny liked it that a Knight of Kerry was living in Dingle not so very long ago. She wished there were still knights around. As the crowds cleared, she and Joanna walked toward the front vestibule. The priest was talking with a sour looking young man who stood with his head bowed.

"How do you explain your rude behavior last night?"

"I was as drunk as the devil, I was, Father. It couldn't be helped."

Father Owen took the young man's arm. "You are mistaken, son. The devil does not drink. He keeps a cool head to watch out for the likes of you."

The man shook his arm free from the priest's touch. "How is it you know so much about the devil, Father? Have you been spending time with him yourself?"

"That I have, son. Living here in Dingle, I have no choice."

As the young man slunk off, Joanna looped an arm through Gunny's and pulled her toward the priest. "Father Owen, please meet Gunny Malone. Gunny is working for us at the shop and is helping me with Jamie. Gunny, please meet Father Owen O'Sullivan."

The priest reached out to take Gunny's hand. He was tall and had wide shoulders and a thick stock of grey hair. Gunny ducked her head to one side and looked away as he took her hand. Father Owen held her hand in both of his until she looked him in the eye.

"Gunny Malone from Dunquin," he said. "Father Jessey told me to be on the lookout for you. And here you are."

True to his word, Father Jessey was haunting her here in Dingle just as he had in Dunquin. Gunny grimaced and tried to pull her hand away but the priest held on with a strong grip. He smiled warmly. "That Father Jessey," he said, squeezing Gunny's hand. "He is an old fellow, don't you think?"

Gunny was confused. Father Jessey was much younger than Father Owen. The priest smiled and released her hand. "Not old in body, mind you, but in spirit," he said with a chuckle. Gunny slowly shook her head in agreement. Father Jessey was old in spirit. Old and decrepit. "Here in Dingle," the priest continued, "we try to get along as best we can. I welcome you, Miss Malone."

Gunny smiled and breathed her first truly deep breath in a month.

James sat on the back counter and told Gunny about each of the regular customers who came into the shop. "Now him," he said in a quiet voice pointing at an old wrinkled patron. "He's always looking for a bargain. If he was going to buy a penny he'd want to pay a half-penny for it." He pointed at a short woman with bright red hair carrying a large basket of goods. "And her, she'll only buy the best meats—the belly of the pig, stuffed sheep intestine from the Blaskets, the loin from the cow. And she sniffs everything."

Gunny laughed as the woman leaned over the barrel of pickles and took a long sniff.

"And watch out for that man," James continued, pointing with his elbow at another patron. "His name is Mr. Carlson. I don't like him. When he's had too much to drink he turns awfully mean."

"Who's the pirate?" Gunny asked, pointing discreetly at a middle-aged man with long black hair and patch over one eye who was deep in conversation with Daniel near the stove at the back of the store.

James smiled. "Oh, that's Morgan O'Connell. He's the best smuggler in town. Everyone loves him."

"I thought smuggling was illegal."

"It is. That's why everyone loves him. Since the English no longer allow us to sell wool to the French, Morgan smuggles it out and comes home with silks and brandy in return. Any man who breaks the English law is a hero around here."

116

Gunny grinned at her small interpreter. "What happened to the shy James I used to know?" she asked.

James frowned. "I was never shy. I just didn't have anyone to talk to. Follow me, I have an idea," he said sliding off the counter and heading up an aisle toward the front of the shop. "I've been watching our customers. I think we should move the food to the back of the shop."

Gunny laughed. "But that's mostly what people come in to buy."

"That's my point," the boy said. "We make money selling necessities but people want to see new things. So pickles go to the back, fishing gear moves in the front. Candles move to the back, lanterns go to the front." James stopped and stared wistfully out the front window. "And this window should be more wonderful," James continued. "We could put items there that everyone dreams of but no one can afford."

Gunny shook her head. "Where do you get these ideas, James?"

"I watch. And I listen," the small boy said. "Then it's a matter of using your head."

Gunny went to tousle his hair, but he pulled away. Gunny stuffed her hand into her apron pocket. "I could learn a lot from you, James Murphy. I think we all could."

Gunny took James with her to the shore to collect reeds. James did not like getting wet, so he sat on a rock while Gunny carefully selected and cut her reeds. When they returned to the house, James watched as Gunny put the reeds in a bucket of water to soak and was soon twisting a piece of rope.

"Why do you make rope?" he asked.

Gunny shrugged. "I used to make it to use around the farm." She set the twisted reeds down in her lap. "Here in Dingle there doesn't seem to be as much need of it."

"We could sell it."

Gunny glanced up from her work. "At the shop?"

"Why not? It looks like fine rope. Do you want me to ask Daniel about it?"

Gunny set the reeds down again. "Are you my agent then?"

James looked puzzled. "No, I'm your friend."

It was midsummer when Daniel asked Gunny to make her first delivery to Lord Ventry's estate. She had heard about the Old Lord's estate all her life—in her mother's stories about growing up in Ventry, and her father's stories of work in the Ventry stables. But neither had been into the Big House. She stood outside the shop and looked at her reflection in the glass. Her cap was on straight. Her hair was smooth and pulled into a tidy bun at the nape of her neck. Her apron was clean and wrinkle-free. And she was wearing a new pair of boots. Gunny grinned at her image in the glass.

"Remember—don't talk to Lord Ventry unless he asks you something directly," Daniel said as he loaded thirty pounds of fresh mutton into a small barrow.

"You already told me that," Gunny said.

She had seen the Old Lord several times in Dunquin. He was arrogant, and rude, and burped and spit like a peasant. Gunny liked him. If she saw him at Ballygoleen, she would greet him in the hopes that he would tip her for her delivery of the meat. His son was another matter. Lord Henry had come into the Murphy's shop several times since she'd been there. He was old, not as old as the Old Lord, but seemed more stern, more critical—even with his own father. If she saw Lord Henry she would follow Daniel's advice and keep away.

"The cook will take your delivery," Daniel continued. "Don't stay to talk to her or you'll be there all day. Come straight back once the delivery is made."

Daniel loaded the last bit of meat into the barrow and Gunny smiled at him. "I'll behave myself," she said. "Don't worry."

Daniel had a flash of Gunny's first week at the shop and shook his head. "I'm trusting you."

Gunny smiled. The two mile walk to Ventry on a mild summer day would be a treat. She lifted the handles of the heavy barrow and headed up the road along Main Street. When she reached the old bullan stone, she hopped onto the large rock and unlaced her boots. She pulled the hot leather off of her cramped feet, peeled off her stockings, and dipped her feet in the small rain-filled craters on the rock, then stashed her footwear in the barrow and continued on her way. She assured herself that she would put her boots on again before she arrived at Ballygoleen.

She continued west on the road out of Dingle and onto the road by the shore that went to Ventry. The air was cool and the sun warm. The ocean on her left sparkled with flecks of sunlight all the way to the horizon. She felt important making a delivery to Ballygoleen. And there was always the chance that she would see her father working in the stables. Robert had stopped by twice to see her at the shop but she hadn't seen him recently and missed him.

Gunny followed the road along the coast. Daniel told her to watch for a long, curving drive that branched off on the left just before the village of Ventry that would take her to Ballygoleen. She spotted the drive and could see part of the roof of a large house that sat between the road and the shore.

"This must be the place," she thought to herself. She took in a deep breath of cool sea air and pushed the barrow down the drive. The drive curved around in front of a huge yellow house set on a wide lawn of green grass which banked down toward the shore. The house was two stories high and had three tall glass windows on the first floor, each trimmed in white and bordered with tall black shutters. There were three smaller windows along the second floor. Gunny stood at the base of the broad stone stairway that led to two huge black doors.

She heard horses approaching fast behind her and scrambled to move her barrow off the drive. Dust lifted around her as a shiny black coach with brown leather trim pulled to a sharp stop. Two sweaty black horses eyed her as they pawed at the dirt. The coachman waved her away with the tip of his horse whip and slid down from the box. He pulled open the door of the coach. The man who emerged from the coach was neither the Old Lord nor Lord Henry. This man was young and attractive, perhaps in his late twenties. He was short and had a stiff right leg and climbed down awkwardly from the coach. Gunny was so captivated by the man's light hair, square chin, and deep blue eyes that she forgot to curtsy. He glared at her as she stood by her barrow and she dipped in a short curtsy.

"Excuse me, sir," she said in a breathy voice. "You're not the person I expected to see."

The man signaled for the driver to leave, then limped past the girl, self-consciously rubbing at his right leg. He glanced back at her. "Are you staring at me for any particular reason?"

Gunny bowed her head. "No, my Lord. My deepest apologies. I came to deliver mutton from the Murphy's store in Dingle." She looked up. "Shall I give it to you?"

Thomas laughed. "You must not know who I am. I am Thomas Milliken," he paused. "Lord Thomas Milliken? Take your packages out to the kitchen. I assume you know where the kitchen is."

"No, sir, I don't," Gunny said, clearing her throat and standing up to her full height. She realized she was taller than the Lord and slouched slightly to meet his gaze. His skin was pale and he had tiny lines around his deep blue eyes. He smiled at her and she felt her heartbeat against her chest. "I used to come to Ballygoleen with my Da, and my Mam grew up in Ventry," she stammered, "but I've never been in the Big House."

Thomas chuckled. "Who is your Mam?" he asked, amused to be having a conversation with the barefoot shop girl.

Gunny looked into Thomas' eyes. "Eileen Malone of Dunquin," she whispered. She cleared her throat and started again in a louder voice. "She was Eileen Fitzgerald when she lived in Ventry. That was before she married."

"I grew up here and used to know a few Fitzgeralds," Thomas said. "I don't remember anyone named Eileen."

"She left Ventry twenty years ago when the Old Lord evicted her family from their house and farm. I believe that land is now part of your formal gardens."

The man looked down at his polished shoes amazed at the girl's directness. "I see. That would be my grandfather who evicted your mother's family. And it's my uncle Henry who is next in line to inherit all of this. So the formal gardens are theirs, not mine."

"Oh," Gunny said, not knowing what else to say.

"Who is your father?" Thomas asked, wanting the conversation to continue.

"Robert Malone of Dunquin."

"Robert Malone, the horseman?" Thomas asked, eyebrows raised.

Gunny laughed. "I usually call him Da. But I suppose others might know him as Robert Malone, the horseman."

"Your father knows horses better than anyone I know. He has broken many a horse for me. He is a good man."

"Yes," Gunny said taking a deep breath. "He is."

Thomas eyed the girl's full wheelbarrow. "Well...I suppose I should show you where the kitchen is." He limped to the top of the stone stairs and beckoned for Gunny to follow. Gunny looked at the heavy packages of meat in the cart. Blood was seeping out through the rough brown paper and string. Thomas watched her struggle to lift the bundles but did not offer to help. It wouldn't do to mess his best suit and he didn't trust his right leg. Trying to minimize his limp, he hopped ahead of Gunny and opened the double doors into an airy black and yellow tiled entry hall.

Gunny walked inside. To the left, a merry turf fire burned in a small fireplace. The ceiling in the wide hallway was twice as high as the Murphy's ceiling. Thomas scooted around behind her and closed the heavy front doors. His boots clicked and echoed on the tile floor as he walked to the right past a long stairway that led upstairs. He signaled for her to follow him through a wide arched doorway into the next room.

She gasped. She had never been in a room that large. The plaster walls went up and up and were topped with tight white trim where they met the ceiling. The tall front windows spilled summer sun onto wide, polished wooden floors. Along the far wall, a strong wood fire burned in a massive fireplace. In front of the fireplace, a plump sofa and two reading chairs awaited company. Beyond this room she saw a formal dining room with a table large enough to seat twelve. She gave a low whistle which made Thomas grin.

He pointed her toward a door to the left of the dining room. "The kitchen is through there, across the hallway," he said.

Gunny tried to curtsy but the meat bundles were heavy and her arms were aching. "Thank you, sir," she muttered and moved toward the far door.

"Girl," he called after her.

Gunny turned, struggling to keep hold of the heavy, wet packages. "Yes, sir?"

"What is your name?"

Gunny smiled. "It's Gunny, sir. Gunny Malone."

"Pleased to meet you, Gunny Malone," Thomas said.

"Yes," she said, trying again to curtsy and nearly dropping the meat. "Yes, it was nice meeting you," she said and blushed as she backed out the door and across the hall. She bumped open the kitchen door with one hip and dropped the soggy meat packages onto the nearest table.

The cook was shocked to see a delivery girl enter from the inside hallway and admonished her for her error. Once the meat was inspected, the cook pointed the way out through a back door.

"If Mrs. Needham ever catches you coming in the front door, you'll get an earful. That's the door for the family. I could tell you stories about servants who have used the front door," she started.

Gunny opened the outside door. "It's good I'm not a servant then," she closed the door behind her before the cook could engage her farther. She ran through the lush grass in the yard to retrieve her wagon.

Thomas was sitting under a tree near her barrow reading a book. "Delivery made?" he asked.

"Yes, sir," she said with a quick curtsy wiping her blood-stained hands on her apron. "You will have mutton tonight."

Thomas set his book on the grass and pulled himself awkwardly to his feet. He brushed off the seat of his pants. "So you work in Dingle?"

"Yes, my Lord. I work at the Murphy's shop. Do you know the Murphy's?"

"I used to. I've been away for ten years or so. Fighting." He puffed out his chest and continued in a deep voice. "I was a lieutenant of the seventh Regiment of Foot in the Peninsular War. I served under the Duke of Wellington."

"The Duke of Wellington," Gunny said. "He sounds important."

"We fought with the army of Portugal against the French Army. You've heard of Napoleon Bonaparte, I assume."

"No, sir." Gunny shook her head.

"You haven't heard of..." Thomas sighed. "I was at Busaco—in Lisbon? And I fought at Albuera in Spain. That's where I took a shot to the leg. You may not have noticed that I have a slight limp. I bought myself a captaincy after Albuera and fought at the Battle of New Orleans. I was shot there too." He hesitated and his face clouded slightly. "After that battle, the army gave me half pay to go home."

"I can see why—since you kept getting shot."

Thomas laughed. "You're a bold thing, aren't you?"

Gunny blushed and curtsied. "I'm sorry if I've offended you, sir. I'm not used to being around Barons."

Thomas leaned forward and touched her lightly on the arm. "You didn't offend me. Your honesty is refreshing."

Gunny looked up at his kind face and he smiled. "All my wounds have healed except for this one," he said rubbing his right leg. "I'm hoping time at home will help. Then I'll head back to fight again."

Gunny eyed Thomas' book. "I should think that walking about would help your leg heal faster than sitting around reading."

Thomas looked at the girl with the wild, black curls and the blood smears across her apron. She was tall for a peasant, taller than him, with full hips and long legs. Her cheekbones were set high on her face. Thomas realized he was staring and looked down at the girl's feet.

"Where are your shoes?"

Gunny glanced at her bare feet and curled her toes in the grass. "In the barrow. I meant to put them on before anyone saw me."

"You carry your shoes rather than wear them?"

"Why would anyone wear shoes on a nice day like this?"

"Don't your feet hurt when you are walking on the road?"

"Sometimes. But then I walk in the grass. It's splendid to walk in the grass with bare feet." Gunny brushed one foot across the soft grass. Her dark brown eyes danced. "You do go barefoot from time to time, don't you?"

Thomas looked down at his polished boots. His feet were hot and cramped inside the tight leather. He shook his head and laughed.

Lord Henry Milliken thundered out the double doors at the front of the house and stopped short. "Nephew," he snapped. "Why are you talking to that girl?" He glanced at Gunny. "Aren't you the shop girl from the Murphy's? Did you deliver the mutton?"

Gunny curtsied. "Yes, sir. Your mutton's in the kitchen. Cook said it was exactly what you ordered."

Henry Townsend Milliken was fifty-nine but that didn't prevent him from admiring full hips and high cheekbones. He reached into his pocket and pulled out a few pennies. He handed the coins to Gunny. "Be on your way."

Gunny curtsied, turned and sprinted up the driveway, the boots in her small barrow bumping along in front of her.

"Watch out for that one," Henry said as they both watched Gunny race off. "Her mother is haughty and that runs in families."

"I do hear that it runs in families. So you know her mother's family?"

"The Fitzgeralds. They've moved on. They're too proud for peasants. I never liked them."

"We evicted them."

"Did we? It's hard to remember one eviction from another."

Gunny stopped on her way into town to pull on her stockings and boots. Back at the shop, she took off her blood-stained apron and took a fresh one from a hook behind the counter. She was kneeling to get a fresh cap from under the counter when she heard a familiar voice. She pulled on her cap and peeked over the top of the counter. Matt McCrohan was in the back of the shop talking with Daniel Murphy. She ducked down. How humiliating it would be to have Matt see her like this—working for a stranger and wearing a cap and clean apron—and new boots. If she made a quick dash, she could make it out the front door before he saw her. She crawled along behind the counter. James stood at the end of the counter blocking her way.

"Scoot, James," she whispered. "I have to get out of here."

"Why are you whispering?" the boy asked in a loud voice.

Gunny held her finger to her lips. "Shhh! I don't want that man to know I'm here."

James stepped away from the counter and pointed. In an even louder voice he asked, "That man? Over there?"

Matt and Daniel Murphy looked over at the counter as Gunny attempted to crawl past James toward the door. "Gunny, is everything all right?" Daniel asked. "Did you drop something?"

Gunny looked across the store and smiled weakly. She rose to her feet, dusting off her hands and knees. "I dropped my cap, sir."

Daniel looked at the flushed girl. "Your cap is on your head, Gunny."

Gunny felt the top of her head. "Oh, there it is. I have to run an errand," she announced, jerking the front door open to a clash of bells. She dashed out around the corner and ducked into the turf room under the side steps. She pulled the door nearly closed and stood in the dank room. After a few minutes, she peeked out the door. Matt was sitting on the side steps waiting for her. She stepped back inside and pulled the door closed. Matt pulled the door open and she squinted at the light.

"What're you doing in there?"

"Go away," Gunny said pulling on the door to close it.

"I'm not going away," Matt said putting his foot near the door jamb to keep it open a crack. "I'm a customer. What if I need something?"

Gunny kicked at his foot and pulled on the door. "You don't always get what you want, Matt McCrohan. You told me that yourself. I'm not coming out until you go away."

"And I'm not going away until you come out. I want to see you in your new clothes." He pressed his face up the crack in the door. "I've missed you. Come out and talk to me."

"I don't have anything to say to you," Gunny said keeping both hands on the latch of the door. "I look ridiculous."

"You can't stay in there all day," Matt chided her.

"You have no idea what I can do and can't do, Matt McCrohan," Gunny said, kicking his foot clear of the door and pulling it closed. She kept a firm grip on the door latch for fifteen minutes, then pushed it open to peek outside. She blinked at the light. The side yard was empty. Matt was gone.

Gunny was dreaming. She was sitting in front of a cozy hearth fire listening to stories, the faces around her shifting in deep shadows of yellow and red. Someone was singing a quiet jig. She awoke with a start and lay still under the warm covers, her head clearing as the dream faded. She'd had the same kind of dream many times before but this time it seemed so real. The tune started up again. She sat up. Someone outside was singing one of John McCrohan's old songs. She pushed herself up off the squeaky bed as quietly as she could and tip-toed to the window. She pushed it open and leaned outside. Someone was down by the turf house singing in a rich, tenor voice. She spotted a head of thick brown hair in the moonlight.

Matt glanced up at Gunny and continued to sing, signaling for her to come down. She shook her head but knew he couldn't see her in the dark. He started singing a little louder. She pulled the window closed, grabbed her shawl and quietly but quickly descended the two flights of stairs. She opened the kitchen door and slipped outside into the cool night air.

"What're you doing here? You'll wake everyone with your singing," Gunny said in a hushed voice.

Matt laughed, then shushed himself. "I've been down by the pier with some gentlemen from the Blaskets. Those boys can drink, I tell you."

Gunny looked around. Where could they talk without waking anyone? "Cow shed," she said pointing. "Now." She grabbed Matt by the arm and led him, stumbling, into the shed. The two cows glanced up at the intruders then returned to chewing their cud.

Matt grinned and tried to twirl Gunny around. "I wanted to see you and here you are! You were rude to me last time I was here. You wouldn't talk to me."

"I didn't have anything to say," Gunny said, pulling away from his loose grip.

Matt leaned close and touched the end of her nose. "I thought you liked me."

She looked at his face and blushed, annoyed at how handsome he was. "How did you get here? Where's your horse?"

"Nella's at the stables at Ballygoleen," Matt said, proud that he could remember where he left his horse earlier that day.

"That's good," Gunny said, watching him sway slightly. "You are in no condition to ride. You should walk to Ventry and sleep this off in the stables."

"I can't walk to Ventry. I'll never make it."

"Then go back to the pub with your Blasket friends."

"Can't," Matt slurred. "The Peelers closed the place when the talk turned to revolution."

"Revolution?" Gunny said with a furrowed brow.

"I told you there was some drinking going on." Matt pulled a small white pipe from his pocket and held it to his lips.

"When did you take up smoking?" Gunny asked.

"I didn't," Matt said pointing the pipe stem at her. "I told a fellow from the Blaskets I'd hold on to this for him when the fight broke out. Then I forgot to give it back."

Gunny took the pipe from Matt. "You can't smoke in here. You'll light the cows on fire."

Matt grinned and took hold of Gunny's hand. His hand was warm. He slid the pipe out of her grasp and put it back into his pocket. He leaned against the wall and slid to the floor. "I'm tired," he said, yawning deeply.

Gunny ran her fingers through her loose curls. "I don't know what to do with you. You should go home."

"Don't tell me what I should do," Matt said, pointing at her, his heavy lids closing.

"I'm not telling you what to do."

"Yes, you are," Matt argued from behind closed eyes. "You are not my Mam. You are not my landlord. You are only the girl next door and I don't have to listen to you."

"How can I get you to go home?"

Matt took a small flash of whiskey from his jacket pocket. He took a long swallow and gasped as the burning liquid seared his throat. "I'm not going home," he said resolutely. "I hate that forge."

Gunny squatted by him on the floor. "Then why are you still there? You know Mac can run the forge."

"Because I'm the oldest," he said loudly, slapping the floor with an open palm. A cow mooed and Matt shushed her. "Because my father made me promise. Because it's my job even though working there makes me stink like a pig."

"Your father loved that forge."

"I don't think he did," Matt said waving the flask at her. "He loved the role of Smithy. Now Mac is a different story. I think he actually likes stinking like a pig."

Gunny shook her head. "Then go. It's better to leave than end up a bitter old man who wanders around telling everyone, 'I wish I had done something different.'"

Matt corked the flask and stashed it in his jacket pocket. "Now you're being mean. You should be nice to me."

Gunny leaned forward and took Matt's hands in hers. "I'm trying to be honest," she said in a gentle voice.

Matt looked into Gunny's eyes. "You are always honest, aren't you, Gunny?"

"I just don't understand you, Matt. Your family has some money. You have choices. Go to America. Make a different life for yourself. No one ever expected you to stay in Dunquin."

"I can be normal," Matt insisted, enjoying the warmth of Gunny's hands around his.

"Can you, Matt? And be happy?"

"I'm happy when I'm with you," he said closing his eyes again.

Gunny sighed and stood up. "I suppose you can stay here tonight. But you must be out in the morning before the Murphys get up. Do you understand?"

Matt nodded, then slumped forward with a loud snore. He was asleep sitting up. She sighed and pulled a woolen blanket from the stall wall. She tucked the blanket gently around his shoulders and pushed him to one side. He stirred and mumbled in protest, then pulled the blanket tight around him and wiggled into a small nest on the floor. He looked like a little boy with his blanket tucked up around his face. Gunny touched his wavy brown hair and ran a finger along his sleeping cheek.

"You are trouble all wrapped up in a beautiful package," she muttered. She pulled the door of the cow shed closed behind her and tip-toed upstairs to bed.

She was still awake at dawn. She crept back down the stairs and out to the cow shed to rouse her guest. The two cows stared at her blankly and mooed. Matt's blanket was draped neatly between the two stalls as if no one had ever been there.

The Old Lord sat at the dinner table with his eldest son after the rest of the family had retired for the evening. He loved to spend hours after dinner sitting around the table drinking and talking business. "Son," he said to Henry. "Pour me another glass of the naked truth."

Henry poured two small glasses of clear red claret and passed one to his father. He raised his glass in a toast. "To my father, who refuses to die."

The Old Lord raised his glass. "To my son, whom I love despite his many faults."

Both men drank.

"God, I love France. Claret is the elixir of the Gods" the Old Lord said through clenched teeth as he set down his glass.

Henry leaned back in his chair and wiped a napkin across his mouth.

"What is it, Henry? I can see you are troubled."

Henry folded his napkin carefully on the table and looked at his father's weathered face. "You did not collect rent again from most of the peasants this spring. We have land but no money and you have given me no authority to change that. We need more discipline around here. Last week, I caught young Thomas flirting with a peasant girl on the front lawn."

The old man laughed. "Don't worry about Thomas. Best to get original sin out than keep it in, I say."

Henry winced. "Your favorite grandchild is always the one who is the least well-behaved."

126

The Old Lord roared with laughter. "That is true, very true."

"Father," Henry continued, "we have hundreds of acres of land and nothing to show for it except grumbling tenants who are as likely to shoot us as pay rent. I could accept that if we had more to show for our efforts. But the peasants are exploding in numbers and the soil is depleted. What is going to happen to these farms over the next ten years if the peasants keep dividing them and dividing them?"

"You worry too much," the Old Lord said taking a sip of claret. "We have good wine and food on our plates. What more could a man ask for?"

Henry pushed away from the table and paced. "The problem is the damned Catholics. It seems they have a High Mass holiday every other week." He mimicked a peasant farmer, "We can't be working today, my Lord. Today is a high holy day." We'd get a lot more done if our farmers were Protestant."

The Old Lord chuckled. "Excellent point, Henry, except that there are very few Protestants in Dingle, and none of them are farmers."

Henry stopped pacing and leaned across the table. "What if we could turn Catholics into Protestants?"

The Old Lord waved a wrinkled hand in front of his face. "And after we do that, let's spin straw into gold."

"Listen to me, Father," Henry said, sliding his chair in closer to the old man and sitting down. "Everyone wants a better life. What if we offered to reduce rents if a farmer converted?"

"You said you want more money coming in, not less."

Henry's face lit up. "But with fewer high holy days, everyone would work more. In subsequent years, we could raise rents even higher than today because our peasants would have more that we could take from them." He smiled broadly and finished off his glass of claret with a quick swallow.

The Old Lord dabbed at the corners of his mouth with Henry's folded napkin. "When you are Baron of Ventry, you can do as you wish."

Henry slumped back in his chair. "I'm sixty years old, Father. When do you suppose that is going to happen?" Henry asked, exasperated.

"Are you putting a curse on my life, Henry?"

Henry sighed. "Must you always be so dramatic? You don't have to die to make me Baron. You know I have been waiting patiently for a long time."

The Old Lord slapped his hands on the table and stood, leaning toward Henry. "And you'll have to wait a little longer. I have no intention of making you Baron while I am alive." He stepped away from the table and ran a hand through his thin, grey hair. "It's time for me to take the dogs for a walk. Will you join us?"

Henry poured another glass of claret and stared into the class of red liquid. "No."

"Do as you please," the Old Lord said, "but remember that I have lived a long, healthy life, and spending time outside hunting for hares rather than inside hunting for wealth may be part of the reason."

It was the first Saturday in August and the shop was crowded with customers. Gunny heard a horse thunder up outside and knew it was Matt on Nella. She peeked out the front window and watched as Matt tied the large, sweaty work horse to a post and walked into the shop.

The bells above the door jangled. "I'm here to take Gunny out for Height Sunday," he announced to anyone who was listening. Gunny cringed at the unexpected attention as customers turned to her and smiled. Joanna signaled Matt and Gunny to follow her out to the kitchen.

Matt continued in a loud voice. "A group of us from Dunquin are going to Brandon Mountain on a pilgrimage," he explained as they exited the shop into the Murphy's living quarters. "If Gunny doesn't go with me, God will punish her."

Joanna turned and looked at Gunny who shrugged. Joanna handed Matt a mug of tea. "Brandon Mountain is a half-a day's walk from here and a mighty climb after that. Have you asked Gunny if she wants to go?"

Matt looked at Gunny who smiled and shook her head no.

"You don't want to go?" he asked.

"No," she said. "You didn't ask me."

Matt blushed. "Gunny. Will you go with me to Brandon Mountain tomorrow to celebrate Height Sunday?"

Gunny looked at Joanna who nodded her head.

Matt joined the Murphys for their evening meal, regaling them with quips about his oddest customer requests, and tales of illegal fishing and hunting excursions that started and ended at O'Leary's pub. They all laughed so hard their stomachs hurt. Only James seemed less than amused by their guest.

While Gunny and Joanna cleaned up the kitchen, Matt put Nella in the cow shed for the night, and made a nest for himself in the folded blanket.

At first light he slipped into the kitchen. Gunny was already up, the fire stirred, and a pot of tea warming over the fire.

"Are you ready for a long hike?" he asked as Gunny poured him a mug.

"It does sound a bit far off."

"The farther away the pilgrimage, the fewer old people and children who will tag along."

"I see you've thought this through," Gunny said with a smile. "I've never hiked as far as Brandon Mountain. I've seen him far off there with his head in the clouds."

"The perfect spot for me," Matt said.

Gunny cut four slices of thick oat bread and coated them with butter. "We won't go hungry."

"Perfect. And I have whiskey," Matt said, patting the flask in his jacket pocket. "Will you bring your tin whistle?"

Gunny patted her apron pocket. "It's right here."

They walked the cows and Nella down Goat Street and onto Upper Main. The August sun was barely up in the sky but the day was already warm. They turned the animals loose in the upper field. The cows wandered off to graze but Nella stood resolute by the gate.

"Sorry, girl," Gunny said, patting the horse's long cream nose. "Height Sunday is a day for walking."

"Leave her be," Matt said. "She'll be fine without us."

The two teens spoke little as they walked north along the narrow road that led up into the hills. One or the other would occasionally point out a cluster of wildflowers or an unusual rock formation. When they finally reached the base of the mountain, Gunny was surprised to find the other teens from Dunquin there. Even Ellen had joined in; they'd knocked at her door as they passed through Ballyferriter and she had slipped out for the day. Gunny hadn't seen Ellen in years. She hadn't changed much—she was still small with her mousy face and thin brown hair. She, Gunny, and Ashling fussed over each other while Cornelius, Mac, and the Burke twins teased Matt about being out all night without them. When the greeting and teasing was done, each teen made three turns around the well of the Virgin Mary and tossed in a small stone.

Their obligation to the virgin fulfilled, they turned to the mountain which loomed above them. They cut through several stony fields and passed through the gates of local farmers, then started up a steep dirt path. As they got close to the top, the path grew steeper and rockier, and the group grew quieter as they concentrated on the climb. They were soon walking single file in the fog that shrouded the mountaintop. Gunny stumbled on a rock and Matt caught her arm.

"Let me help you," he said.

"I'm fine," Gunny said. "I'm just a little out of breath."

"Then let's stop for a minute. The rest of you go on. We'll catch up."

Mac stopped to wait with his brother, but Matt signaled him to go which Mac did with a shrug. Gunny smiled at Matt. She felt silly needing help but liked it that Matt was there to hold her arm and to wait with her. When they were alone, she studied his profile and long, wavy brown hair. "You know when we get to the top we won't be able to see a thing with all this fog?"

"So what," Matt said. "We'll be on top of the world."

Gunny took a deep breath. "I'm fine now. Let's catch up with the others."

"Walk ahead of me," Matt said. "I want to be sure to catch you if you stumble again."

Gunny stepped ahead of Matt and continued up the steepest part of the climb with Matt admiring the view from behind.

It was a little past noon when the path flattened and Matt and Gunny neared the top. The sun infused the grey air around them with a bright, ghostly glow. They could hear the others ahead of them, talking in small groups. Matt pulled Gunny back against a worn, grey boulder and reached across his body to shake her hand.

"Nice climbing, Miss Malone."

Gunny took Matt's extended hand. "Nice climbing, Mr. McCrohan."

Neither pulled their hand away. The cool rock against Gunny's back contrasted with the heat of Matt's hand. The bright mist swirled cold around them. Turning toward Matt, Gunny offered her other hand. Matt smiled, squeezed her hands in his and brought both of her hands to his chest. The two breathed together as one in the still space of rock and fog.

A fresh wind stirred and the mist around them lightened. Ghostly shapes emerged and rocks and tall grasses took shape. Matt stepped away from Gunny and yelled to the group. "Lads! I challenge you to jump over that rock in the field."

Matt took off at a run across the steep, foggy field. He bounded over a large rock and stumbled. Gunny gasped as his feet flew in the air. He rolled twice then sprang to his feet. He steadied himself, then waved his flask of whiskey in the air. "No worries! No whiskey was lost in this exercise."

The boys roared and raced after Matt. Gunny smiled. It felt like they were kids again. While the boys challenged each other to farther tests of strength, Gunny, Ellen, and Ashling set off to collect dried furze branches for a small bonfire and picked wildflowers which they wove into each other's hair. They reminisced about their days in the booley and laughed about collecting fairy thorns for the fire. The boys joined them to help build a fire circle, then sat and passed around a pipe which Gunny recognized from Matt's night with the Blasket men.

As Gunny knelt to light the fire, a strong gust of wind blew her small pile of kindling apart and lifted the fog from the mountaintop. She tossed Matt's fire tools aside and rose to take in the spectacular view. Brandon Bay lay far below them to the north. The black humps of the Blasket Islands were far across to the west past a deep channel of green ocean. The town of Dingle and Dingle Harbor were barely visible far off to the south. Gunny felt her heart race and held out her arms to collect the day around her. She felt small and insignificant and at the same time part of the solid rock beneath her feet with warm sun on her face and clear air around her.

A cold wind roughed the air and Gunny knelt again to light the fire. The group pulled rocks into a circle and Gunny soon had the dry furze burning. The fire snapped and whistled as tiny sparks rose in the cooling air. Matt passed his pipe and whiskey flask around the circle while Gunny played her tin whistle to celebrate the fire and end of day.

Matt cleared his throat and clapped his hands for attention. Gunny let a new tune die in her whistle. Matt held a finger in the air. "I challenge someone to jump across the fire."

Gunny pocketed her whistle and stood. "I'll do it."

"I meant a lad, Gunny," Matt said. He reached up and pulled her hand to try to get her to sit down. "You keep playing."

Gunny pulled her hand away. "You don't think I can jump a fire?"

"I'm sure you can jump a fire." Matt stood, still holding her hand. "Jump with me," he said.

Gunny smiled and lifted her skirts with her free hand. They took a step back, and leapt. The group parted on the far side to give them space to land and they landed without a stumble. Everyone laughed and assured each other that Gunny was as crazy as Matt and that they had all missed her. The wind picked up from the west, and the mist blew back in around them. Gunny shivered.

"Let's pack it up, boys," Mark barked. "We need to get these ladies home."

Cornelius and Mac stamped out the fire as everyone gathered shawls, hats, and jackets. Matt reached over and gently took Gunny's hand. As they walked toward the narrow path down, Matt slowed his pace to let the others go ahead of them. Matt's hand was warm and rough in hers, his grip firm. Gunny felt her heart move up in her chest. She didn't want to breathe for fear of breaking the spell. Ashling turned back and looked at them, then whispered to Ellen. Ellen gave Gunny a raised eyebrow. Gunny smiled. At the base of the mountain, everyone remarked on what a perfect day it had been and how much they had missed Gunny. Then the Dunquin teens headed west toward Dunquin, and Matt and Gunny turned south toward Dingle.

The next morning, Gunny stumbled into a deserted, warm kitchen. Her thighs and toes ached from the climb down the mountain and the long walk to and from Brandon Mountain. She stretched, took the steaming tea kettle from the fire, and poured herself a cup of hot tea. She added a spoonful of sugar and took a long sip, cradling the warm cup in her hands. She and Matt hadn't gotten back to Dingle until well after dark. Matt had left with Nella to sleep in the Ventry stables, and she had practically crawled upstairs to bed.

Daniel bustled into the kitchen from the shop. "I thought you'd never get up! I hope you're feeling rested after your pilgrimage. We have an important delivery. Meet me in the shop and I'll help you fill the barrow." He paused and looked at Gunny, then reached over, pulled a wilted flower from her tangle of curls and handed it to the weary girl. Gunny laughed and tossed the limp flower into the fire.

"You know, the church no longer supports pilgrimages," Daniel said. "They say too much drinking and dancing goes on in the hills."

"What could possibly happen on a pilgrimage?" Gunny said with raised eyebrows and a slight smile. She could see that Daniel was impatient to get the barrow packed, but the tea was delicious and she stalled. "What's so special about the delivery today?" she asked, trying to suppress a yawn.

"The Millikens have guests arriving from Galway and they sent a messenger asking for a quick delivery of baking supplies." He eyed the tired girl. "Are you up for this after your long walk yesterday?"

Gunny stood and stretched. "I am willing and able." She pulled a clean apron from a peg near the door and followed Daniel into the shop.

"Jamie could go with you if you want company," Daniel said as Gunny helped pull sacks of freshly ground flour from the shelves. "He's off with Joanna this morning at the milk market but they should be back soon." Gunny's eyes shone as she took a sack of flour and walked outside to the barrow. Daniel cleared his throat and yelled after her. "Gunny?"

Gunny looked back in the door, the flour sack hanging limp in her arms. "I'm sorry. Were you talking to me?"

Daniel laughed and brought out the last two sacks of flour. "What's got you so distracted?"

Gunny blushed and concentrated on the load in the barrow. She had been thinking about her Dunquin friends, and the views from Brandon Mountain, and how Matt's hand felt in hers. And she was thinking about seeing Thomas Milliken at Ballygoleen. She had not seen the young Lord in a month or so. She looked up at Daniel's concerned face and grinned. "I'm a silly girl thinking about silly things," she said coyly.

Daniel shook his head. "Of all of the things I could say about you, Gunny, I would not say you were silly. I asked you if you want to have Jamie go with you today."

Gunny frowned and shook her head. "Oh, my no," she said. "It's too long a walk for James. I'll take him with me to bring in the cows when I get home."

Daniel looked into Gunny's eyes. "Very well. Remember to not ask the cook any questions or you'll be there all day."

Gunny smiled. "I remember. I'll be quick."

She headed out of Dingle pushing the heavy barrow. A hot August wind blew in across the land and she felt beads of sweat drop between her breasts. She stopped at the bullan rock; the wells of the holy rock were dry. She wiped the sweat from her face with her apron and sat down to take off her boots and stockings. As the road out of Dunquin dropped down toward the ocean, the wind shifted from north to south and a cool breeze blustered in across the water. The temperature change was dramatic. Gunny paused to take in a long breath of fresh salty air. Small whitecaps appeared far off the shore and the wind whipped her hair loose. She felt in her pocket for her whistle but had left it in her soiled apron. She sighed and picked up the handles of the heavy barrow to complete her errand.

She rested the barrow near the kitchen door, pulled on her stockings and boots, and hauled the first two flour bags inside. The cook was excited about the delivery.

"My, my. You have no idea how much work I have to do today. It's good you arrived when you did. The Millikens rarely have outsiders to the house. The family coming in from Galway is practically royalty from what I hear."

Gunny nodded and returned to the barrow for the second two sacks of flour.

"I hope you've brought enough. I'll be cooking all day. I hear the young woman who is coming is very picky about her what she eats. Lord Milliken said everything has to be perfect."

Gunny nodded again and returned to the barrow for a large sack of sugar. She set the sack on the large kitchen table and dusted off her hands.

"So tell me the news from Dingle. Father Owen said I must make a better effort to attend Mass on Sundays but Lord Henry makes such a fuss when I go," the cook said.

Gunny smiled at the small plump woman. "No news. I work most of the time. Must be off!" She ducked out the side door and pulled it closed tightly behind her. She stood outside and took a deep breath. She wondered where Thomas was and felt a flutter of excitement in her stomach at the thought. She left the empty barrow by the kitchen door and walked down the back path toward the stables. Perhaps her father was working. And perhaps Thomas was there too.

Sean Fitzgerald was much taller than she remembered, but she recognized him from his bright shock of red hair.

"Your da was around earlier this week but he's gone home."

"Oh, well." Gunny shrugged looking around the stable. There was no one else there. She ran a hand over the Old Lord's tall black mare. The horse whinnied and nuzzled Gunny's hand. "I guess I'll head back to Dingle to milk the cows. Maybe I'll get in a bit of butter making. Not quite the day I'd hoped for."

Sean looked at her blankly. "How's your dog? Shep, was it?"

Gunny grinned. "He's good, I suppose. He's with Da in Dunquin. I hardly see him now."

"Yeah," Sean said. He turned the mare away from Gunny and continued brushing her.

Gunny wandered back up the path to the large yellow house. There was a note lying in the flour dust in her barrow. She picked it up and studied the neat handwriting. She carefully sounded out the letters then read the note out loud to make sure she had the words right. "Meet me by the boathouse. Thomas." She grinned and sat down in the grass to pull off her stockings and boots. She pulled her hair free of its pins and stuffed them into her apron pocket. The boathouse. It must be along the water. She sprinted down the hill through the formal gardens, and out toward the shore.

Thomas was fishing off the end of a short stone pier. His breath caught in his throat as the tall barefoot girl with a mass of black hair tumbling around her shoulders appeared by the boathouse. He gave her a short wave and she flashed him a smile. Thomas set down his fishing pole and hobbled in off the pier. "I saw your barrow."

"And I saw your note," she said, laughing, hands resting on her wide hips.

"What brings you to Ballygoleen today?"

"Flour, sir," she said adding a deep curtsy and flourish of her hand. "I hear you have company coming."

Thomas laughed. "Don't bow to me. Remember I am not the Lord. I am not even close to it."

"You may not be the Lord but you live here," Gunny said with a sweep of her hand along the shore line and up toward the mansion. "It must be wonderful living in such a big house with beautiful gardens—and look at this. You have a place to fish right here in your own yard."

Thomas glanced around. "I suppose it beats fighting the French or the Americans."

"And getting shot at."

"Yes, it definitely beats getting shot at." He crossed to a bench that ran along the ocean side of the boathouse and sat.

"Your leg's looking much better."

"It's better. Not perfect."

"Not perfect like this place."

Thomas laughed. "The house may be beautiful on the outside, but inside, it's quite crowded. When I was growing up, I shared a room up in the attic with three brothers and two sisters. My cousins, uncle and aunt, as well as my grandfather and grandmother, slept on the floor below."

"I like a big family," Gunny said.

"I'd like it too if we had a little more space and a little more food. Dinner was usually mutton and potatoes in a thin greasy stew. Cook can make a fine loaf of bread but her dinners are somewhat lacking."

"Mutton stew sounds delicious. We had mutton a few times a year when we had a sheep left after we paid our rent. We mostly ate potatoes. Potatoes, and potatoes, and potatoes."

"I can't imagine not eating meat every day," Thomas said, surprised. "Though you seem to have grown plenty tall on potatoes." He pulled a small flask from his jacket pocket. "Would you like a bit of port?"

Gunny squinted. "I don't know what port is."

"Oh, it's wonderful stuff," Thomas grinned, uncorking the flask. "My grandfather has it smuggled in from France." He took a swig and held the flask out to Gunny. "Go ahead. It gives you a warm feeling inside. You'll like it."

Gunny took the flask from Thomas and sniffed. She waved a hand in front of her face and passed it back. "It smells like liquor. I'll pass."

Thomas took another swig and corked the flask. "And why is that?" he asked sliding the small bottle into his pocket.

Gunny grimaced. "I used to take a glass or two of porter down at O'Leary's, but since I've been in Dingle, I have seen too many men feeling warm inside from liquor. I'd say half the crime, half the illness, and more than half the misery I've seen in Dingle can be blamed on drinking. I don't think I've ever seen a fight in Dingle where there wasn't an empty whiskey bottle nearby."

"That's why I only take little sips," Thomas said, patting his pocket.

Gunny sat down next to Thomas, straightened her skirts and stretched her bare toes out toward the water. "Tell me about growing up in this crowded palace."

"Well," Thomas said clearing his throat. "Growing up here was... pleasant."

"More detail, please," Gunny said, wiggling her toes in the soft grass. "I like a good story."

"You like a good story... Then I'll tell you a true story as it was told to me by my grandfather." He leaned back on the bench and looked out across the water. "Back in ancient times, there used to be an old ring fort right here on this land. The Vikings built it to trade with the locals. When I was little, we used to dig around in the gardens looking for ancient Viking treasure."

"Did you ever find any?"

"Not a bone, not a farthing," he said with a grin. "After the Vikings died off, the fort fell to ruins and the Geraldine's built a castle here, called Rahanane. They ruled the peninsula from this very spot until Oliver Cromwell crushed them in the Irish revolt of 1649 and the castle fell to ruins. My grandfather was given this land in the early 1800s as a reward for his military service to the King of England and he built Ballygoleen."

Gunny blinked. She had heard another version of the same story from John McCrohan. "Tell me about your brothers and sisters."

Thomas looked into Gunny's dark brown eyes. "They've all married and have moved away to their own estates. I'm the only one who hasn't settled down. Except for Dayrolles."

"Who's that?"

"He is my oldest brother. He moved to Dublin to study law. He wants nothing to do with Ventry or the Dingle peninsula." Thomas's gaze turned to Gunny's neck and breastplate. "You know your skin is flawless."

Gunny put her hands to her cheeks. "Oh, sir," she said. "You flatter me. You're beautiful too," she added looking Thomas squarely in his deep blue eyes.

He smiled. "Men aren't beautiful, Gunny. We are handsome."

"No," she corrected him. "You're beautiful." He held her gaze. She stopped breathing and felt the grass and bench fall away beneath her. She took a breath, stood, and pushed her curls up off of her face. "I have to get back to the shop. Mr. Murphy will wonder what has become of me."

Thomas took Gunny's right hand in both of his. "Tell him you were listening to Cook tell tales. He'll believe you."

Gunny pulled her hand free and smiled. "I'll do that."

Thomas stood and bowed. "It has been most pleasant talking with you, Miss Malone."

"Yes," she said. "It has been most pleasant talking with you, Lord Thomas."

"It's just Thomas," he reminded her.

Gunny looked again into his blue eyes. "Thomas," she said in a whisper, then with a flick of her skirts ran up the hill and grabbed her barrow. She trotted back to Dingle with her head spinning, never feeling the rough road beneath her bare feet.

When she arrived at the shop, Daniel was chatting with Mrs. McAllister at the back of the shop. Joanna and James were not around. Gunny slipped past Daniel and went out to the kitchen. She spotted Joanna in the backyard pulling weeds from between neat rows of radishes and cabbage. James sat behind her collecting the weeds and dropped them over the low stone fence for the cows to eat when they got home.

Gunny leaned out the back door. "I'm home," she said. "The shop wasn't busy today?"

Joanna looked up startled and shook her head. "Mrs. McAllister is in there making all sorts of demands. I had to escape out here with Jamie. Sometimes I just have to go outside and get my hands dirty."

"I can take James with me when I go to fetch the cows."

"He'd like that." Joanna stood and carefully wiped her hands on her apron.

Gunny noticed that Joanna's hands were slightly shaking and wondered if James was naturally shy or if he had learned it from his mother.

Joanna smiled. "Was the delivery all right? You were at Ballygoleen?"

"Yes, Ballygoleen," Gunny muttered. "It's another world."

* * *

Only a week had passed when Daniel told Gunny she was to go to Ballygoleen again. This time the order was light; a few tools and a length of rope to mend fishing nets.

"The order came from Lord Thomas Milliken. He asked specifically that you make the delivery," Daniel said with a raised brow.

Gunny shrugged as she placed the tools in a pouch. She slung the pouch over one shoulder and across her chest, then heaved the coiled rope, one of her own making, across the other shoulder. She was glad to leave the clunky barrow behind her. "I won't be long!"

"Don't forget about..."

"The cook. I won't."

Gunny headed west with a bounce in her step and a grin on her face. Thomas had requested that she make a delivery. She heard familiar hoof beats and turned and watched Matt thundering along the road behind her. She hadn't seen him in weeks, not since their hike to Brandon Mountain. She turned west and continued walking.

Matt slowed Nella and trotted along beside her. "I stopped by the shop. They said you were headed to Ventry. Would you like a lift?"

"No, I'm fine," she said. "I like walking."

Matt slipped down from the saddle and grabbed Nella by the reins. "Then I'll walk with you."

Gunny had a thousand thoughts in her head but said nothing.

"This looks terrible, me walking and you carrying everything," Matt said. "Why don't you give me that bag and rope? I'll strap them on Nella."

"Nella doesn't have to carry things for me. I've got them," Gunny said clutching at the intersection of bag and rope that crossed her chest and stroking Nella's nose. "They don't weigh much."

Matt shrugged. "You're so stubborn. Do you have to walk at such a fast clip?"

"I'm in a hurry."

"If you're in such a hurry then why won't you accept a ride?"

"Matt," Gunny said stopping in the middle of the road. "I haven't heard from you in weeks. I hope you've been busy with work."

"I have been. Sort of."

Gunny stopped, teeth gritted. "Or maybe you've been busy spending time at O'Leary's with the Wren Boys and Ashling Kavanaugh?"

Matt looked at her with raised eyebrows and no ready answer.

She looked into his eyes. "You flirt with me and then you disappear. You did the same thing in Dunquin—one minute you were my best friend and the next you were too busy to talk."

137

Matt's forehead wrinkled. He scanned the line of the ocean as if he were looking for a Viking ship to come to his rescue.

"Grrr!" Gunny said and started walking again.

Matt matched her pace. "Gunny, I have been busy. Since our hike on Brandon Mountain, I decided to let Mac do more at the forge. We've been working together these past few weeks. I don't know why it took me so long to turn things over to him. He's really much better at running the forge than I am."

Gunny clicked her tongue. "You've known that for ages, Matt. Be honest. Sometimes you have time for us and sometimes you don't."

Matt laughed. "You're just the same. I seem to recall you were plenty busy in Dunquin before you left. Cornelius still reminds me how the two of you used to talk and talk at O'Leary's."

"There was nothing to that and you know it," Gunny said grabbing his arm.

He rested his hand on hers. "I know. You jumped the fire with me, not Cornelius. I'm sorry it took me so long to get back to see you."

Gunny swallowed. "Strange, we never talked like this in Dunquin," she said.

"There are always too many people around in Dunquin," Matt said.

"We had good times when we were younger."

"It wasn't only when we were younger," Matt said, squeezing her hand.

Two gulls flew over them, squabbling as one tried to steal a fish from the other's claws.

"They sound like us. Squawk, squawk, squawk," Gunny laughed.

Matt put his hand over her mouth to quiet her squawking. "No one else in Dunquin can do half as good an imitation of quarreling gulls."

Gunny pushed his hand away and inhaled deeply. "Maybe I'll take you up on that ride."

Matt swung up into the saddle and reached his left arm down to pull Gunny up behind him. She mounted the horse and they galloped off toward Ventry.

"Leave me here at the top of the drive," she said sliding down off of Nella's back. "I have to drop these off with the housekeeper, Mrs. Needham. She might think it strange if she sees me arriving on your horse. I won't be more than a minute."

"It's not like I have to be anywhere," Matt said with a smile. He watched Gunny hurry down the drive swinging the bundle and rope, then swung down from the saddle and led Nella to an open patch of grass by the side of the drive.

"Excuse me, young man."

Matt turned toward the voice. A blond man with a long thin face hobbled briskly toward him from the stables. He was well-dressed and looked angry.

"Yes, sir?" Matt said.

The man looked at Nella. "Who said you could graze your horse on this property?"

Matt glanced over at Nella who was thoughtfully munching away on the lawn. "No one, sir. I'll only be here for a minute. I'm waiting for someone to make a delivery at your house."

"It is not my house," the short man grunted. "And it will most likely never be my house." He turned to face Matt. "I am Lord Thomas Milliken," he said without extending his hand. "I don't believe we've met."

Matt squinted at the man. "I heard some men down at O'Leary's talking about you. They said you were back from fighting in the Peninsular Wars."

Thomas reached self-consciously for his right leg. "That is correct."

"It must have been terrible fighting against the French," Matt said in a big voice.

Thomas looked down the drive toward the house. "It wasn't so bad."

From the haunted look in the man's eye, Matt found that hard to believe. "I hear that Bonaparte is quite an excellent fighter. Did you find that to be true?"

Thomas glared at Matt. "You peasants and your passion for the French," he said with disdain. "You mentioned a delivery. Did you come here with Gunny Malone?"

Matt was surprised the Lord knew Gunny by name. "Yes, sir. I saw her walking here from Dingle and offered her a ride. Gunny and I grew up together in Dunquin."

"So you are headed home to Dunquin now," Thomas said, making this a statement rather than a question.

"I thought I'd give Gunny a ride back to Dingle when she's done," Matt said.

"There's no need to wait," Thomas said, a sharp edge to his voice. "Gunny is used to walking home from here. She's done it many times."

"Has she?" Matt asked with amusement. "As much as this might surprise you," he continued without pause, "a peasant girl might actually prefer riding a horse to walking. I'll wait."

"She may be here for awhile," Thomas said.

"She said she'd only be a minute," Matt corrected.

Thomas had had enough of this tall stranger. "What did you say your name was?"

"I didn't. My name is Matt McCrohan," Matt said offering his hand.

Thomas ignored the proffered hand. "Mr. McCrohan, I ask that you and your horse be on your way."

Matt squared his feet and stood to his full height. "I told Gunny I'd wait. I'll move my horse to your stables if that's what's bothering you."

"They are not my stables!" Thomas snapped.

"Of course, sir," Matt said politely with a slight bow. "I'll move my horse to the Lord's stables and we'll wait there."

"I insist you leave the property," Thomas said loudly. "If Gunny needs a ride to Dingle, I will take her in the coach."

"As you said, sir, Gunny generally prefers to walk."

Thomas and Matt were facing one another, shoulders back, and faces red when Gunny came out of the house. She hurried up the drive and curtsied to Thomas. "Sir."

Thomas gave her a half nod. "Gunny."

"I left your fishing supplies with Mrs. Needham," Gunny said.

"Excellent," Thomas said, continuing to stare at Matt. "I thought perhaps we could fish together today…"

"I think you'll like the rope. I twisted it myself."

Matt broke from the stare and swung up onto Nella. He offered a hand to Gunny. Gunny bobbed again to Thomas, then grabbed Matt's hand and swung up into the saddle behind Matt. "Perhaps another time…" she started as Matt spurred Nella around in the roadway, and the two tore down the road to Dingle leaving Thomas in a thin veil of dust.

"Now that the harvest's in, I've been seeing boys from the village going by on their way to the school on Green Street. Why doesn't James go to school?" Gunny asked Joanna as she diced up a large fresh onion.

"He's too little," Joanna explained, scooping up the chopped onion and tossing it into a large bowl on the table. "And he's not good with large groups of people, as you may have noticed."

Gunny sighed, picked up a hot, boiled potato and cut it in half. "But if he went to school, he could learn how to read and do numbers."

"He says he doesn't want to go."

Gunny set down her knife. "I'd have given anything to go to school."

Joanna sat down to cut up the rest of the potatoes. She added the potato quarters to the onions in the bowl and gave them a quick stir with a long wooden spoon. "You didn't go to school?"

"We don't have a school in Dunquin," Gunny explained picking up her knife again to peel the last potato. "Some of the wealthier farm boys went to school in Dublin, but not the girls, not even the ones with money."

"I didn't go to school either," Joanna confessed. "There were no girls' schools in Dingle when I was growing up. Daniel taught me how to read and to do math after we opened the shop. It's a shame to not know how to read."

"Oh, I know how to read," Gunny assured her employer. "A friend taught me."

"It's a good friend that will teach you how to read. Do you think you could teach Jamie?"

Gunny took the spoon from Joanna to mash the potatoes in with the raw onion bits. "I don't know. It took me a whole summer to learn and I was much older than James."

Joanna smiled. "Jamie told me he is trying to be brave enough to learn to play your whistle."

"I've tried to get him to play. He doesn't want to do anything if it's not perfect. But he's really quite smart," Gunny said.

"I'm glad you see it. Most people think Jamie is addled—or crazy. Or both."

Gunny laughed. "He's is the smartest boy I know. And he's still little."

Joanna added a dollop of butter to the potato and onion mixture. "So you'll teach him to read?"

"I'll try. I need a slate and a bit of chalk. And a newspaper."

After a few weeks learning his letters on a black slate board, James quickly figured out how the alphabet formed words and read everything he could get his hands on. He followed Gunny around the shop sounding out words from the paper, reading labels off of barrels, and pointing out shop signs as they walked the cows to and from the shed. Gunny listened patiently as she worked in the shop by day, and around the fire at night when she was mending clothing or hanging wash in front of the fire to dry. As often as not, when there was a word James did not know, Gunny didn't know it either and they both had to sound it out.

James was soon reading on his own with little guidance. Customers loved seeing the small boy, sprawled out by the stove at the back of the store with the weekly newspaper spread out in front him, intent on reading and understanding every word.

It was late fall before Daniel asked Gunny to make another trip to the Ventry estate.

"Can't you go instead?" Gunny asked.

"I thought you liked making deliveries to Ballygoleen."

Gunny hesitated. She remembered sitting with Thomas behind the boathouse—how he had touched her hand and told her she was beautiful. If she went, she'd make sure to not be alone with him again. She was used to flirting with Matt and the boys in Dunquin, but Thomas was a man and it would be easy to lose control. She pictured herself with a large protruding belly and Father Jessey waving a finger in her face saying, "I told you you'd burn in hell." She shook her head to clear the thought and smiled at Daniel.

"I'd be happy to go. I don't know what I was thinking."

Her stomach felt tight as she headed west out of town pushing a barrow loaded high with fresh meat packages. The ocean to her left was bright and sharp in the slant of the fall sun. The fields to her right were freshly harvested, the grasses just turning to gold. She breathed in the cool ocean air and pulled her shawl tighter around her chest. She looked up and down the road for any sign of Matt but the road was quiet. As she neared Ballygoleen, she heard hunting dogs howling in the woods along the shore. She carefully moved the heavy barrow to the top of the drive as the barks and yips grew louder and closer.

By the time Lord Henry Milliken came flying onto the drive on a large black steed, the dogs had knocked over Gunny's barrow and were tearing open the packets of fresh mutton. Gunny stood clutching a tree by the side of the drive, clear of the frenzy of snapping, barking dogs.

"Don't just stand there," Lord Henry yelled, his face flush as his horse pranced in a tight circle around the dogs.

"What would you have me do?" Gunny shouted over the racket. "Pull the meat from their jaws? They're ravenous."

Henry patted his horse to try and calm her. "You'd be ravenous too if you hadn't eaten for several days."

"You don't feed your dogs?"

"They have to be hungry for the hunt," Henry spat.

Gunny watched the dogs snarl and snap at each other as they licked the last of the blood off of the shredded paper. She pictured a live fox in place of the packets of meat. "That seems a bit primitive to me, sir," she said from the safety of the tree.

Henry could barely hear the girl above the noise of the dogs. "What's that?"

Gunny cleared her throat and looked down. "Nothing, sir."

Thomas thundered up behind Henry on the Old Lord's favorite mare. He yelled and kicked at the dogs to clear the road, then slid from his horse as they scattered, his face pale, and his lips tight. He righted the upset barrow and swallowed hard eying the bloody papers in the road. He ran a hand over his face and closed his eyes.

"Are you all right, Nephew," Lord Henry said. "You look as though you've seen a ghost.

Thomas turned and clutched at the saddle of his horse. "I thought for a moment I was back in France…"

Henry turned his horse toward Gunny. "We won't pay for meat that was never delivered. You should have taken your delivery directly to the kitchen as you were instructed."

"Uncle," Thomas said, blinking his eyes and pushing back a loose shock of blond hair from his forehead. "It's clear your dogs attacked her barrow here in the drive. Surely you are not going to…"

"The meat was never delivered, Thomas. We will not pay a farthing for it." Henry turned on his horse and rode off into the woods whistling for the dogs.

Gunny took a step into the drive eyeing the torn wrappers, her eyes brimming with tears. "How am I going to explain this to Daniel?" she uttered. "I'll lose my wages for life."

Thomas kicked at the dirty papers. "Don't worry. I'll explain everything to my grandfather. He'll be sure Mr. Murphy is paid."

Gunny knelt to collect the mess. Thomas rested his hands on her shoulders. "Leave those." His hands were cold and slightly shaking. Gunny stood and looked into his blue eyes as tears spilled out onto her cheeks.

"There, there," Thomas said, clicking his tongue. "There is no need to cry." He took a monogrammed handkerchief from his pocket and gently wiped her cheeks.

She felt her cheeks burn. She had only cried a few times in her life and hated that she was crying now in front of a Lord. She took the handkerchief and turned her back to him. She took a deep breath and tried to laugh. "That was scary," she said.

"The dogs?" Thomas asked from behind her.

"No," Gunny said turning around and handing him the damp hanky. "Your uncle. Dogs I can handle." She tried to laugh but it came out as a half-wheeze which made her want to cry again.

Thomas looked at her face and winced. "Better keep the hanky."

"Thank you."

"Not a problem," Thomas said. "I have dozens."

"No," Gunny blurted. "Thank you for sticking up for me. Your uncle'll be mad at you. I don't know why you did that."

"I did it," Thomas said, "because it was the right thing to do. You did nothing wrong and I'll make sure my grandfather knows it. Besides," he added, the color returning to his face, "my uncle is an ass. I have no problem crossing him."

Gunny smiled. "You're going to be a terrible Lord. You're much too kind."

Thomas looked at Gunny in mock amazement. "Miss Malone. How dare you call me kind? I am a soldier in the English Army and future Lord of some manor. I may have to punish you for those unseemly words."

Gunny raised her eyebrows. "And what would you do to me, kind sir?" Gunny asked, wiping her nose and pocketing the fine hanky in her apron pocket.

Thomas stepped in close to Gunny and rested his right hand on her cheek. "I could stop you from uttering such improper words, but…"

"But what," Gunny asked, leaning in close to him, feeling heat rising in her chest.

"But I could only do that with a kiss," he whispered, pushing a stray curl from her left cheek.

Gunny rested her cheek against his. His face felt smooth against hers, his hands, soft against her neck. Her quick breathing matched his as she pressed her chest against his. She longed for time to stop.

Thomas brushed his lips across her cheek, then across her lips. "Gunny," he murmured, then took a deep breath and stepped away. He stared at her, then swung awkwardly up onto his horse and rode off into the woods.

The months between harvest and Christmas flew by. Gunny was busy at the shop with no additional calls to visit Ballygoleen. The week before Christmas, business was as brisk as she had ever seen it.

"A wren couldn't find a place to light in this shop," she moaned as she passed Joanna behind the counter. She hardly had time to tie her shoe or to re-pin her hair at the back of her head.

People were in from all of the nearby villages and the Blaskets, dressed in their best clothes, and looking for Christmas gifts to share with their families. Daniel dealt with the villagers who brought an assortment of items to trade: sheep, a basket of fish, a sack of wool, a knitted shawl.

Gunny had seen plenty of drinking in Dingle, but it was nothing compared to what she saw at Christmas. Every shopkeeper kept a bottle of whiskey under the counter to tip a small glass with each paying customer. By late afternoon, tempers flared and fights broke out almost daily.

Robert appeared at the shop around noon on Christmas Eve to walk Gunny home. She grabbed a sack of clothes and waved good-bye to the Murphy's. Outside, Shep danced around her barking and nipping. She knelt to ruffle the dog's silky black head and kissed him on the nose, relieved to be out of the mayhem of the shop. Her father joined her outside holding a small sack of goods.

"We're home to celebrate Christmas then," he said, and they headed off west in silence with Shep leading the way. Robert had never seen his daughter look so beautiful in her freshly stitched dress, clean apron, and soft, polished boots. "So are you talking to me? Or are you still mad?"

"Why would I be mad?"

"You were plenty mad when I dropped you off here."

Gunny shushed him and kicked a rock into the nearby shrubbery. "I was afraid to move to Dingle, that's all."

"And now? What's changed?"

Gunny grinned. "I like working at the store."

"Tell me about it."

Gunny laughed and launched into story after story about what she did and about the customers at the shop, about taking care of the cows and churning butter and selling it at the Mall, and about teaching James to read. She didn't mention Matt's visits or her deliveries to Ballygoleen.

When they crested the last hill and the small village of Dunquin opened up in front of her, Gunny fought back tears. The look and the smells told her she was home. They walked past the forge and up through the hard-packed muddy fields. Gunny pushed the door of her house open and stepped inside. The dark, smoky room seemed much smaller than she remembered. Eileen, Maeve, and Michael turned from their stools in front of the fire to greet her.

After a supper of boiled potatoes and dried fish, the family walked into the village for Mass. They passed The McCrohans' pew on the way to their pew near the front of the church. Matt sat in his father's old place next to Kate. Mac and the girls filled the rest of the pew. Gunny gave them a wave but didn't stop to talk. She sat between her parents and straightened her clean skirt. She glanced back to see if Matt had noticed her, but he was deep in conversation with his mother. Eileen patted her leg to turn around.

As they stood to leave, Gunny was the topic of many comments.

"Look at you. Haven't you gotten so tall!" Bitsy Kavanaugh exclaimed. "And you've filled out so nicely."

"Doesn't she look wonderful in that clean apron and cap," Cate Mitchell said pressing her elbow hard in Eileen's ribs.

Gunny was embarrassed by the attention she might have enjoyed some other year.

Father Jessey looked her up and down as she passed him leaving the church. "How is it that you thrive even when you are being punished?" he asked in a low voice.

Gunny smiled. "One girl's punishment is another's girl's fun," she said in a soft voice, giving the startled Father a wink.

After their evening meal on Christmas day, Gunny walked down to the McCrohans' with her father. The house was as crowded as it had been before John McCrohan had died. She spied Matt in the back room talking to the Burke twins. Father Jessey sat near the fire so there was no dancing, no drinking, no stories. Cornelius tried to talk to her but she found his fishing stories boring. She asked her da if they could make an early evening of it.

At home, she informed him that she would go back to Dingle the next morning. "I didn't give James his Christmas present before I left," she explained.

In truth, Dunquin was dull and quiet after her time in Dingle. She missed James and her work in the shop and her walks about town. She even missed the squeaky bed and tiny window of her cool attic bedroom. And what if

Daniel needed her for another delivery to Ballygoleen? And she hated seeing Matt in Dunquin. In Dingle, she had him to herself—away from family, neighbors, and friends, and away from the prying eyes of the priest. Dingle felt more like home now than Dunquin.

~ **Chapter 7: Love** ~

It was a crisp February morning when Gunny saw Matt again. He and Mac walked into the Murphy's to the familiar jingle of bells. She greeted them as she did all of her other customers. "What can I help you with today?"

Matt matched her formality. "We are outfitting the curragh for the spring and need a new fishing net," he said looking Gunny squarely in the eye.

Mac looked down at the tops of his dusty boots. He did not like seeing Gunny with her hair neatly pulled back in a bun and a cap on her head. He liked her better the old way.

Daniel walked up to the boys. "I can help you with fishing gear. Gunny, why don't you help Mrs. O'Shea with her dry goods?"

Gunny nodded at Daniel and scooted out from behind the counter.

Matt raised his eyebrows as she passed him. "Maybe we'll stop in and see you after we get the new nets down to the boat."

"Maybe you will," Gunny muttered back.

Mac pulled Matt by the arm toward the back of the shop. "We have three orders at the forge that I promised would be done by tomorrow. You said we wouldn't be long."

"Mac," Matt said pulling his arm away. "People will wait for your excellent work. Why don't we stay here and enjoy ourselves? I hear the Dingle Pub has fine fare," he added in a loud voice.

Mac scoffed. "Plenty of porter is more like it. Stay if you want. You can take the boat back by yourself. I'll walk." He crossed to talk to Daniel at the back counter.

Matt shuffled over to join them and ran a lazy hand over a net Daniel had on display. He turned to Mac. "Don't you ever want to have fun?"

"I have fun," Mac said solemnly.

"When?"

"When I'm working at the forge."

"I believe you. When you pump those bellows, it's as if your own breath stirs the fire," Matt said in disgust. He leaned back against the counter and watched Gunny as she scooped crackers from a large barrel into Mrs. O'Shea's bag. "You should see what Mac is working on," he said loudly. "He has the most elaborate designs in place for an iron gate."

Gunny grimaced at Matt and smiled at Mrs. O'Shea.

"I'm telling you," he continued, "the details are tremendous. I could never make gates like these. Of course, I don't know who'll ever buy such finery. Maybe Mac has a secret deal with Lord Ventry...," he finished with a smile.

"Matt," Mac said louder than his brother. "Gunny doesn't want to hear about my iron work."

Matt turned to Mac. "You're right. No one does. I'll race you to the pier. Last one to the boat helps mother with the evening meal." He turned and yanked the door open to a jangle of bells, and sprinted out down Green Street.

Everyone stared after him. Mac cleared his throat. "Thank you with your help with the net, Mr. Murphy," he said standing to his full height and sliding a few coins to Daniel. He awkwardly collected the pile of netting and followed after his brother, pulling the door gently closed behind him. The store seemed particularly quiet in Matt's wake.

"I like Mac," James said from his stool by the fire, carefully folding his newspaper in half and resting it on one knee.

Gunny laughed as she showed Mrs. O'Shea out of the shop. "I thought you were busy reading."

"Who can read with all that racket?" James said, quietly drumming the folded paper against his leg. "Matt is all fire and brimstone. Mac is more like water. Smooth on top and deep below."

She pulled up a stool next to the boy. "I think that Matt is fun and that Mac is a grumpy old man."

James opened his paper and scanned the headlines. "That's one way to look at it, Gunny."

"Hey, you."

Gunny had just walked the cows into the shed when Matt appeared in the doorway behind her. She hadn't seen him for a month or so. She turned and smiled. It was late afternoon and the air in the shed felt tight. "What're you doing in Dingle at this hour?" she asked.

Matt grinned from ear to ear. "I was fishing in the harbor. Come out to the boat with me. It's a moonless night. I want to show you something."

"I can't. The Murphys will wonder where I am."

"It's early. The sun's only now going down. This won't take long. I promise."

Gunny looked at Matt's excited face. "This had better be good."

She secured the cows in their stalls and followed Matt out of the shed and onto Main Street. He hurried down Green Street, out to the Strand, and onto the Dingle pier with Gunny following a few steps behind. There were a few fishermen talking near their boats. They nodded at her as she passed. Her boots echoed on the planks of the wooden pier as they neared the boat.

Matt's little curragh was tied up at the end of the pier. He held out a hand, and she climbed in and took a seat on the rear bench. Matt hopped onto the center seat and grabbed the oars. "Untie that rope behind you," he directed.

Gunny flipped the rope off a piling, and Matt pushed off from the pier. "Twenty minutes," he said as he rowed out into the harbor. "That's all I need. You have to see this."

He rowed out toward the center of Dingle Harbor as the sun slipped down in the western sky. There was no wind and no noise except for the quiet sound of rowing. Matt stopped and slid the oars into their locks. They turned and watched as the sun moved closer to the ocean, hot and red, the surrounding clouds lit with fire.

"Beautiful," Gunny muttered.

"Wait," Matt said. "There's more. Look." He took out an oar and spun the boat to face east as an enormous, orange moon rose across the bay. Gunny's breath caught in her throat.

"It doesn't happen often—the sun setting as a full moon rises."

Gunny felt the earth stop. She looked back as the sun flattened, then disappeared into the ocean. She looked back behind her as the moon lifted above the mountains and turned silver.

Matt scooted down into the bottom of the boat between the center and back seat, bunched up his jacket to put behind him, and pulled Gunny down next to him.

She straightened her skirt and apron and leaned back against Matt's jacket. There was no sound but water lapping gently at the boat and their own steady breathing. Gunny watched as the moon rose in the sky and one by one, the stars blinked on, then appeared in clusters, then in sweeping arrays around the glowing orb.

"We spend so much time looking down. We don't look up enough," Matt whispered near her ear.

Gunny breathed deeply, her mind floating. She felt Matt's warm body along her left side. She reached down and took his hand. It was rough and warm. He squeezed her hand as they lay together in the quiet harbor. Watching. Breathing.

By the time Matt walked Gunny back to the shop, the Murphys had already eaten and had gone to bed. Gunny glanced guiltily at the pot of cold potatoes Joanna left out for her. "Care for a bite before you row back to Dunquin under that full moon?"

Matt grabbed a spoon and scooped a large mouthful of potato from the pot.

"Be civilized!" Gunny said. "I'll put them on a plate."

"Why dirty a plate?" Matt asked talking through a mouthful of potatoes.

Gunny laughed and took up a spoon. "Fine," she said, stuffing her mouth. "That's one less plate I have to wash."

"You have to be practical in this lifetime," Matt said, swallowing a last bite and wiping a dribble of potato from his lip with the back of his hand.

Gunny rinsed the pot and spoons with well water while Matt moved to a stool in front of the fire. He pulled a plug of tobacco from his pocket and cut off a short piece. He stuffed it into the pipe and picked up a live coal from the fire, then sucked air through the pipe until the tobacco lit. Gunny pulled up a stool and sat near him. He closed his eyes and slowly let smoke trickle out of his mouth. Tender wisps curled up around his lips and wove their way up through his hair.

"It looks like you're made of smoke," she said.

Matt opened his eyes. "Try it. You might like it," he said handing her the pipe.

Gunny eyed the small white pipe, then reached over and took it from Matt. All her life she had watched her father enjoy a smoke by the fire. The clay pipe felt warm and smooth in her hands.

"Don't breathe the smoke in," Matt said. "Let it fill your mouth, then let it out."

Gunny held the stem to her mouth and gently sucked in while Matt held a fresh coal over the bowl. She tried to do as Matt had instructed but couldn't help but breathe in. She felt her lungs clutch. She thrust the pipe at Matt and coughed until her throat was raw.

Matt laughed. "I did the same thing my first time. Try again," he said knocking out the spent ash and reloading the pipe with fresh tobacco.

Gunny waved her hands in front of her face and continued to cough.

"Fine. That leaves all the more for me," Matt said as he lit the second bowl.

Gunny finally stopped coughing and caught her breath. Tears were running down her cheeks. "That is an evil weed you are smoking," she said with a hoarse rasp.

Matt raised his eyebrows and let out another slow mouthful of smoke. His face looked like it was on fire. "Evil is as evil does," he said looking into the bowl of the pipe with his mysterious green eyes.

Business was slow and Joanna left Gunny to close up the shop while Daniel was off making one last delivery for the day. The bells above the door jangled and a stranger walked in. He was small with a thin face and a few ragged patches of hair on his chin. His forehead was damp with sweat beneath a greasy hat.

"Good evening, sir," Gunny said from behind the counter. "We're just closing up."

The man stared at her, a vacant look in his eye. "Whiskey," he muttered.

Gunny hesitated, then pulled a jug of whiskey from the shelf under the counter. She poured a short glass and handed it to the man. When he took it, his hand was shaking so badly he could barely get the glass up to his lips. He laid a coin on the counter and turned to leave. He passed Daniel on his way out but did not seem to see him.

Daniel stepped to the side, then closed and bolted the door behind the man. "I thought he left town."

"Who was that? I've never seen him before."

"His name is Edmond Moore. He's the son of Small Tom. He used to be a merchant here in town. He married a successful merchant's daughter from Tralee but then he got to drinking. From the looks of him, it doesn't look like he'll be with us much longer. God knows what has happened to his wife and children."

The next morning, Gunny went out to the cow shed and there lay Edmond Moore. He had passed out in the hay and had apparently been lying on the ground all night. Gunny tried to help him sit up, but his body was stiff and cold. She remembered the tale of Father Begley's departure from this life and hurried inside to find Daniel who in turn hurried to get the sheriff. The sheriff's men hauled the body away but could find no kin to bury Edmond Moore. Father Owen stopped by later in the day and said a prayer over the doorway where Gunny had found the stranger.

"They'll bury him in the pauper's grave behind the church," he told Gunny.

Gunny remembered the stories that friends and neighbors had told at John McCrohan's and Father Begley's wakes, and the long line that followed their caskets through town. It was hard to believe someone could die, alone in the night, and not have anyone around to say good-bye.

Gunny couldn't sleep. The cold spring weather had turned into an unusually hot and muggy May and Gunny was restless. She quietly descended the stairs, stirred the fire, and put on a kettle of water for tea. While she was waiting for the water to boil, she sensed something move behind her. She turned and saw an elderly woman descending the stairs toward the kitchen. The woman smiled at her. Gunny blinked, and the woman was gone. Gunny's heart raced. She had heard of ghosts, but this woman was real—at least until she disappeared.

Gunny swallowed hard and pulled the kettle away from the fire. She smoored the fire with ashes and tried to calm her breathing. When she turned and stepped onto the stairs to go to her room, she felt a chill around her and raced up the two flights of stairs. She tried to sleep but could not warm up under the covers. The image of the old woman smiling at her would not leave her head.

Joanna noticed rings under Gunny's eyes the next morning. "Did you have trouble sleeping? It was hot last night," Joanna started before Gunny interrupted her.

"I saw a ghost," Gunny blurted. "I came down to make a cup of tea and there was an old woman coming down the stairs. Then she disappeared."

Joanna's face went pale. "What did she look like?"

"She was old," Gunny repeated.

"I heard that part."

Gunny tried to remember more about the woman. "She was small. And she had grey hair pulled back tight on her head. And she smiled at me—which I thought was odd for a ghost, don't you think?"

"It's not odd if it is who I think it is," Joanna said.

"You know her?" Gunny asked.

"Did you happen to see the color of her eyes?" Joanna asked.

Gunny thought back. "No, it was dark. I don't remember her eyes. I remember she had a funny little stoop, like her right shoulder was higher than her left."

Joanna clapped her hands. "You saw my grandmother!"

"What was your grandmother doing here in the kitchen?"

"She died in this kitchen. She visits from time to time."

"You've seen her ghost?"

"No, I've never seen it. But Jamie's seen her several times."

"Why do you suppose she was back?"

"You said you were making tea. Grandmother loved tea. She drank it hot, weak, and sweet. She would drink it by the pot full. My grandfather used to say he had to open the shop here to buy enough tea to keep my grandmother happy."

"If I see your grandmother again, I'll not panic," Gunny said. "And if it's tea she's after, I'll offer her a cup—hot, weak, and sweet—the same way I like it."

It was late summer. Gunny was pulling bricks of light peat out of the turf house when Matt thundered into town on Nella and stopped in front of the store.

"Riding along as carefully as usual," Gunny said without looking up from her work.

"How'd you know it was me?" Matt yelled.

Gunny turned from the turf house and kicked the door closed with her foot. She eyed the steaming horse and Matt's flush face. "No one else rides like you, Matt," she said with a laugh.

"I'm sure I made record time getting here from Dunquin," he blurted. "Have you seen the Burke twins?"

"No," she said walking past Matt and Nella toward the shop door.

"I beat them! I knew it," he said swinging down from the saddle and pulling Nella along behind him. He looped the horse's reins over the hitch in front of the shop. "We made a bet. First to town wins the race for the bottle." He wiped his brow on his sleeve. "I could use a drink to celebrate."

"It's not yet midday, Matt," Gunny said pausing at the shop door. "Would you mind getting that door for me?"

Matt blushed. "Sorry about that." He opened the door to the tinkle of bells and followed Gunny inside. "I meant a drink of water," he said innocently following Gunny across the shop floor. "What'd you take me for? A lush?"

Gunny shook her head, nodded to Joanna who was working at the front counter, and continued through the shop into the house. "Come out to the well. I'll pull you a fresh dipper."

Matt opened the door to the kitchen and followed Gunny into the house. He watched her from behind as she dumped her load of turf near the fire.

"You should come out for a ride, Gunny. Let's go up to the Shamrock Cliff and look down at Dingle. You'd like the view."

"That may be true," Gunny said brushing loose turf off her shirt and dusting her hands on her apron. "But I have chores to do, butter to churn, deliveries to make."

Matt pulled out a kitchen chair and sat. He grabbed Gunny's hand and pulled her onto his lap. She lingered for a few seconds, then stood up and straightened her skirt.

"How is it you have so much time to dally?"

Matt shrugged and picked at a fingernail. "Mac has everything in order at the forge. Listen," he said looking up eagerly at Gunny's face. "If you don't have all day, then let's go for a short ride to the ocean."

"I told you I have to work."

"It's the fifteenth of August, the Assumption. The Murphys'll let you go if you say you're going on a pattern to a shrine of the Blessed Virgin Mary. It worked last year."

Gunny looked at Matt's handsome face and broad grin. She smiled. "I can't say that if it's not true. There must be a hot spot in hell for people who lie about the Virgin Mary."

"Then we'll make it true," Matt said, standing and grabbing both of Gunny's hands. "We'll go to a holy well in Dingle, say our devotions, then ride to the strand at Ventry and swim."

Gunny felt herself wavering. She hadn't had a day off all summer.

Matt waited with Nella by the turf house while Gunny went inside to ask Joanna if she could take the afternoon off. Joanna was happy to have Gunny go out with someone her own age. Gunny had spent most of the summer working or entertaining Jamie. Joanna had also heard rumors that Gunny had spent time with Lord Thomas Milliken. It was better for the girl to be with her own age and her own kind.

"Are you sure you'll be all right without me?" Gunny asked.

"We'll get along, Gunny. Somehow we got along without you before," Joanna assured the happy teen.

Gunny raced to the kitchen. She cut two thick slices of oat bread, buttered them, and wrapped them in a large sheet of brown paper. She slid the packet into her apron pocket and raced out the back door to find Matt. As she swung up into the saddle behind him, she saw James and Joanna watching her from

153

the kitchen window. She gave them a short wave as Matt pulled on the reins and thundered off down the street.

"He rides too fast," James said to his mother.

Joanna stared after the departing couple. "Some people are meant to live more daring lives than others, Jamie."

Gunny and Matt made three quick rounds at the well at St. James on Main Street then took off for the shore. Gunny liked the way the horse moved beneath her and the way Matt felt in front of her as she held him tight in front of her with both arms. Matt seemed to barely touch the saddle as he rode. The air rushed past, cooling her face against the hot August sun. They raced to Ventry and down toward a deserted cove near the end of the strand.

"Ready for a splash?"

"Don't ride into the surf," Gunny yelled. "My dress will get wet!"

"Who cares about your dress?"

"I do!"

"I don't," Matt laughed, spurring Nella on toward the water.

"What about the bread?" Gunny yelled, squeezing Matt hard around the middle.

"Now bread is worth saving," he said, steering Nella deftly onto dry sand just before they hit the surf. He slid from the saddle and held out a hand to Gunny.

Gunny pushed her hair back from her face. Her hands were shaking slightly from the fast ride. She took a short breath and slid off the horse without taking Matt's hand. "Don't act like you are a gentleman when we both know you're not." She walked off toward the rocks. "I'm going to eat my slice of bread and watch the ocean. It's a gorgeous day."

Matt followed her. "I'll sit with you."

"You scared me on that horse. Why don't you go find some trouble for yourself while I catch my breath?"

"And what if I'd rather find some trouble right here while you catch your breath?"

Gunny climbed onto a high, dry rock and pulled the bread packet from her pocket. She opened the paper and peeled the two bread slices apart. She handed one to Matt. "Here. There's enough butter on that to keep you quiet for a moment anyway."

Matt grabbed his slice and sat on a rock near Gunny. Green waves trimmed with white foam rolled onto the beach in uneven patterns ahead of them.

"I'm hot. It's time to swim." Matt said, licking a bit of butter from one finger and pulling off his shirt and pants. "Keep an eye on these," he said throwing his clothes to Gunny. He hopped across the rocks, raced into the surf, and dove into the first wave he reached.

Gunny gathered his clothes in her lap and hugged them to her chest. She had seen Matt swim plenty of times as a boy, but his body was different now. She licked her lips and tasted both sweet, cream butter and sea salt. Matt dived through a wave, then jumped up and let the next wave smack him in the back of the neck. He flipped over in the surf and stood on his hands in the water waving his feet at her, then flipped upright and rode a wave to shore. He looked like a dolphin playing in the surf.

He ran back to her perch on the rock, grabbed his shirt and dried his face. She tried to look away from his wet body and felt herself blush.

Matt didn't seem to notice. "The water's cold for the first minute then it's perfect. Come in with me!"

Gunny grinned. "I can't go running around with no clothes on."

"Why not? No one's here."

Gunny shook her head and chuckled. "No doubt I'd have my skirt half way off when Father Jessey would somehow sense my nakedness and would come racing from Dunquin to find us. Then—I'd be condemned to hell," she added dramatically.

Matt pulled his pants on over his large, sandy feet. "So Father Jessey has won? I thought you were more daring. At least tuck up your skirts and we'll go wade into the surf on Nella. My horse needs a dip as much as I did."

Gunny glanced at Nella. The horse was dusty from the ride out and had an eager look in her eye. Gunny wasn't sure she was ready to re-mount the fast steed.

"Come on," Matt pleaded. "It'll be like when we were kids." He stood tall in front of Gunny and reached out one hand. "I am Fionn MacCumhaill, here to steal the French king's wife and run away with her to Ventry." When Gunny hesitated, he grabbed her by the waist and flipped her over his shoulder. She shrieked and tried to wiggle free.

"Put me down!" she yelled as Matt ran with her. "Remember the story of the Fianna ended badly!"

Matt tossed Gunny onto Nella's back and swung up into the saddle behind her. "Hold on."

Gunny swung one leg around to sit upright on the horse and leaned back against Matt's chest. She pulled her skirt up around her in the saddle as they thundered out into the surf.

"Don't sit so stiffly," Matt chided her. "Ride with the rhythm of the horse."

Matt rose in the saddle to show her how just as a rogue wave caught Nella broadside and pushed the two passengers off into the swirling green water. Nella trotted through the surf to shore and looked back impatiently at Matt and Gunny as another wave rolled over them.

Gunny had a moment's flash of the French Queen as she went underwater, then felt hard sand under her feet and pushed up and out of the water. She gasped for air as Matt reached out to grasp her by the waist.

"Are you all right?" he asked, looking with genuine concern at her face and wet head of curls.

Gunny wiped her eyes. She started to answer just as another wave pushed over them. She felt Matt's hands grip her waist under water. She surfaced and pushed him away as the water receded. "You're right. The water is perfect!" She splashed water in his face and dove under the next wave before it could dunk her.

Matt tossed back into the water. "It's the battle of the strand. We'll fight to the finish."

They swam through the waves until Gunny tired from the weight of her sea-soaked clothes and dragged herself to shore.

"So much for the Battle of the Strand," Matt yelled after her. "Are you headed to the Valley of the Mad?"

Gunny looked around behind her. "Are you confusing the Valley of the Mad with the Village of Dingle?"

"That's it," Matt said slapping at the green water and wading to shore. "We're off to the Valley of the Mad, also known as Dingle, to live off of grass and spring water."

Gunny' clothes were so heavy with salt water that Matt had to push her bottom up to get her back onto Nella. Once she was seated, he mounted ahead of her and spurred Nella toward Dingle. The wind blew her tangled curls from her face. She was wet and salty and happy as she hugged Matt's broad, warm back and did her best to rise and fall with the rhythm of the horse as Matt had instructed.

Matt stopped on the way back at the old Dunbeg Fort near Fahan. The Bronze Age fort was set in the hillside overlooking a vast stretch of ocean. Gunny thought about the sister fort buried under Ballygoleen and wondered if it had been similar. Matt tethered Nella as Gunny slid from the saddle. Her damp clothes felt good against the August heat. Matt held her hand as they ducked down a short, low corridor of rough grey rock that lead into the ancient fort. Inside the last wall, a series of rock rings opened up to the sky. The part of the fort near the ocean cliffs had fallen away and the inside rings opened onto rock and surf.

Gunny laid her hands on a thick stone wall and paused.

Matt whispered from beside her. "What're you doing?"

"Feeling the vibrations. These rocks are telling me something," she whispered.

"What are they saying?" Matt whispered back.

"I have no idea. I don't speak rock," Gunny said mischievously.

They sat on the broken rock wall and looked out over the blue green water. White caps stretched to the horizon. Below them, breakers boomed against the rocky shore and bits of foam flew up the cliff past them in updrafts of salty air.

"Nana used to say that the whitecaps were little ships out at sea," Matt said.

"I remember your grandmother."

Matt smiled. "Everything was a joy to her. She used to tell me that someday I'd sail off on one of those whitecap ships."

Gunny glanced at Matt from the corner of her eye. "So you want to sail away? Leave everything here behind you?"

Matt leaned back against the rocks. "I think about it from time to time. Don't you? You know you'd make a wonderful Pirate Queen."

Gunny squeezed his arm. "Those are children stories, Mat. I'm afraid there isn't much of a call for Pirate Queens these days."

"Still, it might be nice to sail away," Matt said. "To discover new places. Meet new people. Hear new stories. If I built a bigger boat maybe Mac would go with me."

"Only if he could bring his anvil," Gunny said.

Matt laughed. "That might be tricky in a fishing boat. You could go with me," he said reaching over and rubbing Gunny's back. "You and I were made for adventure. I can't see either one of us settling down on some small plot of land, kow-towing to some landlord and planting crops that we have to worry about all summer. And imagine a house full of hungry little mouths to feed. I dread the thought of it."

Gunny leaned forward so Matt couldn't see her face. 'It might be enough,' she thought, looking out to sea. 'If the right person were in that house and if those little mouths had the same round shape as their father's mouth.'

Matt was quiet behind her as he traced a pattern on her back. "What shape did I make?"

"I have no idea," Gunny said with a grin. "Do it again."

Matt traced the same pattern on Gunny's back.

"It was a G," she said. She turned and looked at Matt's face. "Did you make a G for Gunny?"

"No, I made a G for Going. And Gone." Matt stood up and shook out his legs. "We should go."

"Go... to Dingle?" Gunny asked with a smile. "Or go sailing away to the edges of the earth and never come back?" she asked with a broader smile.

Matt sighed. "A man has to be practical, doesn't he? I hear rumor you have work to do. And I have to get home. Mac wants me to make a few deliveries."

"I like the look on your face better when you're dreaming."

"And I think I scare you when I'm dreaming. Mam says I dream too much. Are you ready?"

Gunny took a last look out across the ocean. The sun was dipping in the western sky, and the clouds along the horizon were highlighted with red, orange, and yellow light. She caught a bit of foam in her hand as it flew by on a breath from the sea. What looked like a tiny fairy as it blew past was nothing but a little water and crust when she looked at what she'd caught in her hand. She wiped her hand on her apron and turned to follow Matt. They mounted Nella and rode quietly back to Dingle.

As they walked in the door of the shop, the tinkle of door bells was lost to the sound of scuffling and angry words inside. Matt threw an arm up in front of Gunny to protect her from two young men who were swinging wildly at one another near the front counter. Daniel hurried to separate the two men before anything was broken—dry goods or noses—but the two men continued to swing and shout at one another. Both reeked of whiskey.

Father Owen stepped in between the two fighters and grabbed one swinging arm of each man.

"Stop!" he yelled.

The two men finally grew still, faces flushed, harsh words locked behind inebriated lips. Father Owen sighed and continued without releasing their arms. "It's whiskey that makes you not return home to your wives at night." He tightened his grip. "It's whiskey that makes your homes so poor." He tightened his grip again. "And it's whiskey that makes you shoot at your landlords—and miss!"

He released the two men and they scurried to leave the shop, massaging sore arms and sore egos. Daniel turned to the other customers who had stopped to watch the fight. "All right, everyone, let's call it a night."

The shop cleared of everyone except Daniel, Father Owen, Matt, and Gunny. Daniel pushed the front door of the shop closed while Gunny and Matt straightened items that had been knocked over on two of the nearby shelves.

Father Owen leaned against the front counter. "Would anyone like to share a bit of sweet wine before I go?"

Daniel laughed. "You know I don't have sweet wine, Father, but I do have whiskey."

"Ah, whiskey will have to do then," Father Owen said with a sigh. "But only enough to make the heart happy."

Daniel reached behind the counter and pulled out two glasses and a bottle of whiskey. He poured a few fingers in each glass and handed one to Father Owen. They raised their glasses to toast, and each tossed back a glass. Father Owen gasped and pounded his chest. "That hit the spot."

Gunny giggled at the old priest and gave Matt's hand a quick squeeze.

"I'll walk out with you, Father. I have to get back to Dingle," Matt said to the elderly priest.

Father Owen shook hands with Daniel, tipped his hat to Gunny, and looped his arm through Matt's. They slipped out of the shop door to a tiny jingle of bells.

Daniel turned to Gunny. "You look like you went for a swim in your clothes."

Gunny blushed and started to explain. Daniel held up a hand and smiled. "No need to tell me a thing," he said with a wink. "I was young once, you know."

Early September was as hot as August. Daniel loaded two barrows with supplies and Gunny eyed the load. "How am I to take two barrows to Ballygoleen?" she asked.

"I'm going with you. The Millikens have ordered baking goods and meat today."

"Sounds like someone is having a party," Gunny said.

"A party?" Daniel asked amazed. "Didn't you hear? Lord Thomas Milliken is getting married. The wedding is two days from now."

Gunny's breath caught in her throat and her eyes opened wide. "Thomas is getting married?" she asked, her voice wavering. "He didn't tell me."

Daniel looked at Gunny stricken face. "I didn't know that you and the Lord were on a first-name basis."

Gunny blushed. "We're not, of course," she stammered. "He's a Lord and I... only talked with him a few times when I was making deliveries to Ballygoleen."

Daniel finished loading a final sack of flour in a barrow. "Rumor has it that his bride is from a rich family in Galway, that she's the daughter of an eleventh Baron or something like that." Daniel patted the full barrows. "This bit of business will make our month. We'll be in fine shape as we head into harvest sales."

"Harvest sales," Gunny said, her mind a million miles away.

"Are you all right, Gunny?" Daniel asked.

Gunny smiled. "It's funny about people, isn't it? You think you know them, but you don't. I wonder if you ever really know anyone."

That night when she returned from making the delivery, she pulled Thomas' carefully folded hanky from under her mattress, crept downstairs to the kitchen, and tossed it into the low peat fire. She watched as the embroidered initials smoldered, then caught fire, and finally turned to ash.

Gunny washed her face in the basin of water on the small table by her window, and dried her face and hands on her hand cloth. She descended the two flights of stairs to the kitchen and took a brick of peat from along the side wall. After a long, hot summer, the weather had turned cold and wet and the house felt damp. Gunny added a few bog timbers to the fire and fanned the flames, then put a kettle of water on the crane to heat. When she heard the water bubbling, she added a few scoops of tea to the pot and pulled the crane to the side of the fire to keep the tea warm. The smell was delicious. She paused for a moment to say a prayer for Joanna's Nana, then took up the broom and started to sweep the hearth. Even after more than a year in Dingle it still felt luxurious to have a long handled broom. Her broom in Dunquin was made from a few hands-full of heather tied together with a bit of rope.

James came into the kitchen, stretching and yawning. He was dressed in a white shirt, a short tie, long pants, and shoes.

"Good morning, James."

"Morning, Gunny."

"Would you like some toasted bread this morning?"

"Could I have a few eggs as well?"

"A few eggs? You're growing fast, James. I've never seen you eat so much as you have this fall. Soon you'll be as tall as your Da."

James smiled.

Gunny cut two thick slices of oat bread and set them in front of the fire on toasters, then headed out to the yard. The rain had let up, but it was still drizzling in the muddy yard. Gunny pulled off her apron and held it over her head while she felt around in the regular roosting spots for eggs. She found two eggs near a hay-pile by the back door and another one near some dried grass by the door stoop.

She hurried inside, took out the iron skillet, and scooped a spoonful of freshly churned butter from a firkin into the pan. While the eggs cooked, she turned the bread on the little wooden stands in front of the fire so that the second side of the bread browned. She slid the cooked eggs onto a plate and slathered each bread slice with sweet butter. She pulled out two spoons, and she and James shared the eggs on the plate. James ate both pieces of the toasted, buttered bread.

"Gunny, you are the best cook ever. You hardly ever burn anything anymore."

Gunny wiped her mouth on her napkin and frowned. "It doesn't take much to cook eggs and toasted bread." Inside she smiled. She liked the feeling of being appreciated and glowed at James' praise. "You should hurry or you'll be late."

James had announced in late August that he was ready to join the other children at school. Each day when he got home, he explained to Gunny what he had learned, and who had said what. Nothing slipped past him. There was the girl who was always adjusting her petticoats. And the teacher who scratched his head when he wasn't sure of an answer. Over their morning meal, James told her about a shy boy in his class who talked with a slight lisp.

"You should be a writer, James. You're much more observant than most."

James smiled. "I'll think about it." He watched as she cleaned up from the morning meal. "But I don't think I'll go to school today. I don't like it when my face gets wet in the rain."

Gunny frowned. Joanna was at the milk market with Daniel and she had promised to get James off to school. "You don't want to be at the shop on a soft day, James. The farmers won't be able to work in this rain. They'll be here all day crowding in around the fire, sipping at whiskey and not buying a thing."

"You'll hear good stories," James said.

"I'll tell them to you tonight." She handed James his hat and gently pushed him out the door.

Gunny's second fall in Dingle was as busy as the first, but business was slow in the weeks leading up to the Christmas Market. Joanna sat in the sill of the front window and looked across the street. "Everyone's shopping at Packy Dollan's this year."

Daniel joined his wife at the window and shook his head. "The harvest was light. Only a few farmers have money this season. It's hard to compete with Packy's pricing—or with his credit terms."

"How can he sell the same items we do for so much less?" Gunny asked. She had been over to see Packy Dollan's shop. There were no shelves, only barrels and boxes stacked randomly around the shop. Everything was covered in a fine coating of dust. James would not approve.

Daniel sighed. "Packy is under-pricing us and selling to the farmers on credit. He'll lose money now, but if and when a farmer defaults on a loan, Packy'll take their whole farm or all of their livestock. That's when he makes his money."

"He's called a Gombeen man, Gunny. Don't ever deal with the likes of him," Joanna added.

"If we can't compete with price, what if we try something else?" Gunny asked.

Daniel turned to Gunny. "What do you have in mind?"

"Well," Gunny said walking away from the window and wiping her hands on her apron. "James is always reminding me how important it is to have something unique in the front window of the shop."

Joanna and Daniel turned and looked at their son who was sitting on a stool near the woodstove at the back of the shop reading a book.

"Jamie reminds you of that?" Daniel asked.

"Oh, yes," Gunny continued. "James is always reminding me to keep the glass sparkling clean and to have something new on display in the front window."

"I thought that was your idea," Joanna said to Gunny.

"I do the work," Gunny said, "but James is the one with the ideas."

Joanna and Daniel looked quizzically at their son. He looked up from his book and shrugged his shoulders.

"So I, we, thought this year for Christmas that maybe we could create a little snow scene in the front window. Everyone loves it when it snows at Christmas. I was thinking I could set up a couple of little furze bushes and dust them with flour to look like snow. Then we could add red ribbons to brighten the scene," Gunny said. "I've noticed we sell a lot of red ribbons this time of year."

"We do," Joanna said.

"And James thought we could tie little sweets on the bushes. Everyone likes sweets for the holidays," Gunny continued. "I thought I could twist some very fine rope to loop on the trees as garlands, and I could make little stars of straw to hang over the scene."

James closed his book and cleared his throat. "Don't forget the finishing touch."

"What's that, James?" Gunny asked.

"Candles," he said, opening his book again to continue reading.

"Candles! Of course. James is a genius. What's more beautiful than candles burning in every window along the street at Christmas? When the shop is closed for the night, the candles from our little snow scene will glow. Everyone who passes by on the way to the Dingle Pub won't be able to resist stopping for a look."

"Gunny and Jamie, you have my blessing," Daniel said. "Just don't make too much of a mess. And don't catch the shop on fire," he added.

Gunny was excited. She grabbed James' book from him and placed it on the counter. "I'll collect the furze bushes. Can you clear the window so we have a place to build when I get back?"

"You want me to help?" James asked. "I thought I was the one with the ideas and you did the work?"

Gunny smiled. "I need your help. Can you find a few candles and ribbons too? And don't forget that we need flour."

"I can help," Joanna said.

"No, Mother," James said. "Gunny and I are going to work on the window."

Gunny clapped her hands. "I'm off to collect some furze." She grabbed her shawl and sprinted up the street toward the cow field with visions of the perfect Christmas scene forming in her mind.

The next morning, a crowd stood outside the shop talking about James' and Gunny's winter scene. Joanna peeked out the window. "The only trouble is no one is coming into the shop," she said to Gunny.

Gunny opened the shop door with a jingle and greeted the crowd. "Come inside and warm up," she said with a grin.

Mrs. McCallister looked at Gunny's bright face and glanced at the front window. "Maybe you have an idea for my daughter," she said. "She is so hard to shop for. A red ribbon may be just the thing."

Mr. Hansel walked into the shop behind Mrs. McCallister. "That roping in the window reminds me that my father could use a new fishing net."

Soon business was as busy as it had been the year before. Gunny and James straightened the front display each afternoon taking some things out and adding something new. And each night they lit the candles.

"This window tells a story," James said, as he sat with Gunny twisting fresh stars to hang in the window. "That's why people like it."

"James, I know I've told you this before," Gunny said, "but you are one of the smartest people I've ever met."

Robert came to the shop to walk Gunny home on Christmas Eve. He brought Shep with him and the dog danced and yipped around Gunny's legs while Robert picked out a few Christmas gifts for the family.

Business was brisk and it was early evening before Gunny could get away. She finally said her good-byes to the Murphys and sprinted out of the shop with her father. Robert and Shep could hardly keep up with her on the walk home. She had a bounce in her step and talked a mile a minute. She excitedly told Robert about the Christmas windows and about how busy they had been after facing the challenge of Packy Dollan. She did not tell him about the sweets she had picked out for her mother and the flask of whiskey for him— she wanted to have a few surprises. She was also carrying a new blanket for Michael and Maeve she had purchased with her butter money, and had a secret gift for Matt in her apron pocket.

They arrived in Dunquin just in time for Christmas Eve Mass. Shep waited outside the church while Gunny and Robert slipped into the pew next to Eileen, Michael, and Maeve. Gunny grimaced seeing Father Jessey, but his words floated past her. At the end of Mass, she walked with her family to the back of the church, and lingered, awkwardly, near the door.

"Go on without me," she told her family. "I want to talk to the McCrohans for a minute." Robert gathered Gunny's bundles from Dingle and headed outside.

"Don't be long," Eileen said, patting Gunny on the cheek. "Christmas is a time for family."

Maeve sniffed and gave Gunny a knowing look as she looped her arm through Michael's. Gunny reminded herself that she would only be home for a day or two and smiled at the heavy girl as she waddled past her and exited the church.

She caught Matt's eye as he walked toward the church doors with his family. He gave her a wink then leaned down and whispered to his mother.

Kate McCrohan looked over at Gunny and mouthed "Merry Christmas." Mac gave her a nod then left with Kate and the girls.

Matt walked over and held out his hand. "Miss Malone?"

Gunny held out her hand and Matt gave it a warm squeeze. Father Jessey looked over and eyed them critically. "Wait for me at the old graveyard," Matt whispered near her ear, then crossed to Father Jessey to distract him.

Gunny slipped out the wide front doors and waded through the tall grasses into the quiet of the old graveyard. Dim light from the candle-lit church windows reflected off the rough gravestones. A few of the stones had tipped over and lay face-down on the ground. Others tilted left and right, their faces covered in thin layers of black lichen. The edges of a few stone boxes stuck out randomly through patches of dry winter grass.

Gunny felt her way through the scattered stones toward the darkest corner of the yard. She felt a chill and pulled her shawl tight around her as she waited. She was relieved when she heard Matt whistle near the church door.

"Over here," she called quietly.

Matt joined her and wrapped his arms around her. "You're freezing. Do you want my coat?"

"I'm not cold. It's the graveyard that's making me shiver," she said nestling in close to Matt's warm body.

"Sorry, I couldn't think of another spot close by."

"I can't stay long," she said. "My parents'll worry. But I wanted to see you."

"I know. I wanted to see you too. I don't like it that I can't ride up and sweep you off your feet like I can in Dingle."

Gunny looked up as a few flakes of snow landed on her long eye lashes. "It's snowing."

Matt looked up. "The churchyard will soon look as magical as your display window at the Murphys'."

Gunny smiled. She wanted to freeze this moment in time, but instead she shivered. Matt noticed. "Let me warm you up." He slid her arms under his coat and hugged her tight.

She loved feeling the heat of his body against hers. "Thank you, Mr. McCrohan. That's much better."

"My pleasure, Miss Malone." He paused looking at her face in the scattered candlelight of the church window. "You know someday you'll be Mrs. McCrohan."

"Don't tease me. I'm too young to marry." Gunny said.

"I'm not teasing. Ashling married last Shrove."

"What?" Gunny said. She had not heard.

"To Cornelius. They're expecting a baby. I saw her last week at O'Leary's. She's as big as a house."

Gunny tried to imagine Ashling and Cornelius married—and Ashling with a huge belly. "Just because she's married doesn't mean I'll marry anytime soon."

"But you could. You're seventeen and I'll be twenty next week. We're plenty old enough to wed."

Gunny laughed and snuggled in closer. "Wed? I thought you were going to sail away with Mac and his anvil, remember? And you know I don't have a choice about who I marry."

"We all have choices," he said leaning in close to her face and kissing her firmly on the mouth.

Warmth flowed through her body. She tightened her arms around him, then pulled away and took a deep breath. "I should head home. Mam will worry."

Matt reluctantly broke the embrace. Gunny looped her arm through his and they stepped around the rough grave stones and walked out through the tall church gates. Shep was waiting on the road just past the gates. Gunny knelt and patted his head.

"Were you waiting for me, boy?"

Shep gave a yip and set off at a fast trot up the road toward the Malones'. Matt grabbed Gunny's hand, and they walked up the deserted dirt road as gentle flakes of snow fell around them.

"Mam has her heart set on me marrying someone from Ventry," Gunny tossed out. "She was talking about it earlier tonight. She said that Father Jessey approved of her choice."

"Your Mam is crazy and that priest has no right to get involved in your life. I'll talk to your Da. He knows what's right."

Gunny laughed. "Da may know what's right, but he's never been one to argue with Mam about matters of the house. There are some fights a man knows he can't win."

Matt stopped Gunny just outside her yard and pulled her once again to his chest. "Promise me you won't marry anyone but me."

Gunny mimicked Matt's low voice. "I won't marry anyone but you."

Matt shook his head. "I wish you could be serious for one minute."

"Said the man who rode me off a horse into the ocean."

"That was fun, you have to admit it!"

Gunny pulled away, looked into Matt's warm, green eyes, and brushed a few flakes of snow from her thick eyelashes. "You're my best friend, Matt. But I won't make a promise I can't keep." She raised her eyebrows, gave him a quick kiss on the cheek, and went inside.

Shep sat in the yard staring at Matt. He tried to pet the dog but Shep shied away. Matt shook his head and left. When he was finally out of the yard, Shep scratched at the door to be let inside.

Matt trotted down through the fields and walked in his house just in time for a holiday toast by his mother. He tossed his jacket on a stool and a small package fell to the floor.

"What's that," Kate asked.

"I have no idea," Matt said, kneeling and retrieving the small bundle. He pulled off the string and pushed the paper away. Inside was a fresh new white pipe.

"A present from a friend?" Kate asked.

"More than a friend, Mam. I just need for her to figure that out."

~ Chapter 8: Shrovetide ~

Life returned to normal after Christmas. James went back to school and Gunny puttered about the shop and house, helping sell, cook, clean, churn, twist, and mend. Joanna and Daniel now trusted Gunny to watch over everything from food preparation to James' education to counting inventory in the store.

On a late January afternoon, Gunny was alone in the shop. Daniel was making a delivery and Joanna was with James buying salt down at the docks. Gunny finished straightening the shelves and went to bolt the door when the knob turned in her hand and a middle-aged man pushed his way inside.

"I'm sorry, Mr. Carlson," she said, startled. "I'm closing up. Perhaps you could come back tomorrow." If it had been someone at the door that Gunny liked she wouldn't have objected, but she didn't like Mr. Carlson and was happy to ask him to shop another time.

The thin man stared at her and pushed his cap back on his greasy face. "The door wasn't locked so you're not closed," he announced loudly.

"I was just locking it when you pushed your way in. Please come back tomorrow when the Murphys are here."

"I don't want a drink tomorrow. I want a drink now. And we don't need the Murphy's for that, do we?" He pushed the door closed to a loud jangle of bells and looked around the shop. "Seems we're the only ones here. Good. I have your full attention." He leaned in close and she could smell whiskey on his breath. "Be a good girl and pour me a glass." She took a step toward the doorway to the house. He grabbed her from behind and spun her around.

"Where are you going, girl? The whiskey's over there, behind the counter." He held out a few coins. "I'm not trying to cheat you."

"It's just that we are closed, and ..." Gunny turned again toward the house door.

Mr. Carlson gripped her tighter this time around her waist and pushed himself hard against her back. "It's been a long time since I've smelled a woman's hair," he mumbled.

Gunny tried to unclasp his hands from her middle but his grip was tight. He breathed into her ear and she felt the hairs rise on the back of her neck.

"You're a working girl. Maybe you want to earn a few extra coins."

Gunny took a deep breath and thrust an elbow hard into his ribs. He gasped and stumbled back. "How dare you push me away like that?"

"And how dare you hold me like that—and insult me," Gunny hissed at him.

Mr. Carlson took a step forward and slapped Gunny hard across the right cheek. "I never said anything improper to you. And if you say I did, I'll swear you're lying and you'll lose your job."

Gunny rubbed at her cheek, then turned and grabbed a small white pipe like the one she had given Matt from a nearby shelf. She cupped the bowl in the palm of her hand, cracked the stem that was protruding between her fingers against the counter, and punched Mr. Carlson solidly in the right cheek. The broken stem of the pipe slashed a deep cut in his cheek. Blood flowed down his face. He howled and grabbed at his stinging cheek, staggering back against a full shelf. A glass lantern fell to the floor and shattered.

"What did you do that for?" he cried, clutching at his cheek.

Gunny's voice trembled. She dropped the bloody pipe to the floor and shook the pain out of her hand. "Mr. Carlson. I'd like you to leave. Now."

"I'll leave when I am bloody ready to leave," he spat, his eyes glaring red.

The bells jingled above the door. "Hey, Gunny, I..." Matt stopped and surveyed the scene.

Mr. Carlson hurried to the door, one hand covering his slashed cheek. "She'll pay for this," he said as he passed Matt. "I'll... I'll..." he muttered, then pushed Matt out of his way and left the shop.

Gunny ran and slammed the door behind him, then pushed the bolt closed with shaking hands. The little bells jingled above her. She turned to Matt and he pulled her close. She sobbed against his worn jacket.

"That's enough of this," he said.

Gunny looked up at Matt's face and tried to stop the flow of tears. "I'm sorry you had to see that bit of nonsense."

Matt pulled her tight against him. "Bit of nonsense? We have to make this right. It's time for you to come home."

The front door rattled against the bolt. Gunny clung to Matt. "He's back," she whispered.

Matt held Gunny away from him. "Go into the house and lock the door. I'll deal with him, man to man."

"No, Matt," Gunny pleaded. "He's drunk and angry and I hurt him."

The door shook again. "Gunny," a man yelled from outside the shop, moving to the window and peering inside. "The door is bolted."

"It's Daniel," Gunny said, moving past Matt and sliding the bolt open.

Daniel stepped into the shop and looked at Gunny's tear-streaked face and at the mess of glass, broken lantern, and blood on the floor. "What happened?"

Gunny wiped her face on her sleeve and tried to straighten her apron. "Everything's fine. I had a problem with a customer but then Matt came along..."

Daniel picked up the bloody pipe from the floor.

"I owe you money for that," Gunny said in a soft voice. "And for the broken lantern."

Daniel examined the broken bloody stem. "I'm assuming this is not your blood."

Gunny stepped toward Matt and shook her head. "No."

Daniel looked Matt up and down. "And Matt doesn't appear to have a scratch on him. This wouldn't possibly be the blood of Mr. Carlson would it?"

Gunny cringed. "It might be, sir," she whispered.

Daniel laughed his big booming laugh. "That bastard ran past me, as I came up Main Street. I thought he looked spooked." He shook his head. "That jackass is always pushing to get his way. This time, someone pushed back. I'd say justice has been served. You don't owe me a thing, Gunny. In fact, I'm sure I owe you."

All of the shops along Main Street were packed with visitors for the February Shrovetide Fair. Gunny's feet were sore from standing all day, but there was no time to sit as she sold dozens of household goods, bottles of whiskey, and boxes of sweets to demanding customers. She was leaning down to pull a package from under the front counter when she heard a voice that sent a shiver up her spine. Her head cracked against the underside of the counter as she jolted upright. She saw stars as she looked around the crowded shop.

"Mam?"

Eileen pushed her way through a cluster of customers and leaned on the counter, smiling and adjusting the bow on her large black hat.

"Look at you all business like," Eileen said, reaching out and touching Gunny's hand. "Clean hair. Clean fingernails. My, my, you look like quite the lady working here."

Gunny wiped her hands on her apron and pushed a stray curl away from her face. "Mam, you're embarrassing me. What're you doing here?"

"Your father lets me out of the house every once in awhile," Eileen said while she adjusted her hat in the reflection of the store window. "He was coming to Dingle and I decided to tag along. Do you like my new hat?"

"Da's here?" Gunny asked, looking around the crowded store.

"Yes, somewhere. It's a mob scene in town today."

"Don't you usually stay in Ventry when Da comes into Dingle to shop?" Gunny asked.

Eileen's eyes gleamed. "I usually do, but not today. Today I have business to attend to."

Gunny cleared her throat and put on her best customer-voice. "In that case, how can I help you?"

"Oh, that's nice," Eileen said, leaning forward and looking Gunny in the eye. "I'm here to make a bargain for Shrovetide. I have an eligible daughter and I'd like to make a match."

Gunny's face went pale. "Mam, don't tease."

"I'm not teasing," Eileen said. "That is why I'm here. You'll be eighteen in April. Your father and I have decided it's time for you to marry."

Gunny looked around the crowded shop for her father. "Mam, we can talk about this later. I have to work." She turned to a tall woman who approached the counter, purse in hand. "I'll be right with you." She turned back to Eileen and whispered. "Mam, please go shop. Or find something else to do. We'll get a bite at the Dingle Pub tonight. Meet me here at sunset."

Eileen had a sly smile on her face. "The Dingle Pub will be fine. In the meantime, I'm going to buy you a new hat to match mine. I want you to look beautiful tonight. Remember, it's Shrove, Gunny. If you don't marry this week, you'll have to wait another whole year."

"I'm not in any hurry," Gunny yelled after her mother as Eileen turned and melted into the crowd.

Gunny was busy the rest of the day but her mind never strayed far from one thought: Her mother was in town to make a Shrove match for her. She could be married to a complete stranger in two or three days. All day she heard mothers and fathers bickering in the shop with matchmakers, all making wedding bargains for Shrove.

"I want a girl with a dowry."

"Your son must marry the best he can for the money."

"I'll settle for no less than twenty pounds and a cow."

When a match was settled, whiskey was served all around as the most important decision in some poor girl or some poor boy's life was decided over the counter at the Murphy's store. She pleaded with the matchmakers in her mind. "The money goes away. It's the match that remains."

Robert and Eileen stopped in at the Murphys as the shop was closing. The shelves were nearly bare from the day's frenzy of activity. Gunny and Joanna were sitting on flour barrels at the back of the store talking quietly while Daniel swept.

Daniel set his broom down and shook hands with Robert. Eileen made a small curtsy to the big man then waltzed past him and handed Gunny a hat. It was lovely with a broad black rim. Gunny put it on and hurried to the back counter to look at herself in the glass.

"I am Eileen Malone," Eileen said to Joanna. "I hope Gunny has been behaving herself."

Joanna smiled warmly. "It's nice to finally meet you. Gunny has been a tremendous help in the store and with James."

"Who is James?"

"James is my son," Joanna said softly. "He's seven. Gunny has helped him come out of his shell as if he were a stubborn periwinkle. He's off today with a school friend."

Eileen looked skeptically at her tall daughter kneeling in front of the glass counter admiring her hat. "I never knew Gunny to take to children. Well, that's a good sign. I hate to be rude but we must be leaving. We have business at the pub." She turned to her daughter. "Hurry. I've asked a few others to join us and we mustn't be late."

Gunny walked slowly toward Eileen. "A few others, Mam? Please tell me you're not serious about this Shrove matchmaking."

"Oh, I am serious," Eileen said. "I've been talking to my old neighbors in Ventry, the Kennedys." She leaned toward Joanna and said in a soft voice. "The Kennedys're interested in a match for their son, Noel. He's thirty-one and has never been married."

"I wonder why," Gunny said glumly. She grabbed Eileen by the arm and moved her toward the door. "We can discuss this over food. I'm famished." She turned to Joanna. "Is it all right if I take the night off?"

"Of course, Gunny," Joanna said, pale at Eileen's words. "Take whatever time you need."

Gunny walked down Main Street arm in arm with her father. The Dingle Pub was packed with Shrove revelers. Gunny pushed her way through the crowd and found a table in a smoky back corner of the room. She sat with Eileen while Robert went to the bar to order food.

Gunny sat, quietly fearing the start of a conversation with her mother. Finally, Robert returned with two bowls of steaming lamb stew. The women ate in silence until Robert returned to the table with his own bowl of stew and a few slices of heavy oat bread. When they were done eating, Robert gathered the bowls, took them to the bar, and returned with three glasses of porter. Gunny was surprised that she was included in the round of porter but eagerly took a short sip, then leaned back and polished off the glass. She wiped her mouth with the back of her hand and burped.

Eileen shook her head. "I should have known better than to think you'd become a lady."

"Sometimes a girl needs a drink. So, you haven't told me anything about how things are at home. How are Michael and Maeve?"

Robert looked at Eileen to let her answer. "They're fine," Eileen said stiffly

"That's good." Gunny took a deep breath. "Da, you are being awfully quiet tonight."

Robert grunted.

"What do you think of this match making idea of mother's?" Gunny asked.

Robert took a long swig of his porter, then sat back in his chair and picked at a fingernail that seemed to be bothering him. He had a few more wrinkles around his eyes and the hair around his temples was greying. She hadn't noticed it when she was home at Christmas.

"Your father agrees that you should be married. Don't you, Robert?"

"I do agree that Gunny should be married," Robert said, sticking out his chin, finishing off his glass of porter, and setting the glass down loudly on the table.

Gunny was shocked. "Da, I thought you needed me to work? Don't we need the money?"

Robert picked again at the rough fingernail. "The oats and potatoes were plentiful last harvest. And I've been getting pressure from a certain someone to get you wed."

"From Mam," Gunny said sharply.

It was a statement, not a question. Gunny was surprised when her father shook his head no. She frowned. "If it's not Mam then it must be Father Jessey. Is he back to his old prodding?"

"No," Robert shook his head. "I am not talking about Father Jessey. We hardly see the priest anymore now that you're not around."

Gunny was confused. "Surely you are not talking about this Noel Kennedy fellow from Ventry? I don't even know him."

Robert slammed a fist on the table. Nearby patrons turned at the sound. Robert grimaced and waved to let them know everything was all right.

"The last thing I want is to see you disappear to Ventry for the rest of your life," he said in a quiet voice. "It's been hard enough having you out of the house these past two years. If I thought you were never going to return to Dunquin, I…" He hesitated.

"You'd miss me?" Gunny asked with a grin.

Robert looked Gunny in the eye. "Of course I'd miss you. I miss you now."

"How can you miss me," Gunny asked slyly, "when you have Michael to work with?"

"I don't miss your help on the farm, as good as that was."

Robert looked at Gunny's skeptical face and continued in a quieter voice. "I miss your stories. I miss how you used to sing about the house all the time. I even miss that damned tin whistle!"

"Don't be sentimental, Robert," Eileen snapped. "It doesn't suit you. Go get yourself another porter."

Robert looked at Eileen then at Gunny. Gunny held up two fingers. Robert nodded and headed to the bar.

"I've missed Da too, though you must know, I've made a nice life for myself here in Dingle. I love the Murphys, and James is my favorite little lad on earth."

Robert returned with two glasses of porter and set them down on the table. "James is your favorite lad?" he queried, pulling out his chair and sitting down close to Gunny.

"Oh, yes," Gunny assured him sipping at her fresh glass of porter.

"Then there are no other favorite lads we might talk about?" Robert asked her, eyebrows raised.

Gunny blushed and pictured her hikes and talks and rides with Matt. She looked her father in the eye. That's when she knew. "Are you talking about Matt McCrohan?"

Robert sighed with relief. "Aye. He's the one that's been pressuring me. Every time I'm down at O'Leary's having a quiet glass of porter, he's there telling me what a good match he'd be for you." He winked at Gunny and tipped his glass toward her.

"Matt McCrohan is an insolent boy," Eileen said. "I told your father that he's no match for you and that you'd have none of him. You can do better than marry a Dunquin boy, much less a McCrohan."

Gunny's heart raced. She reached out and took Robert's hand. "Da, do you think I should marry Matt?"

Robert paused and looked at Eileen. "I do. But your mother disagrees with me."

Gunny scooted her chair up tight next to Robert. This was too good to be true. "Da, you must listen to Matt. He and I are a good match. I didn't want to admit it, but we're a match of the heart. I know we are. Please, please, you have to make this happen."

Robert looked across the table at his wife's angry, red face. "A match of the heart," he muttered wondering what that would be like.

Eileen looked away from Robert toward a parting of the crowd. "Oh, here are the Kennedys." She stood and smiled at an elderly couple as they approached the table.

Gunny let go of her father's hand and stood to greet the strangers. They smiled at the tall girl. She was stunning for someone not quite eighteen. Gunny smiled back and put out her right hand. "I'm Gunny," she said in a warm voice. "I'm so pleased to meet you."

Mr. Kennedy looked surprised at Gunny's bold offer to shake hands but held out his right hand. She squeezed it tightly, then turned and squeezed Mrs. Kennedy's until she winced. Gunny dropped her hand and stood to her full height, smiled again sweetly and smoothed her apron. "Why don't we all sit down?"

When all of the chairs were pulled up to the table, Eileen started to talk about how she had grown up in Ventry when Gunny interrupted. "Excuse me, Mam. Before you get to the bargaining part of this discussion, I need to share something with the Kennedys." She turned to the couple, put on her most angelic face and lowered her voice to nearly a whisper. "You seem like lovely people so I must be honest with you. I'd be a dreadful wife. I may look clean and pretty but it's all a show." She chuckled a strange, deep chuckle, pushed her hat back from her face, and continued. "I can't keep a house clean for the life of me and I spend every bit of money I can get my hands on for tobacco and drink."

She raised her glass, downed the porter, wiped her mouth with the back of her sleeve, and burped. "Most days, I sleep until noon and I burn nearly everything I try to cook. I'm terrible with children—I have an incredible urge to slap them. And I have spells where I wander about in the hills for days at a time. Do you have any questions for me?" she asked, eyebrows raised.

Mrs. Kennedy pulled her shawl tight around her shoulders. "I told you she wasn't good enough for our Noel," she hissed at her husband.

Eileen opened her mouth to object but Gunny leaned across the table and squeezed her mother's hand hard, then turned toward the Kennedys and added in a whisper. "You can't believe a thing my mother says about me." Gunny took a breath and slyly pointed to the glass in front of Eileen. "You know... she drinks more than me," she said with a wink.

Eileen's mouth fell open and she pushed her glass over in front of Robert. Robert tried to cover his laugh with a cough.

Gunny stood before the amazed couple and opened her arms wide in front of them. "I can't wait to meet your son," she said clutching dramatically at her head. "Oh, I feel a spell coming on ..." She snapped to attention as if some invisible person was talking to her. "Yes, I must fly," she said loudly. She grabbed her shawl from the back of her chair, gave her father a quick hug, and raced out the door of the pub with her shawl flying out behind her like a cape.

Outside, she giggled, leaning back against the front wall of the pub. She took a huge breath of cool evening air. Her head was spinning from the two porters. Or maybe it was from the crowded, smoky pub. Or maybe it was because her father wanted her to marry Matt McCrohan. She pulled her new hat down tight on her head and howled up at the rising moon, then turned at the unmistakable sound of thundering horse hooves. The Fianna had arrived to rescue the French Queen but it was too late: The French Queen had rescued herself.

Matt pounded up beside her and swung down from Nella as the Malones emerged from the pub with two strangers. He scanned their faces. He saw relief on the woman's face, embarrassment on the man's face, raw anger on Mrs. Malone's face, and a broad smile on Mr. Malone's face. He grabbed Robert's arm. Robert shook his head yes, smiled, and reached out to shake Matt's hand.

"She is all yours, Matt McCrohan. I hope you know what you are getting yourself into."

Matt turned to Gunny and swept her up in his arms. Gunny kicked and laughed in his embrace. He set her down and kissed her gently on the mouth. "Do you want to marry on Shrove Tuesday or Shrove Wednesday?" he asked his bride-to-be.

Gunny grinned. "Shrove Tuesday is supposed to be luckier."

"Then we'll marry tomorrow," he shouted. He expertly swung up onto Nella's back. "I'm off to tell Mam the news. I'll see you at the church—tomorrow!" He kicked on Nella's side and thundered west toward Dunquin.

Joanna rose early on Gunny's last morning at the shop. She stirred the fire and added a brick of turf to help crisp a pan of sizzling potatoes. Her eyes filled with tears as she watched the potatoes brown. She wiped her eyes with the back of her sleeve, then caught herself, thought of Gunny, and laughed.

Gunny was surprised to see the fire going and to smell food cooking when she walked into the cozy kitchen. Joanna rose and took up the tea kettle to fill it with water.

Gunny reached out for the kettle. "I'll get that."

Joanna pulled the tea kettle away from Gunny. "No, you are a free woman today, and I'm serving you."

Gunny was embarrassed as Joanna carefully ladled water from the bucket into the kettle and hung it on the crane. "You don't have to do that."

"I know I don't have to," Joanna said. "I want to. Now be quiet."

James and Daniel walked into the kitchen. James glumly pulled out his chair and plopped down at the table. Daniel stood awkwardly, then sat and signaled for Gunny to sit as Joanna spooned pan-roasted potatoes onto everyone's plates. They all silently took up spoons and ate the crispy treats. James finally broke the silence.

"This seems awfully sudden to me," he said in his small voice. "Is this really what you want?"

Gunny sighed and smiled at James' perplexed face. "I think it is."

"You think it is," he repeated.

Gunny reached over and took his small hand. He did not flinch at her touch.

"I don't want to leave," she said looking around at the beloved faces at the table. "But Dunquin is calling me and it's time for me to go home." She smiled weakly. "The good news is that I'm not marrying a stranger."

Joanna pushed her half-eaten meal away. "From the way you told us the story, your good news may not be something your mother is so keen on. This could be a long walk home followed by a lifetime of criticism."

Gunny grinned. "It's only my Mam, Joanna. And I'll only have to bear her glares for a short time before I move in with the McCrohans. Mac will be my brother, and the little girls my sisters. I always wanted a big family. And I'll be with Matt. I'll be happy."

Gunny insisted on helping clean up after the morning meal, then brought her things down from her room and set them on the kitchen table. Joanna helped her fold her clothes and pack them neatly in several cloth sacks. The bells in the shop jingled and she heard Daniel greet her parents. She took her bags outside and placed them in her father's small hand wagon. She set her new black hat on top of the load.

Joanna joined her outside and added two large packages in the wagon.

"Are those for Mam?" Gunny asked.

"No, they're for you. They're wedding gifts, Gunny. You can open them now if you want."

Gunny lifted the first package from the wagon. It was heavy. She pulled off the string and brown paper. It was a clean, new iron pot with three small legs. Gunny held the pot out in front of her. She had never seen anything so beautiful. She set the pot in the wagon and hugged Joanna. "What else could you possibly have gotten me?" she asked eying the second package. "This is already too much."

The second package was even more spectacular. It held a new tea kettle and several bundles of loose tea and sugar. Gunny cried and hugged Joanna again. "I promise to always drink my tea hot, weak, and sweet, Joanna."

The others joined them outside, and after promises to visit were made and tears were wiped away, Gunny turned to James who stood alone in the doorway of the shop and knelt in front of him. "James, I'll never forget my time here with you. You were my first friend. I can't thank you enough for believing in me when you did."

James whimpered, then threw himself into Gunny's arms and wound his arms tightly around her neck. "I'm going to come and see you some day," he whispered in her ear."

Gunny hugged him then held him in front of her. "I know you will. Maybe when I have children, you'll come and teach them all the fine things you've learned in school."

James wiped his eyes with his hand. "Sure, Gunny. I can do that."

"Then there's one more gift we have to take care of before I go." She stood and reached into her apron pocket. She pulled out the tin whistle and handed it to James. "This is for you."

James body went stiff. He looked from the whistle to the dirt road and jammed his hands deep into his pockets. "I can't take that. I don't know how to play it well enough yet."

Gunny reached down and pulled his right hand free of his pocket. She placed the whistle in his hand and wrapped her hands around his. "This whistle belonged to my grandmother. It's the best thing I own and I need to make sure it's in a safe place. I can't think of any place safer than with you, James. And you know the notes. All you need to do now is add the tunes you hear in your head."

James opened his hand inside Gunny's hands and looked at the whistle. "I'm going to learn how to play this thing," he promised.

"I know you will. You're the smartest boy I know." She tousled his hair, then smoothed it down and kissed him on the top of his head. She wiped one last tear from her eye and pulled on her new broad-rimmed black hat.

"We're off then," she said. "I have a wedding to attend!"

She bobbed out of town with her parents, full of joy and sorrow. Partway home, she reached into her apron pocket for her whistle, then patted the empty space and hummed the rest of the way home. As they crested the last hill near Dunquin, she smelled the west sea air and looked down at her sleepy little village shrouded in fog. She heard a yip from Shep, and as the dog bounded out of the fog ahead of her on the road, she knew she was home for good.

~ Chapter 9: The Wedding and the Accident ~

Maeve and Michael sat by the fire giggling and sharing a pipe full of tobacco after a night alone at the house. The door flew open as Robert, Eileen, and Gunny bustled in all energy and silence. Shep slunk in behind them and curled up on his mat in front of the fire.

"How did the Shrove matchmaking go?" Maeve asked with a smile, pulling her shawl tight around her from the blast of cold air. "Will there be a wedding this week?"

Eileen glared at Maeve, pulled off her hat and shawl and threw them onto the table. Gunny carefully untied her hat, hung it on a peg by the door, and waltzed past Maeve to the back room juggling several large bundles. Robert took off his hat and jacket and sat heavily on a stool. He pulled his hat and jacket onto his lap with a sigh and scratched the dog's head.

"So?" Michael searched his father's face for a clue. "Was it good trip?"

Eileen paced around the fireplace. "I don't want to talk about it."

Robert nodded his head toward his son. "The wedding is on," he said in a soft voice with one eyebrow raised. "Gunny is to marry Matt McCrohan this afternoon."

Maeve's mouth popped open. "Matt McCrohan?" She turned on her stool toward Eileen. "I thought you said you were making a match with the Kennedy boy?"

Eileen stopped pacing. "I said I don't want to talk about it," she hissed. She looked around. "This house is a mess. Michael. Knock out that pipe and go clean the yard. Robert, we need a keg of porter for the wedding party. And Maeve..." Eileen paused and sniffed at the air. "What're you cooking?"

"Michael slaughtered a sheep this morning like you asked. I'm boiling mutton for stew. And I am making a cake. I used the last of the sugar. I hope you brought more from Dingle."

"It's Shrove Tuesday, Maeve. We won't be eating sugar again until Lent is over. No sugar, no eggs, no milk, no flour, no butter... Remember? All of the tasty food goes into the dung pile tomorrow unless we eat it. So cook everything we've got. We might as well feed everyone as throw food away."

Maeve licked her lips at the thought of it.

Eileen crossed to the fire, wrapped her hand in her apron, and lifted the top of the large iron pot to look inside. "When will the cake be done?"

"It won't be done if you hold the lid open like that," Maeve said leaning forward and pushing the pot lid closed with the toe of her boot.

Eileen stood and held out the broom. "Start sweeping. We have two hours to get this house spotless."

Maeve took the broom and leaned it against the hearth then squatted in front of the fire and stirred the simmering pot of mutton. Michael packed his pipe with tobacco and watched his wife as she cooked.

"I don't know why you're making such a fuss, Mam," Michael said, stifling a yawn. "It'll be dark after the wedding and no one will care about anything except food and drink and a place to dance. Then you'll break the cake over Gunny's head, crumbs will fly everywhere, the hens will go crazy, the sheep will be butting the door to come inside..."

Maeve guffawed at Michael's humor.

Eileen stared at the two of them. "What do you two know about weddings?"

Michael looked down at his boots and Maeve turned back to the fire, snickering, to stir the pot of meat.

"This wedding party must be perfect," Eileen murmured. "Matt's not the man I picked for Gunny but he's enough of a man to make the neighbors jealous. For once, I want to be proud of this family and of this nasty little house."

"That stew smells delicious," Michael said to Maeve, reaching over and patting his wife on the rump. "This'll be a day of high feasting."

"Don't get any ideas about sampling, you two," Eileen snapped. "Michael, I thought I told you to clean up the yard. And you," she said pointing at Robert. "O'Leary's. Now."

Robert stood and stretched. He had his orders and was glad for an excuse to be away from the house. He pulled on his jacket and cap and pushed Michael out the door ahead of him. The fog was thickening. Michael stood glumly looking about the yard as Robert headed off down the steep road to O'Leary's.

Bitsy Kavanaugh knocked at Kate McCrohan's door and walked in. "Kate?" she said with a concerned look on her face. "Did I hear correctly about a McCrohan wedding today?"

"God bless you, Bitsy. Come in," Kate McCrohan said, setting her broom aside.

Bitsy pulled off her shawl and walked to the fire to warm her hands. "Is it true? Matt's to marry Gunny Malone?"

Kate brushed away a quick tear and nodded.

"How did this happen?" Bitsy asked, clutching Kate's arm. "I thought Gunny was in service in Dingle?"

Kate had been awake most of the night after Matt burst in with the news and her eyes were red and sore. "I'm trying to make sense of it myself. Matt didn't tell me much except that his dearest wish had come true. He took off early this morning to be with his lads. He's so excited—I don't think he slept a wink."

Bitsy lifted the lid of the large pot on the fire. The steamy aroma of boiled potatoes and fish filled the room. "Why're you cooking when the wedding party'll be at the Malone's?"

"You know how everyone ends up here. I thought I'd cook a few things. It's damp out. We'll be looking for something to warm to fill us after the wedding."

"You're not baking one of your cakes, are you?" Bitsy asked.

"No, I wouldn't take that away from Eileen."

"You're twice the baker she is," Bitsy said with pride.

"I've had more occasion, that's all. Eileen has a small house and a small family. She's done the best she can, God bless her."

"She's a hard woman," Bitsy said shaking her head. "I've never heard anything but criticism come out of that mouth of hers."

"Imagine having to leave your childhood home after an eviction. There must be such bitterness. And then to have your parents pass early and end up here in Dunquin. Her life hasn't been easy."

"None of our lives have been easy," Bitsy said, chin raised.

"Still, Matt's marrying Gunny, not Eileen, and we'll welcome the girl," Kate said.

Bitsy sat down on the bench near the table. "So you're happy to have Gunny as part of your family?"

Kate shrugged and sat down next to Bitsy. "She's a little wild at times but that may be what Matt loves about her."

Bitsy reached over and took Kate's hand. "But what about you? Do you like her?"

"Matt loves her," Kate said firmly. "A mother couldn't ask for anything more."

"Hmpf," Bitsy said pulling her hands into her lap. "You certainly could ask for more. Need I point out that Gunny is an empty woman, that she has no dowry? You should be collecting a fine bride's dowry for Matt," she added sharply. "He has this house to offer—and the forge."

Kate shook her head. "He chose Gunny. I had no part of it. He says they're kindred souls."

"Kindred souls!" Bitsy stood and walked to the fire. "What nonsense." She squatted in front of the fire and gave the turf a few pokes. "He could be just as happy with an ugly girl with a large dowry. You'll regret this decision when you have to pay dowries for your own girls." She pointed the fire poker at Kate. "You're not thinking of the future, Katie."

"When John died, I stopped thinking about the future. Somehow we survived that and we'll survive this."

Bitsy hoisted herself upright with the fire poker and straightened her apron. "I still say Matt would be just as happy with a rich girl. Lust passes—money is forever."

Kate stood. "Who knows what lasts, Bitsy. I only hope that Matt has found true love with Gunny."

Bitsy rested the poker against the fireplace and gave her friend a quick hug. "I only want what's best for you," she said pulling on her shawl. She gave Kate a smile and pulled the door closed behind her, heading out into the fog to spread the word of the upcoming nuptials.

"You do know the best part about getting married at Shrove?" Matt asked. Cornelius, Mac and the Burke twins looked at him blankly from their favorite table at O'Leary's. "No one is allowed to visit during Lent which means starting Thursday, Eileen Malone can't visit us for forty-six days. Yes, gentlemen," Matt said placing both hands on the table and standing. "Today is the start of my marital bliss."

"Alone with Gunny—and Mam, and me, the girls," Mac said raising his glass.

"Marital bliss," Cornelius chuckled, drinking. "I remember hearing that last year. It's all bliss until the baby arrives."

Matt shushed Cornelius and raised his glass. "I'll hear none of that. To Shrove!" he yelled.

"To Shrove!" the boys yelled in response, then drank and bounced their empty glasses down on the table.

"Micky!" Matt yelled. "Bring us another pitcher of porter."

Micky filled a fresh pitcher and brought it to the table. "You may want to slow down a bit," he said, setting down the pitcher. "You do want to make it to your wedding night, don't you, Matt?"

Matt filled the glasses at the table and raised his glass to Micky. "To my wedding night!"

The boys laughed again. Micky shook his head and returned to the bar. Edmond Burke looked thoughtfully at Matt. "You're going to live off of wedding cake for the next week while the rest of us eat nothing but potatoes for Lent."

"To wedding cake!" Matt said with a grin.

Robert pushed open the door of O'Leary's. Cold fog swirled in around him. "Micky, we need a keg of your finest porter." He looked toward the back table. Matt and the Wren boys were there singing a raucous version of an old Shrove song. He caught Matt's eye, and Matt raised his glass.

"None of this would've been possible without you, Robert Malone," Matt said loudly from the back table. "You're a fine man. Let's toast the bride's father!"

"To the bride's father!" the boys yelled and drank again.

Robert shook his head and rolled the keg out to his wagon. The pub door closed behind him with a bang and he trudged back up the hill pushing the loaded barrow.

Gunny emerged from the small back room of the house carrying a long loop of dried flowers. She laid it on the table and started to sort the flowers by color.

"Is that what you're wearing?" Eileen said eying Gunny's dress.

Gunny looked up from the flowers. She had on her best dress from Dingle. Joanna had helped her make it over the winter. It was dark grey and had a small white collar and long black sash.

"I don't have much to choose from," she said. "You don't like it?"

"I suppose it'll do," Eileen said with a wince.

Maeve glanced over from the steaming pot of mutton stew. "Where'd you get the flowers?"

Gunny smiled. "I picked them in the fields last summer and dried them in my room in Dingle. Their dusty colors remind me of warmer days."

Eileen stepped to the table and roughly pushed a few of the flowers around. "They're all dried out. They're nothing but trash."

Gunny cupped her hands protectively around the dried flowers. "Don't break them. I want to weave them into my hair. Maeve?" she asked. "Will you help me?"

Maeve looked at Gunny as if she had bitten into a sour apple. "I'm busy."

Gunny sighed. "Fine, I'll do it myself." She tied a thin red ribbon loosely around her hair then took a handful of hairpins from her apron pocket and pinned her hair up in the back. She broke off the longer stems from a few of the dried flowers and carefully wove the heads into her thick curls, then pulled a few of the front curls loose around her face. Eileen and Maeve watched in silence.

Gunny patted her head to see if the flowers felt even, then turned to Eileen. "How do I look?"

Eileen stared at her daughter and said nothing.

"You don't like it," Gunny said. "I can see by the look on your face."

Eileen walked a half-circle around Gunny and sighed. "The fog is making everything damp today. Your curls look like they did when you were little—all tight and crazy. Why don't you pull your hair back?" She moved to tuck a loose curl up away from Gunny's face; Gunny pushed her mother's hand away.

"No," she said. "Matt likes it when my hair's loose."

Eileen picked up a dried thistle from the table. "It seems strange to me to put dead things in your hair on your wedding day…"

Gunny ducked down to eye herself in the firelight reflecting off the glass of the front window. She could faintly see the outline of her hair. The curls were going everywhere. She smiled at the reflection. "I like it."

Eileen brushed the remaining flowers off the table and took up the broom. "Suit yourself," she said briskly sweeping the scattered dry petals into the fire. "You always do."

Robert opened the front door and stepped inside. Shep scooted in behind him and Gunny gave the dog a quick pat.

"The keg's out front," Robert announced. "We should head to the church soon. I want to get there early. Is everyone ready?" Gunny swallowed hard and looked at her father. "Are you all right?" he asked.

She took a deep breath and smiled. "I am," she said. "I didn't know it was time." She reached over and took one of her father's large hands in hers. "Truth be told, as much as I want to marry Matt, I just want this day to be over."

Robert squeezed Gunny's hand and looked at his tall, beautiful daughter with her strong, wide shoulders and tiny waist. She looked elegant in her full grey dress with dried wildflowers and a bright red ribbon woven through her dark, shiny curls. "It'll be over before you know it," he assured her. "And we'll be standing in this very spot, saying, 'My, that was fast.'"

Gunny patted her father on the chest and leaned in toward him. "And then we'll all go to Matt's house for a gathering," she grinned.

"Not a gathering and it's not Matt's house anymore. After tonight, it'll be your house too," Robert said sadly.

Eileen snorted as Robert took Gunny's hands in his.

"I wish you could live here. But I'm happy you'll only be a field away," Robert said with a wide grin on his face.

Maeve dumped a bowl of boiled potatoes into the pot of hot mutton. Steam hissed out into the fire. "It's actually been nice and quiet without you these past couple of years, Gunny," Maeve said over the hiss. "Maybe you and Matt could start a new forge a few more fields away?"

Gunny walked out the front door clinging to her father's arm. The sun was trying to break through the fog and Gunny's hair was alternately misty with fog and shiny with sunlight. Her skin was so pale it was nearly transparent. Her deep brown eyes glowed with anticipation.

"Are you ready?" Robert asked.

Gunny smiled and squared her shoulders. "I'm as ready as I'll ever be."

"She's not ready," Eileen announced from behind, brushing imaginary lint from Gunny's shoulder. While Eileen fussed, Robert untied a borrowed horse from the front bench and mounted, then reached down for Gunny.

"Where'd you get the horse?" Gunny asked.

"Lord Thomas Milliken loaned it to me. He told me to wish you a good day."

Gunny blushed as her mother continued to dust her.

"Stop your fussing, Woman," Robert said, "or we'll never get to the church." He glanced around the foggy yard. "Looks like we're in for a wet ride."

Gunny heard a familiar pounding of hooves and turned toward the road. Matt swung into the yard and stopped just short of her father's horse. He was out of breath, but looked handsome in his best suit and jaunty derby.

"What's wrong?" Gunny asked. "Why're you here?"

Matt grinned and reached down to pull her up behind him. Gunny smiled as she swung a leg up over the horse, then sat up to straighten her dress. She leaned against Matt and squeezed him hard around the middle. His back was warm and he smelled of sweat and porter. He reached around and patted her behind to make sure she was seated properly. She laughed and pushed his hand away.

"You're not supposed to see me until I get to the church. I'll meet you at the front gates," she said giving him another squeeze from behind as she started to slide off of Nella's wide back.

"You are going to the church with me," Matt said, reaching back to hold her in place.

Eileen stood in front of Nella and pointed at Matt. "Let Gunny down right now and meet us at the church," she said. "A proper young lady arrives at her wedding riding with her father."

Gunny looked at Robert. He lifted his hands and smiled at Gunny as if to say—I have no say in this. She clutched at Matt's waist and roared with nervous laughter as he kicked at Nella and they tore off toward Mount Eagle. Robert grabbed hold of Shep who squirmed and barked at being left behind.

Eileen's voice tailed off behind them. "Be at the church in an hour. You'd better not be late!"

Matt raced up the dirt road and pounded out into the open fields. The fog was rolling in thicker and it swirled about them as they rode. When they neared Gunny's old booley hut, Matt pulled Nella to a stop and slid down from the saddle. Gunny leaned forward and patted Nella's sweaty neck. She looked down at Matt.

"We're not getting married, are we?"

Matt looked up at Gunny then looked away. "You know I never wanted to marry," he said pacing. "But I couldn't have you marry someone else."

Gunny felt her breath catch in her throat. She swallowed hard. "I know," she said, her voice shaking only slightly. "So the wedding's off?"

"Marriage is so traditional," Matt continued, reaching up and taking hold of her left hand. "I thought it was what I wanted. It's all I've talked about for months with Mac and your father. I wanted you all to myself. But now the wedding is today, and you know I dread the idea of a house and work and babies. I've been trying to convince myself that it's all right to give up my dreams…"

"It's all right, Matt. Somehow I never expected our wedding to happen."

"No, no, you don't understand what I'm trying to say, Gunny. Listen to me. I don't want to get married, but I want you. And if I have to stand up before Father Jessey and all of the people in this damned village to make that happen, I will. But first I had to see you, alone, … to tell you that I love you beyond all of my plans of escaping Dunquin and the forge—beyond all reason."

Matt pulled on Gunny's hand and she slid off Nella into his arms. He wrapped his right arm tightly around her back and ran the fingers of his left hand up to loosen her bun of curls. He kissed her softly, then long and hard on the mouth. The taste of porter was sweet on his tongue. Gunny felt her body melt into his. Her head was spinning from the fast ride and from Matt's words of love. She took a step away and rested her hands on his chest to catch her breath.

"Then we are getting married?" she asked.

Matt laughed and pulled her toward him. Her boot caught and she stumbled. He tried to steady her and they both stumbled onto a thick hillock of damp grass and fell, laughing. He balanced briefly over her, then let his body ease down onto hers. He kissed her deep on the lips and pushed up the grey material that clung to her hips as the wind sighed and the fog closed in around them.

Gunny ran her hands over Matt's perfect face and kissed him lightly on the mouth, the dried flowers in the back of her hair crushed and forgotten, the red ribbon lost in the grasses. He looked at her in mock surprise.

"Girl, do you know what time it is?"

Gunny smiled. "No, Matt. What time is it?"

He sat up and rubbed a hand lightly across her chest and whispered. "It's time for our wedding. If we're late, we'll be the talk of the village."

"We are, no doubt, already the talk of the village."

Matt helped her to her feet and brushed dried grass from her backside. She laughed until Matt cupped her face with his long, slim hands and she quieted.

"We'll journey places together even if we never leave this village. I love you with all my heart." He kissed her again softly on her mouth, then on each cheek and across her forehead. He whistled for Nella and snatched up his derby. He mounted in a single swing and pulled Gunny up behind him. She hugged him around the middle as she had done so many times before, resting her head against his broad back as they flew down the road, her stomach filled with butterflies.

Mac was working in the forge crafting an elaborate pot crane with multiple swinging arms. The last twist on the top of the crane would not go in the direction he wanted.

"Damn! I'll have to try again after the wedding," he said throwing his hammer down in disgust. "I don't suppose they'll notice if their gift is late. I don't suppose they'll notice much of anything today but each other."

Mac studied the unfinished gift. Matt always teased him about his elaborate iron work but he had designed this crane with Gunny's curls in mind. He pictured her slim hands touching the fluted curls, then using it to hang rope from, or to tie up livestock. If she did that, he'd tell her... What? What would he ever say to her face? He'd known her seventeen years, all of his life, and had never been able to find words around her. What would it be like when she moved into their house?

He sighed and pulled off his heavy leather apron. He bent to wash his hands and face in a bucket of water and studied his thick, calloused hands. They were so different from Matt's long thin fingers. Who would ever marry a man with hands like these? He took a nail and tried to clean the dirt out from under his fingernails but it was no use. If he didn't hurry, he'd never get to the wedding. Why go, he thought. Why torture himself seeing Matt up there with Gunny? Because Matt expected him to go, and Mac did what was expected.

He pulled off his sweaty shirt, his muscles tight and his body slick with sweat. He ran water through his thick black hair, put on a clean shirt, and hurried into the yard. He eyed Evin, a new, delivery horse Matt had purchased a few weeks before from a traveling gypsy. He walked up to the huge horse, hand outstretched. Evin put his ears back and raised his lips to show his large yellow teeth.

"Matt says you're the laziest horse on the Dingle Peninsula, but today you have to work. Steady, boy," Mac said as he untied the horse and climbed onto the bench beside him. He tentatively slid a leg over the horse and tightly gripped the saddle. "If I wasn't in a hurry, I'd have no more interest in riding you than you have in carrying me."

The horse shivered with Mac on his back and kicked out his left hind leg.

"There you go," Mac said patting Evin's wide neck, trying to sound more confident than he was. The large horse lumbered out toward the road with a start. Mac closed his eyes and held on with his knees as the horse galloped to a wedding Mac did not want to attend.

As Matt and Gunny tore through the village, she heard a boy yell, "Watch out! Matt McCrohan is coming!" She grinned. Everyone knew to stand clear when Matt and Nella were flying down the road. She saw the church ahead, barely visible in the fog except for the candles shining beautifully from each arched window. There was no one in the yard; the wedding crowd had already gone inside. Matt spurred Nella to a gallop and Gunny did her best to move with the rhythm of the speeding horse. Matt turned in the saddle to tell Gunny they still had time when Gunny spotted a foggy black shadow ahead of them in the road. She screamed and pointed but it was too late. Nella ran directly into Mac riding on the large work horse. Gunny pitched forward on impact and felt Matt fly away in front of her. She grabbed at Nella's mane as the two horses crushed against one another. She felt Nella start to roll to the right and hit the ground hard on her back a second ahead of Nella's large body landing on top of her. Then there was nothing but crushing red pain and swirling black fog.

Mac heard the scream when Nella appeared out of nowhere. He clutched, at his saddle horn white knuckled as the large horse reared and Nella rolled to the ground. When Evin settled and backed away with Mac clinging to his back, Mac looked around in disbelief as neighbors swarmed out of the church, pointing and talking all at once.

"Who screamed?"

"What happened?"

"Oh, my God."

Nella lay kicking and screaming on the ground to Mac's right, her left front leg bent at an odd angle. He heard Gunny screaming, but couldn't see her. Matt lay just ahead of him, crumpled and still against the iron gates of the church.

Robert ran out of the church and spotted Gunny's long black curls under Nella's thrashing body. "Cornelius! Michael! Help me get this damned horse off of Gunny. Oh, my God. She's crushed!"

The three men rolled the hysterical horse off of Gunny. Stabbing pain flooded through Gunny's body. She felt hot and wet and looked down to see that her grey dress had turned black with blood. She couldn't move her legs and felt her heart shiver inside her chest. Her vision blurred. She heard her father's voice somewhere above her.

"Someone get me a gun." With three quick shots, Nella lay still and silent by Gunny's side.

Gunny looked up at her mother's tear-streaked face hovering above her. "I told you this match was cursed. I told everyone but no one ever listens to me!"

Gunny heard a wail and realized the sound was coming from her. She tried to swallow. "Matt," she whispered. A salty taste filled her mouth and she spit a mouthful of blood onto the dusty road. She moved her head slightly and her vision swam as she looked through the shuffle of legs around her. When she moved her head to see better, a fresh shock of pain raced down her right hip and leg and she felt a rush of warm, sticky blood pour from between her legs.

Robert threw the hot gun to the ground. He grabbed Gunny's shoulders and gently held her still as a chill passed through her body. "Don't move, girl. It'd be best if you don't move."

Eileen appeared over Gunny again, gesturing and screaming but language was no longer clear to Gunny.

"Someone ride to Dingle," she heard as if someone were yelling from the bottom of a deep well. "Get a doctor. Can't you see we need a doctor?"

Then she saw her mother rise and point at Mac. The words were clearer. "Go to Dingle. Now!" She watched as Mac backed Evin away from the crowd and disappeared into the fog.

Robert stood just in time to catch Eileen as she fainted. He laid her down next to Gunny and pulled off his jacket to cover the two of them. Gunny blinked and moved her mother's limp arm away from her face, trying again to spot Matt in the crowd. Legs parted and there he was. She took a shallow breath. Kate McCrohan had her hands on his chest. Tears flowed down to her chin and dripped onto Matt's suit. His sisters clustered behind their mother, weeping. People stood whispering in small groups. Gunny's head swam. Why was Matt sleeping by the church gate, and why was everyone crying? She tried to crawl over her mother to see better. The pain in her leg and hip surged again and took her breath away. She squeezed her eyes shut and felt a chill pass again through her body. She gasped, then her eyes fluttered open as the sun broke through the fog and highlighted Matt's perfect, beautiful face as Kate lifted him from the road and pulled him into her arms. Matt's eyes stared back at Gunny and saw nothing.

"No!" she screamed and her world went black.

Gunny stood laughing on the strand at Ventry. She was the French Queen with seaweed hair flowing around her. She leaned into the wind and felt waves crash over her. Nella dipped above her and flew off into a dark sky. She heard Matt laugh and looked up as he climbed down from the stars on a large fishing net. He reached out for her and fell —down, down into the cold green water. She could hear him laughing as he fell but the sound grew fainter and fainter. She tried to cry out, to tell him to wait for her but she couldn't speak. Then Matt was gone and she stood alone in the cold, still water. She couldn't move, couldn't breathe.

The Burke twins and Ashling helped Robert move Gunny's limp body into Micky O'Leary's cart and carefully wheeled her home while Robert hobbled behind supporting Eileen. Cornelius and Michael sprinted ahead and moved a bed out of the Malones' back room to be close to the fire. Robert helped Eileen inside, then returned and carried Gunny's still form into the house. Her black curls lay tangled and dirty around her pale face. Her eyes fluttered behind closed lids. He thanked the boys and Ashling. They quietly backed out the door and left for O'Leary's.

Maeve helped Eileen strip Gunny of the ruined grey dress. Her right side, from armpit to foot was black and red, crushed and swollen. The bleeding from her mouth and from between her legs seemed to have stopped but she had not opened her eyes. Eileen's face was like stone as she washed the blood and dirt from her daughter's nearly lifeless body. She gently covered her with a blanket and said a prayer over her while they waited for the doctor and the priest to arrive.

A dolphin leapt from the wave next to Gunny. Matt's a dolphin! Of course. The dolphin nudged her then swam playfully away leaping over tiny white-capped ships. Gunny tried to swim after him but her gown and arms were heavy with sea water. She looked down. Her feet were tangled in seaweed. She tried to kick free and an incredible pain shot through her body.

"Hold her down," someone said. "Don't let her kick like that."

Who was holding her? She had to swim, to find Matt. Her world went black again.

The doctor and priest arrived at the same time. Father Jessey looked away as the doctor examined Gunny's bruised and swollen body.

"I don't think the leg is broken," the doctor announced, "but everything is so bruised and swollen right now it's hard to know what damage was done. I have no doubt the bones in her pelvis are broken." He shook his head. "Pelvic bones are like a basket that protects several delicate areas inside a girl," he said to Eileen making a cup-like basket with his hands. "The bleeding you described is from the pelvic area being crushed." He squeezed his hands closed to illustrate and Eileen winced. He tossed the covers over the girl's still form.

"She may never walk again and having children is out of the question," he said, standing and dusting off his hand.

Eileen stifled a sob. "But is she going to live?"

The doctor shook his head. "I can't say for sure. She's lost a lot of blood. All you can do is keep her still and warm. Try to drip a little water in her mouth each hour. If she fights off infection and fever she has a chance. We won't know much more until she wakes up."

Robert handed the doctor a few coins and he left.

Father Jessey moved to the bedside and took Gunny's right hand in his. He gently squeezed her hand and muttered a prayer.

"Thank you for your prayers, Father Jessey," Eileen whispered. "We'll pray by her side now. You can go."

Father Jessey looked at the sleeping girl, tears in his eyes. He squeezed her limp hand once more, picked up his hat, and left.

Gunny looked down from the chicken loft at her sleeping form on the bed in front of the low turf fire. She heard her mother sobbing in the back room. She wanted to tell her that she was all right but she didn't have any words. The room faded in front of her and she was a sheep in the Valley of the Mad. There were no feelings and no pain in the Valley of the Mad. There was no happiness, no misery. She felt numb and quiet. She had to wait. Her job was to wait...

Shep sat by Gunny's side through the night. When her cool hand fell from the covers, he nudged it but got no pat in reply. He scuttled about on the floor through the night trying to find a comfortable place to sleep under the bed. He stared at the sleeping girl as the first light of dawn lit the room. He pawed at the bed and whined. When the girl still did not stir, he scratched frantically at the door. Robert woke up from his nearby stool, and let the dog out. Shep chased the sheep out of the yard and up the road without the girl.

The McCrohan girls woke early to help clean the house for their brother's wake. Kate McCrohan laid her eldest son out on the table, feet toward the fire. She bathed him, then dressed him in his second best suit. She tucked a white sheet up under his arms to cover his legs and feet, and wove black rosary beads through his long, still fingers. She carefully arranged his long brown hair on the pillow, and kissed him softly on the forehead. She would never again look into his bright green eyes or hear his jaunty tunes or hear him pound by on that damned horse. She gently touched a small bruise on his chin.

"Your life taken and no more evidence of it than this. I'll never understand it, Matt. First your father and now you." She wiped her nose on a clean handkerchief and placed twelve candles at the base of the sheet. She lit eleven of them to represent the eleven good apostles. "Rest, Matt, my little boy who was always in a hurry for fear he'd miss something. Perhaps you knew how little time you had."

Kate McCrohan was the picture of calm as friends and neighbors arrived through the day to pay their respects. Each man doffed his cap and knelt by the body to say a prayer for Matt's soul. Each woman squeezed Kate's hand then joined the other women, keening. She greeted each visitor with a warm smile as if she were there to comfort them for their loss. "There, there," she murmured over and over patting arms and hands as neighbors tried to cheer one another with stories about Matt. She smiled but felt only darkness around her.

Mac had returned after delivering the doctor to the Malone house, and had disappeared into the forge. Kate waited all day for him to join them, but he did not come into the house. At sunset, she sent the girls out to the forge to get him. He sent word back that he needed no food, no comfort and would not come inside.

* * *

Gunny slept through the long day of Matt's wake. She stirred a few times and moaned in her sleep but never opened her eyes. Robert insisted that Eileen go with him to attend Matt's wake.

"Maeve and I'll stay with Gunny, Mam," Michael insisted. "You and Da should go and pay your last respects to Matt."

Eileen rose stiffly from her stool by Gunny's side and straightened her hair. She pulled her shawl tightly around her and picked up the untouched wedding cake from the table. "No use letting this go to waste," she said. "Lent will have to wait another day."

Maeve had been waiting all day for the cake to be shared. She slumped down on a stool by the fire and sighed as she watched Eileen walk out the door leaving only the sweet, lingering smell of cake behind her.

Robert grabbed his cap, took one last look back at Gunny's still form and joined Eileen outside. The snap of cool air made him shiver.

Kate McCrohan greeted the Malones at the door. Robert talked quietly with her while Eileen twisted through the crowd toward Matt's body. She gasped when she reached the table, dropped to her knees and clasped her hands tightly in front of her face.

"My daughter will soon be dead like you," she whispered. "I hope you're happy you reckless, wretch." She crossed herself and stood. "Amen," she said loudly.

She turned and looked around the crowded house. The same people would soon be gathered at her house for a second funeral from this accident. She glared at Kate McCrohan talking so easily to Fiona Burke. Kate's composed face fell when she glanced up and saw Eileen staring at her. She gave Fiona's hand a squeeze, and excused herself. She walked across the room and took Eileen's hands in hers.

"I'm so sorry," she said, her eyes filling with tears. "How's Gunny?"

Eileen pulled her hands free of Kate's warm grip.

"How do you think she is? That damned son of yours and his damned horse," she said loudly, then leaned in close to Kate's face. "You should have raised that boy better, Katie McCrohan. It's your fault Matt is dead and Gunny lies dying by my fire. Why did you let your boy ride that way?"

Kate buried her face in her hands and stifled a sob. Robert hurried across the room and took Kate by the elbow. Eileen pushed him away from Kate.

"Don't you dare comfort her when she's the one responsible for a murder. A murder!" she yelled. The room grew quiet. All eyes were on Eileen. "We all know my daughter will die soon and it's his fault," she said pushing through the crowd, crossing to Matt's body, and ripping away the sheet. Everyone gasped as the candles went flying and sputtered out across the floor. "How great are you now, Matt McCrohan? You insisted on marrying my daughter

191

and look what's become of it," she said in a low, snarling voice. Her voice grew softer as she turned from the body and looked around the room at the stunned faces. "How great is he now, laying there without one scratch on him?"

Mr. Hughes had been praying near Matt's body when Eileen's tirade began. He was still kneeling by Matt's side and tried to make himself as inconspicuous as possible. Eileen stumbled back into him, then turned and roughly grabbed him by the lapels and pulled him to his feet.

"You won't speak poorly of the dead, will you, Mr. Hughes?" she laughed manically. "No one will. Everyone's afraid of speaking poorly of the dead because maybe someone will speak poorly of them when they die. Isn't that right, Mr. Hughes?" she asked again, loudly. When he didn't answer, she tossed him aside and leaned over Matt's body. She grabbed his still face in her hands.

"Well, I'll speak poorly of the dead. I hate you, Matt McCrohan, and I hope you burn in hell." Her voice trailed off as she slumped onto Matt's body and wept.

Robert pulled her off of the body and gently wrapped her shawl around her. "That's enough," he muttered in her ear leading her toward the door. "You are fighting with a spirit that is no longer here."

After the Malones left, the house was disturbingly quiet. Kate took a deep breath and placed her hands gently on Matt's chest. She crossed herself, then straightened the rosary beads in the dead boy's hands and carefully pulled the white sheet up and tucked it back in around him. She turned to her girls. "Pick up the candles and re-light them," she said with a steady voice. She turned to the quiet crowd. "This is Matt's wake. He deserves a big send off. Drink up."

Then the drinking and storytelling began in earnest, starting first with stories about Eileen Malone and what a cracked pot she was. Then nearly everyone had a story to share about Matt, of all the crazy times they had had with him. The Wren Boys lead the crowd with challenges of agility and horse-play as the women sang and keened.

Mac listened to the shouts and laughter from the house. He pumped hard on the bellows until the room swam with heat and the sound of the roaring fire blocked out the sounds of the wake. He pulled white hot iron from the fire and pounded it until it shattered into small pieces. His head throbbed and his eyes stung but still he refused to cry. There could be no pity, even self pity, for the true murderer.

The funeral procession from the McCrohan house to the graveyard was set to start at noon the next day. By late-morning, mourners had begun to assemble along the road leading to the churchyard, all speaking softly of the tragedy.

When the back door of the McCrohan house opened the crowd along the road fell silent. Cornelius, Michael, and the Burke twins exited through the back door carrying the hastily prepared coffin. Kate McCrohan and her girls followed as the boys carried the long coffin past the forge and out to the road. Mac bolted the door to the forge closed, and the McCrohan women walked without him. As the coffin passed, men along the roadway removed their hats and crossed themselves, praying for the repose of the dead boy's soul. A few woman wrapped her shawls about their faces and wept. There were prayers and murmurings up and down the lane as men and women crossed themselves and remembered Matt McCrohan.

"I remember when he was this high…"

"Thundering by on that horse of his…"

"Every year the captain of the Wren Boys…"

"Looked after the forge after his father died… "

"I knew he'd meet an early end—his spirits were too high for this life…"

"A boy like that. Maybe he is better off dead than growing old…"

"It's a pity he had to die so young. But when God calls, you answer…"

"God rest his soul."

"God rest his soul."

"God rest his soul."

As the coffin passed, the villagers fell in behind and followed as the Wren Boys took the longest route possible, walking the coffin past the church, down to the strand and out by the pier, then back up the steep hill past O'Leary's pub, and finally in through the gates of the stone-walled church and up the center aisle.

Father Jessey waited at the pulpit until the villagers had all filed in and were seated in the long, hard pews. He glanced at the coffin as it lay at the front of the crowded church, wiped the sweat from his forehead and took a deep breath.

"We are gathered here today to celebrate the life of Mathew McCrohan and to take a lesson of what can happen when you live life too fast. Let us pray."

~ Chapter 10: Bedridden ~

Gunny woke up the third day after the accident, her mind cloudy. She lay still and blinked her eyes a few times. She could hardly breathe for the pain in her back and down her right side and leg. She turned her head slightly and looked at the low peat fire. Her head throbbed at the movement. Her mother was sleeping on a small mat on the floor in between Gunny's bed and the fire.

"Mam?" Gunny whispered.

Eileen stirred, then woke with a start. "You're awake!" she said scrambling to her feet. She felt Gunny's head. No fever. She squatted by the bed and closed her eyes in silent prayer.

Gunny looked at her mother's face in the dim light of the fire. "What happened?" she asked in a hoarse voice.

Eileen eyes filled with tears as she gazed at her waking daughter. She swallowed hard. "You don't remember? You made a fine muddle of your wedding day is what happened," she said, softly brushing a tear from one eye.

"I was waiting in the Valley of the Mad…"

Eileen placed a cool hand on Gunny's cheek. "Don't you remember the accident?"

Gunny's forehead wrinkled. Images flashed through her mind. Tucking dried flowers in her hair. Riding off with Matt into the hills. Making love in the booley. Thundering into town through swirling fog. A shadow in the fog. The feel of Matt's body flying off Nella. The images slowed and Gunny tried to take a deep breath. She closed her eyes and felt herself falling. Nella was falling with her. She felt a tremendous weight then heard three gunshots. She looked into Eileen's tear-filled eyes and felt her own eyes fill with hot tears. "Da shot Nella?"

"Yes," Eileen sobbed. "Your Da shot Nella—after you were pinned under that damned horse."

"And Matt?" Gunny asked softly.

Eileen bowed her head. Gunny tried to shift herself upright on the bed. An incredible pain shot through her right leg and up through her chest. Every muscle and bone in her body screamed out for her to be still.

"Don't move," Eileen said in a panic. "The doctor said you cracked your pelvic bone in the fall. You mustn't move or you'll start bleeding again."

"How long have I been asleep?" Gunny asked wiping her face with one hand.

"You've been in and out of a fever for three days. The doctor told us you might never wake up, that you might die. All I could do was give you little sips of water and keep a wet cloth on your head. You moaned and cried day and night."

Gunny licked her dry lips. Eileen stood and poured a cup of cool well water from the bucket near the door and held it to the girl's mouth. Shep pushed his head up under Gunny's hand. She absently stroked his smooth, black fur and he lay down next to the bed with a grunt.

"Mam," Gunny said in a quiet voice. "I doubted Matt, and God showed me there was more than one way for Matt to cross through those church gates."

"Shh, shh," Eileen said, walking to stir the fire. "What's done is done. All you can do now is rest."

"How can I rest when I…" Gunny paused. "What was that?"

"What was what?" Eileen asked, glancing around at the stuffy room.

Gunny struggled to sit up and winced. "I heard Nella whinny."

Eileen gently pushed Gunny still against her pillow. "Be still, Gunny. Nella's gone. Remember? You'll not hear that horse again."

Gunny looked at Eileen's pale face. "Why did Da shoot her?"

"When she fell she broke her leg. She was crazy on top of you. Your father had no choice." Eileen placed a fresh wet cloth on Gunny's forehead. "Your da's in Ventry today," she said, trying to change the subject. "The old Lord sent for him and wouldn't hear reason about his daughter and wife needing him here in Dunquin. Your da'll be so happy to find out you're awake."

"Where're Michael and Maeve?" Gunny asked listening to the quiet house.

"They're down at O'Leary having a pint. This's been very hard on them."

Gunny's eyes filled with tears. "Mam," she said in the soft, small voice of a little girl. "Where's Matt?"

Eileen took a long breath and pulled the cloth from Gunny's face. "I thought you understood, Gunny. Matt's gone." She looked wistfully toward the fire. "You know, there was hardly a mark on him at the wake. Only one little bruise at the base of his chin."

Gunny's eyes filled with tears. "Matt's wake? You already buried him? Why didn't you wait for me?"

"Because we didn't know… What difference would it make, Gunny. He's gone—that's all there is to it." She squeezed Gunny's slender hand. "I know it's painful when you lose a first love. It's hard to understand and hard to get over, but you have to live with the consequences of your actions," she said giving Gunny a knowing nod.

Gunny closed her eyes tight. "Your first love had a choice when he left. Matt didn't have a choice."

"Oh, Matt had a choice, Gunny. There's no one to blame for this but Matt."

Gunny closed her eyes tight and the tears spilled out onto her cheeks. "No, Mam. It's not Matt's fault. And I'll live the rest of my life knowing that."

* * *

Gunny blinked her eyes. Weak morning light was hazing in through the windows. Had she slept through another day? How many days? The fire smoldered in the hearth. She heard breathing. Someone was sitting next to her on the bed holding her hand.

"Matt?" she whispered.

"It's me, Gunny," Robert grunted in the dim light.

Gunny lay still feeling the heat of her father's large hand wrapped around her long cool fingers.

"I'm sorry I woke you," Robert said. "I'm headed to Ventry again. I wanted to tell you how happy I am that you are getting better. I've never been as scared as I was when I saw you lying there in the churchyard."

Gunny looked at her father's face. "You didn't shoot Nella because you were mad, did you?"

Robert shook his head. "I would never kill a horse in anger."

"But you were angry. I remember," Gunny said.

"Oh, I was plenty angry but mostly I was scared."

"But you shot her out of mercy," Gunny said.

"I did," Robert said. "There was no saving her. And I had to shoot her to save you."

Gunny squeezed her father's hand. "I'm sorry you had to do that, Da. She was a good horse."

Robert wiped his eyes with the back of his hand. Perhaps it was easier for Gunny to talk about Nella than it was to talk about Matt. He patted his daughter gently on the head and rose. "I'll be back in a couple of days. We'll talk more then. Rest and get better."

"I'll do the best I can," Gunny said and smiled weakly at her father's slouched, retreating back.

"Oh," Robert said turning back into the room. "I forgot. I stopped by the Murphy's shop in Dingle to tell them about the accident. The boy said to give you this." He reached into his pocket and pulled out Gunny's tin whistle. Gunny took the whistle from her father's outstretched hand. She wiped a tear away with the back of her hand and rested the cool whistle against her cheek.

"Joanna Murphy said she'd be out to see you as soon as you're up to having visitors."

Gunny shook her head. "Tell her not to come, Da. I don't want anyone to see me like this."

Robert gripped her shoulder. "There's no shame in this, Gunny. It was an accident. Everyone knows that."

Gunny snorted. "Everyone knows that I was to be married and instead I'm a cripple. There is shame in that, Da. I feel it right down to the end of my aching toes."

*　*　*

The doctor returned to examine Gunny. He pulled the covers back and pressed his hands into the black, purple, and yellow tissue that stretched from the base of her ribs across her middle, and all the way down her side to her knee. Gunny gasped in pain.

"That hurts?" he asked.

Gunny breathed out through clenched teeth. "Aye," she muttered. "My hip and leg ache and feel numb at the same time. And every muscle from my head to my toes hurts when I move."

The doctor pulled the blanket back up over the girl and turned to pack his bag. "Then don't move. You are swollen and bruised inside and out. The numbness will pass as the swelling goes down." He stood and turned to Eileen. "She'll be in pain for a month or more but she's healing. She's not to get out of bed for six weeks. Her bones need time to heal. Come April, she can try walking. By harvest time, she'll no doubt be out in the fields harvesting potatoes with the rest of you."

Eileen thanked the doctor and he picked up his small bag and left.

"Peeing in a bed pan for six weeks. How humiliating," Gunny said. Her hip and side ached afresh from the doctor's deep prodding. Why hadn't she just died when Matt died? Death couldn't be worse than being in so much pain. The warm room and blankets felt suffocating.

"When the doctor saw you right after the accident he said you could never have children, that you were all smashed up inside."

Gunny was quiet. "Thanks, Mam. I needed to know that."

Eileen snorted. "I felt you should know. I've been thinking about it ever since he said it. You might as well know all of the bad news now that you're staying awake longer."

Gunny felt a fresh rush of hot tears fill her eyes and pulled a pillow over her head.

"Putting a pillow over your head won't make bad news go away."

Gunny grunted and pushed the pillow away. "Some doctor he is. Of course I can't have children without a husband."

"He didn't say you'd never marry."

"Marry? You thought I was a difficult match before. Now in addition to being poor, I'm a barren cripple. A women who can't have children is no good to anyone."

Maeve sobbed loudly from her stool in front of the fire.

"Now, Maeve. Don't be crying over Gunny," Eileen asked.

Maeve stirred the pot of oatmeal and glanced over at Eileen and Gunny. She wiped her nose on her apron. "I'm not crying over her. Michael and I have been married for three years. Why don't we have children?"

Eileen looked at Maeve's soggy face and red nose. "You're still a child, Maeve. You married young. You have to give it time."

197

"How soon did you have Michael after you and Mr. Malone were wed?" Maeve whined.

Eileen's face reddened. "In our case it was very soon after, but everyone's different. I assume you're taking the necessary steps to have a child?"

Maeve sniffed loudly and giggled. "Oh, yes. We do plenty of that."

Eileen grabbed her shawl from the table and opened the front door. "I'm going out to look for eggs. Make sure the oatmeal doesn't burn," she said, leaving the house in a swirl of skirts.

Gunny listened to Maeve sniffling by the fire. "How I envy my mother. When I can walk again, I'll go out that door and never come back."

Maeve pulled a large spoonful of mush from the pot, blew on it, and licked it slowly off the spoon. Gunny watched in disgust.

"Perhaps if you ate less Michael might find you more appealing," Gunny said.

Maeve's back stiffened.

"All those sweets you ask him to get you when we have no money—you're making us poor and you're making yourself fat and sluggish. It's no wonder you don't have any children."

Maeve turned toward Gunny, her small eyes narrowing to slits. "You're jealous because I have a man and you don't," she said through plump, wet lips, her rotten right front eye tooth now black.

"That's only if you call my brother a man," Gunny said.

Maeve threw the large wooden spoon. It bounced off the wall near Gunny's head and fell to the floor. "How dare you insult my husband?"

"He was my brother long before he was your husband and I'll insult him anytime I like."

"Oh," Maeve said grabbing her apron with both hands as if she were going to tear it in two. "You make me so mad I want to pull that dirty curly hair of yours right off your head."

"Go ahead," Gunny said. "I can't be in any more pain than I'm in right now."

Maeve snatched the spoon from the floor and shook it in Gunny's face. "I don't feel sorry for you one bit. You got what you deserved."

"You're right, Maeve. I did. I had the best man anyone could ever want. One day with him was better than a lifetime with any other man."

"I hope it was," Maeve said, "because that's all you got. No man will ever want you again."

There was soft knock on the door. Eileen set down her mending and opened the door. Gunny felt a welcome draft of cool air, then heard a despised voice.

"I hear our girl's awake," Father Jessey said from the doorway, taking Eileen's hand.

Gunny growled from the bed. "I'm not your girl."

"Come in, Father," Eileen said opening the door wider. "I'm sure Gunny'll be glad for the company."

The tall priest took off his hat and pushed a lock of loose blond hair from his forehead. He set his hat carefully on the table and walked stiffly to Gunny's bedside. The thick layer of covers made Gunny seem small. Her face was ashen; her black curls lay flat and matted across the pillow.

"Go away," she snarled, her voice not nearly as faint as her looks.

"Forgive her, Father," Eileen said crossing her arms. "She's not been herself since she woke up." She turned to Gunny. "Be nice, Gunny. Father Jessey'll only be here for a minute."

Gunny looked up at the ceiling, puffed out her cheeks and held her breath until she thought her lungs would burst, then blew out the air. "A minute's up," she said looking at Father Jessey. "You can go."

"Gunny," Father Jessey started, pushing his blond hair again from his forehead. "I know you are in pain and that you are angry..."

Gunny stared at the slim priest. "Really? How can you tell?"

Father Jessey looked to Eileen for help. Eileen glanced at him, eyebrows raised, then sat on a stool by the fire and took up her mending. Father Jessey walked to the foot of the bed and stood with his eyes closed.

Gunny glared at the priest. "Do you enjoy torturing me?" she asked in a loud voice. "Is the purpose of your life to make me crazy?"

"Shhh. I have something to tell you, Gunny."

"I don't want to hear anything that comes out of that mouth of yours."

"You don't know what I'm going to say," the priest clipped.

"I don't care what you have to say. I want you to go away. I don't want you to ever talk to me again."

The priest closed his eyes. "Gunny, I'm praying for you to listen to me."

"I don't have to listen to you. I don't have to listen to anyone. And if you are going to pray, pray that I'll be able to walk again so that I can walk, no, run away from you. All of you!" she shouted.

Eileen winced from her stool by the fire.

Father Jessey opened his eyes. "If my being here makes you want to run then I am going to stop by every day to see you. The Lord works in mysterious ways, Gunny."

Gunny closed her eyes. "Stop with your prayers and mysterious ways, Father. I don't want to get better. I want to die. I want to be with Matt."

"Gunny," Father Jessey said, "you are not to question the Lord's ways. Matt..."

"Father," Gunny interrupted. "Don't tell me what I should and shouldn't question as I lie here wondering how any God could take away a man as decent as Matt McCrohan and leave me behind, a crumpled, crippled heap."

Father Jessey picked up his hat and ran his hands slowly around the rim. "You should let me speak, Gunny."

"I don't want to. Please go away," Gunny said turning her face toward the fire.

Father Jessey paused, set his hat down again on the table and picked up a low stool from the hearth. He sat next to Gunny's bed and took her right hand in both of his. Gunny pulled her hand away and thrust her arm deep under the covers.

"Gunny, Gunny, Gunny," Father Jessey muttered, folding his hands in front of his face. "Dear Lord," he intoned. "Please help me talk to this girl."

Gunny gasped. "What gives you the right to speak to God on my behalf?"

The priest smiled. "Gunny, aren't you tired of running from the flock?"

"Hah!" Gunny said. "I am no more tired of running from the flock than you are being fettered to the flock. We all know you hate it here."

"God, the Father, protect us," Father Jessey chanted.

Gunny let out a high whistle through her teeth. "God didn't do a very good job of protecting Matt, now did he?"

Father Jessey stood and shook out his loose, black robe. "God has a plan for each of us Gunny. We are not to question the wisdom of God." He scooped up his hat from the table then slowly turned back to Gunny. "As soon as you can walk, I expect to see you in church. You may be surprised what you find there."

"Father, when I can walk, the last place you'll find me is in your church."

"I forgive you for that," Father Jessey said.

"You forgive me for what?"

"You must trust God, Gunny. And trust me."

"Trust you?" She reached up, grabbed the priest's hand and pressed his palm flat against her chest. "Do you feel my heart breaking with each beat? I want Matt back," she said her eyes filling with tears. "Can I trust you to do that for me?"

The priest twisted his hand free of the girl's weak grip. "Come to the church, Gunny, and you'll see what miracles God can perform."

Gunny grabbed his hand again and squeezed his fingers tight together. "Matt died like the heroes of old," she said through clenched teeth. "Like the knights and the kings and the pirates. Maybe your god, your hero, is dead too."

Eileen tossed her mending aside and stood. "That's enough, Gunny. Father, I told you Gunny's not herself. Perhaps you could come back another time."

Father Jessey pulled his hand away. "I'll be back tomorrow afternoon. We'll talk again," he said striding toward the door.

"Careful you don't stumble on the way home and fall into the creek!" she shouted at his departing back.

Father Jessey slowly turned in the doorway and pointed at her. "I will keep coming to see you until I find that you are no longer in that bed. Then you'll come to the church and we'll talk." He pulled his hat down tight onto his head and turned toward Eileen. "Good afternoon, Mrs. Malone, Miss Malone." He left the house pulling the door closed behind him.

Robert sat drinking at a small table at the back of O'Leary's Pub. It was mid-afternoon and there was no one else in the pub but Micky O'Leary. Robert sighed and swirled his glass of warm porter. John McCrohan was gone. Nick was gone. Matt was gone. And Gunny was a cripple. Robert downed his glass and yelled over to Micky for another. The pub door opened letting in unwelcome light. Robert squinted as his wife walked in and approached his table.

"You'll be coming home now," she said in a low voice.

"I'll be coming home when I'm ready."

"Now would be better."

Robert looked at his wife. "Is the fever back? Is something wrong with Gunny?"

"No, nothing's wrong. We miss you. That's all."

Robert sighed. "Why don't you have a drop with me, then we'll walk home together?"

"I would love to sit here and drown my sorrows, but isn't it enough that one of us is cracked?"

Robert sighed and wiped the back of one hand over his mouth. He pushed back from the table and stood with a grunt. "We're off then, Micky. Hold that glass for me till next time, will you?"

Micky smiled and gave a wave as Robert pushed in his chair and stumbled toward the door with Eileen trailing close behind him.

Kate McCrohan hiked up to the Malones' small house with a loaf of warm bread neatly wrapped in a clean flour sack. Eileen greeted her stiffly at the door. She took the bread but did not ask Kate in. The two women had not spoken since the wake.

"Gunny's resting," Eileen explained.

"I'd like to see her."

"She's resting."

"You said…"

Eileen stared at Kate McCrohan willing her to go away.

"Who is it, Mam?" Gunny called hoarsely from the bed.

Eileen turned to Gunny. "It's no one," she said flatly.

"I'd like a visitor," Gunny said in a small voice.

Eileen sighed and opened the door. "Don't be long," she said to Kate, grabbing her shawl from the bench near the door and picking up the water bucket. "Gunny needs her rest."

Kate gently closed the door and turned to Gunny. "I hope it's all right for me to visit."

"Mrs. McCrohan," Gunny teared up. "Please pull up a stool."

Kate picked up a stool and placed it near Gunny's bed. The room was dark and cramped with the bed so close to the fire. Gunny looked pale and thin, not at all herself. Kate took the girl's cool, limp hand in hers. "I'll only stay a minute," she said, gently squeezing Gunny's hand. "I've been thinking about you and wanted to see for myself how you were doing. It's been nearly a month..."

Gunny gently pulled her hand free of Kate's grip and thrust it under the covers. "I still can't walk," she said.

"What does the doctor say?"

"He says to give it time, that I cracked a bone in here somewhere," Gunny said patting the tender area around her right hip.

Kate shook her head. "I'm sure you'll heal, Gunny. You're young. I'm so sorry..."

"Don't be sorry," Gunny interrupted.

"But I am sorry, Gunny. I'm sorry Matt was so crazy with that horse of his. If I told him once, I told him a thousand times to slow down, to be more careful."

"Matt never listened to anyone."

"No, he didn't."

Gunny managed a weak smile. "That's part of what made him who he was."

Kate's brow wrinkled. "His stubborn streak?"

"No," Gunny said, "that he was always so sure of himself. The rest of us scurry around and farm and fish. Matt put himself above all that."

"It didn't work out so well for him," Kate said with a sigh.

"He died trying to marry me, trying to be normal. It wasn't in him," Gunny said, her eyes filling with an hourly spill of tears.

"But you're the one who's paying the price, Gunny. I'll never forgive myself for what Matt did to you."

Gunny laughed. "I am the one who should be asking for forgiveness. If it weren't for me..."

"Shush. If it weren't for you, Matt would've had no joy in life. He hated living here and working in the forge. We all knew that. The only time I saw light in his eyes since his father passed were the days he came back from seeing you in Dingle. The night you told him you would marry him... well, I'd never seen him happier."

Gunny closed her eyes. "When I was working in Dingle, I'd hear Matt come thundering up behind me, then whoosh, I'd be up behind him in the saddle and we'd be off. I still hear Nella sometimes," she said in a small voice.

Kate paused. "You hear Nella?"

"I know it sounds crazy, but nearly every day I hear her whinny and paw at the front door." Gunny no longer mentioned this to her mother. She looked Kate in the eye, then looked away and closed her eyes.

"Well," Kate said standing. "I should let you rest."

"Mrs. McCrohan?" Gunny said, eyes still closed.

"Yes?"

Gunny opened her eyes. "Thank you for coming by. Talking with you… it's the first time I've had even a wee smile since I woke up."

Kate let out a breath she did not know she had been holding. "Any time you want to talk…" She patted Gunny's hand and let herself out. She stopped to lean against the front wall of the house and take a deep breath of the warm spring air. The visit was harder than she'd expected. She saw Eileen at the top of the hill headed back to the house with a sloshing bucket of water. She waved as she left the yard. Eileen looked right through her and did not wave back.

Heavy rain beat against the front window. Gunny's eyes fluttered open. She glanced around the dusky room. Maeve was kneeling by the fire.

"Where's Matt?" Gunny asked.

"Matt's gone," Maeve answered said in a sing-song voice. "You ask me that every time you wake up, and every time I tell you: Matt's gone." She turned to the fire and stirred the embers, then picked out a new turf and pushed it in amongst the hot coals.

Gunny fell back against the pillow. Pain shot through her hip and down her right leg. She shifted around on the bed trying to find a position that was comfortable. "The dreams're so real. I see him. I smell his tobacco smoke." Her eyes teared and she wiped her face with the back of her sleeve. For a girl who never cried, why did she cry now all the time?

"I'm not interested in what you smell, Gunny."

Gunny swallowed hard and sniffed. "It's hot in here."

"It takes away the damp. If you are too hot, kick off some of those covers."

Gunny rested her hand on her immobile right leg feeling the ache deep down inside her. "Open the door, Maeve. Let in some fresh air."

Maeve turned toward Gunny and stood, hands on hips. "Look, little Miss Princess. I'm tired of waiting on you hand and foot with your bed pans and your blankets and your pillows. It's too hot. It's too cold. You need water. You need to relieve yourself. All the while you're sleeping in my bed while Michael and I sleep on a straw mat on the floor. Honestly, Gunny, things were a lot better before you came back from Dingle."

The front door banged open. Both girls started as rain and wind swept in around Eileen's soaked skirts. Eileen pushed the door closed with one foot and set a basket with a few eggs in it on the table. She took off her shawl, angrily shook off the rain and tossed her shawl over a stool near the fire. "You're awake," she said to Gunny.

"Sort of," Gunny mumbled.

"She was dreaming about Matt again," Maeve reported. "Gunny said she could smell his tobacco smoke."

Eileen turned to warm her hands by the fire. "That's Maeve smoking, Gunny."

Gunny rubbed her face with her hands. "No. I smelled Matt's tobacco."

"She's crazy," Maeve said. "I don't know how you can stand her."

Eileen turned on Gunny. "You're making yourself crazy, Gunny. You need to stop thinking about Matt."

"I'll never stop thinking about Matt," Gunny said in a soft voice.

Eileen sighed and absentmindedly ran a finger over her stash of eggs. "Someday the memories will fade."

"Are you talking about Matt, Mam? Or your old love, Moss Barney?"

"Matt, Moss, what's the difference?" Eileen said, her voice rising slightly in pitch.

Maeve covered her mouth with a plump hand to hide a snicker. Gunny stared at the rain drops flowing down the front window. "If I could only re-live that one day or even one moment of that day. If we'd only left a little earlier for the church. Or if it hadn't been so foggy. Or if Mac had decided to walk to the church instead of riding Evin..."

"If, if, if," Eileen snapped. "You're tormenting yourself and making the rest of us miserable. It's over. It's time for you to get back on your feet."

"That's the problem, isn't it?" Gunny said, rubbing a hand down her still leg under the covers. "How am I supposed to live like this?"

"The doctor told you your bones would mend and you'd be able to walk again. Why don't you try putting some weight on that leg?"

"I've tried," Gunny said with a groan. "It hurts too much."

"The doctor said it would be better soon."

Gunny gasped. "How does the doctor know how much something hurts and when it'll stop? Has he ever had his insides crushed by a horse?"

A gust of wind rattled the front window as it pushed blades of rain up hard against the house. Gunny put a hand over her eyes. "Where's Da? He's never around anymore."

Eileen walked to Gunny's side and put her hands on her hips. "He's down at the pub. And if I had a choice, I'd be down there too. We know you're in pain but it would help if you could cry a little less, if you could try and be a little more chipper..."

Gunny pulled her blanket up over her face. "I'm sorry to be such a spoiled child," she said loudly from under the covers. "What a nuisance I must be, lying here in your way all day, messing up your tidy house." She pulled the covers away from her face and stared at the door. "What does it matter that I lost the love of my life and that my legs will never be right again? Why should that bother me so much?"

"This is what I am talking about," Eileen said with a sigh. "It's no wonder your father's never around."

"I'm bored," Gunny said. "Can't someone read to me?"

Robert was sitting in front of the fire puffing on his pipe. The fields were fertilized and planted and it was too early to be at O'Leary's. "You know we're not readers, Gunny," he said through a cloud of smoke.

"Then can you find me a newspaper? John McCrohan always had one. Maybe Mac's been to Dingle and has a paper."

Robert turned to Gunny. "Why do you want a paper?"

"You used to like it when John McCrohan shared the news of the day. And James used to read the paper with me in Dingle. I could read to you. I know the words."

Robert knocked ash out of his pipe and stood. "I'll see what Micky has down at O'Leary's. There's no use trying Mac McCrohan."

Gunny paused. "What's wrong with Mac? I thought you said he was fine from the accident."

"Fine in the body, Gunny, but not in the mind. Mac's hardly spoken a word to anyone since the accident and never leaves the forge from what Kate says. I wonder if he'll ever be right again."

Robert returned an hour later with a stack of old newspapers and tossed them on Gunny's bed. The light was poor in the house. Gunny took a paper from the stack and carefully shifted over in the bed to be closer to the fire. She looked at the large words at the top of the page and spelled them out in her mind: Land Dispute in Co. Kerry. The next print on the page was very small and hard to read in the dim light. She concentrated on each letter of each word, skipping words that were too big to guess at. By afternoon she had finished one column.

She pictured Matt snatching the paper away from her. "Here, I'll read that for you," she could hear him say. She grabbed hold of the paper with both hands and started at the top of the second column. "I've got it, Matt," she said, arguing with herself.

Gunny lay in a messy nest of blankets, pillows and papers dully aware of the activity around her as she looked intently at the stack of newspapers she'd now read through a dozen times.

"If you don't hurry, there won't be any May Day festivities to join in," Eileen complained.

Maeve was having trouble buttoning her dress and Michael was trying to help. "Go ahead without us," Michael said. "We'll be there soon enough."

Eileen gave a snort and practically sprinted out the door dragging Robert behind her.

Gunny listened to Michael and Maeve wrestle in the back room with Maeve's dress. They finally emerged, red-cheeked and laughing.

"I don't suppose you'll be celebrating May Day this year?" Maeve asked Gunny with a sweet half-grin.

"You don't suppose correctly."

"But you don't mind that we're going, right?" Michael asked, uncertain that he was going to like his sister's answer.

"Why on earth would I mind, Michael?"

Maeve grabbed Michael's arm. "She wants us to stay and wait on her, don't you, Gunny?"

Michael squeezed Maeve's arm. "Be nice, Maevey girl."

Maeve pulled Michael away from Gunny's bed and whispered loudly. "I don't know why I have to take care of her. It's not like I'm a servant here. She's not nice. You should hear what she says to me when you're not around."

"I know, Maevey. You've told me. But I'm nice, aren't I?" he asked, giving Maeve's round bottom a quick slap. Maeve giggled.

"I can hear you," Gunny said loudly from the bed, flipping an old paper open to read it once again. "I'm crippled, not deaf."

Michael looked over at his thin sister. "Gunny, can you at least try to be nice to Maeve?"

"She was silly as a little girl and she's even sillier now," Gunny said without looking up from the page.

"We're going out," Michael said.

"You're supposed to stay in the house after a death in the family," Gunny said from behind the paper.

Maeve stuck out her chin and placed her fists on her wide hips. "You never married Matt so we don't have to mourn him."

Gunny folded the paper and set it beside her on the bed. She closed her eyes. "Go to the festival. Go anywhere you want. I don't care."

Maeve took a step toward the bed. "Do you mind if I borrow your hat?" she asked in a perky voice, eying Gunny's broad-rimmed black hat that hung neglected on its peg by the door.

"No, is there anything else you'd like?" Gunny scoffed from behind closed eyes.

Maeve took Gunny's hat from the peg and pulled it down tight on her head. She eyed a wide black ribbon that was hanging behind the hat.

"Since you offered, I'll take this as well." She had Michael tie the ribbon around one wrist then held out her arm to admire the look.

Gunny opened her eyes when she heard the latch click behind the departing couple and let out a long breath.

"Dear Lord," she prayed to the ceiling. "Were Matt and I as disgusting to be around as the two of them? Did we ever put bits of food in each other's mouths? Did we have little pet names for one another? If we did, I could see why you'd take Matt away from me…" Gunny sat up on one elbow, winced in pain and starred at the door. "You two were made for one another!" Her voice rang flat in the still room and she slumped back in bed. "Matt and I were different," she said looking up at the ceiling. "We went hunting and fishing and rode on Nella. We were interesting!" She paused. "God, I'm talking to myself," she said and closed her eyes, then carefully rolled onto one side and stared into the fire.

"God," she said more prayerfully, "I'm locked up in my solitude and there is such a weight in my heart. How is it you make certain there is someone for everyone—and then you take that someone away?"

There was no pop from the fire, no wind at the window to let her know that God was listening. She pulled the covers up around her head and sniffed. "No one will ever understand me the way Matt understood me."

There was a soft knock at the door. Gunny pulled the covers down and listened. Maybe if she was quiet whoever it was would go away. There was a second knock a little louder this time. Gunny grunted. "Come in."

The door remained closed.

"Come in!" she yelled a little louder.

She saw the latch move and the door open a few inches. Mac's face appeared in the crack. "Gunny?" he asked in a small voice.

Gunny had not seen Mac since the accident. "Go away."

"I…," he started.

"I don't want to see you. Go away."

"I…," Mac started again.

"Mac," Gunny said sitting up slightly in bed and wincing at the effort. "I'm not well. I don't want to see you. I don't want to see anyone."

"I have a delivery for you."

Gunny paused. "Come in. Make your delivery then leave. Please," she added, remembering what her father had said about Mac.

Mac remained in the doorway, his hand resting on the door latch. "I'm sorry."

Gunny was quiet. "Is that your delivery? That you're sorry? It wasn't your fault."

"It was. If I hadn't been there…"

"It was an accident, Mac," Gunny said too loudly, then quieter, "You know it was an accident."

"Still…," Mac said.

She looked at Mac standing awkwardly in the crack of the doorway. "Don't just stand there with the door open."

Mac paused, then slipped inside and closed the door behind him. Gunny stared at him.

"Matt's gone and I'm lame… and you don't have a scratch on you, do you Mac?"

Mac looked down, his face red. "I finished this and I wanted to give it to you," he stammered, taking a step into the house and pulling a large iron cooking crane out from behind his back. He held it out toward Gunny with both hands. "It was meant to be a wedding present."

Gunny studied the elaborate cooking crane with its beautiful little curls of metal along the top and down the side. It had three arms at different heights to allow for three pots to heat at once. She'd never seen anything like it. "It looks like something you'd see in the old Lord's house. Why did you make something so fancy?"

Mac's forehead showed a faint sheen of sweat. He placed the crane at the foot of Gunny's bed. "I knew you'd say that," he said with a short laugh.

Gunny reached down and pulled her limp leg away from the weight on the bed. "I don't want it."

Mac shifted awkwardly from one leg to the other.

"Are you deaf from all your hammering?" Gunny asked looking Mac in the eye. "I said I don't want it. Please go away. I have to rest," she said closing her eyes.

Mac backed toward the door without the crane.

"Mac," Gunny said firmly without looking at him or at the crane. "Take that off my bed. I don't want to see it again."

Mac stepped quickly to the bed and picked up the heavy piece of iron work. He walked to the door and left, pulling the door tightly closed behind him.

Gunny opened her eyes and wept.

Gunny whistled softly for Shep. The dog trotted over from a spot near the door and rested his chin on the edge of the bed. He stared at her as Gunny gently stroked his head.

"I know you want to go outside," Gunny said. "You should've gone with Da to the fields this morning. Everyone is out now and I can't get up. I told you my leg is bad." It was funny how even Maeve left her alone in the house now.

Shep put his white, right paw on the frame of the bed.

"No, you can't come up here," she said resting a thin finger on the dog's nose.

Shep put his paw back on the floor. He rested his chin again on the edge of the bed and let out a high whine.

"Stop that," she said. "I wish I could walk with you."

At the word "walk" Shep's eyes brightened and he trotted to the door. Gunny leaned back in bed. She had to be careful what she said around Shep. He knew so many words but apparently he did not understand the word "wish".

"We're not going out," she said firmly.

Shep stared at her then trotted to his mat near the hearth. He circled a few times and plopped down on the floor with a grunt.

"Oh fine," she said. "Now I can't even pet you? I thought you were my best friend. I guess that's only when I can walk with you."

Shep ignored the girl this time when she said the word "walk". He tucked his head between his front paws and closed his eyes.

When Gunny woke the next morning, Shep was at her side, his chin resting on the bed staring at her. She stared into his light blue eyes.

"Stop willing me to get up, Dog," she said. The house was quiet.

Shep continued to stare at her. She reached down and felt her right leg and hip. When she was lying down she mostly felt no pain now but when she tried shifting her legs around on the bed the ache started again. She pushed herself to a sitting position and used her arms to pull her legs around on the bed, then gingerly lowered her legs to the floor. She felt dizzy. She sat still until the spell passed, then leaned forward and put a little weight first on her left leg and then on her right. Her right leg and hip ached but there was no sharp pain.

She grasped the edge of the bed, crouched forward, and stood. The familiar searing pain ripped through her right leg and hip. She caught her breath. "I hate that," she muttered. But then the pain ebbed to a dull throb. She remained standing and slowly straightened. It felt good to stand. She looked down at Shep. His blue eyes were laughing. He raced to the door and stood up on his hind legs as if he were going to undo the latch himself.

"You win," she muttered. "I'm up." She took a tentative step forward. "And I'm moving," she said with a slow smile.

She shuffled to the end of the bed, then grasped a stool to move toward the fire. Her legs were weak from being in bed for so many weeks. She moved slowly toward the front wall, grabbed the sill of the window, and peeked out through the dirty glass. Everything looked as it always had—messy yard, dung hill, green fields beyond. How could it be that everything looked the same when her world had completely changed?

She moved slowly along the wall, braced herself against the frame of the door, and raised the latch. She was shocked at the feel of wind and sun on her face. She squeezed her eyes shut. Shep pushed past her nearly knocking her over in an attempt to get out into the yard. Gunny grasped the door frame to steady herself. "Heat and light," she said, turning her face toward the sun as she stepped through the open doorway. She gingerly slid out onto the wooden bench. She closed her eyes and took a deep breath, relishing the fresh air and feeling of warm sun on her face.

She heard Eileen and Maeve as they approached the house, bickering, their voices raised and biting. She opened her eyes a small slit and watched them walk into the yard, each carrying a bucket of water. When Eileen saw her, it was as if she had seen a ghost. She set down her bucket and ran to the bench.

"How did you get out here?" she gasped.

Gunny chuckled. "I walked, Mam. The dog wanted to go out."

Eileen glared at Shep who tucked his tail between his legs and ran around the corner of the house. She took Gunny's arm and tried to lift her. "Let me help you inside. You shouldn't be out here."

Gunny pulled her arm free of her mother's grip. "You said it was time for me to try my legs again. Remember—the doc said if I didn't try soon I might never walk again. I'll go back in a minute. Right now, the sun feels like a blessing."

Eileen looked at the sun on her daughter's pale, thin face. "The sun's hot," she said. "You should be inside." She held her hand out to Gunny. Gunny sighed, pulled herself up with the help of her mother, and went back to bed.

Bitsy Kavanaugh knocked on Kate's door and stepped inside. "My horse needs a new shoe and Mac won't talk to me. How am I supposed to get Grady shoed if Mac won't do it? Grady's an old horse. He'll never make it to Dingle with one shoe missing."

"Mac is taking Matt's death hard," Kate said with a shake of her head.

"As he should," Bitsy agreed. "But it's been three months and there's work to do. We need our smithy."

Kate sighed. "I'll talk to him, Bitsy."

Mac was in the forge beating at a twisted piece of iron. Kate sat on a stool inside the stuffy room waiting for him to finish. He roughly pushed the hot iron from the anvil into a bucket of water. When the hissing stopped, Kate opened her mouth to speak but paused while Mac tossed two bricks of turf into the forge and pumped angrily on the bellows. Kate walked to her son and laid a hand on his arm.

"We have to talk," she said softly.

Mac shook off his mother's hand and continued to pump the bellows.

"Mac," Kate said in a louder voice, her hand resting firmly on Mac's arm. "Stop pumping those bellows and look at me."

Mac turned and looked at his mother. His face and hair were wet with sweat, his black eyes sunken and haunted. He had lost weight since the accident. He looked down at his worn boots

"I know you hate me," he mumbled.

"I could never hate you," Kate gasped.

"But I killed Matt," Mac said, his eyes filling with tears.

Kate pulled Mac toward her. He reeked of sweat. She held him away. "You need a bath."

Mac looked confused. "What?"

"I'm sorry," Kate laughed. "You're finally talking and all I can do is tell you that you need a bath, but you do, Mac. You really do."

Mac wiped the sweat from his brow and took a step away from her. "I want to die, Mam. I want to take Matt's place."

Kate took his dirty hands in hers. "We don't get that choice, son. Now go wash off in the creek then come back and start talking to our customers again. I managed to do the spring planting with your sisters, but you have to do your share of work too. There's plenty to be done here in the forge."

"How can we go on as if nothing happened?" Mac asked.

"We'll never forget Matt," Kate said. "I ache for him as much as you do. But we're alive and people are depending on us. So work, Mac. Please. I need you to be strong."

Mac started eating his evening meals again with his mother and sisters and began to talk to customers again in the forge. But he would not use Evin, the work horse, to make deliveries. He insisted on making all deliveries himself using a small push cart, and eventually sold the horse to an ecstatic farmer in Ventry for a sum less than half what the large horse was worth.

Robert sat smoking his pipe by the fire as Eileen swept briskly around the posts of Gunny's bed. "There isn't enough room in here with this bed by the fire. Why don't you add another room, Robert?"

"A house two rooms wide is unlucky," Robert stated. "You know that."

"How could our house be any unluckier, Da?" Gunny asked, turning toward her father. "Lord Ventry's house has rooms going in every direction and you can't say they're unlucky."

"Who's to say what's lucky and what's not lucky?" Robert muttered from the fire.

Eileen stopped sweeping and looked at Gunny. "We should move that bed back where it belongs."

Gunny pulled her legs off the bed and set her feet on the floor. "Fine, Mam. Move me away from the fire. Give my bed back to Michael and Maeve so they can produce a grandbaby for you. I'll just sleep over in the byre with the animals."

"I could make a smaller bed and hang it from the wall," Robert said eyeing Gunny's bed. "Then Gunny could sleep by the fire but we could close the bed during the day. My grandmother had a bed like that in our house growing up."

"What if I need to rest during the day?" Gunny asked, frowning.

"Then you'll pull the bed down."

Robert sorted through his collection of bog wood and worked all day in the yard on a hinged drop-down bed. By evening, the large bed was once again in squeezed into the back room, and Michael and Maeve lay snugly together, chatting.

Robert showed Gunny how to lower her new bed and set the feet squarely on the dirt floor. She pulled her nest of blankets off the table and tossed them onto the rough plank bed. Robert wished her a good night and crawled into bed with Eileen in the crowded back room.

Gunny carefully lowered herself onto the new bed. It felt strange and uncomfortable. The back room grew quiet and the fire died low but her mind raced. She could hear Matt singing old songs by the fire in the booley. She hummed along, then heard that now familiar whinny and pawing at the door. A chill moved up her spine. She pulled the blanket up over her head and squeezed her eyes shut. Why wouldn't the horse go away?

She heard a small tap at the front window. She held her breath. A second tap made her look. As clear as if it were daylight, she saw Matt's face in the moonlight. He grinned at her and waved. She blinked and he was gone. She pushed back the covers, shuffled to the door, and opened it a small crack. Outside, the moon cast deep swirling shadows in the misty, empty yard. She clutched at the door frame as a rush of wind blew up her skirts.

"Stop scaring me," she whimpered into the empty yard. "Stop racing about in my dreams. No one wants to hear me talk about you haunting me. No one wants to see me cry over the two of you. You're gone. You're gone," she cried, pushing the door closed and slumping into a heap on the floor.

Father Jessey had business to attend to. He tucked a broken candlestick under one arm and headed off for the McCrohan forge. The midsummer sun was sweltering and the tall priest was uncomfortably sweaty by the time he arrived. He knocked at the door and it swung partly open. He took a deep breath and leaned inside."

"I have a candlestick that needs repair," he yelled. "Could you step out and take look?"

Mac glanced up from his work at the anvil. "Come in," he said roughly from the dark room.

Father Jessey reluctantly stepped inside. The forge was hot and littered with discarded wheels, bits of metal rod, horseshoes and old pots. It smelled of ash, and hot metal, and sweat. The heat and clutter took his breath away. "Your father used to come outside to meet me."

"I'm not my father." Mac took the candlestick from the priest and ran his hands over the cool, shiny metal. The fine silver stem was dented in several places. "What have you been hammering at with this?" he asked.

"None of your business. Can you fix it?"

"I suppose I can. It'll take a minute."

"Hurry, please," the priest said, fanning himself and cocking his head slightly to the side. As Mac turned to pump the bellows, Father Jessey glanced around the forge. A tall structure in the far corner of the room caught his eye. He walked over for a closer look. "What is this?"

Mac glanced over his shoulder. "Nothing," he said. "I started that years ago and never finished."

The priest stepped gingerly around a pile of patched pots and ran his hands over elaborate curled iron spikes. "This is huge. It looks like part of a gate. Such detail," the priest said, breathless.

Mac grunted. "It's too fancy. I meant to take it apart."

"Don't you dare," Father Jessey said protectively. "People would travel from far and wide to see gates like these. How much would it cost for you to build the other half?"

Mac continued to heat the candlestick. "It's not for sale."

"Nonsense. Everything can be had for a price."

Mac looked at the twisted silver stem in his hand and pictured Matt's twisted body lying by the old church gates. He had a figure in mind for what a gate should cost. He doubled it knowing the priest could never pay it.

"I'll see what I can do," the priest said, hurrying out of the forge.

"What about your candlestick?" Mac called after him. But the priest was halfway down the road, his black cloak flowing out behind him.

Shep had not returned home with Robert after a day harvesting early potatoes. Gunny listened for a scratch at the door but the yard was silent. As the late August sun set in the far western sky, Robert slid off his boots and lit his pipe by the fire.

Gunny sat on a stool by her father. "Shep's getting old. Maybe you should go out and look for him."

"He's not that old. He's eleven and is as healthy as the day he was born," Robert said. "He'll be back."

Gunny stared into the fire. "What if he's in trouble and needs our help?"

Robert sighed and pushed up from the stool. He went out into the yard and gave three long whistles but Shep did not appear. He whistled again after the evening meal, and one last time before he went to bed. "I'll be damned if that dog's been taken off by the fairies," he muttered, closing and bolting the door for the night.

Gunny tossed and turned on the small wooden bed and was awake at first light. She hobbled to the door and scanned the yard and nearby fields. Where was the dog? She came back inside, cut a slab of bread and tucked it into her apron pocket, then headed back for the door. She tripped on her skirt and fell hard against the table. She heard her father grunt from the back room at the sound, but no one stirred. She examined the offending skirt. She had lost so much weight, it hung down too long in the front. She synched it up around her waist and retied her apron to keep it tight around her waist, then eyed the tall walking stick propped up by the door. Eileen had pulled it out of the loft when Gunny started to walk again. She said it belonged to Gunny's grandfather.

"I'm not going about like a cripple using that old cane," she told her mother.

Now she limped to the door and took the heavy stick in one hand. She liked the smooth feel of polished wood. She stepped outside, pulled the door closed quietly behind her, and whistled for Shep. Her breath caught when the dog still did not appear and she wanted to cry. Instead, she shuffled through the yard and around the end of the house, leaning heavily on the walking stick. When she reached the road, she looked up toward the fields around Mount Eagle. That was most likely where Shep was but the steep hill looked daunting. She looked down the hill toward the village.

"There's no way that mutt's in the village, but perhaps a trip to the holy well will help." Holding the tall walking stick tightly in her left hand, she made her way down the road and limped toward the village.

A cluster of women were happily talking about the harvest as they circled the holy well across from the church. Gunny crossed to the shadow of the church to wait for them to leave. It irritated her that they were so lively and gay. When they finally left for O'Leary's, she slipped up to the well with a small pebble. She limped around the well three times saying the rosary to herself and running the pebble along the deep lines as she had done when she as little. Her prayers said, she leaned down into the well and splashed water across her face. When the water settled, she looked at the faint outline of her face and hair in the dark water.

"St. Mary," she said quietly. "Matt used to say that you could cure a broken heart. I know you can't bring Matt back, but could you please help me find my dog?" Gunny tossed her pebble into the well. Her reflection rippled into a series of rings.

"Gunny."

The familiar voice behind her made the hair rise on the back of her neck. "Father Jessey," she said, turning awkwardly and straightening her skirt. "I was finishing a pattern and a prayer." She took up her walking stick and limped as fast as she could toward the road. The tall priest followed.

"I see you're walking again, yet you haven't been to church."

"Don't pretend that you were actually expecting me, Father. Lying doesn't become you."

Father Jessey's smile faded. "You must show more respect for the cloth."

"Respect goes both ways," Gunny grunted as she limped onto the road and headed down the hill to O'Leary's.

The pub was only ten houses or so from the well but the journey felt long on Gunny's now sore leg and hip. She pushed open the door and limped in. The crowd quieted for a moment at her entrance, then the conversations began anew. Mac McCrohan turned from a seat at the bar.

"I'm surprised to see you here."

"No more surprised than I am to see you," Gunny said shuffling past him to a table near the window. She carefully lowered herself onto a stiff wooden chair, wincing at the effort, and propped the walking stick against the wall.

Mac grabbed his glass of porter and walked to her table. "Are you supposed to be out?"

"They let me out every once in awhile when I behave," Gunny snapped. Then, regretting her sharp tone, she added in a softer voice, "Shep's missing."

"And you came to O'Leary's to look for him?" Mac asked, heavy eyebrows raised.

Gunny glanced at Mac. "This may be the longest conversation you and I have ever had."

Mac bowed his head. "Matt usually did enough talking for the both of us."

Gunny looked down at her hands and rubbed at a blister that was coming up on her left palm.

"I'm sorry," he said. "I shouldn't have mentioned him."

"No, it's good to mention him. It's just... It's hard to hear his name, that's all."

Mac finished his porter and set the glass on the table. "I just brought some new pots over to Micky. I have to get back to the forge. Do you want me to help you home?"

"No, I don't need your help," Gunny scoffed. "I just need to rest for a moment." She pushed up from the table and a sharp pain shot up her leg and into her chest. She took a quick breath and sat down, her head spinning.

"You're not all right," Mac said. "Do you need a doctor?"

"No, no," Gunny said waving her hand in front of her face. "We can't afford to see the doctor again. I'll be fine once I catch my breath then I'll get back up that hill."

"My hand cart's out front. I can push you home."

"You can't push me in a hand cart."

"Why not?"

"Because I'm heavy and it's up hill all the way."

Mac reached under Gunny's legs and gently lifted her off her chair. "You weigh a lot less than those pots did."

"Mac," Gunny said, shocked. "Put me down. This is embarrassing."

Mac pried the door open with his foot and took Gunny outside. He placed her gently in the small hand cart and stepped away. "You fit quite nicely."

Gunny's looked away. "Get my walking stick."

Mac ducked into the pub and returned with the stick. "You're not going to whack me with this, are you?"

Gunny reached up and grabbed the stick. She knew he was trying to make her feel better but she was in too much pain to laugh. "Can you wheel me home now?"

Mac lifted the handles of the cart and easily pushed Gunny through the village and up the hill toward home.

It took Gunny a full day to get out of bed again and three days to recover completely from her walk into the village.

"You were silly to go so far," Eileen said for the umpteenth time. "And all on account of a missing dog."

"It wasn't just the dog, Mam. I needed to walk. I had to get away. From this house. From everything here."

"That's not... right, Gunny."

Eileen continued to drone on, but Gunny didn't hear her. She was looking at her small drop-down bed. Matt was resting there, leaning back against her pillow. "Wah, wah, wah," she heard him say. "What a baby you are. My leg hurts. I can't walk. I'm so helpless."

"Be quiet, you're dead," Gunny said.

Eileen stared at her daughter. "Did you say I was dead?"

"I wasn't talking to you."

Eileen stood and wiped her hands on her apron. "Perhaps it's good for you to spend time outside. Perhaps it will help clear your head."

Matt raised his eyebrows at Gunny and smiled.

Shep returned home at the end of the week. Gunny cried when she heard him paw at the door and stumbled to the door to let him in. "Where have you been, you naughty dog?" she asked, kneeling and hugging him hard around the neck.

Shep's coat was shiny as if someone had been brushing him, and he only nibbled at the cold potato skins she put out for him that night. He slept on his usual mat curled up in front of the fire but the next morning whined at the door at first light and was nearly frantic to get outside. Through that summer, the dog was often gone for days at a time. After the last of the harvest was in and the sheep and cow returned from the booley, Shep disappeared for good.

Gunny tried to forget about him but was always listening for his familiar yip as she hobbled through the village, or on her first forays up into the high fields. When she heard a rustle in the grasses or heard another dog bark, she was always sure it was Shep. She waited for him most afternoons on the bench in her yard.

"Give it up, Gunny," Robert said. "Old dogs often go off to die on their own."

"I thought you said he wasn't an old dog."

"I was wrong."

The October weather stiffened after a week of light frost. The air was crisp, the sky deep blue and clear. Gunny felt revitalized by the cool, fall air. She pushed up from the front bench with her walking stick and walked around the corner of the house. Sun lit the grasses along the path toward Mount Eagle at an autumn slant, the golden hues contrasting with the deep black rocks in the hills. Gunny gripped her walking stick in her now calloused left hand and headed up toward the booley fields.

Out of breath, she sat on a large rock by the path and looked down across the sprawling empty fields at the village of Dunquin. Low clouds cast deep purple shadows on the blue-grey of the surrounding ocean and tall islands that rose off shore like giant black shadows against the blue sky. Gunny tilted her face to the sun and closed her eyes. She listened to the wind move the dry grasses around her and reached into her pocket for her whistle. She always carried the whistle but hadn't played it since James had returned it to her. She put the pipe to her lips and let out her breath. Her fingers found the notes of a long, slow song of stillness and motion, lightness and dark, love and sorrow.

Eileen tried to cheer Gunny on a misty Hallow E'en by making Champ, but Gunny only picked at the potato mash. She excused herself from the table and moved to her stool, dropping bean after bean into a pot of water.

Robert pulled his stool up next to Gunny and took out his pipe.

"The beans always float," she murmured. "The damned beans always float."

Her leg and hip had started to ache again in the cooler, damp weather. "You know what, Da?" she said chucking a handful of beans into the pot. "Matt's never in pain. He's never sick and has no worries. He'll never be hungry or bored again. He'll never grow old." The ache inside her was deep tonight.

"Why don't you go down and see Mac. He's probably having as tough a time as you are this Hallow E'en."

Gunny sighed. "He might be. I guess there's no harm in stopping by."

"Don't forget your walking stick," Eileen said.

Gunny eyed the smooth, tall stick leaning against the door frame. She rubbed her thumb against the callous on her left palm and shifted her weight back and forth between her legs. "I'm going without it."

She headed down toward the McCrohans' cautiously picking her way across the muddy, uneven potato field. She felt a freedom being out without the walking stick and also felt off balance. As she approached the McCrohan house, she spied Mac through the smoke stained window of the forge, intently pumping the bellows. His shirt was off and his body was wet with sweat. She opened the door and walked in. "You're working tonight?"

Mac glanced up. "Sure. Why not?"

Gunny smiled and pushed the door closed behind her. "It's Hallow E'en. Why aren't you off at a gathering somewhere?"

Mac shook his head and took up his hammer. "I don't remember being invited to any. And I have work to do. I'm working on something for the priest."

Just as he was about to resume hammering, there was a loud knock at the door. Gunny jumped. Mac shook his head and rested his hammer. "Don't answer it. I know who it is."

"Who?" she asked, pulling up a stool near him.

Mac wiped the sweat off his chest and pulled on his shirt. "It's the McCarty boys. They came around last Hallow E'en all moaning down the chimney until Matt chased them off. I heard them at O'Leary's this afternoon planning their evil deeds for the night. I knew they'd come around again."

A low moaning penetrated the door, followed by a loud scratching sound. Then someone started a rhythmic tapping at the base of the front window. Tap. Tap. Tap.

"That's annoying," Gunny said glancing toward the window. "Why don't you tell them to go away?"

"They're only kids. They'll tire soon if I don't play their game."

The tapping continued. "Mac, you have to fight back."

"I'm not going to amuse them by getting angry," Mac said.

The moaning shifted to a low howl, then to laughter.

Gunny looked at Mac. "Come on. We're going outside. Put this over your head," she said tossing Mac her shawl.

Mac pushed her shawl to the floor. "I'm not going to wear that."

"Put it on," Gunny insisted stuffing the shawl into Mac's arms. "If you don't fight back, those boys'll never leave you alone."

She untied her apron, pulled it up over her head, and grabbed the bucket of grimy water Mac used to cool his iron work. She limped to the back door, pushed the debris away with her foot, and opened the door.

"We're not supposed to use the back door," Mac said. "That's only for funerals."

"That doesn't count for forges—only houses," Gunny said shushing Mac and signaling him to follow her out the door. She limped along the back wall of the house carrying a full bucket of water. Mac scooted along behind her. They could hear the boys laughing in the front yard.

"I feel ridiculous creeping around in my own yard," he whispered.

"Quiet," Gunny hissed. "And put that shawl on your head. We're going around front."

"Then what?" Mac asked.

Gunny didn't answer.

"Then what?" Mac repeated, a little louder while reluctantly wrapping the shawl around his head.

Gunny ignored him, rounded the side wall of the forge, and crept up behind the dung hill in the front yard. The three intruders were leaning against the wall under the front window happily howling at the moon. They looked to be between the ages of ten and thirteen, Matt's prime years for haunting.

Mac bumped up behind Gunny and she whispered, "When I count to three, jump out and scream like a Banshee." She didn't give Mac time to object. "One. Two. Three."

She and Mac jumped and screamed. Mac pulled the shawl from his head and frantically waved it about as Gunny slid forward in the mud and sloshed the bucket of dirty water onto the boys. The boys screamed in terror and fell over each other as they scrambled to get out of the yard and sprinted down the road toward the village.

Mac sat down hard on the wet stoop, chuckling, and hugged Gunny's shawl tight to his chest. "I don't know who was more scared when we screamed—them or me." He started to laugh and Gunny joined in.

"I don't think they'll be back next Hallow E'en," Gunny said, sitting down next to Mac to catch her breath.

Mac held out his hand to her. "Nice work, Miss Malone."

Gunny hesitated then took Mac's hand in hers. "Nice work, Mr. McCrohan."

Father Jessey worked feverishly through the fall appealing to his poor congregants to help him finance new gates for the church.

"God will smile on us if we have them."

"This is something we can all be proud of."

"The gates will show that this is not a cursed village."

An extra plate was passed each week. Just before Christmas, Father Jessey returned to the forge and presented Mac with a full basket of coins.

"How could you possibly raise this much in Dunquin?"

"It's a miracle, God be praised. Now go finish your work."

The Malone family had little money that year for Christmas, but Robert took a few hens to Dingle to barter for a Christmas meal and came back with a few small gifts from the Christmas Market.

"I stopped in to see the Murphys," he told Gunny. "They asked after you. You would hardly recognize their boy. He's getting tall."

Gunny bit into a sweet and stared into the fire, her face blank. "I hardly remember the boy," Gunny muttered. "I lived in Dingle a lifetime ago, Da."

On St. Stephen's Day, Gunny walked down to the forge, remembering back on the years she and Michael had chased the wrens and Matt and Wren Boys had paraded through the village.

This year, the Burke twins and Cornelius Foley sat around at the forge with Mac, hardly talking. No one had a story to tell. No one wanted to sing. No one talked of wrens or parades.

"Where's your brother?" Cornelius asked when Gunny walked in.

"Home with Maeve."

"Did you make any masks?"

"No. We're too old for that."

"Mac, where is Matt's wooden horse?" Edmund Burke asked.

"I don't know. It's out here somewhere."

"It's not St. Stephen's Day without Matt," Maurice Burke said with a sigh.

"Matt would want us to go out and have some fun," Cornelius said. "Let's go to O'Leary's and have a glass. We can make a toast to Matt and to Wren Days gone by."

Gunny joined the boys at O'Leary's for a night of heavy drinking and somber chatter.

~ Chapter 11: Life in the Hills ~

The Monday of Shrove, Gunny sat on the bench in the yard watching the sun set over the brown, stubbly fields. She leaned back against the rough stone wall of her house. Her right hip and leg ached and she shifted to try and get comfortable. All day she had been haunted by the activities of the previous year: listening to the Shrove bargaining at the Murphy's, meeting the Kennedys at the Dingle Pub, telling Matt she would be his. She could hardly believe a full year had passed. It was colder this year than last. She wrapped her shawl tight around her shoulders and took a deep lungful of crisp spring air. The cold air made her cough and she limped inside.

On Shrove Tuesday Gunny woke late after a restless night—irritated by the crowded house, irritated by the squawking chickens roosting on her bed, and irritated by the black pit of loss in her stomach. She tried to eat, tried to sleep, tried to pray. She picked up the newspaper a dozen times but could not make out the words. At noon, she headed out for a walk but the light made her head ache and she retreated inside. By sunset she could do no more than sit on a low stool staring into the dim turf fire.

Maeve insisted that Michael take her to a cheerier place to celebrate their wedding anniversary. They headed to O'Leary's and the house became dismally quiet.

Robert coaxed Gunny away from the fire for the evening meal. Gunny picked at a Shrove pancake, then pushed her bowl aside and held her face in her hands. Robert rested a calloused hand on Gunny's rigid arm.

"This is a hard day," he said softly.

"'Tis," Gunny muttered from behind clenched hands.

She got up from the table, wiped her eyes on the back of her sleeve and turned again to the fire. She stirred the embers, added a new brick of turf, and stood watching as the brick slowly caught fire. She listened to her parents talk quietly behind her as she poured herself a cup of tea from the hot kettle and pulled her stool closer to the fire. She cradled the cup in her long, white fingers, rolling it gently between her palms and occasionally taking a sip. She closed her eyes. Visions of the previous year continued to flicker through her mind. Dressing for the wedding. Thundering toward the church on Nella. Lying on the ground in front of the church gates peering through stockinged legs. The wrenching pain. Matt's still body.

The new turf in the fire cracked and split with a loud snap; a large piece of bog wood that was hidden inside the turf flared. Gunny jumped, dropped her mug and backed over her stool. The house door blew open behind her. She gasped and raced to push the door closed. She leaned back on the door as a wisp of fog curled in under the bottom of the door, circled her legs, and moved up her skirt. She kicked wildly. "Is it so difficult for you to stay in your grave?" she yelled. Her head spun. She saw red, then black.

She woke in her small drop-down bed, her father sitting beside her on a stool holding her hand.

"What happened?" she asked looking around the dim room.

"You fainted," he said. "Fell hard. You're thin as a wisp. You need to eat more."

Gunny sighed. "Is the night over? Are we done with Shrove?"

Robert tucked her hand under the covers and crossed the room. He leaned down to look out the small front window. "The moon's about to set."

Gunny turned toward the wall pulling the blanket up around her cheek. Robert walked to her side and rested a hand on her thin shoulder. "You're nearly done with Shrove."

Gunny's eyes filled. "I'll never be done with Shrove, Da," she sniffed. "I ache so badly my chest hurts." She turned and looked up at her father. "Can someone die of a broken heart?"

Robert sighed. "I've known a few who have. If you had died at the church last year, I know my heart would've broken."

Gunny rolled onto her back and studied her father's face in the dim light. His hair was almost completely grey now and was thinning around his temples. The lines around his eyes were deep and angled. She took a shallow breath. "I'm sorry I grieve you, Da."

Robert looked into his daughter's wide, dark eyes. "If I could take this burden from you, I would."

Gunny reached out and squeezed her father's hand. "I know that, Da. I know."

Eileen insisted that Gunny walk with her to Mass the next Sunday. "Your father's away in Ventry and Michael and Maeve left early. Get your shawl. If we don't leave now we'll be late."

"The last place I want to be on Chalk Sunday is in that church."

Eileen pulled on her large black hat and adjusted her shawl. "You used to like Chalk Sunday."

"When I was young, I thought it was funny marking the unmarried women with stripes of chalk. This year, I'll be the one who comes home all marked over."

Eileen bustled to the door. "Do what you want. You always do." She opened the front door and gasped, then stepped outside and pulled the door closed behind her. "I'll see you after Mass," she yelled through the door. Someone had left a little straw bride and groom on the front bench. Eileen picked them up and pushed them onto the dung heap, dusted her hands on her apron, and walked briskly down the road.

When she was certain her mother was gone, Gunny pulled on her shawl and grabbed her walking stick. The sky was grey, the day cool and misty. If she headed down through the village now, she could avoid most of the villagers while Father Jessey droned on through Mass. She walked into the yard but stopped short when she reached the dung heap. She gingerly pulled two straw characters from the pile. She had taught the McCrohan girls how to weave straw and this was most likely their handiwork to celebrate the day. She chuckled and limped down through the fields to the McCrohans.

The McCrohan house was quiet. She heard a hammer beat in the forge and knocked on the door with her walking stick in time to the hammer. The unlatched door swung open. Mac was working at his anvil with his back to the door. Smoky light spilled into the room across bent wagon axles, worn horseshoes, ripped bellows, and rusty iron wagon wheel hoops—just as Matt used to have it. In contrast, Mac's tools were hung as John had kept them on pegs in the walls—the hammers arranged from large to small, the horseshoes lined up in pairs by size, and boxes of nails set on the floor in neat rows.

Gunny listened to the high-pitched ring of Mac's hammer as it struck iron. A spray of sparks flew from the anvil and scattered hot ash on the floor. She studied Mac from behind as he worked in his heavy leather apron. The thick muscles on his arms and chest were wet with sweat as he stepped back to pump the bellows. He beat the hot metal one last time, then picked up an elaborate curl from the anvil with a long pair of pinchers and thrust it into a bucket of black water. The hot metal hissed as it toughened.

"It's hot as hell in here," Gunny said loudly.

Mac jumped, then turned to face the silhouette in the hazy light of the door. "God, woman! Give a man an idea you're in the room," he said wiping sweat from his forehead with the back of his sleeve and pushing a box of iron curls behind him with his foot.

Gunny took a step toward him and tossed the two straw characters onto the dirt floor.

"Didn't your mother tell you it's not nice to pick on the unwed on Chalk Sunday?" he asked.

"I didn't make them," she said, poking at the straw man with her walking stick. "If I did, they'd have much more detail. I am returning them. I assume they're the work of your sisters."

Mac rescued the straw man from the floor and held it out toward the light from the fire. "This is actually pretty good. You're not jealous, are you?"

Gunny gasped and snatched the man from Mac. "This is nowhere as good as the figures I used to make."

"We used to like Chalk Sunday," Mac mused.

"When you're the teaser and not the teased, things are a lot more fun," she said, sitting on a stool and stretching out her right leg. "But you don't have to worry. You could avoid the teasing by getting married."

"Too risky," he said, tossing his hammer from one hand to the other. "Why don't you get married?"

"You know I'll never marry," Gunny said with a blush. "I'll always be a nobody."

"That doesn't sound so good—life as a nobody."

"Don't tease me, Mac."

"I didn't call you a nobody—you did. If you ask me, I'd say you look more like… a witch."

Gunny looked up at Mac's face, wet with sweat. He tried to hold a serious look but could not help but smile. Gunny did not smile back. She stood and angrily tossed the straw man into the fire in the forge and watched as the edges crisped, then flared. "At least a witch is interesting—it's better than a cripple," she said in a low voice. She turned to Mac and cleared her throat. "I need a favor."

"Name it," Mac said without hesitation.

"I need a piece of iron to carry in my pocket. I'm spending more time in the hills and don't want any bad dealings with the fairies."

Mac hesitated. "Matt always said a black-handled knife was the best protection." He stood and pulled a black knife from his belt and held it out toward Gunny.

She took the heavy blade from his hand, felt the weight of it, and touched the sharp tip on an extended forefinger. "This would be good protection against the fairies—and anyone else who crossed me." She handed the knife back. "I don't have money for a knife. I was hoping for an old nail or something."

"I'm not going to charge you. It's mine. Take it."

"And leave you with no knife? I don't think so."

Mac laughed a short, grunt-like laugh. "I'm a smithy. I'll make another."

Gunny looked at the knife in Mac's outstretched hand. "I always wanted a black-handled knife," she said chewing thoughtfully on her bottom lip.

Mac held out the knife again to Gunny. "Take it. I don't think you need protection from the fairies but it's yours if you want it. What would fairies do with the likes of you anyway?"

Gunny frowned. "You suppose even the fairies would reject me as a spinster and a cripple?"

"No, I suppose the fairies wouldn't know what to do when you spun a web of rope around them or scared them with an intricate mask of a giant fairy god or laughed so loudly their tiny ears burst."

Gunny gazed into the forge fire. "I don't make rope, or masks, or laugh much these days," she said, looking hard at Mac. "You don't mind if I take it?"

"I offered, didn't I?" Mac said holding the knife out again to Gunny.

She took the knife and went to slip it into her apron pocket.

"Hold on," Mac said. "An open knife will shred that pocket."

He unstrapped his belt and pulled off the holster. "Might as well have this to go with it."

Gunny took the leather cover from Mac, sheathed the knife and slipped it into her apron pocket. She felt the weight tug at her waist and gave Mac a quick smile.

"Gunny," Mac said hesitantly. "There's just one thing about that knife."

Gunny looked up at his face. "I told you I don't have any money."

Mac shook his head. "What I was going to say was that the knife's a gift. I won't take it back."

Gunny blushed, eying the curled iron crane Mac had made for her which sat dusty and neglected against the back wall of the forge. "Understood," she said looking Mac directly in the eye. She trod across the straw woman on the floor and slipped out the door into the cool morning air.

She turned left onto the road toward Ventry and crossed the bridge over the forge river. The sky began to clear and she felt her mood lift. She passed a tall ogham stone on her right. When she was little, her father told her the slashes on the rock spelled out 'Colman the Pilgrim'. Gunny stopped and bowed with her walking stick across her lap. "Greetings Colman the Pilgrim. Starting today," she said with a smile, "I, too, am a pilgrim."

She hiked off the road to the old church at Templebeg, then walked up through a cluster of nearby tumbled down stone houses from a community long past. She climbed higher, across the ruins of a castle of the Knights of Kerry. She sat on the broken stone wall and looked down at Ventry Harbor. Cool wind pushed at her face and hair and she felt like she was floating.

Her stomach rumbled. She had forgotten to bring a slice of bread. She hiked back down to the old church, knelt by the small stream and slurped several handfuls of sweet water to fill her stomach. She spied an old bullan stone on the edge of the field. Like the bullan in Dingle, this rock was pocked with a series of small, cuplike indentations. She ran her hands along the smooth, large rock and down into the dry cups, then pulled herself up onto the rock and lay on her stomach. Why were the cups there? Was this a magic place to mix herbs, or a place to collect holy water from the nearby stream? She tried to imagine what the world was like when people lived in this clochain and worked at the castle. People long dead and long forgotten.

Gunny sighed and looked across the greening field. Tiny yellow wildflowers were just starting to bloom. A small brown rabbit hopped out from a tuft of dry grasses unaware of her presence. She lay quietly on the rock and watched as he nibbled on a tuft of grass, then busily washed his tiny face and long ears. She listened to the sound of the stream tinkling over shallow rocks and watched the sun dance in small sparks off thin pools of water. She laid her head on her arms and closed her eyes.

Cold wind rustled through the trees and startled her awake. Her arms were stiff from sleeping on the rock. She sat up and stretched to loosen the muscles. The sky above was darkening with thick, heavy clouds. She pulled her shawl tight around her shoulders and slid off the rock with her walking stick in hand. She had just reached the road when the wind picked up in earnest and drops of heavy rain struck her face. As the rain and wind increased, she closed her eyes to slits and walked faster. Circling rain blew up her skirt, against her back, and into her face. Her right leg and hip started to hurt and she slowed.

"Why am I hurrying?" she muttered. "I'm already soaked." A gust of rain pushed her to the far side of the road and she gasped trying to stay upright. A bolt of lightning lit the road ahead of her, followed almost immediately by an enormous clap of thunder that rattled her bones.

She scurried off the muddy road and squatted next to a low rock wall, holding her drenched shawl over her head. The rain pounded down on her back and outstretched arms as another bolt of lightning lit the air around her and thunder shook her. Her hands started to feel numb. She pulled her soaked shawl tight around her head and began to shiver. She wanted to cry. Instead, she took a deep breath and tried to think. If she was going to die of cold or of a lightning strike, why go like a cowering rabbit huddled near an old stone fence?

Using her walking stick, she pushed herself up, limped to the center of the road, and turned to face the skies. The rain poured down on her face. "Why not?" she yelled at the black sky. "Why not take me as quickly as you took Matt?" She closed her eyes, hot tears mixing with cold rain. "Take me now, God," she murmured. "I'm ready."

The rain continued to pour but there was no more lightning or thunder. She pushed long, wet curls from her face and looked through the blowing sheets of rain toward home. She stepped forward. Her tired legs tangled in her wet skirts and she fell hard on the road, her walking stick flying away from her. Her hands and knees stung and she could taste dirt in her mouth. The rain beat down on her back. She struggled to stand against wet skirts and slippery mud as loud horse hooves beat up behind her. She scrambled for footing to get off the road. Her breath caught in her throat as she stumbled and slipped back toward the rock wall, cold hands stretched out in front of her. A gust of wind blew past behind her, pulling at her skirts. She whirled around expecting to see a coach upon her and saw nothing but wind and sheets of rain. She reached into her pocket and shakily pulled out the black-handled knife—but the danger had passed. The wind died down and the rain slowed to a drizzle. A beam of steamy sunshine broke through the clouds and lit the muddy road toward Dunquin.

Gunny wiped her face on a soggy sleeve and laughed at the black-handled knife clutched tightly in her right hand. She slid it back into its leather case, and back into her apron pocket. She tied her soggy shawl around her waist and wiped her muddy hands on her apron.

"You torment me, God," she said in a quiet voice. "Then you pretend to be nice." She took a deep breath, picked up her walking stick, and limped home.

Gunny spent nearly every day outside that spring. From morning light to early evening, she walked, sometimes into the village but more often up into the hills. She woke early each morning, took the animals outside and collected water from the well. Back inside, she swept out the house, washed her face, then packed a few slices of oat bread in her apron pocket along with the black-handled knife. Her leg and hip still pained her, but it was a familiar ache now, a reminder that she was on a pilgrim's journey.

When she headed out the door she let the wind set her direction, going farther and farther on each walk through fields across the multitude of green valleys that surrounded Mount Eagle. She felt each step was a prayer to some mysterious God: "Let me find a path. Tell me why I'm here. Help me heal." When she was thirsty, she stopped at clear running streams to drink, and when she was tired, she sat quietly on lichen-covered grey stones and was quiet. When the wind blew, she reveled at the energy that pushed her tattered skirts around her and swirled her hair in front of her face.

One late spring morning as she was picking her way down through a high, wet valley near the ruins of an old stone house, she took a step over a hillock and felt her right leg disappear down a bog hole. She gasped, pushed up on the solid ground around her, and pulled her soaked leg from the small gap in the stone. She rolled to her side and gingerly felt along her leg and hip. She wasn't hurt but the fall was a reminder that she was alone in this abandoned, wet world and needed to tread lightly.

"I'll pay more attention," she yelled up to the sky, her heart racing. "Thank you for the wet reminder."

On May Eve, Gunny headed to the booley fields to enjoy a quiet day before the village children moved the cattle and sheep to the upper fields for the summer. She sat on a favorite rock and played a soft, sad song on her tin whistle as the sun dipped low in the western sky.

She pulled the whistle from her lips and gasped. It was May Eve. The good people, the fairies, would be out soon, dancing and preparing to move to their summer quarters. This was a night when youth and lovelessness were in particular peril—and she was both young and loveless. She shouldn't have stayed out so late. She turned her coat inside out to hide herself from the sprites and checked to make sure the black-handled knife was secure in her apron pocket before heading home.

As she picked her way down the familiar path to the road, a heavy mist rolled in around her. The setting sun lit up grey rocks with a hazy red light. She shivered and hurried on but the path looked different. What was that looming rock to her right? And why did the path suddenly twist up toward the high hills rather than down toward her house and the village? Should she continue through the thickening fog and risk wandering farther up toward the cliffs of Mount Eagle? She stopped and stifled a sob, then gripped her walking stick and continued at a slower pace. The fog grew thicker, the light dimmer, the path less clear.

Her skirt caught on a furze bush. She heard her skirt rip as she stumbled and landed on her right hip in a thick patch of grass. A sharp pain shot up her leg. She rolled onto her stomach, clutching the dry grass in front of her. The pain in her leg eased and she took a shallow breath. She felt something under her hand and pulled a dirty, faded red ribbon from the grasses. She was lying on the tuft of grasses where she and Matt had made love the spring before. She reached to her right and touched the familiar stones of her old booley house. She had been walking in circles.

She sat up and felt for the black-handled knife in her pocket as the last rays of sun disappeared into the fog and night fell upon her. She leaned on the wall of the booley house and pressed the lost ribbon hard against one cheek. As the air chilled, the wind started to stir and then to whine. She smiled into the vast darkness as the wind whipped mist around her. Then the air grew still and the mist lifted as a huge blood red moon appeared far out across the horizon. She breathed in the dim moon beams and threaded the faded ribbon through her fingers. As the moon rose to a clear silver, the path appeared in front of her. She pushed the faded ribbon into her apron pocket, picked up her walking stick, and hobbled home.

Gunny limped into the house, tossed her damp shawl to the floor, and quietly peeled off her damp shirt. She pulled on a dry shirt, then pulled down the side bed and sat, closing her eyes.

"You look like a hermit returned from the hills," Eileen said, glancing at Gunny over her mending.

"Where've you been?" Maeve asked, knocking ash from her pipe and sauntering over to examine Gunny. "Your skirt's torn, your hair's all wet, and what's this?" Maeve picked a strand of dried grass from Gunny's hair.

"Tell us what happened," Eileen demanded, turning on her stool toward Gunny.

Gunny pushed up from the bed and walked to the fire. She poured herself a cup of hot tea and cradled the hot mug in both hands. "I was in the booley and got turned around in the fog."

Eileen set down her mending and squatted to stir the fire. "You know better than to go out on May Eve. What were you thinking?"

Gunny sighed and looked at her mother. "I wasn't thinking. I was walking."

Eileen roughly stirred the fire and the turf split, shooting out warm flames. "At first I thought all of this walking was good for you, but now I don't know. If you don't have enough sense... Maeve, take the potatoes out to the yard to drain them."

Maeve hurried to obey, not wanting to miss a word of this conversation. "We'll say a prayer for you before we eat tonight," she murmured as she passed Gunny.

"Are you going to pray for my safety?" Gunny asked Maeve's retreating back.

"No," Eileen said from behind Gunny. "We're going to pray that you gain some sense."

Michael and Maeve chose the next day, May Day, to make their big announcement. They asked that everyone gather after the evening meal. Gunny groaned. From the look on their faces, there would soon be a baby in the house. How dreadful, she thought. The baby would have a big round head like Michael and what if he had Maeve's appetite?

Michael stood in front of the fire nervously shifting from foot to foot. Maeve stood next to him grinning from ear to ear. Michael cleared his throat and wiped his large, thick hands on his pant legs while Robert, Eileen, and Gunny looked on.

"Mam, Da, Gunny. Maeve and I... We..."

"Get on with it," Gunny interrupted.

Robert raised an eyebrow to Gunny. "Let him speak in his own time, Gunny."

"I don't know why they're making such a fuss," Gunny retorted.

Eileen shushed both of them.

Michael cleared his throat and started again. "We... I... Maeve has decided. Well, we have decided... We're going to America."

No one said a word. Even the turf fire dared not snap. Eileen was the first to recover. She stood and faced her son. "You're not going to America," she said sharply.

Michael snickered nervously then took Maeve's hand and squeezed it under his arm. "We are, Mam. We've been talking about it for months. Maeve's sisters have a shop in Alexandria, Virginia. We can work there and life will be easier. Last week Maeve's sister Aggie sent us money for the passage."

"Just because you have money for the passage doesn't mean you're going," Eileen gasped. "I can't take care of this house by myself and your father needs help on the farm. No," Eileen said crossing her arms and standing to her full height in front of Michael. "You're not going. I won't allow it."

Maeve squeezed in close to Michael and smiled. "We leave tomorrow."

Eileen reached both hands toward Maeve's chubby little neck. Robert placed a firm arm around his wife's shoulders and pulled her away. He looked at Michael and saw Moss Barney's round face. "Go if you must," he said in a low voice.

Michael looked confused but Maeve grinned. "We are destined to go to America," she said pinching Michael's arm. "I'm going to pack." She reached up and pulled Michael's facedown toward her and gave him a wet kiss on the mouth. "This is so exciting! Everyone'll be jealous of us." She trotted to the back room and noisily started pulling boxes out from under the bed.

Gunny rose slowly from her stool and collected her walking stick from near the door. She turned to her brother. "I envy you the adventure. God speed."

"Thank you. You know I've never been much of one for adventure but Maeve wants to go—so we're going. It's what married people do."

Eileen pushed past Gunny and stood in front of the door. "Robert. Are you going to sit there and do nothing while your son walks out this door? You can't run this farm by yourself. Are you going to work yourself to death like John McCrohan did?"

Gunny moved Eileen aside and unlatched the door. "I'm going out."

Eileen turned on Gunny and put a hand against the door to hold it closed. "You're not going anywhere, Miss," she hissed. "This's your fault. You're the one who's making it miserable for Maeve to live here."

Gunny pushed her mother's arm down and opened the door. She slipped outside and pulled the door tightly closed behind her. She held it closed from the outside as her mother's tirade inside continued, then released the latch when no one followed her into the yard. The full moon lit the cluttered yard with silver light. She turned and shuffled down the hill toward O'Leary's.

Michael and Maeve were packed and ready the next morning, all their goods filling only a few old flour sacks. Maeve pulled on her old brown hat and walked out the door.

Robert took Michael by the hand. "Do you know where you're going?"

"Aggie said to catch a coach from Dingle to Tralee, and to go from there to Cove. We're to buy supplies in Cove after we book our passage."

"And then?"

"Then we sail to America," Michael said with a nervous, high-pitched laugh. "To a village called New York. Aggie said there are coaches that go from New York to Virginia. Maeve'll be happier with her sisters and father. And if she's happy, I'll be happy."

Maeve stepped back inside and pulled on Michael's arm, impatient to be off. Eileen sat at the table wiping her eyes with a corner of her apron. She refused to look at Michael or Maeve.

"We'll pray for both of you," Robert said.

Maeve pulled again on Michael's arm. He took a step toward Eileen.

"Mam?" he said in a soft voice.

Eileen waved her hand in front of her face and turned away with a stifled sob. Michael shook hands with his father and gave Gunny a quick hug, then collected the bags and gave Maeve a smile. The young couple walked out the door and out of Dingle never intending to return.

That night, Eileen insisted that Gunny abandon her bed by the fire and sleep again in the bed in the back room. Her bed wasn't that much farther from the fire but Gunny felt cold and out of place on the lumpy straw mattress, and could smell Maeve's scent. She lay awake for a long time trying to warm up, then dozed. She heard a knock at the door and sat up. She watched as the door opened and thick fog swirled into the room. The fog moved around her face and up through her hair. She felt her heart quicken, the mist moving through her with each breath.

"Matt?" she whispered.

She heard a laugh.

"Matt?" she said a little louder.

She saw Matt's outline in front of the fire, then the image cleared. Matt was wearing his second best suit and derby hat and held out a hand to her. She reached out but he couldn't seem to see her. She heard him call her name, soft, from across a wide field.

"I'm here," she whispered, swinging her legs off the bed, but he was gone. She ran to the door. Her leg did not hurt and she had no limp. She stepped into the yard. "Matt!" she yelled into the foggy night. The mist lifted on a breath of air and he was standing in front of the church gates, arms reaching toward her. She grabbed his hands. They were as cold as black iron. He stepped back and his hands slipped from hers. The ground shifted under her and she grasped at the nothingness of thick, cold fog. She heard the church gates creak, then slam. Then there was nothing but cold, still silence.

"Matt!" she screamed, and awoke in the back room in a cold sweat, tears running down her face.

The next morning, Gunny woke late to an empty house. She washed her face and poured herself a cup of tea, then sat quietly by the fire. Pieces of the nightmare still played in the corners of her mind. She felt drained and had no desire to go exploring though the strong spring sun outside tempted her. Maybe Mac was in. She hadn't seen him in months. She pulled on her shawl and hiked to the forge. Mac was working, pumping the bellows when she walked into the shop.

"What do you want?" he asked without looking up.

Gunny sat down on a stool near the fire and rubbed at her leg. "I'm sure what you meant to say was, 'How're you, Miss Malone? What can I help you with today?'"

Mac glanced at her from behind the forge and grimaced. "Sorry. I haven't been sleeping all that well."

"Same here," Gunny said with a yawn, looking around the cluttered forge. "Looks like you've been busy. What're you working on?"

Mac looked uncomfortable. "As usual, I've been making horseshoes."

Gunny pointed at a pile of twisted metal curls tossed into a wooden box near the forge. "Those aren't horseshoes. What are they?"

"Junk," Mac said, kicking at the box. "When I get mad I take iron and make it into tight little curls."

"It looks like you've been plenty mad." Gunny got up and examined the contents of the box. She narrowed her eyes. "These look like the same kind of curls you used on my cooking crane."

"The crane curls were different. I wasn't mad then…"

Gunny's face went ashen. She looked past the box to a large object pushed up against the back wall. She limped past Mac, her hand pressed against her chest. "Are these the gates from the church?"

Mac looked down and grabbed a new turf to throw on the fire. "They might be," he grunted.

The old church gates were leaning, uneven and broken along the back wall. Gunny ran a hand over the rusted metal. Some parts were brittle. Other parts had been blackened so many times the covering was peeling off in thin layers.

"I don't understand. Why do you have the church gates here?"

Mac glanced up at Gunny from the fire. "Father Jessey commissioned new gates. I finished them just after Christmas. When I pulled down the old ones I didn't know what to do with them—so I brought them here."

Gunny ran her hand over the old metal. "Why is part of this rail missing?"

Mac shook his head. "That's where it was attached to the stone wall."

"No, Mac," Gunny said. "This part, here," she said pointing to a half-bar near the base of one gate.

Mac glanced to where Gunny was pointing and shrugged. "I must have used it for something."

Gunny turned and looked at Mac. "You made something from this gate? The gate where Matt died?" Gunny felt a chill shoot up her spine and cross the back of her neck. Mac stood, awkwardly studying a small nick in his hammer. "You didn't use part of the gate to make the black-handled knife, did you?"

"What?" Mac said letting out a breath and bringing the hammer down against his side. He glanced at his boots.

Gunny pulled the black-handled knife from her apron pocket and took a step toward Mac. "This knife is about the same length as that missing piece of iron." She unsheathed the knife and took another step toward Mac. He stepped away as Gunny turned and knelt in front of the gate. She placed the knife in the missing section of the gate.

"Ah ha! A perfect fit." She turned toward Mac, knife in hand. "You gave me a haunted knife, didn't you?"

"You said you needed a knife. I gave you a knife."

The knife was cool and heavy in Gunny's hand, the blade long and sharp. She gripped the handle. "I love this knife, Mac."

Mac gave a quick nod. "I have work to do."

Gunny slipped the knife back into its sheath and into her apron pocket. She closed her eyes and tightly squeezed the protector in her pocket, then left the forge with a spring wind at her back and no particular destination in mind.

She hiked the familiar path up to the booley and sat to rest on a favorite rock. She'd heard that two of Matt's sisters were living in the McCrohan hut this year but they didn't appear to be around; the booley was quiet except for a few cattle lowing nearby. She looked down across the newly planted fields in the valley below, and beyond at the vast expanse of deep blue ocean. The wind whistled around her. She shut her eyes and felt the warm spring sun on her face. The wind reminded her of a jaunty tune Matt used to whistle. She pictured his face, his green eyes looking at her, his half smile, his laugh. She opened her eyes expecting to break the spell, but the whistling continued as the wind pushed its way through tiny cracks in the surrounding rocks.

She hiked to a higher field and sat on the flat rock she and Matt shared when he'd taught her to watch for rabbits. She glanced down at a tiny rock wall just past her perch and realized she was looking at the remains of a crumbling fairy village. She scrambled down on all fours to study the small structures. The grass parts had blown away, but most of the stone huts she'd built long ago were still standing.

"I can fix this," she said, setting off into the fields to fill her apron pocket with small stones, bits of moss, grasses to weave into mats, and tiny budding flowers. She spent the afternoon rebuilding the tiny village and was startled when she heard voices behind her.

"Gunny?"

She looked up from her work. It was Mary, the oldest McCrohan girl. Two younger girls from the village stood just past her.

"Are you all right?" Mary asked.

"I'm working on a little fairy village," Gunny said, smiling up from her work. "Look. I made a tiny thatched roof from some brown grasses and paved the little street with stones."

"Do you want us to help you home?" Mary asked in the kind of tone used with a sick child or elderly aunt.

Gunny pushed herself stiffly to her feet and all three girls took a step away from her. She dusted her hands on her apron. "I was fixing up a little village I built when I was around your age.

The girls looked from the rocks and twigs at Gunny's feet to her roughly patched skirt, dirty hands, and tangled curls.

"We can help you home," Mary said again, smiling.

"I don't need your help," Gunny snapped. She hesitated, then picked up her walking stick and smashed the newly rebuilt walls and miniature stone houses. She gasped, out of breath, then limped past the startled girls toward home.

When she got to the main path, she changed her mind and headed uphill instead toward the mountaintop. Her hip and leg ached from sitting on the ground all day but she pushed on. When she finally neared the top of a long, narrow ridge, she stopped and flopped down on a large flat stone to watch the sun set. She listened as day sounds turned to night sounds and opened her eyes. One by one, tiny stars appeared in the sky overhead, then dozens of stars winked on as she lay and breathed in the night. It reminded her of floating with Matt in Dingle Harbor, how the waves had lapped against the boat, how the sky that night was clustered with stars, and how Matt's warm body felt lying next to hers. She pictured him hovering over her now and heard his laugh. She smiled when she realized that she was thinking about Matt without crying. What would he say to her now—out wandering in the hills, curls matted on her head, the hem of her dress worn and torn? He would laugh, no doubt, and tell her to clean herself up.

She felt his hand lift her from the rock and listened to his still voice as he guided her home.

Gunny headed into O'Leary's for a bite to eat and a glass of porter. The pub had become a regular stop when she walked in the village. Everyone spent time there. The houses in Dunquin were small. If you wanted to see others from the village or get something to eat, O'Leary's was the only choice. She rarely had money but if Cornelius or Mac were around, they would sometimes buy her a glass or two. And if no one was around to make a purchase, Micky ran a credit for her father to settle at harvest.

"Look Micky," Gunny said above the hum of the regular evening crowd as she sipped at her glass of porter from a stool at the bar, reading over the latest newspaper headlines. "The paper says that Daniel O'Connell, the Liberator, is fighting the English without spilling blood. Matt would have loved this," she said shaking her head. "O'Connell says that if every Catholic contributed a penny a week to him through the church, he could fight the English and the Irish would once again be represented in government."

Micky dried a glass with a worn bar rag. "Sounds like another tithing to me. If you have a penny to spare, Gunny, I'll take it to help settle your account."

Gunny reached across the bar and touched Micky gently on the hand. "You know you love me Micky and would never cut me off. Now get me a fresh glass, will you?"

Micky took her hand and gave it a squeeze. "Only for you, Gunny," he said pouring her a glass of the deep amber liquid.

Father Jessey walked in and sat down next to Gunny at the bar. She pushed her stool away, picked up her glass, and moved to an empty table. The priest followed and pulled out a chair.

"Do you mind if I sit with you, Miss Malone?

Gunny looked up. "Yes, I do. I prefer quiet when I drink."

Father Jessey sat. "I've noticed you spending time here at O'Leary's. Are you quenching your thirst at the cost of your soul?"

Gunny smiled and tipped her glass at the sullen man. "I'm not drinking to quench my thirst, Father. I'm drinking to be merry."

"We've all had our losses, haven't we?" he said with a raised eyebrow.

Gunny snorted and set her glass down. "Have you had losses then, Father?"

The priest tilted his head and looked away. "What I meant was…"

Gunny finished off her glass in a single swallow and stood. "I know what you meant. You were trying to be kind and you're very bad at that." She looked down at him with his neat ashy hair and freshly pressed black robes. "Quite frankly, Father, you're the last person I want sympathy from," she said giving a wave to Micky as she headed toward the door.

"I was trying to be of comfort," the priest said loudly to her retreating back.

Gunny turned. "You're a fool," she said with a wide smile.

"And you are a drunk," he retorted.

Gunny took a step toward him with clenched jaw and fists tight. "Yes, but tomorrow I'll be sober—and you'll still be a fool."

Gunny decided to take advantage of the longer summer days and headed off for the summit of Brandon Mountain. The hike to Ballyferriter, then out through the valleys was long but pleasant. At the base of the mountain, she stopped to take a few turns around the ancient well, then started up the steep mountain path. She couldn't help but think about Matt as she climbed. She could feel the pressure of his hand around hers as she clutched her walking stick, then he was ahead of her, then behind. When she neared the summit, she paused to catch her breath near the rock where Matt had stopped to warm her hands at a time that no longer existed. There was no mist on the mountain today. She closed her eyes and leaned back against the cool rock. Her chest felt tight and her eyes burned. She heard a familiar yip and opened her eyes as a dog came racing down the path toward her.

"Shep!" she cried, bursting into tears. Was this another dream? No, she thought, as a very warm and hairy dog pushed his cold nose against her face. She squatted and ran her hands over the dog's slick coat. He raised his right, white paw for her to shake, then licked her hand. Gunny laughed and cried at the same time. Shep rolled over so she could scratch his belly. She wiped her face with the back of her sleeve and scratched his belly with her free hand.

"You runt," she muttered. "Where've you been? And what're you doing all the way up here on Brandon Mountain?"

Shep flipped to his feet and lowered his head and front paws toward her. It was the posture he took when he wanted something. "What?" she asked, glancing up. A tall, bare-footed man was standing on the path. He was dressed in a faded brown shirt with patched pants belted with a hand-made rope. His wrinkled face was nearly the same color and texture as his shirt. He had a patchy grey beard and wore an old, black derby on a full head of curly, grey hair. He carried a tall walking stick much like hers.

Gunny pushed up on her walking stick and stood awkwardly on the rocky path. Shep trotted over and sat at the man's feet.

"Good day, sir," Gunny said, trying to sound strong and unafraid.

"Good day," the old man rasped.

"Is that your dog?" she asked, pointing at Shep with her walking stick.

The old man shook his head. "No, he's not my dog."

Gunny smiled. "He used to be our dog but he ran off. We wondered where he was. I'm sorry if he's been bothering you."

"He hasn't been bothering me. He lives with me."

"Where do you live?" she asked.

"I live here."

"No," Gunny said, "I meant what village do you live in?"

"I live here," the man repeated.

"On Brandon Mountain?"

"Here," the man said gesturing around him with this walking stick and wondering if the girl was a little slow.

Gunny glanced around. "There're no houses on this mountain."

The man raised his eyebrows. "There aren't?"

"Do you live in the old bee hive huts to the east of the mountain?"

"Maybe," the man replied in a quiet voice.

"By yourself?" Gunny asked.

The man frowned. "Do you see anyone else around?" he asked, firmly planting his walking stick in front of him.

Gunny felt her stomach tighten. There wasn't anyone else around. She reached in and touched the sheathed knife in her pocket. "I should be going," she said with a small curtsy.

"Of course."

The old man tipped his hat to her and headed north off the path across a steep, rocky field. Shep looked at Gunny, then raced off after the old man down some hidden pathway. Gunny sat on a rock and watched them depart, then stood and whistled. Both dog and man turned to look at her.

"Just seeing if my dog still remembers his whistle!" she yelled.

The old man waved his walking stick, then he and Shep disappeared around the side of the mountain.

Gunny pushed open the door at O'Leary's and looked around the smoky, dark interior. Her legs ached from the long hike and she was thirsty for a glass of porter. She waved to the Burke twins sitting at a back table. Father Jessey was sitting at the table next to them with an empty glass in front of him. She'd seen the priest many times at O'Leary's, but she'd never seen him drink.

"Father Jessey," she said in a big voice, approaching the table. "Do I see you drowning your sorrows in a glass of porter?"

The priest looked hard into his empty glass. "I'll have another, Micky," he yelled in the general direction of the bar.

Micky brought a fresh pint to the table and gave the table a quick wipe with a dirty, damp towel. "Are you sure about this, Father?"

"Micky," Father Jessey said loudly. "Your job is to bring me porter. And you have brought me porter," he said taking the full glass. "You may go," he added with a feathery wave.

Micky rolled his eyes at Gunny and returned to the bar. She heard the Burke twins snicker behind her. Father Jessey ran his hands up and down the smooth cylinder then picked up the glass with both hands and took a long swig. He wiped his mouth gently on his sleeve and stifled a burp. "Sometimes, Miss Malone, a man needs to drink," he muttered. He took another sip looking hard into the deep amber liquid.

Gunny sat down next to him and scooted her chair in close. "But you're a priest."

Father Jessey looked at Gunny's slim face and large brown eyes. "Am I not also a man?"

"Now that's a question I can't answer," Gunny said with a grin.

The priest turned his focus back to his glass. "I'm trying to forget something and this porter is helping me."

"Bad day at the church, Father?"

"Bad day...," he whispered loudly. "Ever since I put up those new gates I've been haunted by the devil. My beautiful, new gates," the priest continued, enunciating each word and pointing an unsteady finger at Gunny's face. "They won't stay shut. Every night I lock them and in the morning they are flung open in every direction. How will I ever be made monsignor if I can't keep my gates closed?"

Gunny tried to suppress a smile. This was the most fun she'd had around the priest. "Did you have Mac look at them?"

"Yes, I had Mac look at them. He says there is nothing wrong with the gates. He says the gates are perfect." He slumped in his chair. "I bought perfectly beautiful haunted gates."

Gunny grinned. "Maybe Matt's trying to tell you to leave them open."

Father Jessey blinked at Gunny trying to focus. "Matt's gone. I sent him off ages ago."

"You may have helped bury him, but I don't think he ever left. I feel him around all the time, and he never did like a locked door."

Father Jessey stuck out his bottom lip. "I don't think Matt is anywhere near here." He drew a hand across his forehead, then opened his eyes wide. "Of course, I could leave the gates open. I could tell the Bishop that the gates are symbolic that all are welcome in Dunquin."

"Now you're thinking, Father," Gunny said. "Perhaps you should drink more often."

Father Jessey pushed a coin onto the table and stood, steadying himself on the table, then elbowed his way through the crowd and pushed hard on the pub door. Gunny hurried behind him and pulled the door open. Bitsy Kavanaugh was just arriving. She froze when she saw the clearly inebriated priest.

"What are you staring at?" he slurred. "Don't tell me you've never seen a drunk priest."

Bitsy put her hand to her face to hide a laugh as Father Jessey stumbled past her. She pushed the door closed and turned to Gunny. "That made my day, girl. Let me buy you a drink."

Gunny paced about inside. It was pouring rain for the seventh day in a row. She leaned up against the small front window thinking about Shep and the old man on the mountain. How had Shep gotten so far away? And where did they live? Where could they possibly find turf and grow potatoes that high on a mountain—and in all that mist?

"Find something to do, Gunny," Eileen complained. "You remind me of when you were a little girl and it was too rainy to be outside. If you can't find something…"

"I know, Mam, you'll find something for me."

Gunny had not mentioned Shep or the old man to either of her parents. When she got the dog back, she'd let them know where she'd found him. In the meantime, the mystery was hers to ponder. She put on water for potatoes, swept out the house, and waited.

Finally, she woke to a dry morning, with early rays of sun beaming in through the smoke-streaked front window. She scrambled out of bed, packed two slices of oat bread in her apron pocket, and headed to the mountain. She hiked northeast through the long maze of muddy fields past Ballyferriter, walked three times around the well, and proceeded up the steep path to the summit. She sat on a rock at the peak to catch her breath, the sun warm on her face. The views of the sweeping mountain face and deep ocean below were spectacular—but she wasn't there for the view. She sat quietly for a half hour, waiting. When there was no sign of either man or dog, she stood with a sigh and turned to start back down the path. The old man was sitting on a rock just ahead of her. She felt her breath catch in her throat. Shep trotted over to greet her. She gave his head a scratch then crossed to the old man.

"I've been thinking about you, wondering how anyone could live on this mountain."

The man sat with his eyes closed. "I live as all men live."

"What do you eat?"

"I eat food."

"Are you a mystic?"

The old man opened his eyes and laughed. "A mystic without a monastery? Maybe."

Gunny studied the wrinkled patterns on his face. "John McCrohan used to tell us tales about a barefoot monk community that lived in the hills away from the priests. He said those monks were killed by the Vikings centuries ago. But here you are. Do you mind if I sit with you?"

The man indicated a large rock near him and Gunny scrambled up. She sat quietly, feeling the sun-baked heat of the rock beneath her. "I'd like to live alone on a mountain," she said, finally breaking the silence. "My life has been all crazy for the past year. I'm ready to be done with that."

The old man laughed a deep, raspy laugh. "Chaos is a sign that change is coming. Sometimes when you think you're at the end of a something it turns out you're only at the beginning, Gunny."

Gunny felt the blood drain from her face. "I never told you my name was Gunny."

"Didn't you?" the man asked with a smile. "I am certain you did. Where are my manners?" he added, reaching out his hand. "My name is William Brennan. I am happy to meet you."

Gunny tentatively shook William Brennan's hand. It was large and warm. "You're a little confusing."

"I don't mean to be. I'm simply an old man who had enough of village life and moved to a mountain."

Gunny smiled. "Trouble with the church?"

William cocked his head and smiled. "I used to be a priest in Tralee. How did you know?"

Gunny frowned. "You've the look of a priest about you, sorry to say."

William laughed his big laugh again. "No more sorry than I am to confirm it. I left Tralee to find God on my own terms. Pilgrims used to bring part of their harvest to the top of this mountain to celebrate the equinox of Lunasa. I thought I might catch a glimpse of their Gods if I stayed here long enough."

"Father Owen used to tell us that Brandon Mountain was where St. Brendan launched his campaign to find the new world and spread the word of the church. He never mentioned anything about leaving food here for the Gods."

William shook his head. "The Catholic Church steals all of the good stories. May Day was once Beltaine. Height Sunday used to be called Lunasa. And Hallow E'en and All Saints Day were stolen from Samhain, the celebration of the first day of Winter. The church even took the sun god and turned Christ into the light of the world. There is a thin crust of Christianity over many pagan rituals. Personally, I like the pagan rituals better."

"I don't know anything about pagan rituals," Gunny said.

"You said you were on a pilgrimage. That's a pagan ritual from a time when religion connected more with the earth and less with the church."

"I'm starting to see why you left the priesthood."

"Oh, it wasn't just the rituals. The last straw for me was when the church decided to spend more on gold candlesticks one Christmas than they spent taking care of the poor."

"Our priest just spent a fortune on new gates for the church. Do you think God cares if a church has elaborate gates?"

"No. But do the bishops care? Yes."

"Well the gates are haunted anyway, so it serves Father Jessey right."

William's heavy eyebrows raised. "Father Jessey? Would that be Edward Jessey? From Tralee?"

Gunny shrugged. "I heard he was from Tralee. I never heard his given name. Do you know him?"

William gazed into the mist that was starting to thicken around them. "We found Edward Jessey on the steps of the church when he was but a few days old. The church elders said to take him to the orphanage but we couldn't bear to part with him with his golden hair and blue eyes so we raised him in the church."

"It could be the same man—with the blue eyes and blond hair. Did you ever find his mother?"

"We never did."

"No wonder he hates the thought of unwed mothers," Gunny said.

"Oh, he never got over the fact that his mother abandoned him. Left him with quite a temper as a boy. I'm surprised he became a priest."

"No offense," Gunny smirked. "But he's a perfect priest. He loves telling everyone what to do and what to think. And he loves looking just so in his long, flowing robes with his hair all perfect..."

"Don't judge him," William said raising a finger. "Usually the things that irritate us most about others are traits we don't like in ourselves. Ignore their worst traits—and take on the best ones, I say."

Shep nudged William's arm with his nose. William looked at the dog and turned to Gunny. "Shep is reminding me that we have some business to attend to. And it looks like the mist is rolling back in. We should hurry. We don't want to keep a fish waiting."

"You're going to fish in one of Lord Ventry's streams?"

"What the Old Lord doesn't know won't hurt him."

Gunny was startled to hear Matt's words come out of a stranger's mouth as he slid off the rock and held out a hand to her. She ignored his hand, pushed off her rock and straightened her skirt and apron. William eyed her, then set off toward the back side of the mountain at a brisk clip. Shep raced ahead down an unseen rocky path. The wind stirred a gathering mist as Gunny did her best to keep up. William stopped and waited for her.

"That's quite a limp," he said.

Gunny blushed. "I'm trying to get rid of it by walking."

William laughed. "A limp may be God's way of insisting you slow down."

Gunny took a deep breath. "I thought we were hurrying to see if you caught a fish?" she said with a smile.

"That's my path," William said. "It may not be your path."

He started off again at a slightly slower pace, walking ahead of Gunny to the bank of a low, deep stream. Shep paced on the bank as William lifted a small fishing net from a swift spot at the center of the stream. Inside, a fine, fat trout flipped angrily in the net. William waded out of the stream hauling the net and flopping fish on his back, then turned and headed into a deep, bushy area with the dog at this heals.

"Aren't you going to eat that?" she asked, expecting William to make a fire by the stream as Matt had always done.

"Not without a potato or two," William called out behind him.

Gunny followed, pushing her way through the thick bushes into a small, open glen. Midday light broke through the mist onto a small, early summer garden overflowing with potato plants, pale green cabbages, onions, purple lettuce, climbing pea plants, and herbs. Two chickens were scratching for insects in the garden; another hen sat nesting on a cross-hatch of furze along the roof of a tiny hut just past the garden. A wisp of smoke leaked out of a short, crumbling chimney.

"I like to save the fish guts to use as fertilizer. Fertilizer is difficult to come by this far up the mountain." He cleaned the fish using a sharp black-handled knife and tossed the innards onto a small dung pile near the door of the cottage. "Would you like to come in?" he asked, ducking through the low doorway and disappearing inside.

Gunny followed him. The hut was small but neatly furnished, with a large bed in the back room, and rows of shelves along the far wall that were filled with jars and bottles and books. William stirred the fire with a long poker and added a small turf. He moved a rough board from a deep hole in the floor along the back wall and pulled out a firkin of butter. He spooned butter into a large pan.

241

Gunny watched him as he worked. "Why do you keep your butter in the ground?"

"It's cooler," he said. "I don't get butter very often so I have to make it last."

The butter sizzled in the pan. William cut up an onion from a string he had hanging near the fire and added it to the butter. The smell was amazing.

"What're you doing now?" Gunny asked.

"You haven't had onion before?"

"I've had plenty of onion but we don't cook it. We chop it up raw to add to our potatoes."

"Well then, you're in for a treat."

He dipped the trout fillets in a small pan of oat flour and laid them in with the sizzling onions, then speared a half-dozen potatoes that had been roasting in the fire embers, scraped the ash off them, and tossed them into a large bowl. He flipped the fish once with a long metal flipper, then scooped the hot fish and onions from the pan into three bowls and set them on the table. He added two roasted potatoes to each bowl.

"Who else is coming?" Gunny said eying the abundance of food.

William looked perplexed.

"You served three bowls."

William cocked a thumb toward Shep and said in a low voice. "You don't expect to eat in front of the dog and not share, do you?"

Gunny's mouth watered from the delicious smells that filled the tiny hut. "Now I understand why Shep stopped coming home to the slops from our table. I guess there'll be no getting him back now."

William took a seat on a bench at the table and indicated to Gunny that she should do the same. She sat and reached for a bowl, then stopped when she realized William was praying. She waited for him to finish.

"You must always give thanks for food because it won't always be there," William said, crossing himself.

"You're talking about the hungry days of July before the new crop of potatoes comes in?"

"July. October. March. You never know when the food will run out."

He set one bowl on the dirt floor for Shep. The dog waited for a signal from William, then wolfed down the food in his bowl. Gunny waited for William to start eating before she began. The mix of fish, onions, and potatoes tasted even better than it smelled.

"If you want to live on your own," William said in between bites, "you have to plan ahead—to catch hares, and dry fish, to grow and store what you can, when you can. And even then, sometimes food will run short and you'll have to fast."

"I hate fasting on the holidays. I think about food all day."

"It's good practice to harden you for tough times. Delicious," he added, finishing off a last spoonful.

"Delicious," Gunny agreed, tempted to lick the last crusty bits of fish and onion from her bowl.

William took her bowl and set both bowls on the floor for Shep to clean. "Now," he said standing. "I believe the mist is lifting. You must be off or your people will worry."

Gunny remained seated. "Can I come again?"

William smiled. "Yes, come again. We'll have another talk. I chose a solitary life, but in truth, I like a bit of company."

Shep whined and pawed at William's leg. William scratched the dog's head. "No offense intended." Shep wagged his tail and curled up on a worn mat in front of the fire.

William showed Gunny to the door. "Don't come every day. I require a good bit of silence for my prayers."

"I could visit and not say anything."

"Not talking is not the same as silence." He looked at the girl's disappointed face and grinned. "Come as often as you like."

Gunny held out a hand. William took her long, slim hand in his own rough hand.

"I'm glad you meet you, William," Gunny said with a grin. "Do you suppose we'll be friends?"

William bowed his head. "We already are."

Gunny returned to the mountain nearly every day and William never complained. Sometimes her leg hurt too much for the steep climb and sometimes rain or mist made the climb too dangerous, but each time she arrived, William seemed to know she was coming and either he or Shep was on the pathway to greet her. On a few visits, the weather changed from clear to rainy during the day and she slept overnight on a straw mat in front of the fire. When the night skies were clear, William pointed out clusters of stars and told Gunny their names and their stories. The nights she stayed at the hut were the few nights she did not dream of Matt. When she returned after a night away, her mother glared at her and her father looked at her with sad eyes, but neither asked where she had been; neither wanted to know.

William was an enthusiastic teacher and Gunny an eager student. William taught her what foods to plant and how to fish in a stream with a net. He showed her how to collect seeds, and how to cook, dry, and store food. They spent time in the fields searching for roots, leaves, and bark which William showed her how to mix into healing teas and potions. Occasionally they worked on her reading and arithmetic.

"You're teaching me so much. I don't know how to repay you."

"All I ask is that someday you pass this knowledge on to someone else."

Gunny laughed. "Who would I ever teach?"

William's face was so serious, Gunny stopped mid-laugh and looked intently into his eyes. He took her hand. "Find someone. We're here to give, so teach from a generous place in your heart. And know that when you give things away, the rewards will be one hundred fold."

Gunny smiled. "I taught James how to read and then he used to read to me all the time, if that's what you mean. But when I tried to teach Matt how to twist rope, it was a disaster."

"Matt?" William asked with raised eyebrows.

Gunny hesitated. She and William had talked about so many things over the summer. He knew all about her family and about her time working in Dingle. But she had never told him about Matt. "Matt was a friend of mine," she said with some hesitation. "He's gone." Saying those words brought a familiar ache to her chest.

William paused, lips tight. "And that pains you."

Gunny felt tears pushing at her eyes and blinked. The sides of her throat closed, and she worked hard to swallow. "Yes," she said quietly.

"Did I ever tell you about the man who went everywhere carrying a heavy sack with him?"

Gunny swallowed hard and wiped her eyes with the back of her sleeve. "No," she said. "Tell me the story."

William squatted to stir the fire. "I once knew a man who carried all of his worldly possessions with him everywhere he went. The sack was very heavy but he would not set it down for fear that someone would take it. Finally, the sack became so heavy he could barely lift it, so he decided to hide his possessions on the tallest peak of a far off mountain. He climbed and climbed hauling that heavy sack behind him. When he reached the top of the mountain, he hid the sack in a small cave and finally felt free." William sat on the edge of the hearth and turned to Gunny. "And what do you think happened when he came down off of the mountain?"

Gunny shook her head.

"Someone gave him something new to carry."

Gunny laughed. "I've been carrying a heavy sack for a long time."

"Of course you have. Now," William said, standing and dusting off the seat of his pants. "Let's practice some mathematics. Then I have a few new herbs I want to show you."

They worked through the rest of the summer in the fields, at the stream, and in the small hut. Over meals, they talked about God and pilgrimages and Gunny told William old stories she'd learned from her father and John McCrohan. In the late afternoons, she often played the whistle as William tended the kitchen garden. He had a terrible voice but loved to sing along with Gunny's whistling which made her laugh.

"Don't sing!" she said. "It's very difficult to play a whistle when someone is making you laugh."

"I am singing the wandering soul back home," William insisted. "When we cross to the other side, the only things we take with us are love and music. So love well here, Gunny. Love. And make music. You'll want something familiar with you when you see the face of God."

Gunny would start again and play until William's voice reached a fevered pitch, which made her laugh so hard she thought her sides would split. When William laughed, it made him cough. One afternoon, he started and could not stop coughing, but once he caught his breath, he insisted on singing again. The days she laughed with William, Gunny left the mountain with a smile so wide she had to go straight to bed when she got home for fear her parents would think she'd lost her mind.

Eileen grew more and more worried about her daughter.

"Why must you go out to the hills every day and stay out all night? Look at you. Your hair is a tangled mess. Your shawl and skirt are filthy. Your fingernails are lined with dirt. You should hear what people are saying about you."

"I don't care what people say about me. I'm happy," Gunny said with a wide smile. "Isn't that more important than my reputation?"

"It's not just your reputation. I have a reputation as well."

"And what's that? That you came from Ventry? That you were a Fitzgerald? That's all I heard from you growing up—about your old house in Ventry and the famous Moss Barney who went to America. Who cares about any of that, Mam? Have you ever been happy?"

Eileen's mouth fell open. "Why must you say mean things, Gunny? You should care that we come from Fitzgerald blood and try to act less like a wandering fool."

Gunny sat on a stool in front of the fire and ran her fingers through her tangled, dark curls. "I'm not a fool, Mam."

Eileen paced. "Then stop wandering with no purpose. When someone goes outside, there should be something to fetch, or a delivery to be made. Sensible people move with purpose, with reason. You shouldn't wander about at the direction of the wind. It's not right."

Gunny moved her stool closer to the fire and rubbed at her right leg.

"And look at you," Eileen said sitting on a stool next to Gunny. "You're in pain. That's what makes you crazy. It's the pain."

"I'm not crazy, Mam, and I'm not in that much pain. My leg aches a bit when the weather's damp, that's all. Can't you be happy that I'm happy?"

Eileen stood and snorted. "I'd be happy if you'd settle down and be normal."

Gunny stood and pulled on her shawl.

"You can't possibly be going out again? At this hour?"

"This hike will make more sense to you, Mam. I'm headed to O'Leary's. I'll tell Da hello for you."

When Gunny arrived at the hut the next day after a long, hot climb up the mountain she found William inside his hut roasting a fowl on a spit over the fire. The air inside was cool and close, the smell delicious.

"Why are you cooking your last chicken? What'll you do for eggs?" she asked, pulling a small sack off her back and setting it on the table.

"Today is August 15th, the Assumption. It's a day of celebration... And this bird was making me crazy. When her two sister chickens disappeared, this one got all broody. I'd had enough of her weeping."

Gunny sat on a low stool by the fire. "Matt and I hiked to Brandon Mountain once on the Assumption."

William glanced at her. "Go collect something from the garden to add to our meal, will you?"

Gunny could see that William wanted no weeping today—from her or from a broody chicken. She grabbed a knife from the table and headed outside. William's garden was so full of onions and cabbage it was hard to believe that soon a cold wind would cut up this mountain. She cut off a cabbage head and pulled up a few onions and returned to the hut. William looked pale in the firelight and she noticed a slight tremble in his right hand as he pulled apart the head of cabbage.

Gunny sat on the bench at the table chopping onions. The sun was setting a little earlier each day, the night wind was growing cooler, and the cloud that topped the mountain was thickening. She scrapped the onion into the frying pan with the cabbage leaves. William gave her a nod of appreciation.

When the bowls at the table were filled and a prayer said, they ate in silence. After their meal, Gunny reached into her sack and pulled out a straw man and woman. "I made these last night. I thought you could use a little company up here."

"How clever you are to make something of nothing," he said, admiring her craft.

"They won't be much help when the winter winds set in. How will you survive up here by yourself over the winter?"

William shook his head and pushed his right hand down into his pocket.

"I've spent many a winter alone, Gunny. This winter will be no different. When you're alone in a crowd it's much worse that being alone by yourself."

* * *

Gunny ran to the end of the strand, tossed her skirt and shawl aside, and dove into the waves in her shirt and petticoat. The salty water was brisk as it washed through her clothes and rinsed her long, thick hair. She splashed about until she was out of breath and starting to shiver, then hurried back to the shore, running just ahead of a breaking wave to keep her footing. She shook sand from her skirt and dried her face, then slipped the skirt on over her petticoat and pulled the wet petticoat out from under the skirt. She flipped her hair around a few times to get some of the water out, then wrapped her shawl around her wet shoulders and smiled at the breaking waves.

"Thank you," she said, face raised to the sun. It had been a week since she had been back to Brandon Mountain. She could feel the mountain pull her to return but she resisted. She noticed Mac watching her from the pier and waved. "What's the matter?" she yelled. "You look as if you've never seen a person swim before."

Mac waved back and walked from the pier out onto the strand. "I've seen plenty of people swim but I've hardly ever seen you swim. I thought you didn't like to swim in the ocean."

Gunny shook her head, splashing Mac with fine droplets of water. He jumped away and brushed off his shirt. She laughed. "I don't like being thrown in, but swimming is a delight."

"Are you... all right?" Mac asked.

"Do you mean am I sane? Because that's how you're looking at me." Mac started to reply but Gunny continued. "I was up in the booley this morning catching rabbits. It was so quiet and peaceful up there—and hot. I climbed up onto that flat rock near the booley huts and looked down at this mighty green ocean with the sun beating down on my face and a light salty breeze blowing up through the fields, and I had this incredible urge to dive right right into the ocean."

"You weren't drinking, were you?" Mac asked, his brow furrowed.

"Of course I wasn't drinking. I told you. I was hunting rabbits."

"You know you can't dive into the ocean from the booley fields."

"I know that," Gunny said laughing and pushing on his arm. "I'm trying to describe a feeling I had—that if I had wings, I could have soared right down into the cool water."

"You didn't try to dive, did you?"

"No, Mac, don't be silly. Listen to me. I tossed my hare catch into my yard, then ran as best I could with this damned walking stick down the road and through the village and straight out here. I pulled off my skirt and shawl and dove. I've never done that before—I usually just wade in. Have you ever dived into a wave, Mac?"

"No," Mac said in a low voice.

"I highly recommend it," Gunny said, grinning.

"Do you want me to walk you home?"

"No!" Gunny said with a laugh. "I'm dying of thirst. Buy me a glass at O'Leary's."

Matt hesitated. "I have to pull Matt's boat up onto the rack. Then I'll buy you one glass and walk you home."

Gunny turned her face back to the sun and leaned on her walking stick while she waited for Mac, enjoying the feeling of her wet shirt drying against her cool skin. She opened her eyes to the sound of giggles behind her. Three young girls were playing tag as they ran down the dirt road toward the water. They were in nearly identical dark dresses with dirty white aprons and no shoes. She recognized one of the girls as Mary's friend from up in the booley. She smiled as the girls neared. They stopped short and stared, clutching at one another.

"It's the witch!" the littlest one whimpered.

Gunny took a step toward them and all three shrieked.

"Stop that," she yelled. "I'm not a witch."

"You are a witch," the littlest one said, pointing. "You have a funny walk and you carry a magic stick."

"We saw you up in the booley this morning," the middle-sized girl said. "You had your arms raised and you were looking down the hill cursing the village."

"I wasn't cursing the village," Gunny said with a laugh. "I was looking out at the ocean and praising the sun. Mac," she yelled toward the pier. "Tell these girls I'm not a witch."

Mac nodded and waved but said nothing.

"I was with Mary when you destroyed that tiny village in the booley," the middle-sized girl said. "Mam told me to stay away from you. She said you were up to no good spending so much time in the hills with the fairies."

"My mam said the fairies could give you power to put a curse on the village," the little one said.

Gunny scoffed. "I did not put a curse on the village."

"My father says that no one walks in the booley at night unless they have the power of the fairies," the tall one added, authoritatively.

Gunny put her hands on her hips and stared at the girls.

Mac trotted over from the pier. "Listen, girls," he said. "You know me, right?"

The three girls shook their heads in unison. "You're the smithy," the tall girl said.

"That's right," Mac said. "I'm the smithy. And would the smithy be friends with a witch?" he asked, waving a hand toward Gunny.

They looked at Gunny skeptically. She smiled.

"No," the tall girl said reluctantly.

Gunny grabbed Mac by the arm. Her hands were icy cold on the underside of his arm. He gasped and pulled away. The girls squealed again.

"I'm not going to hurt him," Gunny said taking a firmer grip on Mac's arm. "I need his help, that's all. I carry this walking stick because I hurt my leg a few years back. There's no magic in this stick," she said waving the walking cane in front of them. "See? It's just a stick."

All three shook their heads, yes, but they didn't look like they believed her.

Gunny could not resist. She stamped her good foot toward them. "Then scram!" she yelled waving the cane at them.

The girls shrieked and ran back up the steep road.

"You couldn't leave well enough alone, could you?" Mac asked.

Gunny smiled. "I'd rather have those girls think I'm a witch then think I'm some poor old cripple."

Mac sighed and squeezed Gunny's hand on his arm. "How about that glass at O'Leary's?"

Gunny pulled her arm free of Mac's grasp. "I was trying to show those girls that someone wasn't afraid of me," she said quietly.

"I didn't mean to pull away from you," he said. "I was just surprised at how cold your hands were."

"You looked at me like you were afraid."

"Well, maybe I am, a little" Mac said with a grin.

Gunny shrugged and they headed up the road toward O'Leary's. The girls were standing a few houses past O'Leary's chattering away with a woman. The tall girl pointed down the road toward Gunny.

"Oh, God," Gunny said. "Now one of their mothers is involved. If that woman dares say anything to me, I'll give her an earful."

"Now you sound like your mother. That's Mrs. Foley. Cornelius' Mam." Mac waved at the woman. "You've never met her? She likes to gossip but she's harmless."

"Maybe it's good Mam kept us away from the village," Gunny said as they approached the door of the pub.

They entered and looked around the dim, smoky room. Hardly anyone was there. Gunny pulled out a chair at a table by the front window. Mac went to the bar and ordered two glasses of porter from Micky.

"I have a newspaper here if you want it," Micky yelled over to Gunny.

Gunny missed his words as she peeked out the window up the street. The three girls were still there; Mrs. Foley was gone.

Mac returned to the table. "Ignore them," he said setting the glasses down and tossing Micky's newspaper on the table.

"Ignore them?" Gunny said sipping at the porter and scanning the headlines. "They started it. They called me a witch."

Mac lightly clinked his glass against hers to draw her attention. "Why does it bother you what anyone says about you?"

Gunny took a sip of the frothy brown liquid. "That's an excellent question."

Mac took a swallow of porter and pulled the paper toward him. Gunny studied his wide face and thick black hair as he scanned the headlines. He had a cowlick at the center of his forehead that created a wave of black hair up and away from his face. She looked at his brown eyes, heavy lids and dark lashes, and at his soot-stained hands as he ran a finger over the words on the page. She drained her glass and peeked again out the window.

"The girls are gone. I should head home," she said pushing her chair from the table.

"Gunny," Mac said, gripping her arm. "I need to ask a favor."

Gunny was shocked and sat back down. "It's usually me who does the favor asking."

"It's about Matt," he said in a soft voice.

Gunny felt the blood drain from her face. "What about him?" she asked in a small voice.

Mac hesitated. "Will you go with me to see his grave?"

"His grave?" Gunny said a little too loudly as the few occupied tables around them suddenly quieted. "It's up in the churchyard," Mac continued in a quiet voice.

"Well of course it's in the churchyard," Gunny said, "where else would it be. But why go there? Why now?"

"I want to see it," Mac said. "I want to see where they buried Matt."

Gunny rubbed her hands together to warm them. "You must know where they buried him. You were at the funeral."

"I didn't go."

Gunny paused. "You didn't go to Matt's funeral?"

"I couldn't. I didn't believe he was dead. I heard the Wren Boys pounding his coffin together, but I couldn't help. Then I watched as they walked out the back door of the house with him, but I couldn't go. I never left the forge that day."

"And now?"

"Now I need to know... I...," Mac said with hesitation. "You'll think this's crazy but it still doesn't feel like Matt's dead to me."

Gunny felt the room grow silent around her. "What're you talking about, Mac?"

"I used to dream about the accident," Mac stammered. "I'd see Matt riding toward me and I'd be shouting 'Stop!' but no sound would come out of my mouth. Then I'd see him again farther away from the gate riding toward me, again and again..."

Gunny nodded her head and swallowed hard.

"I've stopped dreaming about him," Mac said. "But I still see him, I mean it's not him, but I catch little glimpses, like he's gone around a corner right as I get there." Mac looked hard into Gunny's face. "And I smell the smoke from his pipe…"

"But no one's smoking, right?" Gunny said, slapping her hand against the table.

"Right. How do you…?"

Gunny shook her head. "I've seen him too, Mac. Ever since the accident. And I've smelled the smoke." Gunny paused. "And sometimes, I hear him laugh."

"Yes! I've heard that," Mac said. "Sometimes I hear Nella too, and I pound even harder on whatever I'm working on but I can still hear them. You wouldn't believe how many horseshoes I've made trying to block that sound. I hardly have room for all of them."

"Sometimes I forget you miss Matt as much as I do."

"Don't ever forget that."

Gunny took a deep breath. "I've never visited his grave either. Maybe it's time."

Mac paid Micky and they headed up the street toward the large white church. When they neared the corner by the gates, Gunny froze. Her head was spinning and she felt short of breath. She reached for the black-handled knife deep in her pocket. Mac continued on a few strides past her then turned and looked at her pale face.

"Are you sure you're up to this?"

"Maybe I'm not."

"We don't have to go. It was probably a bad idea."

"No, it's a good idea. I should have visited his grave before."

The new gates before them were incredible—tall and black with intricate filigree detail along the top and down each bar. Gunny paused, then grabbed Mac's arm and pushed through the partially open gates and sprinted as best she could around the side of the church and into the graveyard. She stopped to catch her breath near her grandparents' gravestones and dropped Mac's hand. The stones in the yard were tipped every which way with rough stones poking through matted, tangled grass.

"Over there," Mac pointed. "Mam said they buried Matt next to Da."

The graveyard was unusually silent as if the ground inside the gates absorbed sound. They picked their way to the far end of the graveyard to the McCrohan plots. Matt's grave loomed in front of them: Matthew Andrew McCrohan. 1805-1825. Rest in Peace.

Mac bowed his head.

"Hah!" Gunny snorted.

Mac opened his eyes. "What?" he whispered.

Gunny pointed at the gravestone with her walking stick. "How could anyone rest in peace in this place? And look at Matt's grave with the stone all tipped and the earth uneven."

Mac shivered. "It poured rain all day the day they buried him. It looks like his grave never settled."

Gunny closed her eyes and swallowed hard, then continued in a quieter voice. "It's Matt who never settled. It's too quiet here for anyone to rest in peace. He must hate being here so he's haunting both of us and haunting Father Jessey and this church." Gunny shivered.

Mac glanced at Gunny. "You're freezing. Your clothes are still wet from your swim."

"I'm not shivering from the cold," Gunny said, but she shivered again as a sharp wind blew through the graveyard carrying the fresh smell of the sea. She grabbed Mac's arm. "Death was Matt's way of escaping Dunquin and all of us. He's not here, Mac, and I don't want to be here either."

After a week at home, Gunny finally headed back up the mountain carrying the heavy length of rope she'd been working on to sell at the harvest fair in Dingle. She was exhausted by the time she reached the top. As usual, Shep was mysteriously waiting for her at the top of the path, and she followed him to William's glen. William was busy pulling the last of the onions from the garden as Shep escorted her in. She presented the large coil to William with a shy smile.

"Sorry I've been away for a bit. I thought you might like this rope."

William stood up and dusted the dirt from his hands. He fingered the fine rope. "What's this for?"

"I thought we should add another layer of rope and sod to your roof before the north winds pick up in earnest."

"There's nothing wrong with my roof," he said, peering through squinted eyes at his small house with the crumbling chimney.

"There's nothing wrong except that it leaks. It's hot today, but it's going to snow up here soon. You'll need a stronger roof if you're going to stay on Brandon Mountain through the winter."

"I don't mind a little snow in the house," William said shaking his head. "We have more important matters to deal with today."

"The furze is starting to dry in the fields. We can use that for thatch," Gunny continued.

"Gunny," William said sternly, taking the rope from her and setting it on the bench outside the house. "We don't have time for that. Today we're going to bring in the last of the harvest. Samhain will be here soon, the day of the dead."

Gunny sighed. There was no arguing with William when he had his mind made up. She sat on the bench next to the rope and scratched Shep's silky head. "Do you think the dead really return on Samhain?" she asked, thinking about her walk through the graveyard with Mac.

"Excellent question," William replied pacing in front of the bench. "But the real question is: Do you?"

Gunny was quiet. "I used to. I used to believe everything my parents told me. But now with Matt gone... Sometimes I'm afraid he'll be back. And other times I'm afraid he won't be back."

William paused. "Did I ever tell you about the time I was hiking along a ridge at night and got lost?"

"No," Gunny said. There was definitely not going to be any work done today on the roof.

William sat next to Gunny on the bench and looked across the drying remains of the summer garden. "I grew up in the hills of Gransha, south of Tralee. One night, my grandmother was gravely ill and my Mam sent me to fetch the doctor. The shortest route to Tralee was north across the mountaintop. My Mam told me to not take that path, but I was in a hurry. I remember that night. It was black and chill with no moon. As I neared the cliffs along the north side of the mountain, I walked slowly, using the stars above me to show me where the path was. I thought I was on solid ground when I felt the earth give way beneath me. I panicked and grabbed at the dirt as I slid. I caught hold of a branch and held on for dear life. All night I kept hold of that branch. As the sun started to rise, I couldn't hold on any longer. I had no strength left and I let go."

Gunny eyes were open wide. "What happened?"

"I dropped a few inches to the ground."

Gunny looked into William's eyes. "Are you telling me that I should stop clutching at a branch, William?"

"I'm not telling you anything, Gunny. It's just a story. The answers are within you."

Gunny shook her head. "When it comes to Matt, I don't have answers. I just feel empty."

William laughed his deep, throaty laugh, followed by a cough. When he finally caught his breath, he pointed a bent finger at her. "You have something to offer the world," he wheezed. "Find something good to do with your life, Gunny. Will you promise me that?"

Gunny grimaced. "You assume that I have a life off this mountain."

"Promise," he repeated, coughing into the back of his hand.

Gunny nodded. "If I can find something good to do, I'll do it. I promise."

William reached out and took both of her hands in his. "Each of us is on a journey, Gunny. I pray that you find the right path for yours."

"William?"

"Yes, Gunny."

"What happened to your grandmother?"

"She visits me every year—on Samhain. Now let's bring in the harvest."

Gunny woke the next morning to a dark house. She pushed the covers aside and went out to stir the fire. A cold heavy rain fell in the yard and blew against the door in gusts. She made tea and pulled her shawl tight around her. She pictured William's leaky roof, heard his cough, and saw his trembling hand, but there would be no hike to the mountain today. She was glad they had least brought some food into his house.

Heavy rains continued for two weeks. When the drizzle finally stopped and the sun broke through thick, departing clouds, Gunny practically sprinted out of the house along her well worn route to Brandon Mountain. She was near the top of the mountain by mid morning and stopped by Matt's rock to catch her breath. Her cheeks were cold from the sharp wind and her eyes watered. She blew on her hands to warm them. Neither Shep nor William came out to greet her. Her heart raced.

"William?" she yelled, scrambling over the rough rocks toward the creek. "William? Shep?"

She jumped across the creek and pushed through the thick bushes into William's glen. The summer garden was bare, the last of the harvest taken in. The yard was quiet. Gunny crossed the glen and opened the small door of the hut. She stooped and peeked inside. Midmorning light from the open doorway lit William's still body on the bed. His eyes were closed, his hands crossed on his chest. There was no fire in the hearth.

She walked slowly toward the bed. "William?" she whispered, seeing her breath in front of her.

William did not stir. She touched his hands and ran her fingers over his cold, grey wrinkled face—then dropped to her knees by his bedside and wept. Deep, wracking sobs shook her as years of untapped sorrow spilled out. She wept until her tears ran dry, then pushed stiffly up onto her feet. She looked around the silent, tidy hut. What should she do? William was too heavy for her to drag outside and bury. She knelt again by the bed.

"Dear, William. I have to leave you as you are, with no one to tell stories at your wake, and no candles to light." She closed her eyes and folded her hands. "Dear, Lord. Please take your servant home. William was a good man." She crossed herself and pushed away from the bed. She backed out the door and closed it tight behind her.

Outside, she took a deep breath of cold air and whistled for Shep. When the dog did not come running, she called and called again, but he was gone. Gunny felt a wave of desperation pass over her, and pushed her way back through the rough bushes toward the creek. Branches caught at her hair and skirt and she stumbled into the icy water. When she finally reached Matt's rock, she paused to say one last good-bye and limped down the mountain toward home.

She arrived in Dunquin shortly before dark and found Mac at O'Leary's sitting with Cornelius Foley and the O'Brian twins.

"Mac," she said sliding in next to him at their table. "I need your help."

Mac stared at her. Her face was puffy and blotchy, her clothes dirty, her skirt in tatters.

"I have to bury someone," she whispered softly in his ear.

"What?" he whispered hoarsely, choking down a swallow of porter. He grabbed her by the elbow. "No. Don't tell me in here," he said guiding her out the door of the crowded pub and around the corner where it was quiet. "Now tell me that again," he said in a low voice.

Gunny grabbed Mac by both arms and looking pleadingly at his face. "I need your help burying an old man on Brandon Mountain."

Mac looked at Gunny and repeated. "You need my help burying an old man on Brandon Mountain." He paused. "What're you talking about?"

"I've been hiking to Brandon Mountain for the last six months. William was teaching me but now he's gone and I need your help burying him."

"You want to bury someone on Brandon Mountain. In October. You can't hike on Brandon Mountain in October. It's not safe."

"Mac, you don't understand. William didn't have anyone but me."

"Gunny, who is this man you're talking about?"

Gunny looked dazed. "William. He's my friend—or he was my friend—until he died."

Mac squinted. "Are you sure that's all there is to this?"

"Don't be crazy, Mac. William is ancient—and he was a friend. Now he's dead."

"Gunny, if this old man is dead then there's nothing you can do for him. You can't go back up there. The snow could start any time."

"Never mind," Gunny said pushing away from him. "I'll do it myself. Can you at least lend me a shovel?"

Mac sighed. "You can't bury someone by yourself. It would take you days to dig a proper grave. I'll go with you and I'll bring a shovel. Meet me at the forge tomorrow morning."

"Tomorrow. At first light," Gunny said with a sad, crazed look in her eyes. "I'll come find you at the forge."

Mac shook his head as Gunny scurried up the road toward home.

Mac slept in the forge that night. He woke several times anticipating Gunny's knock. Light was barely coming in through the window when he heard a soft tap at the door. He pulled on his boots, coat, and hat and grabbed a shovel he had sharpened the night before. Gunny was waiting outside, pacing. Her stride still wasn't even, but she set a stiff pace as they headed out of town.

"Your leg's much better," he said, a little out of breath.

"What?" Gunny said glancing over at him.

"All of your walking this summer—you're hardly limping."

Gunny looked at Mac confused. "I'm not limping," she repeated.

"No," he said.

"Good," she said, hurrying on.

It was midmorning when they reached the foot of the mountain. They paused for Mac to take three passes around the well. Gunny tried to be patient, but headed up the steep path without him. He hurried behind with the shovel. Near the peak, Gunny turned left off the pathway.

"Where're you going?" he asked.

"William lives in a small glen on the backside of the mountain."

Mac followed Gunny over the heavy grey rocks and through the yellowing grasses. Dried furze caught and tugged at his pant legs. Gunny paused ahead of him looking around uncertainly.

"Now what?" he asked.

She shook her head. "I don't understand. There used to be a creek here."

"I don't see a creek."

"I know. I don't see one either. But it was here—I walked into it yesterday. It must have dried up—but it was so deep. It doesn't make sense."

Mac leaned on the shovel waiting for Gunny to decide which way to turn.

"I think this is where it was," she said bending down and examining some smooth, grey stones. "We should go to the right."

"Into those bushes?" Mac asked, but Gunny had already forged ahead, dead branches and small dry leaves catching at her hair and skirt. Mac followed. Past the first row of bushes lay more rocks and dried grasses.

Gunny looked around. "Where's the glen?"

Mac shook his head and waited.

Gunny pointed to another low hedge of bushes off to the left. "There it is. It must be through there."

Mac followed Gunny into a small glen. Gunny stopped short. Past a barren garden lay the ruins of a small hut. It was an old stone structure with a crumbling chimney but no roof. Gunny raced to the wooden door which hung weakly on one broken hinge. The door creaked when she opened it. She ducked inside. Mac heard her gasp and stepped in behind her. There was nothing in the hut but scattered ashes from the hearth and an old broken stool. Rotten thatch from the crumbled roof filled one corner of the room to the right of the door. Weak October sunlight fell through the exposed rafters onto a thick layer of dust along the empty shelves of the far wall. Gunny walked slowly to the back room.

"Where is he?" she said, her eyes wide, a dried bit of spittle at one corner of her mouth.

"Who?" Mac asked softly.

"William!" she said loudly. "The old man I was telling you about. Where is he? Where's his bed?" She raced back to Mac. "Where're his books? His jars of stored herbs? Where is everything?"

Mac looked around the deserted hut. "Gunny, it doesn't look like anyone's lived here for a long time. Are you sure this is the right place? You seemed a little confused back there."

Gunny wrung her hands and looked around. "I don't understand," she said. "I've been coming here nearly every day since last spring. This was a cozy little house, and there was a garden and William grew onions and caught trout..."

"Maybe a really big storm came through and took off the roof," Mac suggested. "It's been stormy lately."

"But where are the stools and the table?" Gunny asked, pointing toward the dusty hearth. "Where're the bowl and spoons, and the big frying pan and the string of onions?" She grabbed Mac by the lapels of his jacket. "Where's the bed, Mac? Where's the body?"

Mac shrugged. "It must have been a really, really big storm, or else..."

Gunny tightened her grip on his jacket. "Or else what?" she whispered. "Or else I'm crazy and only imagined all of this?"

She raced outside. "I worked in that garden all summer," she said, pointing. "And I left a coil of rope right there on that bench. How can it all be gone?" she sobbed.

Mac ducked through the doorway. Straw from the garden blew past him. "You ate something from that garden?" Mac shivered. "It feels like a storm's blowing in, Gunny. We should go." He picked up his shovel and waited as a cold wind whipped around them.

Gunny shuddered and wrapped her shawl tight up across her chest. Mac put an arm around her to help warm her. She looked around the glen one last time, wiping tears away with the back of her hand.

Shep sat watching the activity in the glen from behind a thick, high hedge of furze, his light blue eyes intent on the girl. He let out a soft whine and a large wrinkled hand settled softly on his head. Two gentle clicks of the old man's tongue quieted the dog. Shep and William watched as the young couple turned and pushed their way through the bushes away from the glen.

"You know, Dog," William said. "I've never been any good at good-byes. But it was nice of Gunny to come back to bury me." He shivered in the cooling wind and kicked out the last of the embers from the burnt pile of furniture. "Gunny was right. That roof wasn't safe and this mountain is no place to live in the winter."

He pulled a small sack of goods onto his back. The large frying pan was tied to the outside of the sack; a string of onions tied next to the pan. He hefted Gunny's heavy coil of rope over his head and onto one shoulder, picked up his walking stick, and headed down the back side of the mountain toward Tralee.

~ Chapter 12: The Graveyard ~

In a valiant effort to be more social, Mac had taken his mother's advice and agreed to host a gathering for Hallow E'en. Gunny wished him the best when he told her about his plans but informed him she would not attend. She knew the McCrohan house would be haunted with old memories and hiked to O'Leary's instead. As she headed down the hill past the church, a loud cluster of teens emerged from the door of the pub and headed up the hill toward her. She ducked through the open church gates and stood in the shadows to wait until they passed.

She looked around the churchyard as the setting sun painted the tops of the nearby gravestones red and threw deep shadows along the path leading to the back of the church. She reached into her apron pocket and ran her fingers over the rough leather case of the black-handled knife, then picked her way along the darkening path over the uneven ground and rough, dry grasses. She slipped past the graves of her grandparents and John McCrohan and stood once again in front of Matt's grave, staring at his shadowy name carved deep in heavy grey stone. She fell to her knees on the uneven ground and bowed her head. When she opened her eyes, the last rays of sun were gone and she was alone in the dark, chill evening. She pulled a small flask of whiskey from her apron pocket, a gift from Micky O'Leary the week before. She uncorked the bottle and held it up to Matt's stone.

"Hello, Matt," she whispered. "Seems I can't avoid you tonight." She took a long swallow. The whiskey was harsh and hot as it slid down her throat. A light breeze moved the dry grasses behind her. "And a good evening to you, John McCrohan," she said with a tip of the bottle toward John McCrohan's grave. As she moved the flask to her lips to take another sip, a swirl of dry grasses blew in her face on a sharp burst of cold wind. She felt a chill pass through her. Her heartbeat out of rhythm and she clutched her chest

"That's a fine greeting," she said, standing and dusting grass off her knees. She slapped the cork into the bottle, slipped it into her pocket, and pulled her wool shawl up over her head. "Rest in peace," she said shaking her head.

She picked her way through the dark to the front of the church and slipped out through the gates onto the road. A man leading a tall horse hurried down the road toward her, silhouetted by a full, red rising moon. Gunny made a quick curtsy and stepped to the side of the road.

"Watch where you are going," the man snorted as he brushed past her with the horse, then paused and turned. "Gunny? Gunny Malone?"

Gunny looked up from her curtsy and smiled. "Hello, Thomas."

Lord Thomas Milliken could barely make her out in the dim moonlight, but she was more gorgeous than he remembered, with thick, dark curls spilling down the back of her neck. "Gunny Malone," he repeated. "It's been years. And what did I hear about you? An illness? An accident?"

Gunny stood and pushed her hair from her face. "An accident. I'm fine now."

Thomas leaned forward. "Yes, you are. Though you do smell a bit like whiskey," he added with a grin.

Gunny felt her cheeks warm and waved a hand in front of her mouth. "I've been down at O'Leary's. I must've picked up the smell of the bottle there."

Thomas smiled. "You are lying. I left O'Leary's a short while ago and I'd have noticed if you were there."

Gunny reached into her apron pocket and pulled out the small flask of whiskey. "I'm caught," she said. "Care for a sip?"

Thomas laughed. "I remember these words from a long time past—but I was offering you a flask that time, and as I recall, you were dead set against it."

"Times change," Gunny said with a smile.

"They do, indeed," Thomas said. "Did you hear I have been named the new Lord Ventry?"

Gunny had heard that the Old Lord passed, but had not heard this news about Thomas. "I thought your uncle was next in line."

"He was. But he died of pneumonia two days before my grandfather passed." Thomas chuckled. "Grandfather was ill all summer. He hardly got out of bed and his mind was wandering all over the place. Uncle Henry was a beast knowing that the lordship was finally within his reach. Then he got caught in a sudden rainstorm during a hunt, and died a week later. My grandfather's last wish was that the Lordship pass to me."

"What about your brother, Dayrolles?"

"Oh, he continues to want nothing to do with Dingle, or Ventry, or Dunquin, or farms, or peasants, or taxes. Grandfather wrote to him every week over the summer demanding that he return from his studies in Dublin to fulfill his obligation, but Dayrolles is a stubborn fellow. So Grandfather named me heir. Chrisabella is expecting our first child. I suppose that sealed the deal. It's been quite an exciting summer."

"You never thought you'd end up with the house and the gardens—and now you have all that—and a wife and a baby."

"Yes, I have it all," Thomas said eying the pulsing pale skin at the base of Gunny's throat.

Gunny knew Thomas was studying her. She felt flushed from the attention and the graveyard and the whiskey. She looked up and met his stare. He was as handsome as ever with his thin, pale face, deep blue eyes, and tawny brown hair. She looked down and cleared her throat. "I've been invited to a gathering," she stammered. "I must be off."

"I was trying to leave as well," Thomas said reaching out and touching her arm. "I came here to see that everything was in order for rent collection tomorrow and as I headed home, this damned horse of mine threw a shoe. I'm in desperate need of a smithy."

Gunny stepped past him and stroked the horse's soft nose. The horse whinnied and pushed her hand away. "Come with me," she said stepping away from the horse. "The gathering I'm headed to is at the forge and the man you're looking for is Mac McCrohan. He'll make a decent shoe for your horse. He made these new gates."

"I saw those when I arrived in Dunquin earlier today. You Catholics seem to have plenty of money when it comes to buying nice things for your church."

"Too bad you can't collect rent from the church instead of from the farmers."

"How true," Thomas said, smiling at her.

Gunny looked away. "Come on. I'll show you where the forge is. Now that you're Lord of Dunquin, you should know your way around."

"No worries," he said with a smile. "I have a feeling I'll be visiting here more often. Take my arm. You know I'm a little unsteady on this leg."

"We'll be a matched set," Gunny said shyly slipping her hand through his arm. "I hurt my leg in the accident."

Thomas smiled warmly. "I had not noticed."

They headed down the road with Thomas leading his hobbled horse. As they walked he described improvements to the gardens at Ballygoleen, and talked about his lovely Chrisabella, and how they would name the child after his brother, Dayrolles. Gunny wasn't listening and was relieved when the forge was finally within sight.

"Tie up your horse over there," she directed, opening the door of the forge and looking around the dark room. She grimaced and backed into the yard. "Mac must be inside. I'll go get him."

The McCrohan house was noisy and crowded with revelers, the room smoky and warm. Gunny spied Mac near the hearth, shirt off, dunking for apples in a large bucket of water. It was a shock to see Mac having fun. She caught his eye and he walked over to greet her wiping his face with his hands and pulling his shirt on over his wet hair.

"Look, everyone," he announced loudly. "Gunny's here." A cluster of girls murmured quiet hellos. She recognized a few of the girls from the village but did not know any of their names.

"The new Lord Ventry is outside," she said quietly to Mac. "He needs to have his horse re-shoed."

"The forge fire's out and I'm in no condition to re-start it. He'll have to wait until morning," Mac giggled, resting a hand on a young girl's back as she dipped to bite at an apple in the water bucket.

Gunny walked to the door not sure what to do. Mac slipped up behind her and slipped a wet arm across her shoulders. He held a dripping, partly eaten apple up to her mouth.

"Have a bite?"

Gunny pushed the apple away and looked at Mac. She took hold of his grinning face in both hands, leaned in toward his mouth, and sniffed. "You've been drinking."

Mac pulled away from her. "Aye," he said. "I'm having a wonderful time tonight with my friends." He picked up a glass of clear liquid from the hearth, took a sip, and smacked his lips. "Poteen is much tastier than porter." He hiccupped and smiled, covering his mouth. "Would you like a jar?" He held out his half-full glass to her.

Gunny snatched the jar and downed the contents. Her throat burned from the vile drink. "That's terrible!" she gasped.

Mac grabbed the glass and dipped a refill from the bucket near the hearth. He took another sip and looked at Gunny. "Poteen's not terrible—you just have to sip it," he said wiping the corners of his mouth with two fingers.

Gunny's head was spinning from the mix of whiskey and poteen. She stepped carefully through the doorway and out through the yard. Thomas was sitting on the bench in front of the forge, one foot tapping impatiently.

"Looks like you'll have to wait till morning for any service from the forge."

Thomas frowned. "Is there somewhere I can get lodging and a bite to eat?"

"You have one choice in Dunquin: O'Leary's."

Thomas sighed. "So it's off to O'Leary's again, is it? Will you join me?"

Gunny hesitated. "It looks like the smithy might need my help tonight."

Thomas gave Gunny a short bow. "Have a good evening with your friends," he said and limped off with his horse through the pale moonlight toward the village.

Gunny returned to the house and watched in amazement as Mac clowned with the other boys and flirted with a room full of girls.

"You may want to slow down, Mac," she muttered as she passed him on her way to a stool by the fire.

Cornelius Foley stepped between her and Mac. "Leave him alone, Gunny. Mac doesn't need a girl telling him what to do. He's having fun and we are having fun with him."

"Cornelius Foley. If Ashling were here instead of being home with your babies she might tell you to slow down as well."

Cornelius grinned and slapped Mac on the back. "Mac, we have a little surprise for you."

Mac's thick eyebrows arched. "A surprise?"

"Yes, earlier tonight, the Burke twins put a shilling in a book and hid it in the graveyard. All you have to do to get that shilling is go to the graveyard and find the book."

Mac roared with laughter. "You've been teasing me with that trick ever since we were lads. I'm an adult now. What would I want with your shilling when I run a good business?"

"But what about the book?"

"Aye, is it a good book then?" Mac asked with a serious face. Everyone laughed and Mac was sure he was the funniest one at the party. "You know, boys, I think this is the year I'll go find that book and take your shilling. And I may even bring back the bone of a dead man."

The room fell silent.

Cornelius put his hands on Mac's shoulders. "Mac, if you bring back the bone of a dead man, I swear I'll never tease you again."

"Then I'm off," Mac announced with a salute. "I'll show you I can be as much fun as Matt." He finished off his jar of poteen with a quick swig, handed the glass to Gunny, saluted the group again, and marched out the door.

Gunny set the glass down on the hearth. "Don't worry, Mrs. McCrohan," Gunny said to Kate. "He won't get past the church gates. I was in the graveyard earlier tonight. It's pretty spooky."

"You never know what Mac'll do, Gunny. He's trying hard to fit in tonight."

"He's trying hard to be like Matt and that'll never happen."

Gunny refilled Mac's glass from the bucket of poteen and sat on the stool next to Kate staring at the glowing turf fire and sipping. The buzz of the gathering continued around her. She pictured the house in years past with John and Robert telling old stories, then with Matt and the Wren Boys wearing her elaborate straw masks and getting into water fights. Time and space blurred the shapes around her. She was startled when Kate McCrohan announced it was time to clean up.

"Where's Mac?" she asked, standing and feeling the room spin. She rested a hand on the warm chimney stone as the teenagers in the room said good night and left in small groups.

Kate McCrohan picked up her broom and looked at Gunny. "Are you all right?"

"That poteen packs a punch!" Gunny said, smiling. "I need a little fresh air, that's all. Good night, Mrs. McCrohan." She grabbed an apple from the tub, tossed her shawl over one shoulder, and walked outside.

She took a large bite of the apple. Maybe Mac had gone to the forge, she thought, chewing loudly. That would be more like him than him heading to a spooky graveyard. She walked to the forge and pushed the door open. The room was quiet and cold, the furnace dark. She pulled the door closed and finished off the apple, chucking the core toward the dung hill in the yard of the house. The core landed, instead, only a few feet from her. This made her laugh. She tried, but could not stop giggling. She took out her small flask of whiskey.

"Might as well finish this off and make a night of it," she said, tipping her head back and relishing the feeling of warming liquid as it eased down her throat.

She felt a few drops of cold rain on her upturned face. She tipped her head forward and tried to focus on the ground in front of her. Mac was out there somewhere and she had to find him. She blew out her breath and walked unsteadily toward the village. The earth shifted under her feet as she walked. Sometimes the road was where she expected it to be and other times the road seemed to shift under her as she stepped. She stopped to wipe rain off her face and felt her energy move forward without her.

"I'm drunk," she said out loud to no one. She pointed one long slim finger toward the church. "Forward," she demanded of herself, then giggled as she obeyed. The rain changed from a drizzle to a downpour but Gunny didn't mind. "I like rain," she announced. "Rain is nice."

A sudden clap of thunder startled her and she tripped, falling to her knees in the muddy roadway. Wasn't thunder a bad sign on Hallow E'en? She tried to remember what her father had told her about thunder on Hallow E'en. She pushed herself up off the roadway wishing she had brought her walking stick. The rain picked up in intensity as she staggered forward. She started to feel chilled. She pulled her shawl tighter around her shoulders and walked faster. A heavy mist mixed with the rain and swirled about the new gates as she neared the church. One gate was creaking in the wind. She clutched the cold metal to steady herself. The curling black swirls of the gate under her hands made her feel sick.

"Mac," she screamed into the driving rain. "Are you in there?"

She pushed wet curls from her face with a muddy hand. "Please don't make me go all the way back to Matt's grave to get you. Mac!" she yelled, then whined. "Where are you?"

Her head was spinning and her stomach was starting to ache. She pulled herself past the gates and staggered in the dark toward Matt's grave. A flash of lightning lit the wet gravestones around her and highlighted a shifting black shape in the back corner of the graveyard. Thunder cracked hard against the church wall behind her and she smelled a sharp tang of sulfur.

"What?" she whispered. "Who?"

She took a step forward and stumbled over a loose stone. Water rushed around her feet and she felt herself sliding on wet grass and mud. Her right leg gave out and she felt a ripping pain across her pelvis as her head cracked against the corner of a gravestone. She felt strong arms lift her and hot breath against her neck. She forced her eyes open as lightning lit the steeple of the church and created a glow around the spinning face in front of her. She tried to speak and felt cold fingertips brush her lips. Then her mind went as black as the night.

Gunny's head throbbed. The sound of rain blowing against the window pounded against her eyelids. The dim firelight in the room was too bright even behind closed eyes. Her right leg and hip ached against the boards of the drop-down bed. She opened her eyes a slit. A thin wash of grey light pulsed behind the front window. Her muddy, wet dress was tossed in a corner; her mud-caked boots sat askew near the door.

"Mam? Da?" she whispered, hoarsely, but the house was quiet. She was alone.

She pushed her hair away from her face and the slight movement made her head pound. She looked at her hands and fingernails. They were filthy with dry, caked mud. One touch to her hair told her there was an equal amount of mud in her hair. She ran her fingers along a large, tender lump on her right temple. She lifted the blanket to ease out of bed and saw she was completely naked and had mud smeared along her breasts and stomach.

"How on earth did mud get through my dress?" she thought. She sat up and looked at her body, then looked again. She flipped the covers off and turned toward the weak light of the fire. There was a large, distinctive hand print of dried mud on her upper left thigh.

"My God," she gasped. "What happened to me?"

She thought back on the night. She'd gone to find Mac. She remembered rain and thunder and mud and falling and...

"Oh, my God," she said, clutching her head and sitting up on the small bed. "I saw a man by Matt's grave. Matt, was that you back for Samhain?"

Her eyes filled with tears. Speaking made her head hurt worse.

"No, you're dead," she reminded herself. "It must have been Mac. And he must've helped me home, like the time he wheeled me up here in his cart. Except that Mac was drinking last night and I couldn't find him."

She held her head in her hands. Someone was with her in the graveyard. Someone caught her when she fell. She remembered warm arms around her. And a distinct smell... She pulled at her hair and winched. Why didn't she remember getting home?

She swung her legs to the floor and stood, unsteadily, pulling the blanket tight around her. She stumbled to the hearth and added a turf to the fire. She filled the large pot with water from the bucket and hung it on the crane to heat. When the water was warm, she took a rag from a peg near the fireplace and dipped it in the warm water, then dropped her blanket and ran the cloth slowly over her sore body, soaking the crusty dirt first to create mud, then wiping her skin clean with a second pass of the cloth. The muddy swirls around her breasts and stomach were odd, but it was the hand print that was most confusing. She pulled her left leg up to get a better look at the print before she washed it off.

"Maybe when I came home I pulled off my muddy dress then went to relieve myself," she thought. She put her hand down on her thigh. The fingers on the hand print were facing up. It was not her hand print.

"Who had his hand there?" she thought.

She dipped the rag into the now hot water, wrung it out over the hearth, and scrubbed at the print. The mud washed away but red marks remained where fingers had pressed hard into her flesh.

She lifted the pot of hot water from the stove and mixed it with the cool water in the bucket, then pulled the blanket loosely around her and dragged the bucket and her muddy dress outside. She swirled the dress in the warm water, twisted the water out, and draped it across the bench. The rain would finish the rinse. She lifted the bucket and poured the warm, gritty water over her head. The water tingled against her skin as it passed along her body. She stood, naked, for a moment in the rain, then pulled the rough wool blanket around her and went inside to dress in her best dress—that being her only other choice.

She was pulling on her wool stockings when her mother and father came into the house. She ducked her face away from them behind her wet hair.

Eileen tossed her hat on the table. "You're dressed mighty fancy. You're too late for church."

Gunny swallowed. "I'm sorry if I was noisy last night, coming in so late."

Robert pulled a stool up to the fire and pulled out his pipe. "We didn't hear you come in. We saw your dress outside. Did you get caught in the storm?"

"You didn't hear me come in last night?"

"No. How was the Hallow E'en gathering at the McCrohans?" Eileen asked.

"How was the gathering?" Gunny repeated, her face blank.

Eileen stirred the fire. "Things were a mess inside the church this morning. Father Jessey said he spent half the night scrubbing down the floors after lightning hit the steeple."

Gunny's eyes opened wide. She took a step toward her mother. "There was mud in the church?" she asked in a quiet voice.

"That's what Father Jessey said," Eileen said. "Everything was cleaned up this morning. What's wrong with you? You look as if you've seen a ghost."

Robert eyed his tall, pale daughter. "Are you all right? You have no color in your face."

Gunny hung her head again so that her wet hair covered most of her face. "I'm tired," she said. "It was a long night." She walked toward the door, scarcely breathing, and picked up a soggy boot. She sat on a stool and mechanically pulled it on over her clean stocking.

"You'll want to let those boots dry a bit longer," Robert said, reaching for the second boot to place it near the fire. Gunny grabbed the boot from her father's hand.

"No!" she said. "I have to go see Mac."

With one lace tied and the other one loose, Gunny ran out into the drizzling rain and headed down the hill toward the forge. "You better be there, Mac," she muttered to herself. "And you'd better have a good story about what happened last night in that graveyard."

The McCrohan house was quiet. Gunny knocked lightly at the door. No one answered. She stuck her head inside. "Mrs. McCrohan? Mac?"

Kate McCrohan was scrubbing dirt from the hearth in front of the fire. She turned and looked at Gunny. She did not smile her usual smile. "Mac's not here, Gunny."

"Where is he?"

"I assume he slept in the forge. That's where he was when I checked on him last night, drunk out of his mind and wrapped up around the anvil, snoring."

"You checked on him last night?" Gunny asked. "When?"

"After the gathering," Kate said in a clipped tone, glancing up at Gunny. "Why?"

"I looked for him last night when I left and he wasn't in the forge."

Kate stood and dusted her hands on her skirt. "He was sleeping like a baby when I looked in."

"No," Gunny insisted. "I went to the forge when I left here. He wasn't there."

Kate moved to the table and scooped oat flour out of a bin onto the table. "You're mistaken, Gunny. You must not have seen him in the dark. You'd had a few sips of the poteen yourself last night."

"Yes, but I looked in the forge and Mac wasn't there."

"He was," Kate insisted adding warm water and a little salt to the flour and mixing the bread dough with her hands. "He's probably still there. Go out and see if you don't believe me."

Gunny stared at Kate, then turned and sprinted out to the forge. She burst through the door—and there was Mac, sprawled on his back, his head resting comfortably on an old saddle. She approached his still body and poked him in the ribs with the toe of one boot.

"Wake up," she said.

Mac snorted but did not open his eyes.

"How can you be here?" she murmured, studying his clean, dry clothes. "Damn you," she yelled, kicking at him. "Wake up!"

Mac shifted away from her and blinked his eyes. "What?" he asked, looking up at Gunny glowering above him.

"How can you be sleeping here, warm and dry? You should be as soaked and muddy as I was."

Mac blinked and put a hand over his eyes. "Shhh," he said. "Too loud. "

Gunny paced past him.

"Gunny?" Mac asked.

She whipped around and he smiled at her, head raised. "I had the best time last night."

"And what, pray tell, was so blasted good about it?"

"Please don't yell," Mac said, rubbing his head and leaning back against the saddle. "The night was good because the Wren Boys were here. The house was filled with voices and games again. That was good."

"That was good," Gunny stated. "And what else was good about the night, Mac? Think hard—about the graveyard, Mac? Was there something good about the graveyard you're not remembering?"

Mac looked past Gunny. "I don't know what you're talking about," he said in a quiet voice.

Gunny knelt by Mac's head. "I'm talking about the graveyard. You left the gathering to find a book in the graveyard. Remember? I went after you when you didn't come home—and then it started to rain, and there was thunder and lightning and... mud," Gunny spat.

"I'm sorry you went to the graveyard after me. I never got there. I don't like graveyards."

"Damn it, Mac," Gunny said, grabbing him by the shirt and holding her face near his. "Please tell me you were in the graveyard last night. Please tell me you were there."

Mac looked confused. "I already told you. I didn't go to the graveyard last night."

"Well if you weren't there, then who was?"

Gunny heard the door to the forge open behind them. "Gunny, why don't you leave Mac alone and go home?" Kate McCrohan said.

Gunny spun around. "Kate McCrohan. On Matt's grave do you swear that Mac never left this forge last night?"

Kate McCrohan smiled a sad smile. "Go home, Gunny. Mac has work to do," she said, looking down at Mac. "Lord Milliken is waiting outside to have his horse re-shoed."

Gunny pushed Mac away and sprinted out of the forge past Lord Thomas Milliken and up the hill to home.

Robert was sitting at the table eating a plate of eggs and toast when Gunny burst into the house. He leaned away from the table and studied the girl. "You look like the devil's in you. Where've you been?"

"I don't know," Gunny said, sitting down hard on the bench at the table.

"You should have been at O'Leary's last night," he said chewing a mouthful of egg and warm bread. "The new Lord Milliken was there. He was in a merry mood buying drinks all around. The Old Lord never parted with a farthing for a drink as far as I can remember."

"I saw Thomas last night. His horse threw a shoe and I showed him the way to the forge," Gunny said distractedly. "I told him to go to O'Leary's for his supper."

"Oh, this was well past supper when I saw him," Robert said shaking his head. "He made a dozen toasts to us—to opportunity, to long life, and to hunting rabbits."

Gunny looked up and frowned. "Thomas said he was in town to collect rents."

"Well, he told us he was here to hunt. His boots were muddy as if he'd been out tracking in the storm. He ate two bowls of Micky's lamb stew and downed some porter. He was in a fine mood, I tell you," Robert repeated with a shake of his head. "He may be a good Lord after all."

Gunny could scarcely breathe. The eggs on her father's plate smelled of sulfur and she flashed back to the lightning strike against the church. She gagged and raced outside to the dunghill to vomit.

Gunny felt sick through November and December and had little appetite. She felt pressure at the top of her pelvic bone, her stomach felt tight, and her breasts ached. She had not had her courses since the accident but something was clearly wrong down there. Eileen was worried about her daughter's obvious loss of appetite but the girl didn't appear to be losing weight so Eileen didn't push her to eat more. Since Hallow E'en, Gunny had been spending more time around the house and Eileen was thankful for that.

"Finally got the walking out of your system? Good. I could use your help around here."

Gunny busied herself in any way she could: cooking, cleaning, mending, and looking after the chickens, the sheep, and the cow. She even helped Eileen clean the house from top to bottom for Christmas and insisted they whitewash the inside walls.

"We don't usually whitewash inside until Easter," Eileen reminded her stubborn daughter.

"The house is dirty and needs to be cleaned," Gunny replied, splashing the thin lime water against the dirty stone walls.

Eileen and Robert put on their best clothes for Christmas Eve Mass while Gunny slumped in front of the dim firelight sipping tea.

"Get ready for Mass, Gunny," Eileen said.

"I'm not going," Gunny said softly.

269

"Gunny," Eileen said with a stomp of her foot. "I have put up with you not attending Mass since summer but I insist you go with us on Christmas Eve. Everyone will be there."

"Everyone but me," Gunny stated matter-of-factly taking a long slurp of tea.

Eileen walked to Gunny's stool and stood, hands on her hips. "People will ask about you. What am I supposed to tell them?"

Gunny stared into the low fire. "Tell them I got into a fight with God and that God and I are no longer on speaking terms. I don't want to ever step foot in that building again."

"Gunny," Eileen said shaking her head, "put on your best dress and we'll show everyone that you haven't lost your mind."

"And what if I have?" Gunny asked quietly.

Eileen tossed Gunny's shawl around her and pulled her to her feet. "Nonsense," she said brushing a stray curl from Gunny's face. "Your mind may wander from time to time but it's not lost. Think how pretty the church will look tonight. You've always liked the candles at Christmas." She eyed the girl's dirty dress, apron, and dusty boots and picked at a spot of dirt on her sleeve. "Or you can come dressed the way you are. We'll just keep your shawl tightly wrapped around you. Why do I ever try to change you?" She laced an arm through Gunny's and gave her a squeeze. Gunny meekly complied as Eileen escorted her out the door with Robert following closely behind.

Gunny sat stiffly through Mass, refusing to kneel, refusing to pray. When Father Jessey talked about the birth of the baby Jesus, she started to weep. Her mother squeezed her shoulder and insisted she stop which only made her sob louder.

Mac and Kate McCrohan stopped by the house to wish the Malones good Christmas wishes. Gunny walked outside to fill a bucket of water and Mac followed.

"Where've you been?" he asked. "I haven't seen you since All Saints Day. We've missed you at O'Leary's."

"So you're one of the boys now, are you? Out drinking and creating havoc at O'Leary's?"

"No," Mac said, shaking his head. "I thought I could keep up with them but it's not in me. I have an occasional porter with them at the pub, that's all."

"O'Leary's is a waste of money that we don't have," Gunny said coldly.

"You're sounding more and more like your mother."

"A girl has to grow up sometime, Mac. I need to be more responsible, to help out around the house. Now," she said brushing past him, "I have to get water. I'll see you around."

* * *

Gunny rarely left the house through the winter and into spring. She cleaned to Eileen's delight and twisted strand after strand of heavy rope, her whistle neglected on the hearth. Shrove didn't even seem to upset her and Eileen noticed that she was putting on a little weight. The first really warm day in March, Gunny pulled on her lighter skirt and Eileen gasped at the change in Gunny's body.

"I don't think you're well, Gunny," Eileen stated. "Look at that swelling in your stomach."

Gunny sat on a stool in front of the fire and slumped forward to help cover the bump. "I don't know what you are talking about," she said picking up her basket of mending. "I put on a little weight over the winter, that's all. It's no surprise since I've hardly been outside."

Eileen looked at her daughter. The girl's face was flush, her hair thick and shiny. She was not plump all over—her shoulders and arms were as thin as ever. It was only her middle that had grown large and thick. Eileen reached across Gunny's shoulder and pressed a hand on Gunny belly. The baby inside responded with a light kick. Eileen gasped and jumped away.

"How can this be?" Eileen stammered. "The doctor said... You're not married... How did this happen?"

Gunny looked up at her mother's shocked face. She rested a hand on her belly, her eyes filling with tears. "I have no idea," she said with a sob.

Eileen reached down and slapped Gunny hard across the face. Gunny winced at the sharp sting but hung her head and did not move. She deserved whatever punishment she had coming. Eileen went to slap her again but pulled away not wanting to touch her daughter.

"Damn, child! You've been nothing but trouble all your life. Now we're going to be the laughingstock of the village. No, we already are the laughingstock of the village. This time they may evict us just to be rid of us."

Gunny set down her mending and covered her face with her hands. Eileen grabbed her by the arms and pulled the tall girl to her feet. Gunny's bump pressed against Eileen's ribs.

"Look at me when I'm talking to you," she spat. She glared into Gunny's eyes. "Tell me who the father is."

Gunny looked into Eileen's face then turned her eyes to the floor. It was the question that had been plaguing her ever since the Hallow E'en storm. "It happened on Hallow E'en, Mam. In the graveyard. There was rain and wind and I went to Matt's grave..."

Eileen pushed Gunny away from her. "Are you telling me this was some sort of Immaculate Conception with the Holy Ghost of Matt McCrohan?"

Gunny repeated the only truth she knew. "I don't know, Mam. I honestly don't know."

~ Chapter 13: Catherine ~

By late June, Gunny felt huge. She could hardly sleep at night from the weight across her midsection. She would rest on one side until her hip fell asleep, then she'd shift to the other side until that hip fell asleep. She craved meat but there was no meat in the house. Bread and butter seemed too heavy, the smell of tea made her sick. She tried to make rope to help pass the time but found she could not concentrate.

Eileen could hardly look at her, and her father looked at her with sad eyes. "Next spring, you'll be out planting with me again."

"Aye, Da. Next spring I'll be myself again."

Robert eyed his daughter's enormous middle. "By the looks of things, you'll be yourself again very soon."

Gunny was eating a second morning meal of cold potatoes when she felt her stomach lurch and contract. She held her breath and the pain ebbed. "Mam," she yelled through the open door to Eileen in the yard. "We don't have a cradle yet."

Eileen scurried inside and rested a hand on Gunny's middle. "Your da'll bring a horse collar home from the stable when the baby comes. The baby can sleep there until we build something more permanent."

"Why don't we build something now?" Gunny asked, pushing Eileen's hand away and moving awkwardly to a stool near the hearth. The pain in her abdomen lessened and she took a deep breath.

Eileen shook her head and tossed Gunny's dirty potato dish and spoon into a bucket. "It's best to wait a few weeks to see if the baby lives. Then we'll build a cradle. Maybe Mac could build one for you."

"I'll not put my baby in an iron crib covered with ornate curls," Gunny grunted rubbing a hand across her tight, bulging middle.

"It wouldn't hurt to ask him. Bitsy Kavanaugh says that taking a turn at the bellows helps assure a safe birth."

"I believe the man's work has already been done," Gunny grunted. "The rest is up to me, Mam."

July 15th, 1829, dawned warm and clear. It was St. Swithin's Day, a traditional day of rain and floods. Gunny woke to find her blankets soaked with warm fluid. She called to Eileen who woke Robert.

"Go fetch a horse collar from the stables," Eileen ordered Robert. "We'll be fine here without you."

Gunny looked desperately at Robert as he pulled on his cap to leave. "It's best if I go. Having a baby's no work for a man."

Gunny whimpered as the door closed behind him. "Shouldn't he be off to fetch the doctor?" she grunted from the bed. Her contractions were coming now at regular intervals.

"I had only your father's mother to help me," Eileen said. "And when I had you, I had a toddler to watch over as well."

Gunny leaned forward and tried to breathe through the latest tightening of her abdomen. "But you didn't have a horse crush your insides. I shouldn't be having a baby. The doctor said I couldn't. I want that doctor here to witness this."

"We have no money for a doctor, Gunny," Eileen said clucking her tongue. "You'll have to do the best you can." Gunny pushed up from the bed with a moan and waddled out toward the fire. She stopped and gripped the end of the table. Eileen heard the table squeak and hoped the legs would hold. When the contraction stopped, Gunny took a long breath and started pacing the room, breathing hard through each tightening. She could not imagine that a human being, no matter how small, was going to somehow emerge from her body without killing her along the way.

When the contractions were coming every few minutes, Gunny pulled down the small side bed. She crawled onto the stiff boards and leaned her head against the cool stone wall. Eileen took up the pacing across the stuffy room, occasionally dipping a small wet cloth in the bucket of water and wiping the sweat from Gunny's face. Gunny moaned with each contraction, then took a big breath and slowly let out the air.

"You can scream," Eileen said. "Most women do."

Gunny gritted her teeth and shook her head.

"Whether you scream or not," Eileen said, "it won't be long now. You'll soon be a mother."

Gunny gasped at the thought. When the pain was nearly constant, she felt an incredible urge to push. She lay down on the hard bed and pulled her knees up toward her chest. Eileen waited at the end of the bunk until the baby's head emerged, then with a final push from Gunny, held up a bawling, red baby.

"It's a girl," Eileen said eyeing the tiny newborn. "What a shame."

With the baby out, the pain within her miraculously stopped. Gunny lay back, panting, and watched as her mother pulled the placenta into a bucket and cut the umbilical cord with a sharp knife. She wiped the baby's body clean with a warm, damp cloth, wrapped her in a small blanket, and handed the small bundle to Gunny. Then she roughly pulled the soggy blankets out from under Gunny and tossed them near the door to be washed. Gunny cradled the small, warm body in her arms, then unwrapped the blanket and studied the baby in the half-light of the fire. The baby blinked at Gunny with deep blue eyes. Her eyelids were nearly transparent. Her tiny pink hands and feet were perfect. Her head was covered with fine, white hair.

Eileen squatted by Gunny's side. "You have to keep her warm," she said, tucking the blanket in around the baby and looking at the new little face. "She doesn't look anything like Mac."

Gunny glanced up at her mother's face. "Of course she doesn't look like Mac. Why would she look like Mac?" She stared at the baby's face. "I never thought I'd have a child," she murmured. "She's beautiful."

"Even the carrion crow thinks its baby is attractive," Eileen scoffed.

"Mam, be nice. You do like her, don't you?"

Eileen poured two cups of tea and held one out to Gunny. "You're one medical miracle after another."

Gunny took a cautious sip of the hot liquid. The tea tasted good. Hot and weak. If only they had a bit of sugar.

Through the next day, the baby nursed and slept quietly by Gunny on the small bed near the fire, the horse collar crib Robert had brought up neglected on the floor. Gunny studied the child as she slept. She did not have fairy marks on her; she had no strange discolorations, her eyes matched one to the other and her toes weren't webbed, though with her light fuzz of blond hair and pale skin she looked a little ghostly. Could this be a ghost child from a ghost Matt? Gunny shook the thought away. She continued to dream about the night in the graveyard, but the man's face in her dreams was always soft and blurred against a sharp halo of lightning.

By the second day after the birth, Gunny's breasts were sore from nursing and the baby cried relentlessly. She walked about with the tiny bundle in her arms until the baby was nearly asleep, but as soon as she set her down on the bed, she woke. Her little body would go stiff as she howled, her hands clenched in tiny fists, her little face as red as an apple. Gunny tried nursing her, standing, sitting, rocking and swinging but nothing seemed to calm her.

"You're rocking her too hard," Eileen stated flatly.

"I've tried rocking her gently, Mam. Nothing seems to help! I don't know what else to do."

By the third day, Gunny was weak with fatigue. She handed the howling baby toward Eileen as her vision started to blur. "I think I am going to faint." Eileen grabbed the baby as Gunny collapsed to her knees.

"Put your head between your knees," she yelled. "God knows what else has been down there between those legs."

Gunny leaned forward and did as her mother directed.

"You lost a lot of blood in the birth. You shouldn't be moving about so much."

When Gunny's head stopped spinning, she crawled onto the side bed and pulled the covers up to her chin. The pain in her abdomen was sharp. She felt a chill pass up her spine.

The milk fever lasted two weeks. Gunny could hear the baby crying but could not move, could not help. Her abdomen ached, her pulse raced. She was hot and sweaty and thirsty, but when she drank could not keep down even the smallest amount of water. Eileen had heard of milk fever. Most women died of it. She resigned herself to the fact the Gunny most likely would not live, and that this baby would be hers. She nursed Gunny as best she could, and in between, fed the child cow's milk mixed with the last of the oat flour in an old bottle topped with a preserved sheep teat. She rocked the baby when she fussed and gave her to Robert to walk about the house during her nightly spells of crying.

By the time Gunny's milk fever passed, her breast milk had dried up and she felt she had little to offer the child in the way of food or comfort. She slept most of the time, and only occasionally held the baby. Mostly she tried to stay clear of her mother's routine.

"You are too loud with her, too rough," Eileen would snap the few times Gunny insisted on holding the child. "Let me have her. You don't know what you're doing."

Gunny felt tired and helpless and was more than happy to give in to her mother's demands.

At the end of August, Robert was ready to haul the turf bricks from the upper fields to the yard and asked Eileen to help him. "Gunny's still too weak to be lifting much."

"But I never help you with the bricks. Surely you can ask someone else, Robert."

Robert insisted that Eileen accompany him. He knew it wasn't his place to interfere with women's work and babies, and also knew that Gunny needed time alone with the baby.

"You're sure you can look after her?" Eileen asked Gunny for the tenth time as Robert waited for her in the yard.

"Let them be," Robert muttered. "She's the child's mother."

Gunny smiled at her father and gently rocked the new wooden cradle Robert had made for the baby. "We'll be fine," she assured Eileen. "Go help Da. Since I've been sick, I feel like the babe hardly knows me."

"Perhaps there's a blessing in that," Eileen muttered to Robert as they set off the road toward the high fields.

When Gunny was certain her parents were gone, she gently lifted the sleeping child from the large cradle and sat nestled with her on a stool in front of the fire. She loved the feel of the small, warm bundle and the way the baby's ruby lips pursed and bubbled as she slept. There was a soft knock at the door.

"Come in," Gunny said quietly.

The door opened a few inches and Mac's face appeared in the doorway. Gunny was surprised to see him but was happy for the company. She motioned him inside and held a finger to her lips. She pointed to the sleeping baby in her arms.

Mac tip-toed in and pulled up a stool next to Gunny.

"I heard about the baby," he said softly.

"How did you hear? Is the whole village talking about me?"

"Mam told me. I don't know who else knows. I haven't heard anyone else talking about you."

"That's a surprise. If your Mam knows then surely Bitsy Kavanaugh must know, and once Bitsy knows something..."

"I don't think Mam mentioned it to anyone. I'm not even sure how she found out. All of us have been missing you and wondering if your mother had you locked up here."

"That's what it's felt like. I was too embarrassed to go outside through the winter, then after I had her, I got sick. I think I almost died, Mac."

"Can I hold her?" Mac whispered.

The baby stirred and opened her deep blue eyes. Gunny smiled. "You don't have to whisper. Look, she's awake. Aren't you?" she said in a sing-song voice to the small bundle as she handed it to Mac.

Mac eased himself onto a stool and held the baby in his lap with her feet toward him. He cradled her soft, delicate head in his large, dark hands and looked intently at the child's face. He swallowed hard. "Is this my baby?"

"She was conceived on Hallow E'en, Mac."

"I know," Mac said. "Mam figured back nine months."

Gunny looked at the baby in Mac's arms. "I don't remember what happened that night. I don't know whose child she is."

"This isn't your mother you are talking to, it's me," Mac said. "You must know who the father is."

Gunny shook her head. "I don't. I was as drunk as you were that night."

"What if we both don't remember—and she's mine?"

"I've thought about it and it doesn't add up," Gunny said. "Unless you went to the graveyard in the storm, somehow got yourself home, and then blanked out the whole thing. Even then, you were clean and dry that next morning when I saw you. It couldn't have been you, Mac."

"What if I staggered home from the graveyard and my mother cleaned me up?"

"I've thought about that too. Your mother was acting strangely that morning. But I'm pretty sure you were in the same clothes you'd been in, and you were clean and dry. It was a horrid night. I was covered with mud, my dress soaked. Your mother would have had quite the work cut out for her if she somehow got you home, got me home to bed, and then cleaned and dried your clothes—all by dawn the next morning. And look at this baby, Mac. She doesn't look anything like you."

"So if it wasn't me, then who was it?"

Gunny swallowed hard. "If it wasn't your ghost of a brother, then there's only one other person it could have been—Thomas Milliken. Da said he was at O'Leary's on Hallow E'en, that he showed up there late that night, all muddy and bragging about being out hunting. He told Da he caught a rabbit but let her go."

Mac's face was pale. "Lord Ventry... Do you remember seeing him there?"

"All I remember is falling and someone catching me, then strong arms and a sweet smell. Whoever it was got me pregnant, then somehow got me back here, undressed me, and put me to bed."

"If it was me, it seems like I would remember at least part of that," Mac said, handing the tiny bundle back to Gunny.

Gunny nuzzled the baby's head and kissed her downy hair. "One would hope so," she said with a blush.

"Well, I hope Thomas Milliken steps forward." Mac was quiet for a moment. "What're you going to call her?"

Gunny was quiet, still thinking about the lost night in the graveyard.

Mac nudged her arm. "What's her name?" he repeated.

Gunny stared at him but did not answer.

He spoke slower. "What do you call her?"

Gunny shook her head. "I... we call her the baby. She doesn't know any words yet."

"I know you don't call her anything she recognizes but when you register her with the church what will you say when the clerk asks her name?"

Gunny sighed. "I don't know, Mac. I don't know who she is, or what her name is."

When the baby was eight weeks old, Eileen and Gunny headed off for Ballyferriter to register the birth. All marriages, births, and deaths for the villages of Ballyferriter, Dunquin, the Blaskets, and Ventry had to be registered with the Clerk of the Parish in Ballyferriter. Gunny walked with the baby strapped to her chest in a converted flour sack. The September day was warm, the sky clear as they walked down the main street of Ballyferriter and up the steps of the church. The baby started to fuss, and Eileen insisted that she hold the child until she quieted.

Eileen and Gunny walked inside and crossed the empty, echoy foyer of the church. Gunny sat on a bench outside the church office to catch her breath while Eileen stood and rocked the baby. The clerk finished writing something in a large, bound book, dotted an "i" with a flourish, and signaled the two women to come in. The clerk was a prim little man with a thin band of pale brown hair fringing the edges of a small round head. He had large watery eyes and a pock-marked nose. He sat, pen in hand, looking at the women and baby in front of him.

"Date of birth?" he asked, pen poised.

"July fifteenth. St. Swithin's Day," Eileen said.

"All I need is the date, ma'am. And the child's name?"

Eileen looked at the baby in her arms, then at Gunny. Gunny stared at her mother, shook her head, and said nothing. Eileen turned to the clerk. "The child's name is Catherine Marie," she said, straightening a small white cap on the child's head.

Gunny and her mother had not discussed the child's name and Gunny was surprised at her mother's choice.

"And the family name?" the clerk asked.

"Malone," Eileen stated clearly.

The clerk wrote, "Malone" and looked up at Eileen. "This is your child, Mrs. Malone? "

"My child?" Eileen looked embarrassed. "Why no she's..." She paused mid-sentence. If the baby was hers, the child would have a married mother and a father. Eileen blinked and looked at the clerk. "Yes, she's my child. And after so long, really, it's quite the miracle, isn't it?" she added with a smile.

"I'm the scrapings of the pot myself," the clerk said with a grin. "The last of the litter is bound to be spoiled," he said with a wink.

Eileen brightened. "I'm sure she will be."

"And your name, ma'am?"

Eileen didn't hesitate this time. "Eileen Malone. The child's father is Robert Malone. We live in the Village of Dunquin."

Gunny was quiet on the long walk home. Eileen insisted on carrying Catherine Marie without the sling. "This is an excellent solution," Eileen said for the third time.

"I didn't know there was a problem, Mam," Gunny said in a flat voice, clutching the empty sling in one hand.

"Then you're being naive. People talk about children born out of wedlock. My only regret is that I didn't think of this myself. Your father's going to be so surprised to hear we have a baby."

"No one will believe this, Mam. No one's going to believe you had a baby at your age."

"I'm not that old," Eileen scoffed. "And hardly anyone saw you during your time. Your father and I certainly have not talked about it. And while people may suspect, no one will know for certain."

Eileen bounced baby Catherine in her tiring arms as they walked. She looked at the baby's pretty little face and pouty red lips. "You're my little miracle child, aren't you, Catherine Marie?" she cooed. "Everyone knows late babies were fair and pretty, like you. You are bound to be soiled."

Gunny walked a little faster to get away from the silly banter.

Even the people in the village who had heard rumors that Gunny was with child chose to accept that the new addition at the Malone house was Eileen Malone's miracle child. Baby's were born to older women—and hadn't the doctor told everyone that Gunny could never have children after the awful accident at the church? The girl had gained some weight over the winter, that was all.

Catherine Marie thrived under Eileen's care. When she cried at night, Eileen was there to comfort her. She slept better when Eileen rocked her and ate better when Eileen fed her. Eileen stitched a beautiful white gown to take the girl to church with her, and often took her out with Robert in the evenings to show her off to the neighbors. Everyone wanted to see the pretty little miracle baby with the stark white hair and deep blue eyes. The village women were suddenly interested in visiting with Eileen.

"Look at her skin," Bitsy Kavanaugh said on more than one occasion. "Who does she take after?"

"Oh, she's the image of my dear, departed grandmother," Eileen would answer. "You know, I'm a Fitzgerald from over in Ventry…"

Even Robert was enchanted by the child. As Catherine grew less fussy and started to smile more, he spent less time at O'Leary's and more time at home, often bouncing the little girl on his knee if front of the fire and telling her long stories of heroes and villains while Gunny sat quietly at the table or in the backroom, removed and apart.

The Malone house was merry that Christmas. Robert received a letter from Michael and Maeve in November with a five pound note in it. Michael wrote that he was building houses in Alexandria and Maeve was working as a cook for an English family in Alexandria. They had been able to save a little money and a local bank had converted dollars to pounds for them.

It had been a long time since Robert had seen a five pound note and he splurged on a Christmas meal of roast pork and apples, bought little sweets for everyone, and purchased a fresh stash of tea and sugar for Eileen and Gunny and a pint of whiskey for himself. Little Catherine could sit up by Christmas and had dimples in her cheeks when she smiled at her dear mama and papa as they set her on the table and fed her mashed bits of potato and apple and sweet treats.

As Catherine grew and thrived, Gunny felt smaller and of less and less importance. By the time Shrove arrived in February, Catherine was crawling around the house and sitting up on the table eating mashed potato mixed with the last of their saved butter. Gunny headed outside at any excuse—to take the animals to the nearby fields, to fetch water, or to tend to the crops in the fields or in the kitchen garden. She never fed the child, never pet her pretty head, and rarely smiled. No one seemed to notice.

Mac was surprised to see Gunny sitting crouched by the forge furnace warming her hands, a thick coil of rope slung over one shoulder, an overflowing bucket of goods and a three-legged pot at her feet. She was as thin and pale as he'd ever seen her.

"Gunny," Mac said walking into the forge.

Gunny turned toward him, her dark brown eyes sunken and deeply sad. "I hope you don't mind that I let myself in. I had to get out of my house."

"Why aren't you at O'Leary's?" he asked quietly.

Gunny looked at him blankly.

"It's St. Patrick's Day?" he reminded her.

"I didn't want to go. Mac, I need your help."

"Is everything all right with your baby?" he asked, brow wrinkled.

Gunny wiped at her eyes with the back of her hand. "Everything's fine, I suppose." She sighed. "She's not my baby, Mac."

Mac reached over and turned her face toward his. "Gunny, you know as well as I do that that baby is yours—despite what everyone else believes."

Gunny pushed the coil of rope off her shoulder to the floor and grabbed Mac's muscular hand to help pull herself up. She held the back of his hand to her cheek. "I have a tremendous favor to ask of you," she said in a small, strained voice.

Mac leaned forward and squeezed her hand. "I'll always owe you for what happened on your wedding day. I'll help you in any way I can."

Gunny closed her eyes and leaned slightly forward. "I want you to take me to the west end of the Great Blasket island."

Mac rocked away. "What're you talking about? Why would you want to go there?"

Gunny clung to his hand and pulled him nearer. "You said anything. I have to pay penance for my sins, Mac. I can't live in Dunquin with this lie hanging over me. I'm cursed. Everyone I love disappears. Matt. William. And I'm living through it again with Catherine. I don't think I can bear to have my heart broken again."

Mac pulled his hand gently from Gunny's grip. "So you want to make a pilgrimage to the Blaskets?"

"Not a pilgrimage. I want to move to the west end of the Blaskets."

Mac laughed harshly and shook his head. "You're crazy, Gunny. No one lives on the west end of the Blaskets. What would you do for food?"

Gunny grabbed Mac by the arms, a crazy glimmer of excitement in her eyes. "Remember when we went there hunting seals? I've been thinking about the little cove where we beached the boat. There were old houses—and a spring. I got a chance to explore while you were off hunting." She turned and paced around the forge fire. "I was thinking about moving to Brandon Mountain but I couldn't stay there in the winter, not after what happened to William. But on the Blaskets, I could grow plants much later in the season, and Joanna once told me there are thousands of rabbits there to snare."

Mac crossed his arms. "It's a bad idea, Gunny. A woman can't live by herself. It's too dangerous."

"So you won't take me?" Gunny asked with narrowed eyes.

"No one's lived in those houses for a hundred years, and…"

"And…?" Gunny interrupted him.

"And…," Mac continued, "another name for a house that no one's lived in for a hundred years is a pile of rocks! You can't live in a pile of rocks."

"Mac," Gunny said folding her hands in front of her face as if in prayer. "I'm better off living in a pile of rocks than staying here. You were hurt the day we were on the Blaskets. You don't remember how beautiful it was." She cupped Mac's face in her hands and looked into his eyes. "I've been thinking about this all winter. I want to leave tonight while everyone's at O'Leary's. We can take Matt's boat."

"Matt's boat is too small to take to the Blaskets, Gunny. It's a three mile row to the village on the east side, and the west end is another mile or so along the shore. Matt's boat would never get us there."

"Are you afraid?" Gunny asked, raising one eyebrow.

"No, I'm not afraid," Mac bristled, rubbing at his arm where the seal had bitten him. "I am trying to be sensible and I'm telling you it doesn't make sense to take a small boat to the Blaskets."

"You don't have the muscle to row for four or five miles?" Gunny asked, squeezing his muscle-tight arm.

Mac shook off her hand. "I have the muscle, Gunny," he gasped. "That's not the point."

"Then you're afraid," Gunny said turning her back on him. "Matt would have taken me."

"Matt was as crazy as you are."

Gunny turned and stared at Mac. "You said you'd do anything to help me."

"Anything reasonable. Damn it, Gunny. I want to help you but I don't want to get us both killed." He paused and touched her arm. "Maybe I can find a fisherman to take you, someone who knows the island and knows how to cross the channel."

Gunny pulled away from Mac's grasp. "No."

"Why not?" Mac asked, exasperated. "Because it makes too much sense?"

"No, because then everyone will know where I am. I want my departure to be a mystery. I don't want to be the old spinster witch who lost her mind. I want to be the mysterious beauty who disappeared one night and was never heard from again."

"Suddenly you're a romantic?" Mac asked, shaking his head.

"I'm not being romantic," Gunny said. "I'm being practical. If my parents know where I am they'll come after me. They have a new life with little Catherine and I'm in the way. I don't fit in here, Mac. I never did." She grabbed Mac by the arm as he paced by her. "Today is St. Patrick's Day. It's the end of winter. Tomorrow is the first day of spring. It's time for me to make a fresh start. Keep your promise, Mac, and help me get away."

Mac grimaced. "I'll go pack some things" he said quietly. "Wait here for me."

Gunny sat on the bench outside the forge. She'd felt broken and empty when she arrived but now her stomach was tight with excitement. She looked around the yard and remembered laughing and playing there with Matt and Mac when they were children, climbing through broken wheels and bent hoops while their fathers talked about horses and told old Irish tales. She blinked hard. She thought her father would always be there for her but he had sent her off to Dingle to work, brought Maeve into the house to replace her, and now had a new little girl to take her place.

She rubbed her face. The last two years were a jumble in her mind but one thing was clear—she could not stay one more day in her house staring at her mysterious child, begging God to tell her who the father was, and feeling her heart break each time the little girl called Eileen "Mama."

Mac returned from the house with a small bag slung over one shoulder. "Are you all right?"

Gunny blinked. "No, but I will be. I can't thank you enough for helping me. There's just one more thing."

"Don't ask for one more thing," Mac said waving his hand in front of his face. "You've done that before and it always means trouble."

"When we get to the Blaskets," Gunny continued, "I want to keep Matt's boat. After you drop me off you'll have to walk to the village on the Blaskets and catch a ride home with one of the fisherman."

Mac groaned. "I'm sure no one will ask me questions about how I showed up in a village on an island without a boat."

"If you don't want to do that, you could stay with me on the west end."

Mac looked down at the tops of his boots. "My family needs me," he said with a blush. "People in the village need me."

"Of course they do," Gunny said with a forced smile. "What would a village do without their smithy? I'm sure you'll think of a wonderful tale to tell those Blasket fishermen about how you walked across the water to get there," she said, lightly touching his arm.

"You're assuming we get there," he said squeezing her hand. "Let's load the cart. I want to see what a crazy woman packs when she is about to disappear from her own life."

~ Chapter 14: The Blaskets ~

Mac wheeled his small handcart into the yard. Gunny placed her three-legged pot in the cart, and hefted in her loaded bucket and curl of rope.

"I brought the bucket to haul water and cart sand and seaweed to the fields—and I used it to pack in," she explained.

"Very smart."

Gunny raised an eyebrow and Mac gave her a nod to continue. She lifted several folded wool sacks off the bucket and pointed inside. "I have a sack of oat flour and a small firkin of butter I'd been saving in the bog. I packed a flint for fire, my sewing kit, two tin mugs, two bowls, and two spoons." She tucked the sacks back in around the items in the bucket.

"Are you planning on having company?"

"No, but you can't go away for a lifetime with just one spoon." She cleared her throat and continued. "I packed my best dress and apron and an extra set of stockings in the three-legged pot Joanna gave me for the wedding. I intend to go barefoot as much as possible but I know come winter I'll need socks and boots. Mam'll miss the pot but I left her my tea kettle so she really can't complain. And in here," she said patting her apron pocket. "I have the black-handled knife, packets of seeds from William's garden, and my tin whistle."

"God knows you can't live in the wilderness without a tin whistle," Mac said.

"Do you have an old fry pan?" she asked ignoring Mac's attempt at humor. "And a sack of potatoes I could have?"

Mac stared at her, then pushed open the door to the forge. He re-emerged with a heavy iron fry pan and tossed it into the cart along with several long cooking utensils.

"We're nearly out of potatoes but I'll pull a sack for you from behind the house. You'll need salt—I'll get a small sack of that too. And I'll pack a hoe for you. Do you want oat seeds?" he asked kindly.

Gunny nodded her head and he smiled at her. She had clearly lost her mind. He would help her over to the island, then return to pick her up in a few days when she was ready to return to civilization.

"Oh, and can you get me a box of nails and a few fishing hooks?" she continued.

"You think you're going to fish?" he asked skeptically.

"The Blasket men used to talk in the shop about fishing from the cliffs. I thought I'd give it a try. And once I settle in, I'll make a net to fish from Matt's boat."

* * *

Mac scavenged the last few promised items from the house and finished loading the handcart. He returned to the forge and smoored the fire in the furnace. He looked around the snug, warm room. He hated being out on a boat in open water and prayed this would not be the last time he saw his beloved forge. He closed the door and followed Gunny down the dark road into the village.

When they passed O'Leary's, the sound of fiddles, light, and laughter spilled out through open windows. They crossed to the dark side of the street and wheeled Mac's cart quietly out onto the pier. Matt's curragh looked like a large beetle stored on the nearby rack. Mac carefully lifted the heavy rocks off the top of the boat. Gunny remembered watching Matt toss the rocks off, then flip the craft onto his shoulders to carry it down to the water. She blinked and Mac was standing before her staring at the small black boat, hands in his pockets.

"I've never been good at the flipping part," he said.

"Want me to try?"

"No. I don't want you to try. I won't have a woman carry a boat while I walk behind," he said as Gunny stepped around him and flipped the small boat off the rack and onto her back. She slipped her arms through the side ropes as she had seen Matt do a dozen times. She picked up the two oars that were stashed on the rack underneath the boat and grinned.

"If you wheel the cart out onto the pier, I think we're all set," she said.

"Isn't that heavy for you?" Mac asked.

Gunny grinned and bounced the boat on her back. She paused to adjust the left rope across her shoulder. "No, it feels right," she said. She carried the curragh the short distance to the end of the pier and flipped it upright. She slid the boat quietly into the water and tied the bow and stern ropes around hooks on the pier. The moon was full and high. A path of silver light lit the still water from Dunquin out to the western islands.

"No wind tonight," Matt said. "At least we have that in our favor."

He helped Gunny load her supplies into the small craft and stepped over the center seat. "I'll do the rowing," he said. He fit the oars into the pins on either side of the gunnels and sat down.

Gunny climbed into the stern facing Mac and pulled the aft rope free. She took a short breath and closed her eyes. "Should we say a few words before our departure?"

"I think a prayer is more appropriate," Mac muttered as he pulled the bow rope into the boat. He dipped the oars quietly in the still water and the boat slipped away from the pier.

Behind Mac's black form, Gunny could see the outline of the Great Blasket island against a thick, starry sky and felt a thrill in her stomach. She took a deep breath of salty night air and slowly let it out through open lips. Half way across the channel, she turned to look back at Dunquin. Mount Eagle blocked the stars around the village silhouetting a few lit houses near the pier. The village already looked distant and small. Gunny watched a path of white foam trail out from behind Matt's boat, then dissolve into the black water. She turned back toward Mac and the Blaskets and smiled.

Mac was strong, the seas flat, and the trip swift. The small boat was soon near the glowing white sands of the strand on the eastern shore of the Great Island. Mac slowed as if he were going to pull in along the strand. Gunny grabbed his knee. "West end."

Mac looked at his passenger and shook his head. "The east end makes more sense, Gunny. You'd be near the village and the well. And look, the soil has been worked along those cliffs and you'd be protected from the west winds. Only a hermit would want to live anywhere else."

Gunny pulled her hair free of its pins and said in a commanding voice, "West end, Mac McCrohan."

Mac sighed and took up the oars again rowing parallel to the white strand, then rounding the gob at the tip of the island. Past the gob, the sound of the waves intensified as the black ocean pounded against the impossibly high and rugged rocky shore.

"I don't know how we'll land without killing ourselves," Mac muttered.

"We'll find the perfect spot," Gunny said leaning forward and scanning the shoreline in the moonlight. Mac continued to row and the on-shore cliffs eventually gave way to land that sloped down more gently toward the water.

"Up ahead, Mac," Gunny said excitedly. "That's where we landed when we came to hunt the seals."

Mac shook his head. "I don't know how you could possibly remember. And if you're wrong, there's no changing your mind once we get into the pull of the waves."

"Yes, that's Inish na Bro, the next island over," Gunny pointed. "Your father told me to turn the rudder after we spotted Inish na Bro and that's what he was pointing at."

Mac glanced over his shoulder and made a turn toward the moonlit shore. Gunny spied a short strand of sand hidden in the cove and directed Mac toward it. As they moved swiftly closer to the shore, an unearthly moaning started up. Mac froze.

"Keep rowing," Gunny urged him. "It's the seals. Remember? It means we're in the right place."

Mac remembered the seals all right. He wondered if they remembered him. He pulled hard on the oars and they rode a swell around the rocky bend. Seals bounded past them into the open water wailing and muttering at having been disturbed from their evening slumber. Mac caught his breath and felt a tingle along the scar on his arm. The waves diminished and the boat washed gently up to the shore of a small, protected cove.

Gunny hoisted her skirts and leapt from the boat when she felt sand and rock scraping the bottom of the curragh. She grabbed the rope at the bow of the boat and pulled Mac in the rest of the way. He stepped onto the hard-packed sand and looked around. There was no sound except for the stones on the beach rattling as each wave arrived, then receded. The sky above them was crystal clear and full of stars; the air cold. It felt as if they were the only two people on the earth. Mac shivered and clutched his arms around his chest. He heard Gunny sigh at his side. He looked at her face in the moonlight and saw she was beaming from ear to ear. He had not seen her smile like that in years.

She looked at him, shook her long curls, and said one word: "Home."

"Help me unload," Mac grunted.

They hauled Gunny's possessions up past the high-tide mark. Gunny returned to the boat, grabbed it by the rim, and flipped it easily onto her back. She grabbed an oar in each hand, walked past Mac, and tipped the boat to the ground near the pile of supplies.

Mac looked around in the moonlight. "It's too dangerous to go into the old stone houses now. We'll have to sleep here."

Gunny sat down near the boat and peeled off her wet boots and stockings. Mac slid down next to her, exhausted, and leaned heavily against the boat. Gunny wrapped her shawl tight around her shoulders, tucked her feet up under the driest part of her skirt, and leaned against Mac. A cool breeze whispered around them.

"I doubt I'll be able to sleep," Mac muttered. He looked at Gunny who was already asleep, head on his shoulder, mouth wide open.

When Mac opened his eyes, the sun was breaking across the horizon in a tremendous show of red and gold. He rubbed his eyes and felt at his side for Gunny. She was gone, of course, along with the supplies. He stood and brushed sand from his pants. His neck was stiff from a short night sleeping propped against a boat. His chin felt scratchy.

"Gunny?" he yelled hoarsely.

The early-morning light broke grey along the deserted shore. Waves washed up into the cove which was littered with driftwood and tangled seaweed. Cold wind whipped at his shirt. A ringed plover flew by, balanced against the wind, and landed on a nearby rock. The bird eyed Mac, then started foraging for shellfish on a nearby tide pool. Mac turned inland to look for Gunny. Steep cliffs of purple sandstone rose to his right. The land to his left rolled gently down along grassy slopes to the strand. In the field just beyond the strand were the ruins of several stone houses and the arch of an old stone church. Gunny came running toward him through the tall grasses all smiles, her black curls whipping around her face, her cheeks red, her eyes shining.

"It's even better than I remembered," she gushed. "I've found the perfect house. It looks like someone from the village stays there from time to time, probably hunting for rabbits or seals. There's even turf. And look at all of this wood out here," Gunny said opening her arms wide and dancing in a circle on the strand. "I'll make a fine new roof."

She ran up to Mac. "You remember how to get to the village?" she asked innocently, pointing an elbow gently toward the east.

Mac blinked at her quick dismissal of him, pushed his thick hair from his face, and held his hands over his ears. "The wind out here's incredible."

"Isn't it? "Gunny gushed. "It comes at you from every side and it's nearly constant."

Mac rubbed his hands to warm them. "What about a morning meal? Did you get a fire going?"

Gunny stood in front of him, hands on hips. "I set a few rabbit snares and I have some potatoes on to boil. It'll be awhile."

"Never mind. I'll eat when I get back to Dunquin." He paused. "I don't feel right leaving you here."

"Go home, Mac," she said giving him a soft push. "You have your work and family. I've taken up enough of your time."

Mac stared at Gunny's thin, strong face, her curling black hair blowing across her cheeks and shoulders. "You fit this place, all wild and crazy. You'll end up the witch of this island if I don't come back and fetch you."

Gunny grinned. "I am going to try very hard to not be a witch."

Mac paused. "Before I go, I have to give you something," he said reaching into his pants pocket.

Gunny frowned. She didn't want anything that would remind her of home.

"I made this a long time ago," Mac said cupping something in the palm of his hand. "I know you have the black-handled knife but I thought you might need an iron nail to help you fend off any island fairies." He flipped his hand open.

Gunny looked at the nail in the palm of his hand. It was indeed a nail but Mac had elaborately twisted it into the shape of a heart and had added tiny filigree curls.

"Matt showed me a heart you made for him once from a twist of rope. I tried for years to bend a larger one out of iron."

Gunny gently took the small black heart from Mac. The metal was warm from being in his pocket. She felt a slight vibration as she clutched the beautiful piece. Her eyes filled with tears.

"It's lovely and I'm sure it will be good protection." She slipped the nail heart into her apron pocket and dusted off her hands. "Now go home," she said wiping her eyes with the back of her hand. "I have work to do."

After Mac left, Gunny checked her rabbit snares which were empty. She returned to the shell of the house she'd chosen and spooned out two boiled potatoes onto a tin plate. Her new house was the one closest to the strand. It had four thick, sturdy walls and a working fireplace. A stiff wind blew in from the cove through the open doorway. She hauled the curragh up from the beach and set it in the door frame to use as a wind break. Once the door frame was blocked, she realized she could not get inside, and crawled in through the glassless front window. She looked up at the sun pouring into the small stone structure. A new roof would be her first priority.

She worked for two long days dragging heavy driftwood logs and boards up from the strand and hoisting them across the low stone walls. Once the driftwood was in place, she wove rope across and through the structure to form a net, then made several trips to the fields beyond the village to collect armfuls of dried furze. She laid overlapping bundles of furze on the roof and tied them securely in place.

When the rain started at the end of the second day, she stuffed flour sacks into the open window and stumbled around in the near-dark—the fire in the hearth barely staying lit as the constant wind worked its way inside. The first night of rain was damp and cold. She dozed restlessly, listening to the rain drip in through one hundred undiscovered holes.

She returned to the wet fields the next morning to collect more furze and did the best she could to patch the wind-blown roof with numb hands and a runny nose. She checked on her still-empty empty rabbit snares and settled for partly cooked potatoes roasted in the constantly cooling fire. She tried a few times during the day to play her tin whistle to keep herself amused but her hands and lips were too cold and she was too tired to find the music within her.

The rain continued for ten days. Everything around her was damp, and her nose and lips were chapped and sore. The roof continued to leak, and the rabbit snares remained empty. She lost track of time. Day blended with night as she sat huddled in a corner of the tiny hut, arms laced tightly around drawn-up knees, periodically stuffing cold, partly cooked potato in her mouth and waiting to die.

"Damn you, Matt!" she yelled, hot tears burning in her eyes. "You pretended to be happy with me, but God knew better," she muttered as tears streamed down her damp face. "God knew you wanted to get away from me and he was happy to help you. No doubt if we'd married, you'd have drunk yourself silly and fallen off that horse or you'd have disappeared on some ship to America. Either way, I'd still be left here—alone." She wiped at her nose, and sobbed.

In a moment of desperation, she crawled in a daze to the old church and knelt before the cracked stone alter. "Dear Lord," she prayed, clutching Mac's iron heart in her numb, chapped hands. "Please let Mac sense my distress and come back to get me." She squeezed her eyes shut and listened as the high winds drove the angry ocean to the shore and pushed cold rain down her back. She knew deep in her heart that God was not listening to her, and that Mac was not coming back. But why hadn't her father come to rescue her? Where was her mother? She felt completely alone in her cold, damp misery. She pulled her shawl up over her head, clutching at the altar and sobbing until her chest ached and she could no longer catch her breath. When she finally calmed, she felt empty. She wiped her nose and face with her damp shawl and hiccupped.

"This is all your fault, Matt." She stumbled back to her tiny house, crawled in through the window, and slept a dreamless sleep.

She woke the next morning to warm spring sunlight filtering in around the edges of the flour sack-stuffed window. She scrambled up off the floor and pulled the damp sacks inside. The early-morning light made her squint. She had never seen or felt anything quite so wonderful. She crawled out the window and ran to the strand, pulled off her muddy damp boots and stockings, and set her boots on a rock to dry. She lifted her skirts and waded into the shockingly cold ocean water. The sea pulled at her legs as it receded from the shore, then nearly pushed her over as a new wave came rushing in. She raced up the beach and threw her arms open wide to the brilliant rising sun, humming quietly, then breaking out into louder oohs and ahhs as each wave broke along the shore. She gave a shout of joy and smiled when no one shushed her, then skipped backward along the sand, watching the waves erase her footprints behind her. A school of porpoises passed just past the edge of the cove. She watched as their slick grey fins sliced in unison through the water. She flopped down on the warming sand and leaned back on her elbows to enjoy the delicious feeling of weak morning sun on her face. Maybe God had heard her after all.

She heard deep snorts to her left and turned toward the noise. A large brown seal was watching her from a short distance down the strand. The seal raised one flipper, then rushed at her, flippers flapping and teeth barred. Gunny pushed to her feet and raced back to the stone house. She scrambled in the open window with the seal barking close behind , then turned, out of breath, and peeked through the window. The seal glared at her from the edge of the beach daring her to return. Gunny spied her boots perched on the rock in the cove and wanted to cry. When the tide turned, her boots would be lost. She reached down to finger the iron heart in her pocket and leaned out the window.

"I know about seals," she shouted toward the beach. "John McCrohan used to tell us about you—enchanted princesses trapped in a seal skin, angry at the world, and ready to bite anyone who gets near."

The brown seal watched the girl as she climbed slowly out of the window and leaned against the front wall of the house. "You think you're having a bad day?" she shouted toward the seal. "Try having a bad lifetime!"

The seal looked at the girl then turned toward the ocean and loped slowly along the shore. Gunny followed at a distance.

"Have you ever lost a mate? Have you had to learn how to swim all over again?"

The seal turned to look at the strange being following her and picked up her pace moving toward the water.

"Well, have you?" Gunny yelled, gaining on the seal. "Because that's what happened to me. Then I was raped and my own mother stole my baby." She stopped and stomped a bare foot in the sand. "How about that, Miss Seal. You want to talk about angry? Wouldn't that get you howling?"

The seal splashed through an incoming wave and swam toward deeper water. Her brown head broke the surface of the water only when she was safely in the middle of the small cove away from the raging woman.

Gunny snatched her boots from the rock where she'd left them drying. "You want to see angry, I'll show you angry," she yelled, waving the boots at the seal. She stopped and took a deep breath. "I'll show you angry," she muttered in a smaller voice, but the seal was gone.

The rains came intermittently through April but the sun was warmer each day, and the roof no longer leaked. Gunny made a morning ritual of hauling water from a clear spring past the ruins of the old church. She washed her face, dried it carefully on an old flour sack, and pulled her hair back with a thin strand of rope. Her clothes were stiff with salt from being around the nearly constant spray off the ocean, her black skirt and top were stained white at the seams. She checked over every seam each morning for tears. It wouldn't do to have ruined clothes—she had already come close to losing her boots. She repaired her worn clothes, stitching even the smallest tear with careful, tiny stitches as Joanna had taught her.

She ate sparingly, allowing herself only two boiled potatoes for a morning meal, which she drained in a basket she wove from furze branches, and one roasted potato for her evening meal. She kept the oat flour as dry as she could in a box near the fire and ran her hands through it each morning to drive out the air, promising herself that she would not eat any oat flour until she was starving. As the weather warmed, the rabbits in the fields started to move about and she had as many rabbits to eat as snares set. She skewered chunks of raw rabbit on Mac's fire tongs and slowly roasted the tasty flesh over a driftwood fire on the strand.

During the day, she plotted out a kitchen garden and scoured the nearby fields for the best place to plant potatoes and oats. The kitchen garden and oats needed good soil and she spent hours hauling seaweed and sand to her yard and to the fields. Potatoes preferred rougher soil so she prepared a rockier field past the oat field to set her potatoes. At night, her legs and back ached from the heavy work of hauling and hoeing, but after a week, her small fields were ready for seed. She filled her apron pocket with oat seeds from Mac's small stash, and planted each seed with great care as her father had taught her. When the oats were planted, she set her potatoes in the more distant field in high ridges. The kitchen garden seeds were more of a mystery. William had given her so many, she could only guess at how deep and close together to plant the tiny seeds. But she set matching seeds out in even rows, and waited.

When her kitchen garden began to sprout, rabbits appeared out of nowhere to nibble at the tiny shoots. She shoed them away, then filled her bucket with water and put grasses in to soak and spent an afternoon sitting in the garden weaving a series of tight grass nets. She sorted through her driftwood and picked out sixteen planks and branches that had some height to them and pounded them in around the garden with a large rock. She tied the grass net to the stakes, and buried the bottom of the net in the dirt.

By the time her fields and garden were planted, she felt she'd lived on the island for a lifetime. Every day was different so time passed quickly, yet she could relive almost every moment she'd been on the island because each day was unique. When it felt like it might be Good Friday, she took her bucket and hoe out to the rocks on the ebb of a high spring tide and looked for winkles. Sure enough, the small black snails were plentiful and she collected a few dozen. She boiled the small snails in her three-footed pot and pried the tasty bits out of their shells using a sharp nail. She remembered hating winkles as a child, but these tasted delicious.

When she tired of winkles, she scraped limpets off the rocks and boiled them with the potatoes. When she tired of shellfish, she explored the rocks by the shore for a place to drop a fishing hook but couldn't find a place deep enough to fish. She turned to the purple sandstone cliffs to the east and hiked to the top. The cliffs dropped off sharply into what looked like deep water. Her line was too short to fish from this height. She would have to twist more line—but she had time.

She spent most evenings on the strand, soaking and twisting dried grasses and slivered reeds into rope to keep her patched roof strong against the wind, and she twisted very fine line for fishing. She had saved a few light colored horse tail hairs in her sewing kit and used those as the final strands of line where she would tie a fish hook.

On the nights she was too tired to twist rope, she sat on the rocks and played soft, low tunes on her whistle to accompany the moans of the nearby nesting seals and birds. Most evenings, the brown seal was somewhere along the strand, but the two formed an uneasy truce. As long as Gunny did not sing or dance too loudly, the large creature kept a wary distance on the rocks at the far left end of the cove. Gunny occasionally heard other seals barking, but rarely saw any. The brown seal seemed to be on her own. When the sun set, Gunny played it farewell, then jigged up the moon. On moonless nights, she played out the stars in the thick, black canopy above her.

With her gardens growing and the promise of more food on the way, she decided to make a small pan of bread for an evening meal. She mixed oat flour with salt and slowly added warm water from the three-legged pot. She kneaded the mixture until it was smooth, rolled it out on a clean flour sack on the floor, and cut two thin groves with her black-handled knife to divide the loaf into four farls. After the dough warmed by the fire, she grilled it in butter in her fry pan. When the bread was crisp, she flipped it out of the pan onto the flour cloth, cut it in half, and spread a thick layer of butter over one half. She carefully wrapped the remaining half in the flour sack and took the buttered half out onto the strand. She walked slowly past the brown seal and sat on her favorite flat rock watching the late May sun set over the dark water. She grinned as she chewed the warm crusty bread, then pictured her parents and little Catherine sitting in front of a fire, the baby gnawing on a similar crust of bread. How big was Catherine now? She might even be walking. She sighed and returned to her quiet, empty house.

Gunny stoked the fire one morning and eyed the diminishing pile of turf. There might be a bit more turf to scavenge from the other houses and there was still driftwood to collect from the cove, but to make it through the winter, she'd have to find more turf. She knew there must be a bog nearby—someone had left dried turf in her house—but she had not seen any signs of a bog on her hikes up into the higher fields. She took her hoe and headed east in the direction of the village. After about a half-hour walk, she smelled the damp, rich earth of bog and her stomach raced.

She found a hillside bog, partly cut, but long deserted. The previous cuts were uneven and the soil stiff and dry. She hacked out square sections of bog using her small hoe, then hauling the soggy turf to slightly higher ground to dry. The air on the island was damp but the wind persistent. She hoped the two would balance each other and that by the end of summer, she would have tight, dry bricks of turf. She worked all day and did not have much turf to show for it, but headed home happy, knowing that if nature was kind to her and she found a few more days to cut, that she would have fuel to survive the winter.

The next morning her clothes reeked of bog water. She filled her bucket at the spring and poured the water into the pot by the fire to heat. Then she refilled the bucket and carried it into the yard, peeled off her apron, skirt, petticoat, shirt, shawl, and stockings, and using a smooth stick of driftwood as a beedle, beat and scrubbed each clothing item with a handful of sand in the cold water. She collected another half-bucket of spring water, poured in the hot water from the pot, and rinsed out each item in warm water. Her pale skin turned light pink as she worked exposed to the sun, but she enjoyed the thrill of being outside without clothes on.

She carefully wrung out her clothes and hung them to dry on a long piece of rope she tied from her house to the old church, then decided to take a naked dip in the cold ocean to get her body as clean as her clothes. She ran down to the strand and dove into the water. She splashed about, scrubbing her hair and skin with sand, and chatting with the waves. She floated on her back looking up into the clear blue sky, then closed her eyes and let the ocean gently rock her. When her skin was bumpy from the cold, she hauled herself out of the surf onto the long, black rocks and lay like a seal in the warming sun.

Her shirt and skirt were still damp and a little stiff as she pulled them on, but they smelled better. She left her petticoat, apron, shawl, and stockings to dry a bit longer, and headed barefoot into the fields whistling a jaunty tune. Four years before, she had been bed-ridden wondering if she would ever walk again. Now she'd made a shelter for herself, planted seeds, and cut her own turf. She collected a handful of field flowers in a posy and breathed in the warm spring air. As she neared her house, she was startled to see a man leaning against her front wall looking out across the cove. She felt like the brown seal as she studied the intruder to see if this animal was a threat to her. Then she started to run.

"You're back!" she yelled as she approached the house.

"You're alive!" Mac yelled back, turning to see the laughing woman race down the hill.

After a quick, awkward embrace, Gunny blushed and pushed Mac away. "Happy May Day," she said, grinning. She handed Mac the posy of flowers. "Is it May?"

Mac blushed and looked at the ground. "Nearly so. I'm sorry it took me so long to get back to see you. The ocean was too rough to cross—I couldn't get anyone to take me over. Then when the rains stopped we had to work to catch up on the planting."

Gunny grinned. "It's for the best. If you'd have shown up any earlier, I might have left with you. But now I'm settled in."

"I wasn't sure where to find you or which house you'd taken. This one looked like a large seabird nest with a boat door so I figured it was the place and I saw your clothes on the line. When I yelled no one answered. I thought something might have happened to you."

"It's good you didn't show earlier today," Gunny said pulling her apron and stockings off the line.

Mac glanced at Gunny's glowing face. "You look good. You have freckles and color in your cheeks."

Gunny laughed awkwardly, tying on her still-damp apron and twisted her hair into a loose bun.

Mac cleared his throat and continued. "I brought you something. Now let's see, where did I put it?" he said, setting down the posy of flowers and feeling around in his pockets.

"I don't need anything," Gunny said, trying to remember where she had put the iron heart when she'd washed her apron.

"Of course you don't—you never do." Mac picked up a new firkin of butter from behind him and held it out with both hands. "I don't suppose you could use any butter?"

Gunny grinned and snatched the firkin. "Bless you. You know I like a bit of butter."

"It's from my mother. She also sent you some flour sacks. She thought you might want to make yourself a mattress."

Gunny paled. "I thought you weren't going to tell anyone where I was."

"It's only Mam, and she can keep a secret." He paused and pointed to a small pane of framed glass that was leaning up against the house. "I also picked up a window for you in Dingle."

Gunny gasped and knelt in front of the small, framed pane, her lost secret forgotten. "A real window!" She ran her long fingers over the smooth surface. "It's the best present I've ever had," she said turning to Mac.

"But wait, there's more," he said. "I left them here somewhere…"

Three young hens appeared from around the back of the house scratching in the dirt and clucking at one another.

"You brought me chickens?" Gunny clapped her hands. "Oh, you are my savior. I tried pilfering eggs from the shore birds and it's not easy. The first few eggs I found had chicks inside and I had to throw them away."

"I must say that chickens are not easy to haul over in a boat. Maurice Burke didn't know what he was getting himself into when he offered to row me here today. I had to pack the birds in an old fishing crate to walk them out here. They're all just started to lay so you should have plenty of eggs soon."

"Eggs…" Gunny glowed. "Right now I have toast. Are you hungry?"

"Starving."

"Me too."

"You made bread?"

"Yes," Gunny said with a slight flip of her hand. She beamed, snatched up the flower posy, and climbed into the house through the window.

Mac hesitated and leaned in the open space. "I don't suppose I could use the door?"

Gunny laughed. "Sorry. I've gotten rather used to coming and going through the window."

She pushed the boat away from the doorway. Mac caught the small vessel and leaned it up against the house. Gunny was surprised at how much light came pouring in through the open doorway.

"What's that on the floor?" Mac asked, ducking inside and pointing along the back wall of the house. There was a long plank of wood on the floor mostly covered with dirt.

"I have no idea," Gunny said, stuffing the flowers in a tin cup and adding water. "It's been so dark in here I didn't see that."

Mac tried to pull the wooden plank from the floor but there was too much soil packed on top. Gunny ran outside to get the hoe and hacked at the dirt until it broke up. The plank of wood was large and long. Gunny was delighted. "This'll make a perfect half-door!

She and Mac tried again to move the plank but it still wouldn't budge.

"It feels like it's caught on something." Mac ran his hands over the edges of wood along the base of the back wall and stopped when he arrived at an iron hinge. "Where there is one iron hinge, there're usually two." He ran his hands farther along the wall and found the second hinge. "I believe this's already a door."

Gunny swallowed hard. She had no idea she'd been sleeping on top of a door. Mac cleared off more dirt, then hefted the thick, heavy square open and rested it against the back wall. There was a large hole under the plank with narrow steps leading down. Gunny peered inside. The hole started under the house but looked like it ran out behind the house as well. Dank air rose from the opening.

Mac whistled. "What do you supposed the ancient people used this for?"

"William had a hole in his floor. He used it to keep his butter cool."

Mac waved the stale air away from his hand. "I wouldn't want my butter smelling like that, and this is much more than a hole. Maybe the ancient people used it for something else."

"Like what?"

"I don't know. A place to hide illegal possessions? Or house outlaws? Maybe it's a grave."

Gunny circled around the open space and took a few tentative steps down the steep, soil-packed steps. "The steps seem sturdy."

"Don't go down there," Mac said holding out a muscular arm to block Gunny's way. "Let's close it."

Gunny moved Mac's arm away. "I can't sleep in this house if I don't know what's under me. I wish we had more light."

Mac went to the fire and lit a small furze branch. "This won't last long," he said handing Gunny the flaming branch. "Look fast."

Gunny took the light and ducked down into the narrow passage.

"What's down there?" Mac asked behind her. "What do you see?"

"Come down," Gunny said, her voice muffled. "It's a small room."

"I'll take your word for it," Mac said peeking down the stairs but keeping his feet solidly on the ground above.

"You always were one for adventure," Gunny mumbled as she reappeared up the steps, the fire now extinguished. She brushed a cobweb from her face, and gave a shiver. "There's nothing down there. But it's a cool space. I can store my potatoes there."

Mac moved her aside and pulled the heavy wooden door away from the back wall and let it fall back into place on the floor. It closed with a small puff of dirt. He wiped his hands on his pant legs. "Didn't you say something about toast?"

Gunny rinsed her hands with water from the bucket and unwrapped a half-circle of bread left from her morning meal. She broke it into two pieces and set them in front of the fire on tiny stands she had twisted together from furze branches. She pulled a handful of mushrooms from a box by the door and brushed off the dirt with a corner of her apron. She had collected the mushrooms a few days before on a cool rainy morning. She pulled her knife from her pocket, sliced the mushrooms, and set them to fry in hot butter in the pan. When she slipped the knife back in her pocket, she felt the iron heart and gave it a quick squeeze. How had it gotten back in her pocket? She added a few strands of dried seaweed to the frying mushrooms.

"What'd you add to the mushrooms?" Mac asked.

"There's all kinds of seaweed out here. All the ones I've tried are salty and delicious."

When the hunks of bread were warm on both sides, she topped them with fresh butter, and scraped the browned mushrooms and seaweed into a bowl. She and Mac sat on the floor, side by side in front of the fire, eating warm bread and salty mushrooms with their fingers.

"Sorry I don't have any furniture," Gunny said. "I'll make some stools out of curled up rope this winter."

Mac shook his head. "Stools aren't necessary. It's like living in the booley again. Oh," his face brightened. "I have the perfect thing to add to this meal." He reached into his pocket and pulled out a small flask of whiskey.

Gunny took the corked bottle from Mac and eyed the warm amber liquid. "Funny, I haven't missed this," she said. "The spring water here is delicious."

"I'll take it back then," Mac said, reaching for the bottle.

Gunny hugged the bottle to her chest. "No. Gifts can't be returned, remember? One never knows when one might need a spot of whiskey—for medicinal purposes." She swirled the liquid in the bottle, then bit the cork and pulled it free with a small pop, and spit the cork into her hand. "I guess I could use a medicinal drink right now. Oh wait," she said. "I have to show you my new cups."

She stood and crossed to a large box near the hearth and pulled out two delicate tea cups.

"Where on earth did you get these?" Mac asked cradling one of the cups in his large hands.

"I found them on the strand in this old box. I find all sorts of things on the strand. I even found a plank from a shipwreck that I used for part of my roof. It had the words Santa Ashling de la Rosa carved into it. Do you think it might have been from the Spanish Armada? Remember when your father used to tell those tales... And look at the detail in these cups. I think they look Spanish."

She poured a little whiskey in each cup, then swiftly swallowed her cupful in a gulp and gasped. "Ahh. Tastes like old times."

Mac was quiet, swirling the whiskey in his cup. "Gunny, I want you to come back to Dunquin with me."

Gunny's eyes opened wide. "Is there something wrong with Catherine?"

"No, no. I've seen her out with your mother in the village. They both look fine. Why would you think that?"

"Well, why else would I go back with you?"

Mac paused. "What if something happens to you out here? What if you slip and break a leg or can't find enough food to eat? I never meant for you to stay here this long."

Gunny laughed and shook her head. It was her old, loud laugh. "Mac, I am in the hands of the great sky now. And," she added, "you forget that I have the iron heart AND the black-handled knife." Gunny pulled the heart and knife from her apron pocket as proof that she was protected. "What could possibly go wrong?"

"Aren't you bored?" he asked.

Gunny poured herself a half cup of whiskey and stared into the fire. "I'm never bored. There's always something to be done with the house or collecting food. And when I have any time at all, I make rope. The reeds that grow out here are incredibly strong and this roof has taken every bit of rope I can make."

"You don't miss the company of others?"

Gunny sighed and looked at Mac's fire-lit face. "When I first got here, I kept talking to Matt, but he wouldn't answer so we've been chatting less. There's a brown seal down on the strand. And a poor wild ewe who lives up the hill. Her wool is long and matted and she won't let me near her but she watches me when I'm out in the fields. I've picked her whins off of the furze bushes. Look." Gunny leaned around behind her and pulled out a flour sack filled with scraps of loose, raw wool. "I washed these in spring water. Feel how silky they are."

Mac reached into the bag then withdrew his hand and took a sip of whiskey. "I was talking about human company."

Gunny shook her head. "You're really the only person I talked to in Dunquin. It's not all that different for me here. William used to tell me it was worse to be alone in a crowd than to be alone."

Mac grimaced at the mention of the mysterious, dead William, but Gunny continued.

"When I'm by myself I'm not trying to be anyone, Mac. I don't worry about my limp or how I look, or the fact that I had a baby with no father. I'm just me—thinking about my house or thinking about what I'm going to eat next or how I'm going to make a rope or catch that ewe. No one pities me or judges me out here."

Gunny paused to refill her cup. She took a sip and continued in a gruff voice. "Sometimes I think of an old song or a dance or a story that reminds me of home, but then I sing or dance or tell myself that story, and no one tells me to be quiet or to act sane. My days are filled with sunlight and mist, wind and stone, whistles and work. I have the sea roaring in one ear and the north wind blowing in the other. It's been heaven being here by myself. I believe I was meant to live this way."

"As your mother would say," Mac said shaking his head. "It's not right."

Mac did a fair imitation of Eileen which made Gunny grimace.

"How is my mother?"

"She was frantic when you first disappeared. She sent your father out looking for you. I ran into him at O'Leary's when I got back to Dunquin."

"Mam sent Da out looking for me and Da went to O'Leary's?"

"Where else would he look for you?"

"In the hills?"

Mac shrugged. "He headed to the hills after he didn't find you at O'Leary's."

"Da went into the hills?" Gunny gasped.

"He told Micky O'Leary he went all the way to Brandon Mountain looking for you. Your mother was fit to be tied. She was sure your da's heart would give out on the climb."

Gunny swallowed hard. "It didn't occur to me that Da would go looking for me in the hills."

"He stopped when I told them where you were."

Gunny set her tea cup down on the rough dirt floor. "What? I told you not to tell them."

"I had to—or your father might have kept wandering forever."

"Is there anyone else you told? Father Jessey, perhaps, or Bitsy Kavanaugh?"

"Of course I didn't tell them. Only my Mam and your parents know. And I made your parents promise to give you time. I told them you'd be back."

"Then you told them a lie," Gunny said shaking her head. "I'm not going back."

"But it's strange living in Dunquin without you," Mac said in a quiet voice. "I keep expecting I'll see you hiking in from the booley, or to see you pounding down a glass of porter at O'Leary's with Father Jessey."

"I never pounded down porter with Father Jessey!" Gunny protested.

"Oh, the little girls in the village still talk about the time the witch got Father Jessey drunk."

Gunny laughed. "I suppose those girls miss their witch."

"Catherine must miss you," Mac said.

Gunny squeezed Mac's arm. "Now you are playing with me. Catherine's too pampered and petted by my mother and father to miss me for a minute. Mam said I was too loud and rough with her. And how would it be for her to grow up with a 'sister' who's a witch?"

"But she's your child, Gunny. Don't you miss her?"

"She came from my body, Mac, but she's not my child. She belongs to my parents now."

Mac looked at Gunny's cheeks, flush with whiskey. "I don't have anyone to talk to since you left."

"Mac, the great talker," Gunny snickered.

"I'm quiet, Gunny, but I have thoughts and ideas."

"Then come live on the island with me. This is the perfect place for thoughts and ideas. If you lived here, you could make what you wanted in iron—not just what the villagers ask you to make."

Mac swirled the last bit of whiskey in his cup. "What would be the point of that? And who would shoe the horses and make the nails and mend the pots?"

"Oh, what royal deeds those are, patching up old iron pots for the local gossips…"

Mac shook his head. "Someone in my family has always been the blacksmith, and since Matt…" Mac paused and tossed back the last bit of whiskey in his cup. "I'm sorry," he said standing, setting his tea cup on the floor and dusting off the seat of his pants. "I guess it's time for me to go."

Gunny stood. "Before you go," she said pulling the filigree heart from her apron pocket, "I have a question. We discussed the origins of the black-handled knife. You didn't happen to make this heart from the old church gate, did you?"

"Why do you ask?" Mac said pushing his hands deep in his pockets.

"Why do you answer my question with a question?"

Mac was silent

"I knew it," Gunny said. "I can't get rid of this nail," she said marveling at the small black heart.

"You tried to get rid of it?" Mac asked.

"I didn't try to get rid of it. I've just misplaced it from time to time and it always ends up back on the hearth or back in my pocket."

"Then I guess you have to keep it."

Mac watched Gunny run her long fingers across the smooth, black metal, tracing the heart shape and the intricate filigree. Gunny felt the weight of the heart in her hand. The metal was cold and the points sharp. She slid the heart back in her pocket, finished off her whiskey, and set her cup on the hearth.

"Come outside and see what I planted before you leave."

She took Mac by the hand and led him out toward the fields. A brisk wind whipped up over the hill.

"I don't know how you stand that wind," Mac said.

Gunny laughed. "The wind cheers me. It brings change."

Gunny showed Mac where her oats were coming up and where the potato plants had started to grow. The fields looked stark and small to Mac compared with the freshly worked series of fields in Dunquin.

He smiled. "You always liked farming more than I did. How will you roast the oat heads once you harvest them?"

"I haven't thought that far ahead. But I saw William take a handful of raw oat heads one time and light them on fire. The fire took care of the threshing and winnowing and left a handful of seeds dry and ready to grind."

"That would work for a few oat heads you were going to eat but you'll have to store most of them and they have to be dried. I'll come over at harvest and take them back with me to the kiln in Dunquin."

"No," Gunny said, stubbornly. "I'll figure out a way to dry them here."

"I can help you," Mac said grabbing her hand.

"I don't want help," Gunny said with a shake of her head.

Mac sighed. "You look thin."

Gunny pulled her hand away from Mac and crossed her arms. "There's a lot to do out here—I hardly have time to eat. And truthfully, I ran out of potatoes a week or so ago, but that's no different than it is at home this time of year. There are plenty of rabbits to eat, and there's the shellfish." Gunny said, pointing toward the shore. "It's everywhere."

"You hate winkles and limpets."

"I used to hate them. Now I like them. It's funny how much better things taste when you're hungry. I caught a red crab the other day and roasted him in the ashes of the fire. Delicious. And soon I'll have food from my kitchen garden. I don't even know what I planted, but whatever comes in, I'll eat it."

"Have you been to the village on the east end? When the weather turned bad after I left you, I hoped you went there for shelter and company."

Gunny laughed. "I never even thought about going there."

"You shouldn't be afraid of them. When I showed up in the village after I dropped you off, and asked for a ride to Dunquin, the fishermen were like, 'Aye, Blackie, come ride with me,' and asked nothing farther."

"That's odd. The women of Dunquin would've asked a thousand questions. How many people do you think live out here?"

"When Maurice and I rowed in today there were four or five women watching us from up on a cliff. And a group of children ran to meet me at the stone pier but they ran off laughing before I could talk to them. When I walked through the village, I saw maybe ten or twelve houses with smoke coming out of their chimneys but I didn't see anyone around. I imagine the men are out fishing on a nice day like this."

Gunny shook her head. "I saw a group of men out hunting rabbits once near the bog. I waved to them and one young man yelled over to me that I was living in the houses of the Bright People. But no one's come out to meet me."

"You know who will eventually come out to meet you—Lord Ventry. When he hears about your thriving little farm, he'll definitely want his rent."

"Thomas hasn't tried to contact me since that Halloween. I'm sure he's forgotten all about me."

"I doubt that." Mac shivered. "That wind is cold."

Gunny laughed. "You should see it when it rains! From the top of that hill over there, you can see a storm coming for miles out across the water—maybe right from America. The clouds pile up in dark, tall mountains, with edges of deep purple and red—then lightning flashes inside and the clouds sweep over the island and the rain blows in torrents, whipping around in your face, and down your shirt and up your skirt. Then the storm passes over the island and everything is so still—with long beams of sunlight filtering through the remains of the mist…"

Mac squinted out over the sea. "Yes," he said. "It's cold."

Gunny tucked her hand into the crook of Mac's arm. "I guess you have to be more of a poet than a blacksmith to live out here. I'll walk with you partway to the village. I need to turn my peat bricks and the bog's on the way."

"Pushing me out again, are you?"

"Some are meant to live here and others just to visit."

"Fine. I'll go. Look after my chickens. I'll be back to check on you in another couple of weeks. Like it or not."

They walked in comfortable silence up the hill toward the center of the island. Gunny waved at Mac as he continued on east. Her stomach fluttered. It had been good to see Mac and it was good to see him go. She was different than she'd been in Dunquin but Mac had not changed. She climbed up to the peat bog and turned her dozens of bricks of hardening turf. When she returned home, she moved the curragh back in front of the door and climbed into the house through the window. She cut the new flour sacks open with her knife, and started the slow process of stitching them into a mattress cover.

By midsummer, Gunny had finally twisted enough fine line to try fishing from the high purple cliffs. The summer sun was hot on her face as she sat quietly looking out across her small cove at the white caps that decorated the open ocean. She felt a tug on her line and tugged back. A fish pulled again then took off away from the cliffs. The pull was so strong she nearly slipped over the edge of the cliff trying to hold on to the fine thread of line. At one point, she was sure she was going to lose her grip but refused to lose the line it had taken her so long to twist. She finally hauled a flapping, fat fish up the side of the cliff and speared it with the black-handled knife.

She prepared the fish as William had showed her with oat flour, butter, and roasted early-summer onions. The taste, she decided, was worth the risk of death and she continued to catch fish from the cliffs through the rest of the summer. She fried some and boiled some with new potatoes. Whatever fish she did not eat, she salted and hung in strips in front of the fire to dry. When the fish were not biting, she set snares for rabbits—ate some, dried many, and stored her food in the hole in the floor, cool and safe from the chickens, while she waited for her crops to come in.

In early August, a particularly ferocious storm passed over the island in the night, and Gunny was glad to wake to a clear, sunny sky. She chased the chickens from the house and headed out to collect her usual bucket of water from the spring. She stopped and looked out across the cove. There were several large, dark shapes floating out in the water. She set her bucket down and ran cautiously to the shore. All manner of strange debris was floating into the cove and several wooden planks had already washed ashore on the high storm waves. She feared that a ship had sunk nearby and raced up the purple cliffs for a better view of the ocean. She could see a pattern of planks and debris floating toward her from the west but could see no ship. She stopped to say a quick prayer for any sailors who might have been on the ship that went down, then gave a loud "whoop" of thanks to God for sending her new building materials.

She worked past noon dragging soggy wooden planks up past the high-tide mark. Some of the wood was splintered and damaged but most of the planks were perfect: long and straight. By the time she returned to the house for a farl of bread, her legs were aching and she was soaking wet, salty, and sandy, but was grinning from ear to ear. The day was better than any Christmas she could remember.

When she'd finished the bread she returned to the shore. She had worked earlier to move a large chest out of the water, but it was still mired in heavy, wet sand. Now that the tide was farther out, most of the chest was clear of the water. She picked up a large rock and waded through the shallows toward the chest.

"All right," she said running her hands over the smooth wood and brass locks. "Let's see what you've got inside you."

She pounded the rock hard against each of the two large locks on the chest to no avail. She tossed the rock aside and took out her black-handled knife and unsheathed it. She held it up toward the sky and watched sunlight glint off the blade. "Help me, fairy magic, to open these stubborn locks."

She worked the knife into one lock, which sprang open. She twisted the knife in the second lock and whooped with joy as it, too, opened. The brown seal lumbered off into the water as Gunny pushed open the heavy lid of the chest. The chest was lined with lead and held boxes of a crumbled black substance. Gunny leaned over the trunk and pinched a small amount between two fingers and held it to her nose. The smell was wonderful, like grass but sweeter.

"Tea!"

Her eyes filled with tears as she crossed herself and thanked heaven for the gift. She hadn't missed tea until she smelled it—and now she had a whole trunk of it, rich and black.

"God be praised," she muttered. "I may have no whiskey in this deserted place but I have tea. Wait until Mac hears about this!"

She closed the lid. As soon as the tide was all the way out, she'd try again to move the trunk. In the meantime, she'd take a last patrol down the beach. She noted a few more planks floating near shore; she would collect them later. Then she saw two oddly curved planks bobbing up and down in the cove. They appeared to be moving out to sea. She had a few hours left before the tide came back in. She hurried to the house for the boat, flipped it onto her back, and grabbed the oars from the side wall. It was time to try her hand at rowing.

She set the boat down on the edge of the lapping water, pulled off her skirt and petticoat, and tossed them to shore. She waded out into the chilly surf with the oars in hand, and flipped herself into the boat. Her hands shook slightly as she secured the oars in their dowels, but she rowed steadily through the gentle waves out into the cove. She looked behind her for the floating item but it had disappeared. Then it reappeared just behind the boat, two thin rounded pieces of wood that ran parallel to each other bobbing along on the dark surface of the water. She leaned over the side, and pulled—but the object was too heavy to pull on board.

"I don't know what you are," she said, "but I'm interested enough to find out."

She took the loose end of the rope from the front of the boat and tied it around one of the wooden runners, then pulled hard to row to shore. When sand and rocks scraped the bottom of the boat, she jumped out into the shallow surf, pulled the boat up onto the sand, and stared at the found item floating behind in the shallow water. It was a chair with two bent runners that connected the front legs to the back.

"What were these for?" she asked running her fingers along the smooth, wooden runners. "I suppose I could get Mac to cut them off."

She pulled the chair from the water. The cane seat and back were heavy with sea water and she staggered under the weight as she flipped the chair upright. She paused to catch her breath, then dragged the chair the rest of the way to her yard. She wiped the chair clean of sand and pulled it in through the open doorway to dry in front of the fire.

She ate a quick evening meal of fried eggs and salt fish, then left with her bucket. If she couldn't move the mired trunk ahead of the tide, she'd at least rescue the tea. The trunk was still stuck fast, so she brought bucket after of bucket of tea to the house, filling every pot, dish, and sack she owned with the black fragrant leaves. When the lead-lined chest was nearly empty she closed the lid and found she could now move the trunk about an inch at a time in the clinging wet sand. It took nearly an hour to get the trunk to dry sand and by the time she got there, she was exhausted. She looked at the battered wooden trunk. If she could get it up to the house, she'd have a wonderful place to store her tea. But was it worth the effort? She looked up and down the deserted strand. Of course no one was there to help. Even the brown seal had gone away. She sighed. Perhaps if she waited until morning she'd have more strength.

She grabbed her skirt and petticoat from the beach and walked off toward the house, then turned to look again at the trunk. She wanted it in her house. She pulled on her skirt and returned to the beach to try again. She heaved and shoved until she moved the heavy trunk first onto the rocks, then pulled and pushed until it was safely at the edge of her yard. She wanted to cheer but was too exhausted to even mutter. She staggered inside, smoored the fire, swallowed a sip of water, and fell promptly asleep on her thin straw mat.

She woke early the next morning to bright light pouring in through the doorway. She had forgotten to bring the boat back up from the beach. She laughed at her mistake and decided that her first use of the new wood would be to build a simpler door. She smiled at the thought, washed her gritty face and hands and dried them gently on a sack filled with tea, having no other sacks available to dry her face. She stirred the fire, added a turf, and put water in a pan to heat for tea. Her mouth watered at the thought of tea. She ran her hands over the new chair. The cane seat and back were nearly dry. She sat down gingerly in the chair and leaned back. The chair tipped back with her weight and she quickly leaned forward. The chair moved with her. She slowly leaned back again and the chair rocked back but did not tip over. What a wonderful, strange piece of furniture this was, she thought rocking forward again.

She scooted off the chair and went out to the yard. With renewed strength, she pulled the trunk the rest of the way across the yard and in through the open doorway. She cheered for herself, wishing that someone could see how her hard work had paid off. She propped the trunk open by the fire, and by evening found it dry enough to be filled once again with fragrant tea leaves.

Mac reappeared at her house a few weeks later with a heavy wooden kreel strapped to his back. It was a proper late-summer day with not a breath of wind and his face was red and sweaty from his long hike across the island. Gunny was retying furze to her roof and scrambled down to greet him.

"Welcome!" She moved to hug him, but eyed his sweaty face and shook his hand instead.

He hefted the kreel to the ground and wiped a sleeve across his face. "First it's freezing out here, now it's hot as blazes."

Gunny shrugged.

"Sorry. I should be more chipper. It was windy on the way over. Twice I thought we were going to tip and Maurice said we'd have to go back. I hate that channel crossing."

"You're kind to come and visit your hermit friend."

She shifted from foot to foot, wanting to tell Mac about the shipwreck and her newfound items, but waiting to hear his news first. He emptied the kreel of another pound of butter, more flour sacks, a grater, and a long turf cutter and sharpened scythe. He also pulled a few hinges from his pocket.

"I thought you might make a drop-down bed, and maybe we can piece something together for a door."

"Oh, Mac," she gushed. "Wait till you see my new stash of wood."

He ignored her words and pulled one last gift from his jacket pocket—a fresh corked bottle of amber whiskey. She snatched the bottle from him and grabbed his hand.

"You're wonderful. Now come inside. You'll be so surprised."

She scooped up the new firkin of butter, pushed the boat away from the door, and dragged him into the house. The trunk of tea and oversized chair now dominated her small living space. She pushed a chicken off the new chair, and was thrilled when Mac sat down and leaned back, then forward, until he got the rhythm of rocking. She made him tea from her new stash, which they washed down with a swallow of whiskey.

Then she walked him out along the back of the house to admire her new supply of wood. They picked out several long boards to piece together for a door and found one large plank that would do for a drop-down bed. They worked through the morning using rocks and Gunny's stash of nails to hammer together the new additions to the house. When the door made of layers of mismatched boards was finally squared off and hung, Mac added a rope latch that Gunny could secure from the inside. Gunny swung the door open and closed a dozen times, amazed at how complete it made her house feel.

In the early afternoon they hiked to the cliffs. Gunny showed Mac where she'd been fishing, then disappeared over the edge of a cliff, much to Mac's chagrin. They returned to the house with three dead birds.

"Ever eat a puffin?" she asked as she plucked off the short black and white feathers of the birds she'd dipped briefly in a pot of boiling water. "There are hundreds of nests along the cliffs. I kept seeing birds fly up and disappear into the face of the cliff while I was fishing. If there's dung in the entrance to the hole, there's a bird inside and you reach in and pull it out. The first few times I got bitten and scratched. Now I'm pretty good at grabbing and breaking a neck all in one swift move."

She illustrated her technique with a quick flick of her wrist. Mac swallowed hard.

She speared the gutted plucked birds and propped them up over the heart of the fire. "And," she added. "I'm now the proud owner of a puffin feather pillow."

Mac shook his head in amazement. "I don't know why I worry about you."

Gunny tossed a clean plank of wood on the floor and cut up four potatoes and a couple of onions to fry in a heating pan of butter. She pulled part of a cabbage from her storage place in the floor and added that to the potato and onion mix. The house filled with delicious smells. Mac sat in the rocking chair and rubbed at a blister on his calloused hand. Next time he came over, he'd bring a hammer. When the food was ready, they sat on the floor and feasted on the small, roasted birds, fresh vegetables, and hot tea. Gunny threw the leftovers and potato peals to her growing dung hill in the yard and smiled at the smelly mess of fertilizer piling up for next spring.

Mac slept that night on a mattress stuffed with furze on the floor with the chickens while Gunny pulled a second thin mattress onto the new drop-down bed. They worked together the next day to select a few more long planks to build a sturdy table and bench. While Gunny arranged the new furniture, Mac set the window in place and sealed the edges with two layers of mud. He hoped to be over again before winter, but if he wasn't, Gunny's house would at least have some protection against the chill winter winds. It was late when they finally sat down at the new table to a meal of pancakes made from the last of Gunny's oat flour. It was so late Mac decided to stay another night—though he was sure his mother would think he'd disappeared at sea.

The next morning, they hiked to the high fields and loaded heavy, dry bricks of peat into Mac's kreel.

"You need a barrow," he said as Gunny helped him lift the heavy kreel onto his back.

"Next trip," they both said in unison.

They hiked past Gunny's small plot of ripening oats.

"I may not be back in time to help you with the harvest."

Gunny grinned. "Living out here is making me tough and clever, Mac. I'll figure out how to bring in the oats," she said proudly eying the lush, ripening fields of swaying grass.

They unloaded the peat at the house and Mac slung the now empty kreel onto his back for the walk back across the island. He glanced at Gunny, then stared down at the top of his boots. Gunny could tell he had something to say but would not say it. She did not push. Mac had never been a man of words. He took a deep breath and reached into his pocket. "I've been meaning to give you this," he said holding out a small white object.

Gunny felt the blood run from her face. "Is that Matt's pipe?"

"It is. I found it at the back of the nook last week. I thought you might want it."

Gunny took the smooth, clay pipe and cradled it in her hands. She remembered selecting it for Matt from the shelf at the Murphy's. She sniffed at the bowl and held the pipe up to her lips.

"Are you going to take up smoking?"

"No, but I like it that Matt's lips touched this," she said, running the pipe again lightly over her lips.

"Well, I'll see you," Mac said, and with a short wave, he turned to leave.

Gunny pulled the pipe from her lips and grabbed his arm. "Tell my folks I'm well, will you?"

"Sure, I'll tell them," Mac said. He squeezed her hand on his arm, then with a sigh, turned and hiked east toward the Blasket village.

Gunny shivered and pulled her shawl up higher on her shoulders as she watched Mac's shape grow smaller, then disappear over the hill. Her hip ached. The days were getting shorter and colder; winter was coming. For the first time since she'd arrived on the island, she felt a pang of loneliness. She slipped the pipe into her apron pocket, limped back to her house, and put on a pan of water for tea.

Collecting the ripened oats took two full days, even using the newly sharpened scythe from Mac. Gunny hauled armful after armful of cut oats down to the old stone church yard and sliced off the heads from the straw. She collected the heads in several boxes she'd pounded together from her lumber supply, and tied the straw into tight bundles to save for roof repair and mattress stuffing. She stored the straw in the alcove of the old church and hauled the boxes of oat heads home. It took another two days to knock the seeds out of the heads, rub off the chaff, and lightly roast pan after pan of seeds. When the seeds were finally all roasted, she crushed them with a beedle of driftwood in the three-legged pot, and stored the rough flour in two large sacks in front of the fire. The chickens feasted on the stray seeds that fell to the floor.

Her back was sore and her hands and arms burned with fatigue—and she had not yet lifted one potato. She longed for a cold rainy day to spend at home sipping tea and twisting rope, but when the weather remained clear, she headed back outside to dig up her spuds. It took her a week of shortened days to dig and drag home load after heavy load of potato on a mat she wove of tough marsh grasses. She stored the spuds in the cool earthen cellar along with her harvest of cabbages, onions, turnips, and carefully collected and sorted seeds from her kitchen garden. Each night, she knelt in prayer and thanked the Lord for her father, Joanna Murphy, and William, who had all taught her important skills.

When the fields and garden were finally empty of their bounty, she celebrated with a meal of potato pancakes. She grated her largest potato, mixed in an egg, flour, and a little onion, fried it crisp, and headed to the strand where she savored every delicious bite as cool winds blew in off the water, and the sun slipped into the cold, greasy ocean.

As the weather stiffened, Gunny found she had a tremendous craving for rabbit stew and hunted almost every day. She let the rabbit meat simmer all day in the heavy three-legged pot along with bits of potato and cabbage, then took the hot stew and several farls of bread with her to the strand to eat while the sun set. After she wiped the last bit of stew from her bowl with a last bite of bread, she hummed to the even rhythm of the waves until a canopy of stars appeared over her head. On the first full moon after the harvest, she finished off another bowl of rabbit stew and watched as a heavy red moon rose over the water. Her cold breath mixed with the air around her and she knew it must be near All Hallows E'en.

She was restless that night and woke early to the sound of moaning outside her house. She crept to the door and opened it a crack. A large black cow stood nose to the door. She pulled on her shawl and stepped outside. Her yard was filled with cows and sheep, all milling about chewing on peels and scraps from her dung heap, and trampling down the remains of her empty kitchen garden.

"Where on earth did you come from?" she quizzed a nearby munching cow. "It's a good thing my harvest's in," she said, hands on hips. She looked about for herders but no one was with the animals. She saw that a few of the cows needed to be milked. She grabbed her bucket and set to work. She hadn't had milk in a year and the warm drink was delicious. The animals grazed in the old village through the day. That night, she let a full bucket of milk sit, and the next morning skimmed off the cream and beat the frothy mixture with a driftwood beedle in her three-legged pot. She squeezed lumps of butter out of the milk, and stored the small bit of butter in a firkin she hammered together out of driftwood. She glanced out the window. The cows and sheep were still milling about in her yard. She set out to milk once again.

It was a week before she heard a knock at the door and nearly fell over backwards in the tipping chair at the sound. She opened the door. Several men were standing in the yard, hats in hand.

"I apologize, Miss," said a tall man with lively blue eyes and deep wrinkles across his forehead. "We're from the village beyond the hill. We've come to get our stock. I'm sorry if they've been troubling you," he said holding out a heavily calloused hand. "The name's Donal McCrohan."

Gunny grinned and pulled the door open wider. "You're John McCrohan's brother."

"I am," he said with raised eyebrows. "Did you know my brother?"

"He was a dear neighbor in Dunquin. He used to talk about his brother who married onto this island."

"I married Mary Daly. Been here since 1811. And you are?" he asked eyeing the young woman who appeared to be living in one of the homes of the Ancient Ones.

Gunny blushed. Who was she? She took a hesitant step into the yard. "I'm Gunny Malone," she said, putting out a hand in greeting.

Donal took her hand and gave her a slight bow. "Glad to meet you, Gunny Malone. Sorry again for any inconvenience from the livestock. Lads," he said turning to the others. "Get these cows and sheep back up over the hill." He turned to Gunny. "Lord Ventry's man was by last week to collect rent. We've been sending our animals out here for the past couple of years whenever the Lord's agent comes around. He never thinks to search any farther than the old tower. We forgot we had a guest this year on this end of the island."

"You hide your livestock here?" Gunny laughed.

"A few years ago, Davey couldn't pay his rent so the Peelers took our eight-man fishing boat when we were over to Dingle. The Peelers wouldn't give it back unless Davey paid, and none of us had the money to help him. We had to hitch a ride home. It took us a month to build ourselves a new boat."

"Did the English sell your boat?"

"Worse. They stashed it at the pier in Dingle where everyone could see it. No one would buy it, of course. No one but an island man knows how to handle an eight-man curragh. The sheriff eventually tossed it out into a field and we had the pleasure of watching it rot. So now we move the stock to the west end and say we have none. It saves us a lot on rent since we pay by the head if livestock. No one's usually out here. We apologize again for the intrusion."

Gunny shook her head of black curls. "I am the intruder. I'll expect to see you again next year."

"Aye, no doubt you will—if you're still here."

"Oh," Gunny said as Donal turned to leave. "A few of the cows had to be milked. Would you like the butter?"

"I didn't know any of them were still producing," Donal said. "They must have been quite uncomfortable. You did them and us a favor. You're welcome to the butter."

In November, the ground was hard with frost when Gunny spotted Donal McCrohan and several other men from the village out in their boats near the mouth of the cove. The water around them was black and choppy with fish.

"What's the frenzy about?" she yelled across the cove.

"Pollock," Donal called out, holding up an enormous fish. "Come to the village. We'll have a feast tonight."

Gunny considered the invitation, but did not go to the village.

The weather that winter was unsettled. Some days the wind blew so hard from the north that Gunny could barely leave the house. Other days were still and dry but even on the nicest days, the sun was only out for a short time, the light was weak, and the air cold and gloomy. When the fog rolled in, she walked only to the spring and back for fear of losing her way. She thought the fog worse than the cold snaps or torrential rains. Fog made her feel like she was lost on a ship at sea, mired in low banks of black clouds with no chance of ever reaching shore. Foggy days often led to sleepless nights when she was back riding Nella, then lying helpless at the church gates.

She twisted piles of rope that winter, wove a large fishing net, played her tin whistle, and ate potato pancakes washed down with sparing amounts of whiskey mixed with hot water that warmed her hands as well as her insides. She had plenty of food stashed in her cellar, but ate little. Trapped in the house, she got to know her three chickens on an individual basis. She told them every old story she could think of. They squawked at the most inappropriate times but she was thankful for the company and the eggs, and let them roost in and around her at night on the small drop-down bed.

When she thought it was near Christmas, she ventured up into the windy hills, collected dried grasses and green laurel leaves, then wove them into intricate wreaths to hang on her walls, inside and out. She twisted a loose garland of grass and greens to place around the fire and carved a small village out of a large turnip. She had no candles but set the turnip in the window for old time's sake. She burned the largest driftwood log she had and sang Christmas hymns in front of the fire, sipping at the last of Mac's whiskey until she finally nodded off to sleep in the tipping chair.

One winter day blurred into the next. All were a mix of fog, cold, and damp wind, with periodic bouts of chilly, pouring rain. Gunny stayed inside when she could and skirted around outside when she had to.

~ Chapter 15: Patrick, a Poet, and a Pig ~

When spring arrived with clearing skies and a warmer sun, Gunny could not keep herself inside. She propped the door open, shoed the chickens out into the yard, and cleaned the house of winter dust, feathers, and old smells. She eyed the small curragh in the yard and thought about rowing to Dunquin. It had been a long, lonely winter and she craved company. Wouldn't Mac be surprised to see her? But the seas in the cove were rough with white caps. She sighed and decided to stay put until the ocean calmed—but she dreamed of having a conversation with someone other than a clucking chicken.

As the days lengthened, she carted sand, seaweed, and the contents of her dung pile to the fields and turned the soil for a fresh planting. She sorted out her seeds and seed potatoes; planted oats, potatoes, and a new kitchen garden; and mended her fences. When the fields were planted, she cut turf from the bog with the sharp new turf blade, praising Mac for his excellent smithy skills.

She was intent on her work mending the kitchen garden rabbit fence when she spied a man walking along the high purple cliffs to the east of her house. She rocked back onto her haunches and dusted dirt off her hands onto her apron.

The man waved as he approached her house. He was tall and thin with rounded shoulders, and wore loose pants and a thin black jacket. He wore a dusty black derby on a head of thick, black hair. "Hello, Miss! Good day to you," he piped in a high-pitched voice.

Gunny wiped her right hand again on her apron and held it out to the stranger. He took her hand in a gentle grip. His fingers were long and thin, his fingernails clean, his hand so soft she knew it had hardly known a day of work. His eyes were brown and deep set under bushy black eyebrows. He had dark circles under his eyes. He studied Gunny's face intently before releasing her hand.

"The name's Owen Dooly. I don't believe we've met."

Gunny grinned. "I'm certain we have not met. My name's Gunny Malone. I'm not from the Blaskets."

"Nor am I," said Owen Dooly. "I married into the island. And you?"

"I've been living here for about a year. I am from Dunquin," she said feeling no need to elaborate.

"A fine village, Dunquin," he said. "I'm from Dingle myself."

"I used to work in Dingle," Gunny said. "For the Murphy's."

"I know them well," Owen said.

"Good," Gunny said. She was out of practice chatting and found she had nothing else to say to the stranger. She squatted again by the rabbit fence and took up a long blade of soaked grass. She wove the grass through a freshly chewed hole.

"You don't mind if I watch, do you?" the man asked. "I am writing a poem about a hard-working lass and I may be inspired by your actions."

"You're a writer?" she asked, glancing up from her work.

"I'm a poet," he corrected her. "Everyone on the island knows my work. You might have heard my poem, The Black-Faced Lamb? It's one of my best."

"I'm sorry. I don't know it," Gunny said.

Owen Dooly closed his eyes and cleared his throat. He swayed slightly as he recited the first stanza of his epic poem. Gunny thought it was quite good and was about to make a comment when he started in on a second stanza. She held her tongue and listened as the poet dramatically recited a third, fourth, and fifth stanza. As he started on a sixth stanza, Gunny cleared her throat to get his attention. He opened his eyes and looked at her but continued reciting. He ended the seventh stanza with a large flourish of his hands. Gunny held her breath waiting to see if there was more, then applauded with relief when the poet remained silent.

"That was wonderful," she said. "Very nicely written and spoken."

"As I mentioned, the eighth stanza will be about a working girl. Perhaps you'd like to hear it when I am finished?"

"Of course," she said. "When you're finished. I should work now if that is what you're going to write about."

"Yes, yes, I didn't mean to keep you from your work," he apologized, seeing that his words had not halted her weaving for even a moment. "I'll sit out of your way. Pay no attention to me."

The poet settled in on a bench in the yard that Gunny had built over the winter. He took out a small notebook and pencil from his jacket pocket. After a few minutes, he set the pencil and notebook on the bench and closed his eyes. Gunny watched him as he slept, jaw hanging slack. She finished the fence repairs and chucked the bucket of water and grass over the front wall. As she passed the poet on the way to the spring for fresh water, his eyes popped open.

"Would you like to hear another poem?" he asked hopefully.

Gunny hesitated. "I'm headed off to fetch some water. Perhaps another time," she said with a smile.

The poet stood and dusted off the back of his pants. "I'll walk with you. You'll like this poem. It's about the villagers here on the Great Island."

"I haven't met many villagers," she said glancing down at her bare feet.

"You'll know them by the time I finish this poem," he said. "Come along, Gunny. We will walk together."

By the time the poet said good-bye it was late afternoon. Gunny waved at his departing back, then ran to her house and closed the door and looped the latch closed. As lonely as she'd been, she looked forward to an evening of silence. She'd never heard so many stories and so much gossip in such a short period of time.

Owen appeared at her door every week or so throughout the summer. He seemed to sense when she had work to do and never acknowledged that he was taking up her time. He always showed up with a short wave and a "Hello, Miss!" and launched immediately into a review of his latest writing. If he had nothing new to recite, he regaled her once again with the Poem of the Villagers of the Great Blasket island, or all of the stanzas of the Black-Faced Lamb, which now included an eighth stanza about a woman weaving, weaving, weaving.

Gunny tried to appear even busier than she was when she saw Owen Dooly approaching from the east, though her work never seemed to deter him. Her only guaranteed escape was to be out on the water when he arrived and she became quite good at getting the small curragh up off the beach and out into the breakers by the time he neared her house. If he caught her on the land, he would shake her hand and hold on to tether her, then reel her in to sit on the sand and listen to his gentle words. Occasionally she thought about protesting, but remembered some of the less than gentle words in the Villagers poem and held her tongue for fear of creating a new stanza about the rude fisherwoman who lived on the west end.

When she did make it safely out to sea, Owen would yell out across the water, "I thought we'd have some conversation today."

Gunny would wave and shrug. "I have fish to catch. Perhaps another time."

The poet's visits forced Gunny to spend more time on the water. She soon mastered the feel of the oars but was careful to never go far past the mouth of the cove for fear of being caught in rougher seas. In early July, she saw the poet hiking up along the cliffs and launched the curragh for an unplanned day of fishing. She gave Owen a wave as he walked out on to the strand, and rowed out to the edge of the cove. She tossed out her fishing net, and leaned back to enjoy a quiet day under deep blue skies.

After an hour or so bobbing about and occasionally rowing to keep the boat in the deepest part of the cove, she was startled by a sharp gust of wind that tipped the boat sharply to one side. She shifted her weight to right the boat and looked out along the horizon. Thick clouds were building, tall and black. She started to pull in a heavy net of fish when the wind picked up in earnest. The air cooled and darkened. A jagged bolt of lightning struck Inish Na Bro to her left with a boom of thunder immediately behind it. The skies opened and rain fell down in driving sheets. She knew she was not far out in the cove, but with the wind, rain, and increasing waves, could not decide which direction to row home. The net full of fish weighed down the back of the boat. She pulled out the black-handled knife and cut the net free of the boat. She pushed her wet hair away from her face and pulled slowly at the oars not heading in any particular direction but feeling the need to take some action. As the boat filled with rainwater, she decided it was time to have a serious talk with God.

"Lord above," she intoned through the drum of the rain and backdrop of thunder, "I have sinned but would prefer to not die today in this cold ocean. You know I'm not much of one to strike a bargain," she shouted between pulls of the oars. "But I would appreciate it if there were slightly less wind. Or less rain. I don't think I'm asking for much and could really use a wee bit of help here."

The gale continued to rage about her with no sign of settling, then ended as quickly as it started. She watched, drenched to the skin, as the black clouds raced east along the shore. She wiped the rain from her face with the back of a soggy sleeve and said a quick "Thank you" to the heavens—then added a coda to her prayer—that she had not meant to set her storm loose on some other unsuspecting soul. She peered into the deep water after her lost net. She supposed a net was a small price to pay for being saved, though weaving a new net would no doubt mean more time with the poet. She sighed. There was always a price to be paid for God's good graces.

As Gunny collected seaweed along the shore that summer, she examined each stalk looking for differences. She remembered her mother saying that her grandmother in Ventry had collected seaweed for food and medicine during hard times. Gunny had no idea if the seaweed growing near the strand had medicinal uses but from early spring to early summer, there was plenty around to test and most of it was quite tasty, if a bit chewy.

Back at her house, she sorted the plants by color and size, and dried the weed in batches—in the sun when the days were hot and in front of the fire when the days were rainy or foggy. She found that most of the salty strips added excellent flavor to boiled potatoes, and that one kind in particular helped soothe the start of a sore throat when she ground it and added it to boiled water. She eyed the fields of grasses, roots, and flowers and decided to collect, sort, and test the rest of her wild environment starting first with plants and roots she had learned about from William.

By midsummer, Mac had still not been over to the island to see her, and she decided it was time for a visit home. It made her heart race to think about seeing Dunquin—and Catherine. Her little girl would be two now—walking and talking. She decided to make a St. Bridgit's cross for her and made several small, elaborate crosses which she laid out along the front, stone wall. As she examined her work trying to decide which cross was the best, it occurred to her that a child of two might eat straw and would certainly destroy a delicate cross. She brushed the straw work from the wall and picked up an old root she'd found in the bog. The ancient knot looked a little like a horse. She walked to the strand and sat on her favorite rock, whistled hello to the brown seal, and took out the black-handled knife. She started to carve a face on the horse when the knife slipped and stabbed a small hole in her left thumb.

"Damn!" she yelled tossing the wooden horse to the sand. The cut on her thumb was small but painful. She put her finger in her mouth to stop the bleeding, then untied her apron and wrapped the tie of the apron around the cut. She picked up the root again. The blood from her finger had stained the horse's face. She thought she heard Nella whinny, and sliced away most of the stain to finish her work.

The next day dawned clear and wind-free and Gunny took that as a sign that it was time to travel. She tucked the small horse in her apron pocket along with the black-handled knife and heart nail, then wrapped a loaf of fresh bread in a flour sack and smoored the fire. She tossed some grain to the chickens and left the door to the house open a crack so they could come and go if the weather turned bad. She hauled the curragh to the shore in the dawning light, packed the loaf of bread under the seat, and rowed out to sea. She waved to the brown seal who barked at her as she departed.

"Guard the house!"

The seal leaned toward her and hissed.

"I love you too, Brown Seal," she yelled. "I'll be back tomorrow."

The row to Dunquin was easy on a calm sea, even with a sore thumb. Gunny's arms and legs were strong from days of hauling, planting, cutting turf, and rowing. She rounded the gob and rowed past the strand. Young boys from the Blasket village were wading near the shore. They waved to her and she raised an oar to wave back. An hour later, she pulled the curragh out of the water at the Dunquin pier and stashed the boat and oars in an open spot on the nearby rack. She placed two large rocks on the boat, tossed the bag with the loaf of bread over her shoulder, and headed up the familiar steep road toward home. It was early and the village was quiet as she passed O'Leary's pub. A few women were out in their yards feeding hens and hanging laundry across low stone fences. Gunny slipped past unnoticed. The look and smell of Dunquin took her back in time two years. She'd been running away then but was returning now as a farmer and a fisherwoman with a place of her own.

When she got to her house she wasn't sure if she should knock or walk in. She stood for a moment outside the door. As she was about to knock, the door opened and her mother stepped back with a start.

"Gunny!" she whispered, her face pale. "Why must you startle me like that?" She stepped outside and pulled the door softly closed behind her. "I wasn't expecting you."

"I don't suppose you were." Gunny said. Eileen turned sideways and they had an awkward half hug.

"I made you some bread," Gunny said pulling the bread from the flour sack with a flourish and holding it out as a peace offering.

Eileen looked suspiciously at the fresh loaf. "You made bread?"

"I did."

Eileen reluctantly took the loaf and stared at her daughter. "Why're you here?"

"It's nice to see you too, Mam," Gunny said. "I came to see you and Da. And Catherine."

"Catherine's not awake," Eileen said abruptly.

"That's okay. I'll just take a peek at her." Gunny moved to unlatch the door and Eileen placed her hand over Gunny's hand.

"The child needs her sleep."

Gunny looked at her mother and grinned. "I'm not as loud as I used to be," she said in a low voice, then lifted the handle, opened the door a crack, and looked inside. Through the light of the doorway, she could see the large cradle in front of the fire. She turned to her mother. "She's still sleeping in that cradle? She must be all folded up in there."

Eileen peeked around Gunny. "She likes the coziness."

Gunny tiptoed inside with Eileen trailing close behind. Catherine was small but filled nearly every inch of the wooden cradle. She was sleeping on her back with her mouth open, her head rolled slightly to one side. A mass of blond curls formed a soft halo around a delicate, porcelain face. Her cheeks were rosy from sleeping so near the fire.

"Isn't it too warm to have a hot fire going?" Gunny whispered as she pulled the blanket up off the sleeping child.

Eileen stepped around Gunny and tucked the blanket back in. "You left because you didn't know how to raise a child," she whispered harshly. "Don't pretend you know better now. Catherine's thriving in my care." Eileen paused to touch Catherine's downy head of hair. "I hope you haven't come back with some silly notion of taking her."

"No, Mam," Gunny whispered. "I can see you're doing a wonderful job."

"As far as the neighbors and the priest are concerned, Catherine is my child."

"I didn't come here to take her. I promise. I only came to visit," Gunny whispered loudly.

"Are you sure?"

"Yes," Gunny said, her voice a little louder.

Both women turned toward the cradle at the sound of a small whimper. Gunny stepped forward to pick up her child but her warm smile was met with a shriek. She still moved to pick Catherine up but the terrified girl screeched for her mother. Gunny reluctantly handed the wiggling, crying child to Eileen.

"Why does she always do that around me?" Gunny asked, shaking her head.

Eileen gently patted Catherine on the back and swayed from side to side to quiet her. With her free arm, she set a pan of milk near the fire to warm for Catherine's morning meal. When Catherine stopped sniffling, she craned her neck around her mother's shoulder to peek at the tall stranger.

"You gave us quite a scare the night you left," Eileen said, her back to Gunny. "Your father went as far as Brandon Mountain looking for you. His heart nearly gave out. Two pilgrims had to help him home. He was in bed for weeks, barely able to catch his breath." She turned, still holding the child, and handed Gunny three bowls.

"I'm sorry," Gunny said running a finger along the edges of the heavy, chipped bowls. "Mac said he told you where I was."

"By the time he told us your father had already gone off find you." There was an awkward silence before Eileen continued. "So who're you living with on the Blaskets?"

"I'm not living with anyone. I live by myself out on the far west end of the island. Mac said he told you."

"Mac told us you were on the Blaskets. I assumed a family took you in. Go stir the potatoes and see if they're soft," Eileen said handing Gunny three spoons to put on the table.

"Catherine doesn't know you," Eileen said, gently swaying and patting Catherine's curly blond hair. "I hardly know you myself. Your limp is better, and you look… pretty."

Gunny laughed, juggling the bowls and spoons while she stirred the potatoes. "How shocking, Mam. I look pretty?"

"What I meant to say is that you appear to be taking better care of yourself."

"I'm as happy as I've ever been," Gunny said. "I've fixed up a wonderful house and planted…"

"Your father's due back any time from Ventry," Eileen interrupted. "And I have to get a morning meal ready for the baby."

"I'm trying to help," Gunny said sharply, still clutching the bowls and spoons. "Where's the table?"

"Oh, we raised your old drop-down bed higher on the wall and use it now as a table," Eileen said pointing to the far wall of the house. "Catherine needed more space to play in front of the fire so we burned the old table. The cups are over on the cupboard," Eileen said gesturing with one elbow.

"I know where the cups are, Mam. The table is the only thing that's new in this house." She struggled to balance the bowls and spoons while pulling down the table and kicking out the support legs. "On the island, I have potatoes coming up and a fine kitchen garden…" she started again, but could see that her mother was not listening.

There was a soft knock at the door and a muffled "Hello" from outside.

Eileen smiled and leaned toward Gunny. "That's probably Father Jessey."

Gunny's face fell as she set the bowls and spoons on the table with a clatter. "How could he know I'm here?"

Eileen shook her head and smiled. "He's not here to see you. He comes around as regular as the sunrise to visit with Catherine. He says he's trying to spend more time with all of the children in the village. He wants to get to know them before they become teenagers. He told me last week that he may soon be made Monsignor. The church is finally paying attention to him. It all started with those gates he had the vision to build. Go let him in. Perhaps he'll share our morning meal with us."

Gunny pulled the door open, her tall shape filling the small doorway. Father Jessey took a step back.

"Gunny!" he said holding a hand to his chest. "You're back."

"As always, Father, you make me feel welcome—and in my own home. Perhaps you'd prefer to have this time alone with my mother and the baby?" she said indicating that he come inside.

The priest scurried past her. When Catherine saw the tall priest, she pulled away from Eileen and reached toward him. He swept her into his arms and held her up, giggling, over his head.

"I'll be back," Gunny said stepping out the door.

"But you just got here," Eileen said, feigning sweetness.

"I need air," Gunny said. She stepped into the yard and pulled the door closed behind her. She leaned against the front wall of the house then sprinted down through the fields toward the forge.

Mac was pounding out a horseshoe at the anvil. Gunny stood in the doorway and watched him work. It was as if no time had passed since she the last time she saw him working in the forge. He gave a start when he turned and saw her standing in the doorway.

"Gunny," he gasped, his hammer halted mid-swing. "What're you doing here?"

"Why does everyone keep asking me that?" Gunny gasped.

Mac tossed the hammer to the floor and wiped his hands on his leather apron. "I beg your pardon," he said. "Welcome home."

"I'm not home," she snapped. "I'm here for a visit. I wanted to see Catherine for her birthday."

"Too bad. I was hoping you'd had enough of island life and were home for good."

Gunny sat heavily on a stool and shook her head. "Home for good… You can forget that. Why haven't you been over to see me?" she asked looking up at him. "I was worried about you."

"You were worried about me? That's a switch. I'm sorry I haven't been over. I've been busy." He picked up the hammer and softly beat the head against the palm of his hand.

"And?" Gunny asked.

Mac looked Gunny in the eye then looked away. "And I didn't think it would be appropriate for me to visit," he added softly.

"Not appropriate?" she scoffed. "You've been over plenty of times."

"Gunny," he said, "I got married at Shrove. I'm sorry. I should have come over to tell you."

"You got married?" Gunny repeated with a forced smile. "That's a surprise. But I'm happy for you."

"Are you?"

"Not really," she said scuffing the heel of one boot in the dirt floor. "I thought you weren't ever going to marry."

"I didn't plan on it," he said squatting in front of her. "But I started talking with Sheila Mitchell at a Hallow E'en gathering last October, then we started sitting together at O'Leary's."

"Sheila Mitchell? Ashling's little sister? She can't be more than seventeen."

"She'll be seventeen next October but she's a fine girl, Gunny."

"She's sixteen?" Gunny said standing up and nearly knocking Mac over. "You're twenty-two and took up with a sixteen year old?"

Mac stood. "She took up with me," he said with a grin.

"You could have said no," Gunny said, pacing the room.

"If a sixteen year old took an interest in you, would you say no?"

Gunny walked to Mac. "Of course I would," she said, placing her hands on his chest. "You know I hate children." She continued to pace. "So you married Sheila. And she's moved in here with you?"

"She and Mother have become fast friends. And I hope you don't mind, but Sheila asked if she could have the crane I made for your wedding. She loves the little curls."

Gunny swallowed hard and looked into Mac's deep-set brown eyes. "I don't care about the crane, but I thought you would always be here for me, Mac."

Mac puffed out his cheeks. "You left, Gunny. I think you know how I felt about you but I couldn't wait forever."

Gunny's eyes filled with the hot tears. "I didn't ask you to wait. I asked you to come with me, to live on the island."

"The Blaskets aren't for me and you know that," he said shaking his head. "I'm a blacksmith with responsibilities here in Dunquin. I can't run off like you. I'm not like Matt, Gunny. I never was."

"No," she said looking at the floor then up at Mac's face, tear spilling down her cheeks. "You're not."

"You're never going to forgive me for that awful day at the church, are you?"

"What's to forgive, Mac?" Gunny took a quick breath and eyed the door. "I should be going," she said, her voice breaking.

"No, stay," Mac said touching her arm. "Tell me how you're doing. How's everything in your perfect island world?"

Gunny shook Mac's fingers from her arm as if they were hot pokers. "My island world is fine, Mac. Life there is perfect. It's quiet and peaceful. In fact," she said taking a deep breath, "I'm going home now."

Mac's forehead wrinkled. "You only just arrived."

Gunny walked to the door. "Yes and my visit's done. I'll see you, Mac. I wish you and Sheila the best." She pulled the door closed behind her and ran up the hill, angry tears spilling onto dry soil.

Robert Malone was tying up a borrowed horse in the yard. He had to look twice when he saw his tall daughter racing up the hill. "Gunny!" he shouted as she ran into the yard and fell into his arms. Robert hugged her tight, then held her away from him.

"You're home and in one piece," he said grinning from ear to ear. "I have done nothing but worry about you since you left."

Gunny wiped at her face. "You shouldn't worry, Da. I'm fine."

Robert shook his head. "Mac told me as much. He said you'd fixed up an old house and were thriving running your own farm."

Gunny looked her father in the eye. "Why didn't you come over to see me?"

"Mac said you didn't want to see us. And your mother was angry about your going. I didn't want to make things worse. I knew you'd be back," he said smiling. "And here you are." He placed his hands on her shoulders and squeezed. "You look wonderful," he said shaking his head, then eying her teary eyes. "Are you all right?"

Gunny gently pulled free of her father's grip and took a deep breath. "I'm fine," she shrugged. "I'm not here to stay. I only came to visit."

Robert's face fell. "I thought..."

Gunny shook her head. "I brought you some bread. It's inside. Please tell Mam I said good-bye."

"Stay, Gunny. We've missed you. I want to hear your stories."

"It's difficult being here, Da. With Catherine and Mam, and the news about Mac's marriage..."

"Gunny," Robert insisted. "This is your home. You belong here with us."

"I don't belong anywhere, Da." She kissed her father on the cheek, grabbed the empty cloth bag from the front bench, and ran down the road toward the village.

* * *

When she got to the pier a stiff wind was blowing in from the north and a long line of whitecaps crossed the channel to the Blaskets. There were no boats in the water, no fisherman along the pier. She cursed the wind and walked to the strand and up onto the high rocks. She sat cross-legged and looked across the water, willing herself to be back on the island. By noon, the weather had not improved. She was hungry and walked up the road to O'Leary's. The pub was deserted, for which she was thankful. Micky served her a steaming bowl of lamb stew with a thick slice of oat bread, on the house as a "welcome home." She didn't bother to tell him she was leaving again. She thanked him and took her meal to a table near the window. She watched the white caps race each other across the water and felt the pub walls close in around her.

Eight fishermen bustled in, silent and in single file. Seven faces were dark and weathered by sun, sea, and salt. The eighth fisherman was young with a full head of bright red hair stuffed under a tight green woolen cap. He was as tall as a man but had a young face. Micky greeted the group as they pulled two tables together and sat. Gunny listened as they talked about the tough row in to the Dunquin pier. The men ordered drinks and food at the bar and quietly discussed crossing back to the Blaskets. Gunny looked to see if Donal McCrohan was among the men, but he was not.

Gunny picked at her stew and waited by the window, her eyes glued to the channel. When the wind and white caps looked like they had lessened, she collected her bag and headed for the door with a quick wave to Micky. The young red-head tipped back in his chair. "That's a mean wind out there. You'd best not be crossing yet."

She turned to face the group. "The wind's died back," she said, pointing. "You can see from the window. I have to get home."

"Boy's right. Best to wait," one of the older men said, slurping at a fresh glass of porter.

Gunny smiled. "It's not as windy as it was."

"The wind'll start up again soon," the man muttered, raising his glass to her.

Gunny grunted and headed out the door and down to the pier. High brushes of cloud crossed the grey blue sky. She tossed the rocks off of Matt's boat and pulled it onto her back, carried it to the end of the pier, and dropped it into the green, choppy water at the end of the pier. She stepped carefully across the center seat, sat, and slid the oars into their locks. She rested one hand on the pier and squinted out toward the island, as warm, wet air pushed loose curls across her face. "If I had a sail, I'd be across in no time," she muttered, remembering John McCrohan's frantic sail back from the island after their fateful day with the seals.

322

The young man with the red hair trotted out onto the pier. "Da said I should come and fetch you. You shouldn't leave now." When Gunny did not look up he continued at a slightly higher pitch. "You should listen to my Da. He knows this channel better than anyone."

Gunny looked up at the bold teen from her boat. "I'm sorry. Do I know you?"

The boy grinned. "The name's Patrick O'Connor," he said, lowering his voice. "We saw you rowing over this morning when we headed out to fish. You live on the west end, right?"

"I do. That's where I'm headed now."

Patrick frowned. "You shouldn't be so stubborn, Miss. If you get in trouble you'll need a man to come save you and where will we be? Drinking the afternoon away at O'Leary's Pub."

Gunny snorted. "I may need a man, but I don't need a boy telling me what to do," she said. She pushed away from the pier with an oar and started the long row home.

Partway out into the channel, the wind shifted from north to south and picked up in intensity. Gunny continued to row west, but felt her small boat being pushed up the channel, away from the island and out toward the open ocean. She felt more resistance with each row. She stopped, exhausted, and looked back toward the Dunquin pier. Patrick O'Connor was still standing on the pier, which seemed only a few stones throw away.

"Blasted wind!" she yelled, then noticed water starting to pool under her boots. If she could get home in the next hour, she was sure the boat would not fill. She pulled again at the oars, singing to herself to keep her rowing even. After an hour of rowing, her arms and neck ached, her palms were blistered, the cut on her thumb was throbbing, and the water in the bottom of the boat was up to her ankles. She turned and looked out toward the islands. She was still only about halfway across the channel. She closed her eyes and rowed harder, singing now through gritted teeth. She paused as male voices joined her for the chorus of her song. She stopped rowing and opened her eyes. A large, eight-man curragh was nearing her small vessel. At the front of the boat sat Patrick O'Connor, grinning at her and waving.

"I don't believe you told me your name," he said into the wind.

"Gunny Malone," she shouted, feeling her heartbeat strong in her chest.

"If you'll take in those oars, Miss Malone, we'll pull in close and I'll toss you a line," he said, the pitch of his voice rising and falling with the wind.

Gunny pulled the oars into her boat and watched as the larger boat approached, a sacred medal and bottle of holy water tied to the bow.

Patrick raised his green hat with one hand as the large boat pulled up next to her. He eyed the water in the bottom of the boat. "I see your boat's settling down a bit, Miss."

"I'm not so good at settling down. I'd be much obliged if you were to give me a tow," she said, trying to contain her joy at being rescued.

Patrick tossed her a line. She secured it to the bow of her boat, and the men pulled in unison toward the island. Even with eight men rowing, the large curragh struggled against the strong southern winds, but within the hour, the two crafts neared the landing on the Great Blasket with no hands overboard.

The landing place on the Great Blasket was a small, natural cove on the north east corner of the island, partly sheltered by a series of large, offshore rocks. Gunny felt strong currents pull at her boat as the two crafts rounded the barrier rocks and moved in toward the cove.

"The slip only fits one boat at a time," Patrick yelled. "Once we get our boat in, you can pull in after us."

Gunny untied her boat from the Blasket boat and watched as the eight fishermen expertly maneuvered their large curragh toward a low stone ledge, then sprang in unison from the boat onto the long, flat rock. Their curragh sank away from them for an instant as it rode down the wave. When the water swelled again, the men grabbed at the ropes and pulled the boat onto the stone pier where they proceeded to unload several full nets of herring.

"You're next," Patrick yelled from the ledge as two of the men pulled their empty curragh up over their heads and stashed it on a rack built into the path on the way up the cliff to the village. "Row up here, wait until the ocean swells, then jump."

Gunny maneuvered her floundering boat as best she could toward the large, flat rock. Two of the fishermen stopped picking fish from the net to watch her. Gunny tried to ignore their grins as she rowed in parallel to the rock. She tucked in the oars and tossed the aft rope to Patrick, then crouched and waited for the boat to rise. It rose and fell with Gunny still crouching in a pool of water at the bottom of the boat.

"You'll have to move in again," Patrick shouted as her boat drifted off at an awkward angle. "Don't hesitate to jump once you're in the right spot."

Gunny unlocked her oars, moved her boat in again toward the flat rock, and tossed the tow line to Patrick. She gathered her soaked skirts in her right arm and this time when the tide rose, she leapt. She landed with a grunt on her stomach and looked behind her as her boat disappeared. Patrick held tight on the rope and offered her a hand up, but she pulled herself farther up on the rocky shelf, her right elbow burning from a scrape. She lay panting as Patrick pulled her small boat out of the churning sea, water pouring out the back of the small vessel.

She stood and pulled her wet skirt and petticoats away from her legs just as a large dog bounded past her, nearly knocking her off the rock and into the water. Patrick caught Gunny by the arm to steady her.

"Glad to see me girl?" he said, tousling the dog's head. The dog was completely black with silky fringed hair, long legs and a thin snout. Gunny pulled her arm away from Patrick and clucked for the dog to come to her. The dog backed up behind Patrick, tail between her legs, and looked away.

"Don't mind the dog," Patrick said. "This is Lorcan, the little wild one. She may warm up to you—eventually."

Gunny shook her head. "This is the best place you have for a landing spot?" she asked, wringing out her wet skirts.

"Oh, it's a fine spot once you get the hang of it," Patrick said with a smile. "Just make certain you arrive at high-tide. At low tide, the jump is nearly impossible."

"Why don't you land on the strand? It looks like there's plenty of room there."

"More room, but the current's too strong, especially in the winter. Any boat trying to land on that beach would get swept into shore and crushed."

Patrick worked with Gunny to tip the rest of the water out of her boat. By the time they finished, the older men had hauled the fish away up the steep, rocky path. Patrick easily slung Gunny's small boat onto his back and stashed it with the oars in the rack in the cliff, then expertly lashed the boat to the stays and weighted the boat with stones.

Gunny looked up the steep path and was surprised to see several faces looking down at her from the top of the cliff.

"Don't pay any attention to them," Patrick said in a low voice. "The women gather there any time we're out to sea. They want to be the first to know that we've made it home. No doubt they're up there now talking about who we brought with us this afternoon."

"Every village has their gossips," Gunny said.

Patrick smiled. "Careful, my mother's usually part of the group."

Patrick walked behind Gunny up the winding path to the village with Lorcan close at his heels. Gunny paused at the top of the steep climb to catch her breath and looked back down at the blue-green water in the small harbor. She took a deep breath of fresh salt air and pushed a few curls of wind-blown hair from her face.

Patrick studied her. "I suppose you're the witch that's living on the west end of the island?"

Gunny glanced at Patrick and shrugged.

"You don't seem to be an evil, old witch."

"Well," Gunny said eyebrows raised, "I'm not old." She eyed Patrick critically. "Or maybe I am. How old are you?"

"Thirteen," Patrick said with pride, one eyebrow raised. He was tall for thirteen, Gunny thought.

"I'll help you re-tar your boat tomorrow. Tonight you can stay at our house," the boy said with a sweep of his hat.

Gunny bit her bottom lip. The idea of spending a night in a house full of strangers wasn't appealing but she'd never patched a boat before and knew she needed help. She took a deep breath. "I'm much obliged for the rescue. I thought I could out-stubborn the wind."

"First rule of a Blasket fisherman: Respect the wind."

They crossed a narrow road and started up another steep path. The top of the second climb opened up on the little village of the Great Blasket island. A cluster of twenty or so small, stone houses sat nestled in the dell. Half the houses were painted with fresh white-wash and had tight thatched roofs. The other half appeared to be deserted. Cut deep into the hillside behind the houses lay a series of long, furrowed fields.

A short, plump woman came scurrying down from the cliff and grabbed Patrick by the arm. "I was worried when I saw you dragging along that smaller boat," she said, clutching at her son's cold arm. "What were you thinking crossing in this wind?"

"We thought we could out-stubborn the wind, Mam," Patrick said giving Gunny a wink. "Meet Gunny Malone. The owner of the wee boat we helped over."

Patrick's mother was short and plump with rosy cheeks, deep set brown eyes, and thinning brown hair. She looked at the tall young woman with the long black curls, then squeezed Gunny's arm with a rough, red hand.

"This was no weather to cross the channel, girl. Now, both of you clean up and we'll have a bite to eat. Your father and the other men are down on the strand salting the herring. What a week this was for herring, eh?" Mrs. O' Connor grinned from ear to ear. Patrick laughed as his mother hurried off toward the house.

"Mam is a worrier. If she isn't worrying about us fishing, she's worried about us not fishing."

Gunny was cold and exhausted and had no talk in her. She hoped the O'Connors would accept her as a silent stranger. They approached a small stone house along the right side of a short dirt road. The front door was painted a deep blue, and a merry curl of smoke wove its way up and out the chimney. Patrick grabbed a bucket from in front of the house and pointed up the steep hill behind the house. Gunny was hoping to sit on stool in front of a warm fire, but took a deep breath and followed Patrick up the hill. At the top, Patrick set down his bucket at the mouth of a small spring.

"This is the best spring on the island," Patrick said taking a seat on a nearby rock while the bucket filled. "The water's slow but dependable, which gives us plenty of time to catch up on the news while we're waiting."

Gunny lay back in the grass, exhausted. Lorcan stared at her from behind Patrick. She tried again to pet the dog but the dog ducked away from her outstretched hand.

"I found Lorcan as a pup last year in Dingle," Patrick explained. "She was starving. She doesn't trust anyone but me."

Gunny pushed to her feet and walked up to the crest of the hill. A sharp, chill wind slapped her in the face at the summit. She pulled her shawl tight around her when she realized she was standing next to an old gravestone.

"Is this the village graveyard?"

"No, you're standing at Castle Point. That's where we bury sailors lost at sea. Suicides. Illegitimate babies."

Gunny returned to the wind-protected rocks around the spring. "Where do you bury your friends?"

"We go home when we die. My family's church is in Ventry so I'll be buried there. If you died tomorrow, we'd take you back to Dunquin. When someone's sick, we send for a priest from Dunquin, Ballyferriter, or Ventry—depending on where the family's church is."

"If someone's sick wouldn't it better to call a doctor?"

Patrick laughed. "There's no money for that. But our burials're wonderful. The lead boat carries the body to the mainland and all the other boats follow. Then we walk with the body to wherever the grave is to be dug and drink the night away. A good funeral gets us off the island for a full day and sometimes two."

"Things are a little too quiet when one looks forward to a funeral," Gunny said with a smile.

When the water bucket was full, they hiked back down the hill. One of the older men from the O'Connor boat was waiting in the yard. Patrick poured water into a bowl on the front bench. The man eyed Gunny as he scrubbed fish gut from his hands and splashed water onto his face. He had heard there was the woman living on the west end. From her rescue today, it was clear she had no sense. When his hands were clean, he dried them on his pants and reached out a hand in greeting.

"The name is Timothy O'Connor," he said curtly. "Welcome to our home."

Timothy O'Connor's fingers were cold, stiff, and knotted from years of hard work hauling full nets of fish from the chilly ocean, but his grip was strong. He looked Gunny squarely in the eye as they shook hands. He was tall with liquid blue eyes and a black cap pulled down tight around a fringe of long, red hair. Gunny knew he was irritated with her from her rescue at sea; she would try to not cross his path again.

Inside, the house was crowded with small, red-headed boys who raced about yelling and playing, each trying to get Patrick's attention. Gunny stood awkwardly near the door. "How many brothers do you have?"

Patrick grinned and pretended to try to count the boys as they clustered about him. "I'm the oldest of six boys. And that's my sister, Martha and her husband, David," Patrick said pointing to a couple sitting on stools near the fire who looked to be about eighteen. Martha was small like her mother, with smooth brown hair, deep brown eyes and a large bump tucked under her skirt. David had a smooth round face and dusty mop of brown hair. They gave Gunny a quick wave.

"My other sister, Bridget, left the island when she was eighteen to go to America. She's been gone three years and we've had no word from her."

Mrs. O'Connor clucked in through the front door carrying a large bowl of salt herring. "Plenty of kitchen tonight. Plenty of kitchen. Oh, my!" Mrs. O' Connor stopped and looked at Gunny. "Wet feet. That'll never do—you'll be sick by morning. Take off those wet stockings and dry them by the fire."

When Gunny hesitated, Mrs. O' Connor stared at her, eyebrows raised. Gunny sat on a nearby stool and untied the tight laces of her boots and peeled off her wet stockings. Mrs. O'Connor was back in a blink with a pair of thick wool stockings.

"I'm fine with bare feet," Gunny insisted. "Really I am."

"I'll have no cold feet in my house," Mrs. O'Connor insisted, pressing the fresh stockings into Gunny's hands.

Gunny reluctantly pulled on the warm, dry socks then took a deep breath, relishing the comfort of both heat and care. She heard cackling from over the fireplace and looked up to see chickens nesting in the loft. She looked again. Mixed in with the chickens was a large, white bird.

"Is that a sea gull?"

Patrick laughed. "That's Johnny's pet gully, but don't tell her that. She thinks she's a chicken. Johnny was floating eggs last spring to find the good ones—and out popped this little bird. I told Johnny to quick snap its neck but he wouldn't do it. Next thing we knew, Johnny was raising her, feeding her minnows every hour."

One of the little boys clinging to Patrick's arm made a face and turned to Gunny. "I had to chew up those raw fish and spit them out into my hand before she'd eat 'em."

"Now Gully thinks that Johnny's her mother. She follows him everywhere."

Gunny watched as Johnny took a few steps up the ladder to the loft, pulled a fresh herring from his pocket, and tossed the fish to the gull. The bird snatched the fish mid-air and shrieked in appreciation.

"Can she fly?" she asked as the gull quieted.

Patrick shook his head. "Apparently when you think you can't fly, you can't fly. "

Johnny hopped down from his perch on the ladder and stood in front of Gunny's stool. He thrust his hands deep into his pockets and dug at the dirt floor with a bare toe that looked as if it might never have been washed.

"I got my pants this week," he said.

"How's that?" Gunny asked.

328

"Johnny turned eight this week," Patrick said. "And he is mighty proud to be in his first pair of pants."

Johnny stared at Gunny. "Have you got a penny for me to put in my pocket?"

Gunny looked into Johnny's large blue eyes, then reached into her apron pocket and fingered the small pony she had meant to give to Catherine. "Put out your hand," she said.

Johnny obediently did as he was told.

"I don't have a penny," she explained. "So I'm hoping you will settle for a pony."

She placed the small carved horse on the boy's dirt-creased palm. Johnny's mouth fell open. He had asked every villager that day for a penny and no one had given him a thing. He looked at the intricate carved pony and clutched it to his chest. He had never seen a horse before. "It's the most beautiful thing I've ever seen. I will never forget this, Miss."

"Let's eat," Mrs. O'Connor announced, and the family gathered around the crowded table to share a large plate of fish and small pot of potatoes. Gunny picked out one potato with her spoon and put it in her bowl. Mrs. O'Connor scooped a large chunk of butter from a nearby firkin and plunked it into her bowl. Gunny helped herself to several pieces of the plentiful salt herring, then listened to the chatter around her as she ate. Occasionally, she would catch the eye of one of the older boys watching her. Johnny seemed oblivious to her strangeness, and happily crawled up onto her lap as soon as he saw she was done eating.

When the meal was over and the potato peels and fish heads were added to the dung heap, Mrs. O'Connor shoed the boys outside. Gunny took a stool in front of the fire and sat in awkward silence with Patrick, Mr. O'Connor, Martha, and David. Gunny tried to think of something to say but was exhausted; her mind was blank. She turned to Mrs. O'Connor, who was cleaning off the table.

"Thank you again for sharing your home and a fine meal with me."

Mr. O'Connor glanced over at the stranger. "So you're from Dunquin. Donal McCrohan came over from Dunquin."

Gunny gave a quick nod. "Yes, I met Donal on the west end last fall. His brother, John McCrohan, was a neighbor, and was my Pa's best friend."

"The McCrohans are a fine family," Timothy O'Connor said with a shake of his head. "And what brings you to the Blaskets?"

Gunny paused. "A leaky boat?" she said smiling weakly.

Mr. O'Connor did not seem to appreciate her attempt at humor. Gunny closed her eyes. What brought her to the Blaskets? She opened her eyes and looked at Mr. O'Connor until he looked away. She blinked and picked briefly at a dirty fingernail. Then as if she were in a trance, Gunny started to talk and the room hushed.

"I grew up in Dunquin," Gunny said in a soft voice, "helping my father care for the horses in the village and for Lord Ventry's horses at Ballygoleen."

Mrs. O'Connor wiped her hands on her apron and quietly pulled up a stool to listen. It wasn't often there were new stories in the village.

"My da's one of the best horse men in Ventry," Gunny continued. "He taught me all he knew, from curing a horse's earache to helping deliver a new colt or filly. My da's also a farmer. I learned to plant from him. I'm not too good around the house, but I did learn to make butter from my mother. I left home when I was fifteen to work in Dingle, then returned to Dunquin to marry John McCrohan's oldest son, Matt."

Gunny took a deep breath then continued at a slower pace. "Matt died in a horse accident on the way to our wedding. I was hurt and couldn't walk for a long time. But I made myself walk again," Gunny said with a shake of her long, black curls. "I walked the pilgrim trails and I walked the mountains and I walked the shore until I didn't have any place left to walk. Then I got in a boat and came here to the Blaskets. So to answer your question," she said turning to Timothy O'Connor. "A boat brought me to this island—a leaky, little boat." She grinned. "Oh, and when we have more time, I'll tell you about a haunting, and a graveyard, and a baby."

She took a deep breath. Why was it she could not talk to her family but would tell her story to complete strangers?

Mrs. O'Connor leaned forward and gripped her arm. "I remember hearing about a horse accident at Shrove a few years back. I'm sorry for your loss."

Gunny shook her head. "It was a long time ago. There's no reason to be sorry. Matt's still around. When the wind blows, I feel his breath on my cheek. I feel his tears in the rain, and I hear his whistle in the songs of the birds." She looked at the shocked faces around her. "And what brought you to the island?" she asked with an awkward laugh.

"You're laughing from the teeth out," Mrs. O'Connor said with a shake of her head. "We came to the Blaskets a few years back when Lord Ventry evicted us from our farm in Ventry. Your story is a much better one."

"It'd be a better story if it was someone else's, not mine!" Gunny snorted.

"We all come to this island to escape from something," Mrs. O'Connor said, resting a hand on Gunny's arm. "Have you met Margaret Dunleavy? She lives on Inis Tuaisceart, the island furthest north of here, in an eleven-foot clochain. She's raising eight children out there."

"Oh, and tell her about Miss Gueehin," Timothy prodded.

"Catherin Gueehin's living out on Inishvickillaune, raising eagles. The Rock is the island furthest to the south, down past where you're living. It used to be the only things out on the Rock were an old monastery, a roofless oratory, and a few gravesites. But now Catherin's out there living in a stack of layered stones nestled below the wall at the center of the island."

"The Dalys used to live there," Timothy added.

"They are the sweetest couple you'll ever meet. Mary and Joseph. Isn't that funny? Their youngest girl, Marie, is a mighty fine singer. She and Patrick grew up here together in the village before Joseph got it in his head to move to the Rock. They're back now—living on the south end of the Great Island."

"Mary grew up in Ventry with Charlotte," Timothy said.

Gunny frowned. "Who's Charlotte?"

Mrs. O'Connor roared. "That's me!

"The Rock's full of dead spirits and fairies," Patrick grinned at Gunny. "You'd probably like it if you ever get tired of the west end."

"Please tell me there isn't anyone living on the islands to the west of me," Gunny said. "I've seen them hit by lightning a dozen times."

Mr. O'Connor shook his head. "No one lives on Inis na Bro or on Tearacht. There's no fresh water and nowhere to land a boat."

"It's hard to imagine anyone living in places that are more remote than the west end."

Charlotte grinned at Gunny. "The more remote the better when you can't pay your rent. The Lord's agent rarely goes to any of the lesser Blaskets. Most who come to this island were evicted and have nothing when they arrive. Oh, but how we're filling your ears. You must be exhausted. Would you like a cup of warm milk?"

"I'm tired, but I'd love some milk. I've missed milk."

"After a sip or two, perhaps you could tell us more of your story," Mr. O'Connor said.

"Listen to himself," Mrs. O'Connor said. "The girl needs sleep. She'll come back another time and tell us more. Won't you Gunny?"

Gunny smiled at Charlotte in the warm firelight. "If you'll have me then I suppose I will."

Charlotte took Gunny's hand between her own warm hands. "It's good to meet you, Gunny Malone. You and I are going to be friends."

"Do you think so?"

"I know so. You're part of our family now—like it or not."

Gunny slept soundly that night on a straw mat in front of the fire surrounded by the O'Connor children, a few brooding chickens, and one very noisy seagull. The next morning after sharing a bowl of cold potatoes and herring, Patrick walked Gunny down to the stone pier carrying a large wooden box and bucket of pitch to re-tar her boat. Lorcan sprinted ahead of them and greeted them at the pier.

"Have you met anyone else from our village?" Patrick asked as the tar heated over an open fire.

"I've met your poet, Owen Dooly. He seems to know when I have serious work to do and always chooses that very moment to stop by and chat."

Patrick laughed. "Don't cross him or he'll write a poem about you. I suppose he's recited The Black-faced Lamb?"

"I suppose he has—about a hundred times! I'm the weaver in the eighth stanza."

Patrick laughed again. "I haven't heard that one yet. Owen likes to write about us. Promise you'll only believe half of what he writes about us and we'll promise to only believe half of what he writes about you."

Patrick showed Gunny how to apply the hot tar to the covering of Matt's boat using an old rag. By midday, the tar was dry and hard and Gunny was ready to launch. Patrick slid a wooden box under the seat of Gunny's curragh. "Mam said to send that back with you."

"What is it?"

"Can't you smell it? It's salted fish."

"I can't take that," Gunny stammered. "You have so many mouths to feed at your house."

"You don't take it and Mam'll put a curse on you. We have plenty and Mam likes to share."

"Thank you," Gunny said. "This'll be wonderful kitchen for my remaining potatoes."

Patrick slid Gunny's small boat into the water and held the rope tight to keep the vessel near the stone ledge. Gunny clambered in when the boat came up on a swell, slid onto the center seat, and pinned the oars into the locks. Patrick gave her a push off the rock, and waved as she rowed out into the channel, calm and still now on a windless day.

"Thank you!" she yelled as she paddled away. Patrick stood on the pier with Lorcan at his side. He waved again, then headed home to mend his fishing nets, thinking about the strange woman who lived by herself on the west end of the Great Island.

That night, Gunny fished a salt herring from the box by the hearth and mixed it with a small bowl of boiled potatoes. The mix of chewy, salty fish and warm potatoes was delicious. She praised the O'Connor's resourcefulness and started weaving a small-holed net to catch her own herring.

A week later, Gunny was shocked to see Mac hiking down through the back fields carrying a large wiggling basket. She ran out to meet him.

"I thought you weren't coming over to see me anymore."

"I wasn't but then I got to worrying about you and I was at the Dingle fair and... well, I bought you a pig."

"You bought me a what?"

"I bought you a pig."

"I heard what you said. What I meant was,—why did you buy me a pig?"

"Da used to say that a pig is the gentleman who pays the rent. Just let this pig loose and he'll scavenge till he grows fat. At harvest, I'll come over and we'll take him to market. Then you can pay your rent."

"From what I understand, there're a lot of people here on the Blaskets who don't pay rent. I'm planning to do the same—even if I have to move to one of the smaller islands."

"Fine. Don't pay rent. You'll still have pig money for a rainy day."

Gunny listened to the high-pitched squealing in Mac's basket and grimaced. "So let's say this pig survives the rest of the summer and grows huge. How will we get a full-grown pig back to the market in Dingle in Matt's little boat?"

Mac set down the crate with a huff and brushed the back of his hand over his lips. "I hadn't thought about that. Maybe a fisherman will take us," he said, his heavy eyebrows raised.

"A fisherman's going to take us to Dingle with a full-grown pig squirming around in his canvas and tar boat? I don't think so."

"Then we'll ask someone to slaughter him out here. You're making this too complicated."

The pig squealed loudly from the crate. Mac pulled the lid open and they both peeked inside. Two small, beady eyes looked up at them from a face bristling with stiff white hairs. Mac pushed the crate over on its side. The piglet scrambled to the back of the crate to hide and was quiet.

Gunny squatted down and looked into the crate. "All that fuss to let you out, and now you're scared to come and meet us?" she asked the piggy, clicking her tongue and holding out her hand. She hesitated and pulled her hand slowly from the crate. "Pigs don't bite, do they?"

"I don't know. We never had a pig. Da only talked about a pig being the gentleman who pays the rent."

The pig made a sudden dash out of the crate. Gunny jumped out of the way as the small beast sprinted past her, then raced off and disappeared around the corner of her house. Gunny and Mac watched as his small white shape appeared again around the back side of the house before he raced down toward the shore. The pig stopped short when an incoming wave washed up against his feet. He gave a terrified squeal and turned to race along the beach until he ran directly into the sleeping brown seal. The seal barked and hissed at the small white creature as he rolled away from her in the sand. When the pig finally got his feet under him, he tore back to dry land, raced past Gunny's house, and scurried around the corner and into the old abandoned church. He re-emerged in the church doorway, out of breath, his long, black tongue hanging loosely from of his mouth.

Gunny was laughing so hard her sides hurt. "I'd better get that pig some water," she said wiping tears from her eyes. "Thanks for a wonderful gift, Mac."

"I bought him with the best of intentions," Mac muttered.

Gunny picked up the crate. It was heavy. She looked inside and saw that Mac had brought her a new large pot with a heavy lid.

"What's this?" she asked, pulling it from the basket. "I already have a pot."

"It's a pot oven," Mac said. "Nick O'Leary had one way back. Now everyone wants one. I can't make them fast enough."

"What do you do with it?" Gunny asked, pulling the low, heavy pot from the crate and taking off the large, rimmed lid.

"You bake bread in it. Mam sets the pot in the coals and puts coals on top of the lid. See how the lid is flat and has a lip around it? When the pot and the lid are hot, you put your bread dough inside. You have to move the pot around on the fire a few times to keep the heat even. Mam and Sheila swear by it for making a fine crust on a bread."

Gunny bristled at Sheila's name. "No offense, Mac, but I may use this new pot oven to feed the pig," she said. "Or it would be a fine pot to soak my stockings in before I wash them. Do you want to come in for a bite before you go?"

Mac shook his head. "I should head home."

Gunny shrugged. "Thank you for coming over. Please give my best to your mother and the girls. And to your wife."

Mac blushed. "I'm still not used to hearing that."

"I'll never get used to it," Gunny said. She walked to her house lugging the heavy pot and calling out to the little piggy.

The pig made himself at home in a burrow of straw in the old church. He rooted in the nearby fields for roots and grubs by day, and slept at the church at night. He ignored the bowl of water Gunny set out for him, choosing instead to drink directly from the spring. On hot days, which there were plenty of in August, Gunny liked to watch him splash around in the surf, then roll in the sand to dry himself. Whenever the brown seal was sunning on the beach, the pig would charge at her squealing until she dove into the ocean to get away from the latest nuisance. Then the pig would trot up and down the beach as if he were the proud owner of the entire island.

The pig tried to intimidate the wild ewe as well. Whenever he spied her in a nearby field, he did his best to chase her away, but she ignored him. One day, Gunny spied the two of them sharing a drink together at the spring. By the last days of summer, the old ewe had made a nest of loose straw in the church and joined the pig there every night. It seemed the ewe had finally made a friend.

On the days Gunny worked in the fields, the pig followed her out in the morning and back in at night. He was excellent at discovering mushrooms and sometimes even shared his find with her. As he got bigger, he started rooting around in the potato and oat fields. Gunny went after him with the end of her turf spade and he seemed to understand that the fields were off limits as was her kitchen garden. He was generally a neat little pig. He chose one spot in the fields for his toilet and never varied from his routine. Since he was eating all of her potato peels and table scraps, she was glad to have a growing pile of pig manure for planting the next spring.

The poet was fascinated by the new animal. "That pig follows you around like a dog. What do you call him?"

"He's a pig. I don't call him anything."

"Well, he must have a name," the poet said. He stared hard at the white pig and the pig stared back. "I believe his name is… Gallarus."

The pig looked up at the poet when he heard the name, blinked his small black eyes, and grunted.

"You see? The pig agrees. I shall write of the mighty pig, Gallarus, who lived far, far on the west end of the Great Blasket island with…" The poet hesitated.

"Go on," Gunny said. "I'd love to hear how you describe me in the poems you don't recite to me."

"With… the mystic farmer who lives on the west end."

"Patrick O'Connor asked if I was a witch. Is there perhaps a poem about the mystic witch who lives on the west end?"

The poet pursed his lips and looked up to the sky.

Gunny laughed. "You can call me a farmer or a witch. It doesn't matter. I have work to do." She called out to the pig and they walked off together to weed the high fields leaving the poet behind, scribbling down notes for his latest verse about the mischievous and stubborn pig, Gallarus.

~ Chapter 16: A Calling ~

By late September, Gunny had harvested her oats and most of her potatoes and knew she would survive another winter. She was setting out a small lamp she'd made from a scallop shell and putting on water for tea when she was startled by a heavy knock at her door. She unlooped the rope latch and peeked outside. Patrick O'Connor was in the yard, shifting from foot to foot, hat in hand. His face glowed pale in the low light from her fire. Lorcan paced just behind the boy in the yard.

"Patrick. What a surprise. Come in," she said pulling the door open with one hand and twisting her hair up into a quick bun at the back of her neck with the other.

"Martha's in trouble. Mam sent me to get you," Patrick said without coming inside.

Gunny stared at the boy, confused.

"Mam's hoping you know something about babies. Hurry, please. Martha doesn't look so good."

"Patrick, I'd help if I could, but I don't know anything about babies."

"So you're not a witch?"

"No, I'm not a witch despite what the poet says. I don't know any magic spells that'll help your sister."

"But the night you stayed at our house you said you worked with horses."

"With horses, yes, when I was younger. But your sister's not a horse and I assume she's not having a horse?"

"No," Patrick stammered. "It's just that our old midwife was a horse woman, so Mam thought... Mrs. Peters moved to Ventry and we don't have anyone to help now. We should hurry. Mam said to be quick."

Gunny shook her head. "I'm sorry, Patrick. I can't help you." She could see the worry and fear in Patrick's large blue eyes. "But I suppose I could go just to be with your mother."

"Yes, yes," Patrick said grabbing hold of Gunny's arm. "It would help if Mam wasn't the only woman in the house."

Gunny squeezed his hand. "Come in. Let me collect a few things."

She looked around her snug house. When she'd had Catherine, her mother had hot water to wash up with and plenty of blankets. The O'Connors would have those. She felt in her apron pocket for the black-handled knife. She'd need that to cut the cord. She grabbed a small bag and filled it with tea leaves, then took another bag and put in some roots she'd collected that William said helped with sleep. She piled ashes over the fire in the hearth, grabbed the iron heart off the mantel, and pulled on her shawl.

The sun was setting and the sky was a mix of orange and purple as she and Patrick headed off for the village. Patrick nearly sprinted ahead of her along the cliff path with Lorcan tight at his heels. She had only gone to the village before through the high fields; Patrick insisted that the cliff path was faster—if you knew the way. Gunny did her best to keep up with the boy. Forty-five minutes later, they burst through the door at the O'Connor house, and nine hours later, Gunny helped deliver her first island baby—thankfully with no complications.

Gunny finished cleaning up and sat on a stool in the back room near Martha and the baby as weak morning light tipped in through the front windows. Martha had been strong through the night, but finally drank a weak broth of tea and roots, and dozed off with her new baby boy tucked safely by her side. Gunny finished one last swallow of her own weak tea and slipped the clean black-handled knife into her apron pocket. She walked quietly out to the front fire and rested a hand on Charlotte's back as she stirred the fire and added a new brick of turf.

"I'll be off now."

Charlotte shifted to her knees and clutched Gunny's hand to her chest. "I thank God you were here to help us."

Gunny grinned. "Martha did all of the work."

Charlotte O'Connor stood and wiped her hands on her apron. "You worked hard as well. You knew when to listen and when to push. You are steady in a storm, Gunny. I knew you would be. You were exactly the help we needed."

Mr. O' Connor slipped in through the front door and tipped his hat to the ladies. He had spent the night in the byre with the boys and looked like he'd hardly slept. He walked to the back room, rested a gentle hand on his daughter's sleeping head, and touched the baby's downy soft cheek with one rough knuckle. He walked to the fire and stood in front of Gunny.

"How do we pay you for this?" he asked in a quiet voice.

Gunny chuckled. "You paid me the day you and your son kept me from the cold floor of the ocean."

"I'll wake Patrick. He'll walk you home."

Gunny fingered the iron heart in her pocket. It radiated heat from being in her pocket all night. "I'll be fine on my own, sir. I find that walking's the perfect way to clear my head after a long night."

"I agree," he said, his voice breaking slightly. "Don't be a stranger, Gunny. We'll expect to see you back here soon."

"Yes, sir," she said with a smile. "I'll be back."

She stepped outside and leaned against the rough stone wall of the house. The sun was rising across the channel behind Mount Eagle. The air on the island felt crisp and still. A small brown bird flew down and lit on the stone wall in front of her, picked up a seed, and flew off. Gunny pulled her shawl tight around her shoulders, pushed her hair away from her face and headed off along the dirt path toward the south end of the village. As she neared the cutoff up the steep hill toward the cliffs, she saw a familiar face approaching her on the road. There was nowhere to hide.

"Father Jessey," she said briskly, looking up the hill and trying her best to show the priest she had no desire to talk. The tall priest grabbed her arm as she passed.

"Gunny."

Gunny stopped and looked him in the eye. He looked down and let go of her arm. His dusty blond hair was thinning and fine lines ringed his blue eyes.

"I'm surprised to see you here, Father. I didn't know you visited the Blaskets. Well, good morning," she said starting up the steep hill.

"I come over at harvest to collect for the church," the priest said behind her. "I stayed on the south end last night with the Dalys. You ran away from Dunquin last time before we could talk."

Gunny stopped and turned to face him. "Mam said you were leaving Dunquin, that the church was making you a monsignor."

"The promotion fell through," Father Jessey said through tight lips.

"Well then, you'll have more time to spend educating the children of Dunquin—and you'll have more time with Catherine."

The priest stiffened at the girl's name. "I do not understand how you could leave your baby like that."

"Excuse me, Father. Catherine's not my baby."

"Lying is a sin, Gunny."

Gunny brushed off her sleeve where the priest had touched her. "I'm not lying. Consult the birth records. They very clearly state that her parents are Eileen and Robert Malone. I don't even exist as far as that child is concerned," she said with a short curtsy. "Good day."

Father Jessey took a step toward her and grabbed her by the sleeve. "Gunny."

Gunny pulled her arm away and sprinted up the steep hill toward home.

"Gunny Malone," Father Jessey yelled behind her, but she did not turn, did not answer. "I told you to come and see me at the church. I told you we would talk then," he yelled at her retreating form.

She stopped out of breath, and turned. "You'll see me in hell before you'll see me in your damned church." She crested the hill and ran the rest of the way home.

Gunny welcomed the pig's company as the days shortened and nights lengthened. With less work to do and more time to think, the loneliness of life without Matt, or Mac, or any family around weighed on her. She chatted with Gallarus as she collected water in the morning, skinned a freshly caught rabbit, or chopped vegetables for a stew. The pig stayed aloof of her, but was always nearby in case there was a walk into the fields or a bit of food to be retrieved from the floor.

On a late October morning, Gunny woke early after a chilly, restless night and sat by the fire drinking a cup of hot whiskey and water on a small stool she'd made from a coil of thick rope. She was deeply lost in no particular thought when the door of her small cottage swung open with a low creak. She looked up and was startled to see Gallarus's nose in the doorway.

"Go away," she snorted. "I haven't put the potatoes on yet for a morning meal."

Gallarus pushed the door open the rest of the way and trotted into the small room. A chicken squawked past him with a flurry of wings and loose feathers but the pig continued in, undisturbed. Gunny sat quietly as the beast sniffed around the boxes of food she had stored near the hearth and pushed over a stack of peat with his snout, then sat down in front of the fire directly in front of her. Gunny reached out a tentative hand and touched the pig's back. His skin flinched but he did not leave his post in front of the fire. Gunny laid her hand more firmly on his back and he let out a deep sigh. Gunny let out a breath she did not realize she'd been holding, and scratched the pig's back and up under one ear. His hair was bristly and rough but his white skin was warm and smooth. The pig leaned into her hand as she scratched him, then he laid down and rolled onto his side. He snorted peacefully and she swore he was grinning as he fell asleep in front of the low fire.

Gallarus followed Gunny out of the house at midmorning when she went to collect water from the spring and stayed in the yard that day, but returned that night and scratched at the door to come in.

"Go way, Gallarus. You're not moving into this house. Go sleep with your girlfriend in the church."

That night, thinking it was around the time of Hallow E'en, Gunny set out a plate of bread and bowl of water and left the door open a crack for any spirits who might be wandering about the west end. In the morning the bread and water were gone and the pig was sleeping peacefully in front of the fire.

"Taking advantage of my Hallow E'en spirit, are you?" Gunny laughed.

The pig snorted in return.

"The poet calls you Gallarus. Is that a good name for you?"

The pig looked up when Gunny said "Gallarus."

Gunny laughed. "Maybe the poet knows more than I think he does. At least when it comes to pigs."

Patrick O'Connor stopped by Gunny's house in mid-December to see if she wanted to join the O'Connor family for Christmas.

"Christmas?" Gunny asked. "Won't your house be crowded with all of you, and Martha and David and the new baby?"

"No more crowded than it ever is. And Martha's the one who suggested it. None of us can imagine being alone, especially at Christmas."

"It is a little quiet out here on these dark days," Gunny confessed.

Patrick grinned. "You won't have any quiet at our house and there'll be lots of food and stories around the fire—and whiskey on Christmas Eve."

Gunny felt a deep ache in her chest and pressed a hand against her heart.

"Are you all right?" Patrick asked, startled at how pale Gunny had suddenly gotten.

"I'm fine," she said in a soft voice. "I forgot how much I missed all of that—the company and the food and the stories. Do you go to Christmas Eve Mass?" Gunny asked, thinking of a possible unwelcome encounter with Father Jessey.

Patrick laughed. "The closest thing we have to a church on the Blaskets is the old abandoned church out here. If you're in need of a Mass..."

"No, I'll not miss it," Gunny said quickly then looked down at her hands. "I have nothing to give as Christmas gifts."

Patrick smiled. "Neither does anyone else. No one will expect a thing from you."

Gunny's face brightened. "What about rope? Could your father use this?" Gunny picked up a long coil of rope she'd just finished and handed it to Patrick.

"Where did you get this?" Patrick asked hefting the heavy coil with both hands.

"I make it in my spare time," she said, shaking her head of long, black curls.

"You must have plenty of spare time. Da'll love this. Now you have to come home with me."

"I'd love to," Gunny hesitated. "There is just one thing..."

They both looked over at the eager, staring pig.

Gunny put out the fire and left the house door open a crack for the chickens to fend for themselves, then she and Patrick trudged up over the hill along the cliff path toward the village. Lorcan took the lead with Gallarus trotting close behind her. Gunny and the pig stayed with the O'Connors for two weeks. Days were filled with visits as Gunny was introduced to the other families in the village. Nights were filled with cooking, village stories, candles, Yule logs, music, singing, and dancing. Gunny could not remember a happier time. She slept each night in front of the O'Connor fire nestled between Gallarus and Johnny O'Connor and his pet seagull, exhausted from the company, but thankful to be part of the island world.

Gunny did not see any villagers again until early March. She was intent on spreading manure in her high potato field and jumped when Patrick cleared his throat to get her attention.

"You startled me," she said setting her spade upright in the fresh dirt.

"Sorry about that. Mam sent me. Mrs. Keane is in need of your help."

"Mrs. Keane?" Gunny asked wiping her brow with the back of a dirty hand.

"You met her at the house at Christmas. She's the heavy set one with the thick grey hair and deep dimples. Her daughter's having a baby. Mam said to come and get you."

"But I'm not a healer."

"Mam says you are, and Mrs. Keane needs you."

Gunny squinted and looked across the field at her unfinished work. "Now isn't a good time, Patrick. Tell your mother I'm sorry but I have too much to do here."

"Gunny," Patrick said softly. "Mam says that when you live on an island, you depend on one another to survive. In the village, we plant, and fish, and harvest together. No one cares how much money anyone had before they got here, or who their parents are, or where they were raised. What matters is what skills you have. If you're a good farmer, you help plant and harvest. If you're good at catching fish, then you fish. If you can tell a story, or write a poem, or spin a rope, then that's what you do. And if you can help deliver a baby, then you help deliver a baby."

"But I've only delivered one baby. No one in their right mind would depend on me for anything."

"You live here—and you have skills."

Gunny glared at the stubborn teen, then sighed and jerked her spade from the dirt. "Fine," she said, stomping off toward the house with Patrick, Lorcan, and Gallarus following close behind.

Inside, Patrick eyed more rope in a box near the hearth. "I don't suppose we could beg a little more rope off of you. Father said the rope you gave him for Christmas is the strongest he's ever had."

Gunny grinned and tossed Patrick a heavy coil from the box. "You have to be tough to survive on the west end, even if you're a reed. You're welcome to anything I have."

"When you are done helping Mrs. Keene," he said, "I'll help you finish manuring."

"I can manage on my own," Gunny said, checking her pocket for the black-handled knife and iron heart. She packed a bag of tea and healing roots, and pulled on her shawl.

Gunny, Gallarus, Patrick, and Lorcan walked along the cliffs toward the village. The spring air was clear, the sun warm, and the ocean breeze cool. The odd foursome passed three women sitting on their haunches on the hillside on the south end of the island. They were watching their husbands fish far out off the coast. One woman tucked her skirt in tighter around her feet and waved to Gunny and Patrick as they passed.

"That's Mrs. Sullivan, Mrs. Dunlevy, and Mrs. Shea," Patrick said quietly as they turned onto the road that led to the main part of the Blasket Village. "They grew up together in the village, and now their husbands fish together."

Gunny thought about her time in the booley with Ashling and Ellen and wondered how her old friends were now. She helped deliver her second island baby later that day and became a new, fast friend of the Keane family.

Patrick returned to Gunny's farm the next morning with a small hand cart and walked with her to her high potato field. He helped finish spreading manure, and when the potato field was done, helped spread several cartloads of seaweed and sand in the oat field and in Gunny's kitchen garden. The manuring was finished in about a quarter of the time it would have taken Gunny on her own without help and without a cart.

As a way of saying thanks, Gunny caught two red crabs and roasted the meat over a low turf fire in a fine seaweed mushroom sauce. The sun was starting to set as they finished eating. Patrick suggested he stay overnight to help set potatoes and plant oats the next day, but Gunny had had enough of the talkative youth.

"You've helped me plenty, Patrick. Go home and plant with your father. There're many more O'Connor mouths to feed than I have here."

"There are also many O'Connor hands to plant," Patrick said with a grin. "You don't have anyone to help you—and you don't have a cart"

"I got by without a cart before. Go home," Gunny said with a raised eyebrow.

Patrick looked into Gunny's deep brown eyes and smiled. "Maybe I like helping you more than I like helping my Da."

Gunny lifted the large iron pan she was scrubbing with sand. "Move along, young man. The full moon will see you home."

Patrick raised his hands in surrender and hiked off into the night with Lorcan tight at his heels.

May mackerel were shoaling in patches past Gunny's cove. Gunny watched, fascinated, as the Dingle fishermen brought in the huge creatures in their nets, each fish as long as her arm. She eyed the pig, grabbed two large coils of rope, and hiked to the village with Gallarus following behind. She ventured out onto the strand as Patrick and Timothy O'Connor and the other Blasket fishermen arrived to gut and salt their catch.

"Will you be taking that fish to Dingle to sell?"

"We will," Timothy O'Connor said.

"Would you have room in your boat for a passenger?"

Timothy looked up from his work, covered in fish gut and salt, and grinned. "If you don't mind traveling with the likes of us, we'd be happy to have you in our boat. Or I can get something for you in Dingle. What do you need?"

"I need to see some old friends," Gunny said with a smile.

"Then you'll be joining us. We'll launch in about an hour. Meet us down at the pier."

Gunny promised Johnny a sweet from Dingle if he kept an eye on Gallarus for the day. Johnny was ecstatic and promised to play all day with the pig. Gunny tucked her two rope coils in the boat around her feet as the O'Connor boat pulled away loaded with fishermen and huge, salted May mackerel. She spied Johnny and Gallarus up on the high cliff, the pet gully perched regally on the pig's back.

Gunny had not been back to Dingle since she'd left for her wedding years before and was both excited and nervous about the visit. The wind was brisk across the water. Patrick and Timothy rigged the sail on the large currach and the boat practically flew across the channel. Past the wide beach at Slea Head, they sailed near several large houses along the shore. Gunny spied the dock and tall yellow house at Ballygoleen. She pictured a young Thomas Milliken fishing from the short pier. She blinked at a time long passed and reminded herself that Thomas was now owner of the large yellow house, the short pier, the formal gardens, and all of the nearby villages. She shook her head and the faded image cleared as they pulled down the sail and rowed into Dingle Harbor. Dingle looked much bigger than she remembered with houses and businesses sprawled along the waterfront and lined up along winding streets that cut into the steep hillside.

When the boat was docked at the quay, Gunny scrambled out and pulled her two lengths of rope behind her. Everyone agreed to gather back at the pub on Green Street by late afternoon. As the men unloaded the fish and made deals with the old women hucksters on the pier, Gunny walked into Dingle and up Green Street.

She paused for a moment outside the Murphy's shop to admire an elaborate window display of fishing nets. The small bell over the door tinkled as she pushed open the door. Everything inside looked and smelled the same as she remembered. The place was noisy with buyers and sellers. Daniel Murphy was at the front counter haggling with two men over the purchase of a sheep. He had a few grey hairs at his temples and had gained a little weight but still looked his robust self. Gunny spied Joanna quietly stocking shelves at the back of the store. Joanna hadn't changed at all. Gunny slipped up behind her and tapped her lightly on the shoulder.

"How can I help you," Joanna said as she turned, then gasped and grabbed Gunny by the shoulders. She pulled Gunny close, then held her away, then pulled her close again. "Holy Mary! Wisha! Look at you, such a fine young woman."

Gunny closed her eyes and soaked in the warmth of the greeting. Joanna pulled a clean handkerchief from her apron pocket and wiped her eyes. Gunny took the hanky, wiped at her own eyes, and handed the hanky to Joanna

"You've changed and you haven't changed," Joanna laughed, stashing the damp hanky in her apron pocket. "Let me look at you. It's been too long."

Gunny laid the two heavy coils of rope on the counter and held her arms wide before the grinning Joanna. Joanna's eyes shifted from Gunny to the pile of rope. "Is that for sale?"

"Name your price."

"Your skills are better than ever. Daniel will strike a good deal with you."

A nicely dressed young woman tapped Joanna lightly on the arm. "Mrs. Murphy, your husband said you might be able to help me."

Joanna turned to Gunny. "How long are you here for? Can you join us for our evening meal?"

"I'm to meet up with the lads at the pub on Green Street this afternoon. Why don't I help you till then and we can catch up as we work."

"You're visiting. You don't have to work."

Daniel glanced up from the front counter not noticing Gunny. "Joanna," he yelled. "Can you get me more bagged salt from out back?"

"Market day," Joanna said, shaking her head. "All right," she said, turning back to Gunny. "You know where the salt is. I'll help Miss Gunderson here. Maybe we can close early. Daniel!" Joanna shouted across the store, pointing. "Look who's here!"

Daniel glanced up and gave Gunny a short wave as all three got to work.

Gunny quickly reacquainted herself with the store and surprised several old customers when she popped up to greet them from behind the counter. It was wonderful to be surrounded by the humanity of shoppers again after so many quiet years in her little house on the island, but by early afternoon, Gunny was exhausted. When the afternoon crowds thinned, she slipped out to the kitchen and put on the kettle for tea.

Joanna joined her in the kitchen, carefully hanging her apron on a peg near the door. She pushed a loose strand of hair from her face and pulled two chairs up in front of the fire.

"Your father stops in from time to time and fills us in on your news."

Gunny poured two cups of weak, hot tea and added a rounded spoonful of sugar to each cup. Joanna took her tea and sat, then reached out and took Gunny's hand. "Your Da told us about the accident, Gunny. I'm so sorry."

"It was a long time ago," Gunny said in a quiet voice, sitting down next to Joanna and staring into the swirling steam rising from her cup. "A long time, and still…" Her eyes burned talking of the hard times.

Joanna let go of her hand and wrapped her hands around her own warm cup. "Robert told us about how you pushed yourself to walk again and about how strong you were through everything. Then he said you left for the Blaskets. He worries about you, you know?"

Gunny looked at Joanna. "Did he tell you about the baby?"

"He did," Joanna said. "It was a miracle your mother could have another child at her age."

Gunny stood up and paced to the fire. "It was mysterious," she said softly.

"Is that why you left?" Joanna asked. "Because your parents had another baby?"

Gunny sighed. "I went home to be with Matt. When he died and I was living back in the house I'd grown up in—and it was like I'd never grown up, never moved away. Then Michael and Maeve moved to America and the baby arrived, and well, I felt like a stranger in my own home. So I left. "

"The Blasket people are so strange. Why didn't you come here?" Joanna asked taking a sip of tea.

Gunny laughed. "The Blasketers are no stranger than the rest of us! They're wonderful—kind and warm. They say what's on their minds—there's no time for nonsense on the Great Island. They work hard and mind their own business. Around the holidays, they gather to tell stories and dance and sing. They're used to taking in strangers—so everyone is welcome, everyone finds a place. And you should hear their music," Gunny sighed. "The Sullivans and the Dalys are the risp-raspers, the fiddlers on the island. They play in such a gentle way they could bring someone back from the dead. One night, Michael Sullivan was playing the fiddle as a storm beat down outside. I thought he brought the wind right into the house. And there's an old woman named Lady Sheehan," Gunny continued. "She lives out on the south end and looks to be about a hundred years old. Her face is a map of lines. But when she speaks, her voice is full and she spins tales out of the air like music. She told me that as she gets older she sleeps less, which gives her more time to reflect and remember—and that's what makes her stories keep getting better and better. It almost makes you want to get old."

Joanna laughed. "Listen to you. So many stories. But tell me about what you do all day, about where you live in this wonderful village."

"Oh, I don't live in the village," Gunny said with a shake of her head. "I live on the west end of the island. By myself. Well, not really by myself. I have a pig."

"You have a what?" Joanna asked with a laugh.

"I have a pig," Gunny giggled. "He thinks he's a dog. His name is Gallarus. And there's a wild ewe who lives in the old abandoned church. And a brown seal… This all sounds a little crazy, doesn't it? Gunny said, sitting back down in her chair. "

Joanna smiled. "I wouldn't have said that."

"Only because you're polite."

Joanna grinned warmly. "It does sound a little crazy—and you look happy after all you've been through." She paused. "Are you happy?"

Gunny's brow wrinkled. "I'm content. I love running my little farm and keeping a cozy house. And I try to help out whenever I can."

"It sounds a little bit lonely to me."

"It is at times," Gunny said with a frown. "But there's a safe feeling to that, you know? You can't be hurt by people who aren't there."

"Oh, Gunny," Joanna said shaking her head. "Loss is part of life. It's all heartache but you don't want to miss it. If something happened to Daniel or to Jamie I'd be devastated. But would I give up loving them for a guarantee of no heartache? Never."

Gunny smiled and tucked her hair behind her ears. "You're stronger than me. Maybe someday I'll take a chance again. But for now, I like living on my own, and visiting when I feel like it," she said finishing off her cup of tea. "Speaking of James, where is he?"

Joanna grinned. "He's at school. He spends most of his time there helping out the younger students. He has a gift for teaching. I doubt you'd even recognize him."

James cleared his throat from the doorway, interrupting his mother and the stranger in his kitchen. Gunny turned and gasped. James's face hadn't changed but he was fourteen and was nearly as tall as a man and had a new pair of round, wire-framed glasses perched on his small nose. He was only a little younger now than she had been when she came to work for the Murphys, she thought. She stood and walked slowly toward the tall, thin boy.

"Hello, James."

James glanced at his mother then down at his feet.

Gunny spread her arms wide in front of him, trying to catch his eye. "You don't remember me?"

James looked up and grinned, then pulled a shiny tin whistle from his pocket. "Of course I remember you, Gunny. You taught me how to play the whistle. Daniel bought me this one in Dublin after I sent yours back when we heard about the accident. I still can't play as well as you do, but I practice every day."

"My, aren't you the talker now," Gunny said, grabbing his hand. She could see he felt awkward and let go.

James walked briskly to the fire and poured himself a cup of tea, then stood with his back to her. "You were like a big sister to me. Then you left."

"I left to get married," she said walking to stand next to him.

"I remember," he said. "You left to marry Matt McCrohan." He turned and walked to the table. He pulled out a chair and sat down across from Joanna.

Gunny crossed to the table, pulled out the chair next to James, and sat. "After the accident I couldn't walk for a long time."

"Your father told us. But after you could walk, why didn't you move back here?"

Gunny smiled. "I was just telling your mother about that. I decided to move to the Blaskets."

James looked up excited. "You live on the island? Our teacher's been talking about setting up a school on the Blaskets. Now that the Catholic Laws have been repealed, I can be a teacher. Maybe someday I'll teach out there."

"The Catholic Laws have been repealed?" Gunny asked leaning back in her chair. "I didn't know. We don't get much news on the Blaskets. I'll have to get a newspaper before I leave. Matt used to tell me this day would come. Things'll change now for Catholics. Maybe one day we'll even be able to own land again."

"Things will change," James said. "With Daniel O'Connell's help, we may soon represent ourselves again, have our own government."

Joanna waved her hand in front of her face. "No politics today, Jamie. Gunny was just about to tell me about how she's surviving on the west end of the Blaskets."

"You always had good stories," James said, leaning forward. "I've missed that."

Gunny laughed loudly. "You may have missed my stories, but have you forgotten those first months I was here? I was dreadful."

"You came around," Joanna volunteered.

Gunny eyed the old tea kettle over the fire. "I think about your grandmother whenever I drink tea, Joanna," she said walking over and adding a splash of hot tea to her cup.

"Hot and weak and sweet," she and Joanna said at the same time, and laughed.

Gunny glanced at the waning light outside. "My stories'll have to wait. I have to get down to Green Street to catch my ride back to the Blaskets."

"And I should go help Daniel close up the shop," Joanna said, standing and wiping her hands on her apron. "Make sure you settle up with him about your rope before you go, and grab a few boxes of tea to take with you." She grasped Gunny's hands. "You'll come to see us again, Gunny, won't you?"

Gunny felt a warm rush in the pit of her stomach. "It's nice knowing I'm still welcome here. I promise I'll be back."

* * *

Gunny hurried down Green Street to rejoin the Blasket fishermen. She worked her way through the crowded group of merry-makers in the small, smoky pub. Strong voices and loud laughter filled her ears as local family members caught up with the Blasketers over porter and fresh mackerel pie. Gunny ordered a pint and a pie at the bar, fingering the coins in her pocket. Daniel had been more than generous with her in his purchase of her rope. She sat on a stool next to Patrick and listened while the others talked and sang, ate and drank—and drank—and drank. She glanced outside at the ebbing light.

"I take it we're not sailing back tonight?" she asked.

"I should have warned you," Patrick said with a smile. "A trip to Dingle often takes two days. One day to barter and shop, and a night to drink and sing. We'll row home tomorrow at first light."

"But no one on the island has money," she said. "How can any of you afford a night here?"

"We sold a lot of fish today," Patrick said raising a glass to her.

"And you'll spend all of it on porter and pie?"

"No, we'll spend about half. That's part of the thrill of fishing."

Bar patrons took turns singing and making requests of each other to hear old favorites. Gunny slipped outside around midnight and let herself in the back door at the Murphy's. The house was quiet. She stirred the fire, added a turf, then pulled a blanket off a chair by the fire and curled up for a short night on the floor before sailing home.

Johnny was waiting at the pier on the Blaskets the next morning with Lorcan, Gallarus, and his pet gully. When the boat pulled up near the pier, Lorcan was so excited to see Patrick she nearly jumped into the boat before Patrick could scramble up onto the rock. Gallarus acted cooler around Gunny, but stayed tight at her heels as she and Johnny made the steep climb back up the path to the village. At the top of the path, the pig was clearly winded and Gunny paused to let him rest. She fished three pennies and a sweet out of her apron pocket and handed them to Johnny. He grabbed his gully off the pig's back and skipped home with a loud whoop.

Donal McCrohan passed Gunny and the panting pig on his way down to the pier. "About time to slaughter that one, isn't it?" he asked.

"He's not for slaughter," Gunny said, shaking her head.

Donal stopped, hands on his hips. "What good is a pig if you don't slaughter him? There's enough meat on that one to feed this village for a month. Or you could fetch a fine amount for him at the Dingle fair."

"Keep your eyes off my pig, Donal," Gunny said, jingling the coins in her apron pocket. "I make my money selling rope."

Donal threw his hands in the air and shrugged. "I have fish to catch," he said, continuing past the charming, strange woman and the fat, white pig.

348

Gunny stopped in to visit with Charlotte O'Connor before walking home to the west end. She tapped at the newspaper she had brought back with her. "The Catholic Laws had been repealed."

"What do you think of that?" Charlotte asked.

"What do I think? I think it is wonderful that you want to know what I think."

Charlotte smiled. "Stay with us tonight, Gunny, and read to us from the newspaper. Everyone will want to hear the news from Dingle—and the men will have had too much porter to remember much of the trip. The Catholic Laws are repealed... This will be the seed of conversation for weeks."

After a fine meal of mackerel and potatoes, Gunny read to a packed house of villagers about the repeal of the Catholic Laws, which lead to other stories of Irish rebellions and to recitations of old poems about Irish freedom.

Johnny and the younger boys complained that they'd had enough of the boring news. "Tell us something good," Johnny said, "something about adventure."

Gunny poured herself a cup of tea and thought back on the tales she'd loved when she was Johnny's age. She chose the shortest one she knew. She was tired and her head full after her trip back in time to Dingle.

"Once," she said to the quieting room. "There was a woman whose lover disappeared at sea. She mourned for him for years. She could hardly eat, hardly sleep. She just wanted to die. Then one day, she was walking the deserted beaches past Ballyferriter dreaming of her lover's lost ship, when the shadow of a pirate blocked her way. She looked up at the pirate and saw around his neck the half-shilling necklace she had given to her lover so many years before. She grabbed for the necklace, but the pirate pushed her away, saying he had found the necklace on a dead man, and that it was rightly his. They argued through the night, and into the next morning and all the next day until she had fallen in love with him and sailed off and was never heard from again."

Johnny howled in approval. "Tell us more about pirates," he shouted.

Gunny shook her head and grinned. She should have known she could not get off so easy with Johnny O'Connor. She rubbed her hands together for inspiration, then told a longer tale of a landlord's daughter who fell so deeply in love with an Irish peasant that she followed him off to sea when her father banished the young man from the kingdom.

"She traveled far and wide looking everywhere for her lover. When she was as far from home as she'd ever been, she found him. He was the captain of a ship docked at Rio. He was as tall and as handsome as she remembered. She ran to him, happy at last. But he turned to her as a stranger would. He'd found a new love and sailed off without her."

Johnny snorted. "That's enough love stories. Tell us about the strange things you see out on the west end."

Gunny laughed. "The west end looks pretty much like it does here. I live in a house just like you, and I farm pretty much like you do. Patrick can tell you. He's been there."

"No," Johnny complained. "I want to hear about the fairies who live on the west end."

"There aren't any fairies," Gunny scoffed, trying to end the evening.

Johnny's face fell.

Gunny paused. "But there are wild things," she continued, with a tip of her head.

Johnny's face brightened and he crawled into Gunny's lap. She smoothed his rumpled, red hair.

"Did I ever tell you about the wild things that live under the deep pools in the loneliest marshes up behind my house? They only come out at night when they want to dance with the elf-folk."

Johnny shook his head, his blue eyes open wide.

"When you stand at my spring," she said, "you can hear the wild things whispering. And they play music all through the night while they dance on the reflections of the stars on the water. When the stars begin to fade, the wild things sink back into the marsh and disappear with the morning light."

Johnny blinked and rubbed at his eyes. "How is it you can see these spirits and I cannot?"

Gunny grinned. "I was born at dusk at the moment the first stars appeared in the night sky. Were you?"

He looked at his mother. Charlotte shook her head no. He turned back to Gunny. "I guess not," he said with a sigh. He looked a little sullen, but also deeply relieved. "Tell us another story," he demanded.

The other villagers nodded. Gunny sighed, took a sip of tea, and started in again.

Gunny made frequent trips to the village through the summer. Sometimes she had an excuse—when villagers were in need of rope, or when someone needed a medicinal root. Other times she made the hike seeking company. But as friendly as the villagers were to her, only Patrick and the poet were brave enough to venture out to see her on the west end. Of the two, she preferred Patrick's company. At fifteen, he had become an excellent farmer, builder, and fisherman and she valued his friendship and sound advice.

She was pulling a large kreel onto her back to bring in her first load of dried turf before the harvest when she saw Patrick appear on the high cliff path leading a small, fat donkey with Lorcan racing just ahead of him. She waved to him and was surprised when Lorcan arrived first and leaned against her leg. She scratched gently at the dog's long ears and raised her eyebrows to Patrick as he hiked up with the donkey.

"What a nice surprise," she whispered.

"We've all gotten to trust you a bit."

"It took, what? Only three-and-a-half years?" Gunny laughed. "What brings you to the west end?"

"A sprite told me you might need help hauling turf today."

"A sprite, eh?" she asked with a smile. "I am hauling turf, but I've made myself a fine new kreel so I don't need any help." Gunny had woven her latest kreel from bog timbers and bracken and was quite proud of the latch door she had fashioned at the bottom.

"How can you haul heavy turf on your back like that?"

"I make a lot of trips."

"Well, I brought the donkey. Let's have him do the work," he said reaching behind Gunny and lifting the kreel from her back before she could object. "I'll strap your kreel to this old fellow, and we'll haul twice as much," Patrick said, glancing at Gunny from the corner of his eye as she shook out her shoulders and her long black curls tumbled down her back.

Gunny watched Patrick as he strapped her new kreel onto the donkey. He was about the same height as her these days. Over the past three years, his shoulders had filled out and the beard on his face was rougher.

"You know I don't like to ask for help," she said. "It means I have to say thank you."

"You're welcome," Patrick said, grabbing hold of a rope around the donkey's neck.

They walked the animal up the hill with Lorcan racing ahead and Gallarus following closely behind. It was a cool day for late August and a stiff breeze swept in from the ocean.

"It's windier out here than in the village," Patrick observed.

Gunny thought about Mac and how he hated the wind on the Blaskets. She looked out across the ocean. There were white caps as far as she could see and the waves thundered below them into the heavy black rocks. "See those white caps out there? They're little ships bound from America… They bring the salt wind that stirs the grasses and tells us to prepare for winter."

Patrick chuckled at her explanation. "You and the poet must get along famously…"

When they reached the bog, Gunny squatted next to her first orderly row of peat. She pushed the three bricks apart that she'd left leaning in on each other as her father had taught her. "Bone dry and rock hard," she announced.

"Our turf isn't quite dry yet," Patrick said as he helped Gunny load the heavy dry bricks into the kreels on the donkey's back. "We have another week or so to wait."

"What a shame," Gunny said. "If only you had a little more wind."

Back at the old abandoned village, Gunny opened the bottom of the kreel basket on her side of the donkey and let the turf bricks tumble into the yard.

They unloaded Patrick's kreel by hand and stacked the turf in even rows along one wall of the church.

"Do you want me to take some of this into your house?" Patrick asked.

"No," Gunny said with a smile. "I'll move it later. I already owe you for helping me bring all of this in from the bog."

She looked over at her cozy cottage. Patrick's donkey was standing in her yard calmly munching a long length of rope she'd been working on at her front bench.

"Hey," she yelled, running into the yard. "Stop that!" She reached the donkey just as he swallowed the last bit of rope, then shook his long ears and whinnied. "If I didn't know better, I'd say he's telling me, 'I'll take the thank you for all of the work I did today.'"

"I'm so sorry," Patrick apologized in a low voice from behind her.

"It's not a problem," Gunny said. "I'll make more. It'll be cold soon and all I'll have to do is twist rope."

"Is there anything else I can help you with?" Patrick asked, already knowing the answer would be no.

"There is something," Gunny said.

Patrick was shocked. "Name it."

"There's an old ewe who lives out here. I've been watching her for years. Her coat is so filthy I can smell her whenever I'm downwind of her. I wonder if Lorcan could help bring her in."

"There's no better sheep dog than Lorcan," Patrick bragged.

Gunny grabbed a fresh length of rope from inside her house and they headed north into the back hills. Patrick followed behind as she crept around a huge grey rock near the shore where she knew the ewe liked to rest in the afternoons. The ewe was there but took off at a full trot up onto the cliffs as soon as she smelled the humans.

Gunny shook her head. "There she goes. She's a great climber. Once she gets to the cliffs she always loses me."

Patrick whistled for Lorcan to follow the sheep and the dog took off at a fast clip. By the time Patrick and Gunny caught up, Lorcan had chased the ewe into an open field back toward the center of the island. The ewe was panting from the chase, her long tongue hanging out the side of her mouth. Patrick whistled for Lorcan to stop and the dog did so reluctantly. Patrick made a leap for the sheep and tackled her. Gunny stepped in and tied a rope noose around the animal's front and back feet. When the ewe was bound, Gunny grabbed her front legs and Patrick took the back and they marched with her down the hill to Gunny's cove. Patrick laid the sheep on her side and examined her from head to tail looking for an identifying mark.

He shook his head. "She must've been born in the wild and was somehow separated from her mother before anyone could identify her. She's yours."

"She's mine?"

"She's an unmarked sheep. Finders keepers. It's an island rule."

Patrick used a sharpened knife to shear the ragged, tangled wool from the terrified animal. She bleated angrily at first, then was silent as Patrick completed his work. When he was done, the old ewe looked small and thin with her thick, matted coat lying beside her on the shore. Gunny ran her hand over the ewe's soft black and white speckled skin, then held the sheep's long face in her hands and looked into her strange golden eyes.

"Now you'll have to spend the winter in the old church to stay warm. You didn't think I'd ever catch you, did you?"

The sheep blinked in response and pulled her head away from Gunny's hands. She kicked at the ropes that held her legs. Gunny pulled out her black-handled knife and cut the ropes. The ewe struggled to her feet, gave a buck in the air toward Gunny, and sprinted around the house and back into the hills. Gunny roared with laughter.

"After three years and a half-a-days chase, you're turning her loose?"

Gunny gathered the dirty wool from the beach to clean and card over the winter.

"She'll be back. She likes to sleep with Gallarus and eat my hay. The point was to get some of that nasty wool off that she's been dragging around for years. We'll try to catch her again in another three years if you're up to it."

"Gunny," Patrick said, grabbing Gunny's arm as she started toward the house.

Gunny looked at Patrick's earnest face.

"I had fun with you today." Patrick's blue eyes looked right through her and she looked away.

"Yes, that was fun," she said, re-adjusting her armful of stinky, dirty wool. "Thank you for your help."

"Gunny," Patrick continued. "I could spend more time here. On the west end. With you."

Gunny felt her chest tighten. "Patrick, you're ten years younger than me. I don't think it's appropriate that you spend more time here."

Patrick blushed. "Ten years isn't that big a difference."

Gunny shook her head. "It might not seem like a big difference to you but it does to me. We're friends, Patrick. I truly appreciate your help. Now you should go."

"I'll be back to help you with your harvest."

"Of course you will."

Gunny was ready for quiet time after the harvest but ended up spending several nights in the village with new mothers.

"Why is it so many girls are having babies this winter?" Gunny asked Charlotte over a late-night cup of tea after a particularly long delivery in early December.

Charlotte giggled. "I think you know why…"

"Well, I know that part, but this is the third delivery this winter. Is there something in the air this year?"

"There're so many babies because there were so many marriages last spring. Remember?"

"But why did so many get married last spring?"

"Because last winter was a good winter," Charlotte said matter-of-factly. "We had plenty of food and turf. When we're well-fed and warm we think of things like marriage. When food and turf are in short supply, we don't have many weddings or many babies. I remember a stretch when we had no weddings for about seven years. Then we have years like last year where it seems that every young couple in the village is eager to marry."

Gunny had attended one wedding in the spring that was held in Ballyferriter. She'd sailed over with the O'Connors for a festive day, with fiddlers playing in every pub plus one playing out on the street where most of the villagers congregated. She'd enjoyed a night filled with food, drink, singing, and dancing before they returned late to the island. She remembered one happy couple who were about seventeen as they proudly showed off their first pair of new boots. On the island, no one could afford to buy a youngster a new pair of boots until their feet stopped growing. A wedding seemed like the perfect time to indulge.

She glanced up at Charlotte. "Does Patrick ever talk about marriage?"

Charlotte shook her head. "Patrick has always spent more time with boys than girls. His first love is fishing with his Da and the men in the boat. When he was younger, he used to like to sing with the Daly girl. But these days, you're pretty much the only girl he spends any time with."

"That's probably because I'm more like a boy than a girl."

"I don't know about that," Charlotte said, raising one eyebrow.

"You don't have to worry about Patrick and me," Gunny said. "He's practically young enough to be my son."

Charlotte laughed. "You're a story teller. There've been odder mixes of ages that have married on the island."

Gunny stood and laughed nervously. "Now that would be a story. Give me your tea cup. I'll wash up and be on my way before this chatter turns to nonsense."

Whenever Gunny was in the village she liked to stop in to visit with the children she'd delivered. Watching them grow up helped her mark the years she spent on the island. As the children grew from babes in arms, to toddlers, to little children with their own strong personalities, they treated her as a favorite aunt and always wanted a story. The most requested story was of her encounter with a whale. It wasn't actually her tale—it was a tale she had heard John McCrohan and her father tell numerous times. She supposed the tale was part of some Irish legend but was happy to tell it, tailoring the story to the Blaskets.

"Did I ever tell you about my encounter with a mighty whale?" she would ask. The children would giggle and shake their heads no so that Gunny would have to tell the story one more time.

"I was out fishing one summer day," she would say, "when I noticed a large black shadow moving along in the water at the same pace as my wee boat. I looked down into a deep blue eye as large as a fish barrel. I could see my reflection in this eye and I will tell you that my reflection was tiny. I grabbed my oars and decided to pay that whale no mind. I rowed and rowed but the whale swam beside me blowing out a stream of air and water so foul and fishy I could hardly breathe. I knew this fellow was considering me, a mere morsel, for his meal but I could not out-row him. Still, I kept rowing, ignoring the big brute, hoping he would get bored—which he finally did. But when he dove down under the waves, the pull nearly sucked my tiny boat along behind him."

"I watched and waited—afraid he would come up again under my boat, but he was gone—the water was still and I was safe. The only problem was that I was now so far from shore I didn't know where the shore was! And night was a-coming—a dark, moonless night. When you're lost at sea you can't see anything but the sea and the sky, and while the sea and sky are lovely to look at most days, they don't look quite so good when they're all you have to look at. I had a crust of bread with me which I ate with a handful of seawater to wash it down."

Some child always asked, "How did you get back?"

Gunny would smile. "I'm glad you asked that. I was lucky because as I sat there pondering my fate, a huge eagle flew over and landed on the prow of my boat. Did I mention that I have a tiny boat and that this was the largest eagle you ever saw? "

The children would shake their heads with vigor before Gunny continued.

"The eagle looked me in the eye. 'How do you do?' the Eagle asked."

"Very well, Ma'am, I answered. How could I not answer so direct a question from such a large eagle?"

"Would you like me to lift you up into the sky so you can see where it is the whale has taken you?" the Eagle asked.

"Aye, Ma'am," I answered. "That would be most helpful."

"So I climbed onto that eagle's back and she flew with me up into the night sky. Up and up we went until we were well past the moon. When I mentioned that perhaps that was high enough, the eagle screeched.

"High enough, are we? And were you high enough when you climbed up the cliffs on the north side of the Great Island and stole my eggs?"

Gunny gulped and looked guilty as she explained to her little listeners. "She had me there. I thought she looked familiar. 'I deeply apologize, Madam Eagle,' I said. 'Now what will you do with me?'"

"I suppose I will drop you. Good-bye!" And with that, the mighty eagle shook me off and soared away. I bounced off of the face of the moon and fell to earth... and when I awoke, I was on my own little beach sleeping next to my own little boat. And I'm happy to say that I no longer row so far out to sea, and I definitely no longer snitch eggs from eagle nests."

The children would all pile into her lap at the exciting conclusion, petting her long black curls and thrilling at the touch of her large warm hands resting on their heads.

In the fall of 1838, Gunny was called in to help deliver a baby on the south end of the island. Time had scampered past, and Gunny had now lived on the Blaskets for eight years and had delivered more babies than she could count. She trudged up to a small house perched along the south cliffs and tapped at the door. Mary Daly answered and pulled Gunny inside, stifling a sob.

Gunny grabbed Mary's hand. "Why're you crying? Am I too late?"

Mary sniffled again. "I don't know if you can save my daughter, Gunny. Go and look at her."

Gunny hurried inside and did a quick examination of a pale, thin girl she had not met before. The girl was clearly in labor, but was hardly breathing, hardly moving, and did not make a murmur as her stomach tightened with contractions.

Gunny pulled Mary outside. "What's wrong with her?" she asked. "I don't know if I can deliver a child from a mother who's so weak."

Mary shook her head and pulled Gunny into the back room of their tiny cottage.

"I'll tell you quick," she said glancing out at the girl. "Colleen ran away from the island when she was sixteen to marry a Tralee boy she met at the Dingle fair. We didn't hear from her for five years. Then last year, she showed up on a fishing boat in from Dingle. She had my three little blond grandsons with her. She was in a daze and spoke of a life in Tralee with a husband who drank too much and had an evil temper. She said she'd fled with the boys and hoped we would take her back."

"So this is a baby from the Tralee man?"

"No," Mary said, shaking her head. "After Colleen was back for awhile, she fell in love with Paddy Dunleavy out on Inis Tuaisceart, Paddy had the scarlet fever as a child and a doctor from Dingle told his mother that Paddy could never have children so he never married."

Gunny grinned. "If I can guess where this story is leading, I think I may know that doctor."

356

Mary continued. "Paddy grew up with just his mother and sisters on Inis Tauisceart and was terribly shy but he adored Colleen. They were like two children when he visited here on the Great Island. Then a miracle occurred — Coleen found out last spring she was with child. Paddy was as happy as anyone had ever seen him. They married last May and Paddy moved in with us."

"Isn't Paddy Dunleavy the one who disappeared from a fishing boat last summer?"

"Aye, sauce for the crabs, he was," Mary said clucking her tongue. "All eight men on that boat should've been lost when they went over in that storm, but somehow the other seven managed to hold on to the bottom of the boat until they washed up on the Skillig islands. When the others got back and told Colleen what happened, she nearly lost the baby right then and there, but the baby held on and waited for its time to be born. Which appears to be now."

"Colleen looks more like she wants to be with Paddy than with the new baby."

"Aye," Mrs. Daly said sadly. "And she has the three other boys to think of. They're tucked in bed next door. How will I explain to them if their mother passes in the night?"

Gunny approached Colleen, lips pursed. Colleen turned away from her, her face pale and drawn. Gunny pulled up a stool and sat down. She took the young woman's hand and leaned forward to talk quietly with her as the contractions gained in intensity. Colleen never looked at Gunny but she listened as Gunny talked. As the contractions increased, she focused on delivering the baby and soon a howling little girl with a crown of auburn hair entered the world.

Mrs. Daly cried as she lifted up the small bundle. "She looks just like Paddy," she said, weeping.

Gunny pulled off the bedding and cleaned her knife as Mary handed the tiny baby to Colleen. The young woman blinked and looked over at Gunny.

"Thank you for sharing your story with me," she said in a soft whisper. "I don't know how I'll survive but I'm going to try. I'm going to trust that something will go right in my life and that I'll be able to make something good of this."

The baby nestled in close to Colleen. Gunny wiped a tear from her eye, packed her knife in her pocket, and walked back to her little cove.

~ Chapter 17: Lord Ventry Builds a School~

Charlotte O'Connor tossed the Protestant Bible onto the hot coals. The front door was open to welcome any breeze on a hot August day, but a turf fire burned low and the Bible smoldered in the O'Connor fireplace.

"I'll have no Protestant reading their Bible to my children," Charlotte said, shaking a finger at the smoking book.

"The sad part is that James would have been an excellent teacher," Gunny said, sipping at a cooling cup of tea.

"How dare Reverend Gayer send us a 'Bible Reader' from Dingle. We may be illiterate but we aren't stupid."

"I rather liked that speckled cat on the opening page," Gunny said as she watched the Bible finally start to blaze. "I've never seen anything like that before in a Bible."

"Trying to fool us by adding pictures…Your young friend is lucky our men didn't toss him and his cat-decorated Bible right off a cliff."

"The men were kind to row him back to Dingle. I had no idea it was James Murphy who was here until after he'd left. James always wanted to come to the Blaskets. I wonder if he'll ever come back."

"If he comes back with another trick up his sleeve, I wouldn't guarantee his life. Those Protestants…"

"James is Catholic," Gunny interrupted. "He only went to the Protestant school in Dingle because there wasn't a school for Catholics. He'd be much more than a reader if we welcomed him here. He could teach the children. And think how it would be if your boys could read and do numbers, to live lives less dependent on the land and the sea."

"The poet used to read to our children. What we need is a new poet—not a Bible reader."

"I actually miss Owen Dooly. How do you suppose he's doing in Dublin?"

"I hear he's gotten himself in all sorts of trouble writing poems of revolution… And don't change the subject," Charlotte said. "We're talking about your friend, James Murphy. Mr. Speckled Cat," Charlotte said, clutching at her chest.

Gunny looked pensively at the crisping Bible. "What if we asked Lord Ventry to build us a school instead of sending us another reader? Then the children could learn to read for themselves."

Charlotte howled. "Lord Ventry wouldn't spend a farthing educating a Catholic child."

Gunny had a flash of thought. Would Lord Ventry spend money on a school to educate his own daughter? What if she could get Thomas to build a school on the Blaskets, then she could bring Catherine over to live with her

358

and attend school. Her heart quickened. She knew it was foolish thinking—but to be able to offer her child an education... What if?

Patrick and the other fishermen rowed Gunny to Dunquin. She had not visited her family in nearly ten years and wasn't sure she'd be welcome. She pictured her arrival, walking up through the steep field to her house. Seeing her father and mother again—and baby. Only Catherine wasn't a baby anymore. She was twelve and needed an education. Gunny would tell her parents about her idea to start a school for Catholic children on the island. If she could convince her parents that Catherine should join, then she would walk to Ventry to inform Thomas of the plan—and inform him of his obligation to her—and to the girl.

Patrick let her off at the Dunquin pier then headed out to fish in the channel with the other men. Gunny hiked up the dirt road past O'Leary's pub. When she got to the fork in the road at the church she hesitated. It would be nice to visit with Mac before dealing with her mother and father and seeing her daughter again after so long a time. She grinned and tucked her hair back along her neck thinking how surprised Mac would be. As she approached the forge she heard the sharp ring of hammer against metal. She gave a brisk knock at the door and walked into the familiar hot room, arms open wide. A stout nine-year old boy with a large hammer in his hand glanced up at her from the anvil then returned to his work. Mac stood just behind the boy, a tight grin on his face.

"Gunny!" Mac said, crossing the room and giving her a quick hug. He looked the same as always—his tight black hair curled in the heat; a sheen of sweat dampening his broad forehead and heavy brows.

The boy continued to work, head down, the sharp sound of the hammer ringing loud against the anvil.

"Is that your son?" Gunny asked over the noise.

Mac grinned. "This is Matthew," Mac yelled, then repeated the name in a louder voice as the boy continued to hammer. "Matthew!"

The boy looked up briefly at his father and the tall woman.

"What?"

"Where're you manners, son? Stop for a moment. This is Gunny Malone, an old neighbor of ours."

Gunny grimaced at Mac's barren description of her. Matthew tossed the hammer aside and put his hands on his hips. He had Mac's round face and black curly hair but his feet and hands were large. He was going to be tall like his uncle Matt. Gunny smiled at him. He wiped his grimy hands on his leather apron, then turned and moved behind the forge to pump the bellows.

"I have work to do," the boy said without emotion, turning a hot piece of metal in the forge.

"Well," Gunny said awkwardly. "It was nice meeting you."

Mac signaled to Gunny to step outside. The yard was cool and bright compared with the air in the forge. Mac leaned against the outside wall and wiped his face on his sleeve. Hammer sounds peeled from inside the forge. He glanced up at Gunny. "It's been a long time."

Gunny smiled. "How are you—and your mother and sisters? How's married life?"

Mac grinned and shook his head. "Mam is fine. All but my youngest sister have married and moved away so things are pretty quiet around here. And Sheila... She's fine. She says I spend too much time at the forge."

"And this is news?"

"She likes to dance and sing where I prefer a quiet night by the fire sipping hot whiskey and telling stories. She tells me I live too much in the past."

"Sounds like you haven't changed a bit."

Mac smiled. "I feel old, Gunny, but I appreciate your kind words. It's good to see you. What brings you to Dunquin?"

"I came to see my parents and Catherine—and you. Then I may have some business in Ventry."

Mac looked up the hill toward Gunny's house. "They're not there."

Gunny nodded. "I'm sure everyone's out in the fields on a fine day like this."

"No," Mac said, a concerned look on his face. "Your parents and Catherine aren't at the house. They moved to Ventry."

"What're you talking about?"

"Lord Ventry's been adding to his horse collection and your Da was hardly ever home. He didn't even have time to plant his fields this spring. Lord Ventry wanted his time and was willing to pay for it. Bitsy Kavanaugh said your Mam was as angry as a hornet about all the time he was spending in Ventry, so they put Catherine into service at the Big House and moved. They've been gone about a week."

Gunny felt the blood drain from her face. "Mam put Catherine into service? At Ballygoleen? The girl's only twelve. Are things here so bad ?"

"No, no," Mac said reaching over and touching Gunny on the arm. "Catherine told my boy Matthew she wanted to go. You know how your mam's always going on about how wonderful Ventry is—with the big house and gardens, the horses, the stables... And Catherine wanted to be near your da. Bitsy said your mam's working at the Big House as well."

"So who's living in my house?" Gunny asked glancing up the hill.

"No one. Things have been bad around here since the crops failed in '31. A few other villagers have moved as well. The Moodys, Fiona Burke and the Burke twins..."

The hammer beating inside the forge stopped. Mac walked to the door and looked inside. "Everything all right, Matthew?"

"Don't mind me," the boy shouted as he angrily pumped the bellows to stoke the fire. "I'll keep working while you're out there visiting."

Mac shook his head and turned to Gunny. "Who does he remind you of?"

Gunny laughed. "Matt got nicer as he got older. I'm sure your Matthew will do the same."

Mac studied Gunny's face as she looked up the hill at her deserted childhood home.

She sighed. "I'll go find my folks in Ventry. But first I'll say good-bye to the old house. Take care of yourself—and that young wife of yours." She gave Mac a nod and sprinted off up the hill.

Mac's heart raced. Things changed and they didn't change.

The Malone yard was quiet as Gunny approached the house. There was no smoke coming out of the chimney, no smell of peat in the air. Gunny unlatched the front door and stepped inside. Midday light beamed through the front window into a house as tidy as ever. The beds and dresser were still in place; only the linens and dishes were missing. Three stools sat evenly spaced in front of an empty fireplace. A short broom of heather leaned unused against the front wall. She felt a shiver cross the back of her neck as she ran a hand over the cold chimney stones. She remembered falling as a little girl and hitting her head on the hearth. She pictured her father sitting on a stool and smoking his pipe in front of the fire, telling stories. She looked up to the loft where chickens had roosted and remembered finding her grandmother's tin whistle in an old wooden box.

She pulled the worn fire crane forward. The tea kettle Joanna had given her as a wedding gift had been left behind. The kettle was black from years of heavy use. She lifted it off the crane to take it with her, then thought better and set it back in its place. She turned to the back wall and pulled down the table that had once been her bed. The squeak of the hinges and feel of the heavy, rough wood were so familiar. She remembered how she felt when she'd first awakened after the accident, and how Shep had tempted her to walk to the front window and out the door. It was the bed where she'd given birth to Catherine. She pushed the table back up against the wall. The girl's large cradle sat in the left front corner of the house. There was a small, hand-carved doll wrapped in a brown wool blanket lying in the bed. Gunny picked up the doll and held it in her arms. Catherine must have felt she was too old to bring a dolly with her to her new position. Gunny squatted and carefully placed the doll back in the cradle. She stood and looked around.

"Good-bye, old house," she said to the still space, then turned and pulled the door tightly closed behind her.

Gunny hiked back through the fields past the forge and headed east up the curving dirt road toward Ventry. The late-summer sun was hot but a cooling wind blew in off the ocean. She passed the ogham stone on her right and waved to Colman the Pilgrim. She walked past the old church and relics of the lost village and wound her way down the steep hill into Ventry. She walked through the bustling village and up to the turnoff for Ballygoleen. She thought of the many times she'd walked down that driveway with deliveries from the Murphy's. This time instead of going to the house, she turned left and headed toward the stables to find her father.

As she crossed near the trees by the house, three young serving girls came tripping out the kitchen door, laughing, each carrying a small bucket. Gunny hadn't seen her daughter in a decade but knew the tall, pale girl was Catherine. She was willowy and had long ringlets of neatly combed blond hair, ivory skin, and large blue eyes. She wore a crisp grey dress and clean apron, and wore polished brown boots with high laces. The girls did not see her and she did not call out to them. They skipped past her to the front of the house and she hurried on to the stables. Robert was in the yard, shoeing a large black horse. His hair was almost completely white and his face and hands were deeply wrinkled. He had a slight stoop to his shoulders. Gunny felt tears well in her eyes and brushed a hand over her face.

"Da?"

Robert looked as if he'd seen a ghost. "Gunny!" He tossed down the horseshoe and swept Gunny into his arms, then held her out in front of him. "Let me look at you," he said with a broad grin on his face. "God in Heaven, it's been forever. You look well. I told your mother you'd find us." He looked around warily. "Have a seat. I have to get this beast shoed. The Lord is anxious to take his new steeds out on a hunt. He'll be down anytime."

Gunny sat on the bench and watched her father work. He hadn't lost his touch and the large horse was quickly shoed and returned to the stable. Robert sat down next to Gunny with a huff. "Now we can talk. How'd you find us?"

"Mac told me you were here."

"Of course. Did he also tell you Catherine's working here?"

"He did. I don't like it one bit that she's in service, but I saw her leaving the house just now. She seemed happy enough."

Robert grinned. "It was your mother's idea to put her into service. I objected, but when did that ever matter? Catherine's living up in the attic rooms with the other servant girls. She's a joyous thing, Gunny. Beautiful and sweet and charming. There's very little of you in her," he said with a wink.

The words burned in Gunny's ears. "Da, there's every bit of me in her and you know it."

"I was teasing. Let's not talk about how much of you is in her," Robert said, holding a finger to his lips. "After all these years, Catherine believes she's our daughter and I wouldn't want her to hear anything different."

"Of course not. Why should she know the truth?"

"Now's not the time, Gunny. We're just getting settled in here. It's best she continue to believe that you're her crazy older sister who moved off to the Blaskets."

"Thanks, Da."

"I don't mean crazy like that," Robert said, rubbing a hand along the back of his neck.

"I know what you meant." Gunny stood and straightened her apron. "You had to tell her something. Let's find Mam. I'm sure she'll be happy to see me."

Robert hesitated. "The work here's been a little hard on your mother. It's only been a week and I'm sure things'll get better. Mrs. Needham has made it very clear who runs this house."

"Mrs. Needham? She was ancient when I used to make deliveries here."

"She's still here and still ancient." Robert remained seated on the bench. "I have to get the horses saddled. Go find your mother. She's probably in the kitchen. It's good to see you, Gunny. It's been too long."

Gunny smiled at her father. "It's good to see you too, Da."

Eileen was alone in the kitchen, kneading bread for tomorrow's morning rolls. Her thinning grey hair was pulled back tight in a small dust cap. Gunny stood in the doorway and looked at the fine wrinkles around her mother's eyes and across her cheeks. Eileen froze when she saw Gunny.

"You found us," Eileen said raising her floury hands in the air.

"I found you," Gunny said mimicking her mother's gesture.

Eileen looked across the wide kitchen work table then returned to her kneading. "How's island life?" she asked politely as if she'd seen Gunny only recently.

Gunny pulled out a chair at the table and sat. "Island life's fine."

"Well," Eileen said dusting her hands toward Gunny. "I have work to do. Lord Ventry says that no one can make rolls like I do."

"Mam, I haven't seen you in ten years. Can you stop and chat for a moment?" She looked around the open, airy kitchen. "You must love working here with all this space and light. You always hated our tiny, dark house."

"I never hated our house but this is where I was meant to live."

"As a servant?"

Eileen punched at the bread dough. "Must you always find something mean to say?"

"That was an honest question, Mam. I can't picture you working for anyone—even if it means you get to live in the Big House."

"We don't live in the Big House. We have a fine apartment next to the stables."

"That must smell nice and horsey."

"I spend most of my time here," Eileen said, heavily kneading the bread. "Lord Milliken appreciates my work. Something you never did."

"Mam, I didn't come to argue with you. I came to see you and Da. And Catherine. I was surprised to hear that you put Catherine into service."

Eileen glanced up from her work. "I'd prefer that you not see Catherine."

"I already saw her—on my way to the stables."

Eileen's mouth twitched. "Did you say anything?"

"No," Gunny said loudly. "She doesn't know me and I'm not going to scare her by telling her who I am."

"I think that's best."

"All the same, she is my daughter, Mam" Gunny sparred, one eyebrow raised. "I'd like to know her and for her to know me."

"She's not your daughter. You gave her to me and left."

"I didn't exactly give her to you."

"That's all in the past now. Why are you here?"

Gunny cleared her throat and looked her mother in the eye. "I think Catherine should be in school."

"School? Who put that nonsense in your head?"

"Catherine's still a little girl. She's only twelve."

"Twelve is plenty old enough to work. And anyway, you don't get to make decisions about her. I think you should go now," Eileen said, setting the powdery dough aside and pushing a stray lock of grey hair from her face.

Gunny stood and ran her hands down into her apron pocket. She absentmindedly fingered the black-handled knife. "You're right. I'll go. I have other business to attend to." She looked around the kitchen. "I hope it works out for you being here, Mam. Sometimes it's difficult when a dream comes true."

Eileen turned back to punching the bread dough and Gunny headed outside through the kitchen door.

"Stop right there," a man yelled behind her.

Gunny turned with a start. Thomas Milliken crossed the yard at a fast limp. She had not seen him since that long ago Hallow E'en in Dunquin. She felt a bead of sweat drop between her breasts.

"I thought that was you," Thomas gushed, grinning from ear to ear. "I haven't seen you since... when? Did you hear that Catherine has become part of our household?"

"I heard that," Gunny said looking down at her boots and trying to breathe. "And that my parents are working for you as well," Gunny added.

"Oh, yes, they're here," he said looking distracted. Then his face brightened. "Come see what I've added out front. It's good to see you." He grabbed Gunny by the arm and pulled her along to the front of the house. Gunny cringed at his touch, at the sound of his voice. How could he act as if nothing had ever happened between them?

They rounded the corner of the house. There were five large ogham stones evenly spaced in a row along the drive. She had not noticed them on her way in. Each stone was marked with a cross and slashes of a lost Irish language. Gunny was stunned.

"Where'd you get these?"

"I moved four of them from Kilvickillane on the south shore of Smerwick Harbor. I found the last one in Ballyfeeny. They're part of my new collection."

"Thomas," Gunny said. "Those stones marked ancient graves. You shouldn't have moved them."

"They're just stones and besides, they're mine to move. I sent two more to my nephew at Chute Hall near Tralee. Aren't they magnificent?" he said, a wide grin on his face.

"They were magnificent where they were originally placed," Gunny said frowning.

"I think they add flair to the house. And I am expanding the gardens. I am going to make this estate magnificent."

Gunny shook her head. "Is Catherine part of your beautification project?"

Thomas smiled. "She is fitting in nicely. I will make sure nothing happens to her. You have my word on that."

"I have your word on what?"

Thomas blushed. "I only meant that she is safe with me, Gunny. I'm going to look after her. She'll have an easier time growing up than you did."

"How kind of you," Gunny said coldly.

Thomas chuckled. "You and I were friends, Gunny. I am happy to take in your sister. She's much nicer than you were at nearly the same age and much more respectful. My sons are quite taken with her."

Gunny blinked. "How old are your sons?"

"Dayrolles is thirteen, Thomas is twelve and we have a one-year old, Todd."

"Three boys. You must be happy. Are they in school?" Gunny asked innocently.

Thomas grinned. "I hired a tutor to teach them here at the house. I'd miss them if they were away at school. And it gives us time to hunt and ride together. Dayrolles is quite the athlete. Young Thomas is more of a reader and a dreamer. Maybe I should send him off to school…"

Thomas paused to study Gunny's pale face, thick black curls, and gentle curves. She was a woman, but he could still see the girl in her. "Tell me about yourself, Gunny Malone. Micky O'Leary told me you moved to the Blaskets."

"True."

"I had Reverend Gayer send a Bible reader there. The boy returned saying he was lucky to escape with his life."

Gunny pictured the Protestant Bible flaming up in Charlotte's fire. "That's partly why I'm here, Thomas. The children on the island need a teacher, not a

Bible reader. We need a school and I want you to build it." She decided to not share her plan for bringing Catherine to the island once the school was built. She could see he was charmed with having her by his side and did not want to break the spell if it meant she could get her way.

Thomas laughed. "Why would I spend money for a school on an island of heathen illiterates?"

Gunny pushed a stray black curl from her forehead and worked to keep a controlled voice. "The islanders are not heathens and the only reason they're illiterate is because they've never had the chance to learn. Wouldn't it be better if your future tenants were educated enough to build better houses and to learn better ways to farm and tend sheep?"

"An education wouldn't change anything for that hoard. Catholics are lazy by nature. Do you know how many holidays my peasants take each year?"

Gunny grunted. "Of course I know, Thomas. I'm one of your peasants."

"If only I could get more of you to convert… My uncle used to talk about it."

"I heard Reverend Gayer offering a plug of tobacco to a few of the Blasket men if they converted."

Thomas adjusted his collar. "The Reverend's tobacco campaign in Ventry and Dingle has been quite successful."

Gunny laughed. "If you believe anyone is actually going to stay Protestant after they get their prize then you're more foolish than I thought."

Thomas stomped his good foot. "God, I forgot how you speak your mind."

"Thomas," Gunny said, trying to regain control. "You could bring change to this peninsula. You could make life better for everyone. Build us a school."

Thomas eyed Gunny critically. "You live on the island. Why don't you build your own school?"

Gunny blushed. "I don't have time to teach the children. I have a farm to run."

"You must have a husband to help you."

Gunny felt her cheeks burn. "I never married. I farm by myself out on the west end."

Thomas stiffened. "I've never seen your name on my rent rolls."

"I don't live in the village, Thomas. I'm out in an old abandoned house and barely grow enough food in a few rough fields to feed myself."

"Anyone who has a house and farms on my land pays rent," Thomas said crossing his arms. "I'll send Mr. Thompson over to visit you."

"Reverend Thompson, from Dingle, works for you?"

"He's Mr. Thompson now, not Reverend. He makes more money working for me than he ever did working for the Protestant church," Thomas said, chin out. "I'd had enough of tenant meetings and court cases and evictions. I pay him five percent of every rent he collects. When you see him, you will pay him as you would pay me."

"I will pay him as I'd pay you. And that'll still be nothing."

Thomas stared at Gunny and felt again the deep urge to touch the pulsing skin along her chest plate, to run his fingers through her thick, dark curls and up the back of her long neck. "Why are you cross with me, Gunny?" he said in a quiet voice taking a step toward her. "We were once friends."

She took a step away. "Friends? We were never friends, Thomas. I don't think you know what a friend is." She paused. "Aren't you supposed to be somewhere? My father said he was waiting for you at the stables to go out hunting—maybe for rabbits?" She spat out the final word and turned to leave.

"Don't turn your back on me, Gunny. Mr. Thompson will be over to see you!"

Gunny turned to face Thomas. "Mr. Thompson can collect my rent from my dead, stiff fingers," she said, then stalked up the long driveway.

"If you don't pay me," Thomas yelled behind her, "I can evict the whole island."

Gunny turned onto the road that would take her back through Ventry. Her visit had produced nothing except anger and fear. She kicked at the dirt and broke into a sprint to Dunquin to catch her ride home with Thomas' words echoing behind her.

Gunny heard nothing from Lord Thomas or Mr. Thompson for two years about rent, Bible readers, or schools. She continued to plant potatoes and oats each spring, to haul turf and bring in her harvest in the late-summer and early autumn, and to spend winter days twisting rope and visiting with the Blasket villagers. Then everything changed.

Patrick pounded on Gunny's door, while Lorcan paced behind him, whining, in the yard.

"Gunny," Patrick panted when Gunny opened the door. "Lord Ventry's agent's on the island. He's storming about in the village asking everyone how to get out to the west end. We sent him along the path by the cliffs hoping he'd get lost. I cut through the hills. He could be here any time."

"I knew he'd come here eventually. But what could he possibly take from me?" Gunny asked, calmly wiping her hands on her apron and checking to make sure the black-handled knife was in her pocket. "My harvest isn't in yet and I don't imagine Mr. Thompson is going to go out and pull up the potatoes and grain himself."

Gallarus snorted from the hearth. Gunny and Patrick both turned and looked at the pig.

"Oh, my God," Gunny said. "He'll take Gallarus. What am I going to do?"

"Gallarus is so old, Gunny. If that's what the Lord's agent wants, maybe you should give him the pig."

"Give my pig to that pig? How would you like it if I suggested you give Lorcan to the old Lord to have for his supper? Gallarus is going to die in his own time and be buried here on my land. Quick. We have to hide him."

"Hide him?" Patrick said glancing at the very large pig and the very small house. "Where?"

"No time to explain," Gunny said. "Go outside and stall the agent if he shows up in the yard." She pushed Patrick out the door and looped the hatch behind him, then pulled the wide straw mat away from the heavy wooden door in the floor and yanked it open.

"Come, pig," she demanded.

Gallarus rolled onto his back and blinked his small black eyes.

"Come, Gallarus," she screamed. "Or a big, nasty man is going to come and take you away."

Gallarus grunted again, blinked once, but did not move from his spot in front of the fire.

"I know you understand every word I'm saying," Gunny said, grabbing a fresh loaf of warm bread from the pot oven. "I hate it when you make me revert to bribery." She held out a small morsel of bread in front of the pig's nose. "Come on, piggy. I know you want this nice, crusty bread." She backed toward the open door in the floor. Gallarus huffed to his feet and followed.

Gunny could hear Patrick arguing in the yard as she pulled the straw mat back in place. She quietly unlooped the latch on the door and sat in her tipping chair in front of the fire to catch her breath. When Mr. Thompson pushed the door open, she was sitting quietly smoking a small white pipe. Mr. Thompson took a step into the room, his full frame filling the doorway. He blinked as his eyes adjusted to the dim light.

"So this is where you live. Lord Ventry has bothered me for years to get me to come and find you. Surely this was not worth all of the effort."

Gunny glanced up from her chair and pulled the pipe from her lips. "How is Thomas?"

Mr. Thompson snarled. "He's Lord Ventry to you. One of the boys in the village told me you have a pig out here. Let me have him and we'll have settled on one year's rent."

Gunny stared into the fire. "A pig? The boy was mistaken. You know how uneducated, heathen children lie."

Mr. Thompson sniffed at the air. "This house smells like a pig."

Gunny pulled the pipe from her lips and took a deep breath. "You're right. It does smell a little piggish in here." She knocked the ash out of Matt's pipe onto the hearth and cut a new bit of tobacco, then turned and looked at Mr.

Thompson. "I used to have a pig, but he passed. We buried him up in the high fields last winter."

Mr. Thompson stood with his hands on his hips. "I don't believe you. Lord Ventry wants his rent and I'm not to leave without it."

Gunny shook her head and turned back to the fire. "This house was deserted when I got here. How can I owe rent on something that's of no use to anyone but me?"

"You're farming on Lord Ventry's property and will pay rent just like everyone else."

Gunny stood to her full height facing the burly intruder. "I have no money. I grow only enough food to get by. Tell Lord Ventry he'll get nothing more from me than what he's already taken."

Mr. Thompson did not budge from his position by the door. "I'm not leaving until I have either your rent or your pig."

Gunny squatted by the fire and picked out a live coal with her tongs. She held it to her pipe and slowly sucked in air to get the tobacco lit, then turned her head toward Mr. Thompson. She let smoke eek slowly out of her mouth. Thin tendrils snaked up across her face and through her black curls. She opened her eyes wide and muttered nonsense words starting at a low pitch and working her way up to a long howl, then pounded her hands on the dirt floor and smeared dirt across her mouth and forehead while she rocked and keened, her body weaving from side to side.

Patrick pulled at the agent's arm. "Best to leave her when she's like this," he whispered. "You never know what she'll do next."

Mr. Thompson stumbled back toward the door and pushed his way out into the yard. Lorcan barked furiously and nipped at his heels. Patrick gave Gunny a quick smile, and pulled the door closed behind them. Gunny slammed her body against the closed door, tossed the loop over the latch, and howled.

Mr. Thompson stood in the yard, pale and shaking. "What's wrong with her?"

"Years of neglect," Patrick said shaking his head and reaching out to scratch Lorcan's head to calm her. "You know how we island people are. Uneducated—and a little bit crazy."

Lorcan growled to add emphasis to Patrick's words.

The agent pulled his coat tight around him. "The Lord doesn't pay me enough to deal with you islanders," he muttered as he stumbled out of the yard and back toward the island village.

Patrick watched the agent scurry up the cliff path, then crossed back to Gunny's door and gave it a push, but it was latched from inside. "Gunny?" he said quietly through the door. "The Lord's agent is gone. You scared him good. I've never seen you smoke that old pipe of yours," he added with a chuckle.

The door remained closed. The house was quiet. "Gunny?" Patrick repeated, knocking loudly.

The door opened with a rush. Patrick leapt back with a start remembering how Gunny looked with the smoke circling through her curls and the dirt smeared across her mouth and face.

Gunny stood innocently in the doorway wiping a wet cloth over her face. "Sorry for the delay," she said. "Gallarus was gorging on the last of my old potatoes. I'm afraid he'll be sick all night."

The old pig pushed past Patrick. As he passed, he let out a loud stream of gas. Patrick waved his hands in front of his face and gasped.

"Are you sure you don't want that agent to take him?"

Gunny laughed. "It would serve him right. They would no doubt be halfway across the channel when Gallarus would try to eat part of the boat and they'd sink."

"Or Gallarus would shift that huge pig body of his from one side to the other and they'd tip into the salty brine," Patrick snickered. "But seriously, Gunny. Now that Lord Ventry has found you, you know someone will be back for your rent—even if Mr. Thompson never sets foot here again."

Gunny tossed the ashy cloth on the table and rubbed her eyes. "Well," she said, "I'll worry about that when the time comes."

The mighty Gallarus took his final breath a week later, his death, no doubt spurred on by severe indigestion. Patrick helped Gunny drag the large, heavy pig out of her house and out to a nearby field for burial.

"If you'd given this pig to Mr. Thompson," Patrick said, out of breath. "Your rent would be paid and we'd have saved ourselves a lot of trouble burying him."

"He was my pig. He'll be buried on my land," Gunny said with a grunt, shoveling the first of many spades full of dirt out of the pig's grave. "Are you going to help me or not?"

It took two hours to dig a hole big enough to bury the large beast. When they'd finished digging, they rolled Gallarus' body in and shoveled dirt on top of him.

Gunny leaned on her shovel and closed her eyes. "Good-bye, good pig," she said to the wind. "If only the poet were still around to write a final verse in your honor."

A week after Gallarus died, Lorcan passed. Patrick carried his old dog's thin body out to Gunny's farm and they buried him next to the pig. They said a quiet prayer at sunset over both graves and returned to Gunny's house for a plate of boiled potatoes. After they ate, they sat by the fire until the wee hours of the morning, sharing a half bottle of whiskey and telling each other every story they could think of about the fine times they'd had with the two strange beasts.

It was another year before Mr. Thompson returned to the island with a crew of fisherman from Dingle. It was early October and a blustery wind blew cold waves up over the pier as Mr. Thompson clambered onto the flat rock. He signaled to the nearby Blasket fisherman who were emptying their nets on the pier to draw near.

"Lord Ventry is a fine and generous Lord," he panted, trying to catch his breath. "He is going to build a school and a school master's house here on the Blaskets. Both are to have wooden floors. The Lord will pay you four shillings a day for your work. Every child on the island must attend this school. You are to start work immediately. Good day."

With that, he clamored back into the boat and ordered the Dingle fishermen to row him home. He wanted to spend no more time than absolutely necessary on this island. The Dingle men tipped their hats to the Blasketers, and rowed away.

The Blasket men returned to the village and word spread quickly. The villagers were wary, but the building of a new school meant work on the island—a rarity. The men decided to build on the flat lands at the south end of the island where there was open space and eagerly set about bringing building stones down from the long abandoned castle at Castle Point.

Gunny was as wary as the rest when Patrick ran out to the west end to tell her about Lord Ventry's school plans. She wondered what had made Thomas change his mind after so many years. She was certain it was not her logical words. No doubt there was a sinister plot behind this decision, but it was still welcome news. Catherine was perhaps too old to attend school now, but maybe she could still join Gunny on the Blaskets and they could work together to help at the school. She looked around her small cottage.

"She'll need more room than I have here," she muttered to the chickens who clucked about her. "I could move to the old church. Or we could move into the village. Catherine might be more comfortable there." She chuckled to herself as she sipped at a cup of hot tea. "Thomas, Thomas, Thomas. It's time for me to spend time with that girl of ours, and you are going to help me make that happen."

On a cool April morning, the day the school was to be dedicated, the villagers and Gunny gathered on the cliff to await the Lord's arrival. He appeared at the dock at midmorning. Gunny watched as Thomas Milliken awkwardly tried to pull himself onto the high stone pier, refusing assistance from the Blasket fishermen. He finally got out with Mr. Thompson pulling from the pier and two sailors in the boat pushing from behind. When the Lord was finally safely on shore, Mr. Thompson reached back in the boat and pulled out a small boy in a white sailor hat who looked a little green from his excursion across the deep, choppy channel.

The Lord instructed the two sailors to stay with the boat while he and Mr. Thompson dedicated the school. He assured them they would not be long. Mr. Thompson tucked the four-year-old boy under one arm and followed the limping Thomas up the long winding path to the village.

The villagers followed behind the Lord as he slowly walked down the road to the south end and into the new school building. The village men proudly filled in the front of the room, while the woman and children sat on the floor along the back wall. Gunny squeezed in between Charlotte and Martha O'Connor, tucking her skirt in around her feet and pushing her shawl up around her face.

The Lord stood on a wooden crate of new books at the front of the room and looked across the motley crowd. The men looked at him expectantly, with weathered, sunburned faces, hats in hand. One young mother sat nursing an infant. Several women squatted on the floor pressing long strings of seaweed into their mouths, a new habit on the island. They chewed and spat juice onto the new wooden floors as they waited for the ceremony to begin. None of the women or children wore shoes and most had dirty faces and hands. The crowded room smelled of warm bodies and fish. Thomas's nose wrinkled and he coughed into his handkerchief.

"People of the Blaskets. Your work on this schoolhouse is complete. This is one of many new schools I built this year—in Ventry, Dunquin, Kilmalkeadar and Dunorlin. Before we dedicate this schoolhouse I have two important announcements." He paused and looked around the room. No one seemed to be paying attention to him as they studied the square walls and wooden floors of the schoolhouse. He started again, speaking slowly to try and hold their attention.

"The King of England has granted a Royal License stating that my family was descended from the de Moyleyns family seated at Burnham, Norfolk, as established during the reign of Charles II. To celebrate the King's decision, we have decided to reclaim the name de Moyleyns."

He paused for affect, expecting perhaps a cheer or even a gasp, but the Blasketers simply stared at him. He awkwardly cleared his throat and continued.

"From this day forward, our house in Ventry shall be known as the Burnham House, and you shall refer to me as Sir Thomas Townsend Aremberg de Moleyns, second Baron Ventry. My oldest son will now be known as Dayrolles Blakeney Eveleigh-de-Moleyns, third Baron Ventry, my second son as Thomas Blakeney Eveleigh-de-Moleyns. My youngest son, well, for the time being will simply be known as Todd."

Two men in the front of room clapped briefly, then stopped.

"Thank you," Thomas said, eyeing the two men and picking his boy up off the floor where he'd been happily tearing pages out of a new schoolbook. He righted the small white cap on the boy's head and tried to hold the squirming child up for the crowd to see, but the boy pushed to get down and wandered off into the crowd.

"It's like they're eternal," Charlotte O'Connor whispered into Gunny's ear. "One isn't gone from the earth before the next one is there ready to take his place."

Martha leaned across Gunny. "I'm surprised the Lord doesn't claim to be descended from an Irish King. That'd give him more a right to our land than verifying he's from Burnham, Norfolk, wherever that is."

"No matter what they call themselves they're still cattle lifters and marauders," Charlotte snorted.

Thomas continued in a louder voice over the mutterings in the room. "And now for my second announcement. As you know, my grandfather, the old Lord as you called him, came to Dingle as the bequest of the King of England to oversee this estate."

Donal McCrohan stood at the front of the room. "The King gave your grandfather our land as a prize of war. And what right did your King ever have to rule over us?"

This brought a brief cheer from the villagers. Thomas' face went red. He ignored the question and the cheering.

"Upon my grandfather's death," he continued in a loud voice, "I became the Baron Ventry. I am happy to continue to serve in this capacity, to oversee this land, to be your protector, and to educate your children. I do not, however, intend to die a pauper as my grandfather did. You all know the former Reverend David Thompson."

Mr. Thompson nodded his head briefly to the crowd.

"Mr. Thompson has worked for the last several years as my receiver and land agent. His attempts to collect the proper amount of rent from the Blasket Islands has largely been ignored. As of today, this will happen no more."

The room went silent at the mention of rent.

Mr. Thompson glanced around the room. "Your next rent is due on November first. Catholics must pay in full. For this year only, if you convert to the proper faith and become a Protestant, I will work with you on the amount that is due."

The crowd grumbled and started to talk amongst themselves.

"Mr. Thompson is a serious man; do not cross him," Thomas said over the low din in the room. The Baron Ventry looked around the crowded room. "Has anyone seen my boy?"

Todd had crawled onto Gunny's lap and was happily bouncing on her knees. She looked up when she saw Thomas' familiar boots in front of her.

"Lord Baron de Moleyns," she said, carefully enunciating each name. "I'd stand to curtsy but seem to have my hands full at the moment."

Thomas reached out for Todd. The child pouted and hugged Gunny hard around the neck.

"Bounce again. Again!" he shouted.

Gunny loved the feeling of the little boy's warm hug around her neck.

"You are as popular as ever with the boys," Thomas muttered, then continued in a stern voice. "Todd, come with me."

When the boy still didn't budge, Gunny struggled to her feet, pulling the child up with her. He reluctantly let go of her as she handed him to his father. She stooped to collect his hat. The Baron Ventry paused while she placed it squarely on the child's head, then turned back to the crowded room.

"If you cannot pay your rent, your children will not be allowed to attend school and you must leave the island. We have fifteen houses on Strand Street in Dingle for anyone who is evicted. You will pay no rent to live there and will receive seven shillings a week in wages. That is if you convert to Protestantism. If you convert back to Catholicism, you will be evicted once again and we will offer you no farther accommodation."

"I know people who live in the houses on Strand Street," Patrick said. "What happened to them?"

"They were Catholic—and were evicted," Thomas answered with a smile. "Are there any other questions? No? Very well. I dedicate this school to serious learning. I expect you to take care of the building, to respect the teacher we send over, and for your children to become fully educated members of British society. Good day."

Charlotte O'Connor saluted the Lord as he pushed out the door past her with Mr. Thompson following, struggling to keep the young Todd perched on his shoulders. The villagers watched their guests leave; no one accompanied them on the walk back through the village and down to the pier.

"Well, isn't our Crippled Lord Protector full of something," Patrick muttered.

"He is full of something," Gunny agreed, leaning against Patrick and feeling a chill in the air. She pulled her shawl up around her head and willed herself to breathe. She had waited three years for this day and knew now she was doing the right thing. Once the new teacher arrived and the school was in order, she would bring Catherine to the Blaskets, away from her parents and away from the girl's silly, pompous father.

~ Chapter 18: Maggie & Larry ~

A gust of wind rattled the window frame of the small apartment near the stables at Ballygoleen. The big house was officially called "The Burnham House" now, but only to the Baron, his wife, and the other English on the peninsula. To everyone else, the house was Ballygoleen and always would be. Lightning flashed along the stable walls, followed by a bellow of thunder. Moisture seeped in the bottom left corner of the apartment window and pooled on the sill. Catherine let out a short groan.

"Keep breathing, Cath," Eileen muttered. "I sent your father for the doctor."

Catherine gritted her teeth as the pain ripped along her insides. She gasped and squeezed her eyes closed. Eileen gripped the young girl's cold hand between her warm palms and tried to will strength into the girl's body. Catherine had been in labor for over twenty-four hours and Eileen knew her strength was nearly depleted. Wind pushed against the walls of the apartment and the girl shuddered. Eileen started when the door burst open behind her.

"Robert? Doctor?"

A flash of lightning lit Gunny's large frame as she swept through the doorway into the room on a gust of wind and moisture. She pulled her shawl from her head and slammed the door closed. "Why didn't you send word to me?" she demanded, tossing her shawl across a chair in front of the fire.

Eileen sobbed and turned toward Catherine. "Because I didn't want you to know."

Gunny wiped her hands on her wet apron and strode to Catherine's side. "How long has she been like this?" she asked feeling the girl's forehead and lifting her eyelids. The girl's forehead was cold and clammy, her pale curls matted against her face, her blue eyes large and dilated.

Catherine muttered and rolled away from Gunny's touch.

"Be still, girl," Gunny said in a soft, firm voice. "I'm here to help." She felt along the girl's large stomach. Her muscles were tight in contraction.

"Look at her," Eileen said weeping. "Look at our poor Catherine. He's ruined her."

"How long?" Gunny demanded.

"All night and all day," Eileen sobbed. "Oh, Gunny, she only barely moans now. What's wrong with her?"

"I need more light. Go up to the Big House and get a lamp."

Eileen fled to do as she was told.

"It's all right, Catherine," Gunny murmured. "You're going to be all right."

She lifted the rough, wool blanket that covered the girl and reached between her legs to see if she could feel the baby's head. No luck. She felt again around Catherine's hard abdomen and up under her ribs. She sighed.

The baby was upright and firmly wedged against Catherine's ribcage. She'd had two other deliveries like this. She had to get the baby to turn.

"This may hurt, girl," Gunny said trying to keep her voice calm.

Catherine was pale and non-responsive as Gunny leaned across the girl's still frame and pushed on her distended belly. Gunny felt the baby shift slightly and pushed down harder. Catherine shrieked in pain and Gunny released the pressure as Eileen flew back into the room.

"What're you doing? Stop that!" Eileen hissed, setting a glowing lantern roughly on the wooden floor and shaking the rain out of her skirt.

"Mam, the baby's upright. It can't be born that way. I have to try and turn the child or we'll lose both of them."

Eileen covered her mouth to stifle a cry as she steadied the oil lamp on the floor. "Do what you have to do, but save her, Gunny. You have to save my precious girl."

Gunny knelt on the bed by Catherine's head and using her full height and weight, pushed again on the small head within the girl's body but sensed no movement. She pushed again. Catherine screamed and went limp.

"What happened?" Eileen whispered, clutching at the girl's hand. "Is she dead?"

Gunny shook her head. "She fainted. It's for the best. She won't feel any pain for awhile. I'll work as fast as I can."

Gunny pushed again, firmly but gently, on the hard knot of the baby's head. This time when the baby's head moved slightly from under Catherine's ribs, Gunny was able to hold it in place until the girl's belly shifted sideways, and the baby flipped to a downward position. Gunny let out a soft whoop and placed her large hands firmly across the girl's stomach.

"Don't even think of turning around, you little critter," she uttered to the girl's belly. "Mam, reach down and see if you can see the crown of the baby's head."

Eileen moved the oil lamp to the end of the bed and gingerly lifted the blanket.

"I see the white top of a head," she gasped.

Gunny jumped from the bed and raced around next to her mother, keeping one hand firmly on the girl's abdomen.

"All right," she said reaching between Catherine's legs with her free hand. "Time for you to make an appearance, Little One, but we need some help from your mother. Mam, try to wake Catherine. I need her to push."

Eileen moved to the side of the bed and cupped Catherine's slim, pale face in her hands. "Catherine? Catherine, can you hear me?" she whispered gently.

"Louder, Mam. I know you can do it. I've heard you."

Eileen glared at Gunny, then turned back to Catherine. "Catherine?" she said a little louder. "She can't hear me, Gunny," she sobbed.

"Mam, this is no time to break," Gunny said firmly. "Take a breath, then yell. Slap her face. Do whatever you have to do to get her attention."

"Slap her face? I..."

"Mam, slap her face," Gunny said firmly. "We have to get this baby out and we need Catherine to push."

Eileen gently slapped Catherine's face. Catherine squinted but did not open her eyes.

"Again!" Gunny said.

Eileen slapped the girl a little harder and yelled sharply. "Catherine! Wake up. Please. You have to push, darling. You have to push the baby out." Tears poured down Eileen's face as she pleaded with the struggling mother.

Catherine blinked her large blue eyes. Gunny felt the girl's legs tense, then felt her push weakly.

"Good, girl, Catherine," Gunny said encouragingly. "Take a breath and push again."

Catherine gasped at the pain that rushed in around her, then pushed hard through gritted teeth. The baby's head emerged and Gunny took a deep breath.

"One more push, Catherine, to get the shoulders out. Don't stop now. Push!"

Through a haze of pain and shadow, Catherine bore down as hard as she could and pushed a tiny baby boy into Gunny's waiting hands. The creature stared at Gunny's face, then shrieked in protest. Gunny gasped.

"God, you're just like your mother. You're not in my hands for a minute and you're already crying."

Gunny realized tears were flowing down her cheeks. She wiped her face on the back of her sleeve and laughed. She had a grandson. She delivered the placenta, then tied and swiftly cut the umbilical cord with her black-handled knife. She gently wiped off the baby's face with a nearby cloth and wrapped a pillow cover tightly around the howling child and handed him to Eileen.

"Try to comfort him. You're good at that."

Gunny turned back to Catherine and bunched blankets up between the girl's legs, but she continued to bleed heavily and the blankets were quickly soaked. She reached across the girl's chest to feel her heartbeat. The beat was slow and steady but was very, very weak.

"No," Gunny muttered.

Eileen rocked the new baby who continued to howl. "Quiet, quiet, little one. You don't want to disturb the horses or wake the master."

"Wake the master?" Gunny muttered. "Please don't tell me the master had anything to do with this."

"All right, I won't tell you that Catherine said Thomas was the father."

"No!" Gunny said slapping her hand against the bed. She shook her head in disgust and spit toward the fire. "The bastard. He told me he'd look after her."

Eileen shook her head. The child's high-pitched crying made her head feel as if it would split. "Yes, the father is the young Lord Thomas Blakeney Eveleigh-de-Moleyns. He always liked Catherine. I had no idea how much."

"The young Lord?" Gunny gasped. The boy had slept with his half-sister and did not even know it. She reached up to feel Catherine's cold hands and face. Blood continued to seep from her body, soaking the straw tick. Gunny's face was as pale as the dying girl in the dim light of the oil lamp.

"What is it, Gunny?" Eileen asked looking from Catherine to Gunny. "She'll be all right now that the baby's out. Pray God, tell me she'll be all right."

Gunny shook her head. "Now would be a good time to pray, Mam. I don't think Catherine has long."

Eileen gasped in disbelief. "No, not my Catherine," she sobbed. "Not my perfect little angel."

Gunny took the crying baby from Eileen and rocked him to try and quiet him while Eileen gripped Catherine's hands and ran her fingers over the girl's pale face. The roaring wind outside was matched by a high-pitched moan from Eileen as Catherine quietly slipped on a breath from this world into the next. When the girl's breathing stopped, Eileen's clutched handfuls of her long blond curls as if she could somehow keep hold of the girl's spirit, then turned and stared at Gunny in disbelief. "He killed her. That baby killed my Catherine."

Gunny cupped the small child's head as she swayed. "Mam, it's young Thomas who killed her. This baby's innocent."

Eileen pushed up from the bed and stared at the small bundle whimpering in Gunny's arms. "He's not innocent," she hissed. "He's a killer. He's a murderer! Let me have him."

Gunny turned as Eileen dove at the baby. "Stop it, Mam," she said as Eileen beat on her back. "You're acting crazy."

Eileen pulled at Gunny's arms. "Give me that baby!" she screamed. "If Catherine's dead then that baby should be dead too!"

Gunny hugged the tiny body to her chest. "Mam! Stop! Have you lost your mind?"

"Give him to me!" Eileen screamed, tears pouring down her face. Then she fell to her knees behind Gunny and pulled at her hair. "He killed my precious Catherine," she shrieked. "He killed my little girl."

Gunny grabbed her shawl from the fireside and pulled it up over her head. She stepped out into the cold rain and sprinted across to the kitchen door of the big house. She stepped inside and threw the bolt then pulled her shawl free and looked at the whimpering baby in her arms. She wiped the rain from his little red face with the corner of her sleeve.

"Sorry I had to take you out into the storm. But the storm in the stables was much worse."

She looked around the dimly lit kitchen, knelt to stir the fire and added a turf. The room brightened slightly. She heard a chair scrape behind her and turned with a start. "Who's there?" she asked looking around the shadowy room.

"Hello, Gunny."

"Mrs. Needham," Gunny took in a quick breath. "I'm sorry, Ma'am. I didn't know anyone was in the kitchen."

Mrs. Needham covered her mouth and coughed deeply. "Is that Catherine's baby?"

Gunny clutched the baby protectively against her chest. "No."

"I know it is, Gunny. I heard Catherine screaming in the stable apartment earlier today. I only began to suspect she was with child a month or so ago. She and your mother hid it quite well."

Gunny rocked the baby in the dim light. He was finally quieting, exhausted from the ordeal of birth and flight.

Mrs. Needham coughed again, a deep rattling cough. "This is a bad day for a baby to be born," she said in a hoarse voice. "Witsuntide. The day of the descent of the holy spirit to the apostles. That child is destined to cause death or to die a violent death. The child will murder—or be hanged."

Gunny glanced at the pale shadow of a woman sitting at the kitchen table.

"The child has already caused a death," she said softly. Gunny was surprised at the quaver in her voice as she said the words. Her eyes burned and she blinked. "Catherine was gone before I ever got to know her."

"It's for the best," Mrs. Needham said. "The girl had no life in her since Thomas rejected her."

"Thomas rejected her?"

"What else could he do?" Mrs. Needham went on. "His father would not allow him to marry a servant girl—and a Catholic at that."

"No, of course the mighty Baron Ventry could not allow that," Gunny said. And he couldn't let his son marry his half-sister. She looked at Mrs. Needham. "Did Catherine love Thomas?"

Mrs. Needham coughed again into her handkerchief. "Who knows with young people. Love? Lust? Does it really matter which it was?"

Gunny continued to sway with the sleeping child in her arms. "My mother's frantic at the loss of Catherine. I have to keep this baby away from her."

"Good. Take it away. No one wants it. Are you going to take the other one as well?"

Gunny turned slowly from the fire toward the seated woman. "What other one?"

"The girl." Mrs. Needham paused. "You didn't know that Catherine had a little girl?"

Gunny's head spun. "A girl? How old?"

Mrs. Needham shook her head. "She must be two or so."

"But Catherine's only sixteen. Who's the father of that one?"

"As far as I know young Thomas is the father of both. The little one's asleep over there on the cot," Mrs. Needham said pointing. "Your mother asked me to keep an eye on her earlier today. She said that Catherine was ill. I knew better."

Gunny had not noticed the small cot or the tiny girl sleeping on it. She crossed the room cradling the newborn in one arm and pulled the covers away from the little girl's face. The child was sleeping peacefully, her small red mouth gathered in a tiny pout. A head full of fine curly brown hair surrounded her face.

"She's beautiful," Gunny gasped.

Mrs. Needham waved a wrinkled hand in front of her face. "She's a handful is what she is. She spends most of her time in the kitchen getting under your mother's feet. Your mother doesn't have much patience with her. I'd be glad to see all of you go away."

Gunny sighed and shook her head. "I can't take a child and a baby." She swallowed hard and listened to the storm rage outside. In the hard patter of rain, she thought she heard William's deep voice. "Take on a difficult task. Do something difficult for the sake of someone else. Do something good with your life."

Mrs. Needham stared at Gunny. "Are you all right?"

Gunny blinked and looked at the baby in her arms and at the little girl sleeping on the cot. She reached down to touch the girl's soft curls. The baby woke and started to howl again, his face red and small fists clenched.

"God, I hate babies," Gunny muttered shifting the screaming baby more firmly into the nook of her right arm. The girl's deep brown eyes fluttered open and she stared up at Gunny. "What's your name?" she asked softly.

"Maggie," Mrs. Needham said bitingly from behind her.

Maggie looked at the tall woman looming over her and held her hands over her ears to protect them from the shrieking baby. She did not utter a word.

Gunny tried to bounce the crying baby as she squatted by the cot. If she left the girl she would be raised by this dying witch in the kitchen and Gunny's angry mother, an underclass servant vulnerable to the whims of her master. She took a deep breath and made up her mind in a heartbeat.

"Maggie. We're going on a little trip. Do you understand?"

Maggie gazed into Gunny's eyes. "Momma?" the little girl asked in a soft voice, moving her hands from her ears.

Gunny's throat closed and she worked to swallow. "Momma can't help you now. You're going with me." She retrieved her drying shawl from in front of the fire and pulled it around her shoulders, then scooped up the little girl in her left arm, covers and all. "Would you mind opening the door for us, Mrs. Needham?"

Mrs. Needham shuffled to the door, threw open the bolt, and opened the door to a gust of cold rain. The chill made the old woman cough again and she clutched at the frame of the door. Gunny hesitated. The rain was coming down in sheets. She pulled the shawl up over her head covering the children as best she could, and headed off on the muddy road toward Dingle.

Joanna Murphy was up later than usual. Daniel was off visiting Jamie in Dublin and she had not wanted to retire to a cold, empty bed. At age twenty-six, James had finally found work clerking for a law firm, much to Joanna's amazement and delight. She envisioned her son, dressed as a fine lawyer, as she listened to the rain pouring down outside. She knelt to smoor the fire and was startled by a sharp knock at the back door. She stood, wiped her hands on her apron and peeked out the window. From the weak light of the kitchen window, she could see Gunny Malone standing outside, drenched, carrying a large bundle of wet blankets.

She pulled the door open and helped Gunny into the kitchen. "Come in — quickly. What're you doing here on such a night?"

Gunny blundered in, exhausted, with rain and wind pushing behind her. She stumbled to the fire and carefully set the armload of wet blankets on the floor. The bundle squirmed. Gunny knelt and peeled off layers of wet blankets to reveal a soaked sleepy girl, and a startled red-faced baby.

"My God," Joanna said clutching at her heart. "Who do you have there?"

"It's a long story," Gunny said working swiftly to lift Maggie out of the blanket pile and pulling off her soggy bed clothes. "Can we stay here for the night?"

"Of course you can. But what… Are you in some sort of trouble?" Joanna asked kneeling to pick up the tiny baby who was now whimpering and looked like he was going to howl.

Gunny turned to Joanna. "We're not in trouble but someone may come looking for us. I can't think about that now. I need to get these children dry and warm."

"Of course you do," Joanna said. "Some of Jamie's old things might fit the little girl. And I'll get dry blankets for the baby. God, he's small, Gunny. How old is he?" she asked, hugging his cold, naked body to her chest.

"Get the clothes and the blankets and I'll explain everything."

Joanna handed Gunny the baby and hurried into the shop for blankets then scrambled upstairs to find clothes for the girl.

They soon had the children dried off and tucked in under two soft wool blankets on a small mat in front of the fire. As the children dozed off, Gunny realized how cold and tired she was. She stirred the fire and added a brick of turf, then draped the soggy bed clothes across the kitchen chairs and table. Her arms and back ached as she knelt to rub her hands in front of the fire.

"You're taller than me. I hope you don't mind wearing one of Daniel's shirts and a pair of his pants," Joanna said quietly, offering Gunny a dry set of neatly folded clothing.

Gunny snickered as she pulled off her wet things and changed into Daniel's oversized shirt, pants, and warm wool stockings while Joanna set the kettle on the fire to heat. When she was finished dressing, she sat on the floor next to the sleeping children.

"Heaven," she said when Joanna handed her a hot mug of sweet tea., cupping the tea in one hand and resting her other hand protectively around the baby's sleeping head. As she sipped at the tea, her body stopped shaking and she took in a sharp, jagged breath.

Joanna sat on the edge of her chair surveying the chaos of the room. "You always were one for surprises, but this one beats all."

Gunny's eyes filled with tears. "Thank God you were here. Let me tell you about my night."

Gunny set off early the next morning to make sure Patrick had survived a night of drinking, and that he had enough room in the boat for a few more passengers. He had dropped her off the day before after she'd insisted on an unexpected trip to Dingle. She'd had a dream that she had to get something back she'd lost in Ventry. Patrick had not asked any questions.

By the time she found Patrick and returned to the Murphy's store, Joanna was up, had heated milk for the hungry baby, and sat with him snug in her arms feeding him warm milk from a ceramic piece that looked a little like a slipper. The girl was sitting at the kitchen table doing her best to get spoonfuls of boiled mashed potatoes into her mouth. Gunny stopped in the doorway admiring the calm, domestic scene.

"You're an angel sent from heaven, Joanna," she said. "Look at these children all content. Maybe I should leave them with you here in Dingle."

"I was trying to feed the baby warm milk from a spoon when I remembered my old pap feeder. My mother had it sent over from England when I had James and was too sick to nurse. I can't believe I kept it all these years. James survived on cow's milk and potato starch until he was old enough to eat food. I'm sure this baby will do the same."

Joanna beamed into the baby's small, red face and cooed. "You're going to be just fine, aren't you?"

Gunny felt her chest clutch. What if Joanna wasn't here? She didn't know anything about feeding a baby with a pap feeder. What had her mother used to feed little Catherine when Gunny had the milk fever? She felt her head spin. She couldn't do this. She didn't know anything about raising a newborn baby, yet alone a two-year-old girl. Hadn't she run away from all this once before? Then she pictured her enraged mother and old Mrs. Needham coughing away in the dim light of the kitchen—and about the aristocratic father and grandfather of the children. She pulled out a chair and sat down heavily at the familiar kitchen table.

"I'm going to raise these children on the Blaskets and I'm going to do a damned good job of it. They won't grow up feeling unwelcome or that they're a burden to anyone."

Joanna smiled. "I have no doubt that you'll raise them well, Gunny."

"I don't know how well I'll do but I promise I'll never say, 'You're too loud,' or 'Don't bother me now,' or 'Do as I say and don't ask any questions.' I want these children to know love and joy."

"You want to be careful about saying, 'I'll never say this to my children.'"

Gunny laughed. "I know it won't be easy, but I couldn't leave them at Ballygoleen. Not with those two women. Not in that household."

She leaned over Joanna and studied the content, suckling baby. "Charlotte O'Connor has a cow. I'm sure she'll give me milk for the little boy. And the girl…"

Maggie had been watching Gunny and Joanna as she spooned bits of mashed potatoes into her mouth. She swung her legs hard against the chair and pointed at Joanna and the baby.

"Baby?" she asked, her mouth full of buttery potatoes.

"Yes, that's a baby, Maggie. That's your baby brother," Gunny answered smiling at the little girl.

"Momma?" Maggie asked in the same tone she had asked about the baby.

Gunny pulled a chair up next to Maggie and sat. She wiped a bit of wet potato from the girl's chin with her thumb. "Momma's gone, Maggie. Momma had to go away."

The little girl concentrated on her spoon and the potatoes. "Gone," she repeated.

"Yes, Maggie. Momma's gone. I'm Gunny. I'm your…"

Maggie looked up at Gunny.

"Well, I'm your Gunny," Gunny said weakly.

"Gunny," the small girl repeated then pointed again to the baby. "Baby?"

"Yes that's a baby."

Maggie pointed and repeated again, "Baby?"

"Yes," Gunny replied a little louder, trying to be patient. "That's a baby. That's your baby brother."

"Larry?" Maggie asked with a scrunched up face.

Gunny paused. "Larry?"

"Larry?" Maggie asked again smiling.

"No, that's a baby, Maggie. Not a Larry."

"Larry," Maggie said and turned again to her bowl of potatoes. "Baby Larry." Maggie licked the back of her spoon.

"I think Maggie just named the baby," Joanna said, shaking her head.

"Larry?" Gunny asked. "I've never heard such a name. I suppose we could name him Lawrence."

Joanna looked at the little boy as he stretched and wiggled in her arms.

"Whatever his name is, he's no worse the wear for his strange birth and a night out in the rain. You are going to have your hands full with these two. They are both full of energy. They remind me of someone…"

Gunny looked at Joanna and saw William's twinkling eyes. "I'm up to the task. I swear I am," she muttered. "It might just be the reason I'm here on this earth."

Joanna packed a large box of Jamie's old clothes for Maggie and topped it with the fire-dried blankets from Ventry. She added a stack of old flour sacks to use as nappies and tucked the ceramic bottle into one end of the box. She hung the "closed" sign in the shop window. Daniel would be surprised if he arrived back before she did, but she knew he'd understand. After all, he knew Gunny. The small bells above the door tinkled as she picked up the heavy box and pulled the door shut behind them. Gunny tucked the baby in her right arm and tried to pick Maggie up in her left arm.

"I do it myself," Maggie stated, pulling away from Gunny's grip.

"You want to walk?" Gunny asked. "It's a long way down to the pier."

The little girl was already tottering ahead of them down the street. Joanna hurried to catch up with her. She looked back at Gunny and shrugged, and the four of them hurried down to the docks. Patrick was waiting at the top of pier. He whistled when he saw his arriving crew.

"Did some shopping, I see?"

"Get in the boat, Patrick," Gunny said. "I'll explain as we sail."

Patrick saluted her. "Yes, Captain. We sail at your command."

Gunny stepped into the large boat and placed the baby on a blanket between the seats. Joanna handed Gunny the box of goods which she secured behind her. Gunny reached up for Maggie, who hopped into the boat without a fuss. She tucked the little girl snugly between her legs.

"Stay still and keep an eye on the baby," she instructed Maggie.

"Larry," Maggie stated.

"Yes, Larry. God, that's going to have to change," she muttered.

Patrick untied the boat and pushed off into the harbor. Joanna waved as Patrick locked the oars in place and the unlikely boatload headed home to the Blaskets.

Charlotte O'Connor was ecstatic. "A new baby! Of course I'll help you."

Gunny grinned. "You've already raised so many of your own."

"But we haven't had a baby in over a decade. I'll take good care of him," she said with a smile.

"I don't mean for him to stay here forever. Joanna said I only need milk for him for the next few months."

"And this is where the cow is so this is where he'll stay, the little dear."

"I don't want to leave him," Gunny said.

"He'll be fine," Charlotte said, taking Larry from Gunny's arms. "Take the little girl to the west end and I'll keep the baby until he gets bigger."

Gunny pictured her mother as she took Catherine from her. "No," she said shaking her head. "I'm going to raise the boy. I'll take him to the west end. I'll figure out a way to feed him."

Charlotte shook her head. "That's crazy talk. The baby needs milk. He should stay here."

"Catherine would want me to raise him…"

"You could move into the village," Patrick offered from his stool in front of the low turf fire.

Gunny and Charlotte turned and stared.

"Of course, Gunny," Charlotte said clutching Gunny's hand. "Why don't you move into the McLeary house? No one's lived there since '35. You'd like the south end of the island. It's quiet and you'd be close to the new school. Patrick's right. It's time for you to move into the village."

Gunny's head spun. She'd pondered moving to the village when she thought Catherine might join her. But now the thought left her breathless. How could she leave the little house she'd put so much time into and that had been her home for so many years?

"What about my fields, my crops?"

"Patrick will help you with your harvest. And next year you'll plant in a field that's closer by. The good news is that that old pig of yours died. Gallarus would not have liked living in the village, even on the south end. I'm sure your chickens will adjust."

Gunny shook her head. "Mr. Thompson will find me if I live in the village."

"If Mr. Thompson ever comes looking for you again, he'll head out to the west end while you'll be safely hidden here in the village—with the children." Charlotte reached over and grasped Gunny's hands. "We'll help you, Gunny. You're not alone."

Gunny stayed with the O'Connors off and on through the rest of the summer. Larry slept in a small cradle at the O'Connor's' house, but Maggie insisted on staying with Gunny wherever she went, hiking back and forth to the west end in rain or shine, and toddling along behind her through the fields of oats and potatoes. Gunny talked to Maggie as they collected food from the kitchen garden, explaining which vegetable was which, and explaining how they might cook each one. The only hike that tired the little girl was up into the bog to turn the bricks of peat. Gunny was happy to tote the girl along on her back. Maggie was chipper and had a huge vocabulary for a two year old and loved to hum and sing nonsense tunes as they walked. Gunny enjoyed the child's banter even though it left her feeling exhausted by the time the girl finally fell asleep by her side each night.

The days Gunny was in the village, Patrick helped her clean out the old McCleary place. The house was twelve feet wide and twenty-two feet long, nearly twice as long as her cottage on the west end. When the house was thoroughly swept and washed, Maggie insisted she have her own small rag to help whitewash the inside and outside walls, and watched intently as Gunny tied new, tight bundles of thatch and hauled them up onto the roof. Mrs. McLeary had left a heavy cupboard behind which Gunny kept in place to separate the sleeping area from the living area. She took an old net of rope and decorated it with white shells she and Maggie collected on the beach. She hung it from the ceiling to the top of the cupboard to help divide the large space inside. Patrick helped her build two beds from driftwood which they placed at the far end of the house.

One day while Patrick was working in the fields, she dug up the floor around the hearth and carted in black stones she and Maggie had found on the strand. She arranged the smooth stones, large to small, in an expanding half-circle pattern around the hearth then poured white sand in around the stones to fill the gaps.

"You made the floor all rough where you dug it up," Patrick teased when he arrived at the house late that afternoon. "You'll regret it when it rains and you have a house full of mud."

Gunny stood back and admired her work. "We'll have a gathering to puddle the floor as soon as the house is done. I want a home filled with music and dancing. And if there's also a bit of mud, so be it."

When the house was finally ready, Gunny crated the chickens and moved them to the new house in Patrick's little handcart. She insisted Maggie stay with Charlotte for the final move, and walked back to the west end with Patrick, the donkey, and a larger cart for the rest of her belongings. They hauled out the old tea chest filled with sea-drift dishes, the rocking chair, and her folding kitchen table made of driftwood. There was no room in the cart for the worn stools she'd made of coiled rope, so they hauled them to the strand and set them looking out across the quiet cove.

She gazed along the strand, remembering her first landing there with her father and John McCrohan, and then her second visit with Mac fifteen long years before. She glanced out along the rocks. The brown seal had long since disappeared. "I can always come back," she said, mostly to herself.

She returned with Patrick to the house and finished packing boxes of cooking tools, mats, blankets, pots and fire tongs, which they added to the cart. Gunny draped a speckled blanket over the cart that she'd woven from the fleece of the ewe. She walked back to the house to make sure she had not forgotten anything. The empty house looked much as it had when she'd first found it. She swept the floor one last time and tidied a small pile of turf by the door, then slipped the heart-shaped nail off the mantel into her pocket. She pulled the door closed, then turned and eyed the small, overturned curragh that was propped on an outside wall of the house.

"I don't suppose I'll have much need for that in the village."

"We can come back for it," Patrick offered.

"No, let's leave it," Gunny said. "I know where it is if I ever need it."

She puffed out her cheeks and looked past the house to her fields of potatoes and oats. They'd be back to harvest those. She spotted the old ewe standing just past the oat field, her coat shaggy again with rotting wool.

"I'm headed to the village," she yelled to the ewe. "Come along if you wish."

The ewe raised her head, bleated, then shook her matted coat and trotted up toward the higher fields.

"Stubborn old lady," Gunny muttered, then turned to Patrick. "I'm ready," she said, feeding a piece of rope to the donkey who brayed in appreciation as they hiked east along the cliff path to the south end of the village.

After they'd hauled Gunny's furniture inside, the large house still seemed empty, even with the large rocker and tea chest in front of the stunning black and white hearth. Patrick left and returned with three stools from the O'Connor house and promised to help Gunny make a larger table and a couple of benches. Gunny arranged her Spanish tea cups and tiny saucers along the cupboard, and carefully draped the ewe blanket across the rocker. She stashed her mending in the cubby to the left of the fire and placed Matt's pipe and a plug of tobacco in the cubby on the right. When everything was in as good an order as she could make it, she set the iron heart on the mantel and knelt to stir the smoored fire back to life. Charlotte arrived with Patrick and the children and the house, at last, felt full.

Her first night alone with the children she barely slept. She tucked them into bed next to her and lay awake listening to their little sleeping noises, panicking when they were quiet. She felt along the covers a dozen times to make sure both children were tucked in and breathing. By morning, she was exhausted but headed with the children to the village to leave them with Charlotte, then walked the cliff path with Patrick and his brothers to begin the harvest of her potatoes, oats, and kitchen garden. Within two weeks, her food supply was safely stored under the beds in the back room, along the walls in boxes, and in her loft. The house felt snug. She was ready for winter.

The Baron pushed open the kitchen door. He had avoided Eileen Malone through the final hot days of summer. The cranky, old woman was sitting alone now, rocking in a chair near the fire, staring at nothing. Her face was pale and deeply lined, her eyes red-rimmed. She had aged ten years in the last two months, he thought.

"Excuse me, Mrs. Malone," he said in a firm voice.

Eileen blinked and glanced at the Baron, then looked back at the fire and said nothing.

"I am sorry to hear of your loss," he said, loudly clearing his throat. "The death was a surprise to all of us."

Eileen shook her head slightly and twisted at a corner of her apron.

"Robert was one of the best men in Dingle when it came to horses. He will be missed," the Baron continued.

Eileen cackled loudly. The Baron was jarred by the harshness of her voice. "It's for the best," she said, tears brimming in her eyes. "Robert couldn't live without her, you know."

"Couldn't live without whom, Mrs. Malone?" the Baron questioned. He had heard rumors but had not wanted to know the facts. "Are you talking about Catherine? Has something happened to your daughter?"

Eileen sniffed and looked toward the window. "You know that she's gone," she said in a low voice.

"I thought I had not seen her around," Thomas said trying to sound innocent, taking a step toward the haggard woman. "Did she find work in Dunquin?"

"No," Eileen said flatly turning to look at the Lord. "She's dead. She died in childbirth."

"Childbirth?" Thomas queried, eyebrows raised. "Oh, my." He paused. "And the baby?"

Eileen turned her eyes back to the fire. "Dead," she said flatly.

"The baby died," he repeated with raised eyebrows. Then his face fell. "Well, it's for the best, I suppose."

"I suppose," Eileen said rocking in the chair and staring into the fire.

"And the other child? The little girl?" the Baron asked. "Where is she?"

The Baron saw Eileen's shoulders stiffen slightly as she shook her head. "The girl disappeared the night Catherine passed."

"Disappeared?" he asked with a nervous laugh. "How can that be?"

Eileen turned toward the Baron and wiped the back of her hand across her mouth. "Why are you suddenly interested in Catherine's girl? You never acknowledged her before."

Thomas waved his hand in front of his face. "And I am not acknowledging her now. I am not the least bit interested in your girl's papist brat." He paused. "My wife wants to know. That's all."

"Your son's the one who should want to know," Eileen said coldly.

"My son? Why would Thomas wonder about a servant girl's child?"

Eileen pushed up slowly from the rocker and took a step toward the Baron. She looked at him with sad, watery brown eyes. "Your son loved my Catherine and you kept them apart. He must be mourning the loss of my daughter."

Thomas bit at a nagging fingernail and glanced toward the door to the house. "I admit the boy has been moody of late. I have decided to send him to school in Dublin. He leaves next week. I am thinking of church work for him," he said glancing at Eileen. "We need better leaders in the Protestant church."

"Oh, your boy's a perfect one for the church. He's attractive and charming and has the tongue of a snake. He'll make a fine reverend," she said waving a finger at the Baron's face.

"Be careful what you say," Thomas said. "You work for me at my pleasure. And it doesn't appear that you are working much these days. As soon as we replace Mrs. Needham, God rest her soul, we will reevaluate your position here at the Burnham House."

Eileen dropped her head. "Yes, my Lord," she uttered. "I forgot my manners."

Chrisabella was waiting for Thomas in the parlor. She leaned against the mantel, foot tapping, sipping at a small glass of claret. She eyed Thomas as he walked across the parlor and sat heavily on the large leather chair by the fire to report his findings.

Chrisabella gasped at the news. "You said the little girl would be safe living in the kitchen," she hissed at him. "And now she is gone?"

"Don't blame me," Thomas said rubbing at his eyes. "Mrs. Needham said she would keep an eye on her. Who knew the old woman would up and die. The girl will turn up eventually from wherever they have hidden her. She is probably in Dunquin with a neighbor. Anyway, she is a girl," he said looking at Chrisabella. "And the daughter of a servant."

"And she is our granddaughter," Chrisabella snapped.

"Yes, and the granddaughter of a crazy woman," he added.

"A crazy woman you always speak of fondly," she said, turning in disgust and shaking her head. She paced the room. "Your son is nearly suicidal over the loss of that servant girl," she said with a rustling turn of her skirts.

"He will get over it," Thomas said. He stood and poured himself a glass of claret from the bottle on a small side table. "Youthful passions pass."

"I do not know how you can be so cold," she said.

"Our son fell in love with a servant girl," he said, rubbing at his forehead. "That is unacceptable. The boy needs to learn to control his emotions."

"Argh! At times you are dreadful to be around."

"As are you," Thomas said politely.

"Excuse me, sir." A young servant girl curtsied by the door. "There's a problem in the cellar, sir."

"What is it?" Thomas asked sharply, turning on the girl.

"Someone has opened the taps on two of your favorite wine barrels. There's wine all over the cellar floor. I don't know what to do," she said stammering.

"No one has access to the wine cellar," Thomas roared, "except for me, and..." He turned to Chrisabella. "And you," he seethed.

Chrisabella shrugged her shoulders. "You really must learn to control your emotions, Thomas."

Gunny returned from the booley fields with a bucket of milk from the O'Connor's cow. Charlotte was in the yard with the baby hoping that fresh air would quiet his crying. Gunny took the milk into the house, then returned to the yard with a bucket of cooled milk from the previous afternoon. She carefully spooned the top layer of cream into the butter churn then turned to look at the screaming child in Charlotte's arms. He was dressed like all of the other babies in the village in a petticoat of undressed wool, a loose shirt, and a knitted cap. His small red face and howling mouth contrasted starkly with the soft white of his baby frocks.

Gunny tossed a mat on the ground and took the baby from Charlotte. She laid him on the mat and sat down to churn, nudging the baby gently with one bare toe. The boy stretched and quieted looking up at the sky.

"We'll be fine now," she said. "Thank you for taking him while I milked the cow."

Charlotte eyed the small baby wiggling around on the straw mat. "You shouldn't set a baby on the ground like that," she said. "Someone might step on him."

Gunny laughed. "He's quiet. Are you going to argue with that? And look at him. He loves being on his own where he can stretch out his skinny little arms and legs."

"You have to be careful with little ones," Charlotte said shaking her head. She knelt and swept the baby up into her arms to cuddle him as she had done with her own boys. Larry arched his back against her tender hold and kicked hard at her warm embrace. "Maybe this one does prefer the ground," she said, laying the baby down again on the mat.

Both women watched as little Larry cooed, legs kicking in the air, arms waving.

"Clearly you know best," Charlotte laughed, clapping her hands together over the baby to draw his attention.

Gunny chuckled. "You know I welcome any advice from you. The children and I wouldn't have survived the summer without you."

Charlotte knelt and gently rubbed Larry's belly. "You're a wonderful mother, Gunny. You're rough with the children and they seem to thrive on it."

"Where has Maggie gotten off to?" Gunny asked, looking around the yard.

"Patrick took her to the cliffs to watch the men fish."

Charlotte stood and watched Gunny work the churn. "Patrick's very good with the children, Gunny. Maybe it's time you considered marrying."

"Charlotte, I told you I'd never marry. But Patrick should find himself a wife and have children of his own."

"He says there're no girls on the island his age who appeal to him," Charlotte offered with a raised eyebrow.

"Most men marry younger women and there are plenty of younger girls on this island."

Patrick walked into the yard singing a jaunty island tune with little Maggie perched on one hip. Her head of tight brown curls bounced as he swung her to the ground, full of giggles. Gunny and Mrs. O'Connor beamed. Was there anything more delightful than the sound of a child's laughter?

Maggie ran to Larry and knelt by him on his mat. He looked at his sister's face and started to howl. She put her hands over her ears. "Make it stop! Why did God send us this half-finished boy? He has no hair and no teeth, and he can't walk. Even a puppy or chicken can walk. All he does is cry and sleep and eat!"

Charlotte and Gunny laughed at the apt description as Patrick picked Larry up and tried to cradle the boy's head as his mother had taught him. Larry held his head up away from Patrick's large hand and continued crying.

"He's got control of his neck now, Patrick. You can just hold him," Gunny said.

Patrick awkwardly held the struggling baby. "This one's harder to take care of than that one," he said, reaching over to tickle Maggie's belly who giggled again at his touch.

Charlotte took Larry from Patrick, who was more than happy to hand off the scrappy boy to his mother. She dangled Larry out in front of her and looked him in the eye as he wiggled in her clutches. "Are you hungry?"

"He's always hungry," Gunny chuckled.

"Perhaps it's time we started him on some oats," Charlotte said. "He's growing so quickly. Maybe that's why he cries so much."

"Is that it?" Gunny asked. "I thought maybe he was angry at the world."

"It may be that too," Charlotte sighed.

Charlotte put the baby back on the mat and went inside to heat milk with crushed oats. "This should knock him out for awhile," she yelled from inside.

Larry continued to fuss on the mat. Gunny set the butter churn aside and scooped him up. She paced the yard swinging him in the air and tossing him around to no avail.

"Go?" Maggie asked Patrick, stretching out her arms toward the tall red head.

He swept the girl up onto his shoulders and waved at Gunny. "The girl's smart. We'll be back."

"Where're you going?" Gunny asked with a flash of jealousy that Patrick had the easier of the two children.

"We're off to find adventure. Have fun with that baby."

She shook her head and looked down at Larry's squalling red face. "If the oats and milk don't knock you out, I'm going to put you out to sea in a small curragh and let the waves rock you," she said, tiring from the motion of swinging the child around.

The boy stopped crying and stared at her.

"What?" she asked, amazed at the quiet. "You like the idea of being set off to sea in a boat?"

Larry's bottom lip started to quiver.

"No, don't start again!" she begged. "Did I ever tell you the story about the whale? Or about the little boy whose boat sailed far, far away on the white caps…?"

~ Chapter 19: Life in the Village ~

Gunny and the children adjusted quickly to life on the south end. There were five families living there. Gunny always had a bit of food for those in need, was handy with repairs and herbal remedies, and told wonderful stories at night around the fire. She and the children were rarely without an invitation on the cool fall evenings to spend time at a neighbor's house.

Maggie's only bit of grouchiness about living on the island had to do with horses.

"We don't have horsies or stables on the Blaskets," Gunny explained again and again, but the little girl would not relent with her requests to see the horsies in the 'table.

Gunny finally wrapped the children in wool sweaters and caps and hiked with them and Patrick up the steep hill to the booley fields to see the sheep. Maggie squealed with delight at the "little horsies." Patrick stood next to Gunny laughing as Maggie snuck up behind a wary ewe and tried to pet her. Gunny smiled, swaying the baby on one of the rare occasions when he lay quietly asleep in her arms. She noticed Patrick watching her and stopped rocking. The baby stirred and she started rocking again.

"We visited with the Dalys last night," Gunny said. "What a fine girl that Marie is," she added. "What a voice! Just like her mother."

Patrick pulled a piece of grass from a nearby clump and put it in his mouth. "I've known Marie all her life. There's no need to point out how fine she is."

"She might be well-suited for you, that's all," Gunny said, trying to sound nonchalant.

"She's a fine girl," Patrick confirmed.

"You're twenty-five, Patrick. You should think about settling down and Marie would make a fine wife," Gunny continued. "The Dalys are wonderful mothers. Or have you spent any time with Colleen Dunleavy? She has those three fine young boys, and that little girl of hers…"

"Gunny," Patrick said, turning to his best friend. "We've talked about this a hundred times. The girls on this island don't interest me."

"You know I'll never marry," Gunny said, glancing at Patrick then turning to watch Maggie sneak up behind another unsuspecting ewe.

Patrick shook his head as he chewed on the bit of grass. "You told me from the start that you were too old for me. And," he added, "I never wanted to marry you anyway."

Gunny blinked. "You don't have to be mean about it. Would I be so terrible to marry?"

"No," Patrick laughed. "So now you want to get married?"

"No," Gunny said shaking her head. "I told you I wasn't meant to be married."

"That's what I was saying," Patrick said nodding his head.

Gunny frowned. "I don't want to marry but I want it to be my choice."

Patrick raised one eyebrow. "Of course," he said, reaching out to take Larry from her arms. "Give me the baby for awhile. Your arms must be tired."

Gunny gladly handed off the small bundle and watched as Maggie sprinted around the field trying to pet the tired sheep. Lorcan couldn't have done a better job of herding.

Each morning and afternoon Gunny watched as the village children passed her house on their way to and from the new school. Even Charlotte O'Connor's boys attended. The teacher, Mr. Holden, made a boiler of soup every morning and each child enjoyed a free, hot meal when they arrived.

"A child can't learn on an empty stomach," he reminded the mothers.

"I don't know what my boys will learn that will be of any use," Charlotte replied, "but they do like the soup."

Through the fall when Gunny worked in the kitchen garden, she carried Larry in a sling she'd rigged across her chest. As long as he faced out, he was happy. He was still fussy, especially in the evenings, but she found the more time she kept him outside, the less energy he had to bawl. Maggie wanted nothing to do with being carried and continued to trot along behind Gunny, pulling weeds or searching in the fields for roots. When they weren't in the garden or fields, Gunny took the children to the strand to collect seashells and rocks which she and Maggie stacked in elaborate structures in the yard and along the top of the front wall.

Quiet evenings at home were Gunny's favorite time with the children—with a turf fire burning in the fireplace, the chickens quietly cackling in the loft, and the children playing on the flat black stones that surrounded the hearth. Gunny liked to sit in her rocking chair, mending clothes or stockings or twisting a bit of rope in the dim light of an oil lamp, listening to the still sounds of the night settle in around her. At bedtime, she told the children a tale from her past or from the thread of an idea she'd heard around the village that day. Before she went to bed, she carefully drew ashes up over the peat embers to preserve the fire until morning and said a quick prayer to bless the children and the house.

Her first Hallow E'en with the children, Gunny made Champ, mixing boiled mashed potatoes with green cabbage and chopped raw onion from her kitchen garden. She served it as her mother had in a large bowl with a huge dollop of butter melting at the center. She and Maggie each took a spoon and dipped and ate till their bellies felt like they would burst. Gunny gave Larry a spoonful as he lay in her arms. He worked to get it into his mouth and when the potato fell off, amused himself mashing it into the table with his hands. Gunny thought about Matt as she watched the children, marveling that her visit to his grave had somehow lead to her living on the Blaskets and raising these two little imps.

After they ate, Gunny bundled up the children and walked to the O'Connors for a Hallow E'en gathering. Fussy Larry was passed from lap to lap while Maggie watched, mesmerized, at her first bobbing for apples. Everyone stayed up late telling ghost stories around the fire, and peeking out the window for hobgoblins, headless ghosts, and Puka, the Black Pig. When it was time to leave, Gunny could not get Maggie to budge from her stool in front of the fire.

"What if there are hobgoblins out there and they eat us up?" she asked, her large brown eyes shiny and wide.

Gunny knelt by her side. "It's not the hobgoblins you have to worry about. It's the fairies!" she said, tickling the little girl who burst out in appropriate giggles. "On Hallow E'en, the fairies pack up their fairy houses and move to their winter quarters," Gunny explained.

Maggie's eyes grew large at the thought of wild fairies moving about the now familiar village.

"But don't worry," Gunny said, reaching into her apron pocket. "I have a black-handled knife so we can't be taken."

"But what about me?" Maggie said with a pout. "I don't have a black-handled knife."

Gunny hesitated, then pulled the heart-shaped nail from deeper in her apron pocket and showed it to Maggie. "An iron nail will protect you as well. I carry this one in my pocket when I go outside. Would you like to carry it home tonight?"

Maggie took the blackened heart from Gunny and held it with both hands. She traced a finger around the delicate pattern. "No fairy could lift me with this in my pocket," she said with a grin, carefully sliding the heart-shaped nail into her small apron pocket and offering her other hand to Gunny. "I'm feeling better now. We can go."

Gunny grinned and gently picked Larry up off a mat on the floor, trying her best to not wake the finally sleeping boy. "I'll carry this heavy Larry home," she whispered. "No fairy could possibly lift me with a Larry in my pocket!"

"Next year," Maggie said as they walked south along the dark road. "I'm going to go out with the big children on Hallow E'en. You can make me a mask and I'll beg from door to door for cake with butter like they did tonight."

"You wouldn't be afraid?" Gunny asked as they walked.

"No, I'll be bigger then," Maggie said. "And I'll have my iron heart with me. Did you used to go out begging on Hallow E'en?" Maggie asked as they neared their house.

"We mostly did dares," Gunny explained. "Who could climb a roof the fastest. Or who was brave enough to go into the graveyard. My friend Matt used to drape his grandmother's shawl over his head like this," she said, pulling her shawl up over her head to demonstrate. "Matt's grandma was long past but Matt sounded just like her and it made us all screech."

"Tell me more about when you were little," Maggie said with a wide yawn.

"I'll tell you one more story as I tuck you into bed." Gunny smiled. She hadn't thought about the dares of Hallow E'en for a long time. Being around Maggie gave her fresh eyes on old memories. After the children were asleep, snug in the back room, she set out a bowl of spring water, left the door unlatched, and peacefully lit a candle for Matt and any other wandering spirits, or hungry Puka pigs, who might visit them that night.

On Christmas Eve day, Gunny cleaned the house and whitewashed the walls again inside and out. She scrubbed the table and pots with sand from the strand, then washed the clothing and bedding and hung the linens inside to dry by the fire.

After the house was clean, she took the children up to the fields to collect anything that was still green. She showed Maggie how to twist green grasses and dry heather together into boughs which they draped over the door and along the mantel over the fireplace. Gunny had pulled a large log from the bog that summer and the sweet-smelling wood burned hot and bright throughout the day.

She'd had no time to twist rope that summer, and had little to trade at the Christmas Market in Dingle. Patrick had taken a half-dozen firkins of her butter to the market along with a half-barrel of dried herring and mackerel. He stopped by her house late in the day with sugar, tobacco, candles, and sweets before returning home. As the sun set on Christmas Eve, Gunny carved turnips to use as candle holders and placed a small white Christmas candle in each of the two front windows. Then she made a pudding with the last of her sugar and put it in the pot oven to bake.

There was a heavy knock on the door. Patrick opened the door without waiting for Gunny to answer and poked his head inside. He was smiling and out of breath.

"You already gave us our sweets," Gunny said, eyebrows raised.

"Bridget has returned from America," Patrick announced. "Mother says you must join us for our Christmas Eve meal. Martha and David and the children will be there."

"This is our first year on the south end. I thought we'd stay in tonight."

"Mam said I couldn't return without you," Patrick said, wrapping warm shawls around the children. "She's pretty excited. You'll love our Bridget."

Gunny pulled on her shawl, seeing that no argument would be heard. "Your mother told me last week she received a letter from Bridget with five pounds in it. She didn't mention a homecoming."

"Apparently the five-pound note was Bridget's way of saying 'I'm sorry and I'm coming home.' She showed up at the pier at midday. She's lucky a fisherman in Dingle was willing to travel on Christmas Eve. Hurry. Father has our Yule log lit. It's Christmas, Gunny, and everyone is home."

Gunny pulled her warm pudding from the pot oven and packed it in a flour sack while Patrick hustled the children out to the yard. She smoored her Yule log and pulled the door closed behind her.

Her heart raced as they walked through the village. There were 153 people living in twenty-some houses on the island that winter and every window was lit with candlelight to welcome Mary and Joseph. Gunny soaked in the warmth of island humanity as they walked through the brisk air toward the center of the village.

Charlotte O'Connor greeted them at the door. The house was crowded with Timothy, the six boys, and Martha, John and their three boys—and Bridget, who was still apologizing to everyone for not having written in her long time away. Gunny pulled the shawls off the children and they were introduced to Bridget as the O'Connors' "fine new friends." Bridget was as tall as Patrick with wide shoulders, a full figure, and a long nose and chin. When Gunny shook her hand, she had a firm grip, and just like her brothers and unlike her delicate sister, Martha, Bridget had a full head of bright red hair.

When Bridget smiled at Gunny, her top front teeth extended out far on her face but her smile was genuine. "I'm glad to meet you," she said handing Gunny a hot cup of tea.

"And I'm happy to meet you," Gunny said pulling off her shawl. "I've heard good things about you." She set Larry down on the floor near the fire. The boy was sitting up on his own now and was quite happy with his new independence. Gunny watched as Maggie stacked a large pile of shells which Larry promptly pushed over.

Bridget howled with laughter. "That reminds me of growing up in a house full of brothers."

"You were away a long time," Gunny said, sipping at her tea.

"Seventeen years," Bridget said wistfully. "A lifetime."

"And what finally brought you home?" Gunny asked.

Charlotte stopped setting the table and hovered. No one in the family had been brave enough to ask Bridget this burning question.

Bridget looked at Gunny and chewed gently on her bottom lip. "America wasn't everything I expected," she said with a shrug. "You work hard and make good money, but it's not home. It's not family. I left for America in hopes I'd find a man and settle down. I mean, who on this island would marry me? A girl with such large… feet," she said, standing to her full height and showing off her wide mouthful of teeth. "I gambled my youth on America."

"You could've stayed on the island and married like your sister," Charlotte mumbled behind her. "Look at Martha's fine husband and three strapping boys," she said proudly as she turned to the fire to rotate a roasting goose on a spit.

Martha grinned at her older sister from her stool in front of the fire as she bounced her new little baby boy on one knee.

"So the streets weren't lined with gold?" Gunny asked.

"No," Bridget laughed loudly. "You work hard for every penny and still you're not a welcome part of the community. The family I worked for for seventeen years told me they loved me but I heard Mr. Stevens refer to me as his 'Irish trash' one night when he didn't know I was in the room. That's when I decided it was time to come home."

"I wish my brother would come home. He lives in America, in Virginia. Do you know where Virginia is? Michael wrote that the Irish are also hated there."

"I don't know Virginia, but we're hated the same everywhere. At least we're paid well—compared to what we can make here." She pulled a fat wallet from her apron pocket. "And now I have enough money to marry. If anyone will take an old maid of thirty-five."

Charlotte grabbed at the wallet but Bridget held it high up in the air, safe from her mother's reach. "I'll share with my Mam but most of this is for a dowry. As soon as I find one, I'm going to buy myself a good man."

After a fine evening meal of goose and potatoes followed by Gunny's sweet pudding, everyone sat around the fire sipping cups of hot, weak tea. When Bridget broke out a large bottle of American whiskey, the noise level in the house increased with singing and ribald laughter as Bridget shared story after story of living in the New World.

As the Yule log burned to embers, Gunny held a now sleeping Larry in her arms and watched Maggie's little head droop against her knee.

"We should get home before the cows and donkeys get the gift of speech," she whispered to Patrick.

Maggie's eyes popped open. "The cows and donkeys are going to speak?" she asked rubbing her eyes.

"I thought you were sleeping," Gunny said tousling the girl's head of rich, brown curls. "Yes, the animals speak at midnight on Christmas. They're the ones who were with Christ when he was born—that's his gift to them."

"What do they say?"

"I don't know," Gunny said with a serious face. "No one's ever heard them."

"Why not?"

"It's bad luck! "

"Well, it doesn't sound like much of a gift if you get to talk and no one's around to hear you," Maggie pouted.

"Maybe it's best we don't hear what the animals have to say," Gunny said, launching into her best cow and donkey imitation for the girl: "I want better food. I don't want to be tied up any more. Why do you take my milk and turn it into butter?"

"I want to hear the animals speak and I'm going to stay awake until they do," Maggie insisted, reaching to pull on her shawl.

By the time they'd walked home, the little girl was nearly asleep on her feet and there was no doubt that the animals were safe to speak in private for at least one more year.

Christmas morning was quiet until Patrick came by to take them to the strand.

"Everyone in the village plays barefoot hurley on the strand on Christmas day," he explained. "You've always gone back to the west end so you've missed it. This year, you must come with us. Everyone will be there."

"It's freezing," Gunny said.

"You think this is cold? Try splashing about in the ocean all day. My feet will be numb for a week. Come on now. Bundle up. We don't want to be late."

Gunny dressed the children and they hurried out to the strand, which was already crowded with pink-cheeked villagers. Patrick joined the other men and boys, each armed with a hurley stick made of furze branches, while Gunny and the children sat with the women and children on the nearby rocks. Two captains were selected and each chose a team. The men shouted and jostled each other tossing about a handmade hurley ball of fabric stuffed with wool while the women and children cheered on their favorite players. The men played for hours, racing into the cold surf as needed when a hurley ball went astray. They ended the day with a driftwood bonfire on the beach to thaw cold fingers and toes and discuss the highlights of the game over mugs of hot whiskey.

On St. Stephen's Day, Gunny was happy that no gang of boys knocked on her door masquerading as women, and that she saw no clubbing of helpless wrens in the bushes.

"That's one tradition that can go away," she muttered to herself as she sat with the children over a late-morning meal.

"What's that, Gunny?" Maggie asked innocently.

Gunny pictured Matt parading about on his wooden horse with Mac by his side and the Wren Boys following behind carrying a bush decorated with small, dead birds.

"Today is St. Stephen's Day," she said to Maggie. "The day of the hunting of the wren."

Maggie grinned and blew on a spoonful of hot potato. It was story time. Gunny looked at the child's expectant face and smiled a half-smile.

"St. Stephen's Day is a day to celebrate the wren, the smallest of birds. It's a day when…" Gunny hesitated. "It's a day when everyone must learn to whistle. Did I ever tell you about my grandmother's tin whistle?" she asking, pulling the magical instrument from deep within her apron pocket.

Gunny tidied the house for St. Bridgit's Day. When St. Bridgit visited, it meant January was nearly over and that spring winds would soon start to stir. The holiday still made her giddy.

"Why must every holiday include cleaning the house?" Maggie frowned.

"I used to say the same thing when I was little. St. Bridgit's coming tomorrow. It's the beginning of spring and we want to make sure she feels welcome. If she chooses to stay, the cows will have calves and then we'll have milk again. The seas will be calmer and the winds will be warmer. And we can start to prepare the fields. If you see a hedgehog tomorrow and he stays outside, the rest of the winter will be mild."

Maggie picked up the miniature broom Gunny had made for her and swept around Larry as he attempted to pull himself up on a stool in front of the fire. "If St. Bridgit is so important, it seems like she could ask God to take care of all this housework. And what's a hedgehog?"

"I'll tell you if I ever see one."

Maggie turned toward Larry as he tipped over the stool and started gnawing on one leg. "St. Bridgit is going to visit us," she explained authoritatively to her little brother. "We have to clean."

"Hmm," Gunny muttered as she knocked dust off of the net of seashells that hung over the large bureau at the center of the room. "We also need someone to play St. Bridgit…"

Maggie's eyes grew large. "Someone plays St. Bridgit?"

"It's usually the most beautiful girl in the village."

"That's me," Maggie offered decisively, holding her small broom to one side.

Gunny looked Maggie over from head to toe. "You're certainly the most beautiful girl in this household. All right. I'll make you a St. Bridgit's shield—as soon as we're finish cleaning."

Maggie swept around Larry with greater fury. When the house was finally in order, Gunny strapped Larry to her chest and walked with Maggie to the strand to collect dry grasses. Back at the house, Gunny put the grasses in a bucket to soak and stirred the fire. As Larry napped on a mat by the fire, Gunny sat down at the table and wove a fine, elaborate shield. She handed it to Maggie to inspect and sat down to twist a small St. Bridgit's cross.

"When you hang a St. Bridgit's cross in your home you are protected from fire," she explained, showing the finished straw cross to the girl.

Maggie tossed the shield aside and held the small cross with both hands. She looked up at Gunny with wide, shining eyes. "Another!"

Gunny chuckled and pulled fresh strands of wet straw from the bucket. Maggie clutched at her handful of wet grasses and sat down on the bench next to Gunny. With nimble little fingers, she did her best to mimic Gunny's every twist and soon had a loose straw cross of her own. Gunny admired the girl's work.

"Wait until I show you how to make rope," she said.

They made a half-dozen St. Bridgit crosses while Larry slept. Gunny sprinkled each one with holy water she'd collected from dew on the spring grasses, and hung the crosses over the doorway. With the leftover straw, she made rush lights, which she placed around the house to honor the Saint.

The next morning, Gunny had Maggie stand outside the door.

"Knock three times and I'll open the door," Gunny yelled through the door.

"What?" Maggie yelled from outside.

Larry rolled around on the floor on his mat and cooed at this strange early-morning activity.

"Let the blessed Saint enter," Gunny yelled. "You're a hundred times welcome. Come in!" Gunny opened the latch and Maggie stomped into the room holding the large straw shield in front of her.

"Greetings to the noble woman," Gunny said with a low bow.

Larry giggled on the floor and stretched out his arms to grab at his sister's shield while Gunny chanted the words she'd been taught as a little girl:

"Something for Poor Biddy!
Her clothes are torn
Her shoes are worn
Something for Poor Biddy!"

Maggie pulled the straw shield away from her brother's grip and tried to look serious. When she spied the warm oat bread on the table that Gunny had made in the shape of a cross, she tossed her shield on top of the baby and raced to the table. Gunny casually pulled the shield off of Larry who blinked and cooed, unconcerned.

"St. Bridgit loved birds. You must take care of the birds for St. Bridgit," Gunny said, taking some of the bread and tossing crumbs to several cackling chickens.

"Birds smell bad," Maggie said.

"They do," Gunny admitted. "And they give us nice eggs so we love them."

Maggie held her nose between pinched fingers and obediently tossed her last bit of bread to a waiting chicken.

On the entire Great Blasket island, there were 1,132 acres, but only 62 acres were arable. Each family was assigned a series of named fields. All of the fields were farmed in unfenced, rundale strips. The soil in the top fields was acidic and wet. This land was good for pasture and meadow. The middle fields were mostly sandy loam and were best for planting oats. The bottom fields were sandy and dry and were good for potatoes. Each family had fields in each area. Grazing and turf-cutting land was shared by everyone in the village. Patrick worked with the village elders to move the fields around after Gunny's move to assign her fields adjacent to the O'Connor fields.

Gunny brought the children with her while she worked to manure her middle and lower fields, but once Larry was no longer content being carried around in a sling, found she could not get her work done. Patrick watched as she alternated between manuring and chasing after the children.

"I can finish manuring for you," he offered.

"No," Gunny said. "These are my fields. I'll find a way to work them."

Colleen Daly said that she and her daughter, Frances, would keep an eye on Maggie. Colleen's little girl, Frances, was nine now and loved playing mother to little Maggie. Finding care for Larry was another story. When Gunny left the boy behind, he cried until his face turned bright red, and sometimes purple. And now that he was crawling, he often disappeared and always found trouble. Even Charlotte O'Connor hesitated to watch him since he'd become more active.

Gunny sat sipping tea in front of the fire chewing gently on her bottom lip. Her fields were nearly ready to plant but she needed one more long day of work. She watched the boy crawling around on the floor in his long, dirty skirt.

"You're a handful of trouble, Mr. Larry," she sighed, and envisioned swinging him from a tree in a strong, rope net as she worked. That gave her an idea.

The next day, she dropped Maggie off at the Dalys, then bundled Larry in a large wool sweater and headed to the fields with a full barrow of seaweed and sand, a small mat, and a long coil of rope. She twisted a loose harness of rope across the boy's chest, then tied the loose end of the rope around a large boulder that sat at the edge of her middle field. As she worked the soil with her spade, she watched Larry crawl again and again to the limits of his rope, nearly doing somersaults trying to wiggle out of the harness. She sighed with relief when the boy finally curled up and fell asleep on the small mat.

At noon, she sat down near the sleeping boy and pulled a thick slice of oat bread from her pocket. Larry blinked at the smell of food, rubbed at his eyes and crawled into her lap. She shared the second slice of bread with him and chatted about what she was doing in the field, and how the oat seeds had to be planted with such care. Unlike Maggie, Larry did not seem to hear her. When the bread was gone, he crawled off to the end of his rope and pulled and whined in frustration.

She stood and shook the crumbs off her skirt. "Sorry, little man. My work's not done yet. You'll have to be patient." She returned to her work in the field and by early afternoon the field was finally ready to be planted. She thanked the heavens and returned to the rock. The rope was still there, but the child was missing. She held up the frayed end of rope. It had been chewed clean through.

"How on earth? The boy only has a few tiny teeth," she uttered.

She turned and looked up and down the hill in a panic, then spied the wild ewe trotting along the ridge—with little Larry crawling just behind her. Gunny howled with laughter and raced up the hill after the two wanderers. The wild ewe skittered away as Gunny approached, then stopped and gave Gunny a glare as Gunny scooped up her lost child.

"Welcome to the village, Ewe," she said with a low bow. "You took your time getting here."

The old sheep bleated and shook her shaggy head at Gunny.

"Just because you're free to come and go as you wish doesn't mean you get to free everyone else," she said, holding up the end of the frayed rope on Larry's harness.

Larry squirmed in her arms as the sheep bleated again and trotted over the crest of the field.

"Why're you sad," Maggie asked as Gunny spooned several boiled potatoes into her dish.

"I'm not sad," Gunny said while vigorously mashing potatoes with a bit of butter for their morning meal.

The days were warming. It was the last day before Lent, and Gunny was living through another empty Shrove Tuesday.

"I see your mouth pointing down," Maggie said, shaking her head of brown curls. "Are you sad because today's the last day we get to eat eggs and butter?"

"Yes," Gunny said, handing Larry a spoon to replace the one he had tossed to the floor. "Giving up eggs and butter is no fun."

"Then why do we do it?" Maggie said adding another spoonful of butter to her mash.

"We give up something we love to show we can sacrifice," Gunny said, taking a deep breath. "It's a test of sorts."

"But I don't like giving up eggs and butter. Why don't we test something else?"

Gunny couldn't help but smile. "The problem is that everyone gives up delicious food for Lent. How would it be if we continued to eat delicious food and no one else had any?"

"Oh, that wouldn't be good." Maggie paused in thought. "When you lived in your little house on west end, did you sacrifice for Lent?" Maggie asked, dipping a bite of potato into her pool of melting butter.

Gunny chuckled. "I never knew exactly when Lent was so I didn't have quite so many rules."

"Then let's go live in your old house where there are no rules!" Maggie said, raising her spoon high in the air.

"Wouldn't you miss little Frances Daly, and Colleen, and our other kind neighbors? You'd only have me and little Larry around to play with."

Gunny and Maggie looked at Larry. He'd eaten his potatoes and crawled down from the table. He was now playing near the fire stacking piles of rocks and shells, then pushing them over. Each time a pile toppled, he laughed, and shouted as loud as he could in some incoherent language.

"I guess we'll stay here in the village," Maggie said, smiling at Gunny.

Gunny grinned and gave Maggie a kiss on the forehead. "You're a good sister."

"Larry's a fussy baby but when he laughs, I love him."

Gunny looked at the wiry boy and grinned. "Thank you for seeing the good in him."

Larry smacked over another pile of stones scattering them to the four corners of the house. Two chickens squawked in protest and flew up into the air, wings flapping. Larry grabbed at the chicken nearest to him. She ran past him out the door in a fluff of loose feathers.

Gunny joined Charlotte on the strand in the dawning hours of Good Friday to collect limpets and winkles. As she raked limpets from the black rocks, she nudged Charlotte with her elbow and pointed to Maggie neatly patting piles of damp sand into the crooked spires of a castle. The girl's tangled curls fell around her face and she pushed them back with a sandy hand. Gunny spotted Larry crawling along the shore in his petticoat, heading toward the rocky tide pools.

"She plays so well by herself, and look at that boy. Last week he crawled right into the ocean. He didn't even hesitate when the waves were crashing over him. Watch Maggie, will you while I go fetch Larry?"

Charlotte rested a hand on Gunny's arm. "Leave him be. The worst that'll happen is that he'll fall in the water and come home wet and cold. Babies know how to survive even under water. And you know that boy was never one to be coddled."

Gunny shook her head and blew out a long breath. "He's always on the edge of trouble. Anytime a door opens or a hot ash pops from the fire, he seems to be in the way. He has a constant scrape or new bruise on him somewhere. But for all the fussing he did as a baby, I never hear a cry or whimper when he gets hurt. In fact he never says a thing that I can understand while Maggie can talk your head off."

"He's not one yet. He'll speak when he's ready. Boys're slower to talk than girls."

Gunny ran a hand through the wet shellfish in her apron. "We have plenty of kitchen for our Good Friday meal. Do you have enough food for your gathering?"

"I have plenty. I never did like the little critters, truth be told," Charlotte said, shaking the shellfish in her apron.

Gunny laughed. "I thought I was the only one. I hated eating these when I was a child."

Charlotte scoffed. "I don't think anyone really likes them. But the full moon brings them to us during Holy Week so we eat them."

"I'll tell you when you like them—when you have nothing else to eat," Gunny said remembering her first hungry spring on the west end.

"Then thank the Lord we hate them! It means we have better choices the rest of the year."

"Oh, there he goes," Gunny said pointing at Larry as he pushed to a standing position and edged out toward the water. "I'd better scoop him up before he floats away." Gunny waved to Charlotte as she stepped carefully across the black, slick rocks and pulled a wet, indignant Larry from the edge of a shallow tide pool. He twisted in her arms but she held fast as Maggie skipped along behind them past the school and headed home.

After the house was scrubbed for Easter, Gunny sat Maggie by the fire during Larry's afternoon nap to talk about Christ and the meaning of Easter. "Today's a day we used to visit the dead in Dunquin. We don't have any dead buried out here," she sighed.

Maggie ran a hand into Gunny's lap. "Could we say a prayer for my mother?"

Gunny was quiet. "Of course we can, child. Let's say a prayer for Matt McCrohan too. We don't need to visit their graves to say a prayer for our dead, do we?"

She knelt in front of the fire. Maggie knelt beside her and squeezed her eyes closed.

"Who's Matt," the girl whispered.

"Matt was my friend," Gunny whispered back.

"What happened to your friend?" Maggie whispered.

Gunny opened her eyes and looked into Maggie's inquisitive little face. Her lips tightened. "You're so full of questions."

Maggie sat back down on her stool and folded her hands in her lap waiting for a story.

Gunny took a deep breath and pushed herself up off the floor and back onto her stool. "Matt was a person who was too full of life to live."

Maggie scrunched up her eyes. "That doesn't make sense."

"No, it doesn't," Gunny agreed. She decided to start again and tell Maggie the simplest truth about Matt. "A long time ago, Matt McCrohan and I were to be married. We were riding to church on a horse and we had an accident. Matt fell off the horse and he died."

Maggie eyes grew wide. "But you didn't die."

"No," Gunny assured the girl. "I didn't die."

Maggie was quiet. "I'm glad you didn't die. My mother died."

"Yes, your mother died."

"I don't remember her."

"It was last year. You were little then."

"Tell me about my mother, Gunny."

Gunny swallowed hard. What could she tell Maggie about Catherine? She hadn't really known her. She decided to tell Maggie a story the girl would like. "Your mother was a princess," she said in an animated voice. "She had pale, white skin, long blond curls, and big blue eyes."

"Like me?" Maggie said, lifting her hair with her hands.

"Sort of," Gunny laughed, looking at Maggie's tangled brown curls and a smear of ash across the girl's right cheek.

Maggie bit at her bottom lip. "Why did my mother die, Gunny?"

"I don't know, Maggie. You never know. Maybe it's so you'd end up here with me. Sometimes I wonder if maybe Matt died so I'd end up here with you."

Maggie slid her small hand into Gunny's large, calloused hand. "I'm sad about my mother, but I'm glad I have you."

Maggie and Gunny sat quietly until a large box came tumbling out of the loft. Larry had woken from his nap and pulled himself all the way up the ladder to the loft and was pulling at anything he could get his hands on.

"Larry!" Gunny yelled, trying to pluck the wiry boy from the rungs of the ladder. "What're you doing?"

Larry held on as tight as he could, then finally gave in to Gunny's pull. He smiled at Maggie as he struggled to get away from Gunny's grip, then crawled back to climb the ladder once again.

Easter morning was an occasion with two children in the house. Gunny woke early, washed her face in a small basin, stirred the fire, and added bog timbers to get the fire blazing hot. She woke the children in time to see the sun dance into the sky. She fixed eggs and oat bread for their morning meal. That night they joined the O'Connors for an evening meal of tender lamb. Gunny made a cake and Maggie dressed the cake with early wildflowers from the fields.

On the last day of April, Mr. Thompson arrived by boat and requested that the villagers meet him at the schoolhouse. When everyone was gathered together at the schoolhouse, he stood at the front of the crowded room and waved a brown sheet of paper for all to see.

"The Lord Baron has received a death threat. There is a reward for information that leads to an arrest. Here's the document we received. Please pass this around and look at the writing. It's possible it came from someone right here in this room," he said, handing the paper to Donal McCrohan.

The page was filled with neat writing. Donal showed the page to the rest of the village elders who also could not read. He handed the sheet back to Mr. Thompson. "You'll have to read it to us."

Mr. Thompson snatched the paper and cleared his throat. "Take Notice," he read quickly. "Do right and send Mr. Thompson out of the country, away from a quiet and respectable people who do not want your soup. Or I will send bullets through your carcass by noon today. Signed 'A Right Good Aim.'"

Patrick laughed. "We have no writers like that on the island, and no bullets, Mr. Thompson. This must be over the soup you're serving on the mainland. You best look there for the poet behind this pretty missive."

Mr. Thompson folded the sheet and jammed it into his bag. "Fine. Line up to pay your rent," he stated angrily.

The men nodded and shook their heads. Gunny slipped a few coins to Timothy O'Connor who got in line with the other men from the village. Gunny paid a small amount of rent now under the O'Connor name. Mr. Thompson had never confronted her again about rent, but if he ever did, she wanted to honestly say she felt she was paying what she felt she owed.

"How do you have any money for rent?" Charlotte whispered to Gunny as they slipped out the door.

"Patrick sold a few ropes for me at the Dingle fair."

"We had to sell one of the sheep to pay our rent. It doesn't seem fair that we pay the Baron so much when he does so little for us," Charlotte muttered.

"There is the school," Gunny reminded her.

"That school is a Protestant devil that never should have been allowed on the island," Charlotte stated in a raised voice as they walked up the crest toward the Dalys' house to collect Gunny's children. "It will be our downfall, mark my words. The wind's blowing in cold from the east this spring. Something evil is headed our way. I can feel it in my bones. We're already short of potatoes for this early in the year and will be living on stir-about from now to August," Charlotte said, sticking out her tongue.

"You're a worrier, Charlotte. The cows will start producing milk again soon, the rabbits'll be back, and the chickens will be laying better with the longer spring days. Personally, I'm just thankful that I was able to set my potatoes and get my oats planted without losing a child."

"I wish I could be more help with Larry," Charlotte said.

"Think nothing of it. Larry loves being out in the fields with me," Gunny said with a wide grin.

"Are you still tying him up?"

"With my strongest rope. I tell you, if I didn't tie him up, he'd be off a cliff before you could finish one verse of The Black Faced Lamb."

Charlotte chuckled. "And him still a toddler. What'll he be like when he's steadier on his feet?"

The villagers celebrated May first with a large bonfire set on the highest point on the island. At Patrick's request, Gunny started telling a long, detailed story about the "good people" who come out on May first to honor their favorite human, Aine Alair of Limerick, a woman who was nearly one of the good people..." But with Maggie wiggling in her lap and the need to keep one fist tightly clenched around Larry's shirt to keep him out of the flames, Gunny finally excused herself from the fire circle and took the children home. By the time she got the children to bed, she was irritable and exhausted and decided that raising children was something better left to the young.

June was wet and cool and July was no cheerier. On Larry's first birthday, July 15th, thick grey skies mingled with the cold, grey ocean as stiff waves beat along the cliffs at the south end of the Great Blasket island. Patrick and Charlotte O'Connor sat sipping tea in Gunny's snug little house while the children played on the floor.

"Rain on St. Swithin's Day is a very bad sign," Charlotte said, shaking her head and listening as the wind pushed sheets of rain up against the house.

Gunny stood and stretched, then traced a finger against a rivulet of rain that was winding its way down the outside of the window. "Da used to tell the tale of St. Swithin, a simple monk who was beloved by his fellow monks. When he died the monks buried him in a fancy mausoleum. St. Swithin was so mad at the monks' overindulgence that he sent floods from the heavens to wash away the mausoleum. Da said when it rained on St. Swithin's you could expect forty more days of rain."

Patrick laughed. "That's silly. I remember one St. Swithin's about ten years ago when it rained all day and everyone said we'd have forty more days of rain but we didn't."

"I remember that year as well," Charlotte said. "And it was wet the rest of the summer. It must have been at least thirty days, if not forty."

"Still, it didn't rain every day," Patrick insisted.

"It sounds like either way, we're in for a wet summer," Gunny said, pouring a fresh cup of tea and enjoying the feel of the hot Spanish porcelain against the calloused palms of her hands.

Patrick stared into the fire. "I'm going to remain optimistic."

It rained nearly every day for the rest of the summer. The crops grew poorly and the turf did not dry well in the fields.

In early September the villagers worked together to bring in a small harvest. Gunny released Larry from his harness while she worked and he was soon toddling behind the older Daly boys through the fields. Even with less food to gather this year, she wondered how she had ever brought in a harvest on her own. Everyone gathered together to cut the last few sheaves of oats and to "put out the hare." As the newest member of the village, Gunny had the honor of sprinkling holy water on the last sheaf cut. She collected the blessed oats to take home for supper, and decided to twist the straw into fresh rope to protect the village scythe blades until the next summer. She looked around the mass of villagers.

"Has anyone seen my boy?" she asked.

Everyone glanced around them but Larry was not in the fields.

"He's no doubt run off with the Daly boys. Don't worry about him," Patrick said.

Gunny grabbed Maggie by the hand and set off to walk to the south end to look for the missing toddler. Unsuccessful, she walked back to the village, handed Maggie off to Charlotte and headed into the hills. How could such a little boy be so much trouble? The wind picked up as she neared the crest of the high ridge on the island. She should never have untied him. She could hear Eileen scolding her for having lost a child. She wrapped her shawl tighter around her. Where was he?

As she started down the back side of the ridge toward the bog, she spied Larry playing with two boys from the village who couldn't have much more than five. They were filthy, lobbing wet dirt balls at a large rock. She sighed with relief. Now that she knew he was alive she wanted to kill him. "Larry," she yelled.

He glanced at her and grinned. Gunny marched over and grabbed an old rick that had been left behind on a nearby rock. She loaded it with a few bricks of the driest of the still damp turf, then grabbed the small boy by his jacket and tossed him into the basket. She swung the heavy rick onto her back with Larry shrieking and rocking the rick from side to side.

"Be still," she said loudly. "I promised Joanna that I would be more patient with you than my mother was with me, but I'll tell you that you try a woman's soul." She pointed at the other two boys. "Go home. I'm sure your mothers are worried."

The two boys threw down their dirt clods and took off at a tear toward the village.

Larry muttered behind her in the rick until he fell asleep, exhausted from his day of wandering with the big boys. After a day of harvest and the hike back from the bog, Gunny's legs ached and she was near tears by the time she got home. She shifted the rick off her back, unloaded the now sleeping toddler to a mat in front of the fire, turned the empty rick over on top of him, and stacked the heavy turf bricks on top.

"I'm not going to spend one more minute chasing you today," she said to Larry's small, still form.

She walked back to the village to fetch Maggie. By the time they got back to the house, she was so tired she could hardly stand. Larry was awake and was howling for his supper from under the rick. Gunny bolted the door, moved the bricks off the rick, and pulled the cage off the crying toddler. When she reached down to pick him up, he pushed past her in pursuit of his sister. Gunny watched the children chase each other around the house as she put a few small potatoes in a pot to boil. They'd have to watch their potato stocks over the winter. Her back room held only half her normal harvest. By the time the potatoes were soft, the children were playing quietly in front of the fire. Gunny watched as Larry pointed at various shells and rocks. When he pointed and grunted, Maggie handed him the desired item.

"Maggie, let the boy speak or he'll never learn to talk," Gunny said wearily from the table.

Maggie opened her eyes wide and looked at Gunny. "If I don't get him things, he bites me."

Gunny shook her head. "Come eat."

~ Chapter 20: The Famine ~

It was November 1, 1845. The last of the crops had been gathered and the sheep and cattle were once again foraging in the nearby fields and kitchen gardens of the tiny village on the Great Blasket island. Thrushes, blackbirds, and starlings gleaned the last remaining seeds from spent flower heads in the dry meadows before flying farther south for the winter. Three crows perched along the peak of the O'Connor house. A light easterly wind carried the sound of their cawing around the quiet village. The turf had not fully dried over the wet summer and only a few houses had fires going; heat would be scarce over the long winter months. And rents were due. A group of village leaders trudged off toward the south end of the island and gathered in the new schoolhouse.

Donal McCrohan looked around the room. "As we all know, the harvest was poor and we may not have enough food to get us through the winter. We certainly have nothing extra to sell and most of us will not be able to pay our rent. In the past, we would have explained this to the old Lord when he came to collect. But when Mr. Thompson arrives here with his black book and open wallet there is no doubt he'll evict the lot of us. Someone is going to have to go and talk to the new Lord."

Timothy O'Connor shook his head. "The Baron said there would be no bargaining for rent."

"But if we sell our meager surplus now," Patrick said, "we'll be starving by spring and we'll default on our rent then. Either way, the Baron isn't going to get much from us this year."

"Thomas won't bargain," Gunny stated. "It's not like it was with the Old Lord."

"You know him better than any of us," Timothy O'Connor said, turning to Gunny. "What do you suggest we do?"

She shook her head. "Thomas made himself pretty clear about evictions."

"We'll not convert, not a one of us," Charlotte piped in, clutching Gunny's arm. "Go talk to him, Gunny. The worst he can do is say no."

Gunny sighed. She knew that wasn't the worst the Baron could do. If she went to Ventry to plead their case, she'd not only have to face the Baron but her parents as well. She had not been to Ventry since she'd taken the children. What if her mother insisted she return the children? It was something she'd had occasional nightmares about. But if she didn't go and no one could pay rent, Mr. Thompson would evict the lot of them. She looked at the hopeful faces of her neighbors and friends and swallowed.

"I don't know that it'll help, but I'll go. I'll see what I can do."

Gunny dropped Maggie and Larry off with Charlotte. "Take care of them as best you can," she said. "If the boy wanders off a cliff, I'll understand," she added with a half-smile.

She hiked the familiar path down to the stone pier and carefully stepped into Patrick's waiting boat. They each manned an oar and set out across the choppy, grey channel toward Dingle. The sharp, gusty wind was too erratic to use the sail.

"This boat is so big compared to my old boat," Gunny said as they rowed.

"I can't believe that little boat of yours ever made it to the island," Patrick said, pulling hard at his oar. "You were mighty lucky the day we picked you up."

"I was lucky, indeed," Gunny said with a short laugh.

They rowed the rest of the way in silence. Gunny imagined how it would be to see her parents and practiced in her head what she would tell them—how wonderful the children were doing and how well she was raising them. If her mother insisted she return them to Ventry she would flee; there was no question about giving them back. Then she imagined talking to Thomas. If he asked about Catherine's children, she would deny they existed.

"You're awfully quiet today," Patrick said pulling in rhythm with Gunny's strokes against the stiff wind.

Gunny nodded and matched Patrick's rhythm as they rounded the point of mainland at Slea Head and rowed east past Ventry. They tied up at the end of the Dingle pier which was empty of fishermen and hucksters this late in the season.

"You're sure you don't want me to walk with you to Ventry?" Patrick asked.

"No, I need the time alone to prepare my thoughts. I won't be long."

"You know where to find me," Patrick said, pointing up toward the pub on Green Street. Gunny pulled her shawl tight around her and set off on the dusty road toward Ballygoleen.

The thick clouds over the water cleared as a biting wind picked up and blew inland. Gunny looked out at the pale sunlight highlighting white caps on the choppy sea. She hoped they'd be able to make it back across the channel. Every fiber in her body told her to return to Dingle , to row back to the island with Patrick, to hide with the children while she still could. She spied the roof of the large yellow house through the trees ahead of her and stopped at the top of the long drive. Her stomach fluttered as she remembered an earlier day on this same spot with hound dogs snapping around her. Thomas had been kind to her then. She looked past the house toward the stables and saw herself with her father bargaining with Sean Fitzpatrick for Shep. A gust of wind blew against her back and she felt Catherine pass her on the drive, her fine, light hair lifting, her girlish laughter flowing past the older woman. Gunny blinked and stared at the house. Pieces of her life were tangled around this place.

She walked down the drive and around the house to the kitchen door, gave a swift knock, then entered without waiting for a reply. A low turf fire burned in the fireplace but the room was strangely quiet.

"Good day?" she said to the empty room, her voice echoing off the high ceiling. She wiped her feet on a new mat and crossed the kitchen to the door that opened into the main house. She hesitated. It wasn't right to enter the main part of the house unannounced. As much as she disliked her, she wished Mrs. Needham was standing guard to announce her. She opened the door to the house a small crack and peeked in. Two servants dashed past. She opened the door farther and put out a hand to stop a young chambermaid as she hurried by. The girl's face was puffy, her eyes red with tears.

"What's the matter? Has something happened?"

The girl pushed Gunny's hand away. "It's the Missus," she sobbed. "The Missus has been stabbed."

"What?" Gunny muttered, then spied the Baron through the open door to the parlor. He was sitting alone in front of a smouldering wood fire, calmly sipping at a large glass of amber liquid. She crossed into the room and pushed the door quietly closed behind her. "Thomas?"

Thomas looked up at her with bleary eyes, then broke into a large smile. "Gunny," he slurred. He attempted to stand, but couldn't and sat back down. He laughed. "You'll have to join me. Come sit with me," he said, patting his lap. His hands and shirt were stained with drying, red blood.

"What happened?" Gunny asked as she cautiously approached. She did not see any obvious wounds on him.

The Baron looked up, his eyes filled with tears. "Gunny," he said then looked away toward the fire. "Gunny, Gunny, Gunny...," he muttered, and closed his eyes.

"Thomas," Gunny said sternly. "Tell me what happened to you and to your wife. The servant girl said..."

Thomas turned toward Gunny and shook his head. He set his glass down on the small table near his chair and dabbed at his eyes with a large clean monogrammed handkerchief and took a deep breath. "I killed her, Gunny. I killed Chrisabella," he said with a wheezy laugh.

Gunny gasped. "You killed your wife?"

Thomas' eyes narrowed and he spoke in a soft voice. "She opened all of my taps again. She let my best wines run out onto the floor of the wine cellar. I caught her this time and I locked her in the cellar. She was yelling at me through the door, trying to embarrass me. I went in to make her stop but she wouldn't stop."

"I pray this is some delusion of drink. What you're saying makes no sense."

Thomas wiped a fine sheen of sweat from his brow with his handkerchief and scooted up slightly in the chair. "She would not listen to me. I told her to shut up and listen. I will not have a woman tell me how to run my household."

"So you stabbed her?"

"I didn't mean to stab her. I only meant to scare her. I held out my knife and she grabbed at it. I'm not sure what happened next. There was so much blood."

"You killed the mother of your children."

"My children can go to hell," he said bitterly, taking a quick drink from his glass. "They are always siding with their mother. But that is done now. No one is going to side with Chrisabella anymore." He turned and stared into the fire.

"The court will hang you for murder," Gunny said in a soft voice.

Thomas laughed and shook his head. "You forget that I own the court."

Gunny backed toward the door. "That's not right, Thomas. It's not fair."

"Life isn't fair, Gunny," Thomas said setting his glass down firmly on the small table by his chair. He turned and looked at her. "Look at us. I loved you but you were Catholic and poor and my grandfather said I couldn't marry you. Then you ran away and I couldn't see you anymore. Was it fair for you to go off and leave me when I needed you here in Ventry?"

Gunny shook her head and took a step toward the Baron's chair. "I don't know what you're talking about," she said in a soft voice. "You never told me you loved me."

"I did tell you!" he said loudly, then continued in a smaller voice. "I tried to tell you." He sniffed and rested his head on his hand. "You thought I was flirting but I wasn't. I loved you and you left me."

"Thomas, I didn't leave you," Gunny said firmly, approaching his chair. "I was in service in Dingle then I went home to marry. You had already married Chrisabella. My leaving Dingle had nothing to do with you. You've had too much to drink and you aren't remembering things as they were."

Thomas reached out and took Gunny's warm hand in his red, sweaty hands and rested his damp forehead against her long slim fingers. "I wanted to marry you and you left me."

Gunny pulled her hand away and wiped the damp redness on her apron. "That's not true and you know it. There was never any love between us."

Thomas grabbed Gunny's hand again and squeezed it tight. "Chrisabella hated me. Dayrolles moved to Dublin to live with my brother. Tom won't talk to me. And Todd is never in the house. I tried to take care of Catherine for you, Gunny. I tried." Thomas looked up at Gunny's shocked face, then fell to his knees in front of her and whispered, "You are the only true friend I have ever had."

Gunny felt the blood drain from her face. She leaned forward, her lips nearly touching Thomas' forehead. "Is that why you took me in the graveyard, Thomas?" she whispered. "Because you loved me but couldn't have me?"

"I was drunk that night, Gunny. I tried to help you."

"To help me?" Gunny said shaking her head, her voice raised. "How could that possibly have helped me?" she said, struggling to free her hand from his desperate grip.

"Now you have come back to me," Thomas slurred. "Somehow you knew I needed you with me today."

Gunny wrenched her hand from his grip and backed toward the center of the room. "I came to talk to you about rents on the island," she said, trying not to cry. "The summer was miserable and we don't have enough food to sell and to keep ourselves alive. You must waive our rent and not evict us."

Thomas blinked and fell back against his chair. "What?" he asked, trying to focus on Gunny's wavering form. "My wife died today. I'm not going to talk to you about something as insubstantial as your summer weather." He stumbled to his feet and tried to sit on the chair but ended up sliding to the floor. He waved a hand in front of his face and laughed. "Talk to Mr. Thompson about your rent," he slurred. "I pay him to do my dirty work."

Gunny sighed and looked at the broken man before her. "And where would I find Mr. Thompson?" she asked quietly, trying to keep herself composed.

The Baron roared with laughter and pointed with an unsteady hand. "He's standing right behind you."

Mr. Thompson hurried past Gunny and helped the Baron into his chair. "What happened, Baron? Or do I not want to know?" He moved the Baron's whiskey bottle and glass to the mantel and turned to Gunny. "Leave. The Baron and I have business to discuss." He hated being in the same room with the witch from the island.

"I'm leaving," Gunny said, turning to go, then changed her mind and turned back. "Before you find out that all hell has broken loose in this house, you must know that our crops are too meager on the island to sell anything to pay our rent but we will not let you evict us. That's all I have to say. Now I'll go."

Thomas laughed bitterly and clutched at Mr. Thompson's arm. "Gunny said it was a wet summer and that the islanders cannot pay rent," he chuckled.

"I heard her," Mr. Thompson said flatly, glancing at Gunny. "We've had wetter summers and the rent was paid. Just be happy you don't have the rot."

"What rot?"

"How could you not smell that awful stench on your way in? Most of the potatoes around here are rotten."

"I came by boat to Dingle and the wind was blowing in across the water as I walked here," Gunny said. "The potatoes rotted over the wet summer?"

"It wasn't the weather," Mr. Thompson said curtly waving his hand at her. "There was a thick fog over most of the peninsula last month. It lasted for three days. After that, the potato leaves and stalks lay blackened in the fields. They looked like they had been burned. You did not have that on the island?"

"No," Gunny said shaking her head. "We only had days and days of rain."

"Then you may have the best crops of anyone."

"I may double your rent," Thomas said loudly, pointing at Gunny. "Where is my whiskey? Someone find my whiskey," he muttered to no one in particular.

"Check the potatoes you stored in the pits," Mr. Thompson said to Gunny. "They may have lifted fine but are rotten now, slimy and black. That's what we are seeing here."

Gunny gasped. "If what we have left rots, what then? What're we to eat?"

Mr. Thompson turned on her. "Don't come looking here. No one has enough to get through this winter."

Thomas stood unsteadily and made his way to the mantel. "Here you are!" he announced to the whiskey bottle. He poured a tall class of the clear brown liquid and took a long sip. "Ahhh." He smacked his lips. "The elixir of the Gods."

"I'll check the potatoes on the island when I return," Gunny said. She looked at Thomas leaning unsteadily against the mantel in his blood-stained shirt, a sauced, jaunty look on his face.

He raised his eyebrows.

"What are you looking at?"

Gunny sighed and turned to Mr. Thompson. "Be sure to ask Thomas about the Baroness."

Mr. Thompson went pale. "What about her?"

Thomas staggered forward, "Oh, let me tell him," he slurred. "Mr. Thompson likes hearing stories about the Baroness."

Gunny's head throbbed. "I'm leaving." She hurried into the hallway and pulled the door to the parlor closed behind her. Several of the chambermaids were talking in the hallway in hushed tones.

"Where's my mother?" she interrupted them. The girls looked confused. "Mrs. Malone?" Gunny said. "She works in the kitchen. And where's Mrs. Needham?"

A tall man stuck his head into the hallway from the kitchen. He looked at her sadly. "Mrs. Needham passed away nearly two years ago and Mrs. Malone moved back to Dunquin. Eileen was never right after her girl died and her husband passed so quickly after. Sorry, Ma'am."

The faces around Gunny blurred. She grabbed at the kitchen doorway to steady herself. Her mother was back in Dunquin? And her father had passed? Why hadn't she heard? Her eyes brimmed with hot tears. She pulled her shawl up over her head and fled out the kitchen door into the yard. She cut along a path past the stables and raced madly through the trees onto the roadway to Dingle, then set off at a run to find Patrick.

Gunny burst in on the O'Connor house with Patrick trailing close behind her, and pulled the surprised children to her chest.

"What on earth's the matter, Gunny?" Charlotte asked. "What happened in Ventry?" she added, looking from Gunny to Patrick who only shook his head.

Gunny released the children and stood. She wiped the back of her hand across her eyes and nose, then burst into tears. "My da is gone," she cried, sounding like a little girl. "He's gone," she said again breaking into greater sobs, "and no one told me."

Charlotte pulled the tall woman to her. "There, there," she muttered. "You mustn't cry in front of the children. What happened?"

Gunny wiped at her eyes and sniffed while Patrick called the children to him to play in front of the fire. Gunny continued in a quieter voice. "A man at the Baron's House said Da passed after Catherine, and that Mam moved back to Dunquin. How can my Mam be living in Dunquin, Charlotte? She has no family there. And Mr. Thompson said some blight was affecting the potatoes. No one has enough food to get through the winter."

"Now, now," Charlotte said clicking her tongue. "The Irish help one another. I'm sure your mother will be fine, Gunny. But that is upsetting about your father. I'm so sorry." She paused. "Did you talk to the Baron about our rent?"

Gunny grimaced. "I saw Thomas. He was dead drunk. The Baroness had been murdered in the cellar and Mr. Thompson came in to talk about the potato blight..." She looked up at Charlotte's face. "I have to take the children to the west end."

Charlotte gripped Gunny's hands. "Stop, Gunny. Stop and take a breath. You're not taking the children anywhere. Winter's coming and there's less food on the west end than there is here. We've faced tough times before. We will get through this together as we've always done. Now have some tea and start again at the beginning. Tell me everything you heard."

Gunny sent a desperate note off to Michael in Virginia to let him know about their father's passing. She told him that the potato stocks on the island were sound, but reported what she had heard about the rot on the mainland. She begged him to send money to their mother in Dunquin. Patrick took the letter to the post office in Dingle on his last trip to the mainland before the channel became too rough to cross till spring.

He knocked at her door to let him know the letter had been posted. She let him in and quickly closed the door to keep the cold wind out. She had a low peat fire burning—just enough to keep the house warm. She had moved both beds into the front room so they would be warmer at night. Patrick sat down heavily on one of the beds and pulled off his cap.

"That was rough crossing but your letter's posted. You've done what you can. Let's hope your brother comes through."

Gunny wrung her hands. "It'll take weeks for that letter to get to America, and weeks for a reply. Maybe Mac took my mother in. He always had money from his work in the forge," Gunny said reassuringly.

Patrick shook his head. "I hate to say it, Gunny, but if there's no food in Dunquin then there's no need for anyone to buy new pots. And a broken wagon wheel's not going to be fixed if money is needed to buy food."

Gunny gave Patrick a thin slice of oat bread and sent him on his way. She knew he was right. Her mother was in trouble and there was not a thing that she could do about it until spring.

In late February, Patrick and the other Blasket fisherman chanced an early crossing to Dingle to sell a bit of fish and collect the mail. They had no room for her in the boat but Patrick promised he'd take her on the next trip. She paced on the windy cliff until their large curragh returned, then raced down to the stone pier to greet them.

Patrick handed her a weathered letter with an American postmark. She tore open the seal. It was from Michael. He and Maeve reported they had little money to spare but had sent a few pounds to Eileen in Dunquin. The letter had been written in late December. Gunny clutched it to her chest and wept, then took a deep breath and straightened out the paper to continue reading. Michael wrote that a few other families from the peninsula were living in Alexandria and that they had heard about the potato blight and had gathered food and supplies they'd be sending soon to Ireland. Others in town, hearing news of the scarcity, blamed the Irish for being lazy and poor, saying they had brought it on themselves. He said that all was well with he and Maeve. They had no more money to spare, and hoped she would somehow get by.

Gunny crumpled the letter and tossed it out into the choppy waters.

"Bad news?" Patrick asked.

"No. Michael sent Mam money. It's more than I could do. I'll go with you to Dingle or Dunquin next trip to find her. I'm going to bring her over to the island."

"Gunny," Patrick started, then stopped. "Things are not good on the mainland. I brought you some papers the postmaster saved for you. You can read all about it." Gunny grabbed the stack of papers from Patrick and headed up the steep path to the O'Connor house while Patrick and the other fishermen cleaned and stashed the boat. She helped Charlotte prepare a small meal of potatoes and fish. After both families ate, she scanned the stack of newspapers and read aloud to the crowded room.

The papers reported that the blight had touched nearly every farm in Ireland, but that the worst famine was up and down the west coast. Anything with a leaf on it had the same burnt look as the potato plants so the livestock had nothing to eat. Some farmers were taking out loans to buy potatoes to get them through the winter but many were eating their seed potatoes.

Gunny paused. "Who can believe that we were better off than most this winter?" She continued reading.

The British Prime Minister, Sir Robert Peel, refused to give food away and insisted that Irish farmers work to purchase food. He'd put public works in place to create jobs. Men around the peninsula had been hired to build new roads through the Conor Pass, around Slea Head, and at Monaree. Peel repealed the Corn Laws to allow cheap imports of grain, but few had money for even the cheapest grain so Peel had Indian corn shipped from America. The American whole grain maze had to be chipped in a steel mill, then ground, then pre-soaked, then boiled. None of this was explained when the corn was first imported. The papers reported that the Irish were calling the corn Peel's Brimstone partly because of its bright yellow color and partly because of what the poorly ground corn did to one's digestive track. Families were pleading with relatives living in America for food or for passage money to sail to America.

Gunny closed her eyes and shook her head. Charlotte begged her to continue.

Gunny scanned through the papers. Charity groups on the peninsula were trying to help. A soup kitchen had been set up in Dingle and soup was being sold for a penny a week. A later paper said that soup supplies were running short and that Indian meal stir-about was being distributed from large iron boilers along Main Street. The Baron had hired local men to build an east tower on the Burnham house but that helped only a few and only for a short time. Gunny couldn't find anything in the papers about the murder of the Baroness. In the chaos of massive crop failures, it appeared that the loss of one soul had been overlooked in the calamity of potentially losing thousands of others.

Each paper included a list of Thompson evictions. The lists in the most recent paper were long and many of the names Gunny read out loud were familiar to the families in the crowded Blasket house.

"When we walked through Dingle," Patrick reported, "we saw people living on the streets, in old sheds, and at the church. I talked to a woman living down by the docks. She said she was trying to keep two children warm and fed, and that when Thompson threw her out of her house, he told her if she became a Protestant he would waive her rent and give her soup. When she said she wouldn't do that, he burned her house down and walked away."

Gunny called it a night at that. She couldn't read anymore; couldn't hear anymore. She asked Patrick to let her know when he was crossing to the mainland again.

419

The remaining stocks of potatoes on the island ran out by mid-March. Island women made thin soups of fish and milk but the soup did not stay with the men as they fished through the warming spring days. The men tired easily and fished less. Few had the energy to cut and stack turf, though they knew they would freeze the coming winter if they did not cut the peat. The teacher at the school continued to make a daily gruel at the schoolhouse. Some days only the children on the island ate. There were few spuds to plant that spring, but what the islanders had, they planted.

Throughout the spring and summer, families arrived on the Blaskets from the mainland with reports of eviction, starvation, and fever. Most of those who arrived on the island had relatives there. The island families tried to be as generous as possible, opening up their homes and meager food supplies to their relatives. Everyone eagerly awaited the lifting of the early potatoes in August.

The Baron and a tall stranger arrived unexpectedly on the island in late July. The villagers followed the men to the schoolhouse. Gunny watched as the crowd passed her house, then left the children playing in the yard and slipped into the back of the classroom.

The Baron stood at the front of the room. His hair was thinning and he had started to grey at the temples. He had lost weight and seemed shorter than usual standing next to the robust young man who had accompanied him on the trip. The Baron introduced his son, young Tom, who had his mother's height and his father's strong chiseled chin. He had a full head of wavy brown hair and deep-set brown eyes. Gunny could see why Catherine had been drawn to him.

"We have a new Prime Minister, Lord John Russell," the Baron announced. "Lord Russell is committed to free trade and refuses to continue providing the poor with Indian meal. He says whatever you eat must come from Ireland, and that food is not to be sold for less than market value. That being said, the schoolhouse soup pot is now closed. If Lord Russell will not feed you, then I will no longer feed you."

The villagers gasped.

"The island children are hungry. Can't you keep the soup going at least until the harvest is in?" Patrick asked. "It's only a few more weeks."

The Baron stared at the tall red-haired man. "You have to survive as best you can. Grain is available in Dingle at market rates plus the five percent that goes to the crown."

"No one has that kind of money. Has the crown decided to starve the Irish and be done with us?" Charlotte O'Connor queried.

"Apparently so," the Baron said flatly. "Are there any other questions?"

Gunny slipped out the door. She had heard all she cared to hear.

The Baron and young Tom stayed for two days in the guesthouse at the school, welcoming the escape from the drudgery of the mainland. Gunny moved with the children to the O'Connor's' house to stay clear of them. It wouldn't do for anyone on the island to see young Tom with Gunny's children. The similarities in looks, especially between Tom and Maggie, were obvious. When the Baron and Thomas finally packed up to leave, Gunny hiked with the children up to the cliffs to watch the boat depart. The Baron stoically faced home, but as young Tom rowed away, he caught Gunny's eye and smiled at Maggie and Larry holding hands with her on the cliff. He gave a quick salute before heading east to Ventry.

The few potatoes harvested in August were firm and plump and the Blasket villagers breathed a sigh of relief. They had been short of seed potatoes the prior spring, but what was growing was growing well. But in September, just before the larger harvest was taken in, a low, thick fog settled over the island and left behind blackened, spotted leaves in the fields. When the islanders dug up the remaining potatoes, the smell of rot confirmed the news: blight had reached the island. After the hungry summer of 1846, the islanders looked at their blackened, rotting crops and knew that starvation was upon them.

Gunny counted her small store of August potatoes. Even with what she had from her kitchen garden, she would only be able to feed the children for a month or two. She thought through her first year of survival on the west end. She'd have to go back to snare rabbits. And she could collect shore food and wild birds. As she strategized her menus, her thoughts kept returning to her mother. She had insisted that Patrick take her on his next trip but no fisherman would cross the channel now for fear of fever.

The ocean waters were unsettled through September, but on a windless day in early October, Patrick finally came with the news that they could cross to the mainland. Gunny packed the children off to stay with the Dalys and walked with Patrick to the stone pier. They rowed to the mainland and landed at the pier in Dunquin. The village was quiet as they walked up the steep hill past O'Leary's pub, the air clear and crisp. Doors were closed and windows were shuttered. Gunny sniffed. There was no smell of burning peat.

"This is eerie," Gunny said. "Where is everyone?"

"Evicted, I suppose," Patrick replied.

Gunny looked up toward the hills above the village. A few people were in the fields but they were not harvesting crops. They were dismantling stone fences.

"A man who came to the island from Dingle said the Baron is paying Dunquin farmers to take down their fences. He is going to move his cattle here and needs larger fields," Patrick said.

"My, God," Gunny said shaking her head. "Thomas is taking advantage of the fact that people are starving? He'll be cursed for this."

"The Baron has lived off rents all his life. He has to make his money somewhere."

"The Baron once told me that life wasn't fair," Gunny said, shaking her head.

"It seems fairer for some than others," Patrick said.

Gunny steered Patrick to the right as they passed the open church gates. "I'm afraid of what I will find at my old house if my mam is there. Let's talk to Mac first at the forge."

Mac was sitting on the bench in the yard in front of the forge clutching a frayed rope that was tied to a bitterly thin cow. Gunny was so relieved to see him that she ran the last few yards to the forge.

"Mac," she exclaimed, scooting past the slender cow and squatting in front of her old friend. She looked him over from head to toe. His eyes were clouded, unfocused, his hair grey around the temples. His face was thin, his bare feet swollen.

"Mac," she repeated, trying to catch his eye. "Are you all right? Have you seen my mother?"

Mac glanced at Gunny then looked away. "There's no food, Gunny," he said stiffly. "Do you have any money?"

"Mac. It's me, Gunny. You know I've never had any money."

Mac blinked at the familiar face. "Do you have food?"

Gunny looked at the wrinkles around Mac's eyes. "We have some food on the island. Come with us. We don't have much but we'll share what we have. Bring Sheila and the boy. We'll make room. I came to find my mother. She's going with us as well."

Mac looked down at his swollen feet. "I can't leave, Gunny. Sheila's sick with the fever. We had a baby. We named her Gunny. She was small but seemed strong. Then she died. We didn't have a coffin. We had to bury her in her cradle."

Gunny felt her throat constrict. "Mac, I'm so sorry. Do you want me to go in and see your wife?"

"No, don't go inside," Mac said clutching at her arm. "The fever's spreading. If you go inside, you'll get it too."

"It sounds like your wife needs help."

"I'm helping her," Mac insisted. "I'm bringing her water. People are dying everywhere from the fever. You remember Cornelius? He and Ashling were worse off than anyone knew. They had no food. We didn't know. What little food they had Cornelius gave to Ashling and the children. Then the fever came and they all died together, right there in their house. All seven of them.

No one will go in to bury the bodies. They're just lying in there bundled up in front of the cold fire. Seven of them, Gunny. Dead."

Gunny got a chill. They had walked past Cornelius' house when they came in by the pier. "Mac, I don't know what to say. I feel awful we didn't come over earlier this year. But we're here now. How can we help?"

Mac slumped forward and stared at his swollen hands. "You can't help. The crops failed again this year. There is no food to buy. The chickens are gone. The sheep. The cows. The dogs."

Patrick grimaced. "You ate the dogs?"

Mac looked at Patrick for the first time, confused, his eyes hard with hunger. "When you have nothing else to eat, you eat the dogs."

Patrick took a step away from Mac and put his hands in front of him. "I didn't mean to offend you. Things aren't this bad yet on the island. We still have fish. Why don't you fish here? You don't have to go out into the ocean. The streams must be filled with trout and eel."

"The rivers belong to the Baron," Mac said, sounding as if he were once again eight. "Poaching is a crime."

Patrick looked at Gunny and shrugged.

Mac pushed to his feet. "You grow up thinking people will always be around. Fathers. Brothers. Neighbors. Friends. Then one day, everyone is gone."

Patrick took a deep breath. "Our potatoes were also black this fall."

Mac shook his head. "Then the terrible times are upon you," he said clutching at the thin cow. Her neck was scarred with a series of small cuts. "This cow is our only hope. I bleed her and cook the blood with whatever we find in the fields: wild birds, nettles, mushrooms, nuts. I have a little cabbage and turnip left from the summer. I have to guard the cow. I have to guard all of the food we have. Sheila won't eat anything. She says her head hurts too much from the fever. She sleeps most of the time. She says I have to stay strong and feed the baby. She doesn't remember that little Gunny died."

Gunny sat on the bench. "Where's your son? Where's Matthew?"

Mac looked at Gunny, puzzled. "Matthew? He's out looking for food. My feet are too swollen to walk but Matthew hasn't been sick. Thank God we didn't have any other children or they might have died too. Our beautiful little girl is gone, Gunny. She was so small."

"Mac, do you know where my mother is?"

Mac looked confused for a moment, then blinked. "Your mother."

"Yes, Eileen Malone," Gunny said. She could see that Mac was struggling for a way to answer her question. "If she's gone, Mac, you can tell me," Gunny said gently.

"She is gone, Gunny."

Gunny hung her head.

"She moved to the workhouse over the summer," Mac added.

Gunny's head snapped up. "The workhouse? In Tralee?"

"No, the new one in Dingle. The Baron built it with his own money."

"How kind of him to supply the poor with housing after he evicts them."

"There's food there, Gunny. Many others have gone. At first they wouldn't take your Mam. They'd heard from the postmaster she was getting money from America but the money ran out. She was so thin when she left. I fear she may not have made it to Dingle."

"We'll go look for her," Gunny said, rising and gently squeezing Mac's hand. "And then we'll come back here for you. You and your family must come to the island, Mac."

Mac stared blankly in front of him. "I have to guard the cow, Gunny. She's all we have."

"All right," Gunny said gently patting his hand. "We'll talk when we get back."

Gunny glanced back at Mac as they left. He sat slumped on the bench, eyes staring at nothing, his hand clutching at the frayed bit of rope that tethered him to the thin cow.

Patrick and Gunny passed small clusters of people wandering the road to Ventry. No one looked them in the eye as they shuffled past. A man and two small children sat near the ogham stone of Colman the Pilgrim. The man's face was swollen with starvation. His children leaned against him in the shadow of the stone, their eyes closed.

As they walked into Ventry, they passed a long line of people, each waiting with a Tommy can to collect a quart of porridge from a large boiler set up in front of the church. Gunny eyed the thin gruel that was being served and listened as a server taunted the old man he was serving.

"If you were a Protestant, I'd give you a bit of meat in your soup. Would you like meat in your soup?"

Gunny recognized the voice. "Has it come to this, Mr. Thompson?"

Mr. Thompson scowled at Gunny. "The Baron says it's my fault no rents were being collected. He brought young Tom on as his new agent and left me to serve the poor. The Baron says his brat is a gentleman by birth and will demand more respect. Hah!" He spat as he carelessly slopped hot gruel into a waiting tin can, burning the hand of the recipient "I wish that boy luck. Now move along, Witch," he uttered. "The crown has no food for you here."

"If this crisis happened outside of London more care would be taken," Gunny muttered.

The ocean and fields on the way to Dingle looked the same as they always had but most of the farms appeared to be deserted. A few houses had been toppled. A sleek black coach drawn by two dappled greys raced up behind them on the dusty road. The coachman sat high on the box in front dressed in a black coat and tall black hat. He yelled at them to clear the road. Gunny caught a glimpse of the Baron inside, looking out the window with unseeing eyes.

As they neared Dingle, they passed a gang of men working to build up part of the road that had washed away, and another group taking apart a stone wall in a low field. They walked into town along upper Main Street and asked directions to the new poorhouse. It was up near the fields where the villagers had once grazed their cows. It was a large, grey, square building that looked down on the harbor. Starving peasants, mostly women, wandered outside the high, stone walls. Several women sat leaning against the building staring blankly ahead of them. Gunny saw one woman with a bright shawl wrapped around her head who looked vaguely familiar. Gunny squatted in front of her.

"Mam?" she asked quietly. The woman pulled her shawl from her face at the familiar word—but neither woman recognized the other. The woman lips were stained green from eating grass mixed with hot water. A thin stream of green juice trickled down her wrinkled chin and onto her neck. Gunny patted her on the head and rose. She crossed the yard and knocked at the large double doors of the building. There was no answer. She opened one door and stepped inside. Patrick followed. There were two large rooms inside, one on each side of the hallway. The room to the right was filled with women, the room on the left populated with a few men. There were no beds, only matted, dirty straw on the floor. The stench of urine, defecation, sweat, and death was overwhelming.

"I'll wait outside," Patrick said, trying not to breathe the putrid air.

Gunny pulled the hem of her apron up over her mouth and entered the room of women. The light in the room was dim, filtered through windows thick with hardened dust and cobwebs. She stepped gingerly around seated and sleeping women. Most of the women were wearing only dirty rags. Any money they had over the past two years had clearly been spent on food, not clothing. Their arms and legs were thin, their skin hanging loose from their bones. Their faces were sallow and puffy, their hair heavy with grime. Small groups huddled together to keep warm. Gunny grimaced that those with lice or fever were no doubt passing disease among them.

Gunny looked around the room at the unfamiliar faces. Would she even recognize her mother if she saw her? She rolled a sleeping woman over to see her face. The woman's face was black. Gunny gagged and rolled the dead woman back onto her stomach.

"Is there no one to help?" she asked a woman sitting near to the dead woman.

The woman shook her head but did not look up. "There are too many dead and dying. Someone will come to collect her later."

"And then?"

The woman looked at Gunny blankly. "Then they'll take her to the burial pit out back."

"For a funeral," Gunny stated.

The woman smiled weakly. "There're no funerals, dear. Who would come? They've dug a mass grave for us. We'll all end up in it eventually, covered with a light dusting of lime. That's all the ceremony we have now."

Gunny knelt in front of the woman. She assumed she was old by the look of her but as she studied the woman's face decided the woman was no more than thirty. "What's your name?" she asked softly.

"Mary."

"Mary," Gunny said, "I'm trying to find my mother. Her name's Eileen Malone. She's from Dunquin, though she might say she's from Ventry."

"I'm from Ballyferriter," the woman said shaking her head. "You don't hear many names here. People come and go so quickly. I've heard people talking about Dunquin. There may be some of your villagers around." The woman looked at Gunny's face. "Do you have any food?"

Gunny shook her head. "Don't they feed you here?"

"They give us a thin gruel at night. It's mostly Indian corn, sometimes burned. It's enough to keep you alive. For awhile."

Gunny reached out and brushed a greasy strand of hair from Mary's face and gently tucked it behind one ear. Mary's eyes filled with tears at the gesture of kindness. "I miss my mother, too," Mary said.

Gunny nodded.

"And my children," Mary sniffed. "I should have converted so they might have lived. Or if I'd died, they would have taken them. They said they wouldn't take my children unless they were Protestant or orphaned. Now they're gone. They separate all of us—the men from the women, the women from the children. It's the last cruelty. You die alone and no one knows, no one cares."

Gunny squeezed the women's shoulder and rose. "God bless you," she muttered and walked outside. An attendant in a white cap passed her. Gunny grabbed her arm and told her about the dead woman inside. The attendant pulled away from Gunny.

"We'll get to it when we get to it."

Patrick was standing in the yard talking with a few slumped, emaciated men. He looked up as Gunny approached. "This man's from Ventry. He said he used to know you."

Gunny stared at the man's thin face and dirty red hair. "Sean Fitzpatrick?" she asked, grasping his red, swollen hands. "What're you doing here?"

Sean's face was deeply wrinkled though Gunny was sure he wasn't ten years older than she was.

"I brought my wife here a few months back," Sean said in a hoarse voice. "She had the fever. She's gone now. I stayed on to work the roads in Dingle. I couldn't bear to go back to the stables without her."

426

"I'm looking for my mother. Do you remember her? Eileen Malone?"

Sean scuffed at the dirt with the toe of one boot. "Of course I remember Eileen, Robert's wife," he huffed in a raspy voice. "They had her in the same room as my wife. She wasn't sick when she got here. Then she got the fever and was plenty mad, I tell you. The one power left to her was the right to complain and she took full advantage of it right to the end. She lived for a week or so after she took sick. She was a tough one, your mother. In the end, she was talking to your father and sister as if they were right there in the room with her. She's buried out back with the rest."

Gunny's chest felt tight. "I'll go visit her grave," she said softly.

Sean looked at Patrick and shrugged. "The burial grounds are about a quarter mile up the rocky lane behind the workhouse. You can't miss them. They're marked by two rusty sheep gates."

Gunny and Patrick wished Sean the best, climbed the hill as instructed and entered the graveyard through the two old gates. The grounds were about an acre in size and were enclosed by a rough stone wall with a beautiful view of Dingle Harbor. There were several long, wide trenches of fresh dirt. Gunny pictured her mother's young face, the face she knew as a little girl, buried under mounds of dirt. Her mother was gone with no funeral procession, no wailing women with shawls tied over their heads, no candles burning, no rosaries said. Eileen was just, simply, gone. Gunny knew her mother would have hated that.

They said a quick prayer over the mass grave and walked back down Main Street. Grass was growing in cracks in the road in front of the Murphy's store. A closed sign hung crooked on the door. Gunny peered in through the front window—the shop was dark inside. The Dingle Pub and most of the other shops along the street were also closed, several were boarded up. The only activity on the street was at Packy Dollan's shop. The Gombeen man appeared to be the last one in Dingle with money.

Gunny stopped at the post office and begged a piece of paper and an envelope. She jotted a quick note to her brother. "Dearest Michael. We are orphaned. Do not return to Dunquin. We are lost. God bless you. Gunny." She scribbled the address in Alexandria as best she could remember it. The postmaster helped her seal the envelope and promised her note would go out in the next carriage to Cork.

"Let's go home," Gunny said to Patrick. "There's nothing left for us here."

They barely talked on the walk back. There was a snap of winter in the October air as they approached Dunquin and Gunny shivered in her shawl. When they reached the forge, young Matthew was sitting with Mac on the front bench scraping a last bit of food from a shared bowl. The boy was tall and very thin but appeared to be healthy. He looked warily at Gunny and Patrick as they approached, resting his hand protectively on the cow. Gunny noticed he had Mac's same heavy brows as he gave them a short nod.

"Matthew found a few turnip tops left behind by some soldiers who were patrolling the area," Mac announced proudly, stashing the now empty bowl and spoon protectively behind him. "Did you find your mother?" he asked softly.

Gunny nodded. "She's gone, Mac. And now you must come back with us to the island. It won't be easy but we have rabbits and shellfish that will get us by for awhile. And in the spring, we'll plant again."

Mac blinked and rubbed a hand across his forehead. "I can't leave the cow. And Sheila's too sick to be moved. We can't go without them. And someone has to run the forge."

Gunny glanced at Patrick, who shrugged. Gunny turned back to Mac. "At least let us take Matthew with us."

The tall boy shook his head of scraggly hair. "I'm not going anywhere," he said in a deep voice that cracked with emotion. "I'm good at finding food. Probably better than anyone. I can take care of things here. We're not moving to some island."

Gunny wanted to weep at the boy's bravery but could see that her argument would not be heard. After a few last hugs and handshakes, Patrick pulled Gunny gently away from the forge. They walked down through the silent, smokeless village and rowed quietly back to the Great Island.

Christmas of 1846 was dreary and quiet. A few villagers gathered together to mark the day but no houses were whitewashed, no candles placed lovingly in windows, no bog logs left burning brightly through the day. It was the coldest winter anyone could remember, with fireplaces empty of turf and bellies empty of food.

Gunny spent time through the winter on the west end snaring the few rabbits she could find and collecting root plants. She mixed bits of rabbit meat with turnip and cabbage to make thin soups and did her best to make sure the children did not go hungry. She was often hungry herself. Every few weeks she took in the waist of her skirt a little more and some mornings she had only enough energy to move from bed to fire, then back to bed.

The rainy spring was no more cheering. The remaining animals in the village disappeared—sheep, chickens, and finally the dogs. Few people had the energy to leave their houses. Two groups of fishermen who did not have the money to pay for canvas and tar to ready their boats for fishing decided to leave the island. Each Blasket boat required eight men to fish in deep waters, so the decision to leave was communal. With no means of supporting themselves, sixteen men and their families left the island looking for food and work on the mainland. Gunny stood on the cliff and watched as they loaded up the boats one last time, the fathers grim with worry, and the mothers stashing children and a few household items away in the boats. Gunny had helped bring several of the children into the world and now they were leaving. She'd never know the end of their stories.

Patrick continued to fish sporadically with his father and a few of the remaining men. When they caught fish, they shared what they had with Gunny and the children, and when Gunny snared rabbits, she shared what she had with the O'Connors. She waited for fever, cholera, and dysentery to strike the island, but there was no sickness on the Blaskets—a small blessing in a world tipped toward disaster.

~ Chapter 21: Tom Milliken Pays a Visit ~

Maggie seemed oblivious, as only children can be, to the gross poverty around her. "I'd like to go to school," she announced one morning in late March of 1847.

"No," Gunny said, stirring a meager fire and setting water on to boil.

"Why?"

Gunny always tried to answer Maggie when she asked "Why?" She'd hated it when her mother told her, "Because I said so." But Maggie was the best "why" asker Gunny had ever met. The girl could go on for ten, twenty questions before she was satisfied with Gunny's response.

On this particular blustery March day, Gunny did not want to answer Maggie's "Why?". The truth was she didn't want to the girl to go to the Baron's school. What if he saw her there and recognized her? It had been almost four years since she'd taken the children from Ballygoleen. No one had ever come looking for them but she feared the day the Baron would discover the connection and demand the return of his grandchildren.

Gunny looked at Maggie's earnest face as she repeated her question, "Why?"

"You're too little to go to school," Gunny said taking a deep breath. "Perhaps you can go next year," she added in her lightest voice, standing and briskly wiping her hands on her apron.

Maggie stood when Gunny stood. "Peg Daly goes to school and she's little like me."

"Peg Daly goes to school with Frances, her older sister. You don't have an older sister."

"I don't need a sister to look after me. I can look after myself," Maggie stated, standing as tall as she could. "I want to go."

Gunny felt a chill pass over her as she looked down at the girl's intent face. She hugged her shawl tight around her thinning shoulders, then stooped again to stir the fire and added a half brick of turf.

Maggie squatted next to Gunny and asked quietly, "Do you not want me to go to school because you did not go to school?"

"No. I want you to go to school," Gunny grunted.

Maggie grinned and slipped her small hand into Gunny's lap. "Good. Then I'll go."

Gunny moved the girl's hand from her lap and stood, wiping her hands again on her apron. She spoke quicker this time. "We have some planting to do. Maybe you could start school after we bring in the harvest. Would you like that?"

Maggie stood and mimicked Gunny, wiping her hands on her apron. She looked up at Gunny's worried face. "The harvest won't be until September. It's only March. That's a long time to wait."

Gunny bit her lip. She had done her best to learn to read and to do numbers but she knew that Maggie's world could open up for her with more education. Was it fair to keep the girl out of school? And if no one had come looking for the children in four years, hadn't they been forgotten? She remembered young Tom's glance at her from his boat the summer before. Did he know who she and the children were? Or was that just an innocent glance?

"Maybe Larry can go too," Maggie interrupted Gunny's thoughts.

"No!" Gunny howled. "Larry could never sit through a school day."

She looked again at Maggie's intent face and knelt before the little girl. "If I let you go, you must go by yourself."

"Fine," Maggie bargained. "I'll go this year and Larry will go next year. Will you ask the new schoolteacher how soon I can start?"

Gunny knew she was defeated. "I will ask him."

A new teacher had arrived on the island the week before but Gunny had not seen him yet. She figured now was as good a time as any and tapped lightly at the schoolhouse door.

"We're not ready for children yet," the young teacher said as he pulled the door open, then took a step back. "Gunny!"

Gunny grinned. "So this time you'll admit you know me."

James Murphy laughed and pulled Gunny inside, shaking her thin hand with both of his. "I know you but I hardly recognize you. I hoped you'd still be here. I begged the school in Dingle to let me come to the Blaskets after I returned from Dublin. We have so few children left in Dingle—there was no point in staying there."

Gunny looked James over head to toe. She hardly recognized him either. He was tall with shaggy blond hair and broad shoulders but still wore the small round spectacles she had seen on her last visit, perched partway down on his nose.

"Do you still have the Baron's children here?" he asked.

Gunny cringed.

"Sorry," he said. "Joanna told me about the rainy night you showed up with them at the shop."

"No one can know about the children, James."

"I understand."

"The little girl wants to come to school."

"Excellent!" James pushed his glasses up on his nose and pulled out a large enrollment book with the Baron's seal embossed on the cover and opened the book to a new page. "What's her name?"

Gunny hesitated. "Maggie."

James wrote down the name in neat, small print.

"And her family name?"

Gunny took a short breath. "Maggie's nicknamed like the other children on the island. The children call her Maggie Gunny."

James looked up from the book. "In order to register her, I need a family name," he said with one raised eyebrow.

"I was afraid of that. Let's say she's an O'Connor," Gunny said.

James chewed on his bottom lip and picked up his pen. "Maggie O'Connor," he wrote neatly at the top of the clean page. "That's all I need. Maggie's registered. I won't ask any more questions."

"I always said you were one of the smartest men I knew," Gunny said letting out a breath. "Now," Gunny said closing the large attendance book for James, "tell me about your mother and father. What happened to their shop in Dingle? Last time I was there it was dark."

James shook his head. "The shop's still open from time to time but there aren't many customers so the door is usually locked. Joanna and Daniel had some money saved so they aren't starving. I sent them part of my wages each month from the law office in Dublin and I'll do the same from here. They'll get by, Gunny, we all will. This blight has to end sometime."

Gunny scrubbed Maggie from head to toe for her first day of school and pulled the girl's curly brown hair into two tight, glossy braids. Larry watched indignantly as Maggie got dressed.

"Why Sis goes?" he whined.

Larry spoke so rarely, it was a shock to hear his sharp little voice.

"Maggie's going to school to learn to read and write."

Gunny handed Maggie a bag she'd made out of old flour sacks. Maggie proudly slung the bag over her shoulder. Larry grabbed at the bag, then pulled at Maggie's hair and kicked her when she wouldn't give the bag to him. Gunny grabbed the boy by the armpits and lifted him to eye level.

"Larry," she stated sternly holding the wiggling bundle out in front of her. "Be nice."

Larry kicked at Gunny and she set him down. He took off at a tear for the back room, threw himself facedown on the bed, and let out a muffled scream into the blankets.

"You can go to school when you're older," Gunny yelled after the boy. "If they'll take you."

Maggie shrugged her shoulders at Gunny and Gunny smiled.

"Bring home some new stories for Larry. He'll like that."

Gunny looked Maggie over one last time and opened the door. The girl hesitated. "Aren't you coming with me?"

"You said you were brave enough to go by yourself," Gunny said indicating the doorway.

Maggie took a step outside and stopped. "Maybe I should start tomorrow," she said hesitantly. "You may need me here today."

"There is no day like today to start your education," Gunny said. She gave Maggie a little push on the behind and the girl left the house. Gunny watched from the front window as Maggie walked, then skipped the short distance to the schoolhouse.

Gunny turned to deal with Larry. He lay on the bed, face buried in the blankets. "Do you want to go to the strand with me? I need seaweed for the fields."

Larry grunted and pulled himself off the bed. He grabbed his hat from the table and headed out the door without waiting for his grandmother to catch up. Gunny pushed her small barrow to the strand and spotted the boy up in the dunes building a small village out of rocks and grass. She took up her rake and pulled together a small mound of seaweed. She carted it her barrow, then paused to catch her breath. She watched Larry work. He was nearly four and loved to collect things—rocks, sticks, and shells—which he hoarded in boxes inside the house and in piles outside in the yard. Occasionally, Gunny would trip over long battle lines of sticks opposing rocks or shells facing off against sticks. When Gunny happened on a battle scene, Larry would quickly gather his players as he called them and move them elsewhere. She looked at the village he was building now and thought back on her own fairy villages.

She was startled from her reverie when Larry screamed like a banshee and bashed his latest creation with a large rock. Gunny felt her heart skip as she watched him drop more rocks onto the smashed village, throwing sand and grass in every direction. When the village was obliterated, he grabbed an armful of sticks and raced with them to the edge of the surf.

"Mutiny!" he yelled as he threw the sticks out as far as he could into the surf. "Everyone dies."

A few boys had been playing hurley on the beach. They ran to see what Larry was yelling at in the surf.

"Get away," he screamed at them. "Those are my villagers!"

Gunny gasped and pulled Larry away from the boys who shrugged and went back to playing hurley.

"Why don't you play with other children instead of screaming at them?" she asked.

"I am the High King," Larry said, shaking his arm loose from Gunny's grip. "The High King does not play with children."

"You might have more fun playing with other children than screaming at them."

"I play with them," Larry stated with an angry look on his face. He pointed a finger at Gunny. "I challenge them to duels."

"I'll challenge you to a duel," Gunny said pointing back at the boy. "Be. Nicer," she said, punctuating each word.

Larry glared at Gunny then turned and ran back to the dunes. Gunny shook her head and started raking again. How could her two grandchildren be so different?

While Maggie flourished in school, Larry became known as the bully of the south end. He was rough with the other children, even the ones who were older, and was always looking for a fight. Larry was small but his thirst for battle seemed to never be quenched. And once a fight started, Larry would not give up. When he wasn't fighting, he pushed himself physically: up onto cliffs and out into the surf.

"Larry," Gunny had yelled a thousand times. "Be careful."

"Only cowards are cautious!" was his usual reply.

Larry was only still at night when he was alone with his sister. After he hurried through his evening meal, he insisted that she tell him stories about her school day and about the high kings and the Viking battles of days gone by. When Maggie was tired or didn't want to spend time with her brother, he would lash out at her with a hot temper. Maggie did her best to comply to keep peace between them.

By late April, Gunny's fields were nearly ready for planting. "We'll be spreading manure when you get home from school," she explained to Maggie. "Come find us in the mid-fields."

Maggie nodded her head of curls and slurped at a small morning meal of boiled turnip. "We have a guest staying at the schoolhouse," she announced.

"And who is that?" Gunny asked sweeping chicken feathers from the hearth. They had two of the last chickens left in the village. Gunny had put off killing them. Some days all they had to eat were one or two eggs.

"The guest's name is Thomas. Mr. Murphy said he's going to stay with us for a while."

Gunny's face went pale. "Did you meet him?" she asked quietly.

"I saw him yesterday when he arrived."

"What does he look like?" Gunny asked, sure she already knew the answer.

"He looks nice," Maggie said innocently. "He's tall and has dark curly hair like mine."

"Oh." Gunny said, surprised. "Is he young?"

"Oh, yes. He's plenty young. Mr. Murphy says he's sick and is going to stay in the guest room at the school."

It was young Tom who was on the island, not the Baron. "Mind your manners," Gunny said, trying to sound disinterested. "And stay away from him if he's sick." Her hands were sweaty when she smoothed a stray curl from Maggie's face. She hoped that young Tom would not notice Maggie, that she would be just another starving child in the crowd.

She scooted the girl out the door and walked to the fields with Larry to spread a final load of seaweed. On the way back, she collected a bag of dandelion greens along with a few nettles, some sorrel, and a handful of dock leaves. She would fry up the greens with a little yellow meal and an egg for their evening meal. She knew that some in the village had only Indian meal left to eat. She still had a meager stock of root vegetables but was saving them as long as she could. Charlotte told Gunny that one of the last sheep had been reported missing along with some cabbage, turnips, and seed potatoes from a neighbor's house.

"Stealing sheep, turnips, and spuds. Honest men are brought to this," Charlotte had muttered, wiping a small tear from one eye.

As Gunny and Larry walked slowly back home from the field, she wondered if young Tom was still at the schoolhouse. Larry pulled at her hand and demanded they go to the strand.

She pulled her hand away. "Take these greens home. Then you can go to the strand. I'll meet you in a few minutes." She watched the boy sprint toward her house with the greens and was guiltily happy to see the antsy boy depart. How he still had energy she had no idea. She herself was so easily winded these days. She was in front of the schoolhouse when young Tom walked out the door. He glanced at the little boy racing off down the road, then headed for the strand himself. Gunny followed. Tom was not dressed as a Baron would dress. He had on one of James' old jackets with the collar pulled up high around his face, and had a black slouch hat pulled down tight on his head.

"Good day," Gunny said, catching up with him, a little out of breath. "You're new to the island."

Tom glanced down at her. He was pale and had the sheen of fever about his face. His rough, curly dark hair under the hat was lightly plastered to his forehead. His brown eyes were ringed with dark circles. He ducked his face away from the inquisitive woman and continued walking toward the water.

"I'm a friend of James," he clipped hoarsely to the stranger who was now walking beside him, matching him stride for long stride. "I'm only here for a short time. Good day."

He turned abruptly and walked back toward the schoolhouse at an even faster clip.

Gunny watched him hurry away. "He's ill and he's hiding," she muttered as she turned and walked to find Larry on the strand. "Perhaps there's trouble at home."

After the children were asleep that night, Gunny gathered a bag of herbs and slipped outside. She walked to the schoolhouse and knocked briskly at the door. She heard chairs scraping on the floor inside, then silence. She knocked again.

"James?"

James opened the door a crack. "Oh, Gunny, it's you. I can't talk. Why don't you stop by tomorrow?"

"I want to see your visitor. Maggie said he was sick."

"What visitor?"

Gunny pushed on the door but James held it in place.

"Maggie reports you have someone staying here named Tom," she whispered through the crack in the door. "I saw him today. He looks like he needs a doctor's help."

James looked around behind him then opened the door. "Come in. He does need help and I don't know how to help him."

James led her to a small room at the back of the schoolhouse, gave a soft knock, and opened the door. A candle on top of the dresser cast shadowy light around the room. Tom lay on the bed fully clothed in the same dark suit Gunny had seen him in earlier. A damp cloth rested across his eyes.

"Is she gone?" Tom asked weakly.

"No, she's not," Gunny answered sternly.

Tom pulled the cloth from his face and squinted at the tall woman standing in the doorway. It was the woman from the strand. Tom weakly propped up on one elbow, then grimaced at the movement. He gripped his head and dropped back to the pillow. "Who are you?" he asked flatly.

"My name is Gunny," Gunny said bustling in to the room. "I'm concerned about your fever. We have no fever on the island. You must stay away from others, and most importantly, you must stay away from the children."

"I thought I was sick from the crossing. I'm not much of one for boats. I was retching out the back of the boat all the way over. The seagulls were quite happy with me."

Gunny couldn't help but smile at the image. "Now the nausea has passed and you still feel ill?"

"My head is splitting. I left the school today thinking fresh air might help but the light outside nearly blinded me."

Gunny crossed to the bed and felt Tom's forehead, cheeks and hands. He was hot with fever as expected. She took the cloth from his hands and dipped it in a small dish of water by the bed. She wrung it out and placed it over his eyes, then handed the dish to James. "Get me cool water from the spring and put on some hot water for tea. Then go to bed. I don't want you exposed to this any more than you have to be. I'll take care of your visitor."

James hesitated at the door. "I was trying to help. He said he had nowhere to go."

"Get the water, James. We'll talk later."

Gunny pulled a chair up by the bed and sat, looking at her slim patient. He swallowed hard. "Am I going to die? So many at the Burnham House have died of the fever. We have hardly any servants left."

"Is that so," Gunny asked dryly. "Is it possible you might actually have to cook your own food? To clean your own house?"

Tom laughed weakly and pushed the cloth from his eyes to his forehead with a well-manicured hand. "It hasn't gotten that bad. But I want the good times to return. The town of Dingle should be lively again. What has happened to all of the clever and witty people?"

"Save your energy," Gunny admonished tucking a light blanket up across his chest. "I'm sure the good days will return—for you, anyway."

Gunny pulled a few small bundles of herbs from her bag and set them out on a table next to the bed. She wanted to tame the fever but not kill it. She took a pinch of one herb to help lower the fever and another to bring on a sweat. She thought of Tom's stomach and added another pinch to solve any digestive issues. She mixed the shredded, dry leaves and roots in a tin cup.

James gave a soft knock and came into the room with a pail of cool water in one hand and a steaming kettle of water in the other. Gunny took the kettle and poured hot water into the herb mix and handed Tom the cup.

"Let this cool, then drink it. Slowly. I've made you a potion that should help you sleep tonight while the fever does its work. We're best to let the fever run its course. The heat inside you is what'll make you better. That and sleep are the best cures."

Tom sniffed the hot, fragrant mix and set the cup on the side table to cool. "I would have a lovely funeral," he said softly. "Think of how my father would mourn my loss."

Gunny shook her head. "If you want a fancy funeral, you're best to die another time. There are too many dying now."

Tom was quiet. "You said your name is Gunny." He paused running the name over his thick tongue. "Do I know you?"

Gunny ducked her head into her bag pretending to look for a lost bit of herb. "Gunny's a common name," she muttered into the bag.

"Gunny is not a common name," Tom argued. "But I have heard it before." He closed his eyes. "I remember," he said with a little more energy. He opened his eyes and looked at Gunny in the dim light. "Eileen who worked in the kitchen. She had a daughter named Gunny who lived on the Blaskets. Yes, that is it," Tom assured himself closing his eyes once more.

"You're delirious with fever," Gunny said. "Your tea should be cool enough now. Drink up." She lifted the cup to his lips and he took a sip, studying her face.

"If you are Gunny," he said, peeking out through half-lids. "Then you are Catherine's sister."

Gunny stood and turned to James. "I'll stop in again in the morning. Make sure Tom finishes that tea. I don't want him leaving this room until his fever goes away. We haven't had any fever deaths on this island and I don't intend to start now."

"Can you put out that candle," Tom asked groggily, setting the empty tin cup aside. "The light is too bright."

Gunny crossed to the dresser and blew out the candle while James held the door open for her. Tom sighed loudly as they left the room.

James pulled the guest room door closed behind them and crossed to his desk. He pulled off his glasses and rubbed at his eyes.

"You should never have let him in here with the children," Gunny admonished him.

James looked up at the tall woman. "He didn't look quite so sick yesterday. And how could I say no? He's the Baron's son."

Gunny sat on the children's bench. "I know you had no choice. Hopefully, he'll heal but he mustn't leave that room until his fever goes down. You understand how important that is? Patrick heard that nearly half of the villagers in Dunquin are gone from fever. Have you heard from your mother in the last few weeks?"

James nodded. "A fisherman gave me a note from her just last week. She said more people are dying in Dingle from fever than starvation. She said someone on every block is sick but that she and Daniel are getting by living off of the kitchen garden. She said they might have to turn to Packy Dollan for money soon."

"Packy Dollan. They don't want to deal with him."

"They may have no choice if they run out of money and have to sell off the goods in the store. You can't run a shop with a locked door, but every time they open for business, people steal from them. Joanna said three men were arrested last month for stealing and were sent to jail—now everyone wants to be arrested. At least in jail, you know you'll be fed. It's a strange world when surviving may be worse than dying."

Gunny swallowed hard thinking of Matt. Matt would not suffer from this plague or any other ills. There was some comfort in that.

James interrupted Gunny's thoughts. "How will this end, Gunny? Will we all die?"

Gunny cleared her throat. "Yes, James, we all will die—but there is no telling how or when. I need to scrub off my hands before I leave."

James led the way into his room and watched as Gunny scrubbed to her elbows in a bowl of tepid water, tossed the water out the window, then gathered her supplies and slipped out of the schoolhouse with a small wave.

Outside, Gunny set down her bag and leaned against the cool stone building. A wave of nausea passed through her. Her legs felt weak and her tears filled her eyes. How had it fallen to her to take care of young Thomas de Moleyns? First, he was a Lord, a Baron from Ventry which made him a sworn enemy of sorts. Second, he had brought fever to the island which could kill everyone including her and the children. And third, he was the man who had defiled her daughter not once but twice. Gunny sighed. And he was Maggie and Larry's father.

"He needs help," she muttered to herself. "And I can help." William's face hovered in front of her. "Do something good with your life, Gunny. The returns will be one hundred fold."

She wiped a damp hand across her eyes and pointed in the general direction of Brandon Mountain. "The returns had better be one hundred fold on this one," she muttered. "And don't think I won't be counting."

The next morning, Gunny dragged Larry and a sullen Maggie to the O'Connor's.

"James has taken in one of the Baron's men at the schoolhouse," she explained quickly to Charlotte. "The man's sick with fever and I have to take care of him. Can you keep the children here for a week or so?"

"You know I can't guarantee the boy's safety," Charlotte said laying a hand on Gunny's arm. "But Mags will help me, won't you?"

Maggie sat glumly hunched on a stool by the fire. Gunny knelt in front of her. "The man you saw at the school is sick," she said softly. "I'm going to take care of him. I'll be back to get you as soon as the man is better. Do you understand?"

Maggie hung her head. "I suppose so."

"Good," Gunny said. She lifted the girl's chin and looked her squarely in the eye. "Please look after your brother. I'll be back soon. I promise."

Patrick grabbed Larry who was by the door, waiting to escape. He tossed the boy high in the air.

"How's my little Larry?"

Larry grunted and struggled to free himself from Patrick's grip. Patrick placed the boy awkwardly on the floor. "We'll find something to keep this one out of trouble," he said, giving Gunny a wink.

Gunny gave Charlotte a quick hug and hurried back to the south end of the island. She stopped at her house to collect her bag of herbs and mending basket, then headed to the schoolhouse. William had taught her about so many ailments as they walked the fields near Brandon Mountain. What was she dealing with? Typhus? Cholera? Dysentery? She slipped in the front door of the school. James was doing his best to teach four hungry students. She gave him a short wave and headed for the back room.

She gave a quick knock on the door. "Tom?" she asked quietly. There was no answer. She opened the door a crack and peeked inside. Tom was sleeping, his still-clothed body only partly covered by the brown wool blanket. Gunny walked into the room and quietly closed the door behind her. She sat in the chair beside the bed and pulled out her mending to keep busy until she was needed.

Her patient started fidgeting after about an hour. A fresh sheen of sweat appeared on his face. She left the room to put a kettle of water on the schoolhouse stove. By the time she returned with the steaming pot, Tom was tossing about, groaning in his sleep. Gunny sat and watched until he opened bleary eyes and put a hand to his head.

"Where am I?" he asked.

Gunny leaned forward. There was no need to touch his forehead. Clearly, the fever had returned. She dipped a cloth in the bucket of spring water, wrung it out, and placed it on his forehead.

"You're on the Blaskets, the Great Island. Do you remember coming here?"

Tom studied the woman's face. He blinked hard to clear his double vision. His head throbbed and he felt dizzy. "Gunny. You are Gunny," he said hoarsely.

"Yes, I'm Gunny. I'm going to give you something to help you sleep again. Are you feeling any better?" Gunny turned to mix a potion on the bedside table.

"I feel worse." Tom watched her work. "What are you making?"

"Something I learned from an old, wise man who was an expert healer."

"If that's what you gave me last night, it smelled better than it tasted."

"Sometimes you have to suffer to heal." She turned and studied her patient. "Tell me what hurts."

Tom covered his face with his hands. "My head feels like it is going to explode. And I'm thirsty."

Gunny dipped a cup into the water bucket and held it to his lips. Tom sipped at the cool water then fell back against his pillow. "When will this pass? When will I feel better?"

"Most are sick for a week."

"And then they die," he sighed. "Dying doesn't seem like such a bad option right now. At least the pain and bleariness would end."

"Your family's blessed. No doubt you will survive. William taught me about fevers. If this were typhus, your face would be swollen, your body black, and you would smell of gangrene."

Tom groaned. "Please tell me that's not what you see."

"Have you had any nosebleeds?"

"No nosebleeds," Tom muttered.

"If this is yellow fever, you'd be vomiting along with the fever."

"I haven't vomited since I got off the boat."

"That's a good sign," Gunny said. "If this was cholera, the trouble would begin down between your big toes. Blackness would move up from your feet into your legs and then into your body."

She lifted the covers and pulled off his stockings to examine his feet. He groaned and she tossed the covers back in place. "Your feet look fine. Could this be dysentery?" she asked. "How are your bowels?"

"This isn't dysentery. One of the stable men died of the Bloody Flux so I know what that looks like," Tom said. "He was the best man out there. He was in terrible pain for two days. The priest who treated him died of the same thing. Everyone got scared after that and no one wanted to help those with fever."

Gunny wondered if he was talking about Sean Fitzgerald—or her father. She had never heard the cause of her father's death, but that had been years before the troubles had started. She pressed on Tom's abdomen through the blanket. "Any pain here?"

Tom pushed her hand away. "No."

Gunny turned to finish mixing a new potion and added hot water from the kettle. She stirred the tea with a small stick she kept in her bag and passed the cup to Tom. "Drink that when it cools a bit."

"So what do you think I have? Am I going to die?"

"I don't understand your symptoms. So all I can do is treat your fever and help you rest."

Tom rolled the cup between his hands and breathed in the steamy concoction. "Aren't you afraid of getting the fever from me?"

"Terrified," Gunny said in a calm voice.

"Then why are you helping me?"

Gunny looked down at her hands. "I'm not sure," she said bluntly. "I'm able to help so I do. It's sort of an island rule."

Tom leaned back against the pillow. His head felt a little better from the hot steam of the tea. "If you know my family then you know who I am. Are you doing this for some sort of reward?"

Gunny snorted. "I do know your family, I do know who you are, and I can guarantee you I'm not doing this for a reward." Gunny looked at the familiar face of the stranger as he sipped at the tea. "What brings you to the island, Tom?"

Tom looked toward the window. "A boat?" he said weakly.

Gunny chuckled. "That's what I used to say when people asked what brought me here."

Tom looked at Gunny. "You are different than your mother. Eileen never used to laugh."

"Mam was a serious person."

"Same as mine. Did you know my mother?"

Gunny pictured the Baron sitting by the fire spattered with blood. She shook her head. "I did not know your mother."

"But you know my father?"

Gunny hesitated then looked at Tom. "I used to make deliveries to your house when I was a young woman working in Dingle. When I first met your father, he had just returned from fighting the French."

"Back when he was a soldier. I suppose he was happier then."

Gunny grinned. "I don't know that your father has ever been happy. When I first met him he was dealing with his wounds from the war—and with his uncle and grandfather."

"I didn't know my uncle or great grandfather. Tell me about them."

"Your father's grandfather, the old Lord, he was a gentleman. He used to walk miles every day with his dogs and knew every villager by name. He was the first Lord on this peninsula, and was a country man. If rents weren't collected on time, he understood."

"When I was little, I used to ride with my father's agent collecting rent. Mr. Thompson used to bring two soldiers with us in case there was trouble. One time, an old woman pointed at me and said it was a shame to take a little boy out for such bloodthirsty work. She scared me talking about blood. I didn't like riding with Mr. Thompson after that."

"Did you ever ride with your father?"

"Oh, sure. Plenty of times. Father always preferred riding a horse to walking. He said when he was in the saddle he could sit tall amongst his people."

"Yes." She looked at Tom's pale face. "Now will you tell me now why you're on this island?"

Tom closed his eyes and took a deep breath. Gunny thought he might be sleeping when he continued in a quiet voice. "My job for most of my life has been to do nothing—as handsomely as I could. Father sent me to school in Dublin for awhile. When I came home for the holidays I could ride as I pleased and shoot what I pleased and swim in the ocean whenever I wanted. I had dogs when I wanted to hunt and horses when I wanted to ride, and had the greatest determination to have the best possible time." He paused and took a sip of the herb tea, then cleared his throat and opened his eyes. "Now that I am twenty, everyone has been wracking their brains about what to do with me. Father wanted me to take on Mr. Thompson's work, to collect the rents and to go to court to evict villagers. I told him the work didn't suit me. Father said it was either that or join the ministry. Or the navy. Imagine me out all day in a boat..."

"You said no?"

"I said no most emphatically. We almost came to blows. That's when Father threw me out of the house. So now I am going to America where he will never have to worry about me again."

"So you were headed to America. You know you aren't quite far enough west?"

"I didn't intend to come to the Blaskets. I was riding through Dingle headed to Cork when my father's men came looking for me. I left my horse at a pub on Green Street and ducked out onto the pier. I hid in a fishing boat waiting for my father's men to leave. Then the fishermen returned. I could see they were Blasketers. I told them they had to take me to the island for an inspection of the schoolhouse and they complied." He chuckled softly. "No one listens to me at home but the peasants listen to me." He finished his tea and handed the cup to Gunny.

Gunny snorted and set the cup on the floor. "Now you will listen to me. Until you are over your fever, you are not going anywhere—not to America, and not out of this schoolhouse."

Tom lay back and closed his eyes. "You remind me of Mrs. Needham." His hand twitched slightly and he started to snore lightly. Gunny took up her basket of mending and waiting for his next lucid spell.

Gunny took care of Tom for two weeks, until she was sure his fever had passed. In his wakeful times, he told her stories about growing up at the Burnham House, and attending school in Dublin. She in turn told him about growing up in Dunquin, about her service in Dingle for the Murphys, about William and Mac—and even about Matt. Tom especially liked Gunny's tales about her decision to move to the Blaskets, and about surviving on her own on the west end. Her early stories were filled with detail, but she said little about her current life except that she lived nearby, worked her own fields, and took care of two orphaned O'Connor children.

"I hope I am as industrious as you are when I get to America."

"Where will you go when you get there?"

"I have no idea. We don't have family in America like most of you peasants do. You said your brother Michael lives in Virginia?"

"In Alexandria, the last I heard. I haven't had a letter for him in a year or so. But Maeve's family is there along with other families from the peninsula."

"Then I'll go to Alexandria, Virginia. Of course, the peasants there will probably hate me."

"If you continue to call them peasants, I guarantee they'll hate you. Perhaps you could say you're from the Blaskets. Blasket men are known for being honest and reliable and would be welcome in most homes."

"I don't believe honest and reliable are words anyone has ever used to describe me," he sighed.

James knocked at the door, then entered. His face was ashen. "The Baron and his men are bringing a new boiler to the schoolhouse so we can start serving soup again. The Baron's just arrived at the pier in the Mission's six-oared boat. Patrick O'Connor sent one of his brothers to tell me."

Tom sat up in bed. "I can't be here when my father arrives."

Both men looked at Gunny.

"Get your things," Gunny said to Tom. "You can hide at my house until the Baron's gone."

It took two days to get the soup boiler installed and new food supplies unpacked and sorted out. The Baron took up residence in the quickly cleaned back room while the Baron's men bunked on the schoolroom floor.

"We are getting no help at this point from the Dingle Relief Committee so I had to take this on myself," the Baron told James. "You'll make Indian meal stir-about as a morning meal for the island children, Protestant and Catholic."

James was shocked. "I thought you only fed Protestants."

"It's gotten beyond that," the Baron said shaking his head. "We will feed everyone. If the Quakers can do it, I can do it. I do not like it but if I do not feed the children, there may be no one left to work the fields. I will increase the rents after the harvest to cover my costs."

"I don't know that anyone will ever be able to pay rent again, sir."

"This can't last forever. And I am paying good wages to the men who work on the roads."

"And what about the ones who are too weak to work?"

"I'm feeding anyone who has less than a quarter acre of land—if they give their land to me and take down their walls."

"But what about those who want to keep their land and have no money for rent?"

The Baron shook his head. "I turn them out on the street. Last week we turned out twelve families and burned down their houses."

James pictured twelve empty homes. Twelve fires extinguished. Twelve sets of walls tumbled. Twelve families wandering the streets.

"I only evict the idle and dishonest," the Baron added defensively. "And what choice do I have? There is better money in dairy these days and I need the fields opened up for my cattle to graze. Besides, I have to pay relief for every peasant I am responsible for—so the fewer in my keeping the better. If I am going to pay to feed dumb beasts, they may as well be beasts I can eventually sell to the British."

"Where do the people go when you evict them?" James asked quietly.

"How should I know?" the Baron sputtered. "I suppose they stay with neighbors or go to the workhouse or sail to America. It's all the same to me. I will no longer breed paupers to pay priests."

"My father said some landlords are paying to send farmers to America or to Canada."

"That is not a bad idea. It is probably cheaper to pay the fare than to feed them, the sorry lot," the Baron muttered. He stood to leave. "You come from good, hardworking people, James Murphy. I'll let your parents know I saw you next time I am in town."

"Have you seen them lately?"

"They are well. Their shop is closed but I am purchasing as much as I can from them to keep them in business. Your father is the last man in town who is not drunk most of the time."

"Surely no one has money for drink?" James gasped.

The Baron laughed. "For you Irish, there is always money to spare for a wee bit. A new whiskey shop opened within a stone's throw of the government relief pay office in Dingle." The Baron paused and pulled on his jacket. "We'll start a work program on the island next month. I'll pay men eight pence a day to improve that landing place. Every time we boat over here I am sure I am going to drown trying to get off that damned boat."

Gunny's house was snug and quiet as she and young Tom waited for the Baron to leave the island. Tom slept soundly the first night in the children's bed in the back room. When Gunny awoke that morning, her guest was already up, sitting in her rocker reading old papers in front of a low peat fire.

Gunny draped the speckled wool blanket around his shoulders, then excused herself and walked to the strand to collect winkles. Tom watched half-awake from the rocker when she returned and dumped an apron full of black shelled creatures into a bucket of well water, drained them, then added them by the handful to a few cups of boiling milk, donated by the O'Connor's old cow. When she pulled the boiling, heavy pot from the fire, he rose, pulled his blanket tight around him, and moved to the table. He looked warily at the black shapes floating in the hot milk.

"What are those?" he asked. "They look like snails from the garden."

"They're winkles boiled in milk." Gunny lifted a winkle with a spoon from the pot, plucked the snail from its shell with the point of a nail, and popped it into her mouth. "Delicious!"

"Snails?" Tom grimaced.

"I didn't like them much when I first had them but when they're all you've got they're quite tasty."

Tom fished a winkle from the pot with his spoon. He took a nail from the table, fished out the bit of black meat, and placed it in his mouth. He chewed tentatively then swallowed. "That's not bad," he added picking out another winkle from the pot, pulling out the meat, and popping it into his mouth. "Chewy and salty." He swallowed again and pointed with this spoon. "What is that white stuff in the other dish? It smells terrible."

"That's mashed turnip. One of my last."

Tom sat on the bench at the table and spooned a few winkles into his bowl. "I've never had turnip," Tom said turning up his nose.

Gunny shook her head and spooned a large portion into his bowl next to the winkles. "We have no potatoes, your Lordship. Tonight we dine on winkles and turnips. If you want something else, you will have to dine elsewhere."

"I am sorry to be such trouble. I know you do not have much yet you are willing to share."

"I'm sure you'd do the same for me if our positions were reversed," Gunny said with a wink.

Tom ate and rested until word came that the Baron and his men had left for the pier.

"I'll give him a day or two to get settled back in at Ventry, then I'll try again to get to Cork. I cannot thank you enough for curing me and for hiding me in your house."

Gunny hesitated. "Before you go we should have a celebratory meal."

"I'd like that. But what are we celebrating?"

"We are celebrating the fact that my medicine worked."

"You didn't know if it would?"

"Fevers are tricky. But you survived so we'll celebrate that—and your escape from the Baron and from this way of life."

"I haven't escaped yet," Tom said shaking his head. "I'll send you a letter from America to let you know when we can really give a cheer. If we are going to fix one last meal, can you make winkles again?"

"You really liked them?"

"I really liked them."

Tom decided to join Gunny on the strand. He felt weak and tired but it was good to be outside in the open air. He sat on the rocks and watched Gunny pull winkles from the tide pools. He leaned back on a large rock and enjoyed the sound of the surf and the feel of warm sun on his face. His head and body were finally free of pain and it was good to be alive. He was startled from his muse by the sound of children calling Gunny's name. He looked across the strand through slit eyes to see a young girl and boy racing across the sand to greet her.

"Gunny!" The little girl called as she scrambled out onto the rocks. "Mrs. O'Connor heard the sick man was well and sent us out here to find you. We're home!" she announced. Gunny looked at Tom as he watched her greet the children.

"Who are these two?" Tom asked.

"Well," Gunny said hesitantly.

The children turned to look at Tom. "Are you no longer sick?" Maggie asked.

"I am much better now. Gunny took good care of me. She is even making me winkles."

"Are we having winkles?" Maggie asked excitedly looking at Gunny's loaded apron while Larry stood staring at Tom, hands on his small hips.

"Yes, winkles," Gunny muttered.

"You don't have to include me for your meal if you need to feed these children," Tom offered.

"If you insist," Gunny started, but Maggie interrupted.

"No, Gunny. You have plenty of winkles for four of us."

Gunny swallowed hard and glanced at Tom. "There's no reason for you to not be around the island children now that you are well. Stay to eat. I doubt you'll have winkles this fine when you get to America."

As they walked back to Gunny's house, Tom listened as Maggie chattered away about her time in the village with the O'Connors. Larry raced ahead scraping a long piece of driftwood across the front of each house they passed. When they got to Gunny's house, Tom sat in the rocker while Gunny put the winkles on to boil. Tom watched Maggie as she scurried about setting bowls, cups, and spoons on the table and Larry climbed up into the loft to taunt the single remaining chicken. Tom did not try to talk with the children. He hated it as a child when his father entertained and adults tried to make polite conversation with him.

"You never mentioned any children to me. What are their names?" Tom asked Gunny.

Gunny blushed. Would Tom remember Maggie's name from her early years living at the Burnham House?

"The boy is Larry. The girl is... Sis."

When the winkles were hot, the children sat with Gunny on one bench facing Tom on the opposite bench. Tom and the children slurped at their winkles and milk while Gunny barely picked at her meal. Maggie made timid glances at the stranger while Larry openly stared at him over the top of his spoon.

"Have you been living in my house?" the little boy asked.

Tom cleared his throat and raised his eyebrows. "Gunny let me stay here while I was sick. But now I am better. I will leave soon for America and you can have your house back."

Larry set down his spoon, his eyes opening wide. "You're going to America?"

Tom looked the boy in the eye and smiled. "I am. I am going to Cork to get on a boat and then I will sail away."

"I'd like to sail away on a boat. I want to be a captain," Larry offered.

"Maybe someday you will be a captain," Tom affirmed.

Larry frowned. "When I have my own boat I'll sail anywhere I wish."

"And where would you wish to sail?" Tom asked.

Larry hesitated. "I don't know. But I'll know as soon as I get my boat," he said defiantly sticking out his small chin.

Gunny was shocked at Larry's conversational tone. She hoped he wasn't building up to some sort of challenge for their visitor.

Tom laughed. "I have no wish to be on a boat myself. The ride over to the Blaskets was rough enough and America is a long way off. But I want to get there and it is too far to swim."

Maggie pictured the large pull-down map Mr. Murphy had shown them in school and giggled at the thought of swimming to America, then turned her eyes back to her bowl of winkles.

"Hey, Sis," Tom said. "Did I just see you smile?"

Maggie covered her mouth with her small hand. "No," she muttered from behind closed fingers. She looked Tom squarely in the eye. "And my name's not Sis. It's Maggie."

Tom blinked. "Someone told me your name was Sis."

"No," Maggie giggled. "That's what Larry calls me. My name's Maggie."

Tom stared at the girl's soft curls and tiny nose. "That's a nice name, Maggie."

Gunny let out a thin breath, her heart pounding in her chest.

"I'm Maggie Malone. Everyone knows me."

Tom smiled. "Well, Maggie Malone, I am glad to meet you. My name is Thomas de Moylens..." He hesitated and cleared his throat. "My name is Tom Milliken."

"Tom Milliken," Maggie said rolling the name around in her mouth. "That's a silly name."

"A silly name? I'll tell you what's silly." Tom reached across the table and tickled Maggie's belly. She howled with delight.

"Do mine," Larry said, pulling up his shirt and showing his white belly to the stranger.

Tom reached over and tickled Larry's belly. Larry also howled with laughter.

Gunny was stunned. Too much information had been revealed, and here was Maggie flirting with Tom and Larry letting a stranger touch him without picking a fight. What fairy mischief had come over them? Still, Gunny couldn't help but smile at the sound of the children's laughter. She stood and wiped her hands on her apron, nudging the black-handled knife deep in her apron pocket.

"Children, we must not wear out our guest. In fact, he should be heading back to the schoolhouse. He has a long journey ahead of him."

"But we just met him," Maggie complained. "Perhaps he can join us tomorrow." She turned to Tom. "Tomorrow everyone will be planting potatoes in the lower fields. Patrick will be there to help us."

"Yes," Larry yelled. "Come with us. I'll show you where the bog is and where the sheep used to graze. And where the good spring is."

Tom hesitated. "I could probably wait another day to cross to Dingle. And I'd love to come along—but only if I can help." He turned to Gunny. "And only if it is all right with Gunny."

Gunny hurried to clear the bowls and spoons from the table. "We don't have much to plant," Gunny said. "The seed potatoes are no bigger than a thimble this year and there aren't many of them"

Maggie grabbed her hand. "But you're going to plant tomorrow, aren't you? Patrick said the fields are all manured and ready."

Gunny nodded at the girl. "We have to try again. We'll plant what we have."

"Gunny can show you how to plant potatoes," Larry explained. "She's very good at it. Her father taught her."

Gunny raised her eyebrows to the boy. When had he ever listened to a word she said about her father or planting?

"I am sure she is good at it," Tom said looking at the older woman. "Gunny is a woman of many mysteries, isn't she?"

"Yes," Maggie gushed enthusiastically, wanting to agree with anything the tall stranger said. She grabbed Tom's hand and smiled up at him. Larry grabbed Tom's other hand.

"And after planting, that's when we can explore. I'll show you around. I know this place," Larry said proudly.

Tom freed his hands to pull on his coat and hat. "I'll sleep in the schoolhouse tonight, but I'll be over first thing tomorrow," he said looking each child in the face. "If it's all right with Gunny."

The children looked at Gunny with anticipation. She slowly let out a short breath and shook her head, yes. Tom collected his small bundle of clothes, winked at Gunny, and left. She closed the door behind him and slid the bolt in place.

Tom showed up early the next morning as promised. He climbed with Gunny and the children to the steep, manured fields. Other villagers were already there, each working their own small plot. Tom had never planted anything before. Gunny was strict with her instructions but he caught on quickly and was actually helpful. The children hung around the fields for awhile, vying for Tom's attention, then finally ran off to play with the other village children. It only took a half a day to plant the few potatoes they had. Then Tom headed off to explore the hills with Larry in the lead. No one asked Tom who he was or what he was doing on the island. Islanders had their secrets and if this gentleman wanted to share his story, he would. He shared a meal again that night with Gunny and the children, a small dinner of cornmeal, two eggs, and a little dried fish. They all went to bed a little hungry, but satisfied with a good day's work.

Stiff wind blew in off the water the next morning and Tom had to wait another day before returning to the mainland. Gunny invited him to join them in the high fields to set rabbit snares before they planted oat seeds in the middle fields.

"How do you stand it being so windy up here?" Tom asked as cold gusts of salty wind blew in around them as they hiked along the ridge.

Gunny chuckled. "You should try living on the west end."

When the traps were set, they retreated to the middle fields. Larry worked to build a fort of old field stones, while Maggie insisted she be allowed to help plant oats. Gunny made her an apron from a folded flour cloth as Robert had done when Gunny was little, and explained that Maggie should drop only one seed into each tiny hole.

"Make sure you don't miss a spot. It brings bad luck," Gunny told the girl.

Maggie ran her small hands through the pocket of silky oat seeds. "Gunny," Maggie giggled. "We make our own luck. You told me that."

That evening they returned to the high fields to check the snares. They were in luck, and had one large rabbit to prepare for their evening meal. Tom offered to take the children to the strand while Gunny skinned the rabbit. Larry headed for his favorite tide pool while Maggie walked with Tom along the rocky beach.

"Do you see the white horses out there?" she asked, pointing.

Tom looked out across the water at the tiny white caps racing on the waves to shore. "Yes," he said. "It's windy today."

"That's not wind," Maggie explained in her most adult voice. "Those are white horses."

"They are?" Tom asked, eyebrows raised.

Maggie looked up at Tom. "Those horses are on their way to the Isle of the Blessed, out beyond the western ocean." Maggie waved both arms with a flourish. "Beyond the Isle of the Blessed is Tir na n'Og, the land of Eternal Youth."

"Really," Tom said incredulously.

Maggie shook her head, brown curls bouncing. "Everyone knows that," she said smartly.

"And what's beyond that?" Tom asked, thinking he might have outsmarted the girl.

Maggie smiled. "Beyond that is America."

"How do you know so much?"

Maggie tossed her curls. "Gunny teaches me the stories. And I go to school."

"You are a smart girl, Maggie."

"I know," Maggie said and smiled.

That evening, Patrick stopped by Gunny's house with a half barrel of fish.

"We were lucky with the mackerel today," he said glancing at the tall stranger sitting at Gunny's table in front of a steaming pot of rabbit stew. Tom stood and offered a hand to Patrick. Patrick shook the extended hand.

"I assume you're the visitor from the schoolhouse. We heard you had the fever."

"It's gone now. Gunny saved my life. I am forever indebted to her."

Patrick raised an eyebrow. "As are most of the people on this island."

Gunny offered Patrick a small loaf of cornmeal in exchange for the fish but he refused to take it, insisting she keep it for the children.

"No, Patrick. Give it to your mother," Gunny insisted. "She fed the children for two weeks while Tom recuperated."

Patrick reluctantly took the bread. "Mam is looking a little thin," he confessed.

Gunny was alarmed. "Is she ill?"

Patrick shook his head. "I think she's just tired. Bridget is tending to her. We're hungry, that's all. Nothing stays with you like potatoes."

"We planted all the seed potatoes we had. God willing, we'll have new potatoes come harvest. In the meantime, have a bowl of rabbit stew with us and be glad you still have milk from your cow."

Patrick eyed the small amount of stew and shook his head. "I meant to tell you. The cow passed away last night. She was old and I think we bled her too often. Bridget promised to spend the last of her dowry money to get us a new cow if we can find one." He clutched at the bread. "I'd best get this home. I'll join you for stew another time. Take care of yourself," he said to Tom and slipped out the door.

Gunny called the children to the table and spooned out small portions of stew into four bowls and broke the loaf of bread into four pieces. Tom looked guiltily at the food in front of him.

"How can I eat this when you have to work so hard for everything you have?" he asked.

"We're getting by," Gunny assured him touching him lightly on the arm. "And there is always something to eat if you know what to look for. Roots. Rabbits. Fish... We're a little thinner than we used to be, but we haven't starved yet."

Gunny spooned hot rabbit into her mouth, savoring small bites of the rich, tender meat. Maggie and Larry ate quickly then left the table. Maggie took out a schoolbook and sat reading by the dim light while Larry built a wall of shells and sticks. Tom mopped his bowl clean with the last bit of corn bread, then moved to a stool by the fire. He was weary, but happy.

Gunny glanced over at him as she pulled the bowls from the table. "Are you thinking about America?" she asked.

Tom grinned and shook his head. "No, I was thinking about how you take care of one another here on the island. About how nice a turf fire feels in a snug house. About the rich taste of rabbit stew when you're hungry. Being here gives me the same feeling I have when I hear good news or find unexpected money in a pocket, you know?"

"The good news I know about; finding money in a pocket I don't know about," Gunny said.

Tom squeezed his fingers against his eyes. "Mother used to say that the peasants were swine—rough and dirty. And here I am getting my hands rough and dirty with work and it's the most pleasant time I've ever had. I feel more at home here than I ever did at home."

Gunny's heart ached for the young man. "You can't compare our worlds —they're too different.

Tom leaned forward and braced his head with his hands. Gunny touched him on the shoulder. "Are you all right? You're not feeling feverish, are you?"

Tom blinked away a tear and looked up at Gunny. "You are better to me than my own family. I can never repay you for my health and for my time here. Your warm house. The children and their incessant questions…"

"I told them not to…"

"No, no. I love their questions. Larry asked me today where clouds come from. I had never given it any thought. I've lived a life of ease with no meaning. I'm going to ponder the world more when I get to America."

Gunny knelt to stir the fire and added a small turf. She crouched and watched the turf catch, then pulled up a stool. "You have money for your fare?"

Tom nodded. "Father doesn't know it but his grandfather gave Uncle Dayrolles a stash of guineas when he was trying to bribe him to come home before I was born. When I was in school in Dublin, Uncle Day gave me twenty guineas in case I ever needed them. I have kept them stashed away for years. I read in one of your old papers that American captains want to sail home with a full boat and don't care if they are carrying lumber or peasants. I should be able to get steerage passage for about three pounds."

Gunny shook her heard. "Did you also read that they call those boats coffin ships because so many die on board of fever?"

"I've had the fever. I'm sure I won't get it again."

"My brother Michael also warned me to watch out for trappers when you get to the ports—they'll try to take your money."

"Gunny, I am an educated man. I will not be taken advantage of."

"Perhaps you should spend more than three pounds and travel in class. If you have twenty guineas…"

"I have it but starting today, I'm not landed gentry anymore, Gunny. I want to shake off the curse of money, of stolen land." Tom paused staring into the fire. "Before I go, I have to give you something."

"I don't want anything from you," Gunny said, frowning.

Tom reached into his jacket pocket and pulled out a small cloth bag. He fished out ten gold coins and pressed them into her hand. "Whether you want it or not, take these. If things get worse here, this will get you and the children to Cork and then on to America."

"I can't take the Old Lord's guineas. It's half your money..."

"Because it's the Old Lord's, it is really more yours than mine. Consider it found money stashed in a pocket that you didn't know you had."

Gunny smiled, weighing the heavy coins in her hand. "I have no intention of leaving the Blaskets."

"Of course you don't. But if the potatoes fail again you may not have a choice."

Gunny slipped the coins into her apron pocket. It was more money than she'd ever seen and would easily cover her rent for the next several years. "Thank you, Tom. It's a tremendous gift."

"There is no greater gift than what you gave me—my health restored and a glimpse of family. I'll never forget my time on the Blaskets." Tom took a deep breath and turned to the fire. "There is one more thing."

"No," Gunny said.

Tom ignored her and reached farther into the little bag. He pulled out a gold locket on a delicate chain. He looked at it lovingly then held it out to Gunny. "This belonged to my mother."

Gunny looked at the locket hanging from Tom's long fingers. She shook her head. "I cannot take that," she said softly.

"It's not for you. It's for Maggie. Her mother would have wanted her to have it."

Gunny looked at Tom, her eyes brimming with tears. "You know?" she asked quietly.

Tom nodded. "Your sister Catherine was the most precious thing I knew on this earth. She was my angel. I did not do right by her and now she is gone. I am in no position to help Maggie and little Larry; they are better off with you. For now."

"For now?" Gunny asked tensely.

"Gunny, please consider coming to America. You would be free to live your life and the children would grow up proud of who they are. Not peasants. Not Irish trash."

"These children are not Irish trash!"

"I know they aren't, Gunny, but that's how they will be treated if they stay here in Ireland."

Gunny hung her head and reached for the locket. She rubbed her thumb over the smooth gold surface and sprung the latch. There was no picture inside, but there were six words. They were written in a script Gunny could not read. She held the locket out to Tom. "What does this say?"

Without looking at the locket, Tom said, "The truth will set you free. It was my mother's favorite saying from the Bible."

Gunny slid the gold locket into her apron pocket where it rested beside the black-handled knife. "The truth," she started, then cleared her throat. She looked at Tom's expectant face but could not tell him that Catherine might be his half-sister as well as the mother of his children. "Sometimes we don't know what the truth is," she continued.

Larry crawled up into Tom's lap and leaned against him. "I don't want you to go."

Tom rustled the boy's spiky brown hair and held him tight. "I don't want to go either, but the America is calling me. Will you come to America some day and find me?"

Gunny grimaced. "Now don't go putting ideas into the boy's head."

Larry shook his head enthusiastically. "I will, Tom. I will do that."

Maggie set her book on the hearth and leaned against Tom's leg. He swept her up onto his lap and hugged both children. The firelight reflected warmly off of the three faces. Tom looked at Gunny over the heads of the children. "Don't forget, Gunny. If things get bad…"

"I know, Tom," she said jingling the coins in her pocket. "If things get bad we will come find you in Virginia."

Gunny and the children walked into the village with Tom the next morning and climbed the cliff to watch him depart in Patrick's boat. Patrick had rousted a full crew to go fishing for more mackerel. Tom squeezed into the back of the curragh near the rudder.

"Will we ever see him again?" Maggie asked.

"I don't know, Maggie," Gunny said honestly. "You never know."

Tom looked up at the small family gathered on the cliff. He waved and they waved back. "One day, I'll be back to get you," he said quietly from the rear of the boat.

"What's that?" Patrick asked.

"Nothing," Tom said. "Nothing. And everything."

That summer the days were warm and sunny. The potatoes and oats grew well and the turf dried well in the high fields. In August, Gunny worked with Patrick in the lower fields to bring in a small supply of early potatoes. Gunny knelt and wept as they pulled the first spuds from the field.

Patrick put an arm around her. "The potatoes are sound, Gunny. There's no need to weep."

And still Gunny wept as she clutched at the cluster of rough, brown spuds in front of her. "I never worried about feeding myself, never worried that I'd go hungry. But having to feed two children is a different thing all together. If anything ever happened to those two…"

Patrick helped her up from the ground. "Don't worry. Things're going to be better now."

Gunny wiped the back of a dirty hand across her nose and sniffed. "Of course they are. Things will be better now. We can eat again," she said with a laugh. She shook the dirt from her skirt, took a deep breath, and walked arm and arm with Patrick back to the village.

By Hallow E'en, the small harvest was in and the potatoes and oats were sound. The village let out a collective sigh of relief. There still wouldn't be enough to get them through the winter and they'd need to save as many seed potatoes as possible to plant in the spring, but their food supply appeared to be on the mend.

Gunny made a small bowl of stampy with Maggie and wove masks for the children, but they stayed at home that year on the south end. Even though there was more to eat than there had been in years, no one had the energy to walk about the village. When Gunny smoored the fire for the evening, she sensed clusters of lost souls circling around her—Matt, her mother, her father, the lost villagers, so many gone. Life felt precious and precarious, and she wondered if she would ever feel safe again.

~ Chapter 22: The Loss of a Murphy ~

Gunny and the other farmers on the island scrimped through the winter to save every potato they could to plant. The short winter days and long winter nights were followed by a warm spring in 1848. When the fields were manured and new seeds were in the ground, Gunny relaxed, and she and the children enjoyed an easy spring and long, warm summer. In August, hungry villagers headed to the fields to bring in the first of the new potatoes. Gunny walked merrily with Patrick to the lower fields to begin her work. Every potato she lifted was black with rot. Her head spun. She heard Patrick's cry of anguish from his adjacent field. Across the village other cries rang out—every field on the island lay wasted: the blight had returned.

Conversations that fall in the village were brief. Nightly visits between villagers were few. Evenings of music, poetry, folktales, and fairies were no more. There were no weddings, no wakes, no bonfires. Word came from Dingle and Dunquin that the blight had also returned to the main land. A few new families moved to the Blaskets in search of food but there was nothing to share. With little food to spare and fear of fever everywhere, most people stayed in their houses day and night, wary of friends and strangers alike. Doors that had never been locked were now bolted.

Gunny insisted that both children attend school. Larry complained every morning that school was boring, but the soup at the school was the children's only guaranteed source of food. Gunny had a small store of oats and kitchen vegetables, but she grew thinner and thinner through the winter as even rabbits on the island began to grow scarce. To conserve energy, she only left the house to collect reeds and grasses to twist rope. If there was any commerce at all in Dingle, she hoped to sell the rope in the spring to get enough money for seed potatoes, though she couldn't imagine finding the energy to manure the fields.

She worried all winter as she obsessively twisted long strands of rope, carefully thinking through how she would sell the rope to get enough potatoes to plant. Her first stop would be at the Murphy's. If their shop wasn't open, she would deal with the likes of Packy Dollan.

On the first clear day in March of 1849, she piled three long lengths of finely twisted rope into the schoolhouse wagon she had borrowed from James and walked with the children to the center of the village. While the children quietly joined Charlotte's younger boys for the day, Gunny and Patrick and a small crew of fishermen hiked down the steep path to the Baron's newly built boat landing that sloped gently down toward the water. For the first time, Gunny was able to board Patrick's boat without making a leap.

"This may be the only good thing to come from these troubled times," she said to no one in particular.

After a slow row across the channel, the fishing boat arrived at the Dingle pier with nearly empty nets. Gunny pulled herself out of the boat, but had no energy to pull her rope from the boat. Patrick pushed it up onto the dock and promised to keep an eye on the precious stock until her return. They promised to meet at the pub on Green Street. Gunny gave a short wave and hiked slowly up the road toward the Murphy's store.

She had to stop to catch her breath when she reached Main Street. A cold wind whistled around the corners of the grey, stone buildings and stole her breath. She glanced around her. Main Street was deserted. She walked to the Murphy's store and lifted the latch on the heavy front door. The door was bolted from inside as James had predicted. When her knock went unanswered, she stepped to the dark, empty front window and cupped her hands around her face to peek inside. She saw Joanna and waved. Joanna frowned, then recognized Gunny and hurried to unlock the door. The familiar jingle of bells over the door greeted Gunny as Joanna pulled her inside, then pushed the door closed and quickly bolted it. Joanna gathered Gunny in a tight grip but said nothing.

"Thank God you're here," Gunny murmured over Joanna's shoulder. "I feared I'd be dealing with Packy Dollan today." Joanna's shoulders were stiff and she did not release Gunny from her grip. "Jamie sends his best," Gunny added waiting for Joanna to pull away.

Joanna finally held Gunny away from her, tears running down her face. "It's good Jamie is on the island with you," she whimpered, wiping at her eyes.

Gunny clutched her old friend's arms. Joanna looked much older than the last time Gunny had seen her. Her hair was thin and grey, her face lightly wrinkled around her eyes and across her cheeks. Joanna coughed and the sound rattled around in her chest.

"He's gone, Gunny," Joanna said with closed eyes. "Daniel is gone."

Gunny searched Joanna's face. "Gone... away?" she asked hopefully.

Joanna shook her head.

"Fever?" Gunny asked.

Joanna shook her head again. "The doctor said it was his heart—that his heart stopped. Oh, Gunny," Joanna said sobbing. "What am I going to do without Daniel?"

Gunny had rarely seen her friend show even the slightest emotion, and she had never seen her cry. She held Joanna in her arms. She wanted to say "There, there," to be some comfort, but all she could do was weep. So many others had passed, but for the first time in a long time, Gunny cried until she thought her heart would break.

* * *

The two women sat quietly at the kitchen table sipping at matching cups of hot, weak tea.

"Father Owen held a small funeral, then we buried Daniel next to his parents. I always thought I would go first. I never got to say good-bye."

"Daniel wasn't here when he died?"

"He was delivering exotic plants to the Baron for his new gardens when he collapsed. They said it was sudden."

Gunny gasped. "Why is Thomas buying exotic plants?"

"The Baron's our last good customer. He's the only one with any money to spend. He's had new walls built everywhere on his estate. And all of the roads around here are now in first rate order. Once the walls and roads were finished, he started adding onto his house and gardens. The work keeps the men busy—at least the ones who are not evicted or too hungry to work."

"Thomas has continued to evict families?"

"It's dreadful, Gunny. I was coming up from the pier last week and passed Mr. Thompson and his men evicting a family of eight from their house on Bridge Street. They hauled out the furniture then set the thatch roof on fire so the family could not reoccupy the house. A red-coated soldier stood with Mr. Thompson and demanded a key to the house—and of course there was no key. The family bolted the house with an iron bar from the inside when they slept at night. The soldier did not believe them. Finally they gave him the iron bar and he seemed satisfied and went away."

"Where did the family go?"

"I don't know. Everyone's afraid of the fever, and no one has food to spare. I feel guilty mourning Daniel when so many are suffering. I should be glad I still have a home. The paper reported last week that the number of recent evictions from Lord Ventry's property near Dingle is one hundred seventy. There are so many now without a roof over their heads, and during such awful times."

She tried to stifle a cough, but continuing coughing till her face changed from red to white. Gunny feared she would not stop.

"How long have you been sick?"

Joanna waved a hand in front of her face, trying to catch her breath. "I'm not sick," she said hoarsely, clearing her throat and dabbing at her mouth with her handkerchief. She pulled an old newspaper into her lap and scanned the headlines to distract herself until she could breathe again.

"Joanna, put that down. You never read the papers."

"There's not much else to do, Gunny, locked in this shop all day and night."

Gunny reached over and pulled the paper away. "I'll tell James about Daniel when I get back to the island," she said quietly. "He'll come back here to help you run the shop."

"No," Joanna said, vigorously shaking her head and clutching Gunny's hand. "Jamie is not to know."

"What? He must know. You can't keep this from him."

"If you tell him—what then? He'll leave his teaching position on the island to come home—and all for nothing. No one has money to shop. Last week we had the door open for a brief time on Saturday and a group of men came through grabbing armloads of whatever was in reach. Daniel tried to fight them but there were too many. It was right after that that Daniel collapsed. I can't have Jamie facing the same terror. Jamie is safer with you on the island than he is here with me. And where would I be if Jamie wasn't sending me what little money he can spare?"

"We heard on the island that there was food here."

"There is food but you have to go to the poorhouse to get it and the poorhouse and auxiliary sheds are full to the point of suffocation. Through the winter I tried to spend a day a week there helping but I don't go anymore. Fewer are dying of starvation but more are dying of fever, dysentery and scurvy. Everyone is weak with hunger. There are five thousand buried in the pauper's burial ground now."

"My mother was among the first to be buried there," Gunny said.

"I'm sorry," Joanna said. "I heard about your father as well."

"So many gone," Gunny said, and sipped at her cooling cup of tea.

Joanna picked up the paper from the floor. "Did you hear about the queen?" she asked with a queer look on her face.

"Has the queen passed as well?"

Joanna could not help but smile. "No. Queen Victoria heard of our troubles and came to the Cove of Cork with Prince Albert. She wanted to see the famine firsthand and thought a visit might inspire us."

"The Queen of England was here in Ireland? She should have saved the money and sent relief instead."

"She announced on her visit that England has no more funds to help the Irish. After she left, she made a personal donation of 1,000 pounds. The paper reported the Sultan of the Ottoman Empire offered to donate 10,000 pounds but the queen suggested that 1,000 pounds was more appropriate."

"How lovely of the queen to keep things proper at a time like this."

"The town of Cove spent a fortune on a fireworks display to greet her and ended up setting a nearby forest on fire."

"Good God."

"And now Cove has been renamed Queenstown."

"Good. Maybe the new name will remind people of her ridiculous visit and hard-hearted policies."

Joanna stood and added water to the kettle. "I want Jamie to move to America," she said in a flat voice.

Gunny stared at Joanna's back. "Has James ever mentioned wanting to move to America?"

"No," Joanna shook her head and squatted to stir the fire. "He's never talked about it but I've been thinking about it. They're talking about cholera in Tralee. It won't be long till it's here in Dingle. Even the Quakers have stopped helping. It's hopeless, Gunny." Joanna stood and turned to Gunny, her eyes brimming with tears. "I don't want Jamie to die too."

Gunny crossed to Joanna and squeezed her cool, thin hands. "James is healthy and strong. You should see him on the island. He's so good with the children."

"Yes, but how long can that go on? You said the potato crops were bad there. How long can any of you stay?" Joanna turned and pulled the kettle from the fire. She poured water into the tea pot and scooped in her last few spoonfuls of tea. She coughed again, a long rattley cough that shook her body.

"I don't like the sound of that, Joanna."

"It doesn't matter, Gunny," Joanna said loudly clearing her throat. "What matters is Jamie." She stared at the tea pot. "My grandmother would have hated drinking tea without sugar."

Gunny managed a smile. "You know that James will never leave Ireland without you."

Joanna turned and stared at Gunny. "If I told him to leave... If you told him to leave..." She had a crazy look in her eye. "The papers say that the ships to America are getting better. They're cleaner and the food is better and they have rules to help keep the fever from taking a ship. Jamie is young. He's strong. He could survive the trip."

"He has to want to go, Joanna, and I don't see that happening."

Joanna set the hot pot down heavily on the table. "Then I'll have him join the British Army. Others have. At least he would have food."

"That's a crazier idea than sending him off to America. James is no more the army type than I am."

"Other men from Dingle are joining up. The army pays a shilling a day and after fourteen years you can retire and get a pension for life."

"James is a teacher, Joanna, not a soldier, and fourteen years is a very long time."

"He could teach British children. Yes, if he doesn't want to go to America, then he will go to London to teach. He's got to get away, Gunny. He's got to get away." Joanna pulled a large handkerchief from her pocket and wiped her eyes. "Don't you understand, Gunny?" Joanna said in a frenzy. "Things will never be as they were. The Lords everywhere have started dairies and are selling whatever products they can to London to make money even though people here are starving. The farms are gone, Gunny. The farms and the families... Talk to Jamie. Please. He has to get away. You have to make him understand."

Joanna started to weep again, which made her cough. Gunny held Joanna tight in her arms.

"I'll talk to James. He must know about his father's passing. And I'll encourage him to stay on the island. James is the smartest man I know. He'll know the right thing to do."

~ Chapter 23: The Fire ~

When a letter from Thomas Milliken arrived at the Dingle post office in late May of 1849, the postmaster summoned Mr. Thompson to collect the missive.

Mr. Thompson scanned the envelope. "This is not for the Lord Baron."

The postmaster looked over the counter at the letter. "It's addressed to Thomas Milliken. Oh," he realized, taken aback. "This is from Thomas Milliken. I saw Thomas Milliken and thought the Lord...," he said reaching out to take the letter.

Mr. Thompson held on to it. "This is from young Thomas and it's addressed to that witch out on the Blaskets." He unceremoniously popped open the seal with a long yellow thumbnail and pulled the letter out of the envelope.

The postmaster reached across the counter. "I'll have that back, please. That's not for you. I see now that it's for Miss Gunny Malone."

Mr. Thompson turned his back on the small postmaster and leaned against the counter. He opened the letter and pulled out a five pound note. "Well, well," he said smiling and waving the note. "How nice of Tom to send us money."

"He did not send that to you or to the Baron," the postmaster said reaching again for the letter.

Mr. Thompson looked at the envelope. "Why would Tom be writing to that crazy woman on the island?"

"It's none of your business."

"You're right. It is not my business," Mr. Thompson said turning to the postmaster, "and yet it is so intriguing. The Baron has been worried about young Tom ever since he disappeared." He scanned the text of the letter. "Tom writes that he is in Virginia. Interesting. He fought somewhere in Mexico. Sailed to San Francisco... And he concludes: The enclosed money is for the children." He looked at the five pound note and then at the postmaster. He tilted his head slightly to one side. "What children?"

The postmaster was indignant, his face red. "You are not to read other people's mail. I insist you give me that letter."

Mr. Thompson held the missive high above the postmaster's head. "Or what? You'll report me to the sheriff? Or to the Baron? I'm sure both would be quite interested to know what other letters you have shuffled through here that contain money from America. You probably know better than anyone who can pay their rent on this beleaguered peninsula."

"I know no such thing," the red-faced postmaster insisted, a faint sheen of sweat on his brow. "But I do know my job and that is to deliver letters to the person whose name is on the envelope." His voice rose to a high pitch. "And in this case that letter must go out to the Blaskets, to Gunny Malone."

"Of course," Mr. Thompson said, roughly folding the letter and shoving it into the envelope.

"And the money," the postmaster insisted.

Mr. Thompson slid the five pound note into the envelope. "Now that I know the money is there, it is as good as mine. I'll have the sheriff's men row over tomorrow to collect rent from Miss Malone. She owes me ten times this amount for the amount of trouble she's given me with the Baron."

The postmaster snatched the missive from Mr. Thompson and did his best to flatten and re-seal the envelope.

Mr. Thompson tipped his hat at the postmaster. "Thank you for calling me in on this matter," he said, leaving the building with a swagger.

The postmaster rubbed a hand across his face then sent his assistant scrambling down to the docks to look for a Blasket fisherman to make the delivery.

While the Irish on the mainland starved that spring, the Blasket Islanders were sent food by none other than God himself. Just when many of the last remaining families were considering leaving the island to find food and work, a shipwrecked offshore—and the Blaskets were blessed with bales of wheat. The first bales washed up on the strand just after the spring planting was done. When the discovery was made, every remaining boat on the island headed out to sea to collect the treasure. Islanders soaked the raw wheat kernels in spring water, then dried the kernels at a huge bonfire on the strand. The salvaged wheat, boiled into a softened thick mash, was manna from heaven. A pact was made to tell no one of the find. After all, one should not be taxed on a gift from God.

Patrick found Gunny in the high fields cutting turf. It had been a few weeks since the wheat was discovered and everyone on the island was chipper and had more energy to work. Faces seemed fuller, smiles broader.

"Something for you. From America," Patrick said, puffing up the hill and waving the letter at Gunny, teasing.

Gunny was puzzled. She had not heard from Michael in years. She wiped her hands on her apron and took the envelope from Patrick. She smiled when she saw the name on the envelope.

"It's from our guest, Mr. Thomas Milliken," she said excitedly. "Looks like he made it to America after all. It's been two years. I wondered…" She wanted to savor the surprise and tucked the letter into her apron pocket. "I'll read this after our evening meal."

"I don't get to hear the news from America?"

"I'll tell you later. Thank you for the delivery."

Gunny and the children ate their wheat mush with great speed. Once the table was cleared, Gunny sat in her rocker, took off her boots, wiggled her toes in front of the fire, and ceremoniously opened the crumpled letter that seemed only partly sealed. She scanned through the text and started to read with both children sitting intently at her feet.

"Greetings and may this letter find you in good health. I am happy to report that my time on board the ship was uneventful. The ship landed after four weeks in New York City, a huge place I could never even begin to write about."

Gunny paused trying to picture a place too large to write about, then continued.

"I caught a coach first to a place called Philadelphia, and then traveled to Virginia as you suggested. When I arrived in Virginia I stayed briefly with your brother and his wife in Alexandria. They were shocked when I told them who I was, but accepted me as your friend. Alexandria is a fine little town with bustling industry and an active port."

"Michael is my brother and Maeve is his wife," Gunny explained to the children. "They live in America, in Virginia."

"You told us about them before," Maggie said impatiently. "Go back to the letter!"

Gunny cleared her throat and continued.

"Michael and Maeve live in a near hovel, no really, it is a hovel even by a peasant's standards. The place is a wreck."

Gunny paused.

"Why does your brother live in a hovel? Why doesn't he live in a house?" Larry asked.

"Good question," Gunny said. The last she had heard from Michael and Maeve they had jobs and helped run a fine shop. "Maybe Tom explains." She turned again to the letter.

"Michael and Maeve live over a small shop on Oronoco Street near the fish pier. The area is called Fish Town and it smells of it. The Irish are not welcome in Alexandria. Most businesses here will not hire the Irish and many will not make purchases at an Irish shop."

"Well, that explains it," Maggie said. "No one wants to shop in Fish Town."

"Yuck," Larry added holding his nose. "Smelly."

Gunny continued reading.

"Michael is well. Maeve seems a bit tipsy most of the time. Maeve's father Nick passed a few years ago. Maeve asked that I tell you about Nick as she knew you would want to hear."

"What's tipsy?" Larry asked.

"Who's Nick?" Maggie asked.

"Tipsy is, well, silly. Maeve was always silly—that's nothing new. And Nick O'Leary used to own the pub in Dunquin. I didn't know him, really," Gunny said.

"Then why would Maeve want you to know about him?"

"Because," Larry explained with a serious look on his face, "Maeve is tipsy. Remember?"

"Read more," Maggie implored.

Gunny cleared her throat and continued.

"No one will hire the Irish, even me, so I signed up with the United States Army to fight the Mexicans in Texas. I met all sorts of great chaps there."

"Tom's a soldier!" Larry shouted. "I want to go to America and be a soldier."

Gunny patted him on the head and continued.

"I returned to Alexandria when the war ended last February. Now gold has been discovered in California and I am headed to a place called San Francisco to make my fortune. There are many Irish headed there so I'll be in good company. We are going by boat to a place called Mission Dolores. We'll be two to three months on the water as we must sail around the tip of Africa to get to California. I am dreading the time on the boat, but will be in touch when I strike it rich!"

Gunny placed a finger on the page to mark her spot. "Imagine that," she said. "Our friend Tom is digging for gold."

"He's going on a boat. I want to go on a boat," Larry said.

"Finish," Maggie demanded.

Gunny cleared her throat and continued.

"I enclose with this letter a five pound note I exchanged from American dollars. The army paid me well. Please spend the money on the children as necessary. Hope all is well with you, Maggie, and Larry. With love and highest regards, Tom Milliken."

Gunny clutched the letter and money to her chest. Her eyes filled with tears at their second blessing of the year.

"Why are you crying?" Larry asked.

Gunny had no words. She pulled both children to her and hugged them close. There was a sharp knock at the door. Gunny released the children and crossed to open the door. It flew open before she reached it and Patrick burst into the room.

"Gunny," he said, out of breath."Can I see you for a minute?" He eyed the children. "Outside."

Gunny smiled. "Of course, I have the best news," she started to say when Patrick pulled her outside and closed the door behind them.

"The letter…," Patrick started.

"Yes," Gunny said. She clutched the letter and five pound note in her hand. "That's the news, you see…"

"Gunny," Patrick interrupted her, "the postmaster wasn't going to say anything then thought better of it. He sent word with one of my brothers. When that letter arrived the postmaster thought it was for Thomas Milliken, not from Thomas Milliken."

Gunny was confused. "The letter was for me, not the Baron. The letter was from Tom…," she started to explain, then felt the blood drain from her face. "Are you telling me that the postmaster delivered this letter to the Baron?"

"Not exactly. He showed it to Mr. Thompson who read the letter before the postmaster could get it away from him. The postmaster said to tell you that Mr. Thompson said he would tell the Baron of its contents—including the five pound note which he said was his."

Gunny swallowed hard, remembering the last intimate details of the letter. Tom had mentioned the children by name. "Good, God," she muttered.

Patrick held her arm. "I knew you'd be worried that the Baron knew about the five pound note."

Gunny shook her head. "It's not the money, Patrick. I have to get the children off this island. How quickly can you get your boat ready?"

"I don't understand. Where're you going?"

"It doesn't matter. He can't take them, Patrick. Not now."

"Take who, Gunny? Why would the Baron be interested in your sister's children?"

"There's no time to explain. Get the boat ready. I'll pack. Oh, my God. How does one run away at a moment's notice? What should I take?" She looked at Patrick, her eyes large with fear. "Stop listening to me!" she yelled. "Go get your boat. We'll be right behind you."

Patrick left the yard at a sprint. Gunny flew into her house. "Children!" she yelled. The children were playing together quietly, for once, in front of the fire.

"You don't have to yell, Gunny. We're right here," Maggie said.

Gunny felt tears well up in her eyes. She blinked them away and ran her hand over her face. "Sorry, little one. We have to hurry. We're going on an adventure."

Maggie stood and put her hands on her hips. "At this time of night?"

"Don't argue with me, Maggie. And for once in your life, please don't ask any questions."

"But why," Maggie started. Gunny grabbed Maggie's book bag and shook the contents out onto the floor.

"That's my school work!" Maggie cried.

"You won't need it now," Gunny said, stuffing Tom's letter and five pound note into the empty school bag. She scrambled under the bed and pulled out an old worn box. She took out the last letter she had from her brother Michael, Tom's ten gold guineas, and the iron heart from Mac. She had wrapped the locket Tom left her in a small piece of cloth. She took the tiny cloth bundle from the box and carefully placed it in the book bag, then pushed the empty box back under the bed.

"Food," she said. She grabbed two loaves of wheat bread she had baked that morning and wrapped them in an old flour sack. "We'll have to buy anything else we need along the way." The children watched, stunned as Gunny scurried about muttering to herself. "I should take my medicines but there's no time and no telling what we'll need." She looked around. "What else?"

"What're you doing?" Maggie asked.

"I told you. We're going on an adventure. Patrick is going to take us on his boat. Get your shawl. Larry, put on your jacket and hat."

Gunny sat down in her rocker and pulled on her boots. She laced them quickly and tightly.

"It's too hot tonight for a jacket," Larry complained.

"Put on your jacket," Gunny said loudly from the rocker. Larry's eyes grew large. Without another word, he pulled his jacket down from a small peg near the door.

"I'm sorry I yelled at you but we have to hurry," she said tying a tight bow on her boot. She paused by the mantel eying her long-neglected tin whistle, then grabbed it and jammed it into her apron pocket.

She heard a noise in the yard and froze. Were they already here? Was the Baron in the yard? She ran to the door and opened it a crack. There was no movement outside; the yard was quiet. She turned and looked around her cozy house, clutching at the hurriedly packed bag. She was taking so little with her. She looked lovingly at her rescued rocking chair, at the old sea chest, at her Spanish cups and saucers on the cupboard. She felt in her apron to make sure she had the black-handled knife. It was nestled in its usual spot. She gave it a quick squeeze and pulled on her shawl.

"All right, children," she said herding them out the door. "We have everything we need. We're off to find Patrick."

As they neared the path that led down to the pier, Gunny's heart sank. The Baron's distinctive voice echoed up from the new landing. She reached out to stop the children and listened.

"No one is to leave this island until I say so." The Baron's voice echoed off of the nearby rocks.

"You see," she heard Patrick explain in a quieter voice, "there is a certain mackerel running tonight..."

"No one!" she heard the Baron yell. He ordered one of his men to secure the landing area.

"Plans have changed, children," she said eying the steep hill behind them. "We're going to the west end till things settle down."

"The west end?" Maggie questioned.

"Rabbits!" Larry said loudly.

"Shhh. No questions. I'll race you both to the top of the hill. Ready, set, go."

Larry took off at a sprint. Maggie started off at a slow trot next to Gunny. "I don't like this game, Gunny."

"It's not a game, Maggie. Keep going, girl, up the hill. Let's hope my old house is good for one more night of visitors and Matt's old curragh is good for one more sail."

The Baron, Mr. Thompson, and two of the sheriff's men climbed the steep path from the pier and walked down the moonlit road toward the schoolhouse. When they arrived, the Baron pounded on the door until James answered. The Baron pushed his way inside and drilled James about Tom Milliken's relationship to Gunny Malone.

"He was here two years ago," James explained as the Baron paced about the room. "He arrived sick with fever. Gunny helped nurse him back to health. He might have died it if hadn't been for her."

The Baron stopped and blinked. "Mr. Thompson reported that Tom sent Gunny five pounds. He said the money was for the children."

"Tom was a caring fellow. He probably wanted Gunny to help purchase food for the children," he shrugged then added, "here at the school."

"If he was sending money for the children at the school, then why wouldn't he send the money to you if you housed him while he was sick."

James blushed. "I don't know, Sir. Tom had his own way of doing things."

"Tell me about it," the Baron spat. "It doesn't make sense. Mr. Thompson said Tom mentioned two names in the letter but he didn't recall what they were. Does Gunny have children here on the island?"

"I'm not sure, sir."

The Baron growled and roughly pushed the books from James' desk onto the floor. "You're the bloody schoolmaster. You must know every child on this island. Where's your attendance book?" he demanded. "I want to see the names of every child who has ever attended this school."

James reached up to the shelf behind the desk and with a shaky hand pulled down his large, red attendance book. He pushed his glasses up on his nose and handed the book to the Baron. "Here, sir. Mr. Thompson reviews this with some regularity. Everything is in order. The school is full and I am feeding all of the children as best I can."

"I don't care who you are feeding," the Baron muttered, flipping open the heavy book. "I want to know if…" He pointed at the very first name in the registry: Maggie O'Connor. He looked at James. "Maggie O'Connor. This entry is from three years ago. How old is this girl?"

"She's might be about… eight."

"Maggie O'Connor," the Baron said, pouting his lips. "Maggie was the name of Catherine's daughter who disappeared." He looked at James. "And she'd be about eight now. But O'Connor? Was this child registered by Gunny Malone?"

James slowly nodded his head.

"Damn it," the Baron said with a raised voice. "Maggie is Tom's daughter. I was told she had gone off to live with Eileen Malone's people. I didn't look for her after Chrisabella died. Gunny never told me she had the girl."

"Then Larry is your grandson?" James asked thinking of the resemblance between Larry and the Baron.

The Baron went pale. "There's a boy?"

James swallowed hard. "I didn't mean, sir…"

The Baron sat on the children's bench, stunned. "The baby didn't die? I have a grandson?" He looked at James. "I didn't know," he said shaken. "I would have looked harder for a boy."

James hung his head. The Baron grabbed him by the collar. "Where does Gunny live?" the Baron demanded.

The Baron and his men tore Gunny's house apart looking for clues.

"Look at this place," the Baron muttered. "How can anyone raise children with so little? One room, a few beds, a dirty fireplace… These island people are savages."

"She can't have gone far," Mr. Thompson said. "The tea kettle is still hot."

Mr. Thompson and the Baron looked at one another and said at the same time: "The west end."

"You've been there before. How do we get there?" the Baron asked.

"It's a long walk," Mr. Thompson said. "I'm not sure your leg…"

"Then get me a horse," the Baron demanded.

Mr. Thompson hesitated. "There are no horses on this island."

"What?" the Baron asked. He shook his head. "Primitives. How else can we get there?"

"I saw a cart out in front of the schoolhouse," Mr. Thompson said. "But I'm not sure how we'll pull it without a horse." Mr. Thompson asked.

"You can pull it," the Baron stated. "Go get it ready for me."

Mr. Thompson's face went red but he did as he was told. The Baron ordered his other two men to wait, one at Gunny's house and one at the schoolhouse.

"If Gunny shows up, keep her here until I return. We won't be long. The island isn't that big."

Mr. Thompson did his best to sweep out the schoolhouse cart with an old broom James gave him, but the bed of the cart still smelled of dung and rotten seaweed.

"Animals," the Baron muttered as he awkwardly climbed in. He sat as upright as he could, touching as little of the cart with his body as possible. There was no road to the west end, only a bumpy pathway lit by a half-moon. The going was slow and Mr. Thompson had to make frequent stops to catch his breath. The Baron yelled at him each time they stopped. "Move! Move!"

Waves boomed against the hard black rocks on the cliffs below the men. A cold wind whistled around them. As they neared the west end, the path sloped gently downwards and they heard an unearthly moaning rising from the shore.

"Stop the cart, Mr. Thompson," the Baron demanded. Then in a quieter voice, "What is that?" The Baron felt a shiver move up his spine. "It sounds like someone is hurt."

"Or dead," Mr. Thompson said. "I heard that once before. The O'Connor boy said it was seals."

"It's an un-Godly sound. Seals don't howl like that."

"Apparently the ones out here do."

The Baron shook his head and said in a muted voice. "Only a crazy person would live out here. Move on!" he insisted above the wailing of the seals and the wheezy whistle of the north wind.

Mr. Thompson resumed pulling the cart. Around the next bend dim silver moonlight highlighted the remains of a small, rocky village in the cove below them. Rock rattled against rock as cold black waves pushed into the shore, then dragged smaller rocks back out to sea. Mr. Thompson pulled the cart to a stop. An old curragh lay near the breaking waves, tipped to one side, partly filled with water.

"Last time I found her in one of those houses," Mr. Thompson said pointing inland.

"Those aren't houses," the Baron muttered, "they are piles of rock."

A blast of sharp wind whistled through the loose stones of the ancient houses and tottering walls of an old church. The Baron shuddered and pulled his jacket close around him.

"That one has a roof," Mr. Thompson said pointing in the dim moonlight. "And I smell a turf fire."

"Hah," the Baron laughed. "We've got them."

Mr. Thompson helped the Baron out of the cart. He was stiff from the ride and reeked of manure. Mr. Thompson coughed uneasily into his sleeve.

"Don't bother trying to hide your distaste, Mr. Thompson. The feeling is mutual."

The Baron limped toward the only house with a roof and pressed his ear against the closed door made of a mish-mash of found boards. "I don't hear anything. They must be asleep," he whispered to Mr. Thompson and smiled. "We've caught them napping." He felt a flutter in his stomach. "I haven't had this much fun since my days fighting the French."

The Baron reached up and slowly lifted the latch on the door. The door did not budge; it was latched from inside. He moved quietly to the front window and pushed against it. It was sealed tight with mud. He peeked inside. He couldn't see anything but the dim glow of a turf fire. He took a step away from the house and yelled in a deep voice. "Gunny Malone! Come out of that house! I know you have my grandchildren in there."

There was no response. The wind continued to howl around them.

"Gunny!" the Baron yelled again moving closer to the door. "Come out now. You can't hide from me any longer. I insist that you and the children come out this instant. And," he added winking at Mr. Thompson, "I want that five pound note you got from my ingrate son."

There was still no response from inside.

"Gunny," the Baron shouted again, pounding on the door. "Open this door. I am your Baron and I demand it. Do you hear me?"

Gunny's voice was muffled behind the closed door. "Get away from the door, Thomas. You can't have these children. They are the product of incest and should never have been born."

The Baron turned and looked at Mr. Thompson. The large man's face was pale, his eyes wide with fear. He pictured the woman as he'd last seen her in this house, with ashes smeared on her face, eyes rolled back in her head and smoke curling up through her hair. "She's a witch, Baron. We should go."

"Gunny," the Baron shouted again, ignoring Mr. Thompson and beating again on the door. "Open this door. I want to see Maggie and the little boy. You've kept them from me for too long."

"I'll never give them to you," Gunny yelled from inside. "They are the spawn of your son Tom and our daughter Catherine. I should have sent them to your workhouse so they could starve and be tossed into the mass burial pit with the rest of the pauper children."

"Gunny," the Baron said quieter into the door. "Come out and talk to me. I've tried to feed the children, you know I have. And these children are not the product of incest. Catherine was not my daughter. I told you that years ago."

"If Catherine was not your daughter," Gunny demanded through the door, "then why did you insist that she come live at your house?"

"You disappeared," the Baron yelled. "Someone besides your crazy mother had to look after her."

"Liar!" Gunny yelled through the door, then continued in a quieter voice. "You bought her new clothes and kept her clean... I hardly knew her. She didn't know me at all..."

The Baron listened to scuffling sounds from inside the house.

"Gunny!" he pleaded to the door. "At least let me have the boy. I'll raise him. He'll want for nothing. And we'll find a position for the girl. We can call her Margaret. The children will be safe and well fed. And one day, the boy will inherit all of this. Are you listening to me?"

"No," Gunny muttered from inside. The Baron heard her drag something across the floor. Then he heard a sharp bang. Then nothing.

"Gunny," he said quietly into the door. "You are wrong about Catherine." He paused and took a deep breath. "I am not her father, but I know who is." The Baron rested his head against the door. "I was in Dunquin that night. I was leaving O'Leary's pub when I saw you go into the graveyard. I followed you. I'd never seen you drunk before. You were staggering about, then there was a flash of lightning and I saw you slip in the mud. I caught you as best I could on my bad leg but I couldn't hold you. I dropped you and you hit your head on a gravestone. I touched your lips to make sure you were still breathing. I thought I'd never see you again."

The Baron paused. "Gunny? Are you listening to me? You were hurt," he explained in a firm voice, bracing himself against the frame of the door. "Then Father Jessey appeared from out of nowhere. We carried you into the church and laid you on a pew. The priest promised he would get you home safely. Gunny?" The Baron beat on the door again. "Are you listening to me?"

There was no response.

"Gunny," Thomas yelled again, hands on the door. "It was the priest who was with you that night. Father Jessey is Catherine's father. Not me..."

Thomas smelled smoke and took a step away from the house. A bright glow of fire danced from under the crack at the bottom of the door as black smoke curled up through the thatched roof against the star-lit sky. Thomas pounded desperately on the door but it would not budge. "No," he cried kicking helplessly at the door. "I love you, Gunny!" he sobbed, then turned from the house. "Mr. Thompson!" he yelled. "She's set the house on fire. Help me get the children out."

The Baron looked behind him into the empty black night. Mr. Thompson had fled long ago. He ran to the stone wall at the front of the yard and strained to free a large rock. He limped back to the house and heaved the stone against the front window. The glass splintered into a hundred pieces. Cold wind whistled through the broken glass. The fresh air farther ignited the flames and the house went up with a roar.

The Baron and the two sheriff's men returned to the pier just before sunrise. Patrick helped the Baron into his boat. His hair had turned completely white and he had ash smeared across his face. His eyes were sunken and hollow. Just as the boat was about to leave, Mr. Thompson hurried down the steep pathway and pushed his way onboard.

The Baron stared at his right-hand man. "You no longer work for me, Mr. Thompson. When we get back to Ventry, I do not ever want to see you again on my property." No one said a word as the sheriff's men rowed the boat out into the channel and headed east to Ventry.

James arrived at the pier just as the boat was leaving. He squeezed Patrick's arm and held back a sob. "Patrick. When the Baron returned to the schoolhouse he told his men that he'd found Gunny and the children on the west end—and that her house burned. All were lost in the fire. I'm so sorry."

Word traveled fast through the village that the Baron and Mr. Thompson had set fire to Gunny's house with Gunny and the children sleeping inside. James and the O'Connor clan gathered to make the long walk west toward the column of black smoke rising from Gunny's old cottage.

Morning sun lit the smoldering rubble. The front door was half-burned, the front window shattered. The roof was dry and had burned quickly. Patrick and James walked around the smoking embers. Part of the back wall had collapsed and everything inside the house was blackened right down to the rock walls.

Charlotte O'Connor knelt and wailed. "How can one human being do this do another?"

"And to children, no less," Patrick added.

Timothy O'Connor shook his head and pounded one fist into the palm of his other hand.

Bridget shook her head. "Burning out a family and starving all of the others. As much as they hate the Irish, this would not happen in America."

"No," James said. "This would not happen in any civilized place."

Charlotte O'Connor sobbed. "I never thought I'd live to see anything as terrible as this," she moaned. "A woman so good and children so sweet."

Patrick looked at his distraught mother and raised his eyebrows.

"I was getting to like little Larry. Honest, I was," Charlotte offered.

Patrick climbed over the rocks of the collapsed back wall and signaled for James to follow. James picked up a long piece of driftwood and the two men poked through the smoky rubble.

"Look, Patrick," James said, picking up the charred remains of a St. Brigit's cross near the half-burned front door.

"Gunny made the most elaborate crosses," Charlotte wept as the blackened straw crumbled in James' hands. "But even St. Bridgit could not stop this fire."

Something caught Patrick's eye in the charred embers near the fireplace. He took out his handkerchief and lifted out a hot iron heart. His eyes filled with tears. "I remember the children's first Hallow E'en on the Blaskets. Gunny gave this to Maggie to carry on the walk home. Gunny said this bit of metal would protect the girl from the fairies."

"Heaven help us with the fairies," Charlotte sobbed, "but who will save us from the English?"

Patrick wiped the scrolled heart clean and slipped it into his pocket. "We'll take our revenge on them. Someday." He shook his head and wiped his eyes with the back of a blackened hand.

Charlotte gathered everyone into a small circle "God bless this little family buried here for all time," she intoned.

They bowed their heads in silent prayer.

Patrick raised his head, eyes closed, and listened to a faint tapping sound. The sound stopped, then started again.

Tap-tappity-tap-tap.

He opened his eyes and stared at the house.

Tap-tappity-tap-tap.

Charlotte O'Connor started keening and was shocked when her son hushed her.

"Listen," he said, waving his hands to silence everyone.

They were all quiet and listened. The rhythmic tapping started again.

"What is that?" Charlotte asked, her heart beating in time with the sound.

Tap-tappity-tap-tap.

This time the tapping was followed by a rasping sound of wood moving against rock.

"This place is haunted," Bridget said in a whisper. "We should go. Even the wind feels haunted out here..." she added with a sniff.

Patrick moved closer to the house where the sound was slightly louder. He signaled to his mother and sister again to be quiet. He grabbed the long piece of driftwood from James and stirred the smoldering ash. A pile of rocks in front of him shifted and he jumped back.

"Morning," came a muffled sound from under the smoking pile.

"Gunny?" Patrick asked, knowing it could not be Gunny. No one could have survived this blaze. He signaled to James and they kicked the hot ash and blackened rock off of a heavy wooden door in the floor of the house.

Gunny pushed the door open a few inches and squinted at the morning sun. She waved wisps of smoke from her face and gasped at the hot air.

"You're alive!" Patrick said, pulling the charred door the rest of the way open and grabbing hold of Gunny's hand. "How can this be?"

The children stretched and yawned as they sprinted up the sod stairs past her. Larry scrambled onto Patrick's back to avoid the hot embers.

Maggie stopped at the top of the stairs and looked around. "What happened here?"

James scooped Maggie up, laughing, and carried her across the hot rubble while Patrick pulled Gunny out of the hole, juggling the boy on his back. She emerged clutching the loaded book bag and let the heavy door close behind her with a slam.

"Well," she said, lifting her skirts and stepping across the hot coals, "that was the longest couple of hours of my life. That is one dark hole."

Charlotte and Bridget reached out to Gunny, grinning and squealing and hugging her from both sides.

"Gads," Gunny said. "I must smell like a pig and old potatoes and smoke." She looked at the amazed faces around her and pulled the children in close. "Sorry for the scare, everyone."

"The Baron is a monster," James said. "How could he have done this to you?"

"Oh, the Baron didn't do this. I'm the one who set fire to the house."

Everyone gasped.

"I always said she was crazy," Timothy O'Connor muttered to Charlotte.

Gunny laughed. "I'm not crazy, Tim. It was the best I could do on short notice. My plan when we headed here was to sail off in Matt's old boat, but it was too leaky, as you may well remember. So I brought the children into the house and put them to bed in a hidden underground room. That's been the handiest place for stashing illegal things. The children were exhausted and went right to sleep. I knew Thomas would find us but I didn't think he'd be quite so persistent once he got here. He was going on and on about Catherine, and something about the priest. That's when I knew he wasn't going to give up and decided to start the fire. I could hear him yelling away at me while I pulled the door shut and waited for the fire to catch."

"But why, Gunny. Why would you do this?" Charlotte asked.

Gunny rubbed her eyes. "Thomas must think the children are dead. I knew it was the only way he'd go back to Ventry without them." She turned and looked at the smoldering remains behind her. "Of course I didn't anticipate the back wall collapsing on top of the door."

"You could have died down there," Patrick said. "What if we hadn't been here to help get that door open?"

"But you were here. God was watching over us, Patrick. And now the children are free."

Everyone was joyous on the walk back. They settled in at the O'Connors' house and Charlotte passed around cups of warm milk from the new cow Bridget had purchased in Ballyferriter the week before. Patrick cleared his throat and presented Gunny with the nail heart.

"I can't seem to lose this thing," she muttered, slipping the metal heart into her apron pocket where it rested beside the black-handled knife. "Children," she directed. "Go off to the strand and play hurley with the O'Connor boys. The adults need time to talk."

Maggie and Larry noisily left the house, happily telling the older boys about their midnight adventure, how they had tried to sail off in an old leaky boat, and how they'd spent the night instead sleeping in a hole in the ground. After they left, Bridget broke out her last stash of whiskey and poured everyone a short glass.

Gunny stared into the fire. "Now that the Baron thinks the children are dead, they must leave Ireland. They must go to America."

"You're leaving Ireland?" Patrick asked quietly.

Gunny shook her head. "No, not me. I'm forty-one years old and too set in my ways to live anywhere but here."

"But how will the children get to America?" Bridget asked.

Gunny turned to James. "James is going to take them."

James looked up from his glass of whiskey. "What?" he stammered, pushing his glasses up on his nose.

"You're going to take them. You're young and strong, and you'll be able to find work in America. Every town needs a good teacher."

"But I can't go. What about my mother in Dingle, and the school here…"

Gunny set down her glass and knelt in front of James. She took his glass and set it on the floor, then took both of his hands in hers. "James, I wouldn't ask if there were any other way. We have been friends for a long time and I couldn't trust anyone more with these children."

James swallowed hard. "I'm honored, Gunny, but my mother…"

"Your mother wants you to go to America. We talked about it the night she told me about your father passing."

"Gunny. I agreed with her that I should stay and work on the island after Daniel passed but I never agreed that I should move to America. That's her dream, not mine. And besides, someone has to look after her. She's getting older, and she has that cough…"

"I'm going to take care of her, James. She is going to move to the Blaskets and live here with me."

"But the store…"

"She's done with the store, James. There's no business in Dingle. Even if the potatoes come back next year there aren't enough people left in town to sustain so many shops. Here on the Blaskets, I can look after her. And she'd make a wonderful teacher. We'll need someone to take your place at the school."

James bit his bottom lip. "When I was growing up, everyone used to talk about going to America, but I never wanted to go."

"James, if I don't get the children off this island and on a ship to America, the Baron will find them and take them away forever."

"But at least they'd still be here in Ireland. You could still see them."

"Ireland is their past, James. America is their future. You must take them to my brother Michael and then find Tom. Maybe by the time you get there, Tom will have found gold and will be back in Alexandria and you'll live a life of luxury. Will you do this for me, James? Will you take the children to America?"

"I have to talk to my mother first."

She turned to Patrick. "Time is of the essence. Can you take us to Dingle and then continue on with James and the children to Cork?"

"I've never sailed to Cork before, but yes, it can be done."

Gunny turned back to James. "When we get to Dingle, I'll stay hidden with the children on the boat until you return. The Baron thinks we're dead which gives us a little time. If Joanna approves of our plan, and I know she will, you'll come and get me and we'll swap places. By the time the Baron discovers the truth, it'll be too late."

"After I drop James and the children off in Cork, I'll come back to Dingle to get you and James' mother," Patrick offered with a smile. "Then we'll all come back here to the island."

James looked pale. "I guess if Joanna approves, I can do this. We're going to America," he said, breaking into a broad smile.

"I'll get the boat ready. We'll leave as soon as it gets dark," Patrick said, taking a deep breath.

Gunny spent the rest of the day on the south end. The Baron's men had left her house a mess but nothing had been destroyed. She righted her rocking chair and swept the ashes from the house. She re-stoked the fire and put on bread to bake, then sat in her old rocker and stitched two flour bags into large satchels for the children. She made two small sewing kits and packed one in each bag, then added a blanket, a pillow stuffed with wild bird feathers, a set of spare clothes, and two pairs of stockings for each child. She added the children's boots. They hardly wore them on the island and she wasn't sure they even fit but they were the only shoes she had for them. She put a tin cup and spoon in each bag, then wrapped three handkerchiefs around a bar of soap and put that in Maggie's bundle along with a spare bonnet. She added a cap to Larry's bag. The bags were nearly as big as the children, but they weren't too heavy.

She picked up the book bag she had taken with her to the west end. She would give this to James to carry. She wrote a note to Maggie explaining that the enclosed locket belonged to Maggie's grandmother. She'd let Tom fill in the rest of the details when he felt Maggie was ready to hear the truth about who he was. She folded the note into the cloth, tied it with a small piece of rope, and placed the tidy bundle back in the bag.

When the bread was cooked, she wrapped three loaves in clean cloths and placed them in the book bag. She pulled the nail heart from her pocket and ran her finger over the delicate filigree one last time, then placed the heart in Maggie's bag. She muttered a short blessing and tied the bag shut. Then she pulled out the black-handled knife. She had carried the knife with her for so long it felt like part of her hand when she held it. She pulled the blade from the worn leather case and thought about Mac and the church gate and Matt... She held the cool knife up to her chest and gave it a final squeeze.

"You've protected me well. Now protect these children." She took a deep breath, slipped the knife into Larry's bag, and tied the bag shut.

James knocked at the door. Gunny handed him the heavy book bag, which he added to his own satchel. Gunny carried the children's bags and they walked to the strand where the children were still playing hurley with the O'Connor boys.

"Maggie Larry!" Gunny called, the names blended into one. "Come over here. I have something to tell you."

The children came at a run. Gunny set down the bags and squatted in front of them. Maggie eyed the bags and shook her curls at Gunny. "Don't tell me we're going on another adventure."

Gunny feigned surprise. "You didn't like the last adventure?"

"Being stuck in a dark hole all night? With Larry?"

Larry punched his sister on the arm. "Let's do it again! I liked that stinky hole."

Maggie pretended her arm hurt and rolled her eyes at Gunny.

Gunny's chest felt tight as she thought about the best way to break the news to the children. She swallowed hard. "Children," she said, her voice wavering. She cleared her throat and started again. "Children," she said with more determination, "you are going to America to find Tom Milliken. James is going to take you."

Larry leapt into the air and let out a loud whoop. "We're going on a boat! I knew it. I'm off to conquer the world!" he shouted, and raced off to brag to the O'Connor boys.

Maggie looked out across the wide beach. "We're going to America? Past the Isle of the Blessed?"

Gunny pointed toward the horizon. "Past the Isle of the Blessed and past the land of Eternal Youth."

Maggie turned to face Gunny. "Why?"

Gunny was ready this time. She stood to her full height in front of the girl. "Because I said so," she stated as firmly as she could.

Maggie giggled. "No," she repeated. "Why are we going to America?"

Gunny looked at the girl's determined face and slumped. She squatted again and held Maggie's hands in hers. "All my life, Maggie, I've seen people leave Ireland to go to America to find a better life. And that's what I want for you and Larry. I want you to have more than what I can give you here in Ireland."

Maggie's face hardened. "You're not going with us?"

Gunny looked up at James, then back at Maggie. "No," she said softly. "I am too old for the trip. James is going to take you."

Maggie pulled her hands away from Gunny and took a step back. Her eyes brimmed with tears. "I'm not leaving without you."

"I want to go, Maggie, I do. I've always wanted to sail off to see the promised land—but you don't always get what you wish for. And I have important business here. You remember James' mother, Mrs. Murphy?"

"Yes," Maggie said hesitantly. "She has the store in Dingle. She gave us hot cider once when we visited."

"Yes, Mrs. Murphy is a very important lady to me and to James. And in order for James to travel with you, I need to stay here with Mrs. Murphy."

Maggie looked puzzled. "Why don't you both come with us?"

"I wish we could, Maggie, but travel is for the young."

"You are sort of old," Maggie admitted.

"I'm very old," Gunny agreed. "And Mrs. Murphy is even older. You trust James, don't you?"

Maggie nodded.

James smiled at her. "We'll watch out for each other, won't we, Maggie?"

Maggie smiled and nodded again.

"You'll live with my brother, Michael. You'll go to school in America and you'll write to me every month to tell me how things are."

"I'd rather stay here," Maggie said softly. "We have the wheat from the shipwreck. Perhaps we'll be lucky and there'll be another shipwreck. And at harvest, maybe we'll have food again."

Gunny squeezed the little girl's hands. "We can't depend on shipwrecks, Maggie. In America, you won't have to worry about where your next meal is coming from. And things are changing here. Even if this harvest comes in, there are cattle grazing now where we used to grow food. The fever is everywhere. So many people are evicted and gone. I want you and Larry to live where people dance and laugh—and where you'll be safe."

Maggie pouted. "If things are so awful here then you should come with us. What if something bad happens to you here?"

Gunny laughed. "Bad things happen, Maggie. And sometimes the best times come from the worst times. I'll be fine. I have the O'Connors, and our snug little house on the south end. I'll get by—and knowing that you and Larry are safe and have food will put my mind at ease."

Larry came tearing across the sand. "Let's go!" he said hopping about on one foot. "When're we leaving?"

"I'm glad at least one of you is upset about the departure," Gunny said winking at Maggie.

"Oh, that's just Larry," Maggie said in her most adult voice. "You know how he is. Larry," she said, turning to her little brother. "James is going to travel with us. Gunny is going to stay here and take care of Mrs. Murphy. We're going to live with Gunny's brother, Michael in Virginia."

"Hurray!" Larry shouted. "And Maeve. We get to live with tipsy Maeve."

"You may not want to call her that to her face," Gunny said as Larry ran up onto the rocks.

"Hurry," he yelled, brandishing an invisible sword and slashing out at invisible enemies.

"I hope America is ready for him," Gunny said to James.

"I hear it's a big place," James said.

~ Chapter 24: On Board ~

It was a perfect night for a long row to Dingle harbor. James sat with the children in the back of the boat with the full satchels tucked in around their feet. Patrick and Gunny each mounted an oar, and Patrick pushed off of the new Blasket pier as a full, orange moon rose mysteriously over the still ocean waters. Maggie sang a song of farewell to the island until she could no longer see the black silhouette against the moon-lit sky. Then she snuggled in next to her brother, and both children slept.

The town of Dingle was quiet as the black curragh slipped up to the end of the dark pier. Patrick secured the boat and helped James up onto the dock. James slipped from the boat and headed up into the village.

"Think he'll be back?" Patrick asked quietly.

Gunny stared up the street after James. "I'm sure of it."

About an hour later, they heard footsteps on the pier, and James reappeared, a sour look on his face.

"Well?" Gunny asked tentatively.

James stood for a moment on the dock chewing gently on his bottom lip, then took a deep breath and pushed his glasses up on his nose. He stepped into the boat and took a seat along the center plank. Gunny and Patrick leaned in toward him.

"Mother approves of the plan," he said in a whisper. "She gave me ten pounds. We'll be in fine shape to travel with that plus the five pounds and ten guineas you gave us."

"Then you're ready to go?" Patrick asked.

James' eyes filled with tears. He turned to Gunny and she saw him again as he was when she first met him, a shy little boy with big eyes and words that would not leave his mouth. "I want to go and yet it breaks my heart," he muttered. "My excitement from yesterday is gone. You know my heart will always be here in Ireland."

Gunny reached out and took his cool hands in hers. "A wise man once told me that if you do something good the rewards will be a hundred fold. You're doing something very, very good, James. You're going to help these children find their father and make a new life for themselves in America. And once they're settled, you can always come home. Ireland will still be here. We'll all still be here." She knew that last part might not be true but hoped the words would be of comfort.

She looked at the children sleeping against their stuffed bundles. She leaned over and kissed each one gently on the head, then closed her eyes and said a silent prayer over their heads before gathering her long skirts and climbing out of the boat.

"Aren't you going to wake them to say good-bye?" James whispered.

Gunny shook her head no and wiped the back of her hand across her face. "Never wake a sleeping child," she said. "And anyway, I'm not so good at good-byes." She held out a hand to James. "God speed. I love you for all you've done for me in this lifetime. For believing in me when I was a teen—and for believing in me now." She cleared her throat and stood up straight. "You have the money? And you know where you're headed once you get to New York City?"

James nodded. "Don't worry, Gunny. I'll take good care of them."

"And I'll take care of your mother," Gunny whispered, squatting by the boat and looking James in the eye. "Write to us."

The two clasped hands.

"Grab an oar," Patrick said to James. "We have a long haul to get to Cove by sunrise."

James unlocked his oar as he had seen Gunny do, and the two men rowed unevenly out into Dingle harbor. Gunny's heart ached as she watched the small craft pick up speed, and melt into the black night. She gave a final wave and reached into her apron pocket for the black-handled knife. But the knife was gone.

She walked slowly up Green Street and onto Main. She pushed open the unlocked door of the Murphy's shop and was greeted by the jingle of door bells—and the open arms of a weeping, coughing Joanna.

The morning sun was high and the children were wide awake by the time the small boat reached the harbor at Cove. The fishing boat was dwarfed by dozens of three-masted ships tied up in slots along the twenty-two long piers of Cove Harbor. The piers were noisy with the business of loading and unloading ships. Patrick expertly maneuvered around the larger ships and pulled into an open slip at the end of a long pier. James was surprised when Patrick climbed out onto the dock and tied up his boat.

"I thought you were going straight back to Dingle?"

"My arms are aching and I need to rest. Besides, Gunny and your mother will be sorting and packing all day. I might as well take a look around. I've always wanted to see Cove," he added with a smile.

"I believe it is called Queenstown," James said as he collected his gear.

Patrick shook his head. "What nonsense. Someday, we'll change that back."

James lifted Larry out of the boat and handed him his bundle. "Don't run off," he said pointing at the boy. Larry smiled and slung his large satchel over his shoulder. The bag hung down nearly to his feet.

James went to lift Maggie out of the boat but she pulled away from him.

"I can do it myself," she said in a steady voice. Patrick reached out a helping hand from the dock which she also ignored. She was clearly nervous but pulled herself up onto the dock as she had seen Patrick do. She stood and reached back to James for her satchel. She slipped her large bag over her shoulder and dusted off her hands on her apron.

James pushed himself up onto the dock and pulled his bag from the boat. Patrick whistled behind him.

"This is the largest town I've ever seen. Look at all these ships. How do we find one that's sailing to America?"

James squinted in the early-morning light and sighed. "I have no idea."

Patrick caught the eye of a sailor who was loading a ship near their slip. "Excuse me," he said in a low voice. "Do you know where we can find tickets to sail to America?"

"If you find any tickets to America, let me know," the sailor said, gruffly dragging a heavy load toward the gangway to his ship.

Patrick grabbed the man by the arm. "No nonsense, Lad," he said in an even deeper voice. "We want to purchase tickets to sail to America. Where do we do that?"

The sailor jerked his arm way. "Talk to a shipping agent," he said pointing toward shore. "Top of the quay."

"God bless you," Patrick said. The sailor snorted, and returned to his work. "Let's go find an agent," Patrick said to his small crew and they headed in off the pier.

The quay was tangled with sailors moving freight, with merchants buying and selling goods, and with gaunt souls, moving about in clusters seeking passage out of Ireland. Some of the weary traveled alone; many seemed to be traveling in family groups. Everyone was thin and no one looked well. James kept a firm grip on Larry's collar and Maggie's hand to make sure he didn't lose the children before the journey began. For once in his life, Larry did not seem inclined to run off. Both children observed the bustle of the port with wide eyes. None of them had ever seen so many people in one place.

Patrick instructed James and the children to wait at the end of the quay, then headed into the crowd. They watched him stop and talk to several groups of people before he returned.

"Why did you ask so many?" James queried. "Did no one know about tickets?"

"As a sailor, I've learned to ask directions from no less than three people," Patrick said in a sophisticated voice. "Most times all three are a wee bit wrong but with three answers you can usually figure out the way."

"So where do we go?" James asked.

"Well, it seems there's a different agent for each ship and different ships sail to different ports. Do you want to sail first to Liverpool and then on to America? Which port in America? Or should you go to Canada? Tickets to Canada are cheaper, but the British ships are more crowded than American ships. But American passage costs more. And are you sailing first-class or steerage?"

"You heard all that and you still have no idea where we should go, do you?" James asked.

"No idea whatsoever," Patrick confirmed.

"Well," James said, his eyes narrowing. "Sailing straight to America sounds better than making another stop in Liverpool and having to buy tickets all over again. Yes?"

Patrick agreed.

"And we want to sail to New York City because we want to try and trace Tom Milliken's steps to get to Alexandria in Virginia. Yes?"

Patrick agreed again.

"And first-class tickets will cost more so I think we should sail steerage. The children won't mind one way or the other and the less we spend now the more money we'll have later for food and coaches. Yes?"

Patrick nodded again and smiled. "You are smart, James. Gunny always said you were the smartest man she knew."

"So we'll get on the first boat we can find that is sailing straight to America," James said with as much conviction as he could muster.

An old man was sitting on a beaten trunk listening to the discussion. He tapped James on the leg with a long walking stick. "Watch out for bad captains," he said, eying the children.

James brushed at his leg, and pulled the children closer to him.

"A bad captain'll charge you six pence for a drink of water. Worse than that, some captains are abusive," the old man continued leaning forward, bracing himself with his walking stick. "Used to be the ships only sailed in the good months. Since the troubles began, the ships sail year round and it makes the crews edgy. Any disagreement with the captain and he'll have you thrown overboard for mutiny. Or hung from the highest mast," he added with wide eyes pointing a bent finger at the children.

James turned his back on the man and shrugged at Patrick. Patrick studied the old man, then squatted down to face him. "How do we avoid a bad captain, old man?"

The man leaned in toward Patrick. "Ask around on the docks. If a crew won't sail again with a certain captain, best to avoid that ship."

"Thank you, sir," Patrick said tipping his hat. "We are much obliged."

The old man smiled, pushed up on his walking stick, and whistled for his dog. He walked into town dragging the trunk behind him. A black dog with one white paw followed closely behind.

"I'm going to mix it up with the sailors down on the docks. When I find a happy crew headed to New York, we'll know which ship you should be on."

James nodded and sat with the children on their bags to wait.

Patrick was back within the hour. "I've found your boat. It's the *Constitution*. It's an American packet ship."

"Did you ask three sailors?" James queried.

"I asked four just to be sure," Patrick said. "They said the ship's agent for the *Constitution* is up in that long row of offices. Let's go get your tickets."

They found the agent's office and confirmed that the ship was sailing directly from Queenstown to New York, then got in line and made their way slowly to the front. The booking agent hardly looked up from his work as yet another group of dirty peasants approached his desk.

"Three tickets to New York on the *Constitution*," James said, sounding more sure of himself than he felt.

"First-class or steerage?"

"Steerage, please."

"Nine pounds," the agent muttered. "One adult with full rations, two children with half rations."

"Half rations for the children?" James questioned. "Clearly you've never seen this boy eat."

The agent continued with his paperwork, saying nothing.

"Very well," James said, fingering the gold coins in his bag. "How long will the trip last?"

"Anywhere from four weeks to three months," the clerk said without affect. "Depends on the weather. If you hit a still spot, you'll sit until the winds pick up. If there's fog or icebergs or storms or you hit a sandbar, the trip'll run longer."

James swallowed hard and took out nine gold guineas. He handed them to the agent with a trembling hand. The agent tumbled the gold coins in his hand.

"Don't see many of these anymore. They stopped making them in 1815."

"They're still good, aren't they?" James asked.

The agent chuckled. "They're good as gold, sir, and will do just fine." He looked at James and the children and smiled. "Are you sure you don't want to upgrade to first-class?"

"We're happy with steerage," James said with a grim smile.

"You may be less happy by the end of the trip. If you're delayed the ship may run short of rations."

"This is a sound ship, isn't it?"

"Sound as they come. She used to carry slaves up until twelve years ago. The ship's owner is first rate. Mr. Cain. An American. The captain's new, only twenty-nine, a Mainer from a long line of Maine captains and comes highly recommended. Do you have any other questions, or can I get on with my work?"

The agent handed James three tickets. "You'll have to pass inspection by the surgeon before you board. His office is at the top of the quay," he said pointing toward a long line of immigrants queuing up behind a sign that said Government Medical Inspector's Office. Hours 10-4.

"Perhaps we should have been inspected first," James muttered, "rather than spend money on tickets we can't use."

"Doesn't work that way," the agent said briskly. "You buy your ticket, then the inspector verifies you aren't traveling with any infectious diseases and stamps the damned thing. The government inspects you to protect you. Now move along," he said eyeing the growing line behind James and the children. James still did not move.

"You sail out of Lynch's quay at high-tide. Wait near the base of the quay. Someone will call out when the ship is ready. Don't be late or she'll sail without you." He waved his hand at the small party. "Next!" he yelled, and reached around James to take money from the next starving peasant.

The children were antsy waiting in line to see the surgeon. Larry was hungry and Maggie had to relieve herself.

"Go with the children," Patrick said. "I'll hold your place in line. But hurry. The line is moving at a fast clip."

"Can't you wait until we pass inspection?" James asked the children.

"I'm hungry," Larry whined.

"We have bread with us," James remembered. He set down his satchel and pulled out a loaf. He broke off a large chuck and handed it to Larry who devoured it and reached for more. James doled out a little more bread, then looked at Maggie. Her hands were on her hips, her lips set in a thin line.

"All right," he said. "We'll duck behind a building somewhere."

Patrick reached down and grabbed Larry by the collar. "Hurry," he said as James and Maggie headed off into the milling crowds.

They made it back to the line just as Patrick and Larry were nearing the surgeon.

"How am I ever going to watch the two of them when it's just me?" James asked.

Patrick shook his head. "Someone will help you."

James was first up for inspection.

"What's your name? Are you well? Hold out your tongue." The surgeon stamped James ticket. "Next!"

The children were inspected just as quickly and their tickets stamped. Patrick walked with them to the end of the quay. He said a quick good-bye, hoping he wouldn't cry, then returned to his small, empty boat to wait until the large ship set sail.

James insisted that they wait right at the end of Lynch's quay. He did not want to miss the call to board above the din of the crowd. They watched as sailors and merchants pulled load after load of Canadian wood from the *Constitution*.

When the steward finally announced that the ship was ready to board, James and the children scrambled down the long pier to board. A young sailor stood at the end of the gangway with his arms outstretched.

"Wait for the captain, please."

A young captain crossed behind them, followed closely by his first and second mate. The captain was berating the first mate for the time it had taken getting the ship unloaded.

"Mr. Cain is on board. If this voyage isn't perfect I'll never hear the end of it from my father."

The first mate laughed. "It must be difficult having a captain for a father."

The young captain stared, unsmiling, at the first mate. "No more difficult than having a captain for a father who also happens to be best friends with the owner. I learned everything I know from my father sailing from Maine to the Orient. Let's hope I remember it now."

James tipped his hat at the captain as he passed. The young sailor who was blocking the gate stepped aside to let the officers onboard.

"He seems the friendly sort," James said to the young sailor who continued to hold the line at the bottom of the gangway until the captain and the first mates were on board.

"Captain Cooper? He's all right. He's nervous because the ship's owner is sailing today." He glanced up the gangway waiting for the signal for the passengers to board.

"You look young for this work," James said watching the nervous sailor.

"I'm the youngest mate on this ship. I'm sixteen. It's my first trip." He held out his hand. "Billy Kelley, ship's apprentice," he said and smiled. "I'm working for free passage. My mother arranged it." He winked at Maggie and looked up again toward the ship. A bent, older sailor at the top of the gangway signaled to let the passengers board. Billy collected their tickets, and James and the children hurried up the steep gangway and onto the ship's wide, sprawling deck.

"Down you go," the old sailor said waving them toward a large hatch. "Down you go. Three to a bunk. Move along. The captain's ready to sail."

James and the children climbed cautiously down the worn wooden steps into the dark hatch. The lower deck was dimly lit by lanterns hanging from pegs set along the posts of the ship. They paused while their eyes adjusted to the light. A series of wooden bunks stacked three high extended along both sides of the boat with another row built down the center of the ship. Each bunk was six square feet, giving each passenger about two feet across for sleeping. James chose a second-tier bunk along the front left side of the ship and stashed the three bags to mark the space as theirs.

Passengers of every age and occupation flooded in behind them filling every bunk and cranny in the 'tween decks. The air buzzed with conversation as two hundred and twenty passengers unloaded chests, bundles, barrels, and old, worn luggage onto the stacked bunks for the long voyage to America.

The steward called everyone on deck for the sailing. Passengers scrambled up the wooden steps for one last look at their native land and lined the railings waving at teary relatives along the quay. As the deckhands started to hoist the gangway, a tall, thin teenager with wavy black hair bit his lip and sprinted past Billy Kelley. He tossed his small bag onto the deck and scrambled after it, tucking himself in behind a little girl with brown, curly hair. Maggie eyed the tall boy squatting behind her and spread her skirt slightly to help hide him. He held a finger to his lips and smiled. She turned her back on him and squeezed with Larry into a spot closer along the railing.

Young Matthew McCrohan sighed. He knew he'd done wrong running away from his father, but the old man refused to leave, not caring if he lived or died. But Matthew was determined to live. He only hoped the sailors wouldn't be able to find him until they were too far from shore to throw him back. He grinned and wiped a sheen of sweat from his face. He was sailing to America.

Maggie spotted Patrick's small boat tied up at the end of a long quay. She and Larry waved furiously. Patrick waved back and watched as a large steam ship towed the three-masted *Constitution* down the river Lee toward the open ocean. The ship moved with good speed as the tide pulled it toward the ocean. Patrick noted a moderate southwesterly breeze. A fine day for sailing, he thought. He untied his boat, hoisted his own sail, and headed back to Dingle.

Captain Samuel Cooper stood on the top deck of the ship looking across the mangy crowd on board the vessel. "I preferred our cargo of lumber to this crowd."

The ship's owner pulled a large cigar from his mouth and let out a slow breath of smoke that eked its way through his greying, brown curls. "It's all the same, Sam. It's all paying cargo."

Sam dipped his head and took a deep breath. "Perhaps, Mr. Cain. But look at these people. They have nothing."

Matthew Cain shook his head. "They're still better off leaving. Perhaps they'll find peace in America."

"Father said you used to live here. Are you from Cork?"

Mr. Cain snorted, his sharp green eyes flashing. "No. I'm from a cursed place. Dunquin. I've been gone over twenty years."

"That was well before the lean times. Why did you leave?"

"I had no choice. I caused an accident and a young woman died. A priest smuggled me out. I still send him money to repent for my sins."

"That priest must be plenty rich by now."

"He uses the money to look after my mother so it's worth every penny."

"Are you sure he and your mother are still alive after so many years of famine and fever?"

"Who knows, but until his mail comes back marked 'Undeliverable,' I'll continue to send him my tithing. It's the least I can do." He eyed the shore along the River Lee. "We are nearly out of the cove. Think you can get this ship home for me as well as your father used to do before the accident?"

"Aye, Sir. I'll get you home."

~ Chapter 25: Home ~

Gunny worked with Joanna for two days packing up the remaining inventory from the Murphy's store. Patrick recruited two additional fishing boats from the island and helped load three boatloads of goods—lanterns, tea, whiskey, barrels of crackers, candles—to ship over to the island. Joanna said it was the least she could do to say thanks for taking her in as she sadly closed up the shop and hung out the "closed" sign for the last time.

They walked in silence to the pier. Gunny helped Joanna into Patrick's boat but remained on the pier.

"Aren't you coming with us?" Patrick asked. Gunny didn't look well. He knew her heart must be as weary as his at the loss of the children.

She wiped a hand across her eyes. "Would you mind coming to get me in Dunquin ? I want to try one more time to get Mac and his family to join us on the island. With all of this bounty plus our found wheat, I don't feel right leaving him here. Can you come back and get us at the Dunquin pier this afternoon?"

Patrick smiled. "I'll meet you there, but I doubt Mac will be with you. He's a stubborn one, and that boy of his is cut from the same cloth. But if he wants to come, we'll figure out a way to haul his anvil and tools. Tell him that. We've always wanted a smithy on the island."

Gunny knelt by the boat. "Joanna. Stay with Patrick's mother tonight. Charlotte will take good care of you. I'll be over in the morning to get you moved in and show you around the schoolhouse."

Joanna shook her head, stifling a cough behind her hand, and gripped the railing of the boat with a white hand as the three boats of Blasket fishermen rowed out into Dingle harbor and disappeared over the horizon.

Gunny could not stop thinking about the children as she walked west out of Dingle. She knew they were safe with James but kept feeling that she had forgotten something, that she had left the children behind somewhere. She said a silent prayer for their safe journey as she ran her fingers through the cups of the old bullan stone on Upper Main. She continued down the dusty road toward Ventry, walking past deserted farms and wide fields. The new sound of lowing cattle mixed with the familiar sound of pounding waves along the rocky southern shore.

As she passed the drive to Ballygoleen she hesitated. If Thomas saw her he'd think he she was a ghost. She wanted to taunt him, to laugh in his face, to tell him that the children were alive and free of him. Instead, she slipped past and continued west toward Dunquin. She was done with Sir Thomas Townsend Aremberg de Moleyns, second Baron Ventry. He was as dead to her now as she was to him.

She thought about her return to the Blaskets, how empty her house would be without the children. But she wouldn't be alone. Joanna would be with her, and she'd spend time with Mac and his family, and with Patrick and the O'Connors. As soon as she got home, she'd clean out the schoolhouse and make sure the boiler was working for the remaining children on the island. Then she'd set a few rabbit snares and bake bread with the found wheat. She had put in a new kitchen garden in April, and had planted what she had for potatoes and oats. Surely the harvest of 1850 would be sound and potatoes and oats would again be in full supply. Families would move back to the Blaskets. Johnny O'Connor and the other O'Connor boys would be able to stay on the island to live out their lives farming and fishing. Bridget would get married and raise a brood of her own under the sharp eye of Charlotte O'Connor. She'd spend her evenings again sipping sweet, hot tea and whiskey, telling tales and playing old tunes on her tin whistle. There'd be no more evictions, no more starvation, no more fever.

She wondered how long it would be before she heard from James. She pictured the cheerful letter she'd receive from him, saying that he and the children had arrived in Virginia after a short and uneventful voyage, and had easily found their way south. That the house Michael and Maeve lived in in Alexandria was quite nice despite what young Tom had said about it. That James had found work, and that the children were happily enrolled in school.

When she crested the hill and the village of Dunquin came into view, she stopped short. There was no smell of peat in the air; not one house with smoke curling gently from the chimney. She trotted down the hill toward the forge, her heart tight in her chest. The McCrohan house was dark, the forge quiet. She tapped gently at the door of the house but no one answered. Fearing the worst, she lifted up on the latch. It was unlocked. She pushed the door open and tentatively looked around the neat room where John McCrohan and her father used to sit side by side, sipping at whiskey and telling tales. She could hear the stomping of feet dancing into the night at a gathering, and smell Kate McCrohan's fine Easter cake. The elaborate crane Mac had made for her wedding day sat unused by the hearth. No one was inside, dead or alive. Gunny let out a short breath and pulled the door closed.

She walked across the yard to the forge. The forge was also deserted, the room unnaturally cool. Mac's hammers, chisels, punches, files, and rasps hung in perfect order along the left wall. An array of old pots, broken rakes, and an old wagon tongue remained unmended along the far wall. She sighed. She was too late. Mac, Sheila, and young Matthew were gone. She wondered if they were dead or alive. She bit at her bottom lip and walked into the yard. She glanced up at her childhood home then continued into the silent village. A breeze stirred the dust on the road ahead of her and she felt a chill move down her spine. Was everyone in Dunquin dead or gone?

She stopped at the church and leaned heavily on one of Mac's scrolled gates. The unlocked gate creaked open, inviting her into the churchyard. The yard was still and filled with shadows. She thought about making one last visit to Matt's grave when she saw a tiny flicker of light in the priest's quarters. Could it be that someone was living in the rectory? She hurried to the priest's door but it was bolted from inside. She raced to the front of the church and pushed open the large wooden doors. Her footsteps echoed across the nave as she raced between the pews, then took a right to the side door that lead to the rectory. She pushed open the door to the priest's rooms and peeked inside. It was just as she remembered—a large room with no furniture and no rugs. A small turf fire burned low in the fireplace. Beyond the front room was Father Jessey's sleeping room. The light of a single, white candle, set awkwardly in a bent, silver candlestick, reflected off of a body lying still under a worn, red blanket on a mat on the floor. She walked across the room and lifted a corner of the blanket.

Father Jessey blinked up at her. His eyes were completely black in the dim light. He had a faint sheen of sweat across his forehead. His blond, neat hair was a dirty brown and plastered in clumps around his face. He smelled of urine, and sweat, and death. He groaned and Gunny took a step away.

"Don't leave me," he muttered.

Gunny turned toward the door to flee. He moaned again behind her.

"Water," he muttered. "Water…"

Gunny turned back to the prone figure. She couldn't bring fever back to the island. Not now.

Father Jessey reached out a claw-like hand. "Gunny? Is that you? Gunny Malone?"

Gunny swallowed. "I'll get you water but then I'm leaving. You have the fever and I don't have any medicine to help you." She turned and raced through the church and over to the holy well. She pulled up a dipper of water and walked quickly back to the rectory. She stood as far away as she could as she held the dipper to the priest's thin lips. He was too weak to lift his head much and water trickled over this lips, down along his cheeks, and behind his neck.

"God," she said, "can you not help out?" She knelt by his mat and gently lifted his head. She held the dipper once again to his lips. He drank greedily then sank back onto the mat.

"Bless you, Gunny. Bless you Gunny Malone."

Gunny snorted. "If your last act is to give me the fever, I'll never forgive you, Father. I'm going home to the Blaskets. Patrick's meeting me down on the pier. Good-bye."

"Gunny," Father Jessey said weakly. "Don't go. I want someone to be near me when I pass."

"And how does this fall to me? How is it that I should be the last one on earth to hear your words?"

Father Jessey chuckled then coughed at the effort. "God works in mysterious ways, Gunny. I told you that after your accident but you wouldn't listen. I had something to tell you then. I will tell you now if you stay with me."

"You're like the devil, Father, tempting me to bargain away my life to hear your story."

"Get me more water, Gunny, and you'll hear my final confession."

Gunny grabbed the dipper and reluctantly walked back through the church. She felt like she was fifteen again under the thumb of the village priest. She'd bring him one more dipper of water, then leave. She owed him nothing.

She collected the water and returned to the rectory, kneeling again by the mat and helping the priest drink. She found an old red alter cloth and soaked up the rest of the water in the dipper to wipe the sweat from his brow. "You've had your water. Let's hear that confession."

The priest coughed again and closed his eyes. He was so still she wondered if he had already passed. She reached out to lightly touch his forehead when he snaked a hand up from under the covers and grabbed hold of her wrist. She winced at this touch but did not pull away. He didn't have long.

"Gunny," he started again, his eyes tearing. "I have to tell you that I..." He hesitated. "I am Catherine's father." He let out a short breath and released his grip on her.

Gunny felt her soul lift out of her body. "It was you that night in the graveyard? Not Thomas?"

He wiped at his eyes. "A tremendous passion washed over me when I saw you lying there in the church after Lord Milliken left. The devil got me, Gunny. It wasn't my fault. You were drunk. I didn't think you'd even know. I never thought about a baby..."

"You never thought about a baby? You just thought you could have your way with me and it wouldn't matter? You defiled me, you sanctimonious son-of-the-devil?" Gunny could hardly breathe. She thought back on the time she had visited at the house when he'd been there with Catherine. She pictured him tossing Catherine in the air, their blond hair mingling. She stared at the diminished man.

"You loved her when she was a baby, didn't you?"

"With all my heart," he said in a whisper. "Catherine was the most precious thing I'd ever seen. She was an angel, Gunny, but I could never tell her I loved her. And then she died in Ventry. God took her away from me because of my evil ways."

"God took her from both of us, Father. What did I do to deserve her loss?"

"God works in mysterious ways..."

"Yes, yes, I know about God's mysterious ways, Father. But in this case, you're the one who was responsible, not God. You can't go blaming God for everything. I tried to blame God for taking Matt. But it was an accident. I've made my peace with God. You should do the same—own up to your mistake and pass over in peace."

"There's something else, Gunny," the priest continued in a weak voice. "About Matt."

Gunny sighed. She did not want to hear one last lecture about Matt. She dabbed the soggy cloth again and ran it roughly over his forehead and cheeks. "You've said enough, Father. Now be quiet and pass. Please."

The priest's body shook. Gunny watched as he struggled for breath. She tucked the blanket in around his shoulders and stood. "Good-bye," she whispered. "Give my best to God when you see him." She turned again to leave and was near the door when she heard the words.

"Matt is alive, Gunny."

Gunny froze in place as a wave of heat passed through her. The priest was clearly delirious, imaging himself in the past. Or he was talking to those who had passed. She turned to face him. "Don't let the last words that cross your lips be a lie, Father."

The priest shivered again. "Come here, Gunny," he said in a weak voice.

Gunny took a step closer, her eyes filling with tears. Would there ever be a time when she heard Matt's name and did not cry? "Why do I listen to you?" she said, kneeling again by the sodden mat.

Father Jessey reached out a cold, boney hand. "Hold my hand."

"Why?"

"So you can't hit me."

Gunny grinned. "That's actually funny. I don't think I've ever heard you say anything funny."

Father Jessey's blue eyes rolled back in his head. She squeezed his hand. "Tell me that you're seeing Matt as you pass. Tell me how he looks. Tell me what he's telling you from the other side."

The priest blinked and struggled to focus on Gunny's face. "Matt is not on the other side. That's what I'm trying to tell you, Gunny. Matt didn't die in the accident."

Gunny smiled. "Of course he didn't die, Father. And you didn't bury him out there in that graveyard."

"Oh, we buried him all right. And for two days, he stayed buried. Then I heard the knocking, quiet at first, then louder. I thought it was the Wren boys trying to scare me, but it kept up through the night. If it hadn't been so rainy when we buried him I never would have found him alive, but the ground was all washed out around the end of the coffin. He'd been in there, paralyzed for two days, but he was kicking now. I heard him kicking...," he gasped, out of breath from the effort of talking.

Gunny's brow furrowed. Was this nonsense he was muttering? She remembered Mac talking about the rain after the funeral, and she'd seen Matt's grave all topsy turvy. "So Matt was kicking and you let him out?" she asked skeptically.

"Exactly. He had about pushed out the end of the coffin by then. Good thing those Wren boys weren't so good at hammering. If Mac had made the coffin Matt would have never gotten out. When I pulled him free, he was a fright, all pale and crazy and weeping. I helped him inside. He was afraid to go to sleep, afraid he'd wake up again buried alive, but he finally dozed off. I went to tell you, but you were so rude to me, Gunny. So rude. You told me to go away, to never talk to you again. I knew then and there that you two would be better off apart."

"And?" Gunny asked, amazed.

"And I smuggled him out of town and got him passage to America," the priest said with a thin smile. "He's been there ever since. He sends me money for the church. I keep his letters in this box." He pulled back the rough red blanket to reveal a tarnished silver box. "Matt helped pay for the new gates, though they never did close right. The barricades in life are so often in the wrong places... That's what I had to tell you, Gunny. Now I can die in peace."

Gunny stared at the priest as he took a deep, raspy breath and closed his eyes.

"Wait," she yelled. "You can't tell me that and then go," she said pulling the blanket back. "If Matt was alive he never would have left me. How can you say that?" She clutched at the priest's cold hand and slapped his pale face. "Father, wake up. I don't know if what you said is true. Father Jessey!" she yelled. But Father Jessey did not answer. He was gone.

Gunny felt the blood drain from her face. Matt was alive? It couldn't possibly be true. She felt the walls lean in toward her. She pushed away from the still body.

"God rest your wicked soul," she muttered over the corpse. "I hope you find the peace in death that you never found here on earth." She bent down and snuffed out the single, white candle and picked up the silver box.

"I hate what you do to me, Father Jessey," she said, wiping away a tear with the back of her hand. She turned to the low peat fire, set the silver box down on the dirty, wooden floor, and stirred the ashes. A new turf lightened and warmed the room as she opened the box. Inside was a heavy stash of gold coins—and a yellowed stack of letters addressed to Father Jessey in Matt's neat handwriting. She pulled the top letter out of the ribboned pack and opened it with a shaky hand. It was dated October 1825. Eight months after the accident.

"Take care of my mother and family." That was all it said.

She looked at the return address on the envelope. Matthew Cain. New York City. Matthew Cain? She looked again at the writing. It was Matt's hand.

She could picture him writing out letters for her on the smudged black slate. She poured the coins from the box into her apron pocket and grabbed the stack of letters. She fled from the rectory leaving the door wide open and raced to the pier. Patrick was sitting on the dock, waiting.

"I have to get to Cork," she said, her face ashen, her hands shaking. "I'm going to America."

Patrick stared at her. "I thought you were coming back to the Blaskets. What about Joanna? What about running the school?"

"Patrick, sometimes things change and you wonder if it is a beginning or an ending. I thought today was an ending, I was sure of it. But now something has changed and I have to go."

Patrick shook his head and rubbed at his aching arms. "Get in. I'll take you—but I'll never understand you."

Gunny laughed, a bold, strong laugh. "I'll never understand me either, Patrick. All I know is that I did something good and now the favor has been returned to me one hundred fold." She scooted into the large curragh, grabbed an oar, and rowed with Patrick out into the channel as the blazing red sun dipped into the oceans of the west, and a full, orange moon rose in the east.

~ Epilogue ~

"Help me outside," the old woman insisted. I want to hear the sound of the ocean."

The writer set down his pencil and offered her an arm. They walked slowly down to the strand. He helped her up onto a large, flat rock. She took a deep breath of salty air and looked out to sea. Small white caps blew toward shore on a stiff October breeze. The air was damp and cool, the slanting fall sunlight warm on her face. A grey curl blew across her face. She tucked the stray curl behind one ear, wiped the back of one hand across her closed eyes, and bowed her head, thankful to have one more day on the earth.

"You know I can't leave here until you tell me the end of the story. Did you get to America? Did you find Matt? What happened to the children and James, and your brother, and tipsy Maeve? And Tom? And what happened here in Dingle—to the O'Connors and Mac and to the Baron? You can't stop now."

Gunny laughed. "I'm tired and those stories will have to wait for another day. Come see me tomorrow and I'll tell you the rest of the story. Or you could ask your father. He knows."

The writer smiled. "My father told me to ask you."

Gunny laughed again until it made her cough. She cleared her throat and looked at the writer with bright eyes. "James is one of the smartest men I ever knew. Will you give him something for me?" She reached into her apron pocket and pulled out an old tin whistle. She held it up to her lips and played a few sweet notes in time to a wave crashing against the shore. The wave receded and she pulled the whistle from her lips. She took a deep breath and handed the whistle to the man.

"I'm not sure my father can play a whistle."

Gunny grinned. "Don't let him fool you. I gave him this whistle once before and he gave it back. Give it to him again. He'll be amused."

"It's hard to believe I'll be back home in Virginia in just a few short weeks."

"Your steamer ship sounds much more civilized than a sailing ship, but two weeks? Where is the romance in that quick a sail?"

"Do you want me to help you inside before I go?"

Gunny shook her head. "I'm fine here. I like sitting near the ocean and watching the stars come out. Go back to your room. We'll talk again before you leave in the morning."

Gunny did not slept well that night. Telling the old stories stirred up too many memories. She woke early, washed her face in a basin of well water, and carefully dried her face on an old flour sack. She knelt to stir the fire, added a new turf, and put on a kettle for tea. When the tea was steaming hot, she poured a cup into her favorite Spanish porcelain cup and added two spoonfuls of sugar.

She eased carefully into the old rocker, then reached her free hand into her worn apron pocket and pulled out Matt's pipe. She had tied the faded red ribbon around the pipe's worn, white stem. She pushed the ribbon aside and held the pipe to her lips. As she rocked she pictured Matt perched on Nella's back racing to the strand and heard the village children yelling, "Look out! Look out for Matt McCrohan!" Then she saw herself running through the surf to meet him. Running, running, her long curls thick and black, running on legs that didn't ache. She felt the hot touch of Matt's hand in hers as he swept her up behind him onto Nella's back. It was all so familiar—the warm press of her chest on his back, the smell of his hair, the sound of his laugh. She felt the spray of cold as they thundered through the surf. She heard booming laughter and realized she was the one who was laughing. She slipped under the white cap ships into the warmth of swirling stars, laughing, laughing as she and Matt dissolved into a tail of moonlight crossing the ocean and rode off to the west.

The writer paused outside the small stone house and listened. He could hear Gunny's low voice, deep in conversation with someone inside. He sat on the low bench in the yard, chuckling when he heard her laughing loudly. When the house grew quiet, he stood and knocked gently on the door. There was no answer. He opened the door a crack, and peeked inside.

"Miss Gunny? It's Jim."

The old woman was sitting in her still rocker in front of the low turf fire, a speckled wool blanket draped loosely across her lap, a cooling cup of weak, sweet tea on the floor by her side. It looked like she was napping with an old clay pipe clutched tightly in one hand and an odd half-smile on her face. There was no one else in the room with her.

He knelt by the rocker and gently pressed her hand against his cheek. It was cold. She was gone. He wiped the back of one hand across his eyes. Gunny Malone's story was over. He would have to find the missing chapters in America.

~ Until we meet again... ~

About the Author

Janie Downey Maxwell grew up in Alexandria, Virginia, the descendant of Irish immigrants who fled the Irish Famine in the late 1840s. She has a degree in History from the University of Virginia. She is married and lives outside of Portland, Maine where she is active in local theater as a writer, producer, singer, and actor. She is currently working on the sequel to this novel which takes place in Alexandria, Virginia in the years leading up to the Civil War. You'll find Janie on Facebook and on Twitter under Janie Downey Maxwell.

Books used to research this novel

20 Years A-Growing by Maurice O'Sullivan. Translated by Moya Llewellyn Davies and George Thompson. Oxford University Press, 1933.

44 Irish Short Stories; An Anthology of Irish Short Fiction from Yeats to Frank O'Connor. Edited by Devin A. Garrity. Old Greenwich, CT: The Devin-Adair Company, (no copyright date).

A Year in Ireland; Irish Calendar Customs by Kevin Danaher. Minneapolis MN: Mercier Press, 1972.

An Old Woman's Reflections; The Life of a Blasket Island Storyteller by Peig Sayers (1873-1958). Oxford University Press, 1962.

Famine Echoes by Cathal Poirtein. Dublin: Gill& MacMillan, 1995.

Famine Diary; Journey to a New World by Gerald Keegan. Dublin: Wolfhound Press, 1991.

Field & Shore; Daily Life and Traditions, Aran Islands 1900. O'Brien Educational Ltd., Dublin, 1977.

History of Cobh (Queenstown) Ireland by Mary Broderick, 1994. (No publisher listed).

Ireland Photographs 1840-1930. Compiled by Sean Sexton. Laurence King Publishing, 1994.

Irish Folkways by E. Estyn Evans. London & New York: Routledge, 1957, 1988.

Out of Ireland; The Story of Irish Emigration to America by Kerby Miller and Maul Wagner. Washington DC: Elliott & Clark Publishing, 1994.

Peig, the Autobiography of Peig Sayers of the Great Blasket Island. Translated by Bryan MacMahon. Talbot Press, 1983.

Tales of Old Ireland; Edited by Michael O'Mara. Seacaucus, NJ: Castle Books, (no date).

The Famine Ships; The Irish Exodus to America by Edward Laxton. NY: Henry Holt & Co., 1996.

The Irish Famine; An Illustrated History by Helen Litton. Wolfhound Press, 1994.

The Islandman by Thomas O'Crohan. Oxford University Press, 1937, 1943, 1951.

The Lively Ghosts of Ireland by Hans Holzer. New York, Avemel, NJ: Wing Books, 1967.

Traditional Irish Recipes by John Murphy. New York: Kilkenny Press, 1988.

Walking Research

I spent two weeks driving around Ireland with Debbi Pierce until Dingle drew me in as the setting for this novel. Then I spent another two weeks hiking the Dingle Peninsula with a group of artists from the University of Southern Maine. On the second trip, I got to spend time in the hills of Dingle, Dunquin and Ballyferriter, walked the Blasket Islands, and spent evenings in the lively town of Dingle. I also spent time in the Blasket Visitor Center, in the Dingle Library, at the Diseart Centre for Irish Spirituality, and at the former Lord Ventry Estate, which is now Colaiste Ide, a boarding school for girls.

32748445R00286

Made in the USA
Lexington, KY
31 May 2014